MABUHAY!

BY ZACHARY STERLING

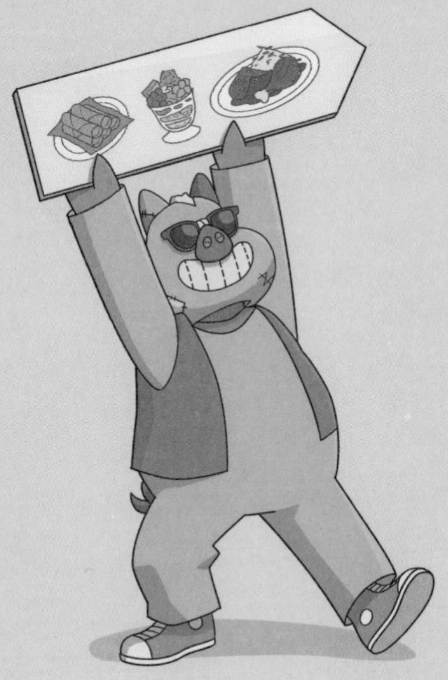

graphix
An imprint of
SCHOLASTIC

All rights reserved. Published by Graphix, an imprint of Scholastic Inc., *Publishers since 1920*. SCHOLASTIC, GRAPHIX, and associated logos are trademarks and/or registered trademarks of Scholastic Inc.

Library of Congress Control Number: 2022943224

ISBN 978-1-338-73864-3 (hardcover)
ISBN 978-1-338-73860-5 (paperback)

10 9 8 7 6 5 4 3 2 1   23 24 25 26 27

Printed in China 62
First edition, October 2023

Color Flats by Rice Gallardo
Color Assistance by Aaron Polk & George Williams
Edited by Megan Peace
Book design by Carina Taylor
Creative Director: Phil Falco
Publisher: David Saylor

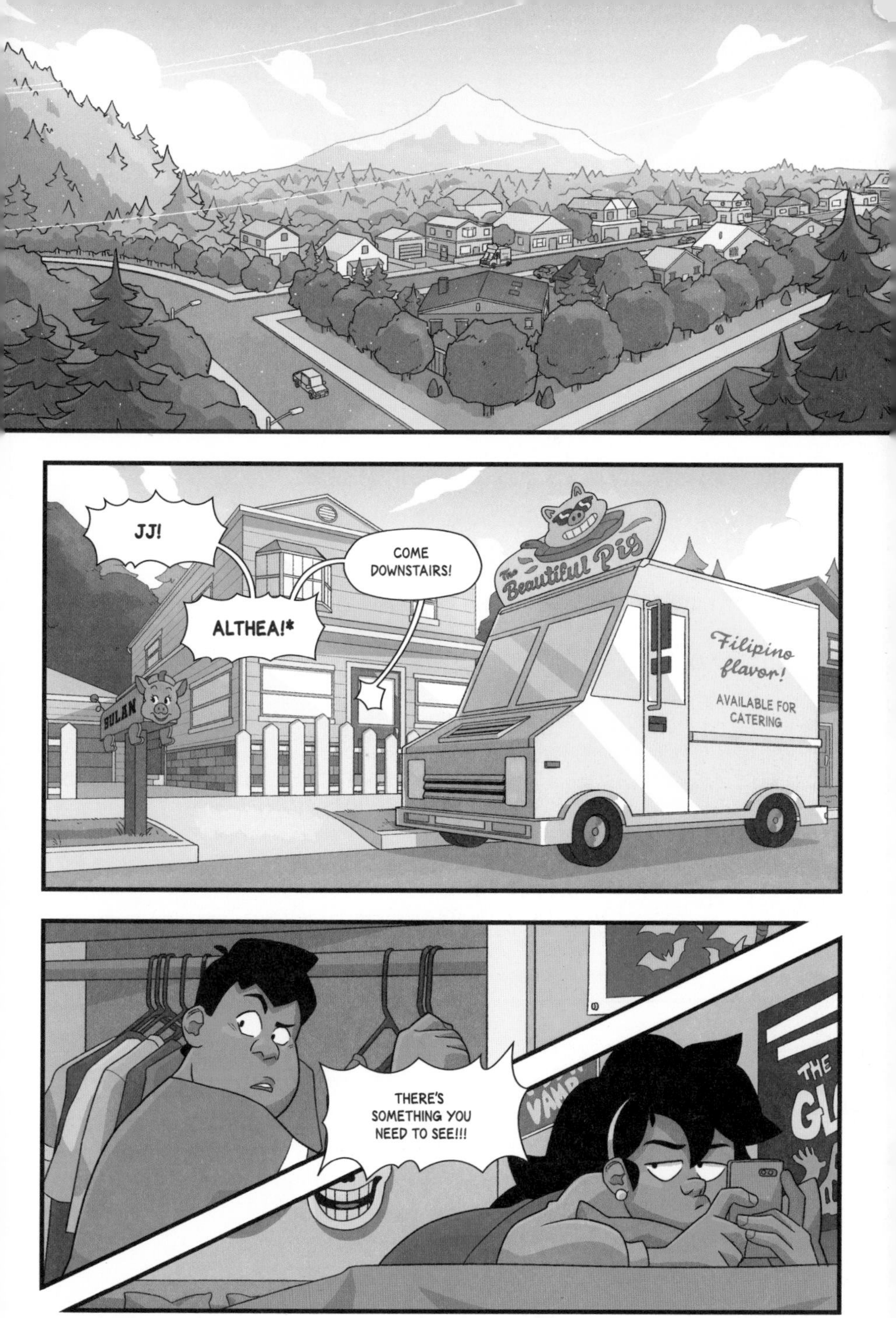
JJ!
ALTHEA!*
COME DOWNSTAIRS!
BULAN
The Beautiful Pig
Filipino flavor!
AVAILABLE FOR CATERING
THERE'S SOMETHING YOU NEED TO SEE!!!

*ALTHEA (AL-TAY-AH).

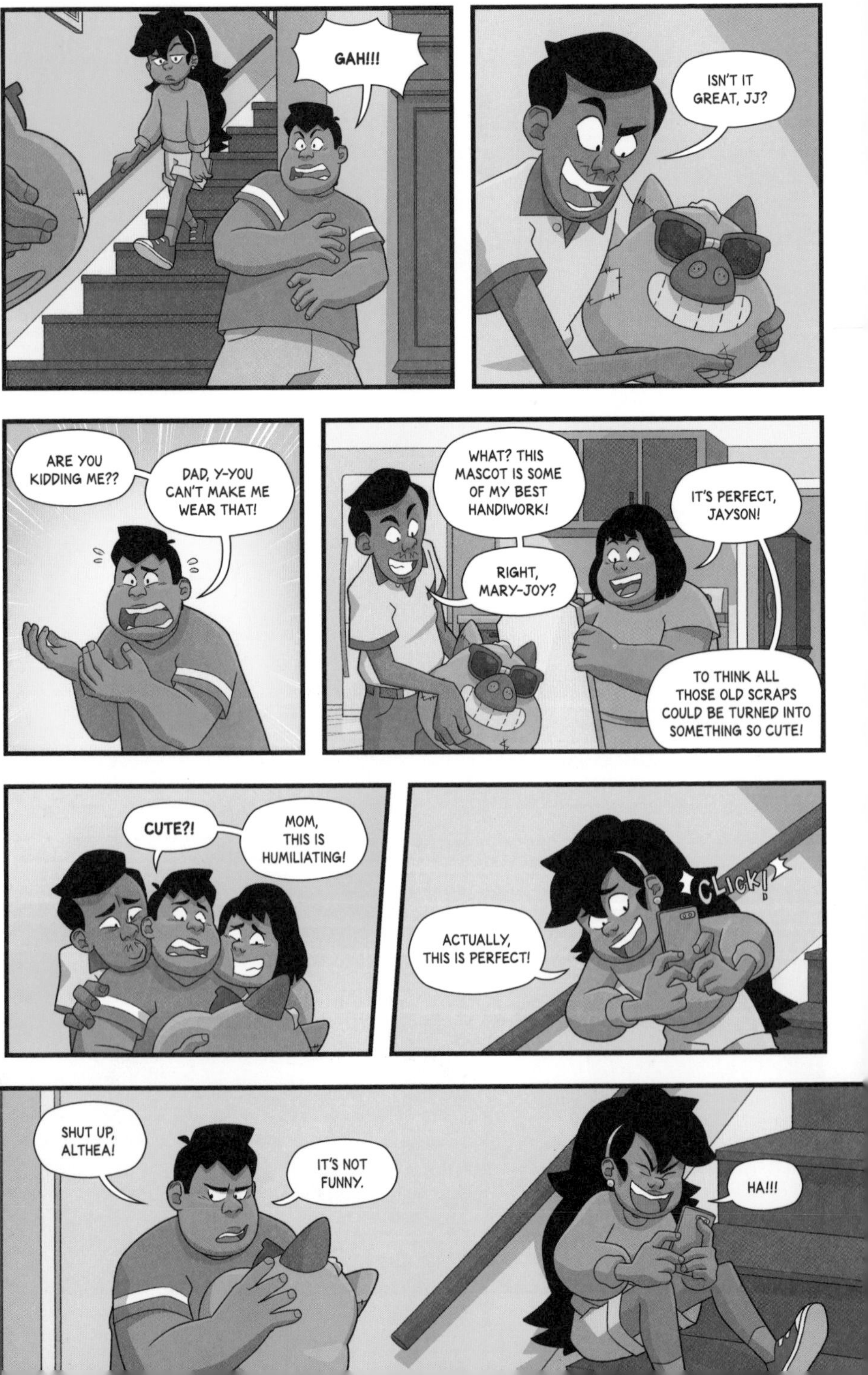
GAH!!!
ISN'T IT GREAT, JJ?
ARE YOU KIDDING ME??
DAD, Y-YOU CAN'T MAKE ME WEAR THAT!
WHAT? THIS MASCOT IS SOME OF MY BEST HANDIWORK!
RIGHT, MARY-JOY?
IT'S PERFECT, JAYSON!
TO THINK ALL THOSE OLD SCRAPS COULD BE TURNED INTO SOMETHING SO CUTE!
CUTE?!
MOM, THIS IS HUMILIATING!
CLICK!
ACTUALLY, THIS IS PERFECT!
SHUT UP, ALTHEA!
IT'S NOT FUNNY.
HA!!!

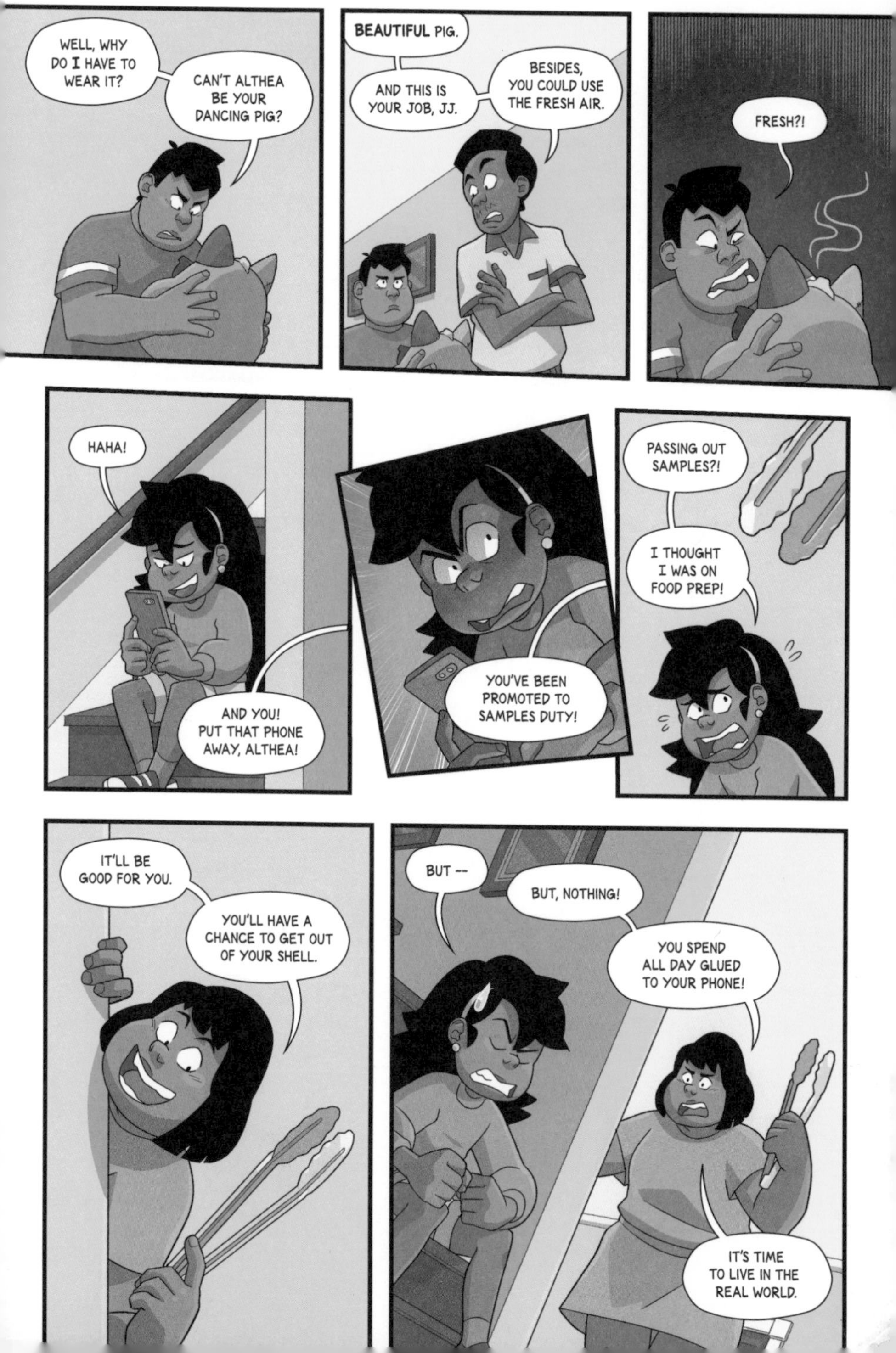
WELL, WHY DO I HAVE TO WEAR IT?
CAN'T ALTHEA BE YOUR DANCING PIG?
BEAUTIFUL PIG.
AND THIS IS YOUR JOB, JJ.
BESIDES, YOU COULD USE THE FRESH AIR.
FRESH?!
HAHA!
AND YOU! PUT THAT PHONE AWAY, ALTHEA!
YOU'VE BEEN PROMOTED TO SAMPLES DUTY!
PASSING OUT SAMPLES?!
I THOUGHT I WAS ON FOOD PREP!
IT'LL BE GOOD FOR YOU.
YOU'LL HAVE A CHANCE TO GET OUT OF YOUR SHELL.
BUT --
BUT, NOTHING!
YOU SPEND ALL DAY GLUED TO YOUR PHONE!
IT'S TIME TO LIVE IN THE REAL WORLD.

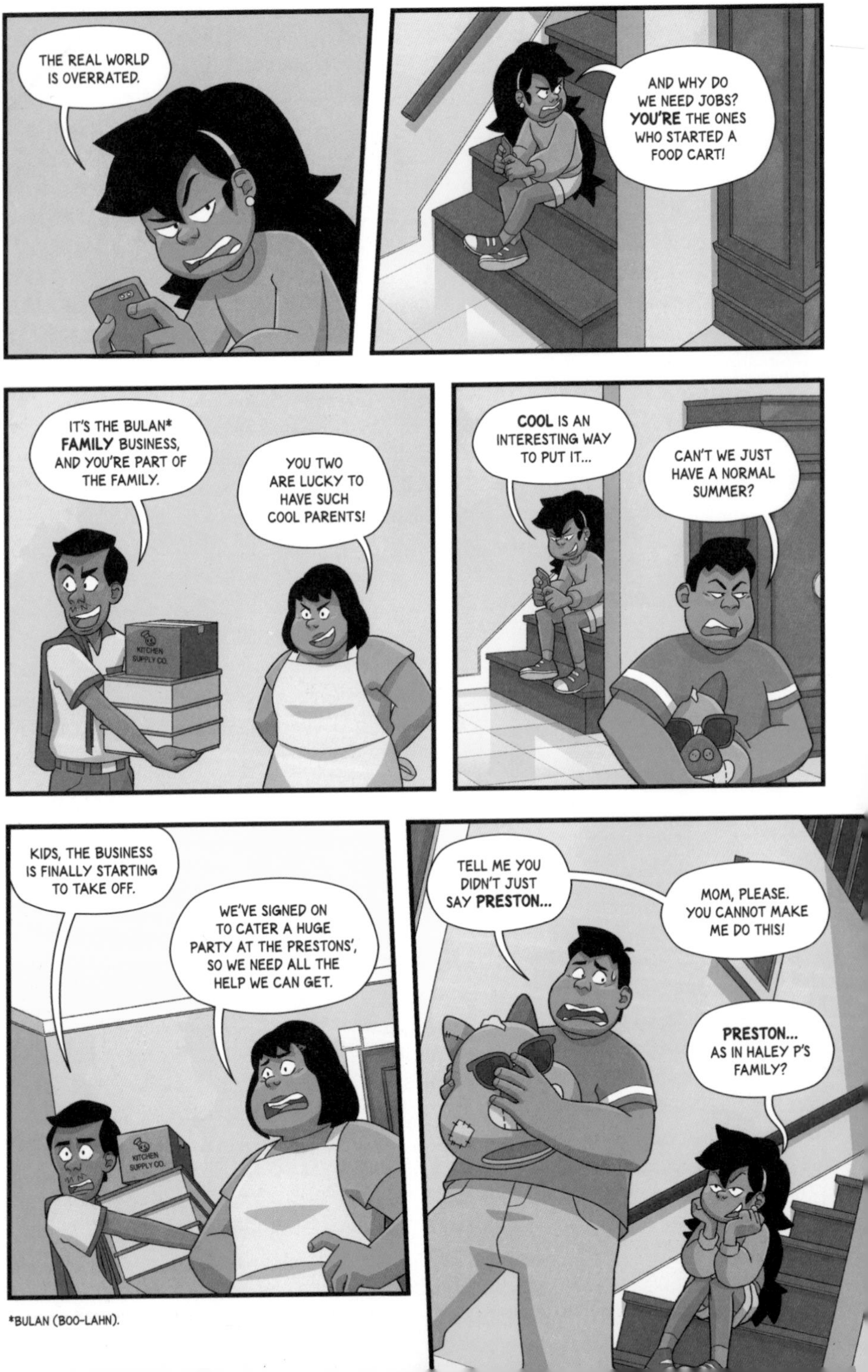

THE REAL WORLD IS OVERRATED.
AND WHY DO WE NEED JOBS? **YOU'RE** THE ONES WHO STARTED A FOOD CART!
IT'S THE BULAN* **FAMILY** BUSINESS, AND YOU'RE PART OF THE FAMILY.
YOU TWO ARE LUCKY TO HAVE SUCH COOL PARENTS!
KITCHEN SUPPLY CO.
COOL IS AN INTERESTING WAY TO PUT IT...
CAN'T WE JUST HAVE A NORMAL SUMMER?
KIDS, THE BUSINESS IS FINALLY STARTING TO TAKE OFF.
WE'VE SIGNED ON TO CATER A HUGE PARTY AT THE PRESTONS', SO WE NEED ALL THE HELP WE CAN GET.
KITCHEN SUPPLY CO.
TELL ME YOU DIDN'T JUST SAY **PRESTON...**
MOM, PLEASE. YOU CANNOT MAKE ME DO THIS!
PRESTON... AS IN HALEY P'S FAMILY?

*BULAN (BOO-LAHN).

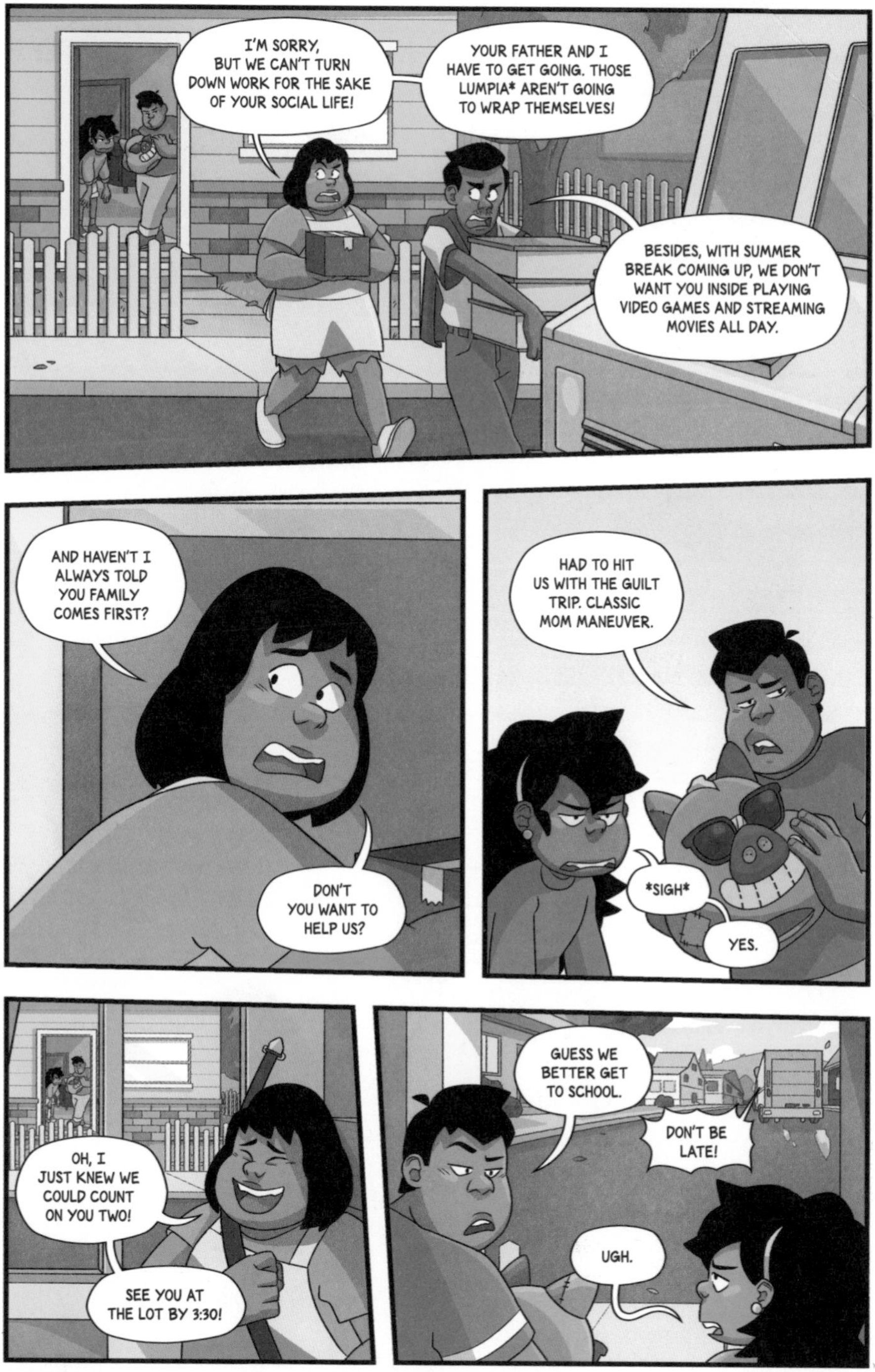
I'M SORRY, BUT WE CAN'T TURN DOWN WORK FOR THE SAKE OF YOUR SOCIAL LIFE!
YOUR FATHER AND I HAVE TO GET GOING. THOSE LUMPIA* AREN'T GOING TO WRAP THEMSELVES!
BESIDES, WITH SUMMER BREAK COMING UP, WE DON'T WANT YOU INSIDE PLAYING VIDEO GAMES AND STREAMING MOVIES ALL DAY.
AND HAVEN'T I ALWAYS TOLD YOU FAMILY COMES FIRST?
DON'T YOU WANT TO HELP US?
HAD TO HIT US WITH THE GUILT TRIP. CLASSIC MOM MANEUVER.
SIGH
YES.
OH, I JUST KNEW WE COULD COUNT ON YOU TWO!
SEE YOU AT THE LOT BY 3:30!
GUESS WE BETTER GET TO SCHOOL.
DON'T BE LATE!
UGH.

*LUMPIA (LOOM-PEEYAH): CRISPY FRIED SPRING ROLLS, OFTEN FILLED WITH GROUND MEAT, VEGETABLES, AND AROMATICS, AND THEN DIPPED IN A SWEET CHILI SAUCE.

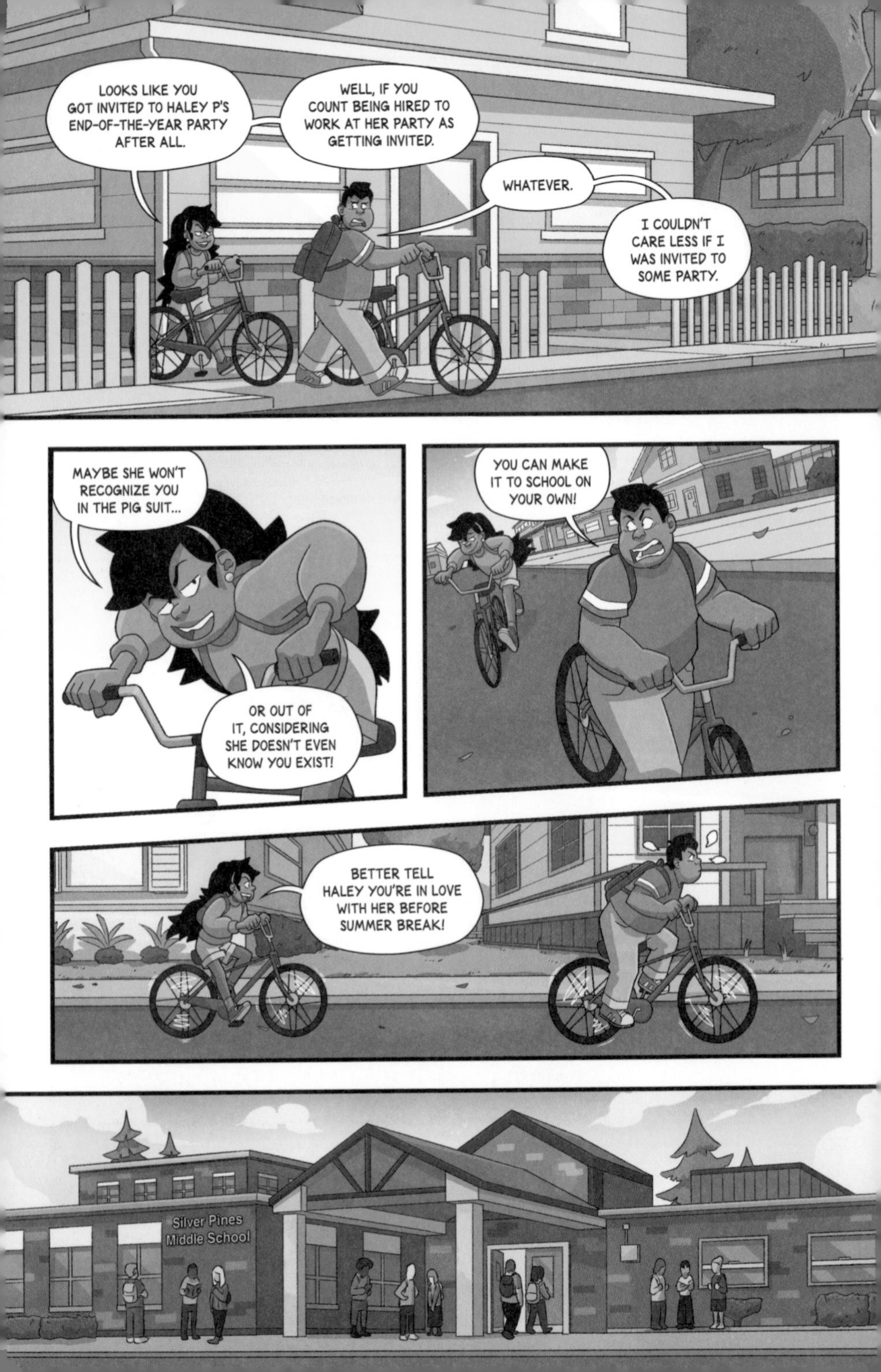
LOOKS LIKE YOU GOT INVITED TO HALEY P'S END-OF-THE-YEAR PARTY AFTER ALL.
WELL, IF YOU COUNT BEING HIRED TO WORK AT HER PARTY AS GETTING INVITED.
WHATEVER.
I COULDN'T CARE LESS IF I WAS INVITED TO SOME PARTY.
MAYBE SHE WON'T RECOGNIZE YOU IN THE PIG SUIT...
OR OUT OF IT, CONSIDERING SHE DOESN'T EVEN KNOW YOU EXIST!
YOU CAN MAKE IT TO SCHOOL ON YOUR OWN!
BETTER TELL HALEY YOU'RE IN LOVE WITH HER BEFORE SUMMER BREAK!
Silver Pines Middle School

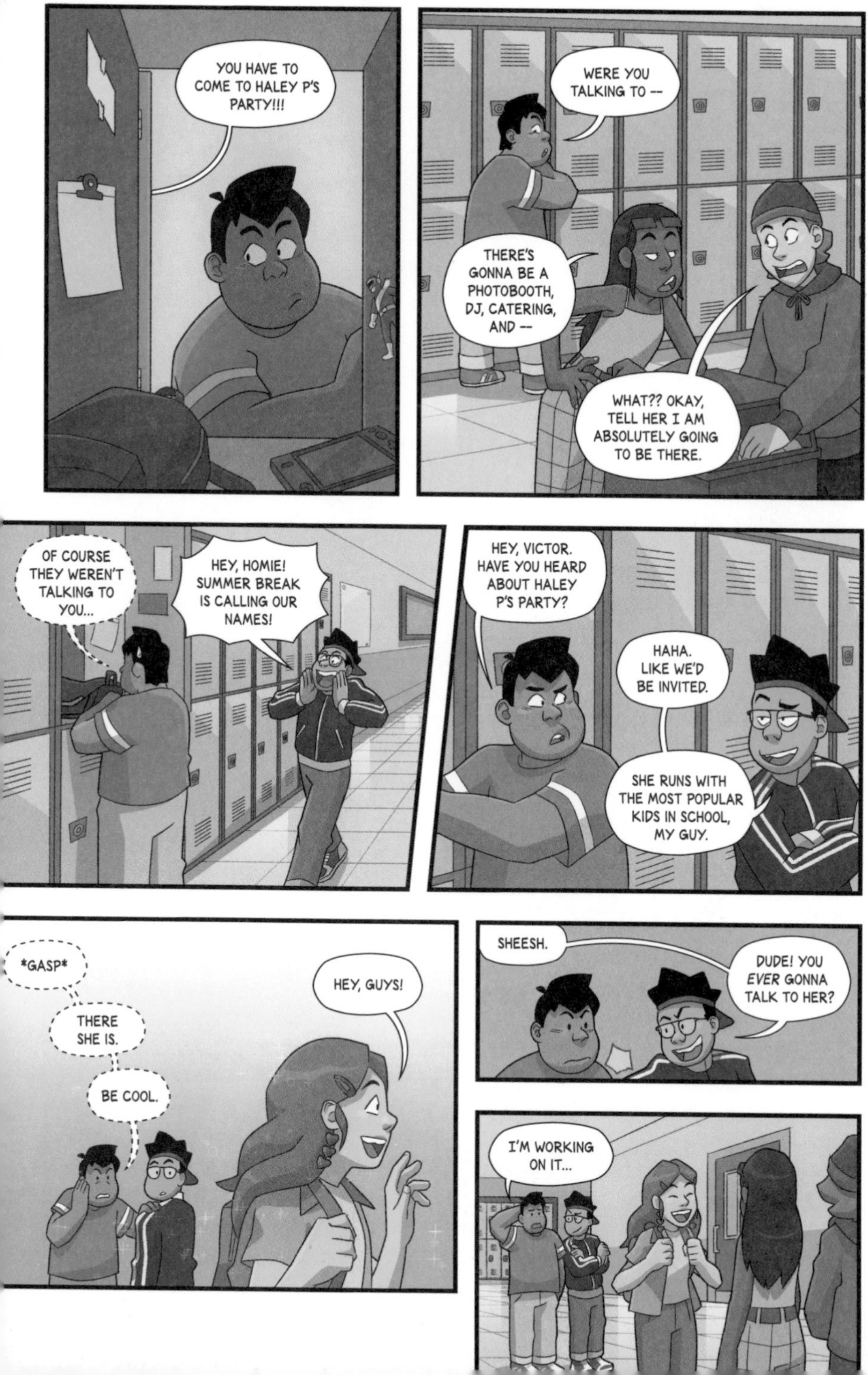
YOU HAVE TO COME TO HALEY P'S PARTY!!!
WERE YOU TALKING TO --
THERE'S GONNA BE A PHOTOBOOTH, DJ, CATERING, AND --
WHAT?? OKAY, TELL HER I AM ABSOLUTELY GOING TO BE THERE.
OF COURSE THEY WEREN'T TALKING TO YOU...
HEY, HOMIE! SUMMER BREAK IS CALLING OUR NAMES!
HEY, VICTOR. HAVE YOU HEARD ABOUT HALEY P'S PARTY?
HAHA. LIKE WE'D BE INVITED.
SHE RUNS WITH THE MOST POPULAR KIDS IN SCHOOL, MY GUY.
GASP
THERE SHE IS.
BE COOL.
HEY, GUYS!
SHEESH.
DUDE! YOU *EVER* GONNA TALK TO HER?
I'M WORKING ON IT...

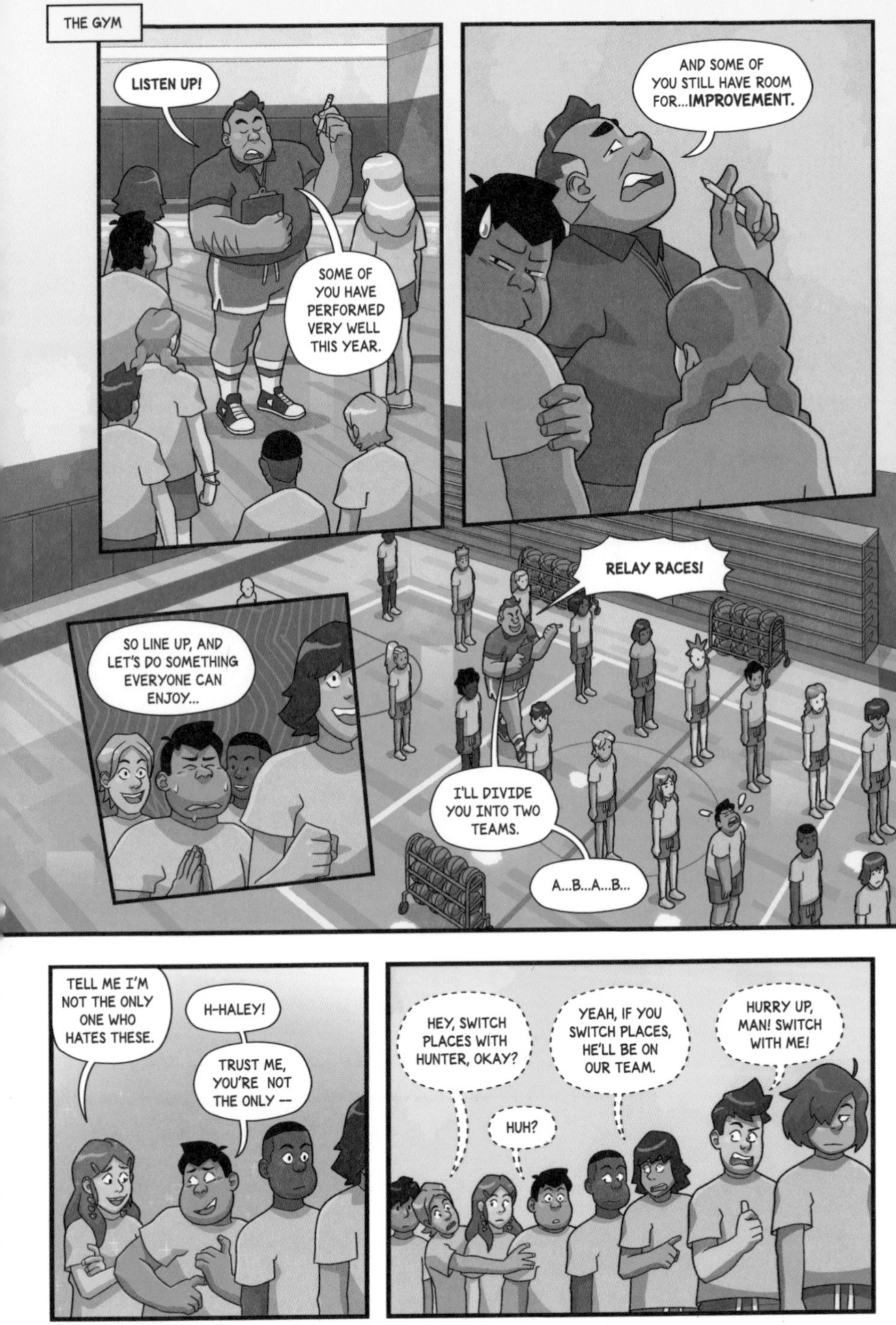
THE GYM
LISTEN UP!
SOME OF YOU HAVE PERFORMED VERY WELL THIS YEAR.
AND SOME OF YOU STILL HAVE ROOM FOR...IMPROVEMENT.
SO LINE UP, AND LET'S DO SOMETHING EVERYONE CAN ENJOY...
RELAY RACES!
I'LL DIVIDE YOU INTO TWO TEAMS.
A...B...A...B...
TELL ME I'M NOT THE ONLY ONE WHO HATES THESE.
H-HALEY!
TRUST ME, YOU'RE NOT THE ONLY --
HEY, SWITCH PLACES WITH HUNTER, OKAY?
HUH?
YEAH, IF YOU SWITCH PLACES, HE'LL BE ON OUR TEAM.
HURRY UP, MAN! SWITCH WITH ME!

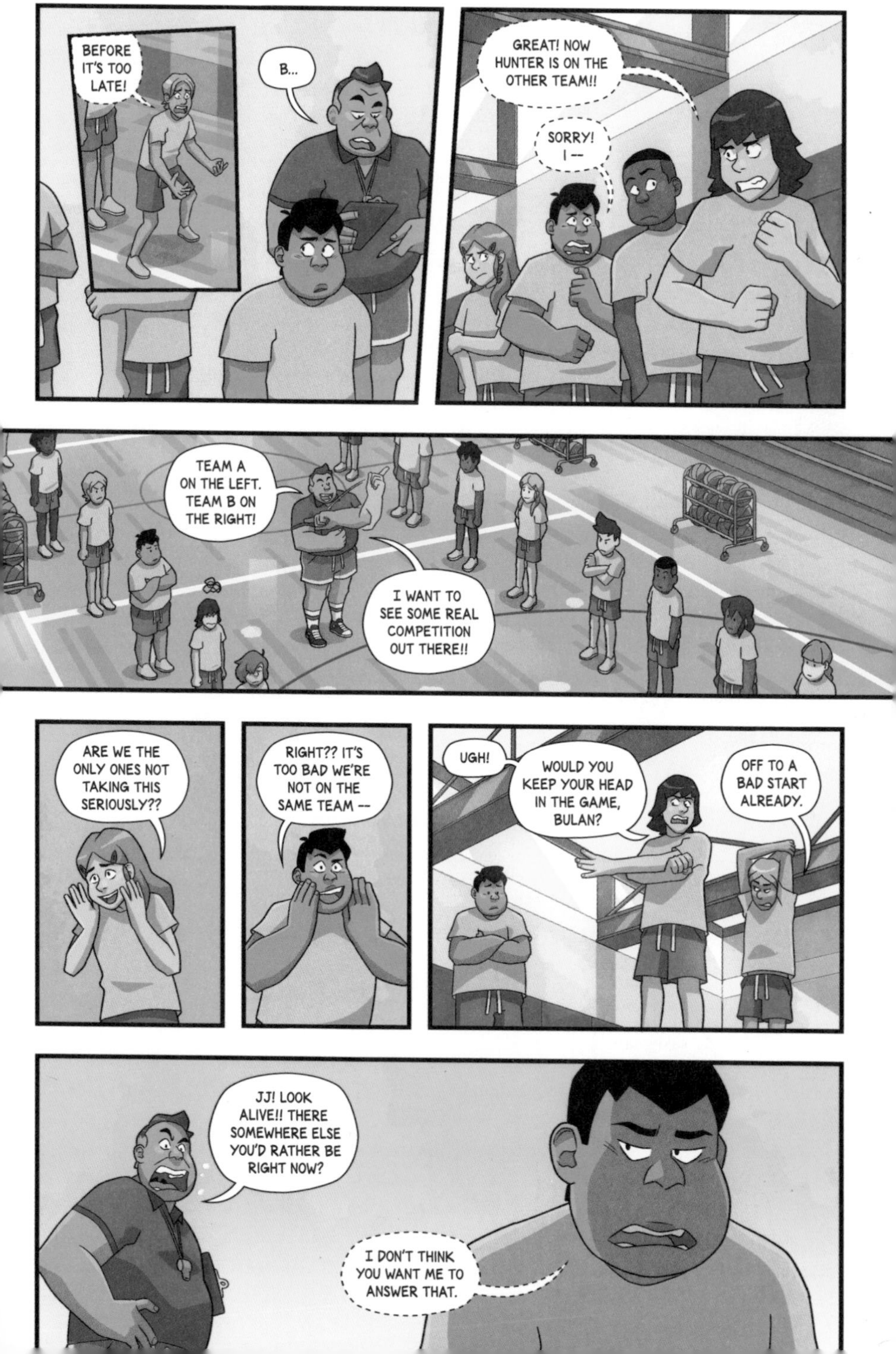
BEFORE IT'S TOO LATE!
B...
GREAT! NOW HUNTER IS ON THE OTHER TEAM!!
SORRY! I --
TEAM A ON THE LEFT. TEAM B ON THE RIGHT!
I WANT TO SEE SOME REAL COMPETITION OUT THERE!!
ARE WE THE ONLY ONES NOT TAKING THIS SERIOUSLY??
RIGHT?? IT'S TOO BAD WE'RE NOT ON THE SAME TEAM --
UGH!
WOULD YOU KEEP YOUR HEAD IN THE GAME, BULAN?
OFF TO A BAD START ALREADY.
JJ! LOOK ALIVE!! THERE SOMEWHERE ELSE YOU'D RATHER BE RIGHT NOW?
I DON'T THINK YOU WANT ME TO ANSWER THAT.

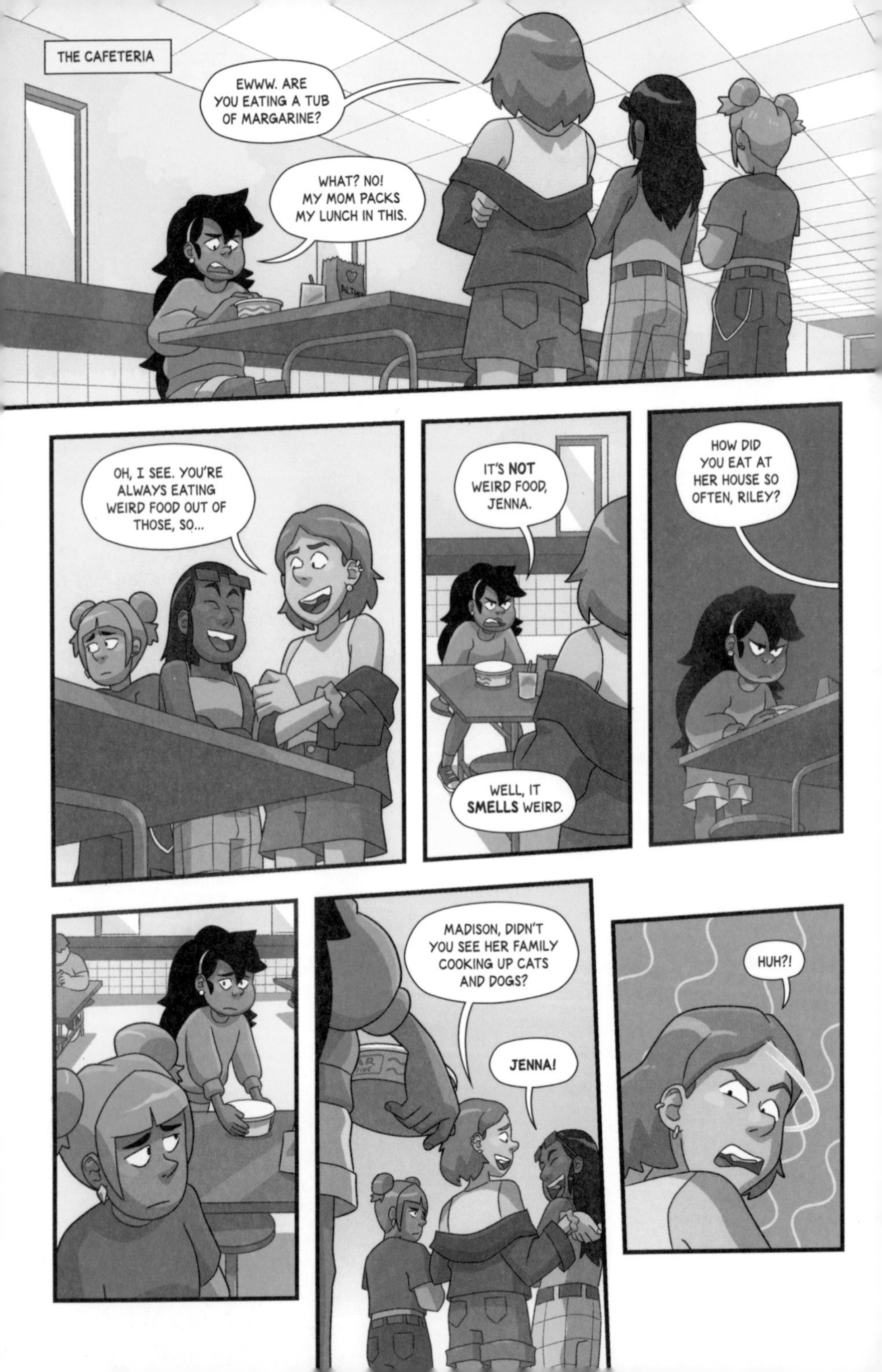
THE CAFETERIA
EWWW. ARE YOU EATING A TUB OF MARGARINE?
WHAT? NO! MY MOM PACKS MY LUNCH IN THIS.
OH, I SEE. YOU'RE ALWAYS EATING WEIRD FOOD OUT OF THOSE, SO...
IT'S NOT WEIRD FOOD, JENNA.
WELL, IT SMELLS WEIRD.
HOW DID YOU EAT AT HER HOUSE SO OFTEN, RILEY?
MADISON, DIDN'T YOU SEE HER FAMILY COOKING UP CATS AND DOGS?
JENNA!
HUH?!

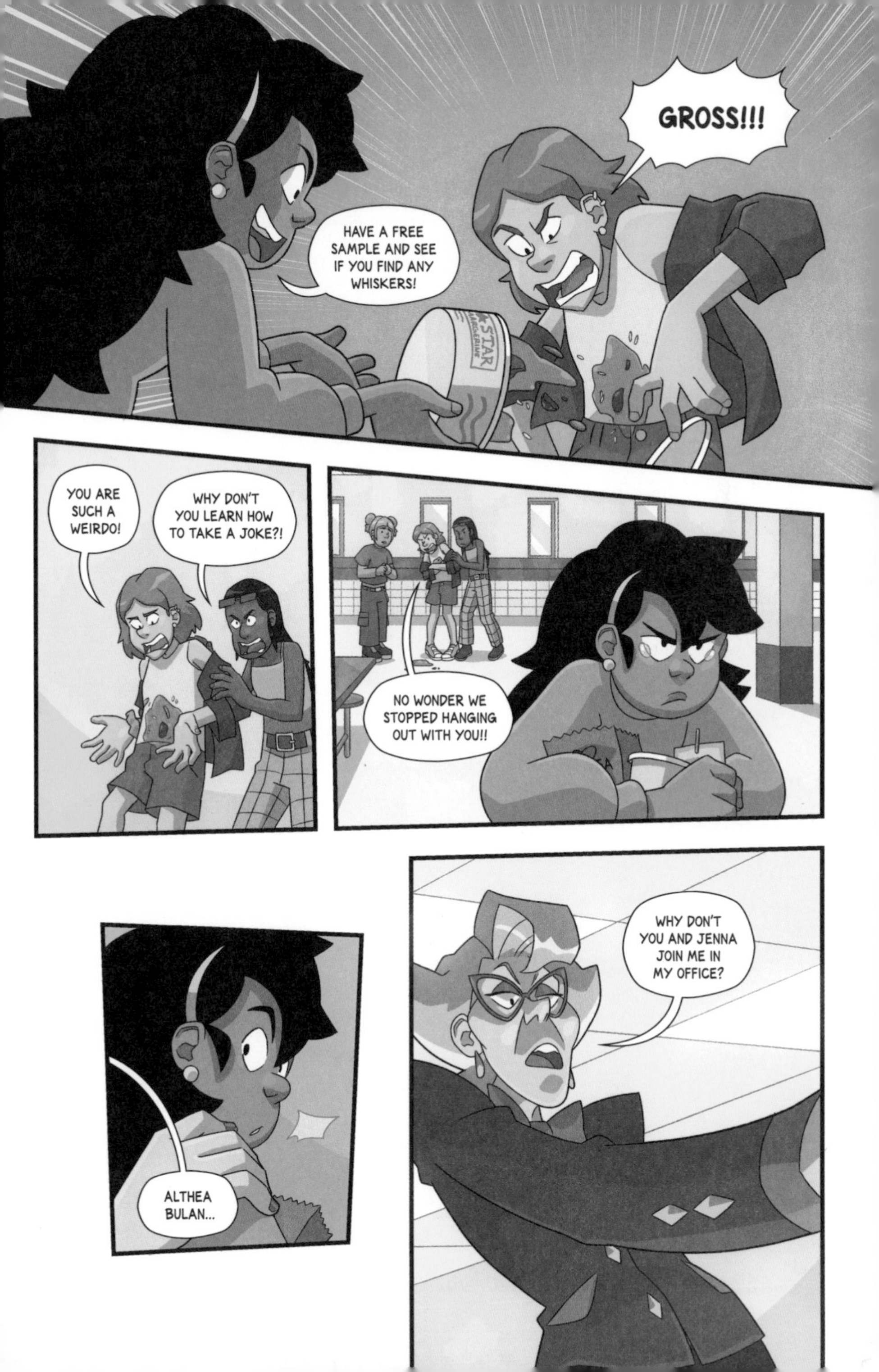
GROSS!!!
HAVE A FREE SAMPLE AND SEE IF YOU FIND ANY WHISKERS!
YOU ARE SUCH A WEIRDO!
WHY DON'T YOU LEARN HOW TO TAKE A JOKE?!
NO WONDER WE STOPPED HANGING OUT WITH YOU!!
WHY DON'T YOU AND JENNA JOIN ME IN MY OFFICE?
ALTHEA BULAN...

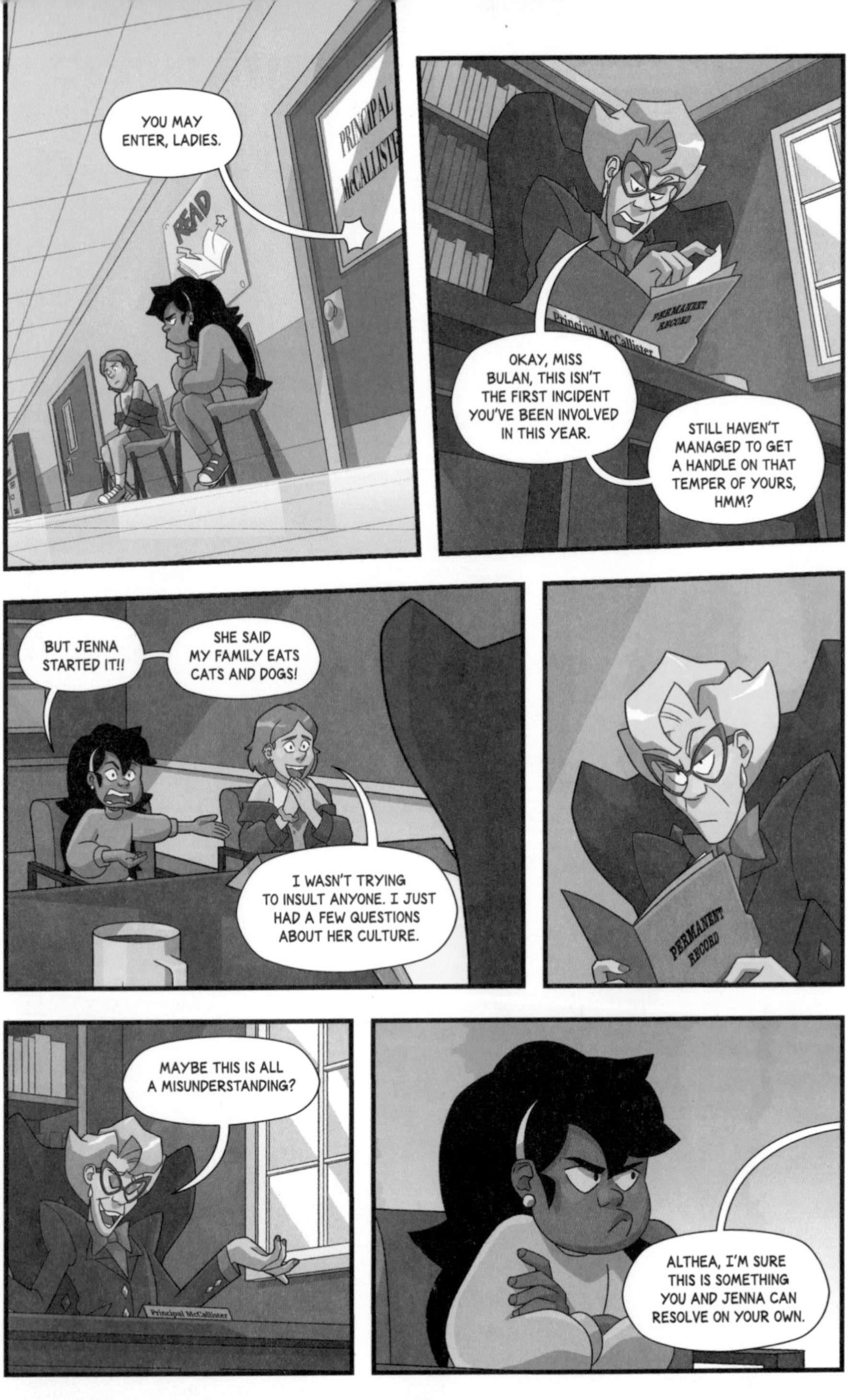
PRINCIPAL McCALLISTER
READ
YOU MAY ENTER, LADIES.
PERMANENT RECORD
Principal McCallister
OKAY, MISS BULAN, THIS ISN'T THE FIRST INCIDENT YOU'VE BEEN INVOLVED IN THIS YEAR.
STILL HAVEN'T MANAGED TO GET A HANDLE ON THAT TEMPER OF YOURS, HMM?
BUT JENNA STARTED IT!!
SHE SAID MY FAMILY EATS CATS AND DOGS!
I WASN'T TRYING TO INSULT ANYONE. I JUST HAD A FEW QUESTIONS ABOUT HER CULTURE.
PERMANENT RECORD
MAYBE THIS IS ALL A MISUNDERSTANDING?
Principal McCallister
ALTHEA, I'M SURE THIS IS SOMETHING YOU AND JENNA CAN RESOLVE ON YOUR OWN.

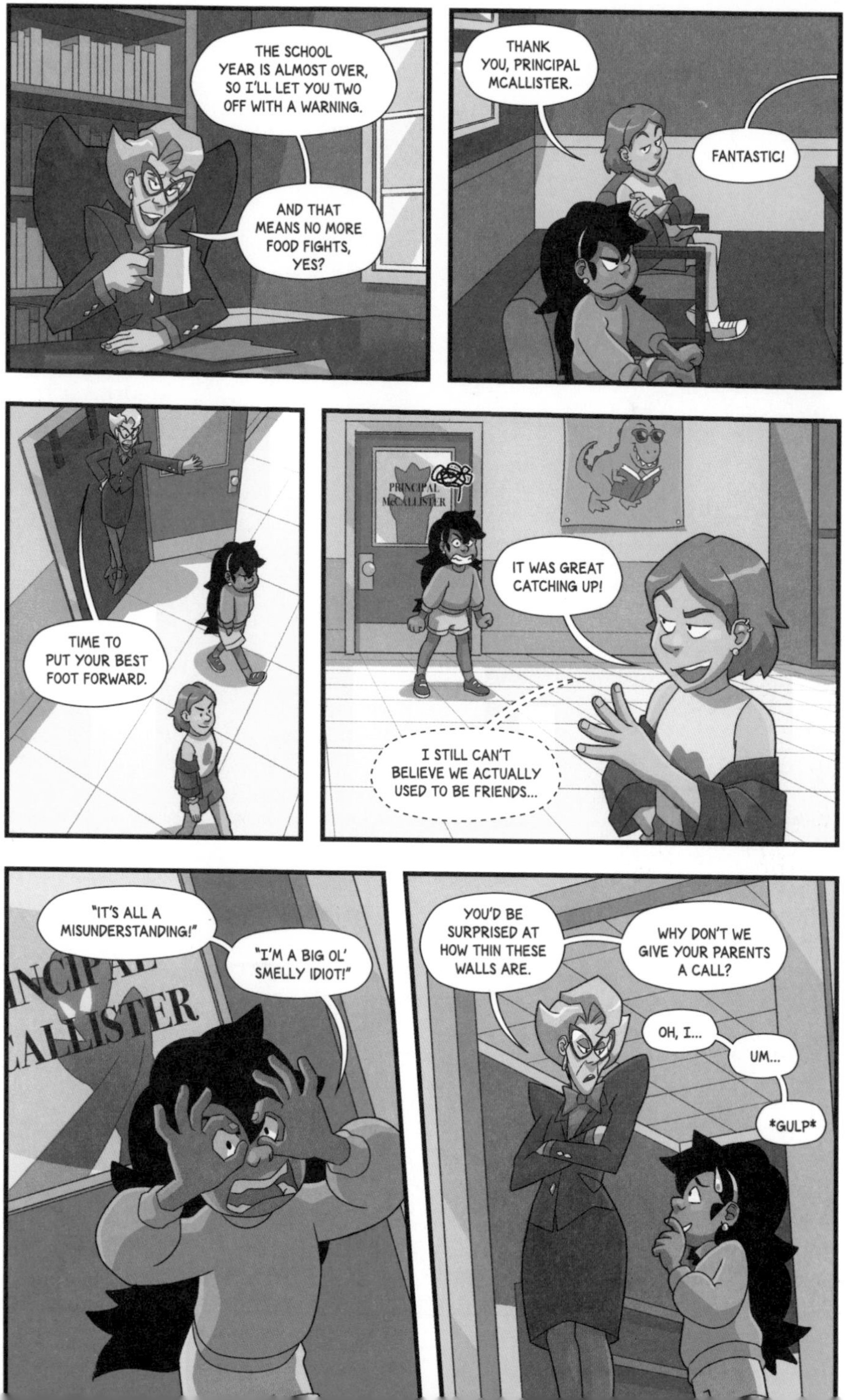
THE SCHOOL YEAR IS ALMOST OVER, SO I'LL LET YOU TWO OFF WITH A WARNING.
AND THAT MEANS NO MORE FOOD FIGHTS, YES?
THANK YOU, PRINCIPAL MCALLISTER.
FANTASTIC!
TIME TO PUT YOUR BEST FOOT FORWARD.
PRINCIPAL McCALLISTER
IT WAS GREAT CATCHING UP!
I STILL CAN'T BELIEVE WE ACTUALLY USED TO BE FRIENDS...
"IT'S ALL A MISUNDERSTANDING!"
"I'M A BIG OL' SMELLY IDIOT!"
YOU'D BE SURPRISED AT HOW THIN THESE WALLS ARE.
WHY DON'T WE GIVE YOUR PARENTS A CALL?
OH, I...
UM...
GULP

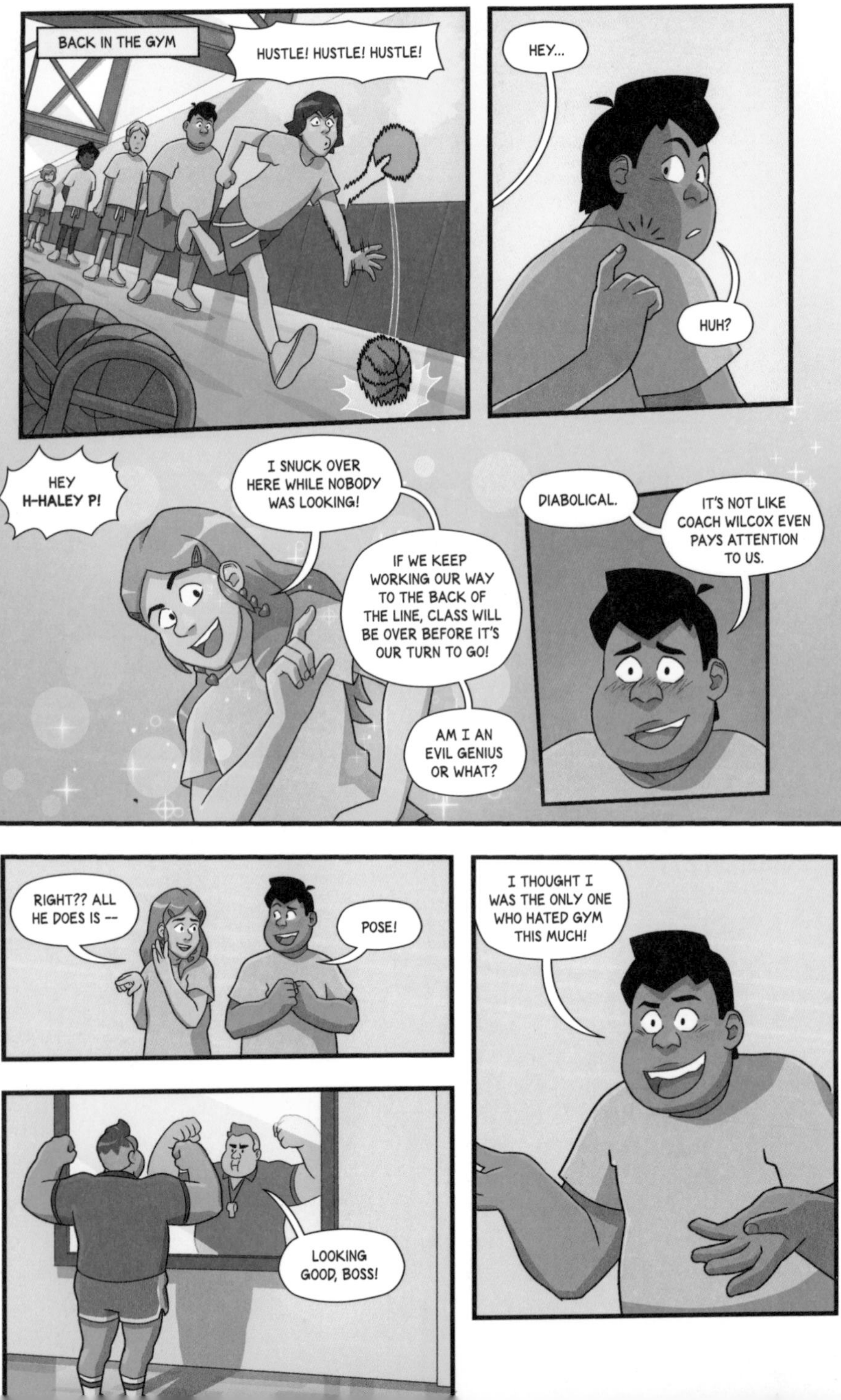
BACK IN THE GYM
HUSTLE! HUSTLE! HUSTLE!
HEY...
HUH?
HEY H-HALEY P!
I SNUCK OVER HERE WHILE NOBODY WAS LOOKING!
IF WE KEEP WORKING OUR WAY TO THE BACK OF THE LINE, CLASS WILL BE OVER BEFORE IT'S OUR TURN TO GO!
AM I AN EVIL GENIUS OR WHAT?
DIABOLICAL.
IT'S NOT LIKE COACH WILCOX EVEN PAYS ATTENTION TO US.
RIGHT?? ALL HE DOES IS --
POSE!
LOOKING GOOD, BOSS!
I THOUGHT I WAS THE ONLY ONE WHO HATED GYM THIS MUCH!

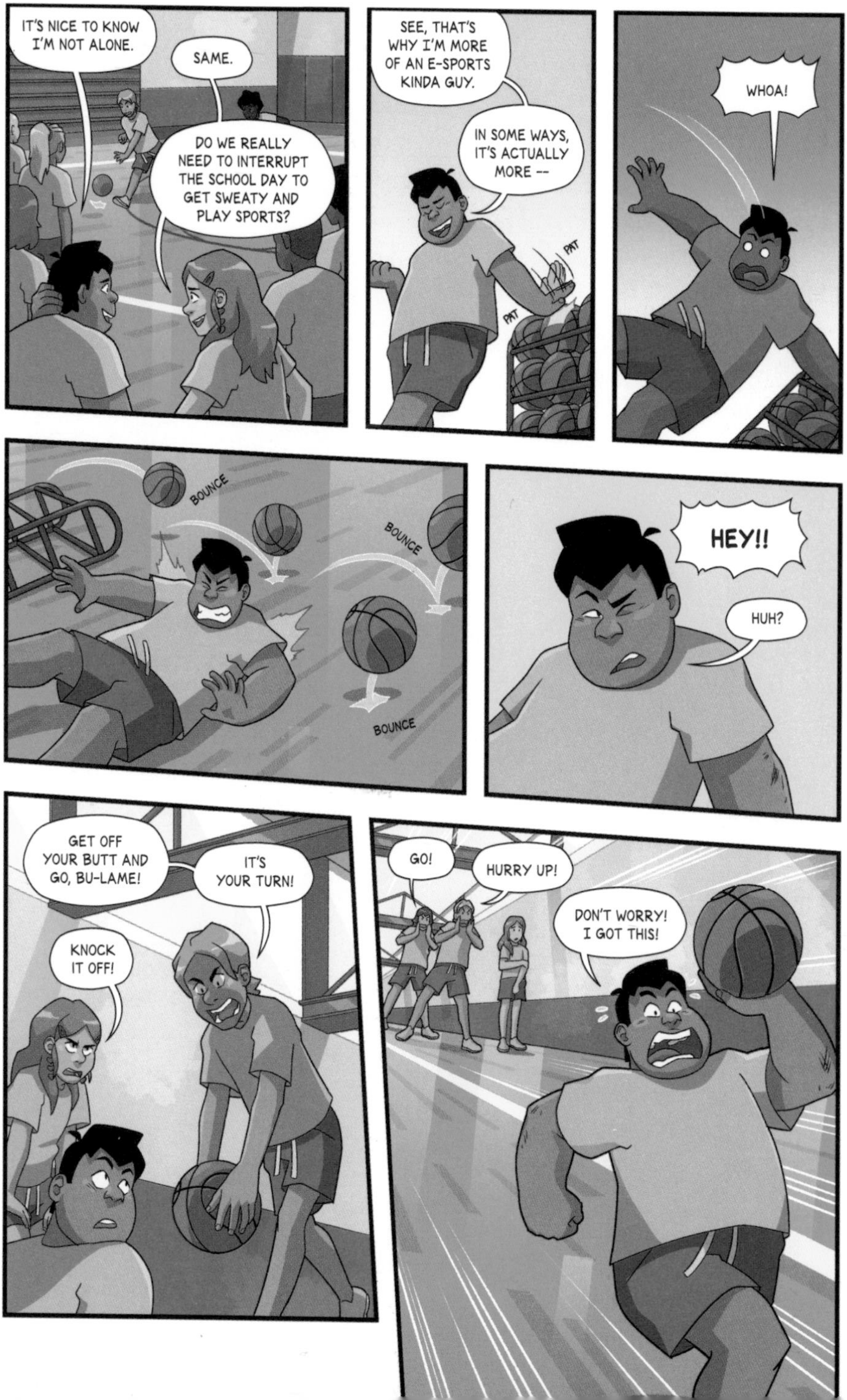
IT'S NICE TO KNOW I'M NOT ALONE.
SAME.
DO WE REALLY NEED TO INTERRUPT THE SCHOOL DAY TO GET SWEATY AND PLAY SPORTS?
SEE, THAT'S WHY I'M MORE OF AN E-SPORTS KINDA GUY.
IN SOME WAYS, IT'S ACTUALLY MORE --
PAT
PAT
PAT
WHOA!
BOUNCE
BOUNCE
BOUNCE
HEY!!
HUH?
GET OFF YOUR BUTT AND GO, BU-LAME!
IT'S YOUR TURN!
KNOCK IT OFF!
GO!
HURRY UP!
DON'T WORRY! I GOT THIS!

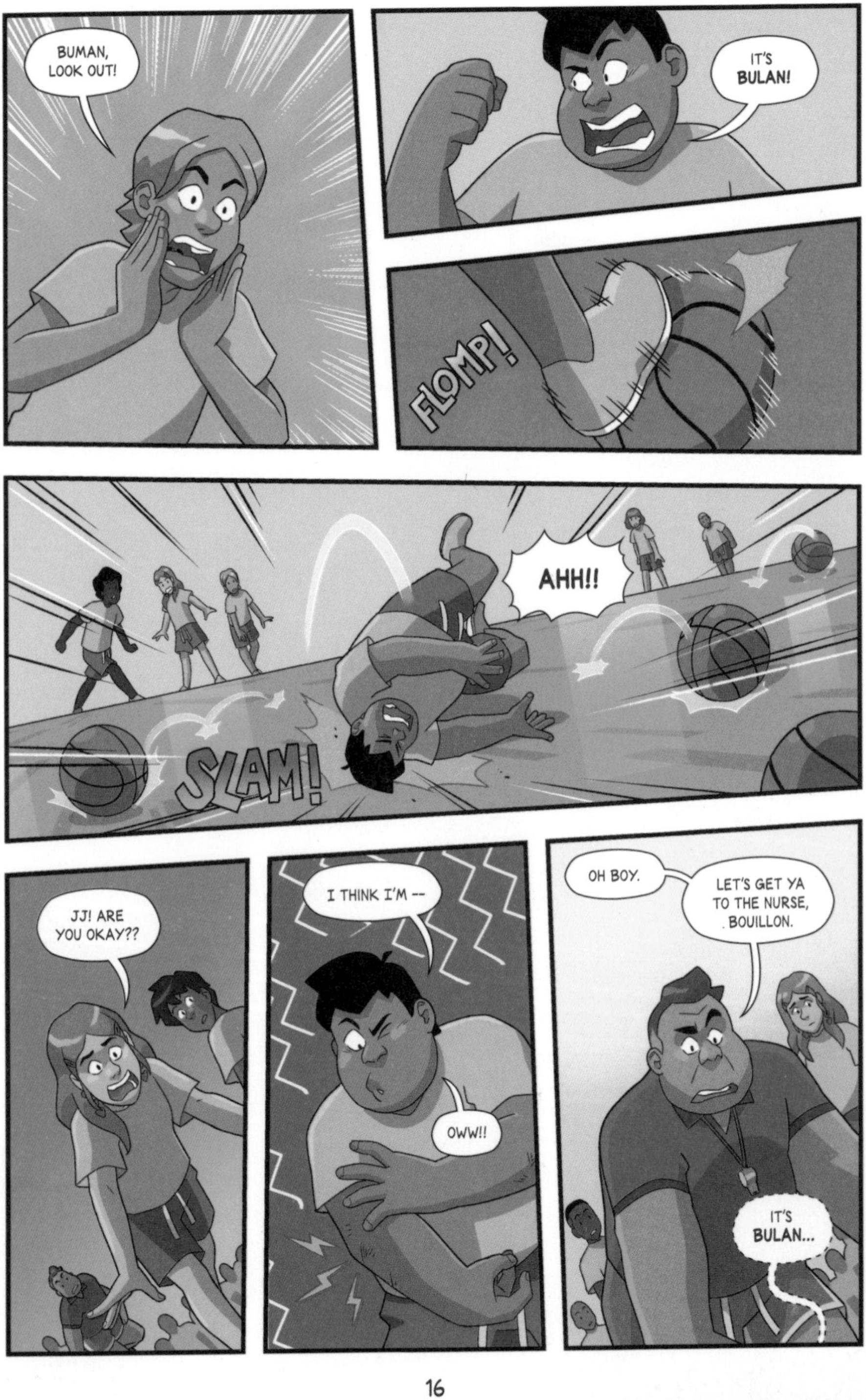
BUMAN, LOOK OUT!
IT'S BULAN!
FLOMP!
AHH!!
SLAM!
JJ! ARE YOU OKAY??
I THINK I'M --
OWW!!
OH BOY.
LET'S GET YA TO THE NURSE, BOUILLON.
IT'S BULAN...

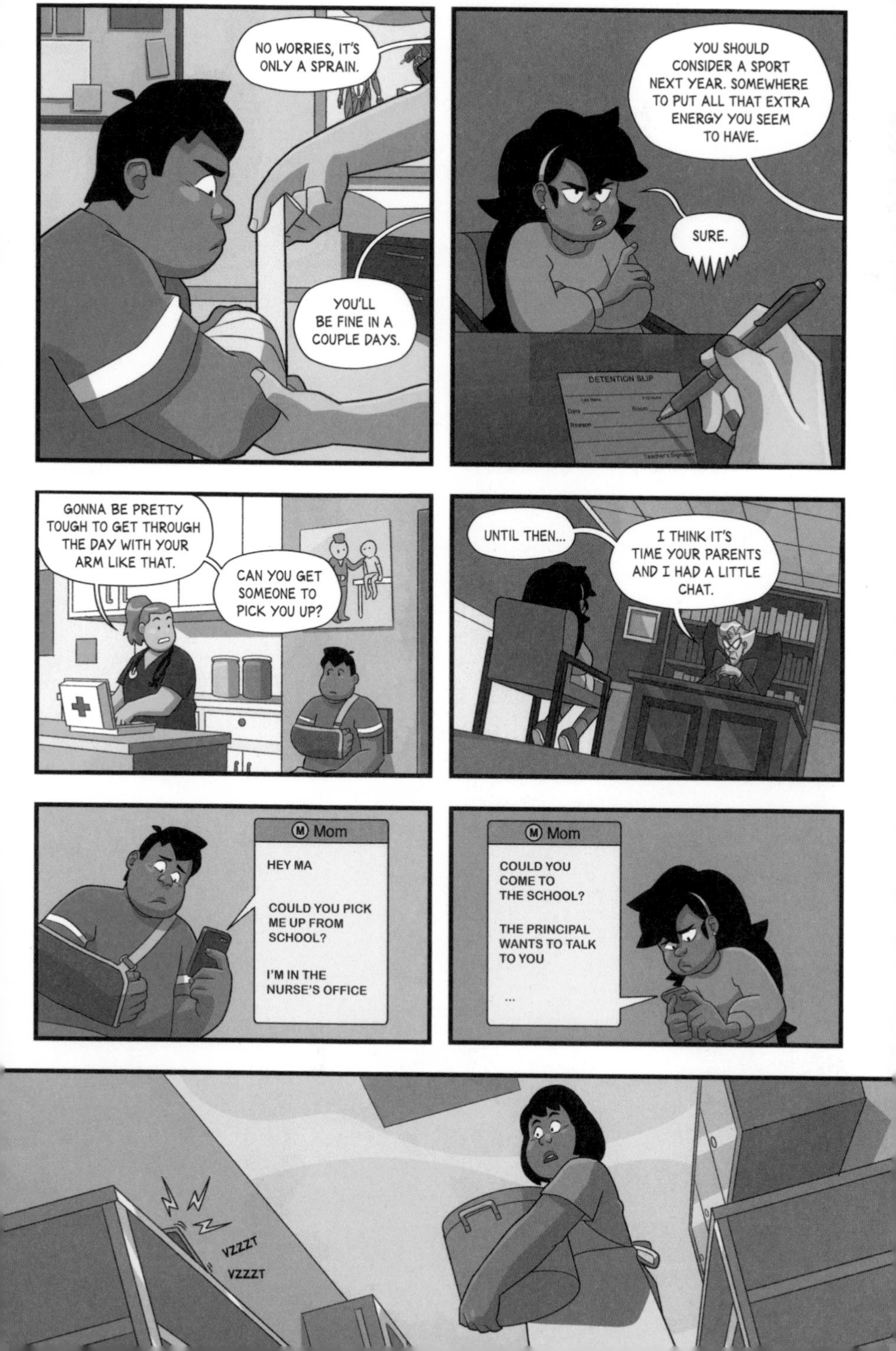
NO WORRIES, IT'S ONLY A SPRAIN.
YOU'LL BE FINE IN A COUPLE DAYS.
YOU SHOULD CONSIDER A SPORT NEXT YEAR. SOMEWHERE TO PUT ALL THAT EXTRA ENERGY YOU SEEM TO HAVE.
SURE.
DETENTION SLIP
GONNA BE PRETTY TOUGH TO GET THROUGH THE DAY WITH YOUR ARM LIKE THAT.
CAN YOU GET SOMEONE TO PICK YOU UP?
UNTIL THEN...
I THINK IT'S TIME YOUR PARENTS AND I HAD A LITTLE CHAT.
M Mom
HEY MA
COULD YOU PICK ME UP FROM SCHOOL?
I'M IN THE NURSE'S OFFICE
M Mom
COULD YOU COME TO THE SCHOOL?
THE PRINCIPAL WANTS TO TALK TO YOU
...
VZZZT
VZZZT

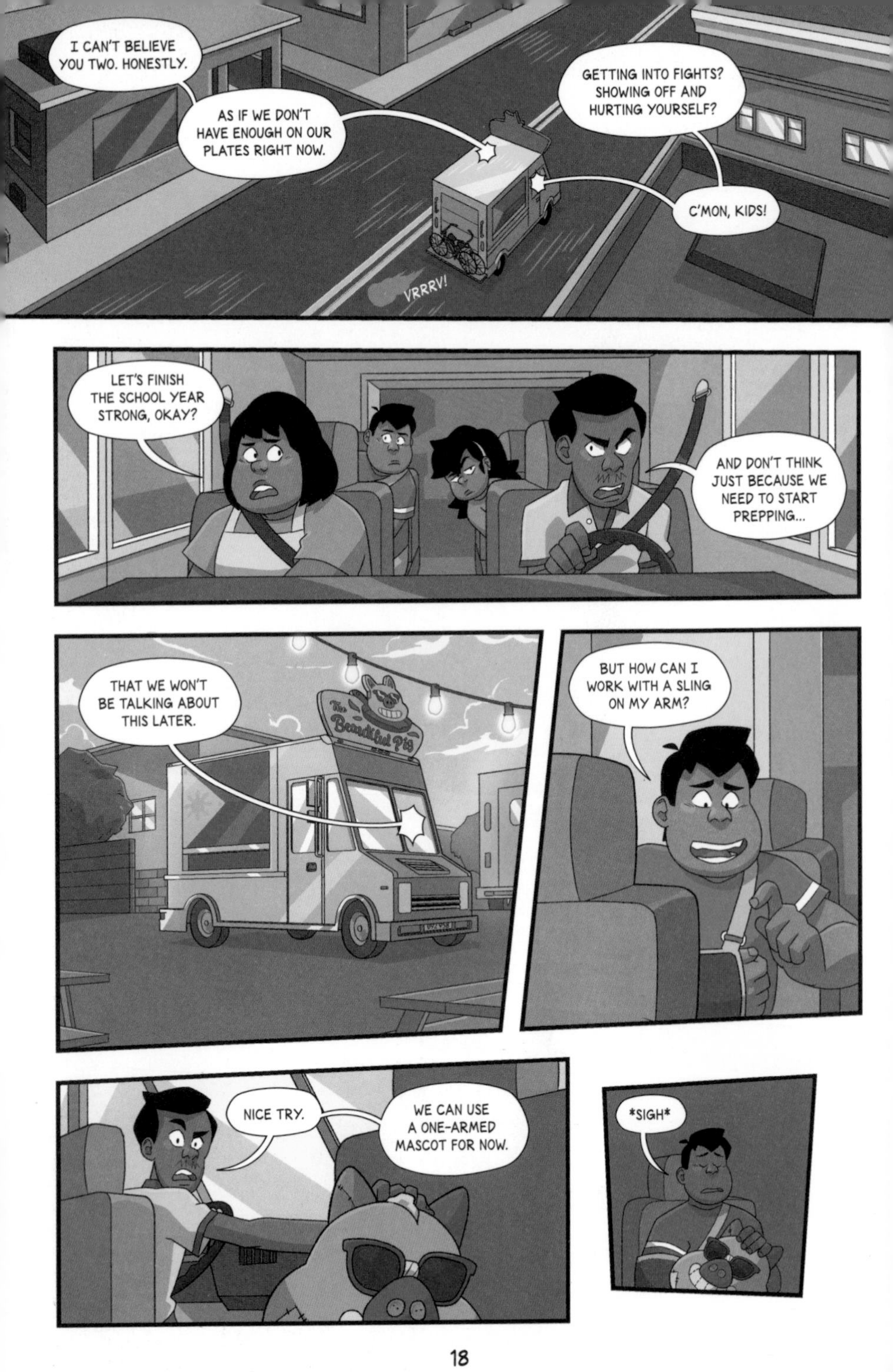
I CAN'T BELIEVE YOU TWO. HONESTLY.
AS IF WE DON'T HAVE ENOUGH ON OUR PLATES RIGHT NOW.
GETTING INTO FIGHTS? SHOWING OFF AND HURTING YOURSELF?
C'MON, KIDS!
VRRRV!
LET'S FINISH THE SCHOOL YEAR STRONG, OKAY?
AND DON'T THINK JUST BECAUSE WE NEED TO START PREPPING...
THAT WE WON'T BE TALKING ABOUT THIS LATER.
BUT HOW CAN I WORK WITH A SLING ON MY ARM?
NICE TRY.
WE CAN USE A ONE-ARMED MASCOT FOR NOW.
SIGH

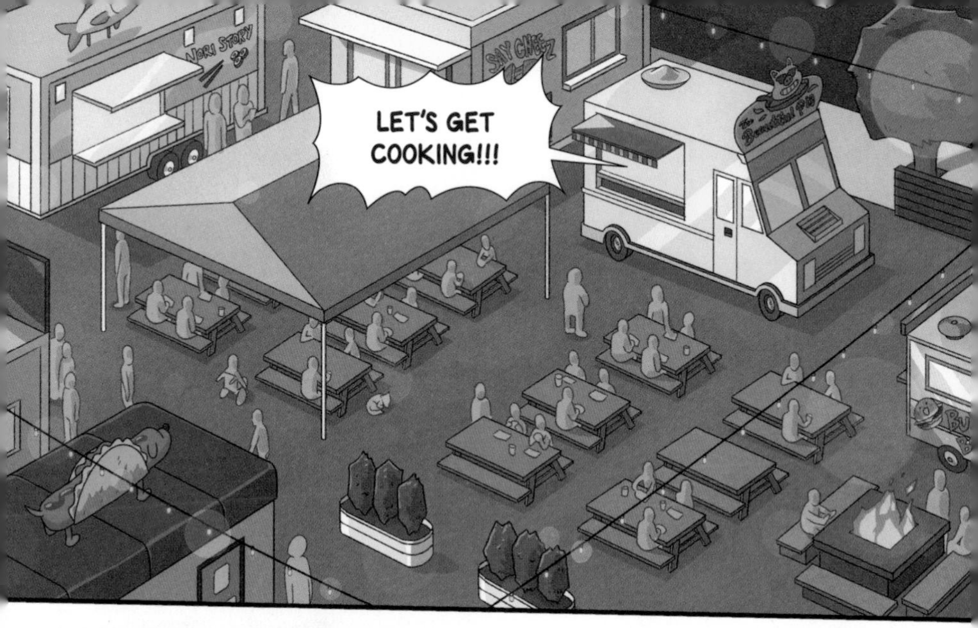
NORI STORY
SAY CHEEZ
LET'S GET COOKING!!!

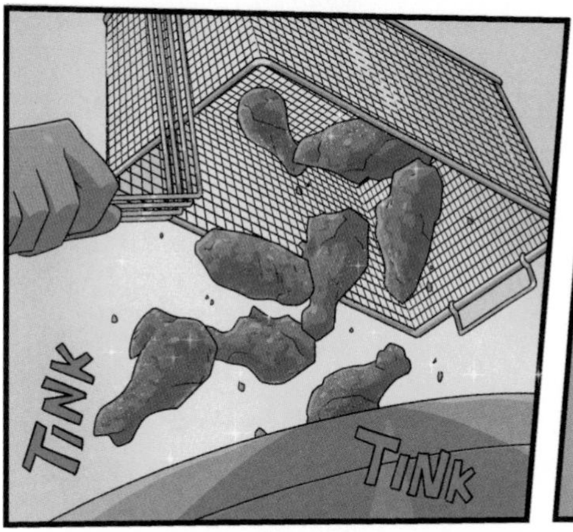
TINK
TINK

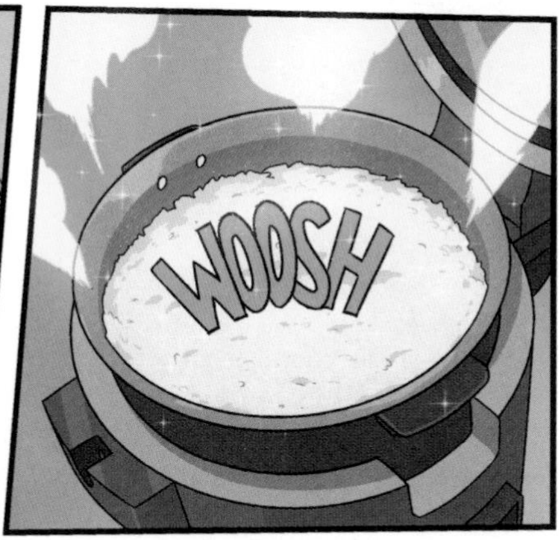
WOOSH

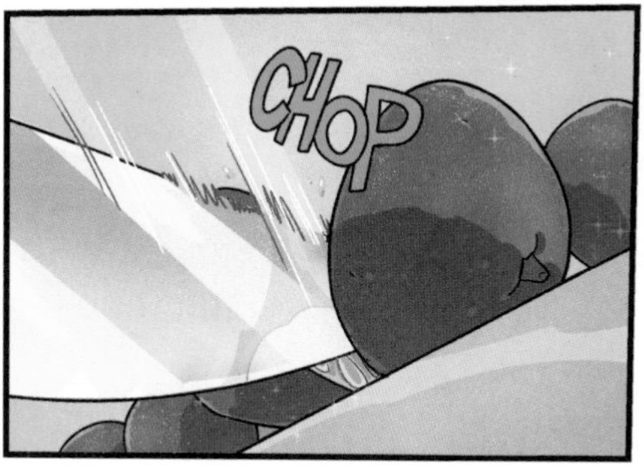
CHOP

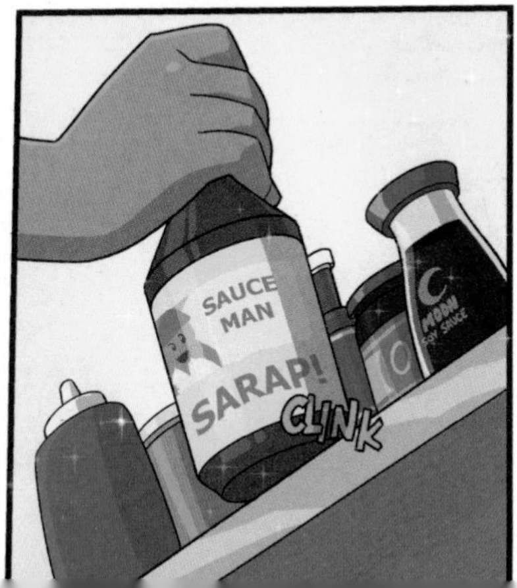
SAUCE MAN
SARAP!
CLINK

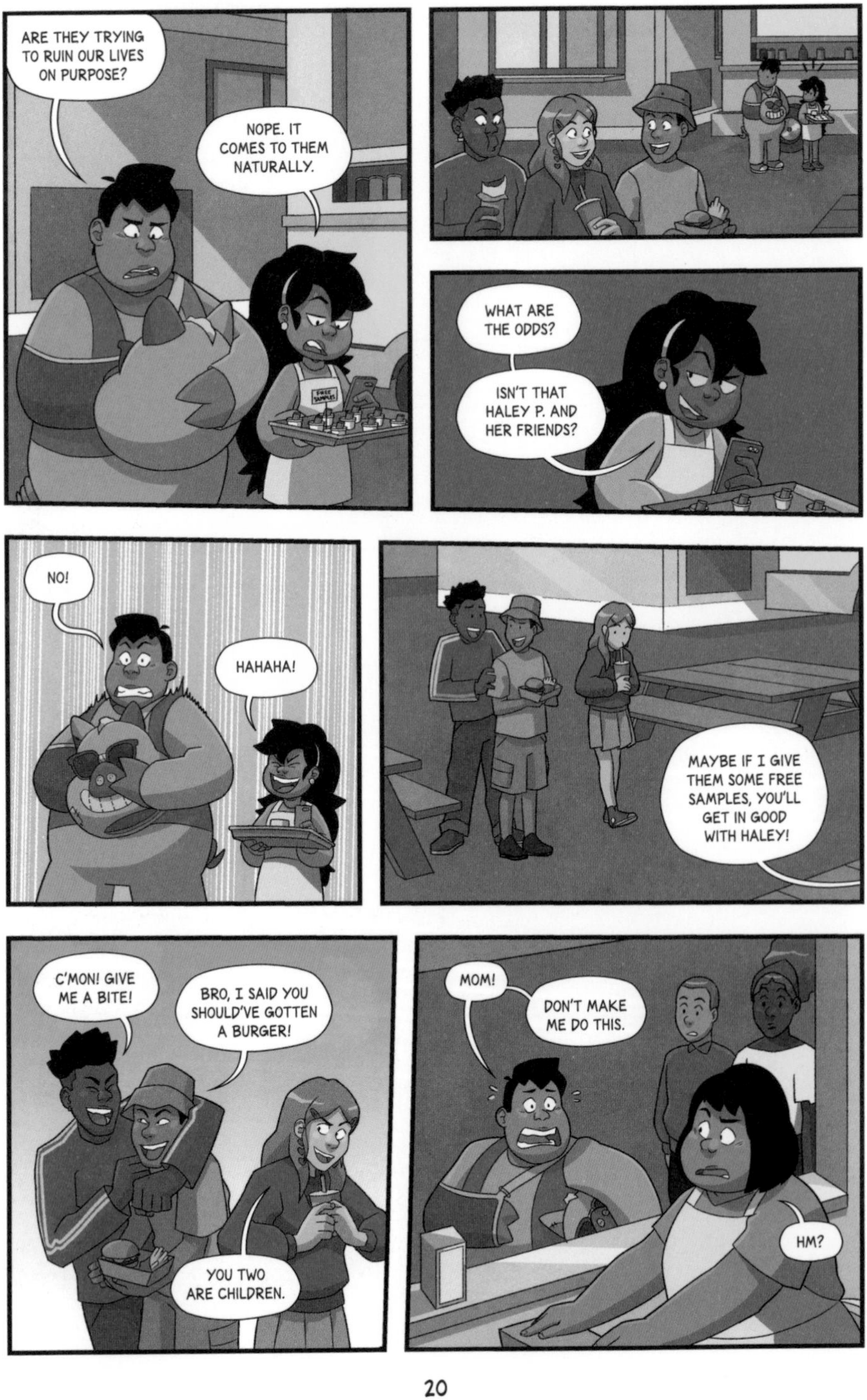
ARE THEY TRYING TO RUIN OUR LIVES ON PURPOSE?
NOPE. IT COMES TO THEM NATURALLY.
FREE SAMPLES
WHAT ARE THE ODDS?
ISN'T THAT HALEY P. AND HER FRIENDS?
NO!
HAHAHA!
MAYBE IF I GIVE THEM SOME FREE SAMPLES, YOU'LL GET IN GOOD WITH HALEY!
C'MON! GIVE ME A BITE!
BRO, I SAID YOU SHOULD'VE GOTTEN A BURGER!
YOU TWO ARE CHILDREN.
MOM!
DON'T MAKE ME DO THIS.
HM?

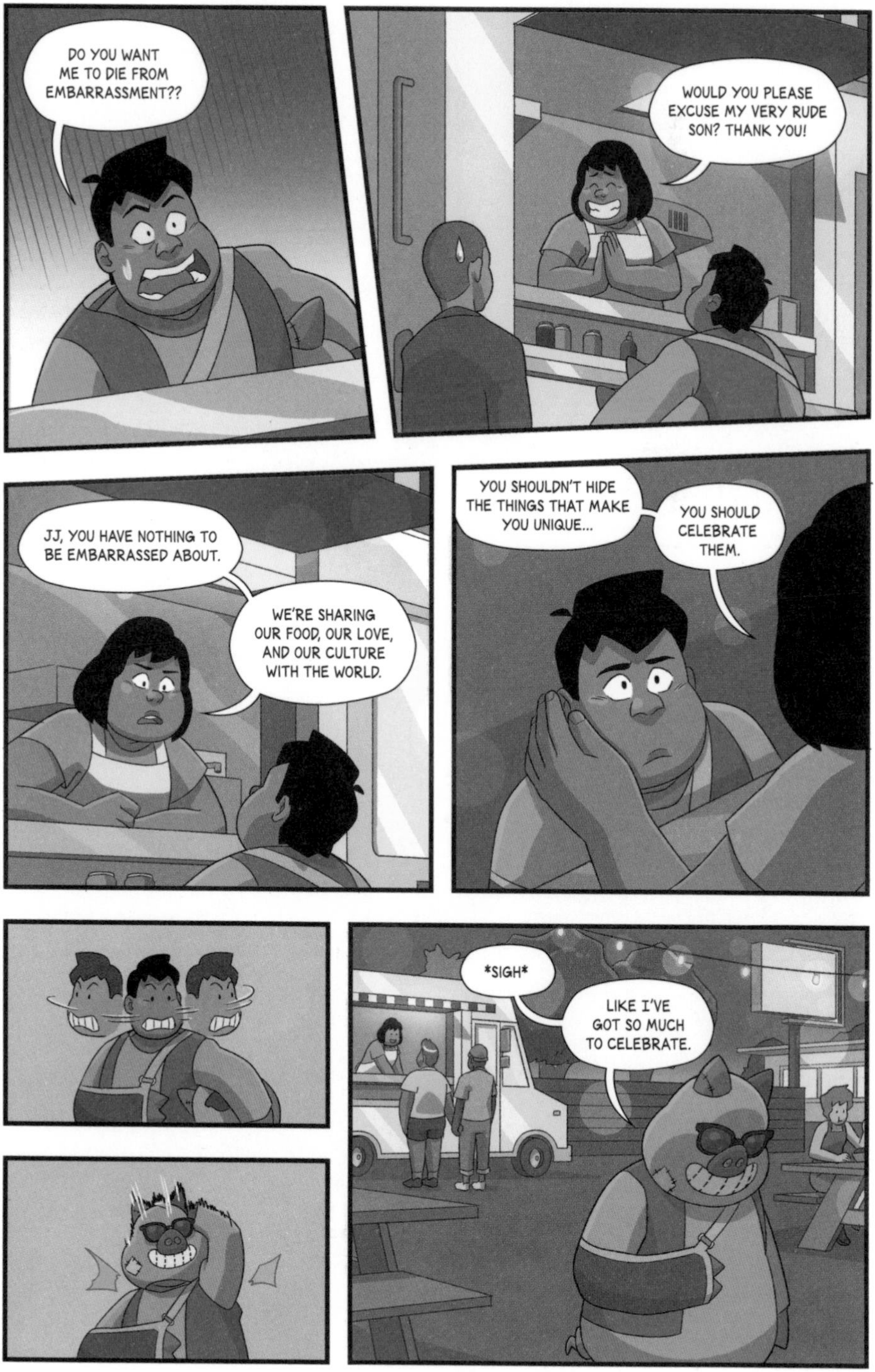
DO YOU WANT ME TO DIE FROM EMBARRASSMENT??
WOULD YOU PLEASE EXCUSE MY VERY RUDE SON? THANK YOU!
JJ, YOU HAVE NOTHING TO BE EMBARRASSED ABOUT.
WE'RE SHARING OUR FOOD, OUR LOVE, AND OUR CULTURE WITH THE WORLD.
YOU SHOULDN'T HIDE THE THINGS THAT MAKE YOU UNIQUE...
YOU SHOULD CELEBRATE THEM.
SIGH
LIKE I'VE GOT SO MUCH TO CELEBRATE.

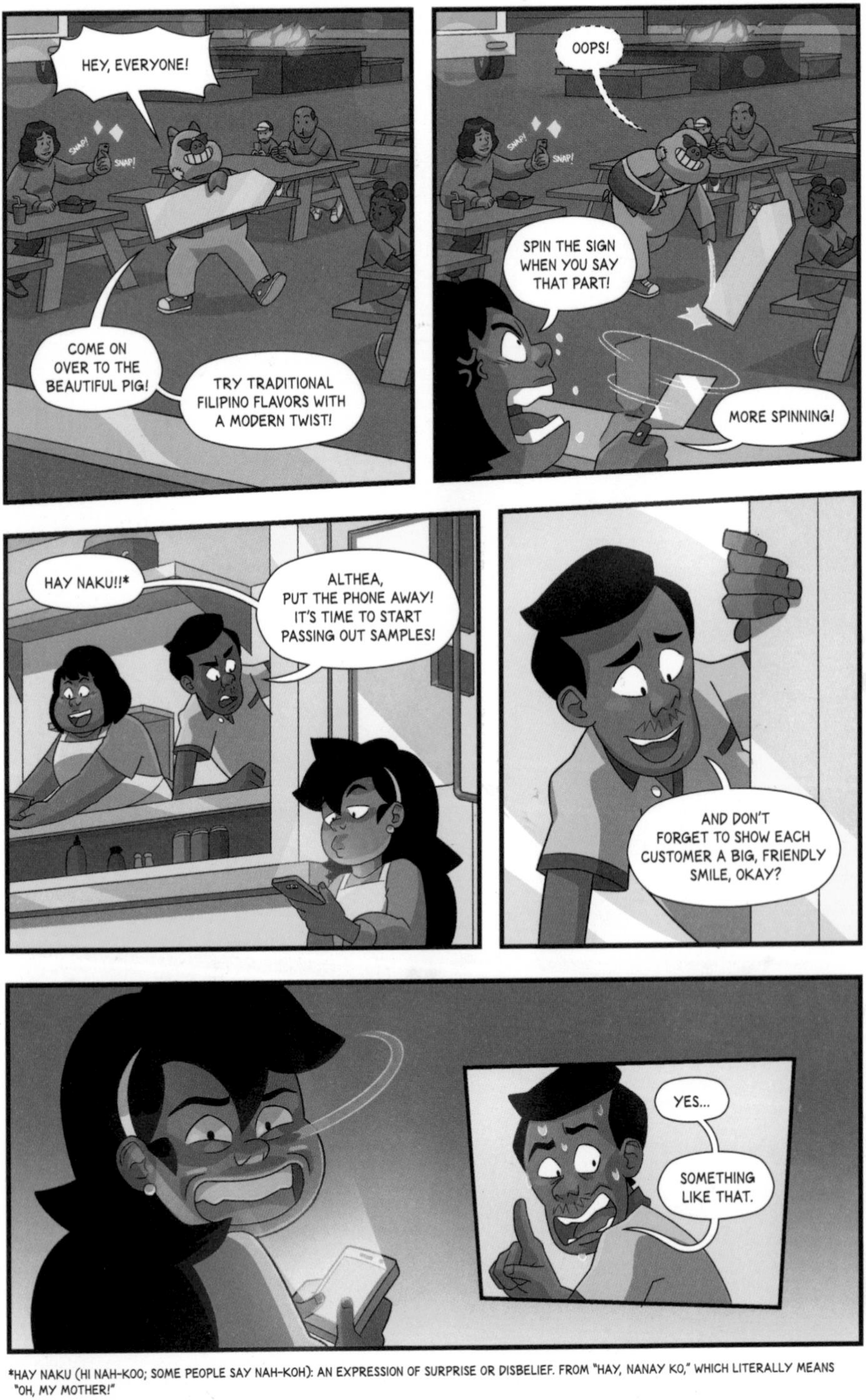
HEY, EVERYONE!
SNAP!
SNAP!
COME ON OVER TO THE BEAUTIFUL PIG!
TRY TRADITIONAL FILIPINO FLAVORS WITH A MODERN TWIST!
OOPS!
SNAP!
SNAP!
SPIN THE SIGN WHEN YOU SAY THAT PART!
MORE SPINNING!
HAY NAKU!!*
ALTHEA, PUT THE PHONE AWAY! IT'S TIME TO START PASSING OUT SAMPLES!
AND DON'T FORGET TO SHOW EACH CUSTOMER A BIG, FRIENDLY SMILE, OKAY?
YES...
SOMETHING LIKE THAT.

*HAY NAKU (HI NAH-KOO; SOME PEOPLE SAY NAH-KOH): AN EXPRESSION OF SURPRISE OR DISBELIEF. FROM "HAY, NANAY KO," WHICH LITERALLY MEANS "OH, MY MOTHER!"

WAIT A SECOND...

WHAT ARE YOU USING THAT OLD KNIFE FOR?

WHAT HAPPENED TO THE STATE-OF-THE-ART, ALL-IN-ONE MULTI-TOOL I MADE FOR YOU?

OH, THAT?

UM...

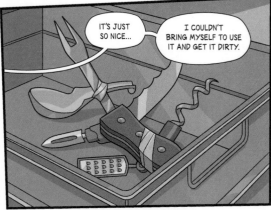

IT'S JUST SO NICE...

I COULDN'T BRING MYSELF TO USE IT AND GET IT DIRTY.

WHY IS MY GENIUS ALWAYS SO UNDERAPPRECIATED?

HUH? THAT'S WEIRD.

NO NAME ON THIS TICKET.

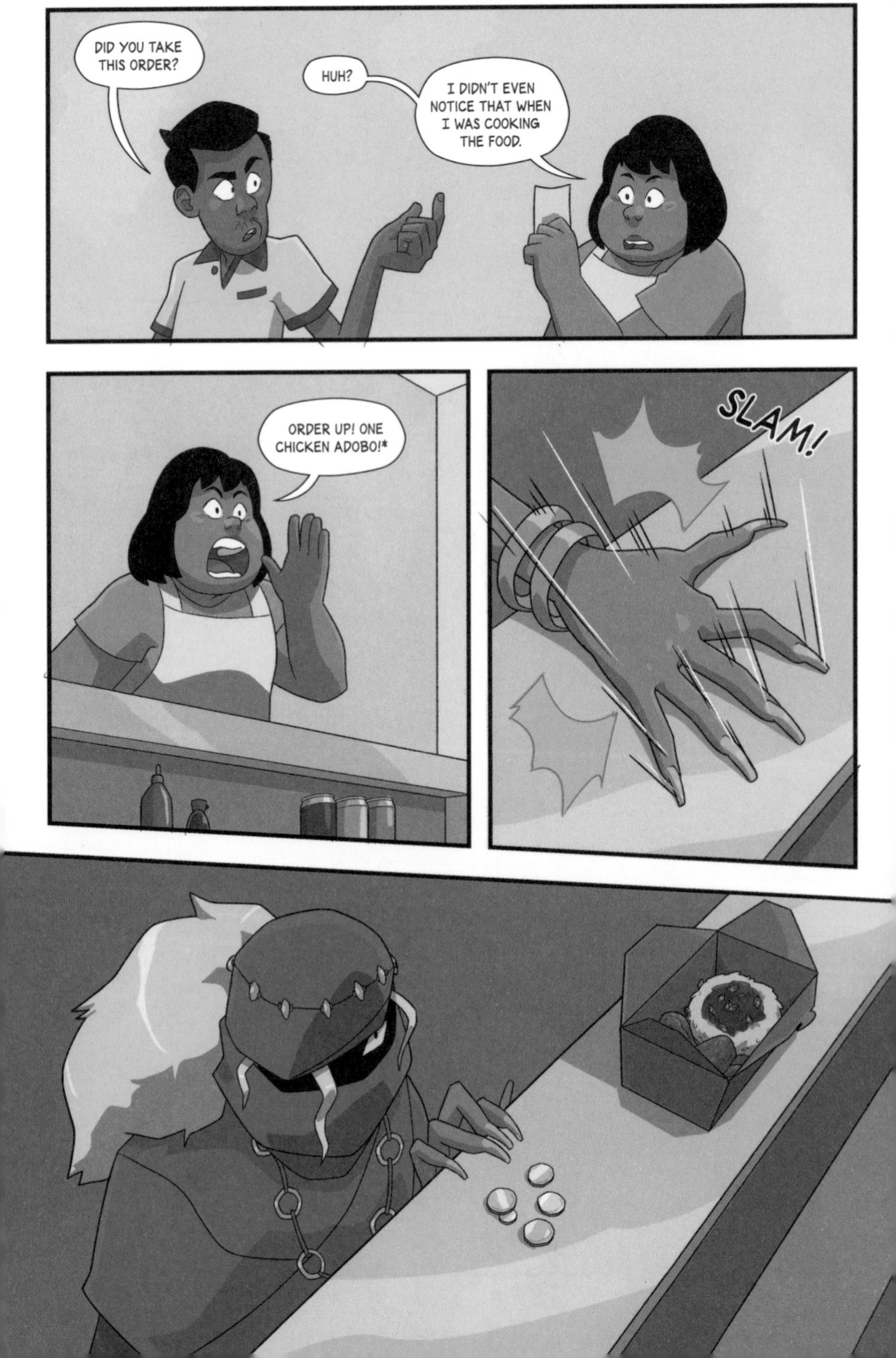
DID YOU TAKE THIS ORDER?
HUH?
I DIDN'T EVEN NOTICE THAT WHEN I WAS COOKING THE FOOD.
ORDER UP! ONE CHICKEN ADOBO!*
SLAM!

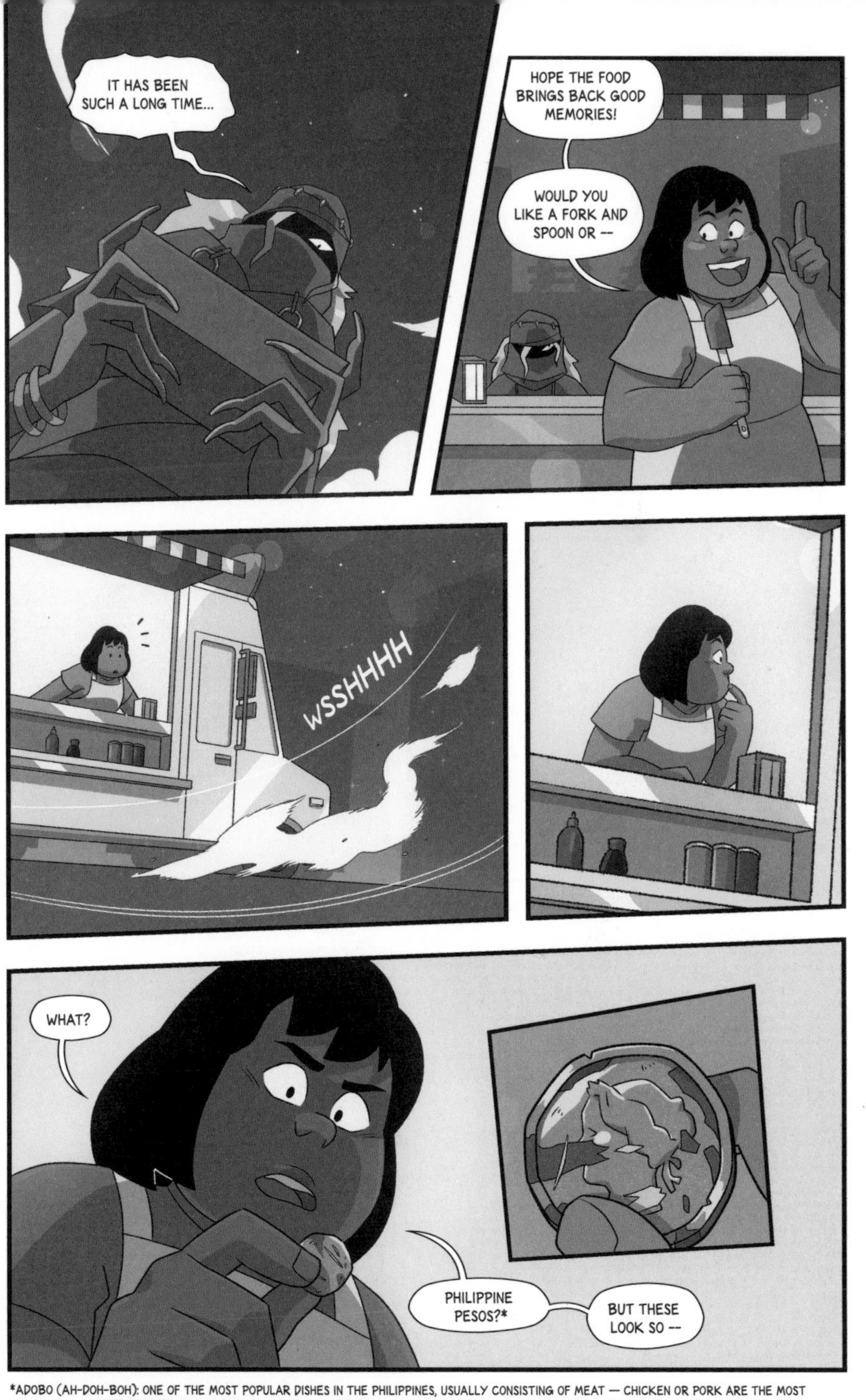
IT HAS BEEN SUCH A LONG TIME...
HOPE THE FOOD BRINGS BACK GOOD MEMORIES!
WOULD YOU LIKE A FORK AND SPOON OR --
WSSHHHH
WHAT?
PHILIPPINE PESOS?*
BUT THESE LOOK SO --

*ADOBO (AH-DOH-BOH): ONE OF THE MOST POPULAR DISHES IN THE PHILIPPINES, USUALLY CONSISTING OF MEAT — CHICKEN OR PORK ARE THE MOST COMMON — COOKED IN VINEGAR, SOY SAUCE, GARLIC, PEPPERCORNS, AND BAY LEAVES, SERVED WITH A SIDE OF STEAMED OR FRIED RICE.

*PESO (PEH-SOH): THE PHILIPPINE PESO IS THE OFFICIAL CURRENCY OF THE PHILIPPINES.

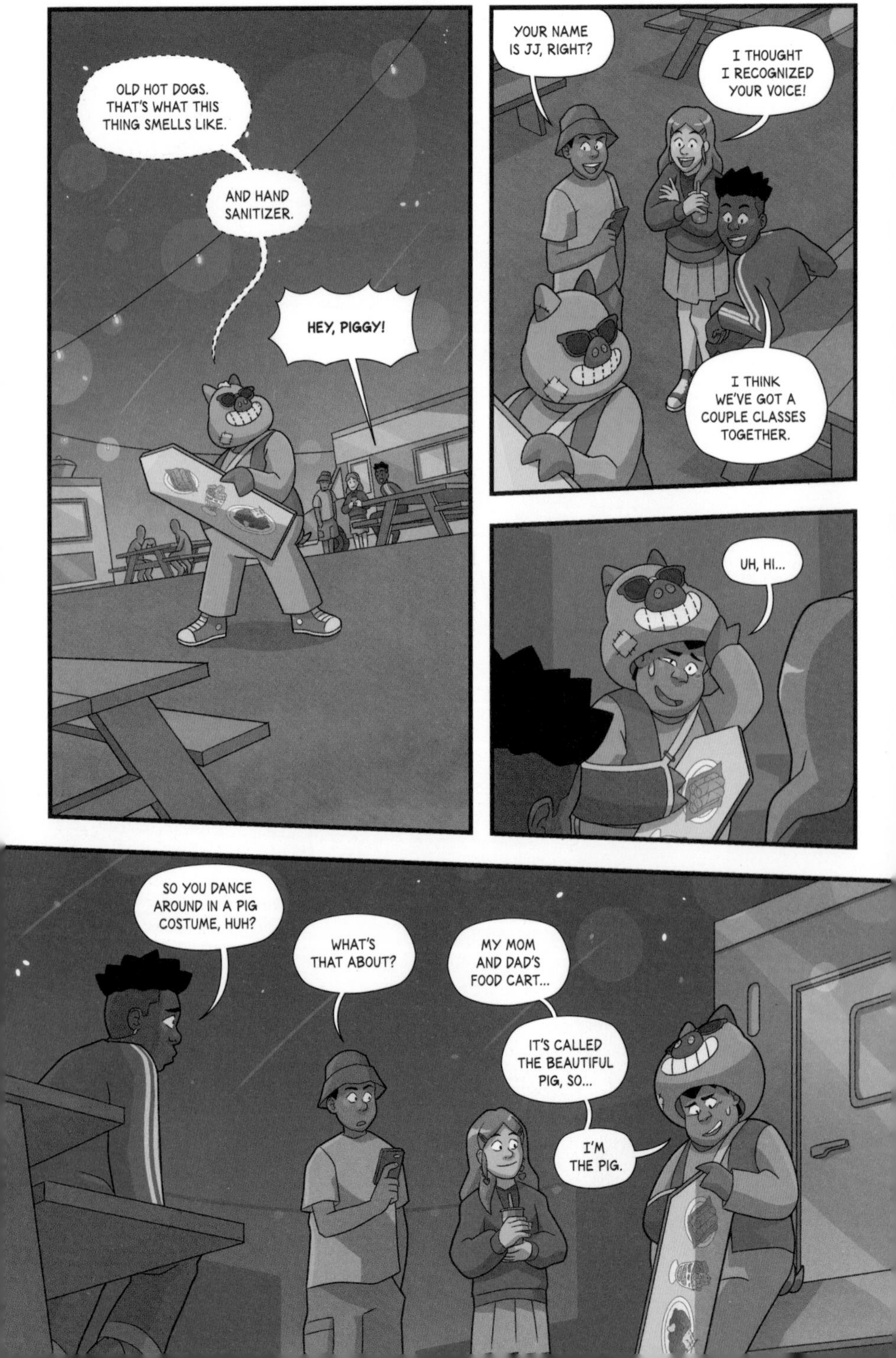
OLD HOT DOGS. THAT'S WHAT THIS THING SMELLS LIKE.
AND HAND SANITIZER.
HEY, PIGGY!
YOUR NAME IS JJ, RIGHT?
I THOUGHT I RECOGNIZED YOUR VOICE!
I THINK WE'VE GOT A COUPLE CLASSES TOGETHER.
UH, HI...
SO YOU DANCE AROUND IN A PIG COSTUME, HUH?
WHAT'S THAT ABOUT?
MY MOM AND DAD'S FOOD CART...
IT'S CALLED THE BEAUTIFUL PIG, SO...
I'M THE PIG.

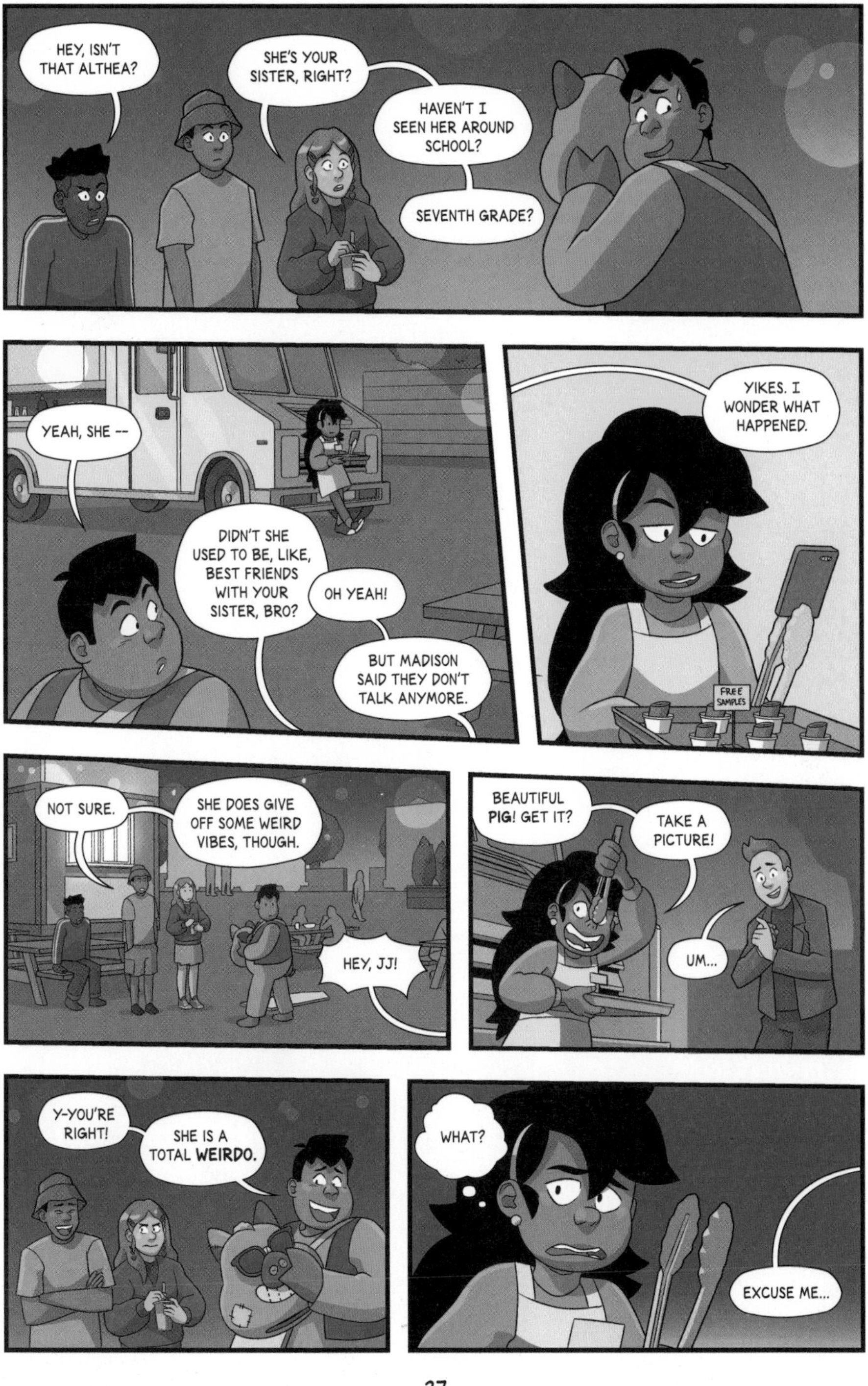
HEY, ISN'T THAT ALTHEA?
SHE'S YOUR SISTER, RIGHT?
HAVEN'T I SEEN HER AROUND SCHOOL?
SEVENTH GRADE?
YEAH, SHE --
DIDN'T SHE USED TO BE, LIKE, BEST FRIENDS WITH YOUR SISTER, BRO?
OH YEAH!
BUT MADISON SAID THEY DON'T TALK ANYMORE.
YIKES. I WONDER WHAT HAPPENED.
FREE SAMPLES
NOT SURE.
SHE DOES GIVE OFF SOME WEIRD VIBES, THOUGH.
HEY, JJ!
BEAUTIFUL **PIG**! GET IT?
TAKE A PICTURE!
UM...
Y-YOU'RE RIGHT!
SHE IS A TOTAL **WEIRDO.**
WHAT?
EXCUSE ME...

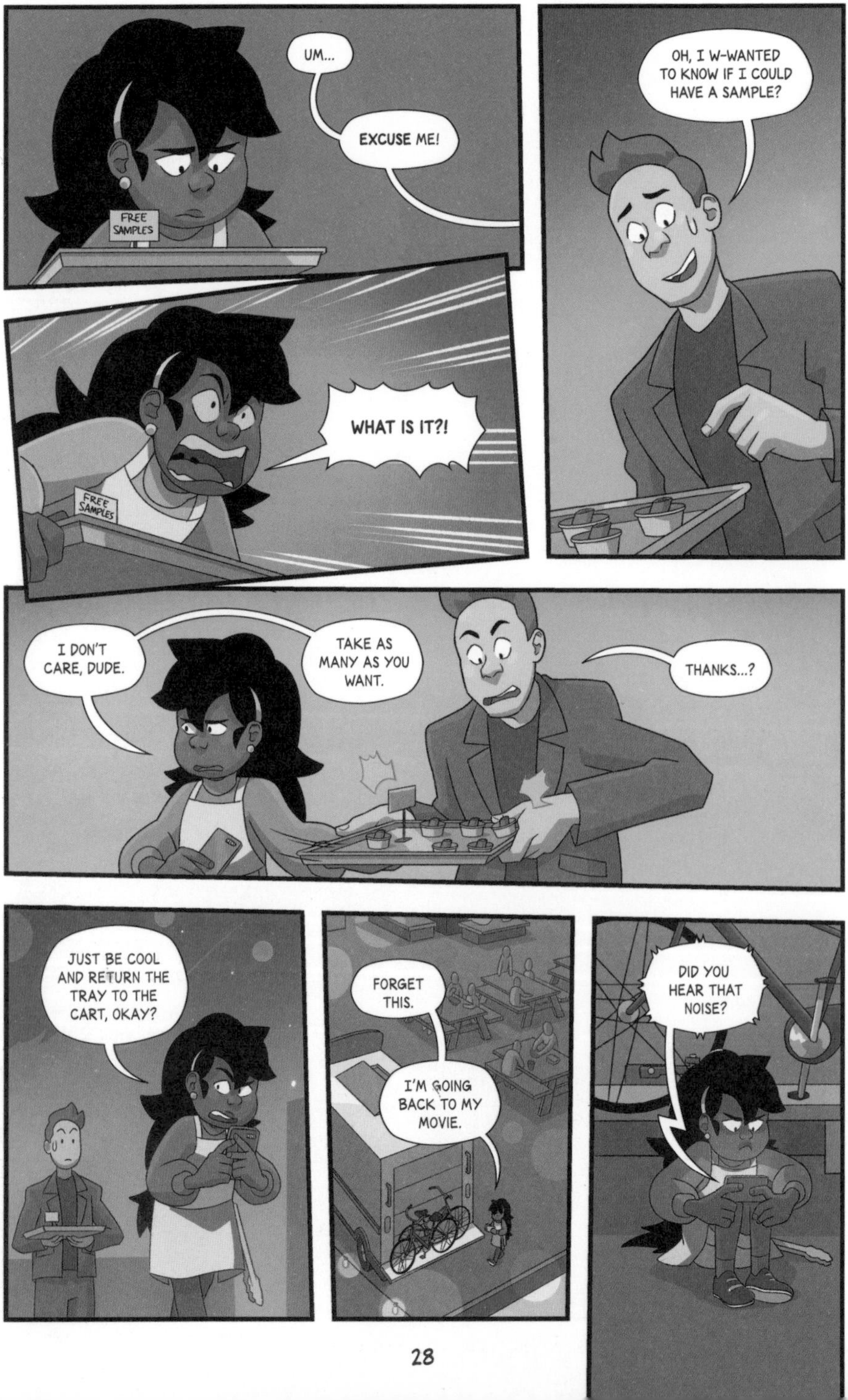
UM...
EXCUSE ME!
OH, I W-WANTED TO KNOW IF I COULD HAVE A SAMPLE?
FREE SAMPLES
WHAT IS IT?!
I DON'T CARE, DUDE.
TAKE AS MANY AS YOU WANT.
THANKS...?
JUST BE COOL AND RETURN THE TRAY TO THE CART, OKAY?
FORGET THIS.
I'M GOING BACK TO MY MOVIE.
DID YOU HEAR THAT NOISE?

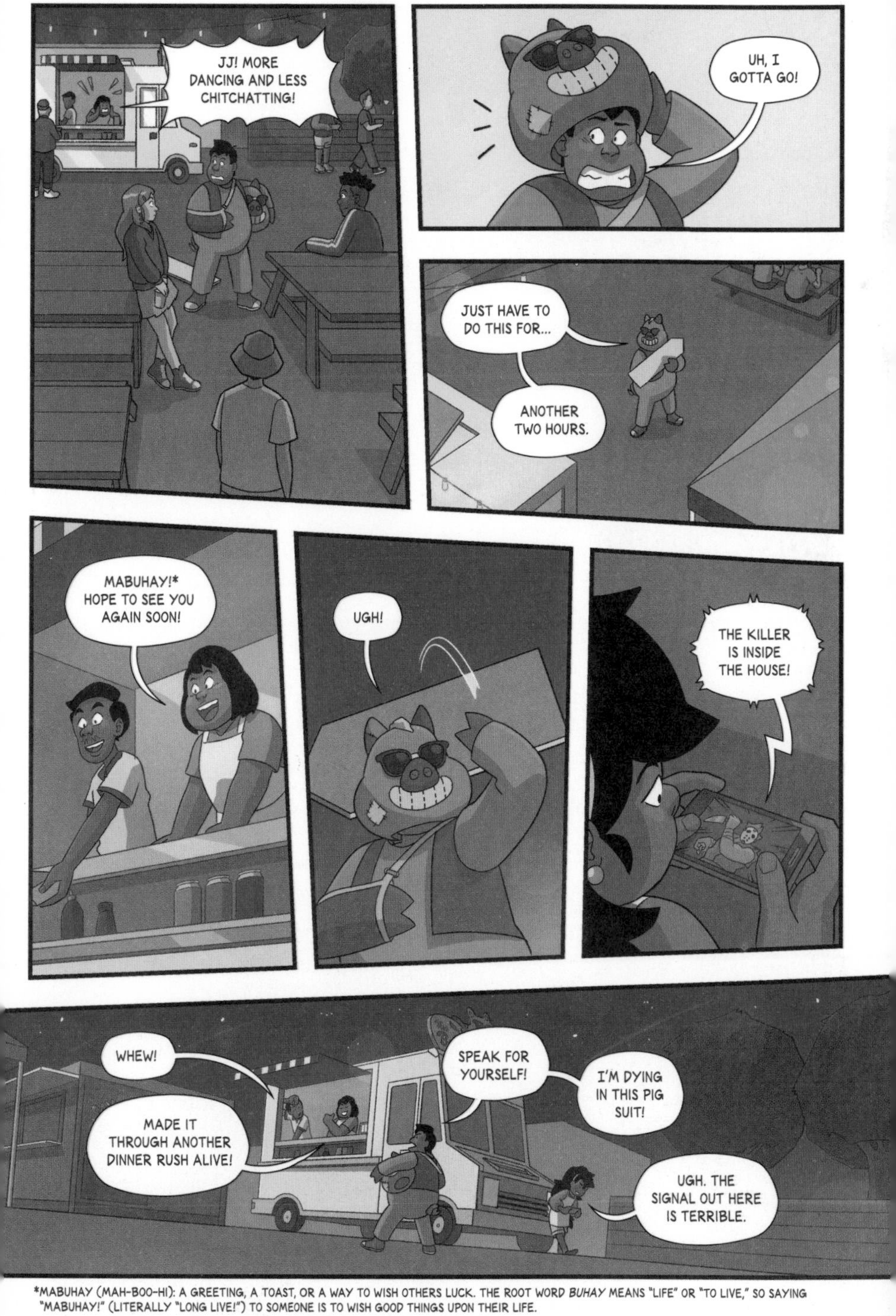
JJ! MORE DANCING AND LESS CHITCHATTING!
UH, I GOTTA GO!
JUST HAVE TO DO THIS FOR...
ANOTHER TWO HOURS.
MABUHAY!* HOPE TO SEE YOU AGAIN SOON!
UGH!
THE KILLER IS INSIDE THE HOUSE!
WHEW!
MADE IT THROUGH ANOTHER DINNER RUSH ALIVE!
SPEAK FOR YOURSELF!
I'M DYING IN THIS PIG SUIT!
UGH. THE SIGNAL OUT HERE IS TERRIBLE.

*MABUHAY (MAH-BOO-HI): A GREETING, A TOAST, OR A WAY TO WISH OTHERS LUCK. THE ROOT WORD *BUHAY* MEANS "LIFE" OR "TO LIVE," SO SAYING "MABUHAY!" (LITERALLY "LONG LIVE!") TO SOMEONE IS TO WISH GOOD THINGS UPON THEIR LIFE.

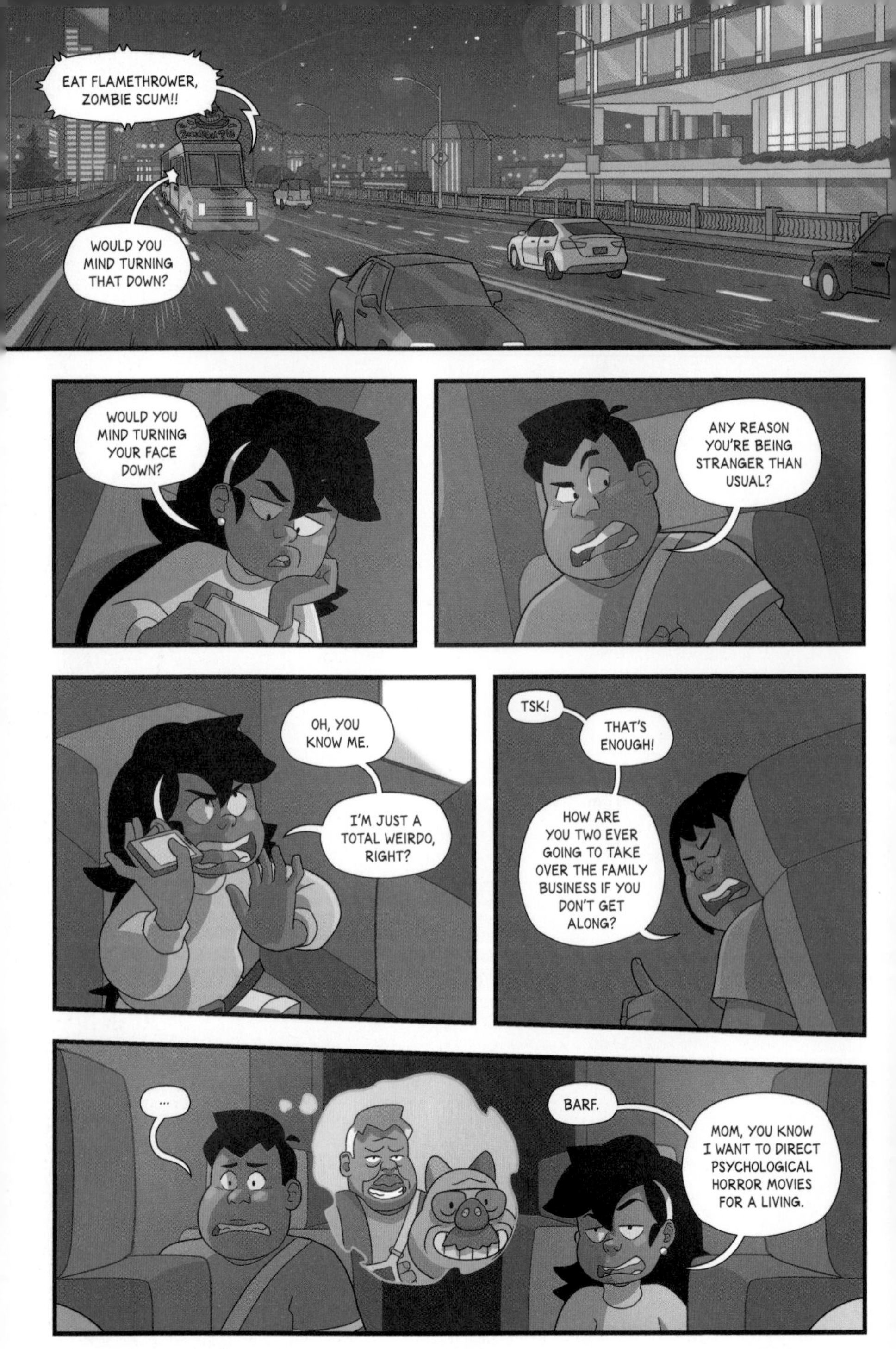
EAT FLAMETHROWER, ZOMBIE SCUM!!
WOULD YOU MIND TURNING THAT DOWN?
WOULD YOU MIND TURNING YOUR FACE DOWN?
ANY REASON YOU'RE BEING STRANGER THAN USUAL?
OH, YOU KNOW ME.
I'M JUST A TOTAL WEIRDO, RIGHT?
TSK!
THAT'S ENOUGH!
HOW ARE YOU TWO EVER GOING TO TAKE OVER THE FAMILY BUSINESS IF YOU DON'T GET ALONG?
...
BARF.
MOM, YOU KNOW I WANT TO DIRECT PSYCHOLOGICAL HORROR MOVIES FOR A LIVING.

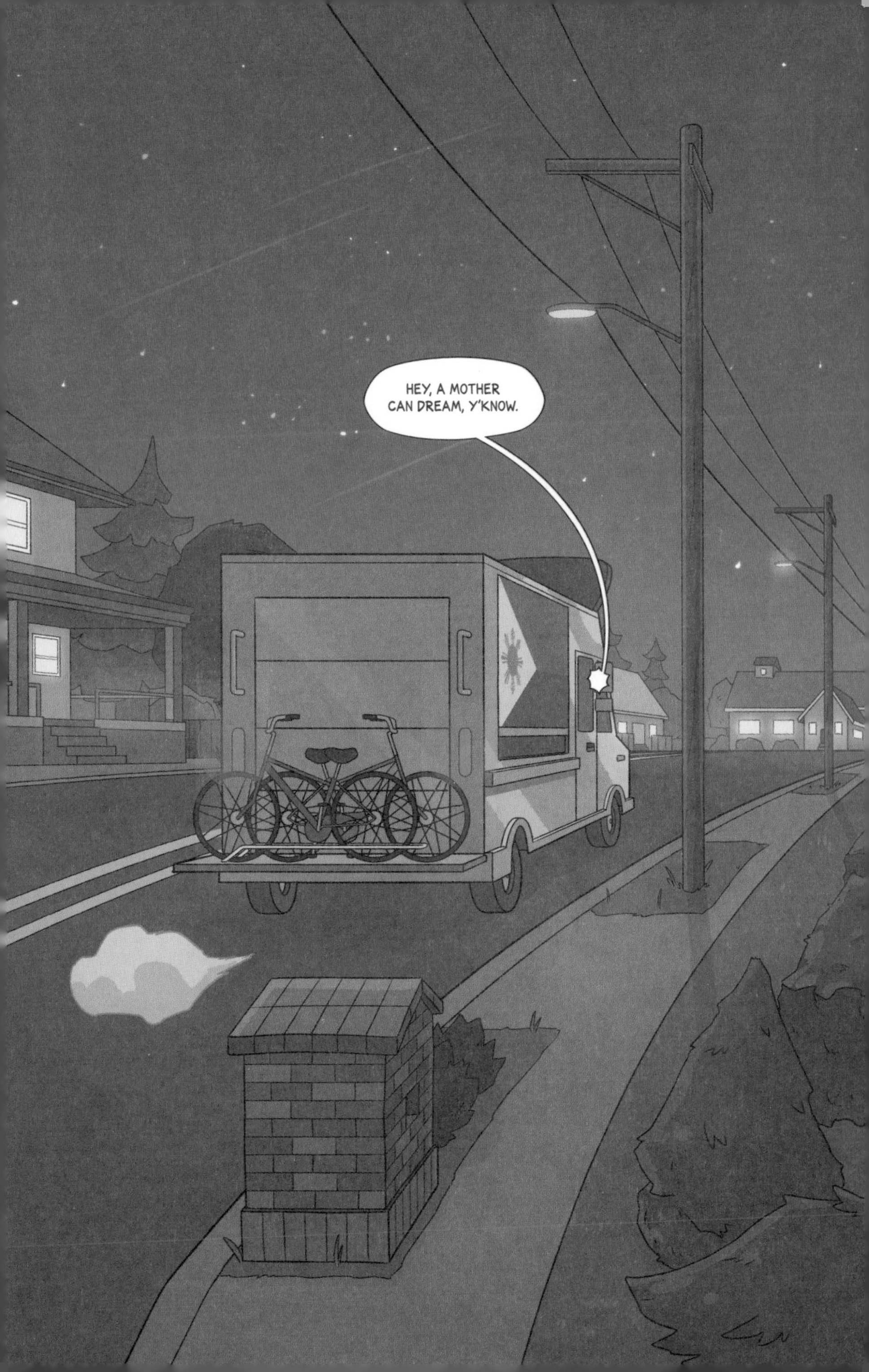
HEY, A MOTHER CAN DREAM, Y'KNOW.

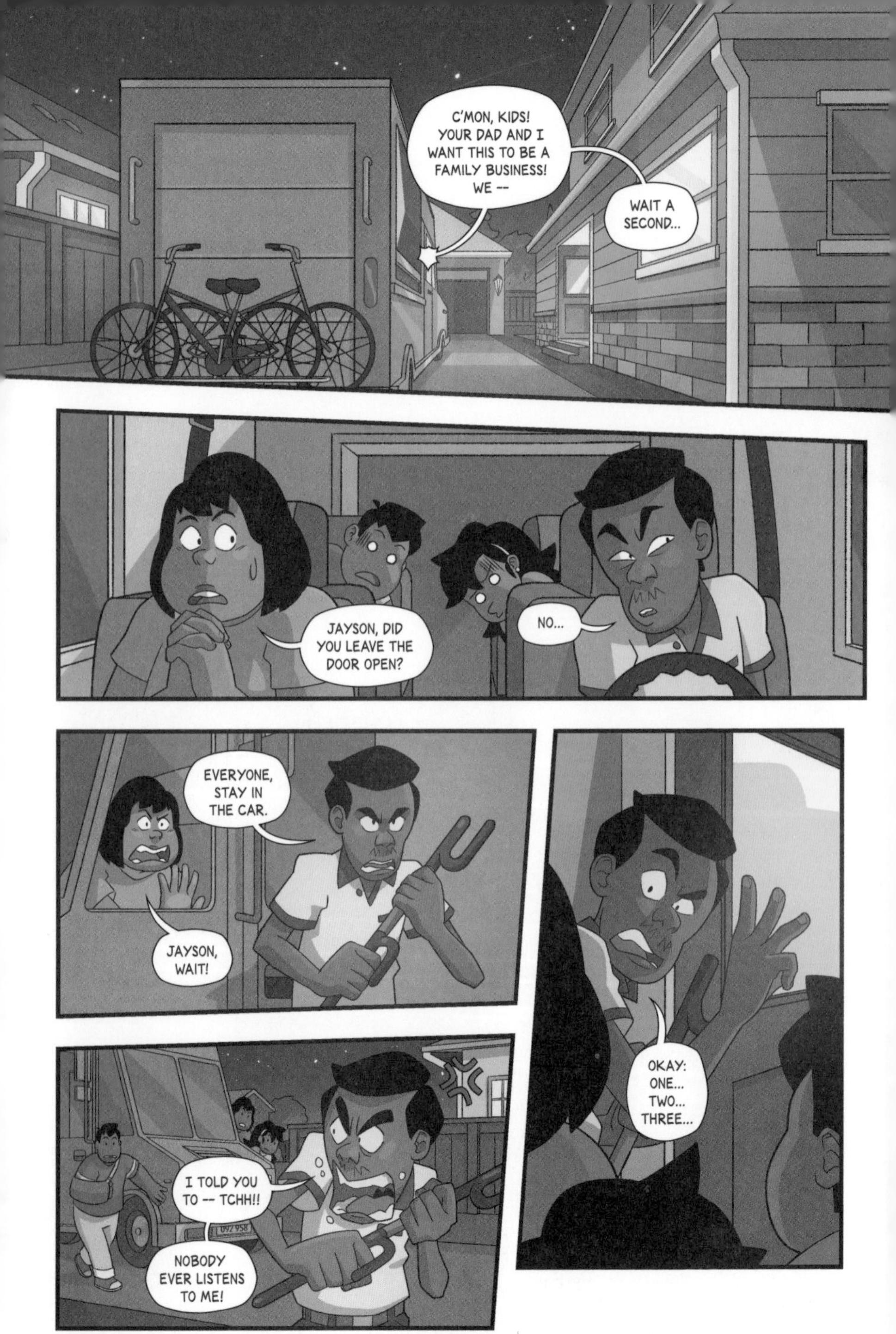
C'MON, KIDS! YOUR DAD AND I WANT THIS TO BE A FAMILY BUSINESS! WE --
WAIT A SECOND...
JAYSON, DID YOU LEAVE THE DOOR OPEN?
NO...
EVERYONE, STAY IN THE CAR.
JAYSON, WAIT!
OKAY: ONE... TWO... THREE...
I TOLD YOU TO -- TCHH!!
NOBODY EVER LISTENS TO ME!

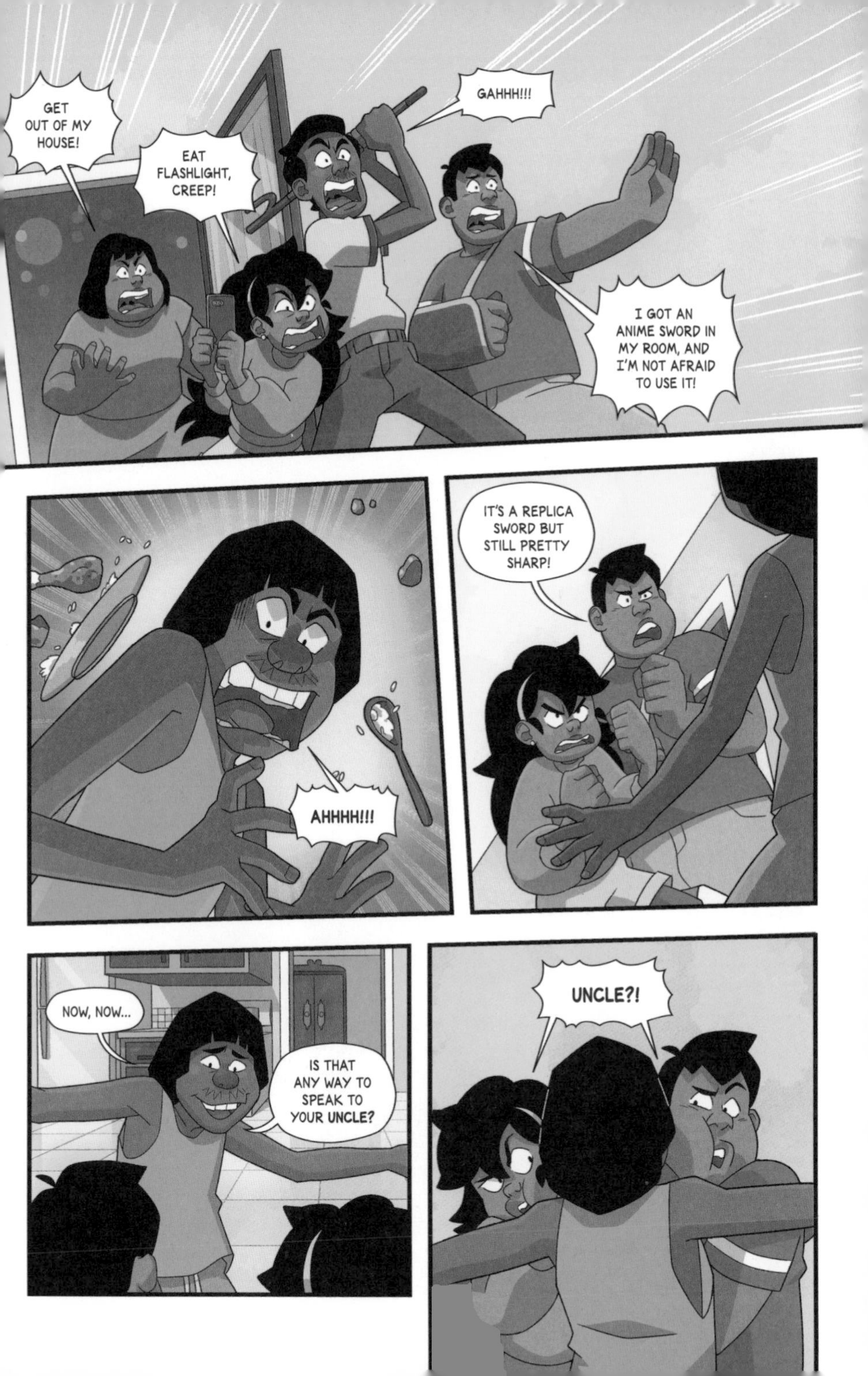
GET OUT OF MY HOUSE!
EAT FLASHLIGHT, CREEP!
GAHHH!!!
I GOT AN ANIME SWORD IN MY ROOM, AND I'M NOT AFRAID TO USE IT!
AHHHH!!!
IT'S A REPLICA SWORD BUT STILL PRETTY SHARP!
NOW, NOW...
IS THAT ANY WAY TO SPEAK TO YOUR UNCLE?
UNCLE?!

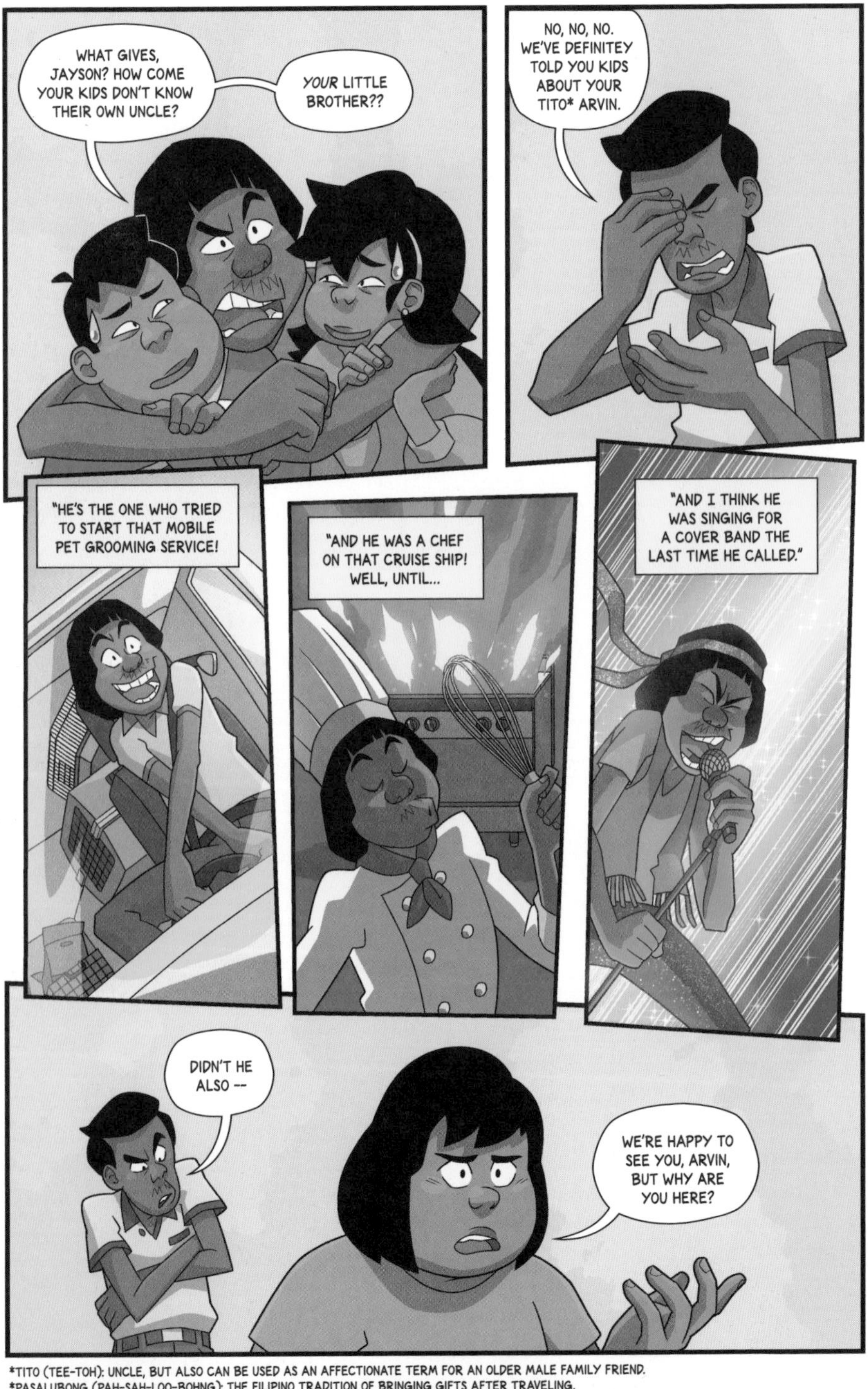
WHAT GIVES, JAYSON? HOW COME YOUR KIDS DON'T KNOW THEIR OWN UNCLE?
YOUR LITTLE BROTHER??
NO, NO, NO. WE'VE DEFINITEY TOLD YOU KIDS ABOUT YOUR TITO* ARVIN.
"HE'S THE ONE WHO TRIED TO START THAT MOBILE PET GROOMING SERVICE!
"AND HE WAS A CHEF ON THAT CRUISE SHIP! WELL, UNTIL...
"AND I THINK HE WAS SINGING FOR A COVER BAND THE LAST TIME HE CALLED."
DIDN'T HE ALSO --
WE'RE HAPPY TO SEE YOU, ARVIN, BUT WHY ARE YOU HERE?

*TITO (TEE-TOH): UNCLE, BUT ALSO CAN BE USED AS AN AFFECTIONATE TERM FOR AN OLDER MALE FAMILY FRIEND.
*PASALUBONG (PAH-SAH-LOO-BOHNG): THE FILIPINO TRADITION OF BRINGING GIFTS AFTER TRAVELING.
*UBE HALAYA (OO-BAY HAH-LI-AH): A SWEET JAM MADE FROM UBE (A PURPLE YAM), CONDENSED MILK, AND BUTTER.

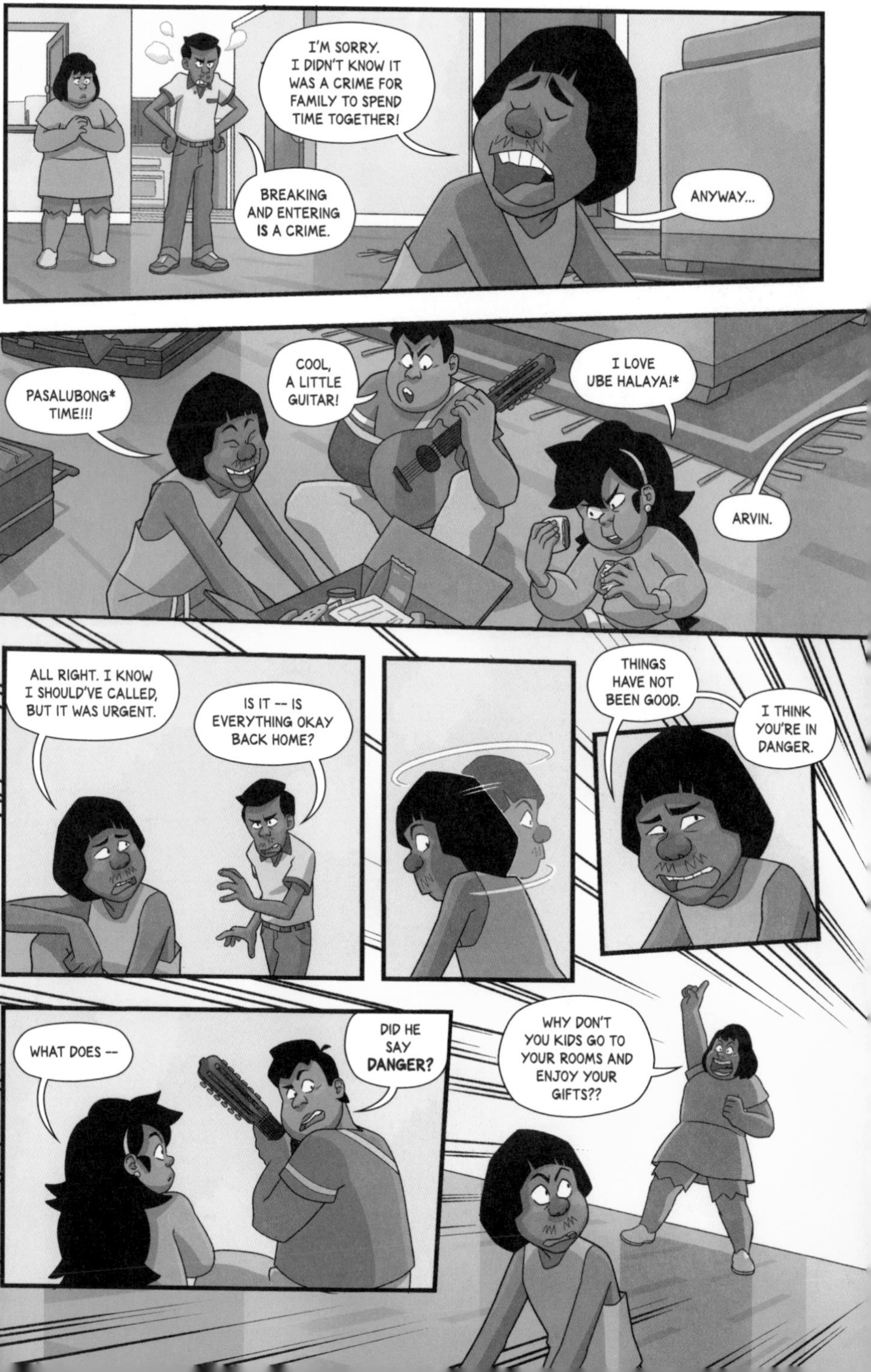
I'M SORRY. I DIDN'T KNOW IT WAS A CRIME FOR FAMILY TO SPEND TIME TOGETHER!
BREAKING AND ENTERING IS A CRIME.
ANYWAY...
PASALUBONG* TIME!!!
COOL, A LITTLE GUITAR!
I LOVE UBE HALAYA!*
ARVIN.
ALL RIGHT. I KNOW I SHOULD'VE CALLED, BUT IT WAS URGENT.
IS IT -- IS EVERYTHING OKAY BACK HOME?
THINGS HAVE NOT BEEN GOOD.
I THINK YOU'RE IN DANGER.
WHAT DOES --
DID HE SAY **DANGER?**
WHY DON'T YOU KIDS GO TO YOUR ROOMS AND ENJOY YOUR GIFTS??

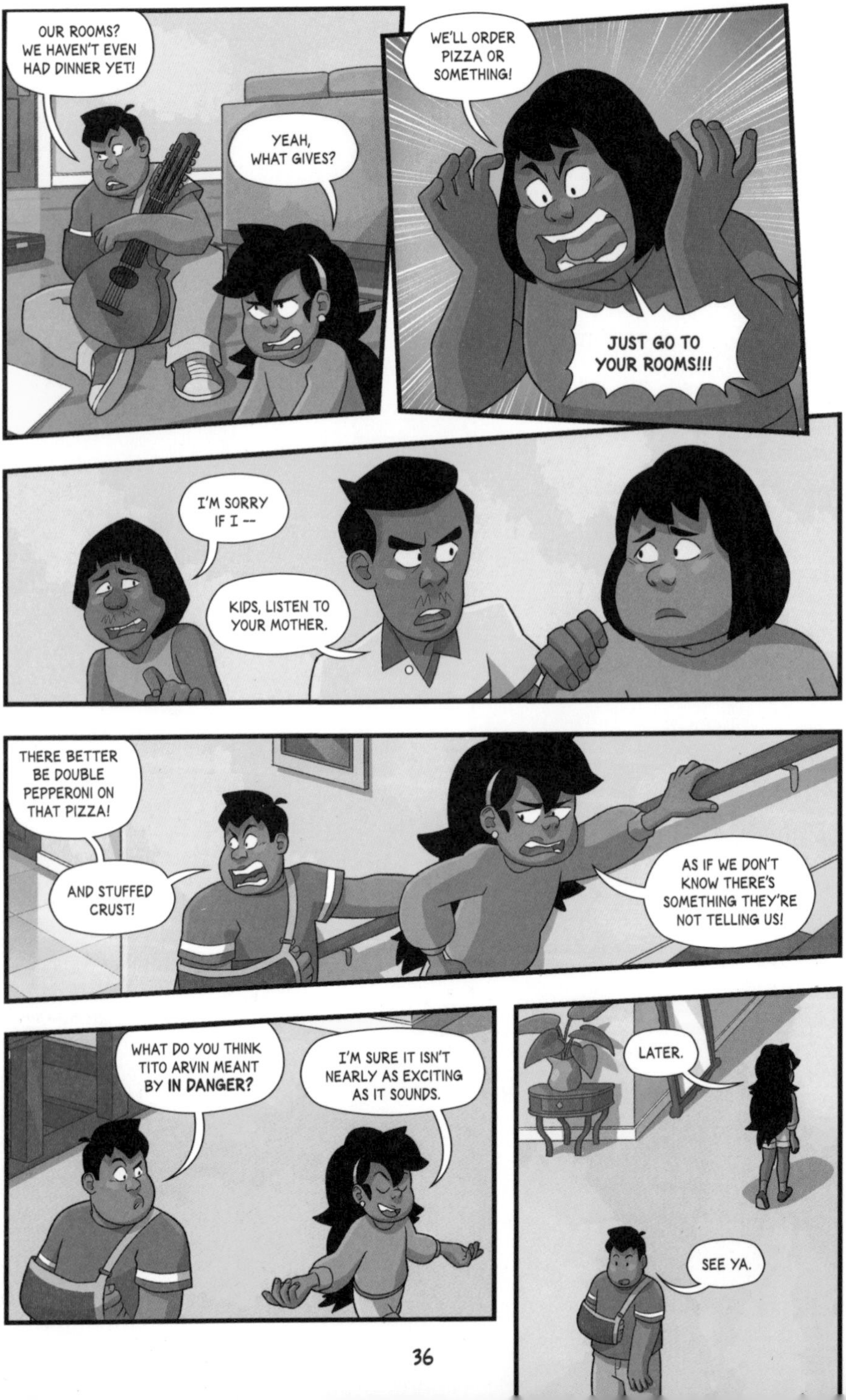
OUR ROOMS? WE HAVEN'T EVEN HAD DINNER YET!
YEAH, WHAT GIVES?
WE'LL ORDER PIZZA OR SOMETHING!
JUST GO TO YOUR ROOMS!!!
I'M SORRY IF I --
KIDS, LISTEN TO YOUR MOTHER.
THERE BETTER BE DOUBLE PEPPERONI ON THAT PIZZA!
AND STUFFED CRUST!
AS IF WE DON'T KNOW THERE'S SOMETHING THEY'RE NOT TELLING US!
WHAT DO YOU THINK TITO ARVIN MEANT BY IN DANGER?
I'M SURE IT ISN'T NEARLY AS EXCITING AS IT SOUNDS.
LATER.
SEE YA.

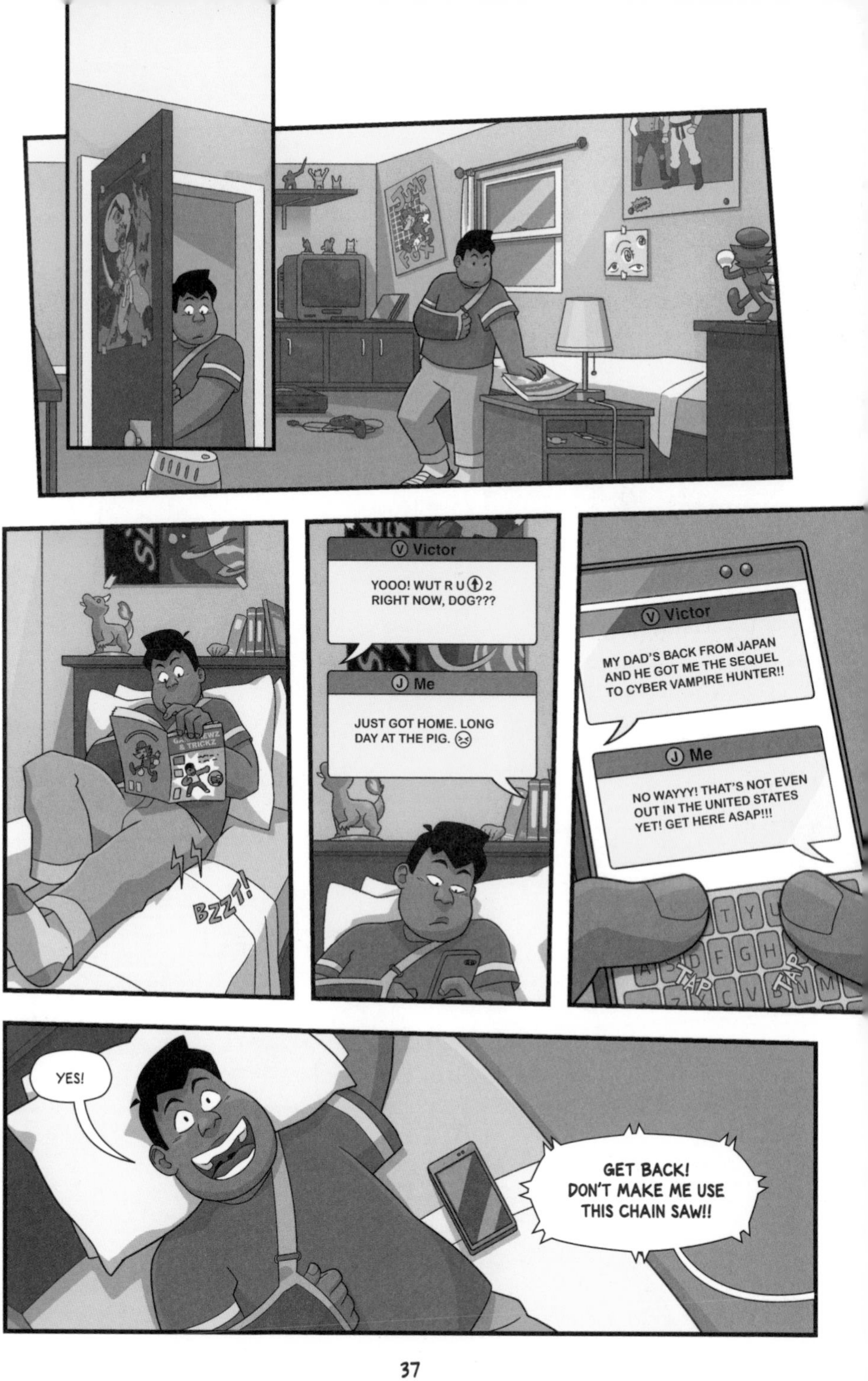
Victor
YOOO! WUT R U ⬆ 2 RIGHT NOW, DOG???
Me
JUST GOT HOME. LONG DAY AT THE PIG.
BZZT!
Victor
MY DAD'S BACK FROM JAPAN AND HE GOT ME THE SEQUEL TO CYBER VAMPIRE HUNTER!!
Me
NO WAYYY! THAT'S NOT EVEN OUT IN THE UNITED STATES YET! GET HERE ASAP!!!
TAP
TAP
YES!
GET BACK! DON'T MAKE ME USE THIS CHAIN SAW!!

ALL RIGHT, YOU ASKED FOR IT...

AHHH!!!

TURN IT DOWN!!

WHAT A BABY.

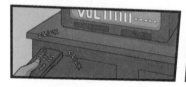

CLICK CLICK

PING!

Riley Johnson

HEY! YOU HAVEN'T BEEN ONLINE IN FOREVER!

REPLY

Althea Bulan

SRY. BEEN BUSY.

REPLY

Riley Johnson

BTW I'M SORRY ABOUT JENNA AT LUNCH TODAY. SHE NEVER KNOWS WHEN SHE'S TAKING A JOKE TOO FAR.

REPLY

Riley Johnson

SHE'S BEING WEIRD BECAUSE WE ALL HAVEN'T HUNG OUT TOGETHER IN SO LONG.

REPLY

Riley Johnson

MAYBE WE COULD ALL GO TO THAT MOVIE WE WERE SUPPOSED TO SEE.

REPLY

SNAP!

HEY, MR. AND MRS. B! IS THAT PIZZA I SMELL?

38

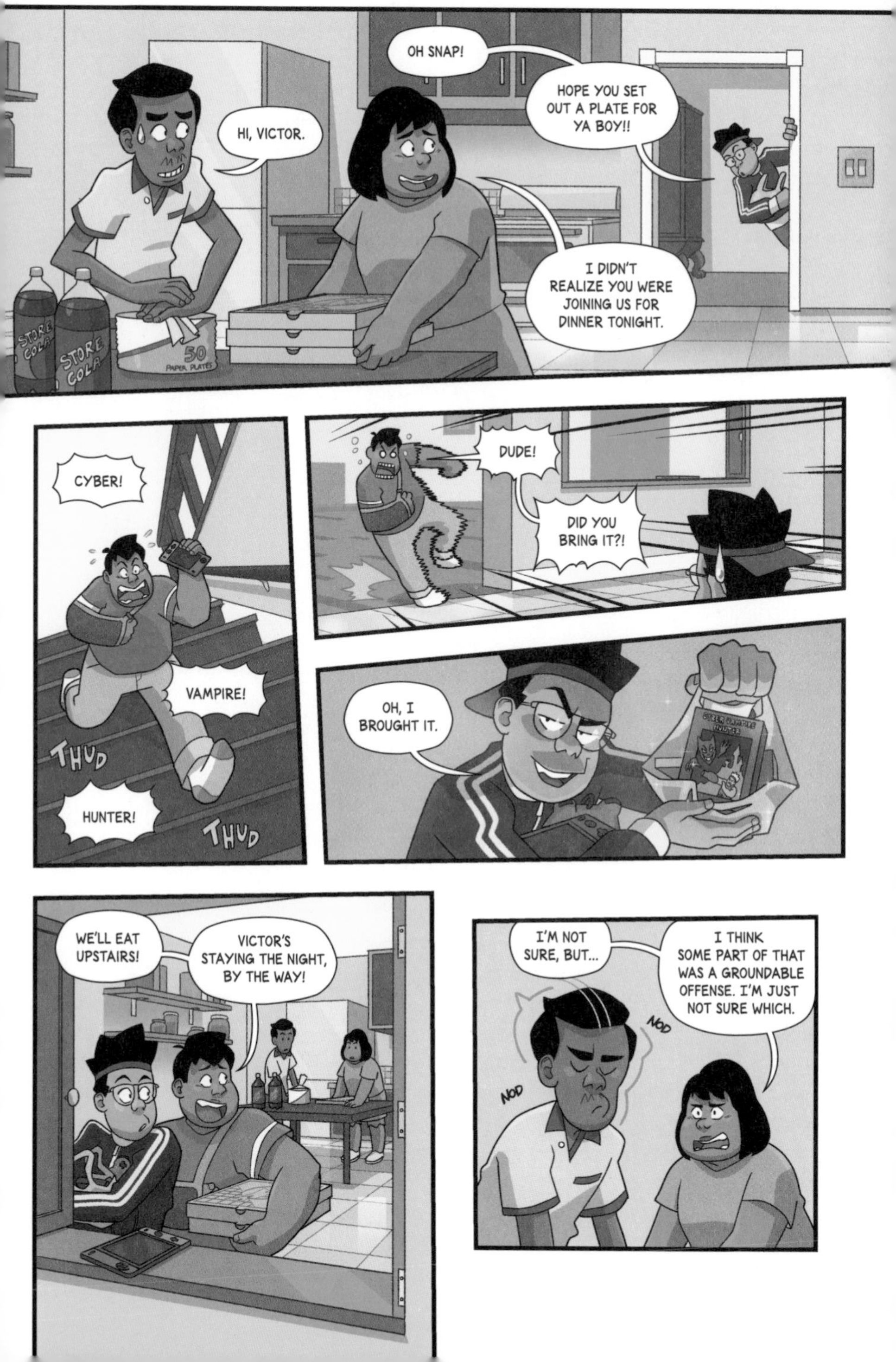
HI, VICTOR.
OH SNAP!
HOPE YOU SET OUT A PLATE FOR YA BOY!!
I DIDN'T REALIZE YOU WERE JOINING US FOR DINNER TONIGHT.
STORE COLA
STORE COLA
50 PAPER PLATES
CYBER!
VAMPIRE!
THUD
HUNTER!
THUD
DUDE!
DID YOU BRING IT?!
OH, I BROUGHT IT.
WE'LL EAT UPSTAIRS!
VICTOR'S STAYING THE NIGHT, BY THE WAY!
I'M NOT SURE, BUT...
I THINK SOME PART OF THAT WAS A GROUNDABLE OFFENSE. I'M JUST NOT SURE WHICH.
NOD
NOD

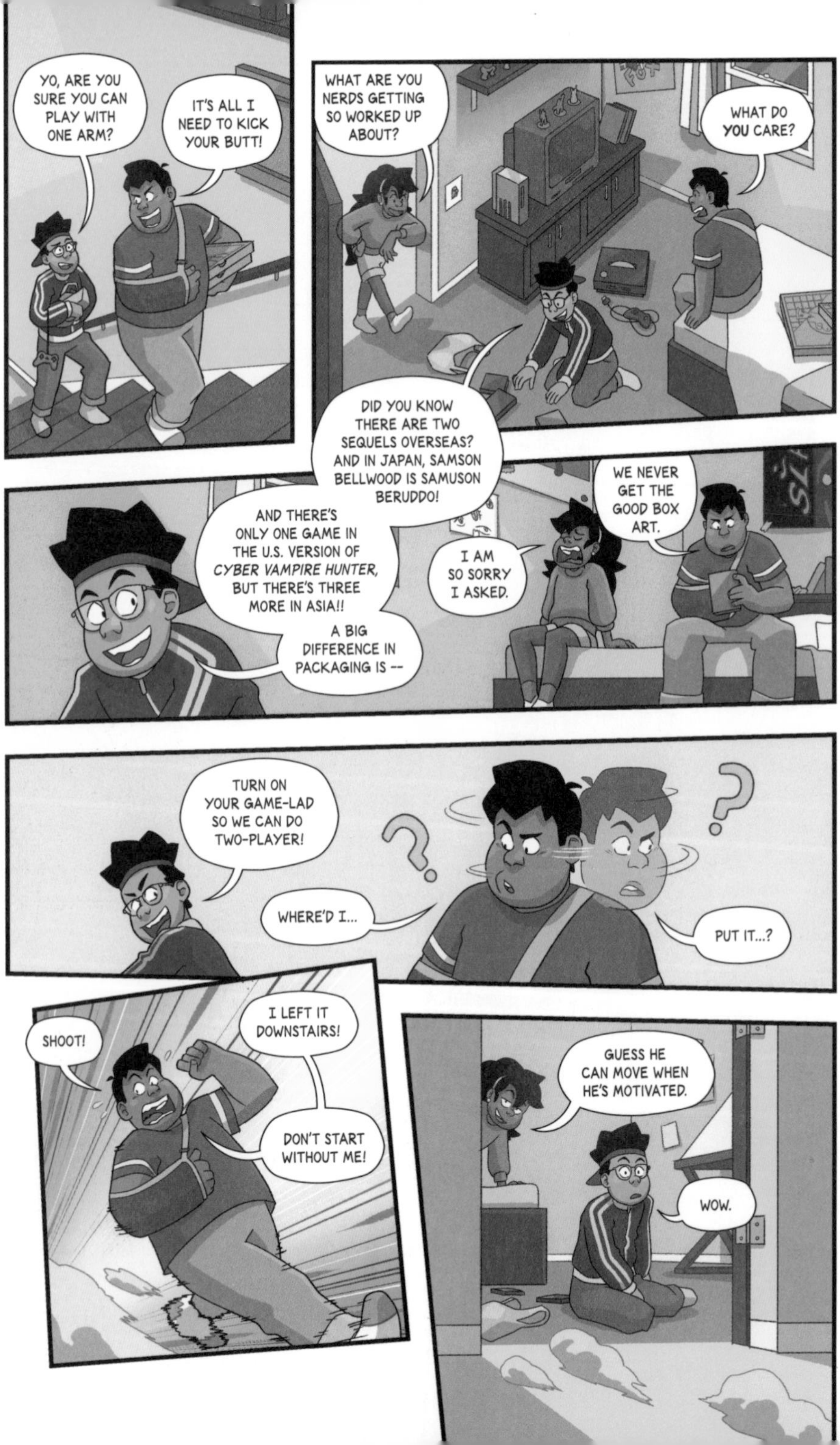
YO, ARE YOU SURE YOU CAN PLAY WITH ONE ARM?
IT'S ALL I NEED TO KICK YOUR BUTT!
WHAT ARE YOU NERDS GETTING SO WORKED UP ABOUT?
WHAT DO YOU CARE?
DID YOU KNOW THERE ARE TWO SEQUELS OVERSEAS? AND IN JAPAN, SAMSON BELLWOOD IS SAMUSON BERUDDO!
AND THERE'S ONLY ONE GAME IN THE U.S. VERSION OF *CYBER VAMPIRE HUNTER*, BUT THERE'S THREE MORE IN ASIA!!
A BIG DIFFERENCE IN PACKAGING IS --
WE NEVER GET THE GOOD BOX ART.
I AM SO SORRY I ASKED.
TURN ON YOUR GAME-LAD SO WE CAN DO TWO-PLAYER!
WHERE'D I...
PUT IT...?
SHOOT!
I LEFT IT DOWNSTAIRS!
DON'T START WITHOUT ME!
GUESS HE CAN MOVE WHEN HE'S MOTIVATED.
WOW.

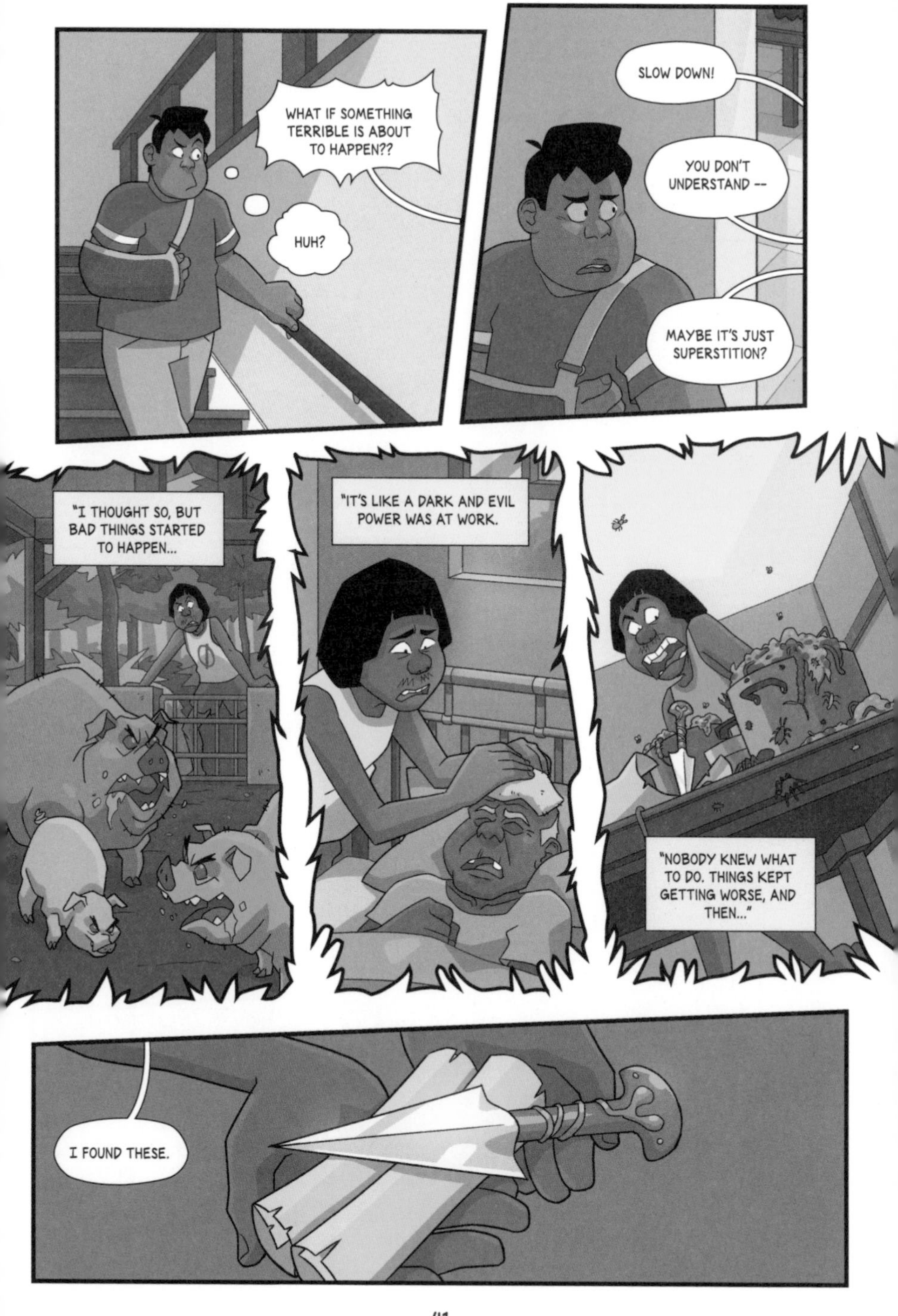
WHAT IF SOMETHING TERRIBLE IS ABOUT TO HAPPEN??
HUH?
SLOW DOWN!
YOU DON'T UNDERSTAND --
MAYBE IT'S JUST SUPERSTITION?
"I THOUGHT SO, BUT BAD THINGS STARTED TO HAPPEN...
"IT'S LIKE A DARK AND EVIL POWER WAS AT WORK.
"NOBODY KNEW WHAT TO DO. THINGS KEPT GETTING WORSE, AND THEN..."
I FOUND THESE.

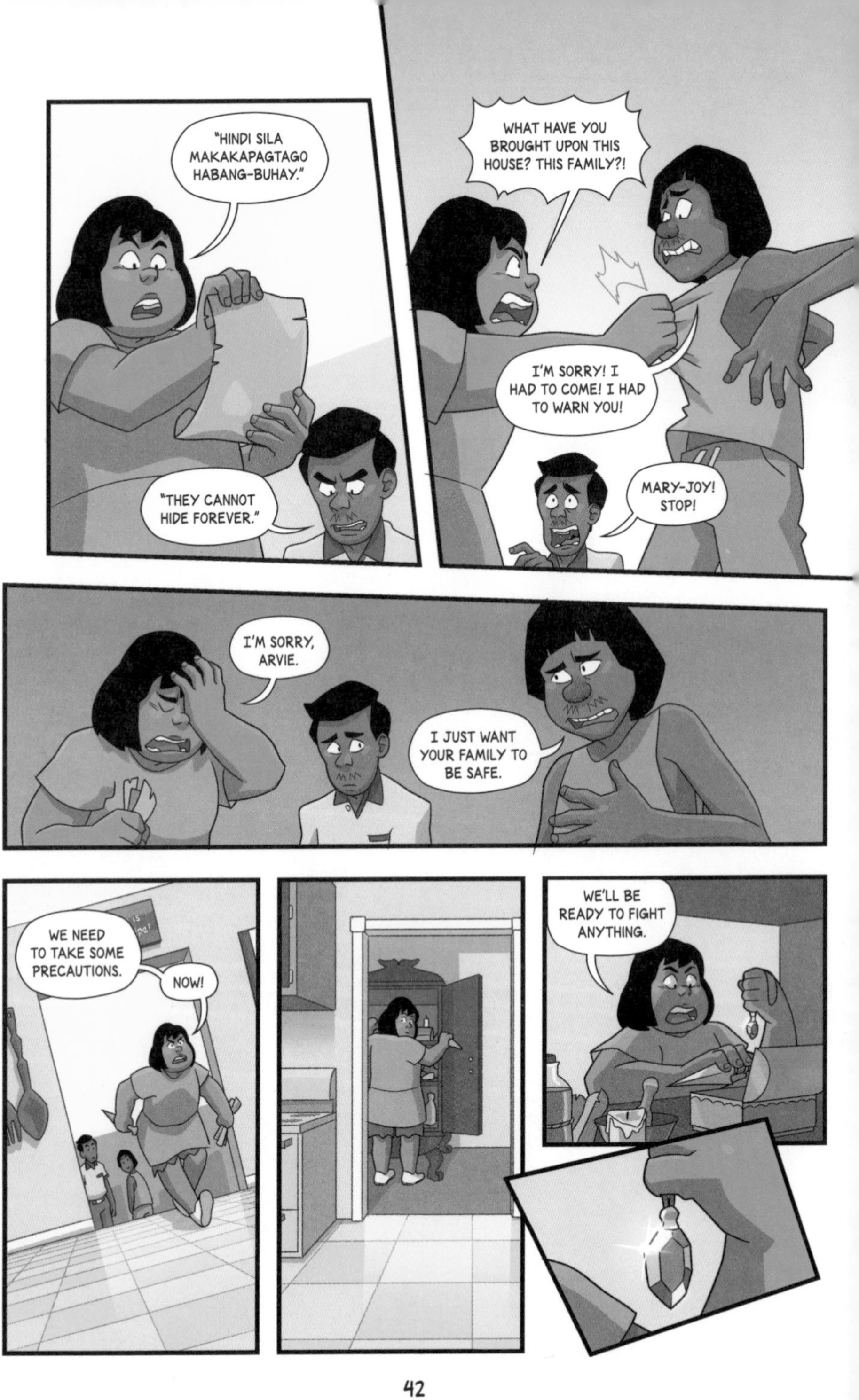
"HINDI SILA MAKAKAPAGTAGO HABANG-BUHAY."
"THEY CANNOT HIDE FOREVER."
WHAT HAVE YOU BROUGHT UPON THIS HOUSE? THIS FAMILY?!
I'M SORRY! I HAD TO COME! I HAD TO WARN YOU!
MARY-JOY! STOP!
I'M SORRY, ARVIE.
I JUST WANT YOUR FAMILY TO BE SAFE.
WE NEED TO TAKE SOME PRECAUTIONS.
NOW!
WE'LL BE READY TO FIGHT ANYTHING.

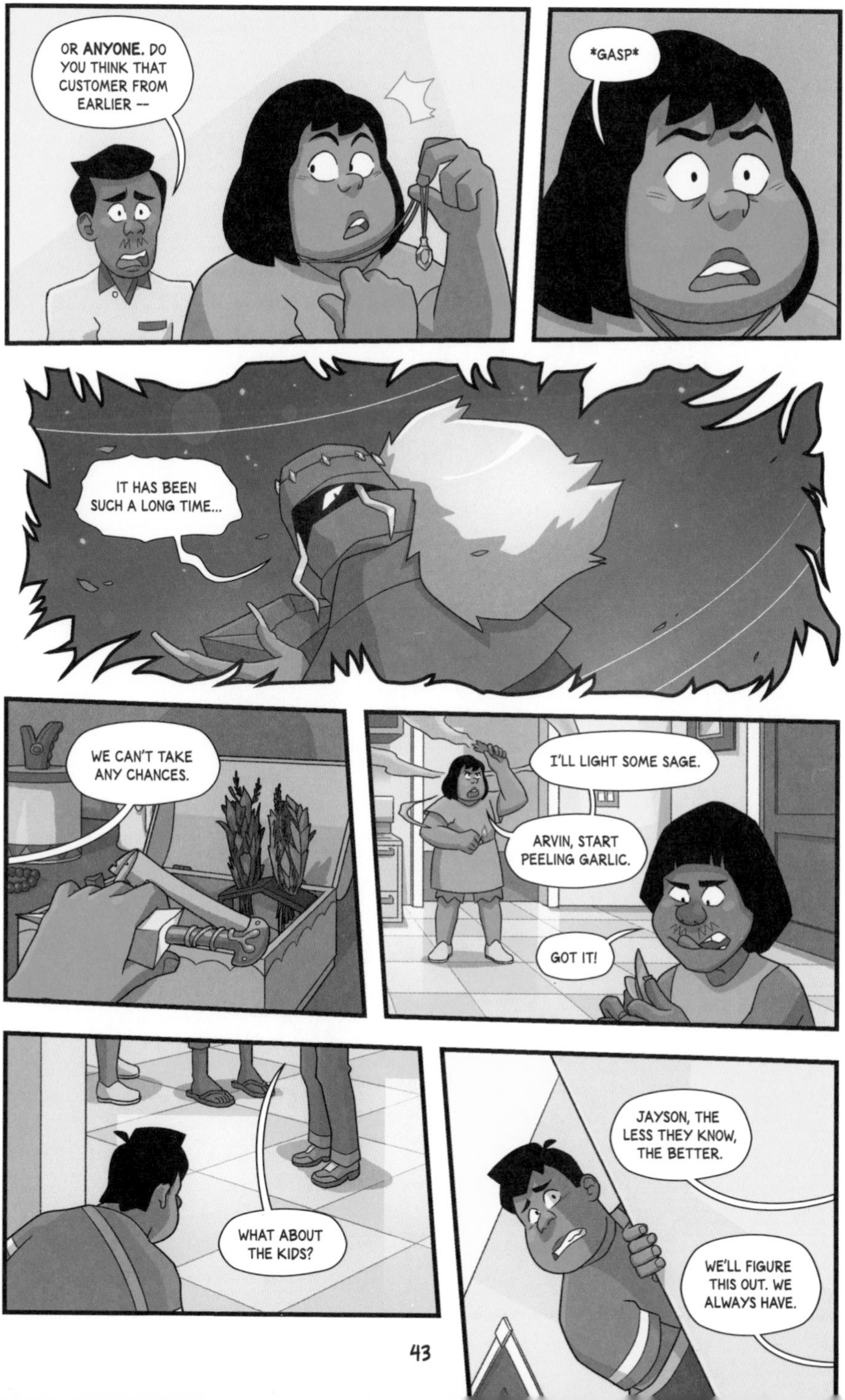

OR ANYONE. DO YOU THINK THAT CUSTOMER FROM EARLIER --
GASP
IT HAS BEEN SUCH A LONG TIME...
WE CAN'T TAKE ANY CHANCES.
I'LL LIGHT SOME SAGE.
ARVIN, START PEELING GARLIC.
GOT IT!
WHAT ABOUT THE KIDS?
JAYSON, THE LESS THEY KNOW, THE BETTER.
WE'LL FIGURE THIS OUT. WE ALWAYS HAVE.

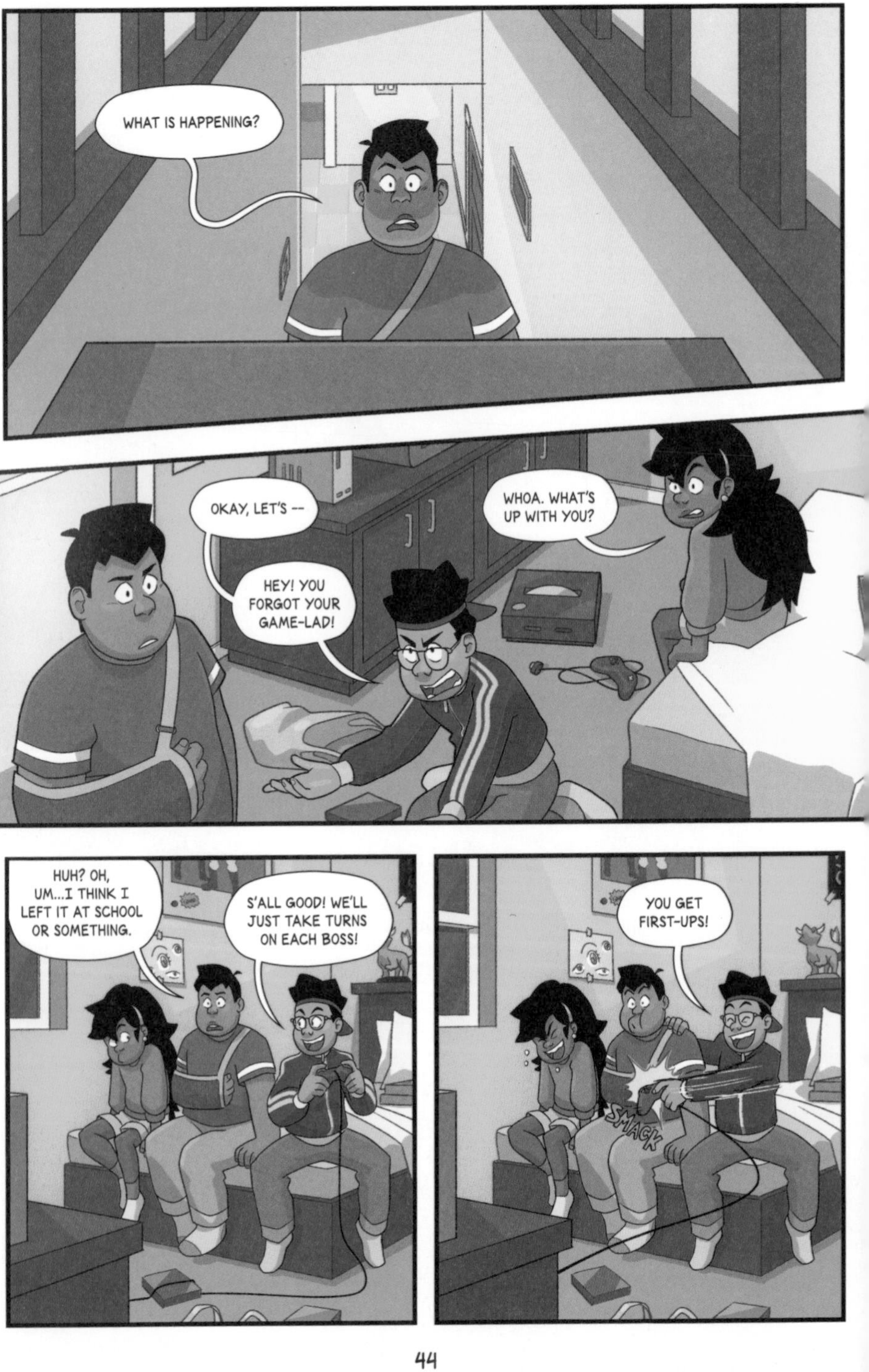
WHAT IS HAPPENING?
OKAY, LET'S --
HEY! YOU FORGOT YOUR GAME-LAD!
WHOA. WHAT'S UP WITH YOU?
HUH? OH, UM...I THINK I LEFT IT AT SCHOOL OR SOMETHING.
S'ALL GOOD! WE'LL JUST TAKE TURNS ON EACH BOSS!
YOU GET FIRST-UPS!
SMACK

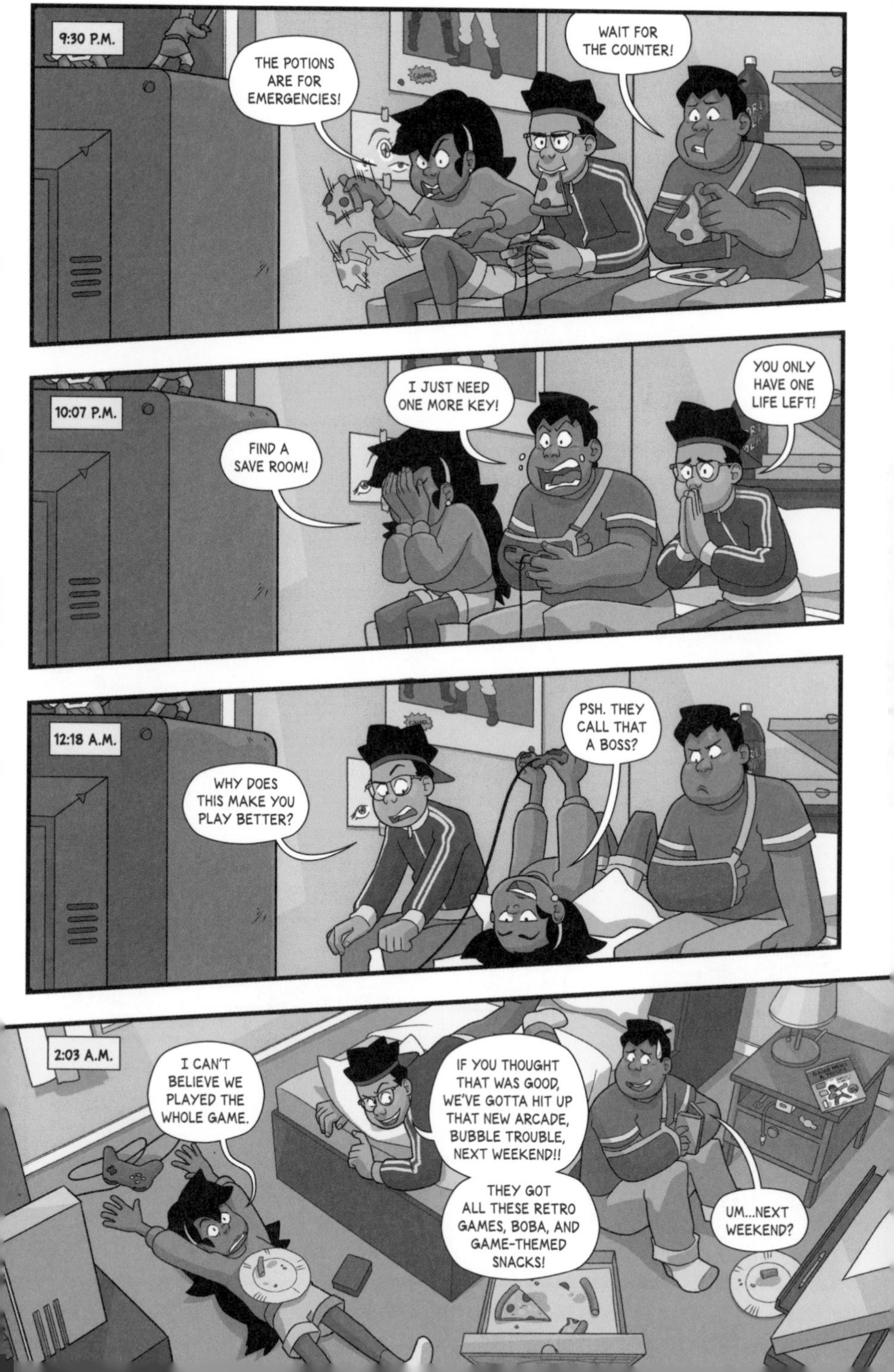
9:30 P.M.
THE POTIONS ARE FOR EMERGENCIES!
WAIT FOR THE COUNTER!
10:07 P.M.
FIND A SAVE ROOM!
I JUST NEED ONE MORE KEY!
YOU ONLY HAVE ONE LIFE LEFT!
12:18 A.M.
WHY DOES THIS MAKE YOU PLAY BETTER?
PSH. THEY CALL THAT A BOSS?
2:03 A.M.
I CAN'T BELIEVE WE PLAYED THE WHOLE GAME.
IF YOU THOUGHT THAT WAS GOOD, WE'VE GOTTA HIT UP THAT NEW ARCADE, BUBBLE TROUBLE, NEXT WEEKEND!!
THEY GOT ALL THESE RETRO GAMES, BOBA, AND GAME-THEMED SNACKS!
UM...NEXT WEEKEND?

I WOULD, BUT... HALEY P'S END-OF-THE-YEAR PARTY IS NEXT WEEKEND.

I KNOW. I THOUGHT WE'D GO AFTER.

YOU WON'T BE BUSY THEN, RIGHT?

HE TOTALLY THINKS HE'S GONNA HANG WITH HALEY P AND HER PALS WHEN THE WORK IS DONE.

EVERYONE AT THAT PARTY IS A HUGE SNOB OR TOTALLY WACK!

COMPLETE WADS.

WHAT IF THEY WANTED TO HANG OUT OR SOMETHING?

THEY'RE NOT ALL BAD. HALEY P IS NICE, AT LEAST.

WHATEVER! LET'S JUST DROP IT AND GO BACK TO FIND ALL THE UNLOCKABLES!

THAT'S WHAT I'M TALKING ABOUT!

I WANNA PLAY THIS UNTIL MY BRAIN TURNS TO GOOP.

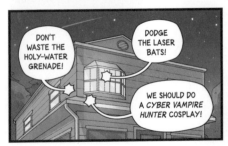

DON'T WASTE THE HOLY-WATER GRENADE!

DODGE THE LASER BATS!

WE SHOULD DO A *CYBER VAMPIRE HUNTER* COSPLAY!

BREAKFAST!!!

46

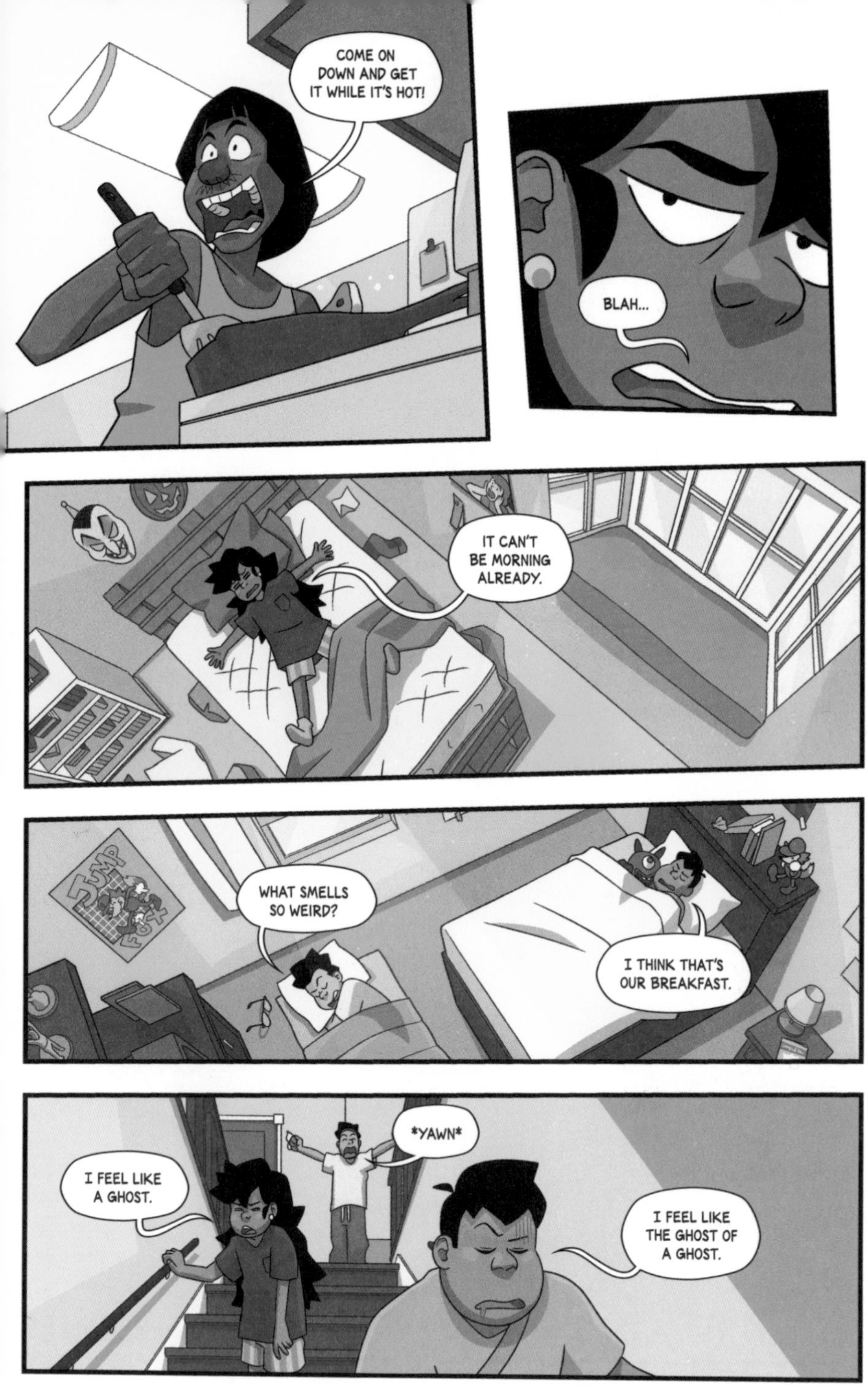
COME ON DOWN AND GET IT WHILE IT'S HOT!
BLAH...
IT CAN'T BE MORNING ALREADY.
JUMP FORCE
WHAT SMELLS SO WEIRD?
I THINK THAT'S OUR BREAKFAST.
I FEEL LIKE A GHOST.
YAWN
I FEEL LIKE THE GHOST OF A GHOST.

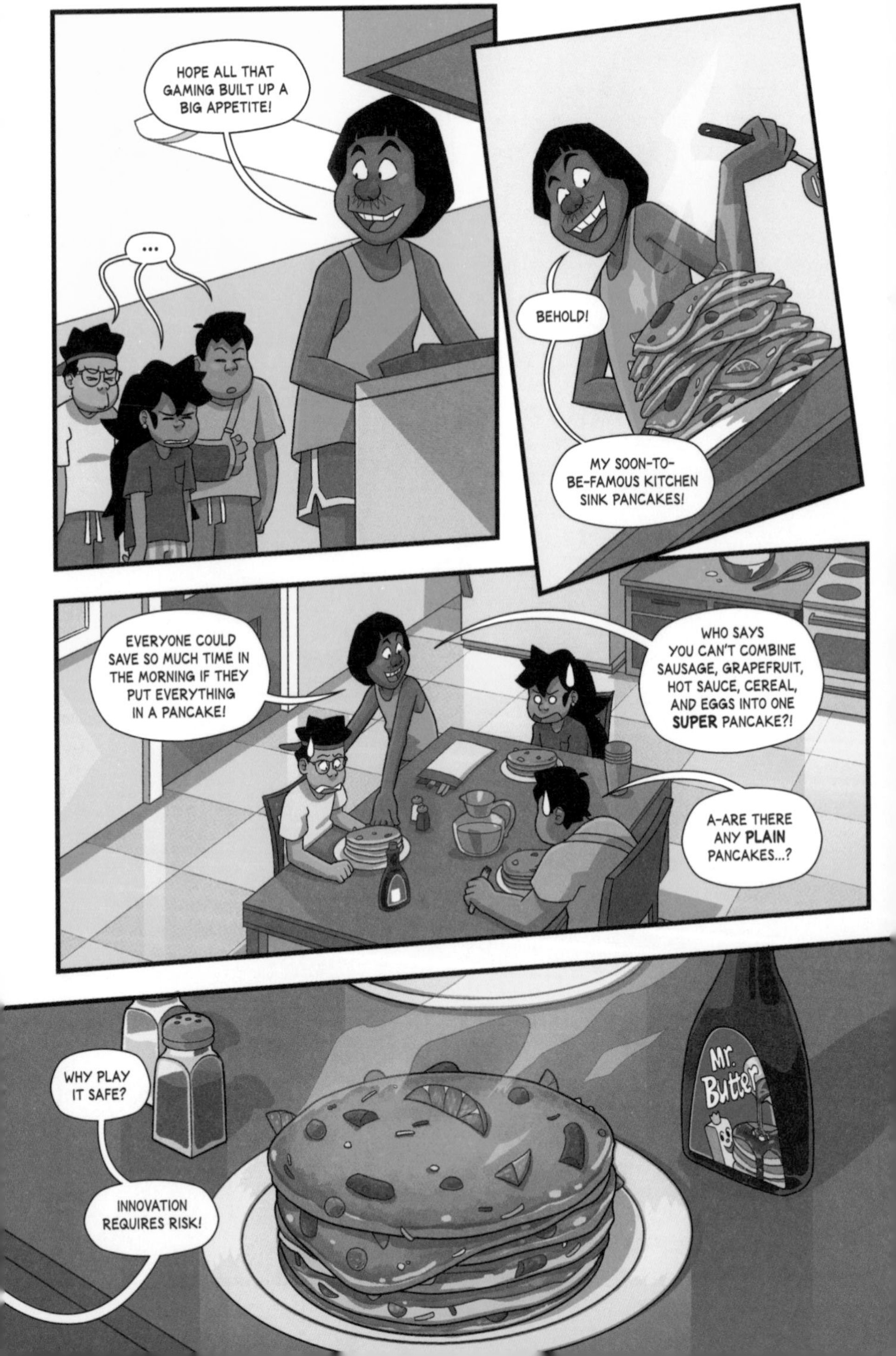
HOPE ALL THAT GAMING BUILT UP A BIG APPETITE!
...
BEHOLD!
MY SOON-TO-BE-FAMOUS KITCHEN SINK PANCAKES!
EVERYONE COULD SAVE SO MUCH TIME IN THE MORNING IF THEY PUT EVERYTHING IN A PANCAKE!
WHO SAYS YOU CAN'T COMBINE SAUSAGE, GRAPEFRUIT, HOT SAUCE, CEREAL, AND EGGS INTO ONE **SUPER** PANCAKE?!
A-ARE THERE ANY **PLAIN** PANCAKES...?
WHY PLAY IT SAFE?
INNOVATION REQUIRES RISK!
Mr. Butter

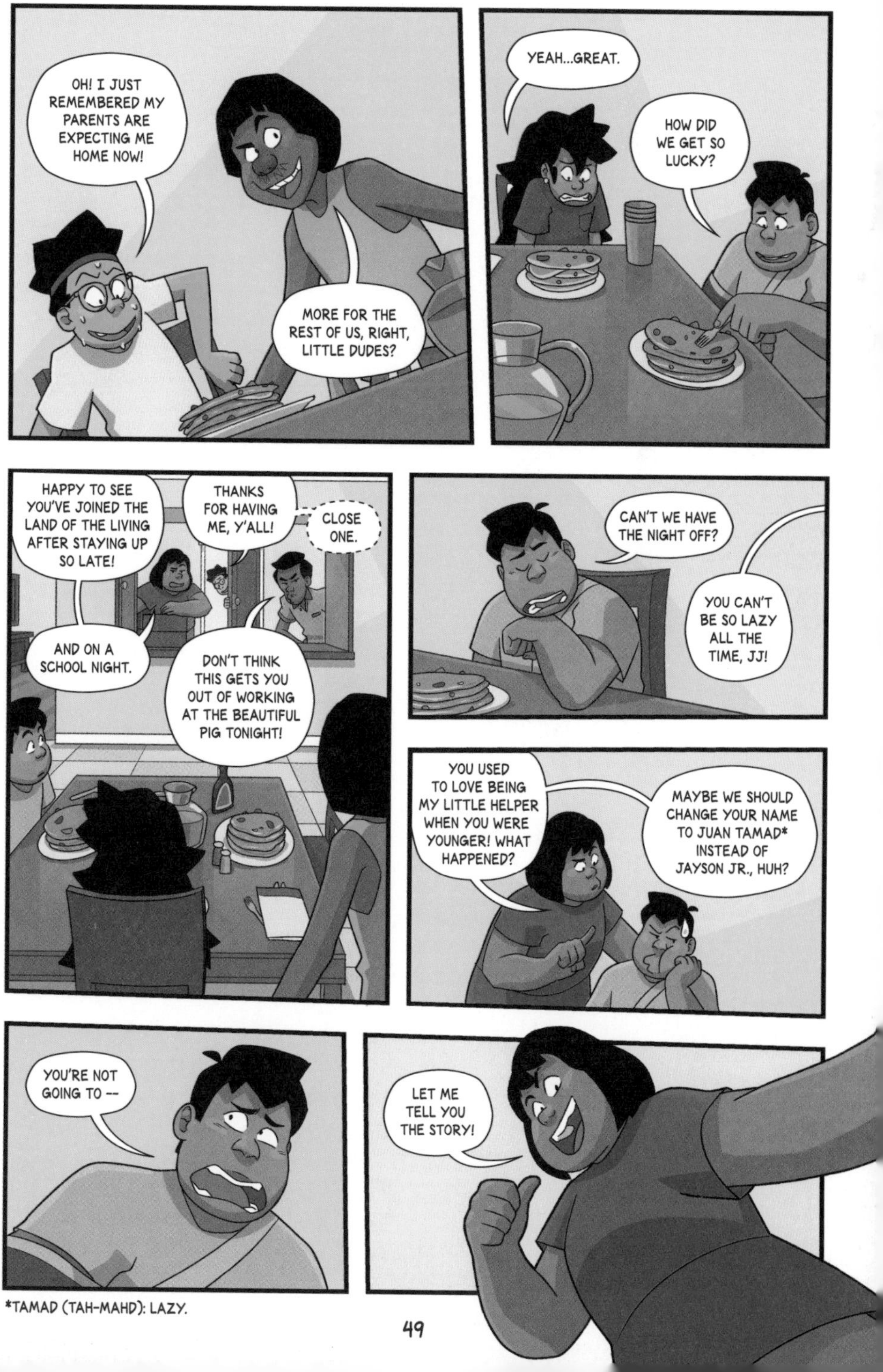
OH! I JUST REMEMBERED MY PARENTS ARE EXPECTING ME HOME NOW!
MORE FOR THE REST OF US, RIGHT, LITTLE DUDES?
YEAH...GREAT.
HOW DID WE GET SO LUCKY?
HAPPY TO SEE YOU'VE JOINED THE LAND OF THE LIVING AFTER STAYING UP SO LATE!
AND ON A SCHOOL NIGHT.
THANKS FOR HAVING ME, Y'ALL!
CLOSE ONE.
DON'T THINK THIS GETS YOU OUT OF WORKING AT THE BEAUTIFUL PIG TONIGHT!
CAN'T WE HAVE THE NIGHT OFF?
YOU CAN'T BE SO LAZY ALL THE TIME, JJ!
YOU USED TO LOVE BEING MY LITTLE HELPER WHEN YOU WERE YOUNGER! WHAT HAPPENED?
MAYBE WE SHOULD CHANGE YOUR NAME TO JUAN TAMAD* INSTEAD OF JAYSON JR., HUH?
YOU'RE NOT GOING TO --
LET ME TELL YOU THE STORY!

*TAMAD (TAH-MAHD): LAZY.

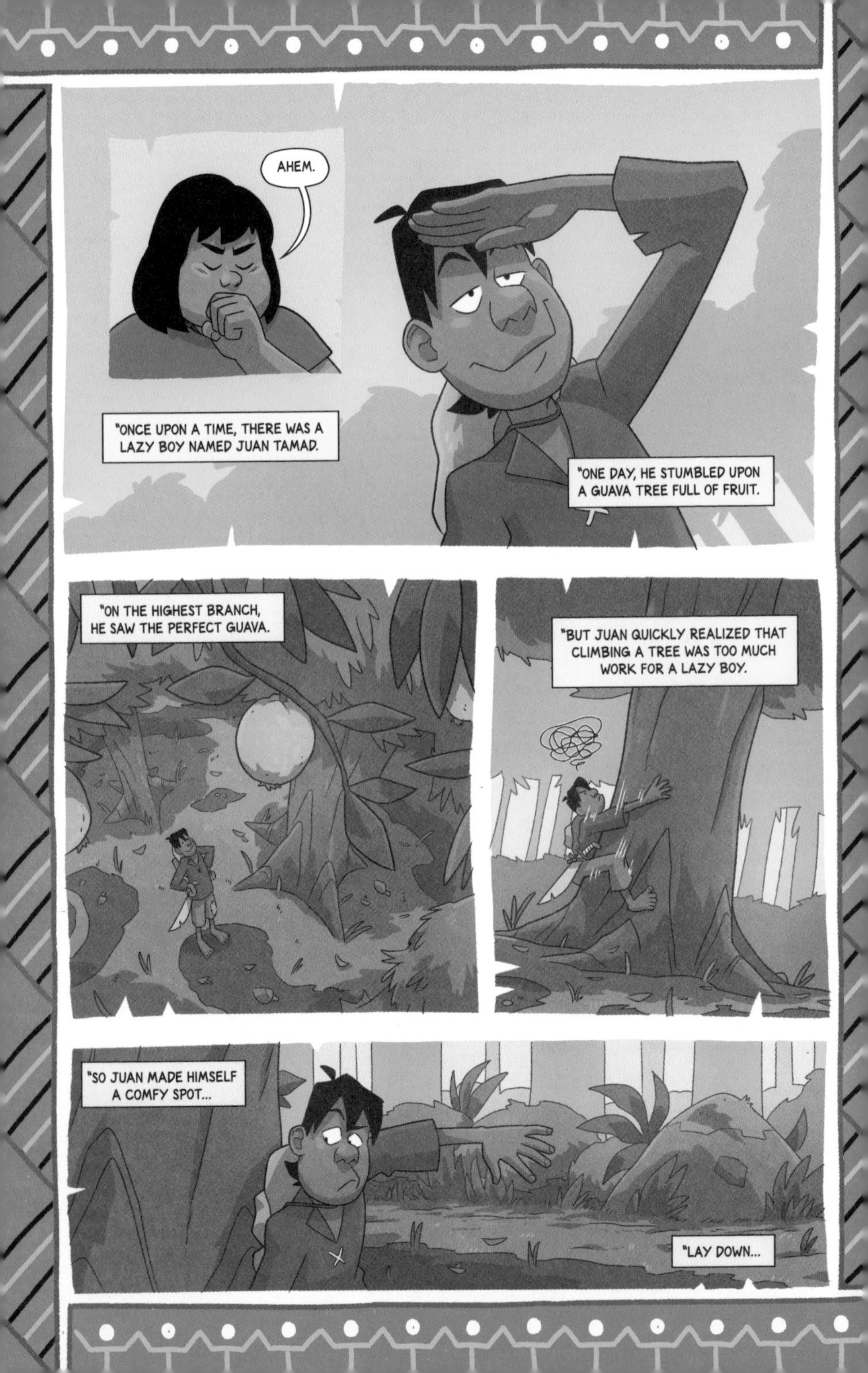
AHEM.
"ONCE UPON A TIME, THERE WAS A LAZY BOY NAMED JUAN TAMAD.
"ONE DAY, HE STUMBLED UPON A GUAVA TREE FULL OF FRUIT.
"ON THE HIGHEST BRANCH, HE SAW THE PERFECT GUAVA.
"BUT JUAN QUICKLY REALIZED THAT CLIMBING A TREE WAS TOO MUCH WORK FOR A LAZY BOY.
"SO JUAN MADE HIMSELF A COMFY SPOT...
"LAY DOWN...

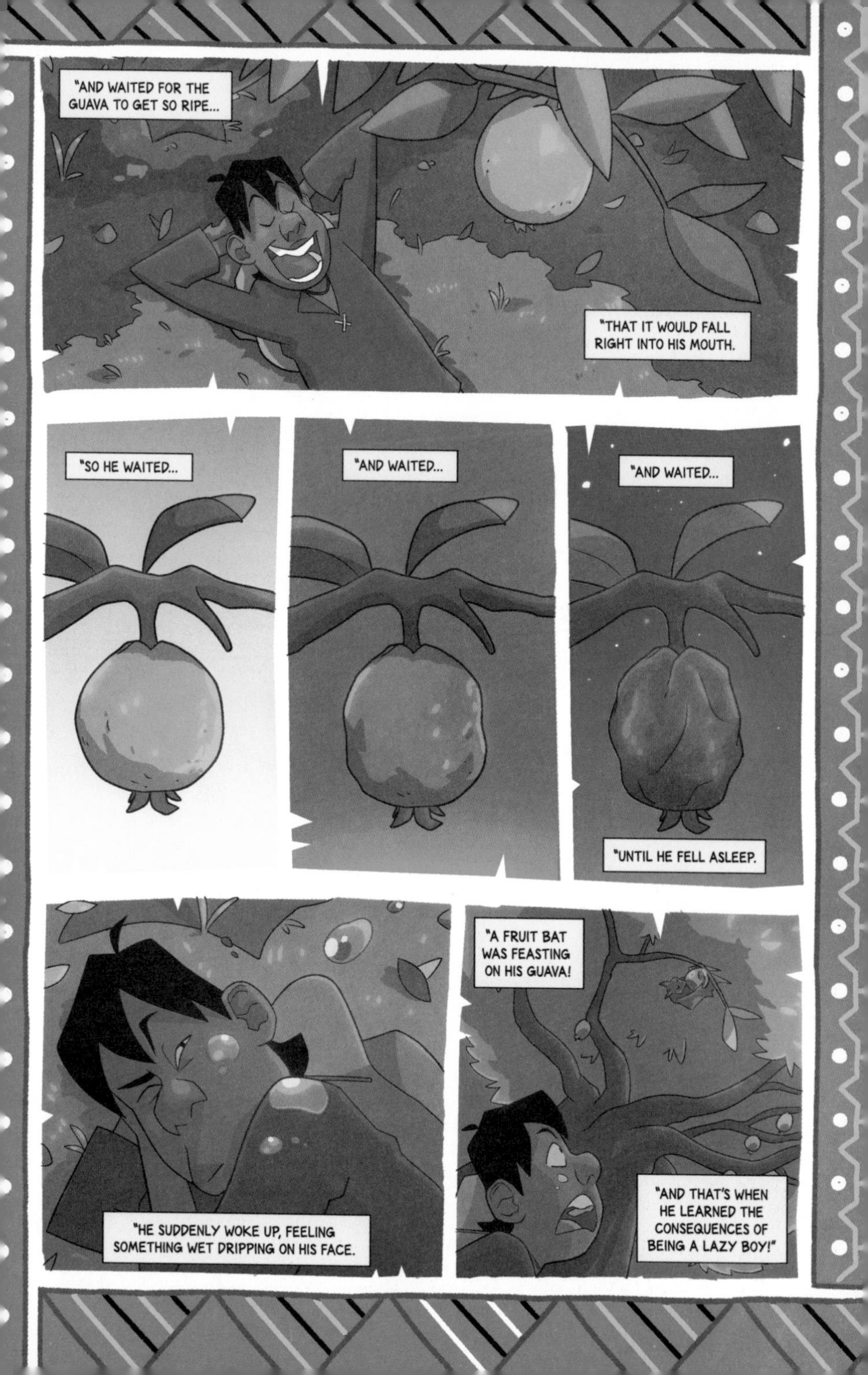
"AND WAITED FOR THE GUAVA TO GET SO RIPE...
"THAT IT WOULD FALL RIGHT INTO HIS MOUTH.
"SO HE WAITED...
"AND WAITED...
"AND WAITED...
"UNTIL HE FELL ASLEEP.
"HE SUDDENLY WOKE UP, FEELING SOMETHING WET DRIPPING ON HIS FACE.
"A FRUIT BAT WAS FEASTING ON HIS GUAVA!
"AND THAT'S WHEN HE LEARNED THE CONSEQUENCES OF BEING A LAZY BOY!"

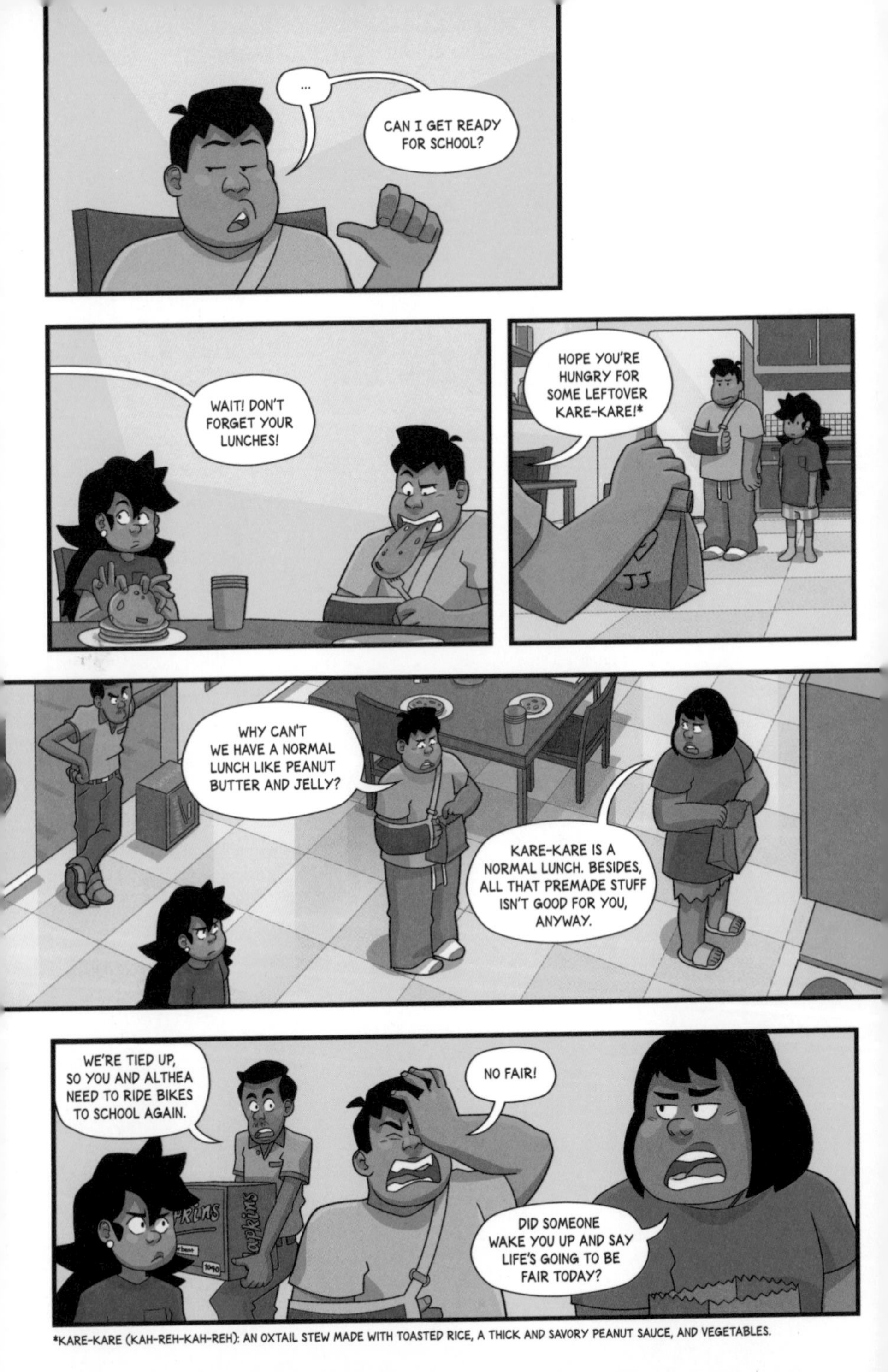
...
CAN I GET READY FOR SCHOOL?
WAIT! DON'T FORGET YOUR LUNCHES!
HOPE YOU'RE HUNGRY FOR SOME LEFTOVER KARE-KARE!*
JJ
WHY CAN'T WE HAVE A NORMAL LUNCH LIKE PEANUT BUTTER AND JELLY?
KARE-KARE IS A NORMAL LUNCH. BESIDES, ALL THAT PREMADE STUFF ISN'T GOOD FOR YOU, ANYWAY.
WE'RE TIED UP, SO YOU AND ALTHEA NEED TO RIDE BIKES TO SCHOOL AGAIN.
NO FAIR!
DID SOMEONE WAKE YOU UP AND SAY LIFE'S GOING TO BE FAIR TODAY?
Napkins

*KARE-KARE (KAH-REH-KAH-REH): AN OXTAIL STEW MADE WITH TOASTED RICE, A THICK AND SAVORY PEANUT SAUCE, AND VEGETABLES.

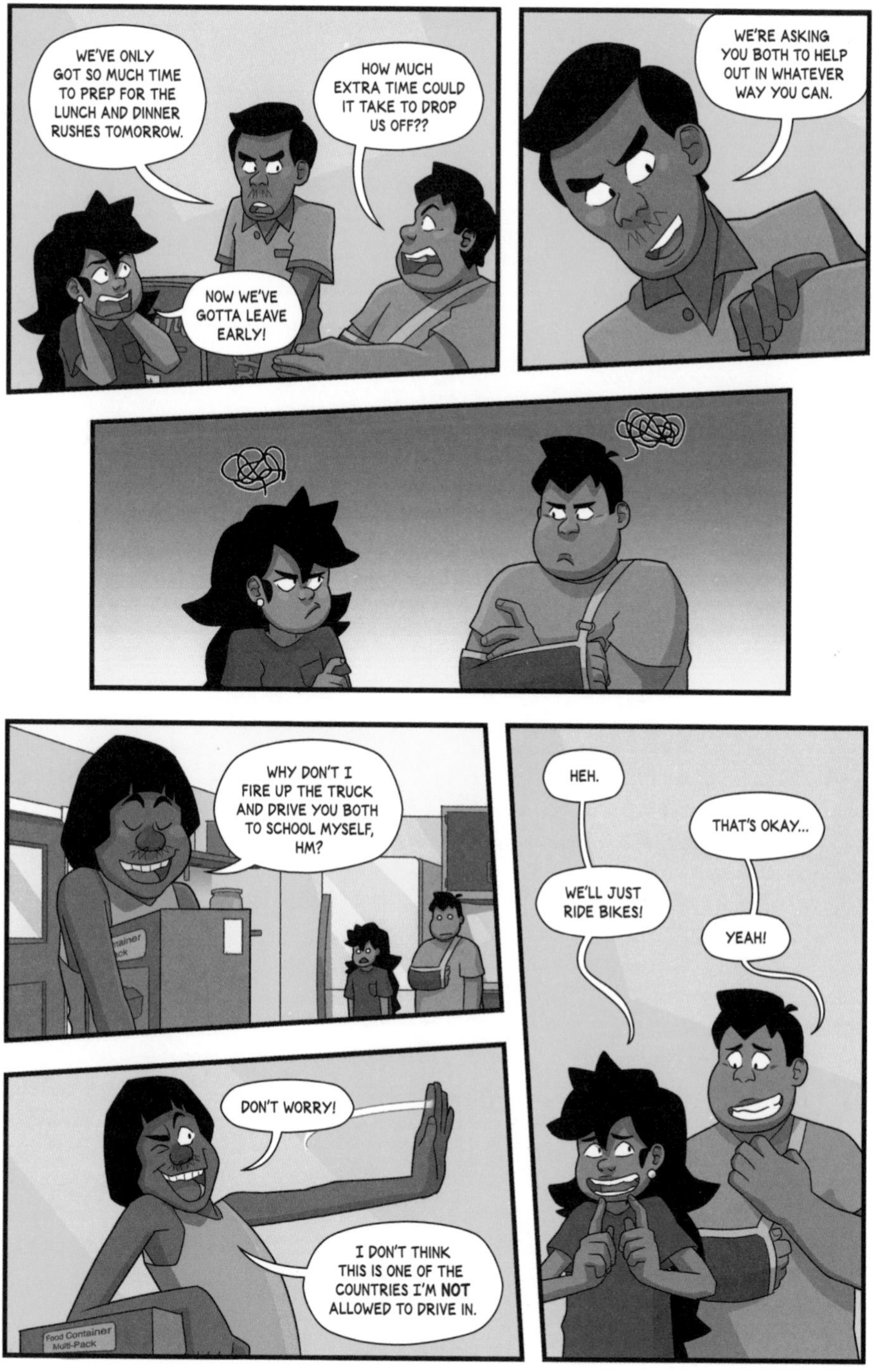
WE'VE ONLY GOT SO MUCH TIME TO PREP FOR THE LUNCH AND DINNER RUSHES TOMORROW.
HOW MUCH EXTRA TIME COULD IT TAKE TO DROP US OFF??
NOW WE'VE GOTTA LEAVE EARLY!
WE'RE ASKING YOU BOTH TO HELP OUT IN WHATEVER WAY YOU CAN.
WHY DON'T I FIRE UP THE TRUCK AND DRIVE YOU BOTH TO SCHOOL MYSELF, HM?
DON'T WORRY!
I DON'T THINK THIS IS ONE OF THE COUNTRIES I'M **NOT** ALLOWED TO DRIVE IN.
Food Container Multi-Pack
HEH.
THAT'S OKAY...
WE'LL JUST RIDE BIKES!
YEAH!

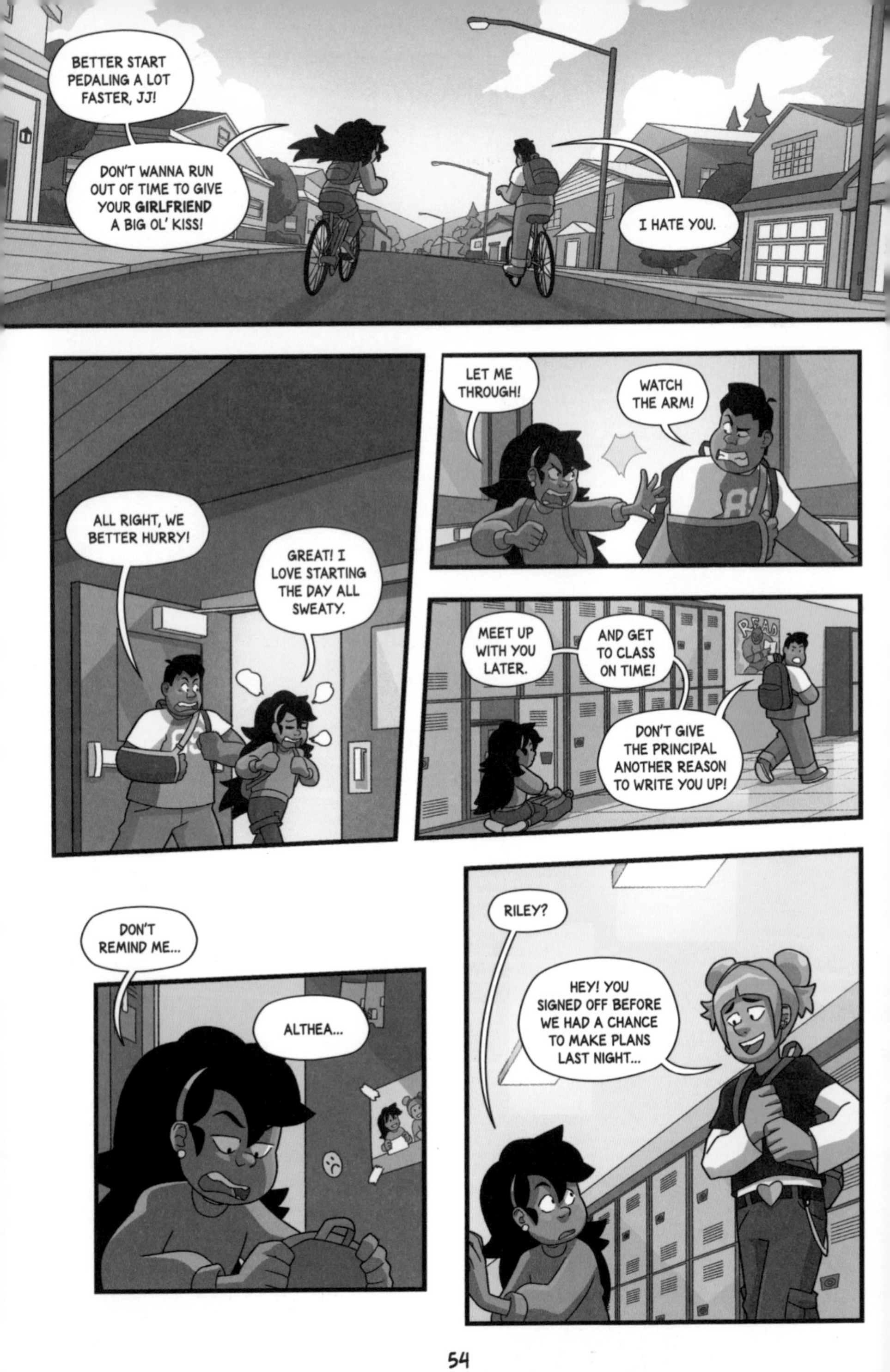
BETTER START PEDALING A LOT FASTER, JJ!
DON'T WANNA RUN OUT OF TIME TO GIVE YOUR **GIRLFRIEND** A BIG OL' KISS!
I HATE YOU.
ALL RIGHT, WE BETTER HURRY!
GREAT! I LOVE STARTING THE DAY ALL SWEATY.
LET ME THROUGH!
WATCH THE ARM!
MEET UP WITH YOU LATER.
AND GET TO CLASS ON TIME!
DON'T GIVE THE PRINCIPAL ANOTHER REASON TO WRITE YOU UP!
DON'T REMIND ME...
ALTHEA...
RILEY?
HEY! YOU SIGNED OFF BEFORE WE HAD A CHANCE TO MAKE PLANS LAST NIGHT...

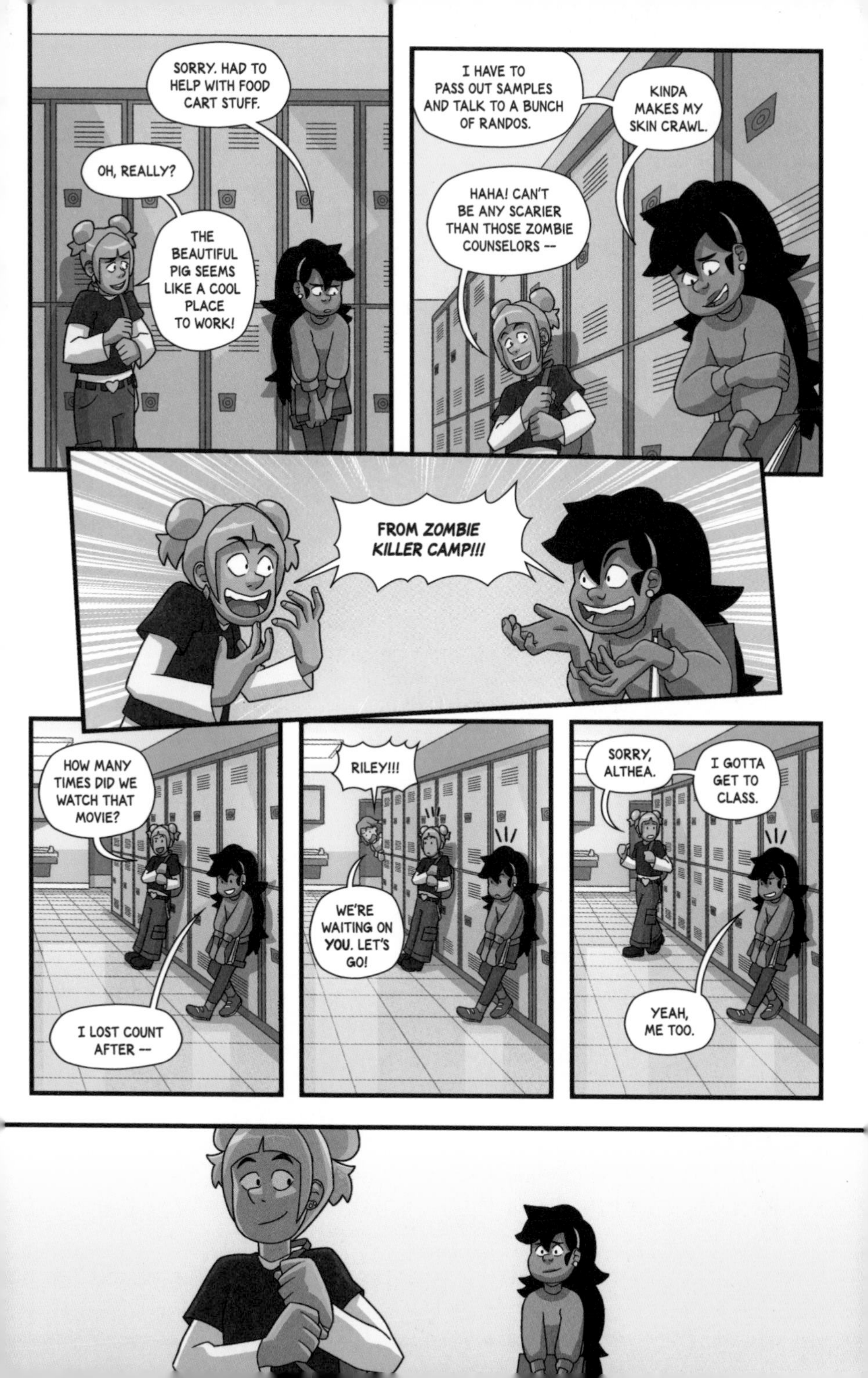
SORRY. HAD TO HELP WITH FOOD CART STUFF.
OH, REALLY?
THE BEAUTIFUL PIG SEEMS LIKE A COOL PLACE TO WORK!
I HAVE TO PASS OUT SAMPLES AND TALK TO A BUNCH OF RANDOS.
KINDA MAKES MY SKIN CRAWL.
HAHA! CAN'T BE ANY SCARIER THAN THOSE ZOMBIE COUNSELORS --
FROM ZOMBIE KILLER CAMP!!!
HOW MANY TIMES DID WE WATCH THAT MOVIE?
I LOST COUNT AFTER --
RILEY!!!
WE'RE WAITING ON YOU. LET'S GO!
SORRY, ALTHEA.
I GOTTA GET TO CLASS.
YEAH, ME TOO.

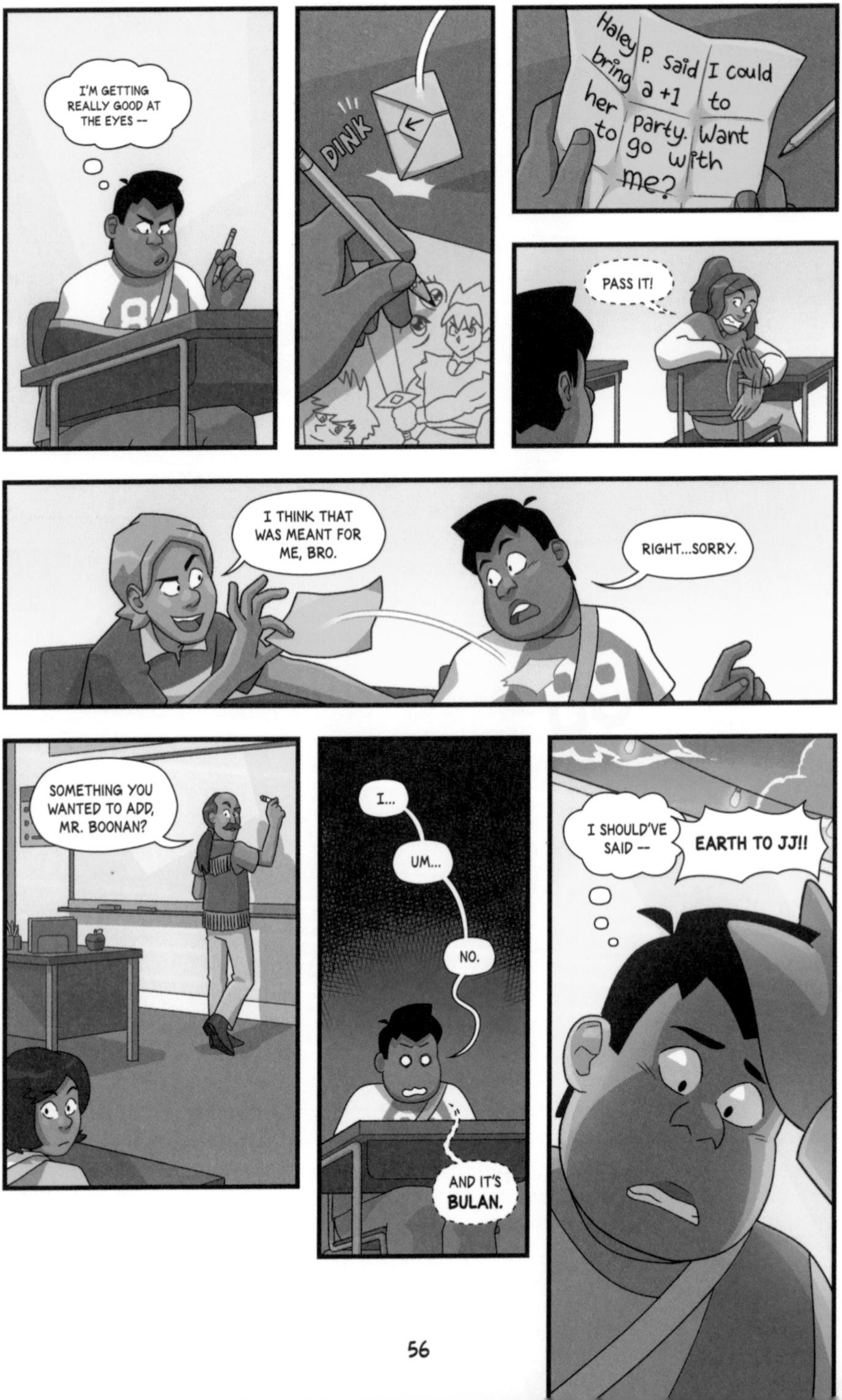
I'M GETTING REALLY GOOD AT THE EYES --
DINK
Haley P. said I could bring a +1 to her party. Want to go with me?
PASS IT!
I THINK THAT WAS MEANT FOR ME, BRO.
RIGHT...SORRY.
SOMETHING YOU WANTED TO ADD, MR. BOONAN?
I...
UM...
NO.
AND IT'S BULAN.
I SHOULD'VE SAID --
EARTH TO JJ!!

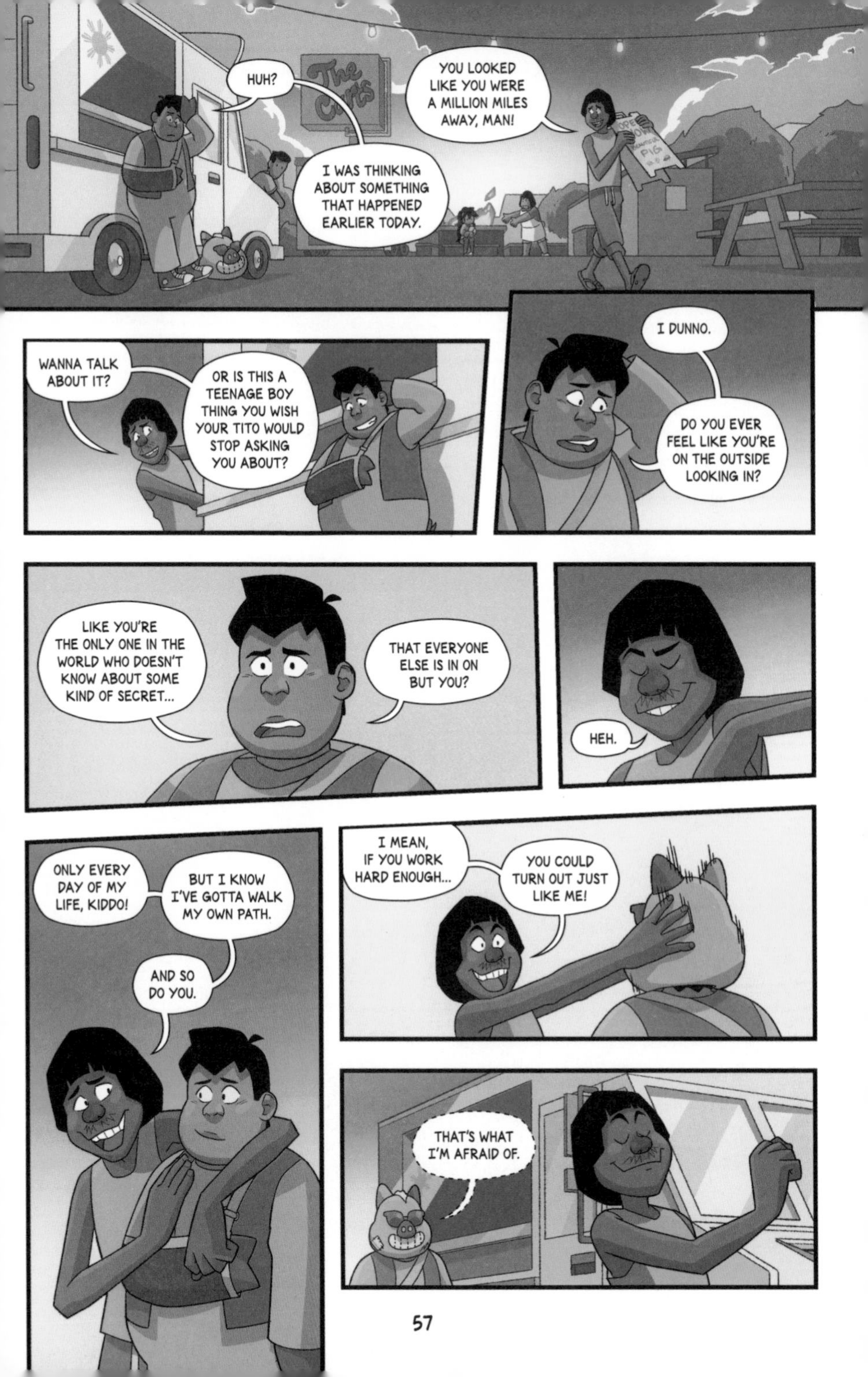
The Carts
HUH?
YOU LOOKED LIKE YOU WERE A MILLION MILES AWAY, MAN!
I WAS THINKING ABOUT SOMETHING THAT HAPPENED EARLIER TODAY.
WANNA TALK ABOUT IT?
OR IS THIS A TEENAGE BOY THING YOU WISH YOUR TITO WOULD STOP ASKING YOU ABOUT?
I DUNNO.
DO YOU EVER FEEL LIKE YOU'RE ON THE OUTSIDE LOOKING IN?
LIKE YOU'RE THE ONLY ONE IN THE WORLD WHO DOESN'T KNOW ABOUT SOME KIND OF SECRET...
THAT EVERYONE ELSE IS IN ON BUT YOU?
HEH.
ONLY EVERY DAY OF MY LIFE, KIDDO!
BUT I KNOW I'VE GOTTA WALK MY OWN PATH.
AND SO DO YOU.
I MEAN, IF YOU WORK HARD ENOUGH...
YOU COULD TURN OUT JUST LIKE ME!
THAT'S WHAT I'M AFRAID OF.

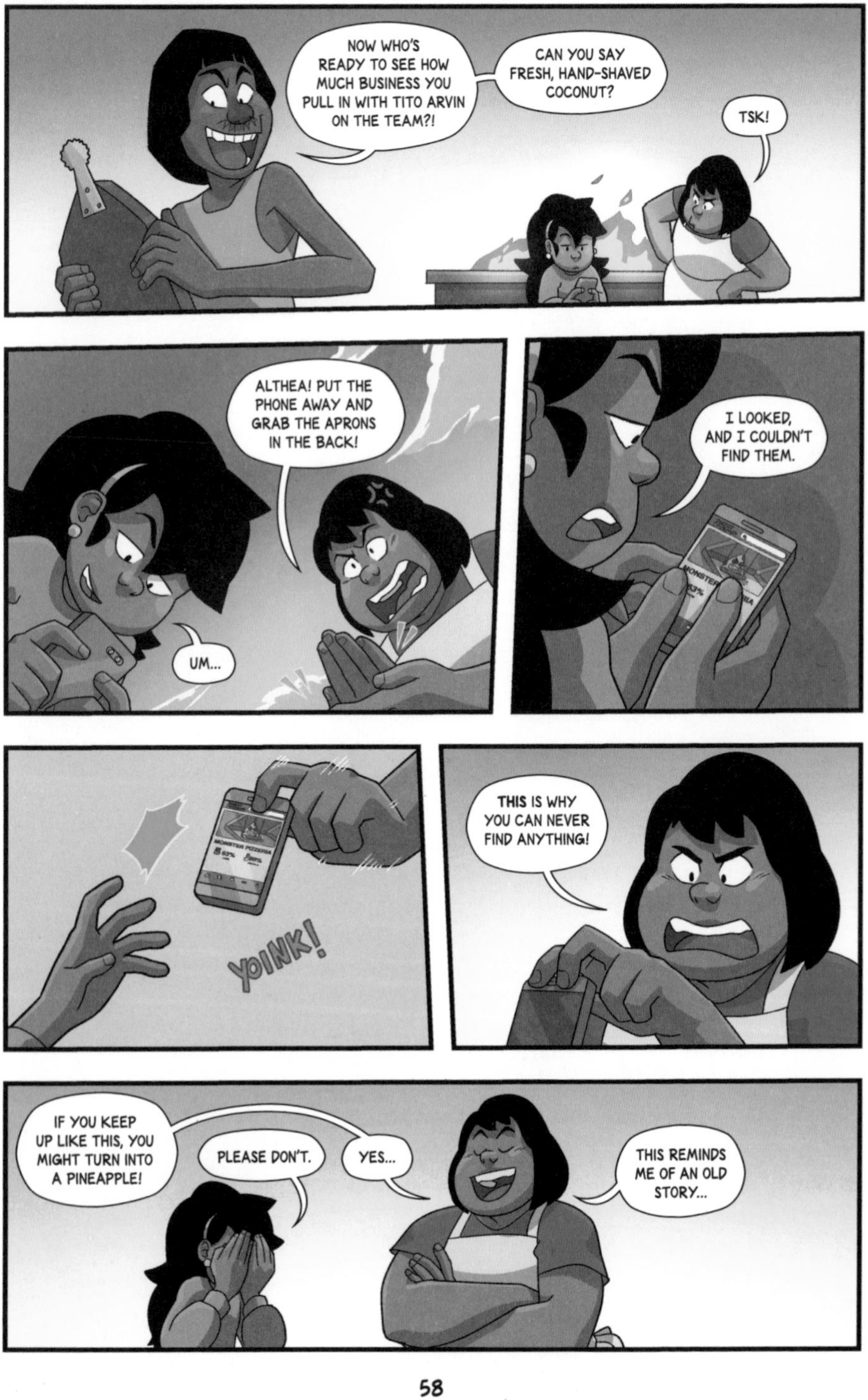
NOW WHO'S READY TO SEE HOW MUCH BUSINESS YOU PULL IN WITH TITO ARVIN ON THE TEAM?!
CAN YOU SAY FRESH, HAND-SHAVED COCONUT?
TSK!
ALTHEA! PUT THE PHONE AWAY AND GRAB THE APRONS IN THE BACK!
UM...
I LOOKED, AND I COULDN'T FIND THEM.
MONSTER PIZZERIA
YOINK!
THIS IS WHY YOU CAN NEVER FIND ANYTHING!
IF YOU KEEP UP LIKE THIS, YOU MIGHT TURN INTO A PINEAPPLE!
PLEASE DON'T.
YES...
THIS REMINDS ME OF AN OLD STORY...

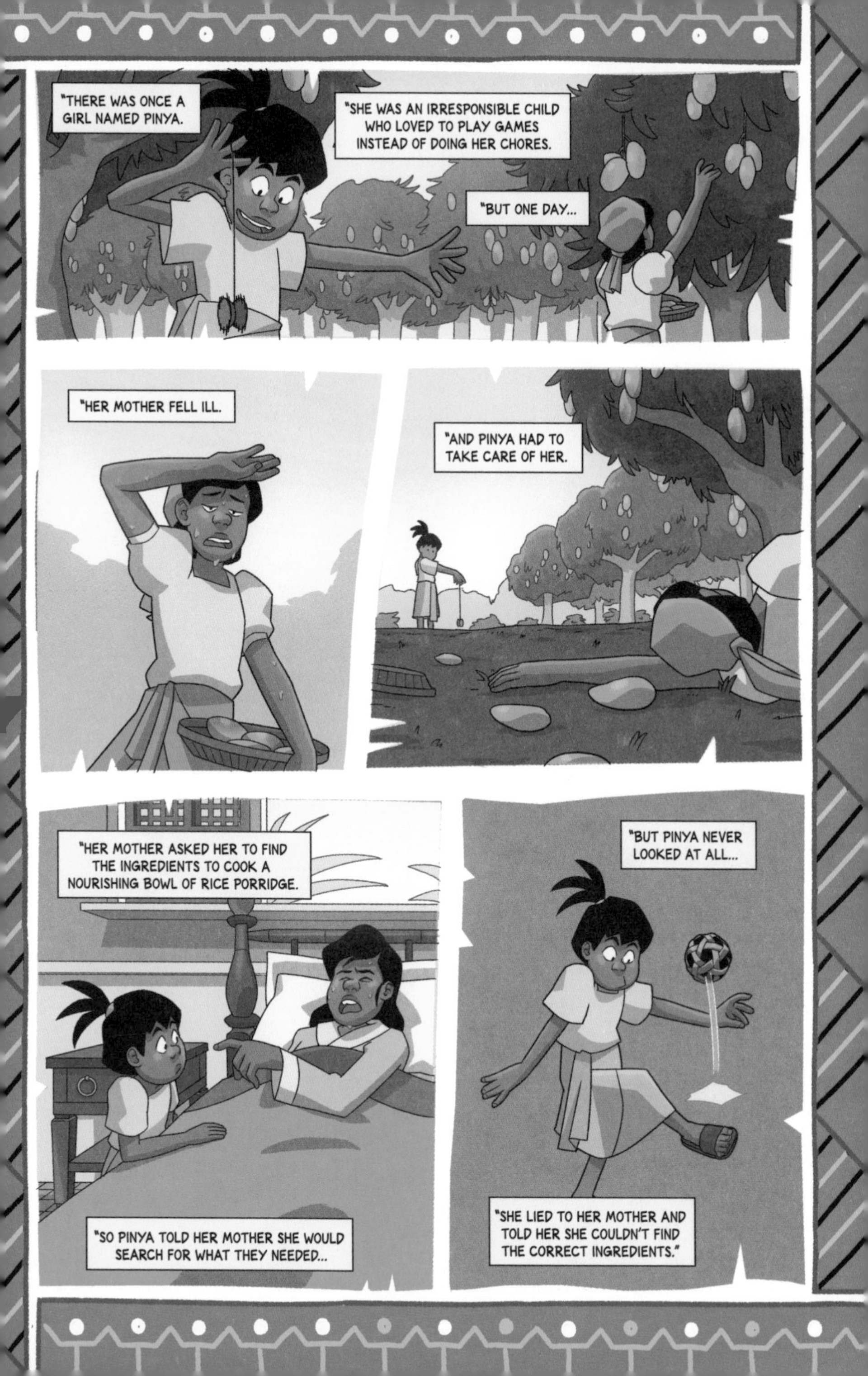
"THERE WAS ONCE A GIRL NAMED PINYA.
"SHE WAS AN IRRESPONSIBLE CHILD WHO LOVED TO PLAY GAMES INSTEAD OF DOING HER CHORES.
"BUT ONE DAY...
"HER MOTHER FELL ILL.
"AND PINYA HAD TO TAKE CARE OF HER.
"HER MOTHER ASKED HER TO FIND THE INGREDIENTS TO COOK A NOURISHING BOWL OF RICE PORRIDGE.
"SO PINYA TOLD HER MOTHER SHE WOULD SEARCH FOR WHAT THEY NEEDED...
"BUT PINYA NEVER LOOKED AT ALL...
"SHE LIED TO HER MOTHER AND TOLD HER SHE COULDN'T FIND THE CORRECT INGREDIENTS."

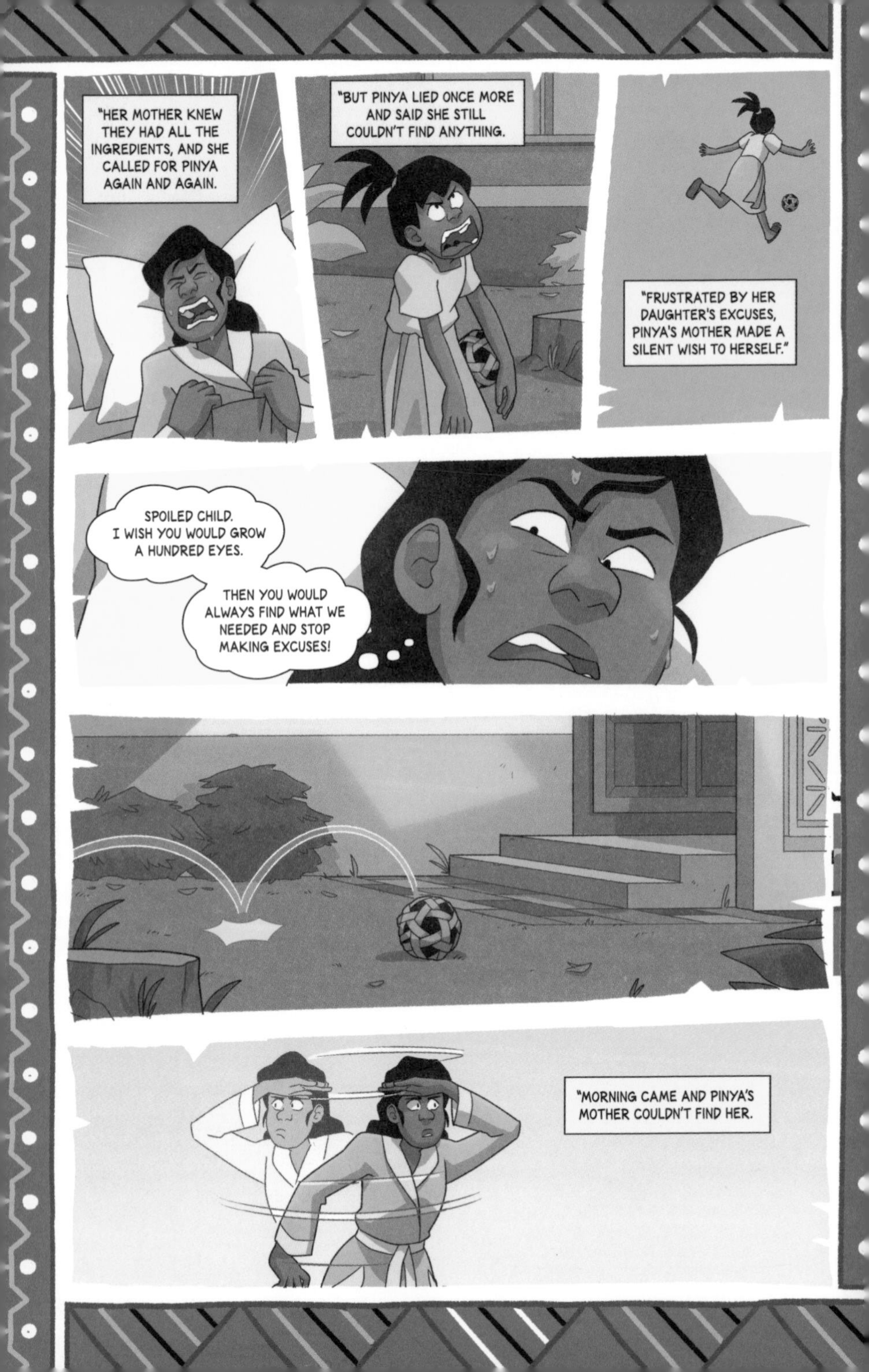
"HER MOTHER KNEW THEY HAD ALL THE INGREDIENTS, AND SHE CALLED FOR PINYA AGAIN AND AGAIN.
"BUT PINYA LIED ONCE MORE AND SAID SHE STILL COULDN'T FIND ANYTHING.
"FRUSTRATED BY HER DAUGHTER'S EXCUSES, PINYA'S MOTHER MADE A SILENT WISH TO HERSELF."
SPOILED CHILD. I WISH YOU WOULD GROW A HUNDRED EYES.
THEN YOU WOULD ALWAYS FIND WHAT WE NEEDED AND STOP MAKING EXCUSES!
"MORNING CAME AND PINYA'S MOTHER COULDN'T FIND HER.

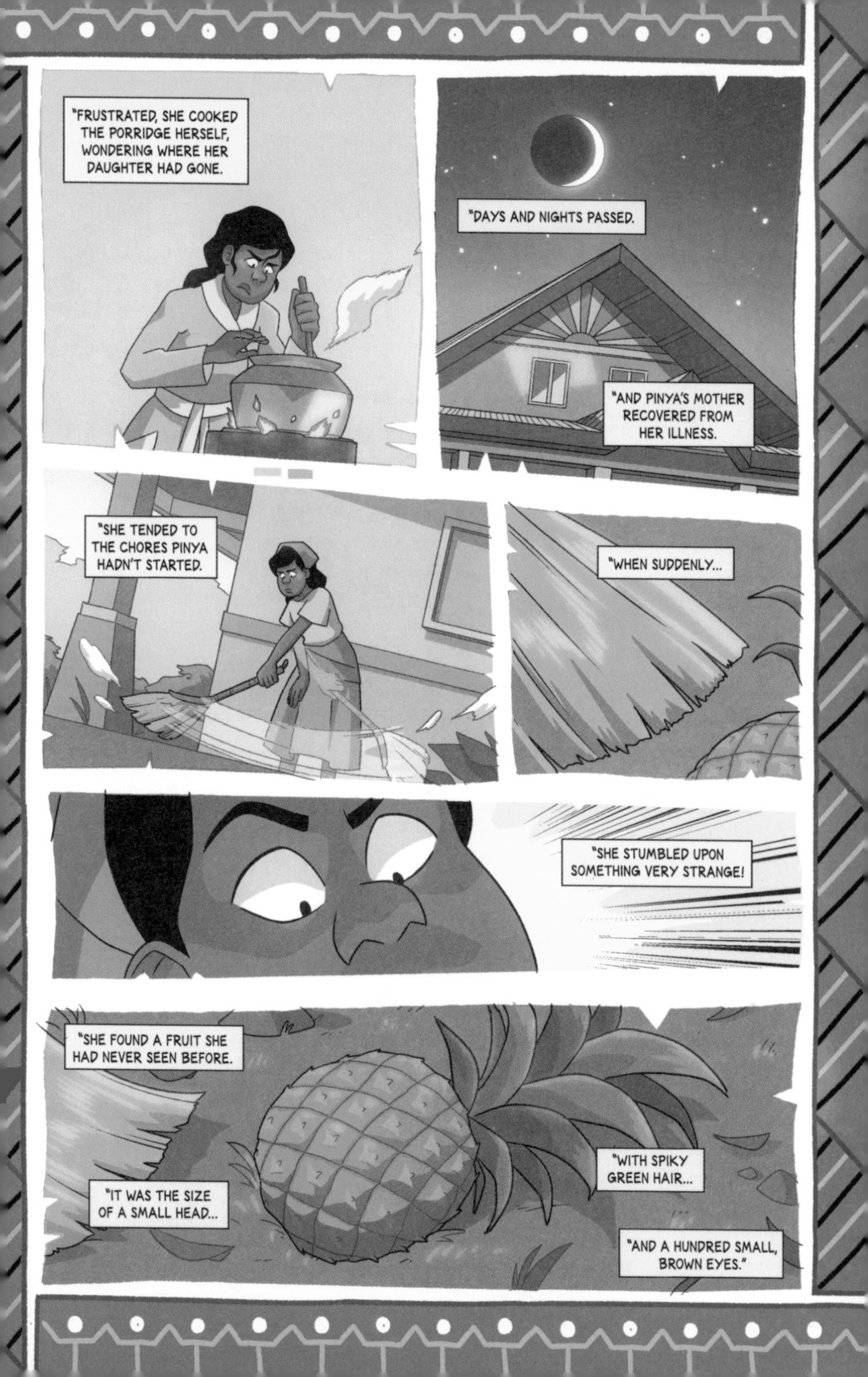
"FRUSTRATED, SHE COOKED THE PORRIDGE HERSELF, WONDERING WHERE HER DAUGHTER HAD GONE.
"DAYS AND NIGHTS PASSED.
"AND PINYA'S MOTHER RECOVERED FROM HER ILLNESS.
"SHE TENDED TO THE CHORES PINYA HADN'T STARTED.
"WHEN SUDDENLY...
"SHE STUMBLED UPON SOMETHING VERY STRANGE!
"SHE FOUND A FRUIT SHE HAD NEVER SEEN BEFORE.
"IT WAS THE SIZE OF A SMALL HEAD...
"WITH SPIKY GREEN HAIR...
"AND A HUNDRED SMALL, BROWN EYES."

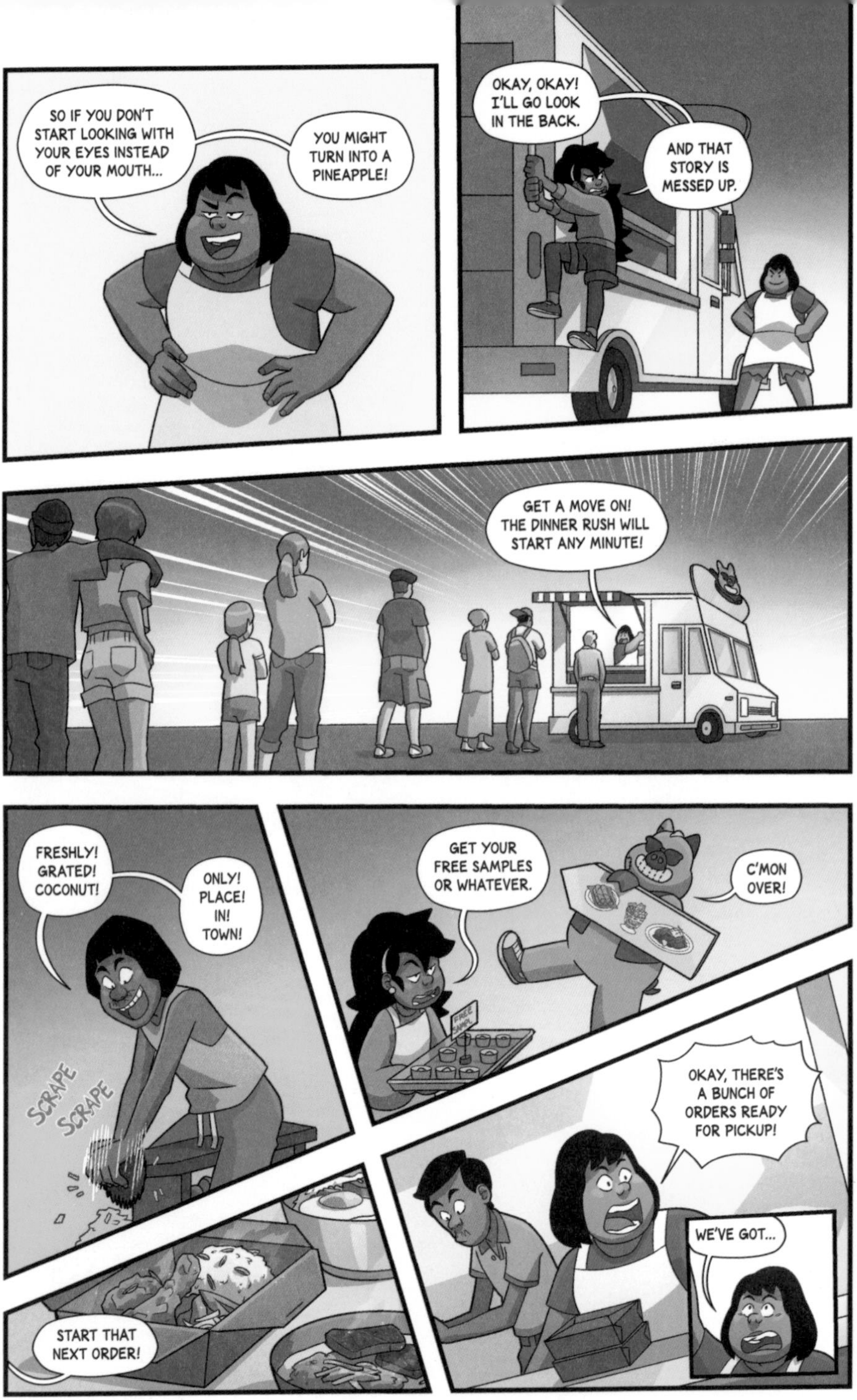
SO IF YOU DON'T START LOOKING WITH YOUR EYES INSTEAD OF YOUR MOUTH...
YOU MIGHT TURN INTO A PINEAPPLE!
OKAY, OKAY! I'LL GO LOOK IN THE BACK.
AND THAT STORY IS MESSED UP.
GET A MOVE ON! THE DINNER RUSH WILL START ANY MINUTE!
FRESHLY! GRATED! COCONUT!
ONLY! PLACE! IN! TOWN!
SCRAPE
SCRAPE
GET YOUR FREE SAMPLES OR WHATEVER.
C'MON OVER!
OKAY, THERE'S A BUNCH OF ORDERS READY FOR PICKUP!
START THAT NEXT ORDER!
WE'VE GOT...

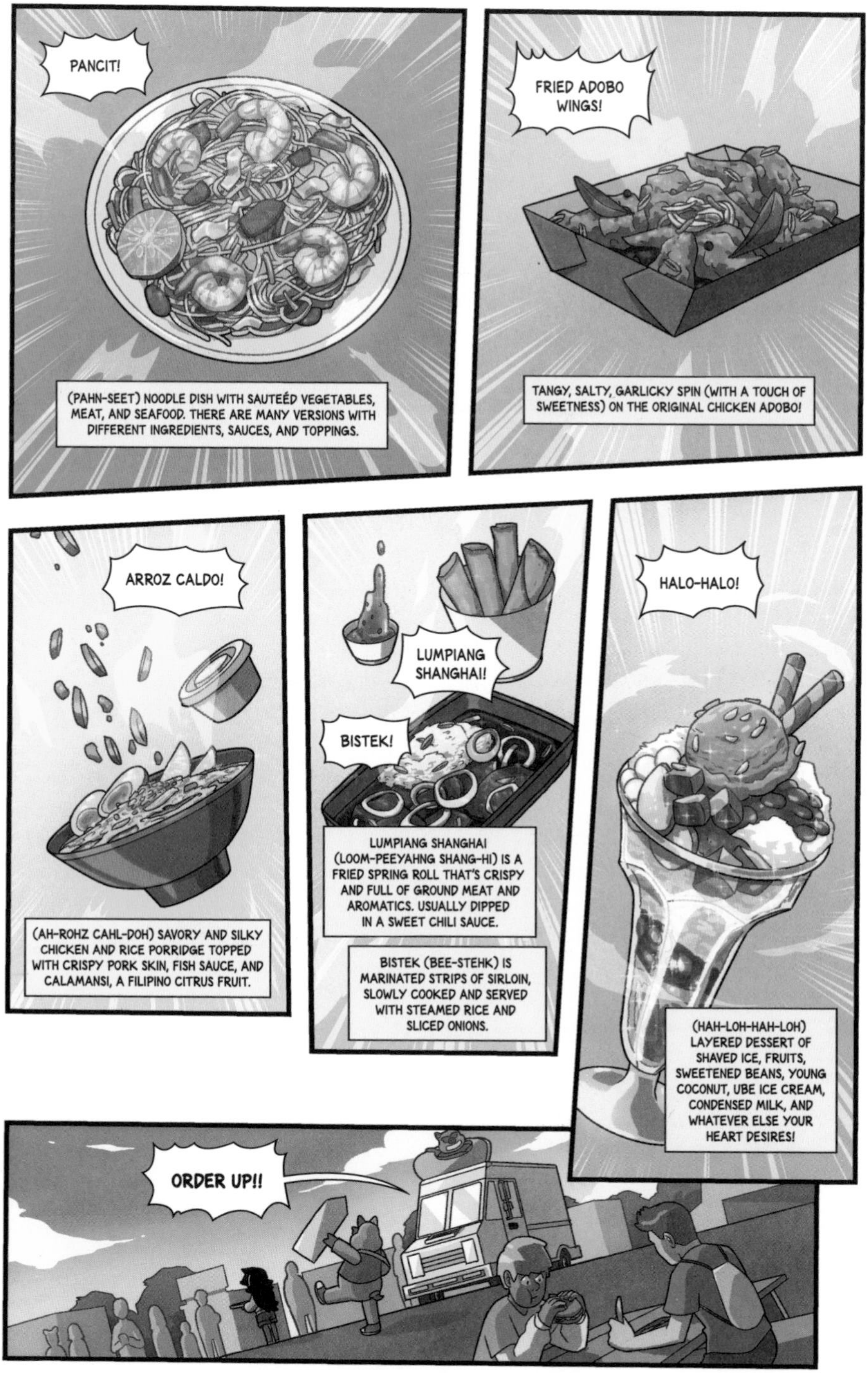
PANCIT!
(PAHN-SEET) NOODLE DISH WITH SAUTEÉD VEGETABLES, MEAT, AND SEAFOOD. THERE ARE MANY VERSIONS WITH DIFFERENT INGREDIENTS, SAUCES, AND TOPPINGS.
FRIED ADOBO WINGS!
TANGY, SALTY, GARLICKY SPIN (WITH A TOUCH OF SWEETNESS) ON THE ORIGINAL CHICKEN ADOBO!
ARROZ CALDO!
(AH-ROHZ CAHL-DOH) SAVORY AND SILKY CHICKEN AND RICE PORRIDGE TOPPED WITH CRISPY PORK SKIN, FISH SAUCE, AND CALAMANSI, A FILIPINO CITRUS FRUIT.
LUMPIANG SHANGHAI!
BISTEK!
LUMPIANG SHANGHAI (LOOM-PEEYAHNG SHANG-HI) IS A FRIED SPRING ROLL THAT'S CRISPY AND FULL OF GROUND MEAT AND AROMATICS. USUALLY DIPPED IN A SWEET CHILI SAUCE.
BISTEK (BEE-STEHK) IS MARINATED STRIPS OF SIRLOIN, SLOWLY COOKED AND SERVED WITH STEAMED RICE AND SLICED ONIONS.
HALO-HALO!
(HAH-LOH-HAH-LOH) LAYERED DESSERT OF SHAVED ICE, FRUITS, SWEETENED BEANS, YOUNG COCONUT, UBE ICE CREAM, CONDENSED MILK, AND WHATEVER ELSE YOUR HEART DESIRES!
ORDER UP!!

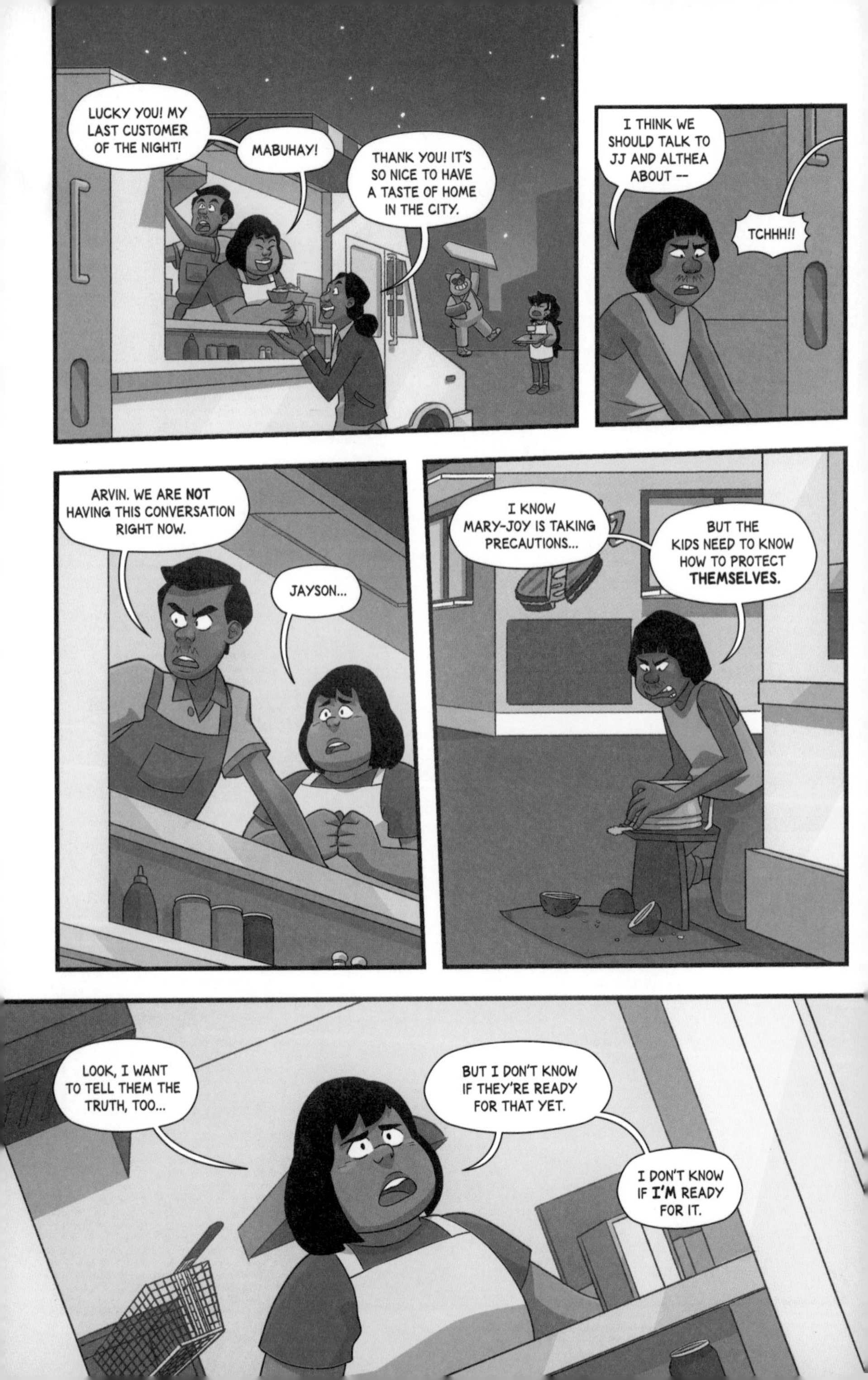
LUCKY YOU! MY LAST CUSTOMER OF THE NIGHT!
MABUHAY!
THANK YOU! IT'S SO NICE TO HAVE A TASTE OF HOME IN THE CITY.
I THINK WE SHOULD TALK TO JJ AND ALTHEA ABOUT --
TCHHH!!
ARVIN. WE ARE **NOT** HAVING THIS CONVERSATION RIGHT NOW.
JAYSON...
I KNOW MARY-JOY IS TAKING PRECAUTIONS...
BUT THE KIDS NEED TO KNOW HOW TO PROTECT **THEMSELVES.**
LOOK, I WANT TO TELL THEM THE TRUTH, TOO...
BUT I DON'T KNOW IF THEY'RE READY FOR THAT YET.
I DON'T KNOW IF **I'M** READY FOR IT.

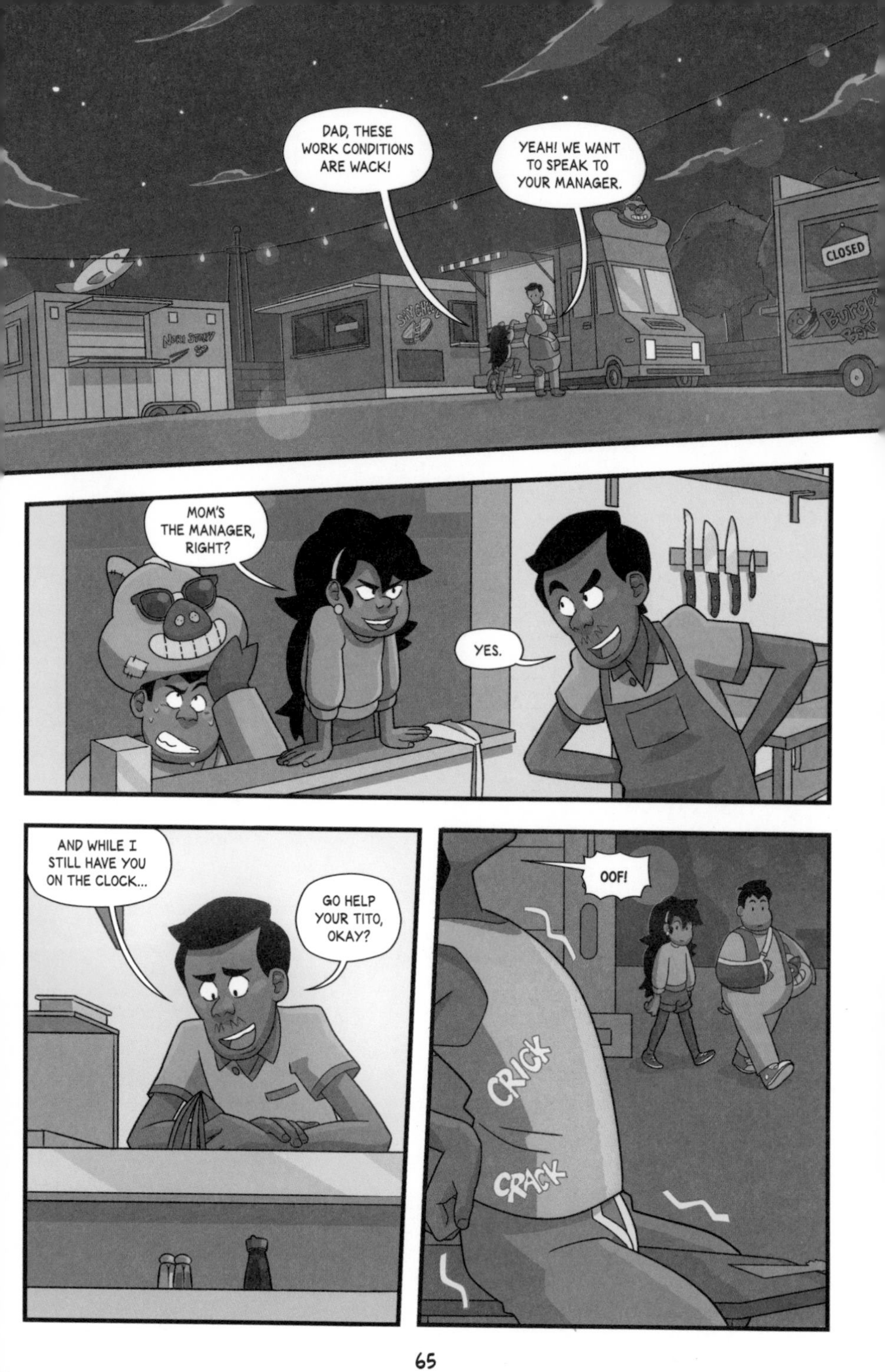
DAD, THESE WORK CONDITIONS ARE WACK!
YEAH! WE WANT TO SPEAK TO YOUR MANAGER.
CLOSED
MOM'S THE MANAGER, RIGHT?
YES.
AND WHILE I STILL HAVE YOU ON THE CLOCK...
GO HELP YOUR TITO, OKAY?
OOF!
CRICK
CRACK

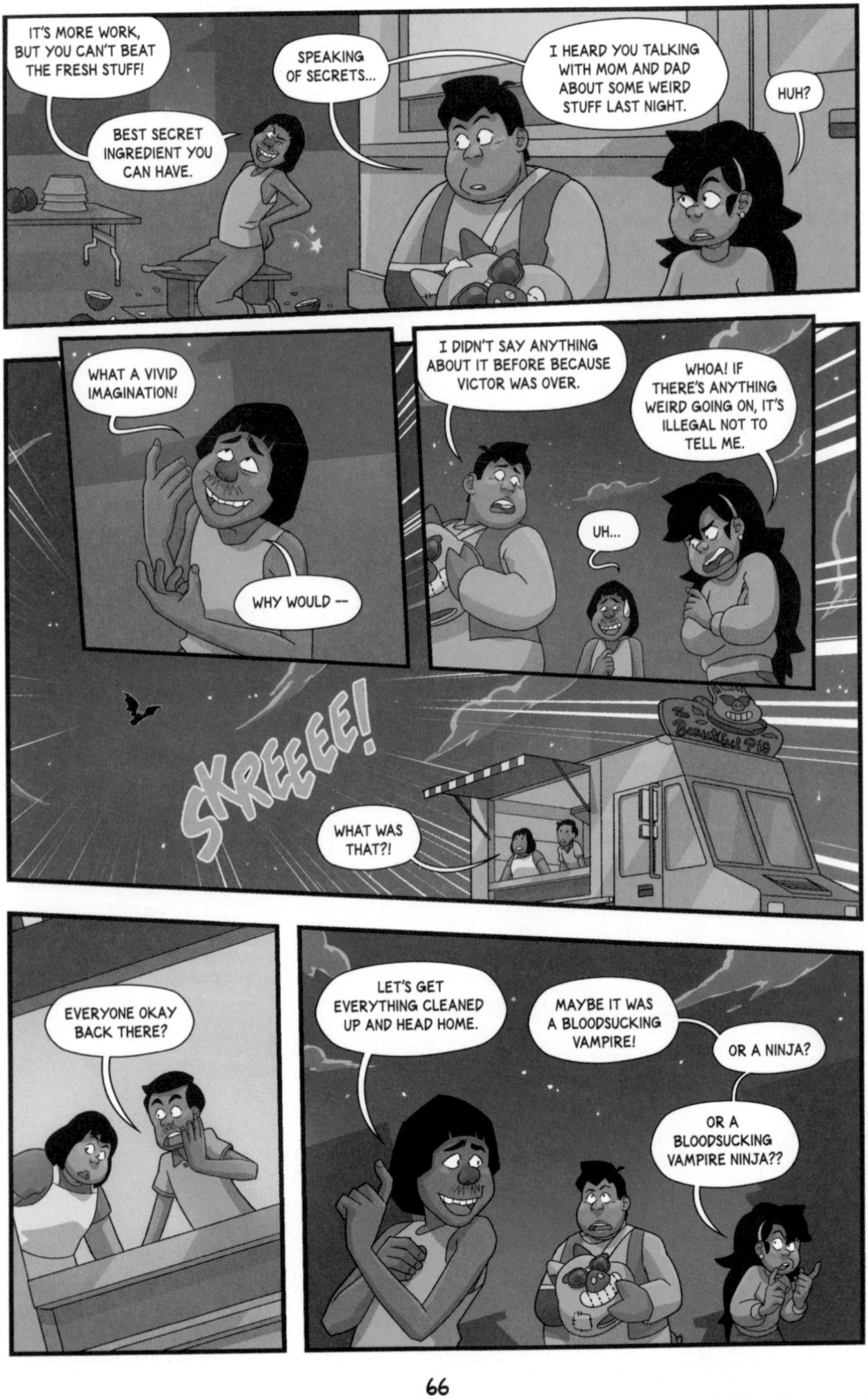
IT'S MORE WORK, BUT YOU CAN'T BEAT THE FRESH STUFF!
BEST SECRET INGREDIENT YOU CAN HAVE.
SPEAKING OF SECRETS...
I HEARD YOU TALKING WITH MOM AND DAD ABOUT SOME WEIRD STUFF LAST NIGHT.
HUH?
WHAT A VIVID IMAGINATION!
WHY WOULD --
I DIDN'T SAY ANYTHING ABOUT IT BEFORE BECAUSE VICTOR WAS OVER.
WHOA! IF THERE'S ANYTHING WEIRD GOING ON, IT'S ILLEGAL NOT TO TELL ME.
UH...
SKREEEE!
WHAT WAS THAT?!
EVERYONE OKAY BACK THERE?
LET'S GET EVERYTHING CLEANED UP AND HEAD HOME.
MAYBE IT WAS A BLOODSUCKING VAMPIRE!
OR A NINJA?
OR A BLOODSUCKING VAMPIRE NINJA??

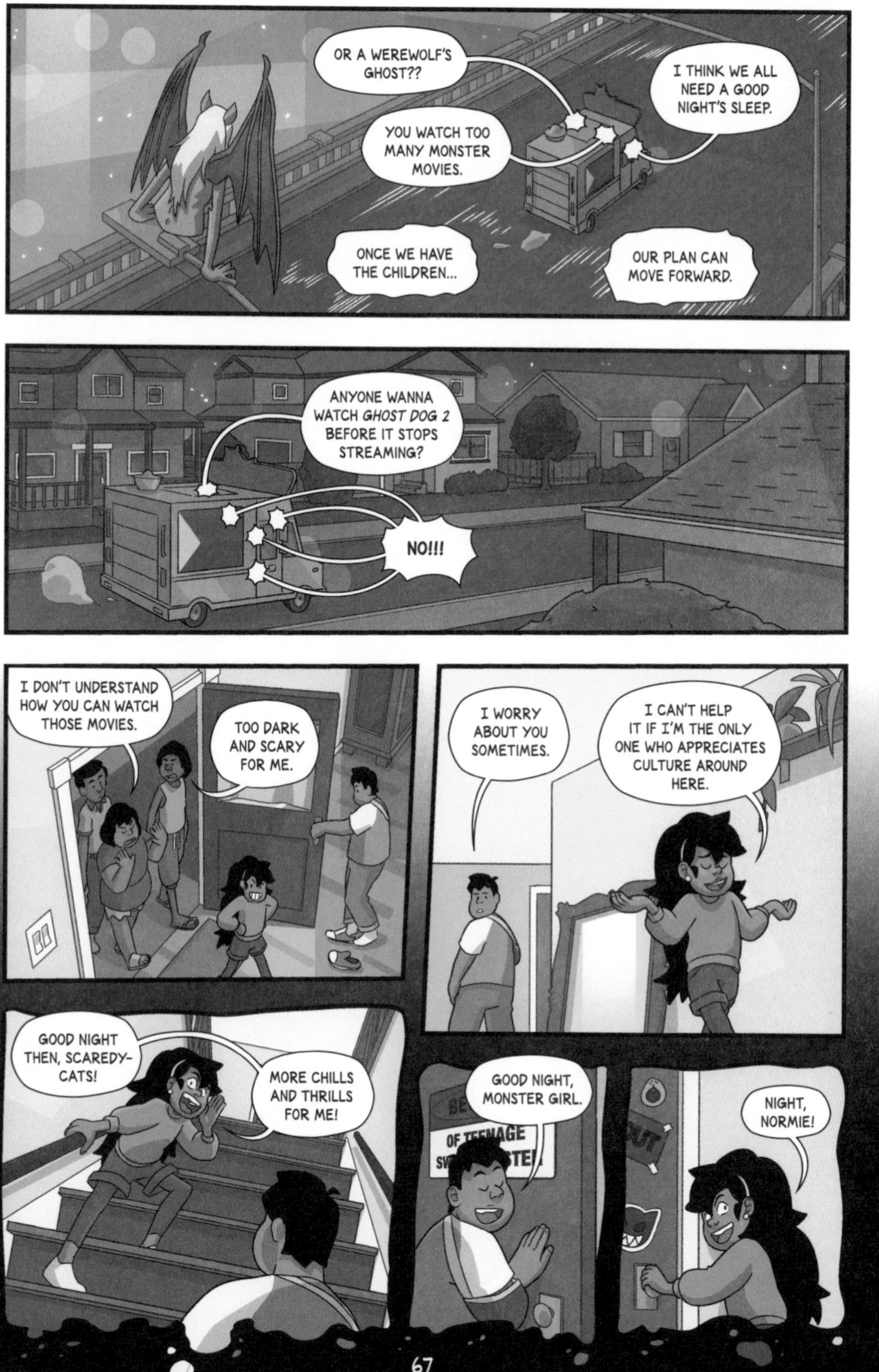
OR A WEREWOLF'S GHOST??
YOU WATCH TOO MANY MONSTER MOVIES.
I THINK WE ALL NEED A GOOD NIGHT'S SLEEP.
ONCE WE HAVE THE CHILDREN...
OUR PLAN CAN MOVE FORWARD.
ANYONE WANNA WATCH *GHOST DOG 2* BEFORE IT STOPS STREAMING?
NO!!!
I DON'T UNDERSTAND HOW YOU CAN WATCH THOSE MOVIES.
TOO DARK AND SCARY FOR ME.
I WORRY ABOUT YOU SOMETIMES.
I CAN'T HELP IT IF I'M THE ONLY ONE WHO APPRECIATES CULTURE AROUND HERE.
GOOD NIGHT THEN, SCAREDY-CATS!
MORE CHILLS AND THRILLS FOR ME!
GOOD NIGHT, MONSTER GIRL.
NIGHT, NORMIE!

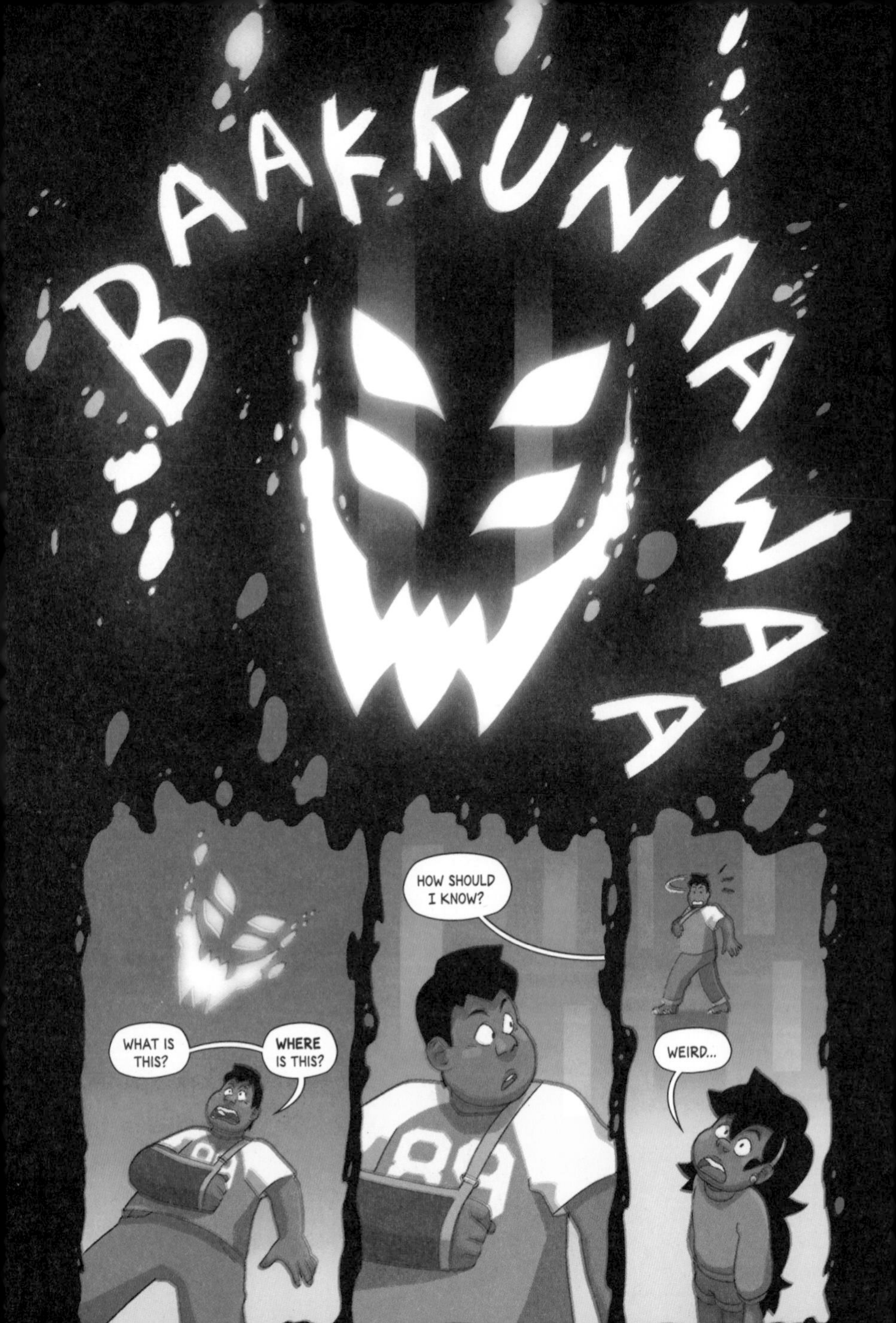
BAAKUNAAWAA
WHAT IS THIS?
WHERE IS THIS?
HOW SHOULD I KNOW?
WEIRD...

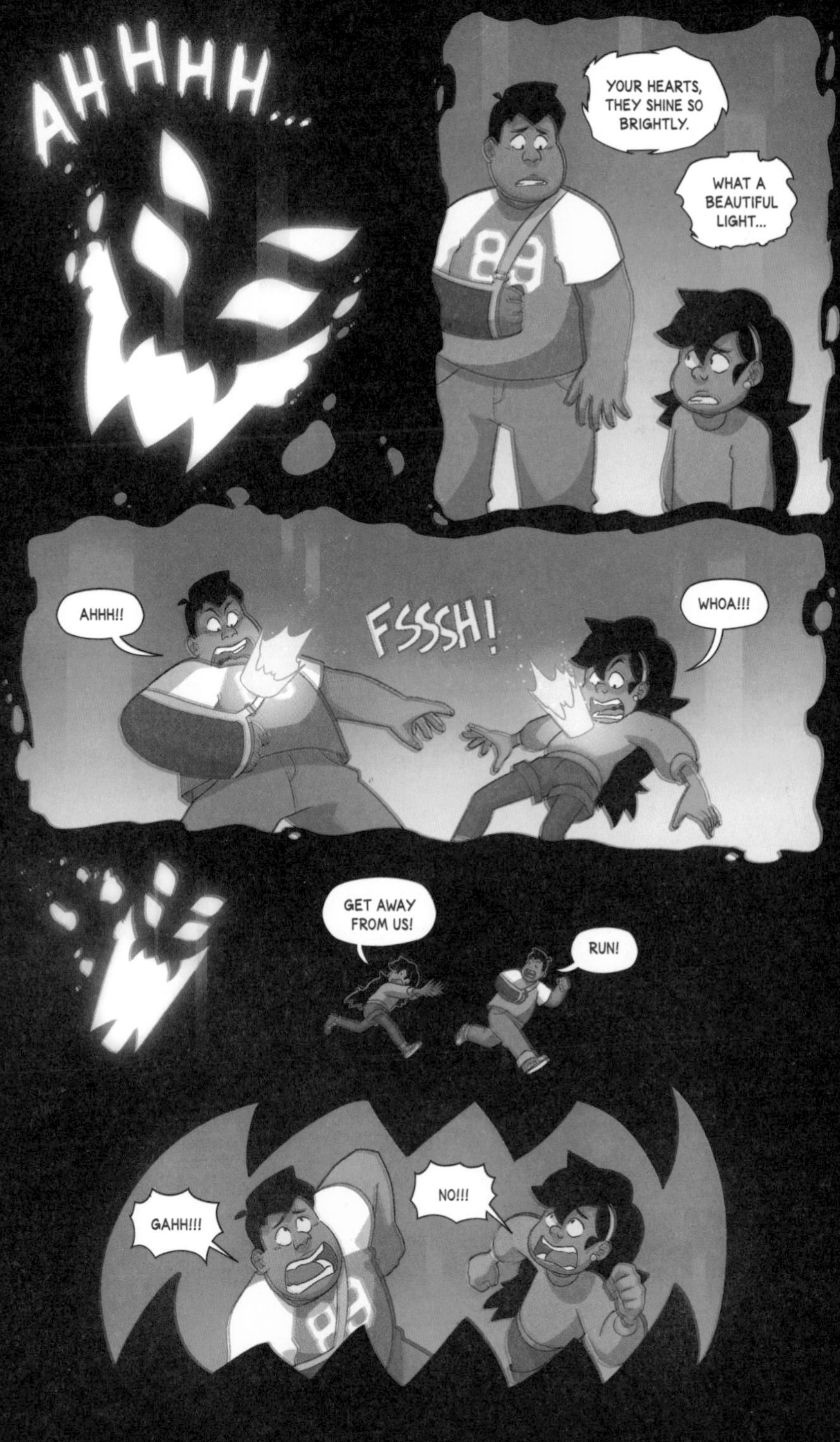
AHHHH...
YOUR HEARTS, THEY SHINE SO BRIGHTLY.
WHAT A BEAUTIFUL LIGHT...
AHHH!!
FSSSH!
WHOA!!!
GET AWAY FROM US!
RUN!
GAHH!!!
NO!!!

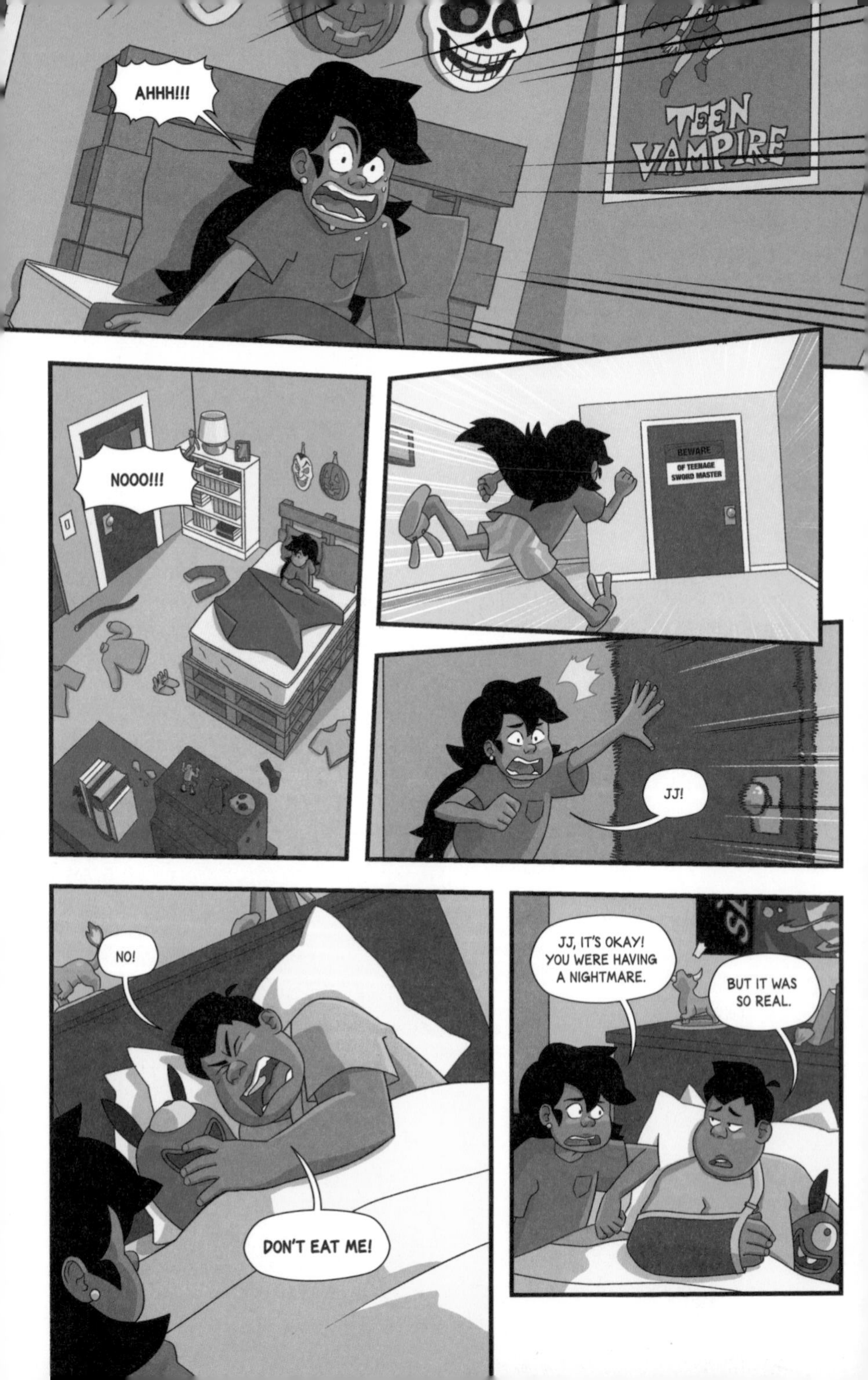
AHHH!!!
TEEN VAMPIRE
NOOO!!!
BEWARE
OF TEENAGE SWORD MASTER
JJ!
NO!
DON'T EAT ME!
JJ, IT'S OKAY! YOU WERE HAVING A NIGHTMARE.
BUT IT WAS SO REAL.

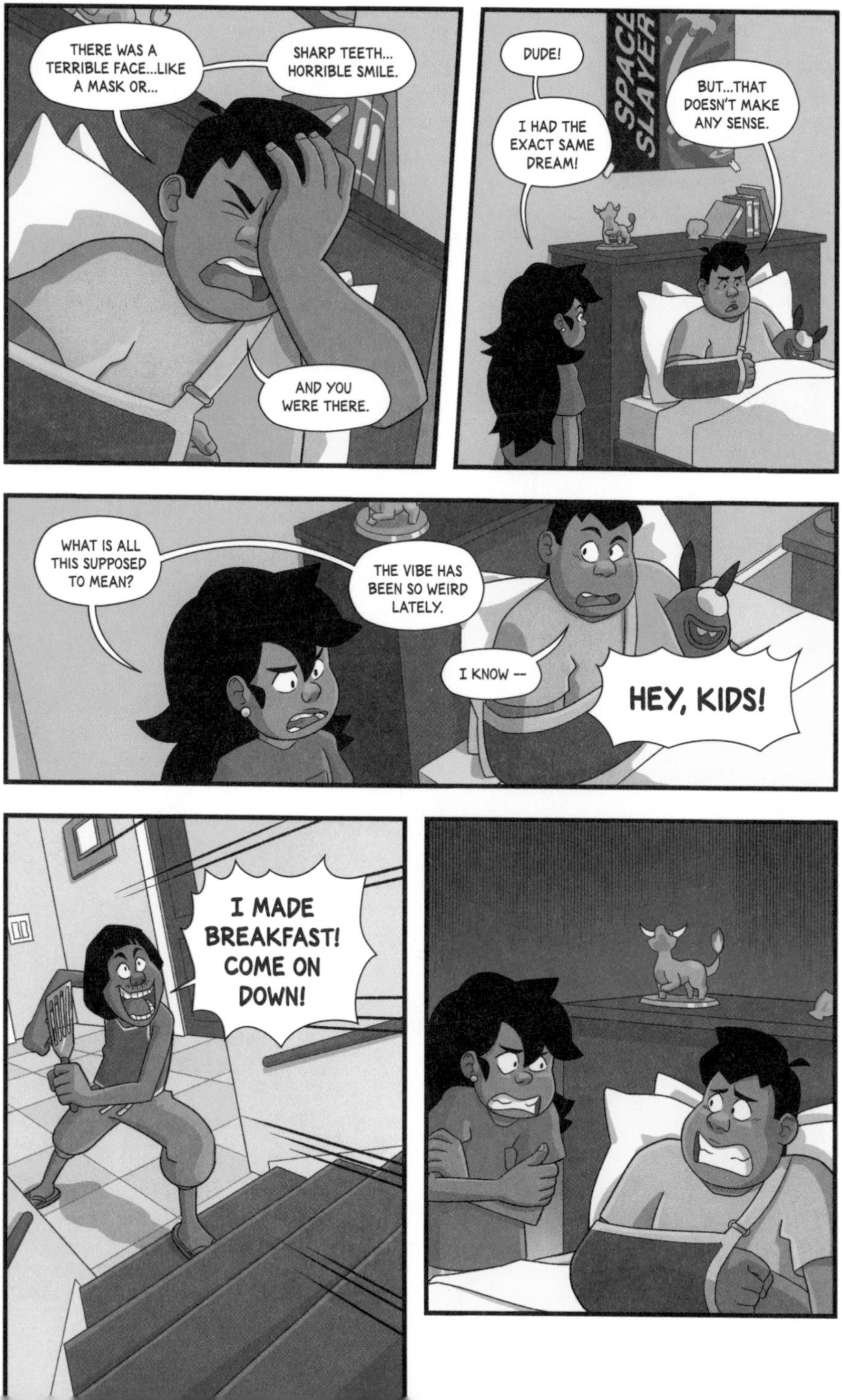
THERE WAS A TERRIBLE FACE...LIKE A MASK OR...
SHARP TEETH... HORRIBLE SMILE.
AND YOU WERE THERE.
DUDE!
I HAD THE EXACT SAME DREAM!
SPACE SLAYER
BUT...THAT DOESN'T MAKE ANY SENSE.
WHAT IS ALL THIS SUPPOSED TO MEAN?
THE VIBE HAS BEEN SO WEIRD LATELY.
I KNOW --
HEY, KIDS!
I MADE BREAKFAST! COME ON DOWN!

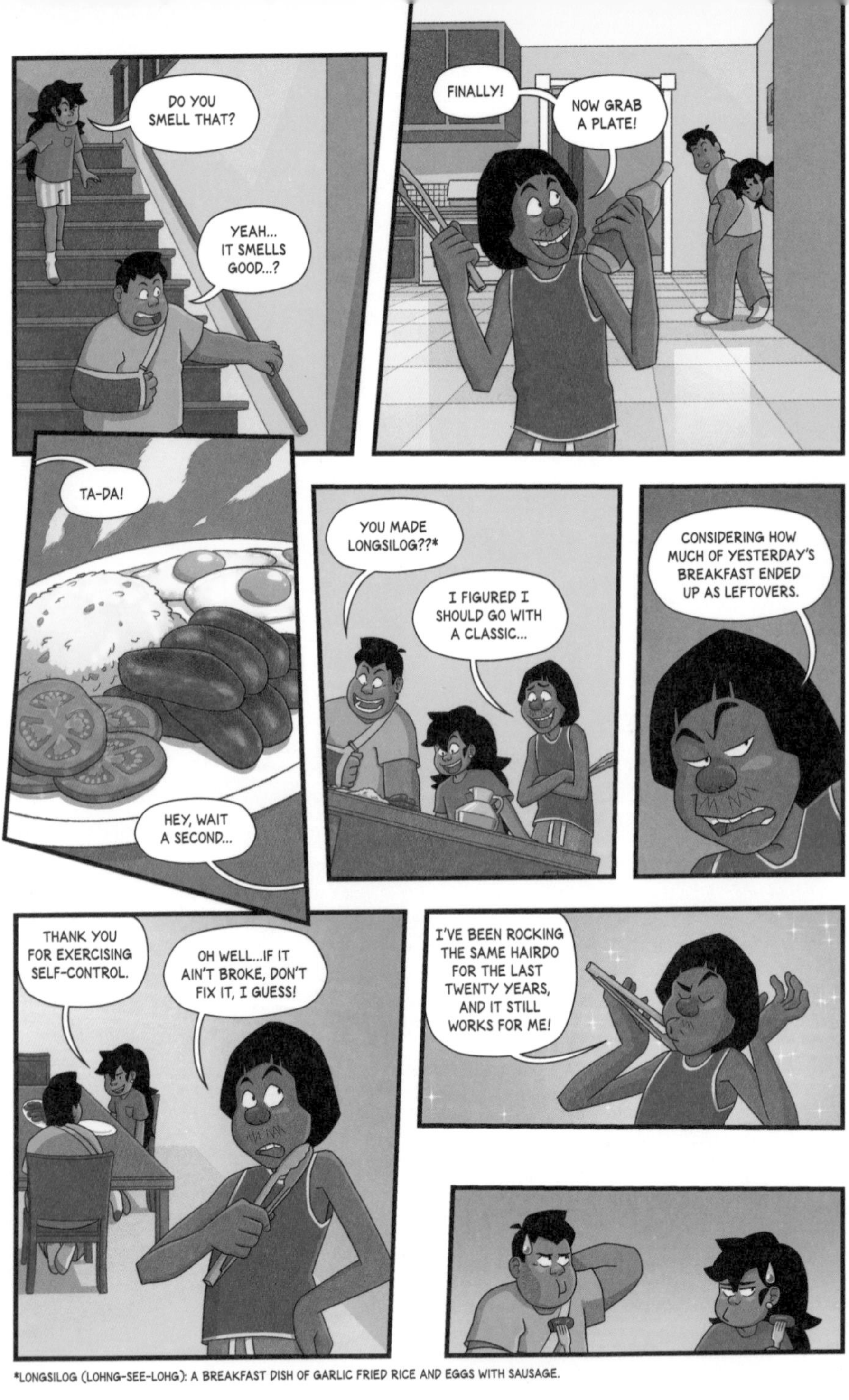
DO YOU SMELL THAT?
YEAH... IT SMELLS GOOD...?
FINALLY!
NOW GRAB A PLATE!
TA-DA!
HEY, WAIT A SECOND...
YOU MADE LONGSILOG??*
I FIGURED I SHOULD GO WITH A CLASSIC...
CONSIDERING HOW MUCH OF YESTERDAY'S BREAKFAST ENDED UP AS LEFTOVERS.
THANK YOU FOR EXERCISING SELF-CONTROL.
OH WELL...IF IT AIN'T BROKE, DON'T FIX IT, I GUESS!
I'VE BEEN ROCKING THE SAME HAIRDO FOR THE LAST TWENTY YEARS, AND IT STILL WORKS FOR ME!

*LONGSILOG (LOHNG-SEE-LOHG): A BREAKFAST DISH OF GARLIC FRIED RICE AND EGGS WITH SAUSAGE.

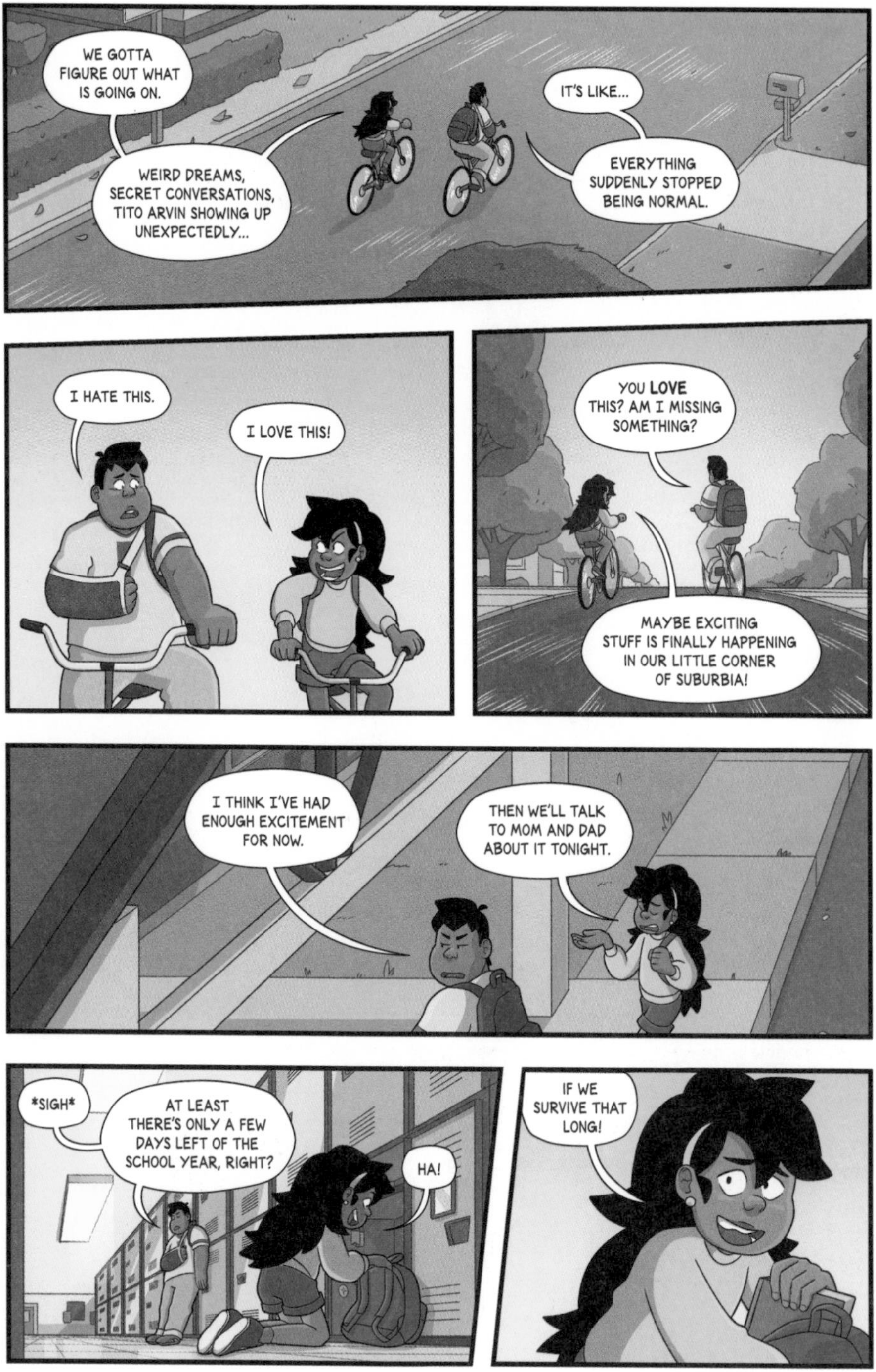
WE GOTTA FIGURE OUT WHAT IS GOING ON.
WEIRD DREAMS, SECRET CONVERSATIONS, TITO ARVIN SHOWING UP UNEXPECTEDLY...
IT'S LIKE...
EVERYTHING SUDDENLY STOPPED BEING NORMAL.
I HATE THIS.
I LOVE THIS!
YOU **LOVE** THIS? AM I MISSING SOMETHING?
MAYBE EXCITING STUFF IS FINALLY HAPPENING IN OUR LITTLE CORNER OF SUBURBIA!
I THINK I'VE HAD ENOUGH EXCITEMENT FOR NOW.
THEN WE'LL TALK TO MOM AND DAD ABOUT IT TONIGHT.
SIGH
AT LEAST THERE'S ONLY A FEW DAYS LEFT OF THE SCHOOL YEAR, RIGHT?
HA!
IF WE SURVIVE THAT LONG!

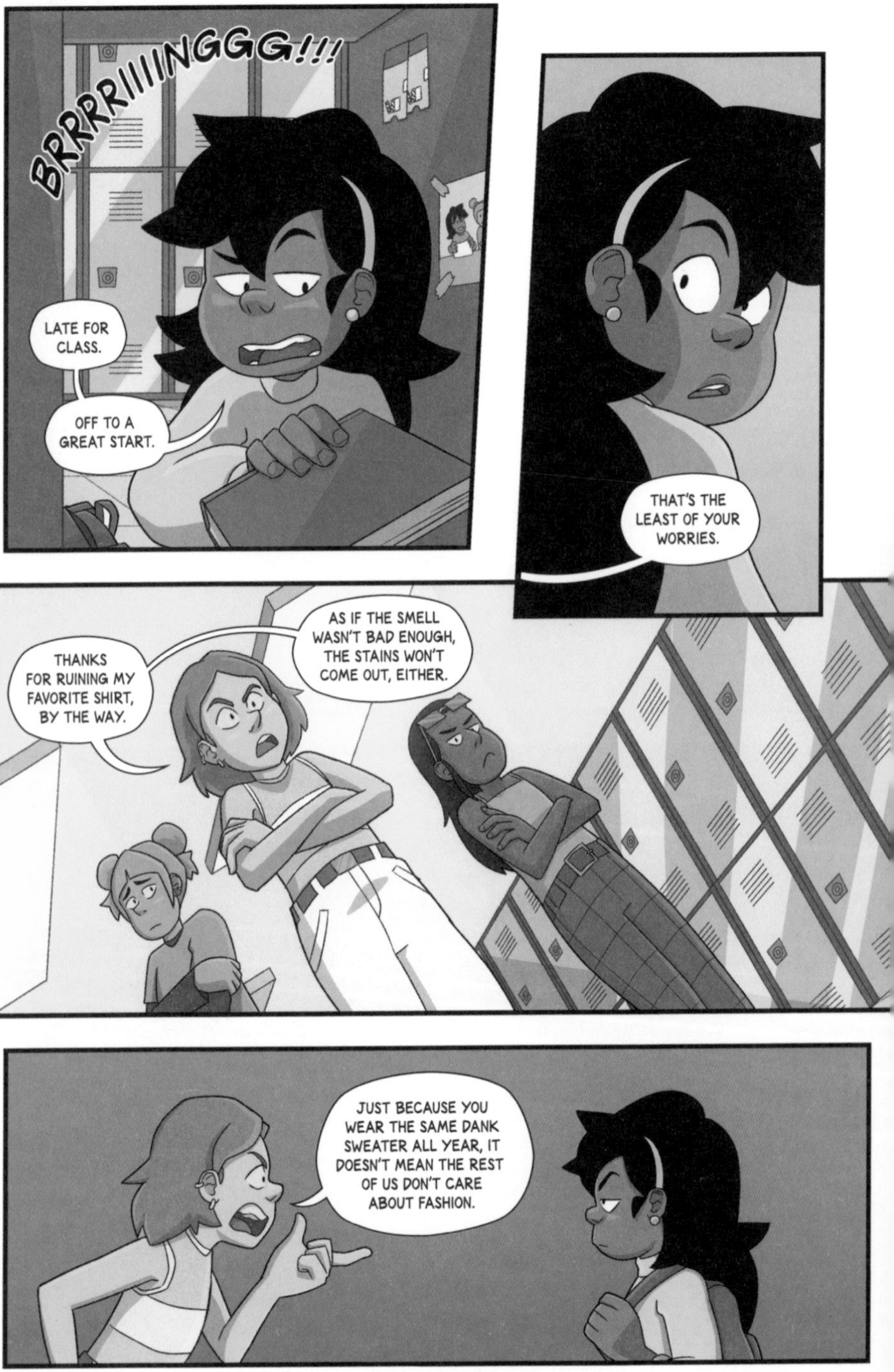
BRRRRIIIINGGG!!!
LATE FOR CLASS.
OFF TO A GREAT START.
THAT'S THE LEAST OF YOUR WORRIES.
THANKS FOR RUINING MY FAVORITE SHIRT, BY THE WAY.
AS IF THE SMELL WASN'T BAD ENOUGH, THE STAINS WON'T COME OUT, EITHER.
JUST BECAUSE YOU WEAR THE SAME DANK SWEATER ALL YEAR, IT DOESN'T MEAN THE REST OF US DON'T CARE ABOUT FASHION.

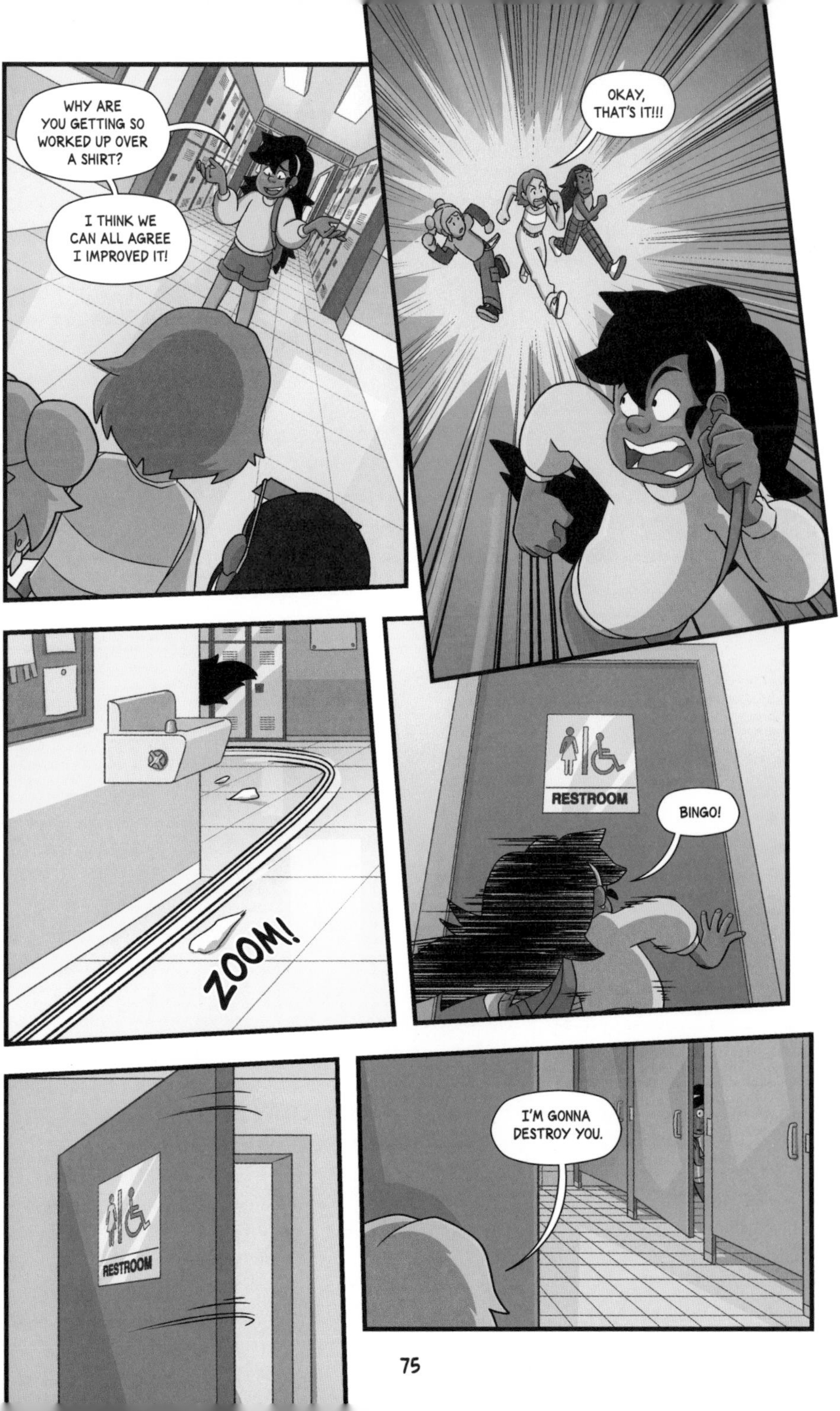
WHY ARE YOU GETTING SO WORKED UP OVER A SHIRT?
I THINK WE CAN ALL AGREE I IMPROVED IT!
OKAY, THAT'S IT!!!
ZOOM!
RESTROOM
BINGO!
RESTROOM
I'M GONNA DESTROY YOU.

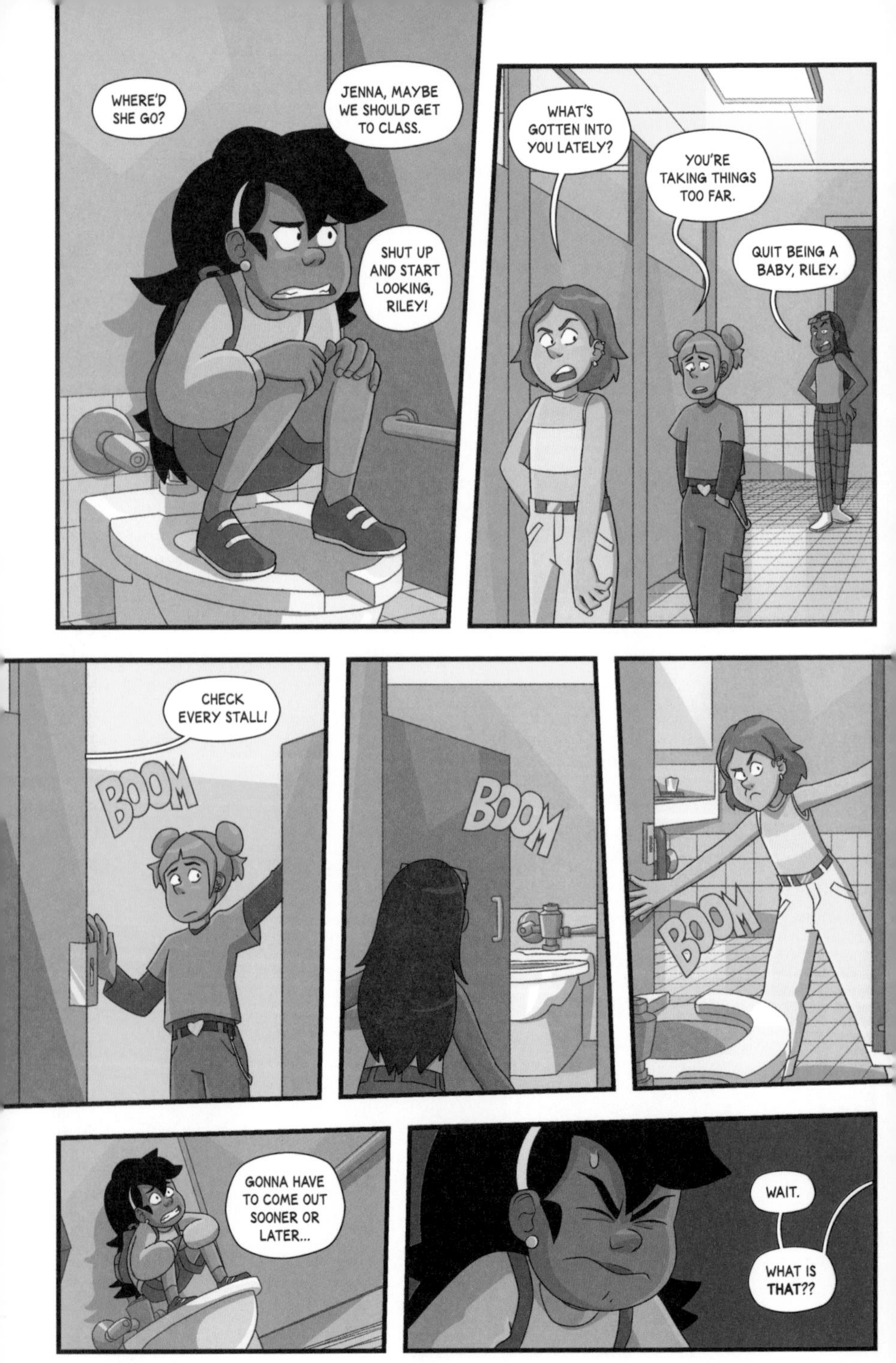
WHERE'D SHE GO?
JENNA, MAYBE WE SHOULD GET TO CLASS.
SHUT UP AND START LOOKING, RILEY!
WHAT'S GOTTEN INTO YOU LATELY?
YOU'RE TAKING THINGS TOO FAR.
QUIT BEING A BABY, RILEY.
CHECK EVERY STALL!
BOOM
BOOM
BOOM
GONNA HAVE TO COME OUT SOONER OR LATER...
WAIT.
WHAT IS **THAT??**

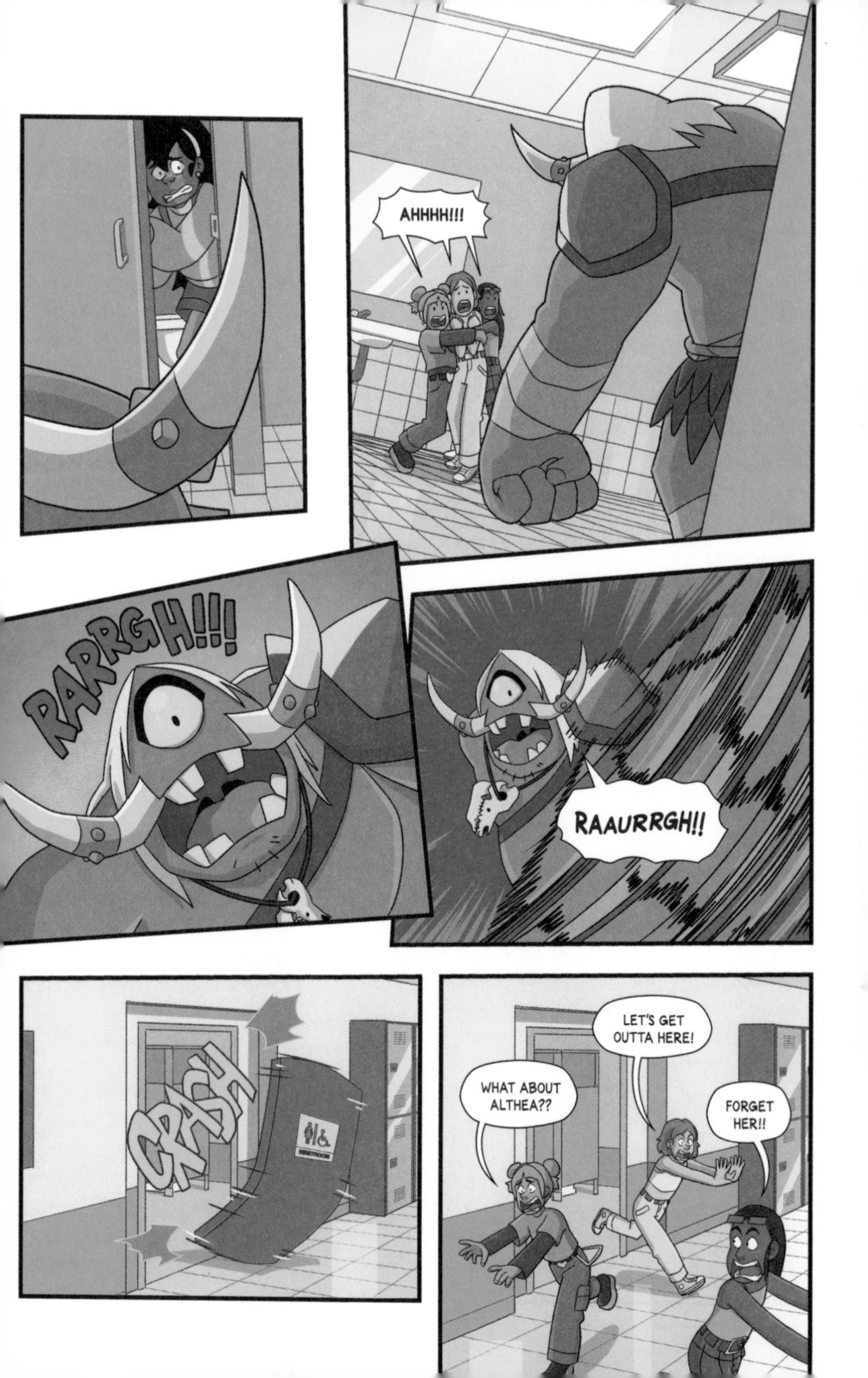
AHHHH!!!
RARRGH!!!
RAAURRGH!!
CRASH
LET'S GET OUTTA HERE!
WHAT ABOUT ALTHEA??
FORGET HER!!

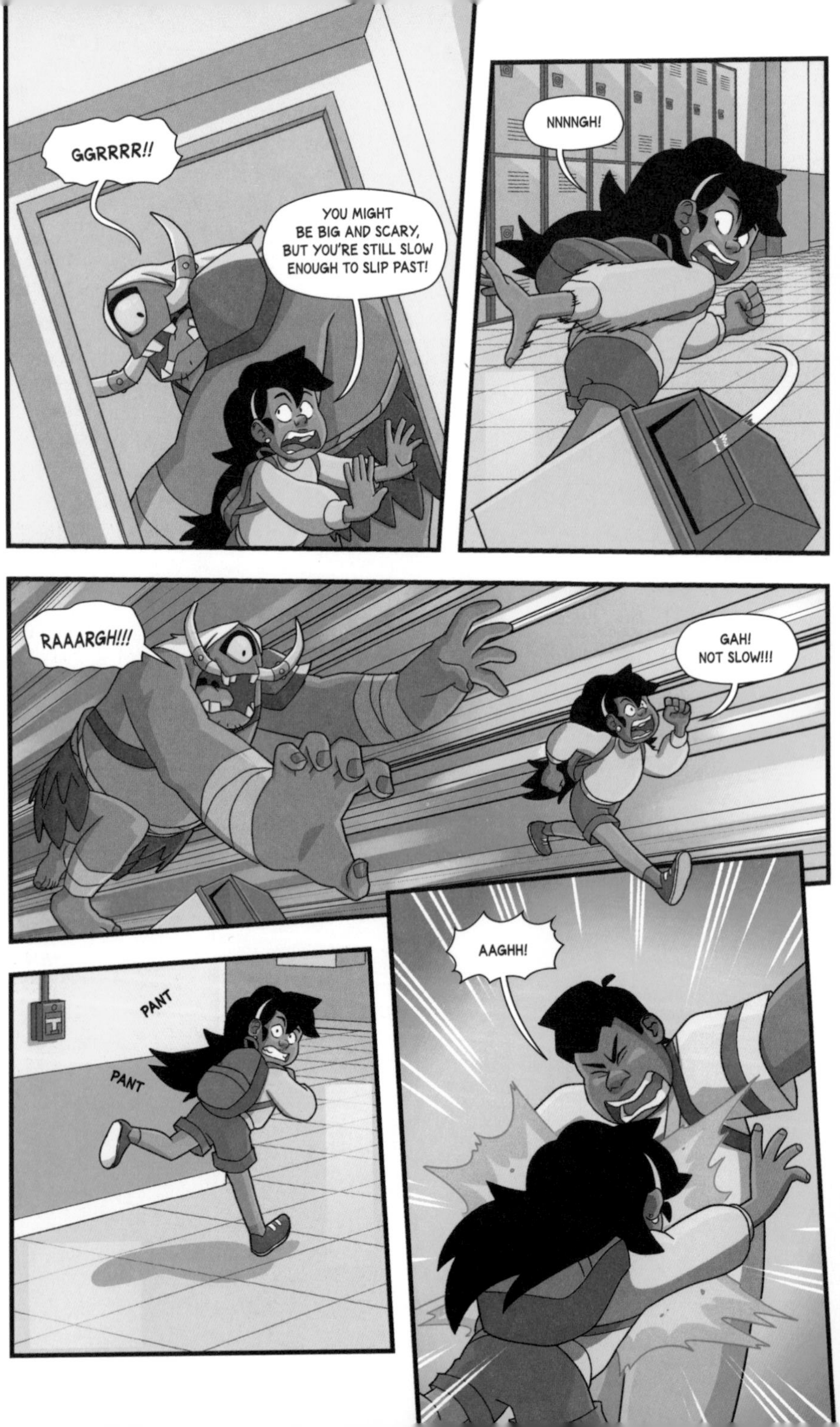
GGRRRR!!
YOU MIGHT BE BIG AND SCARY, BUT YOU'RE STILL SLOW ENOUGH TO SLIP PAST!
NNNNGH!
RAAARGH!!!
GAH! NOT SLOW!!!
PANT
PANT
AAGHH!

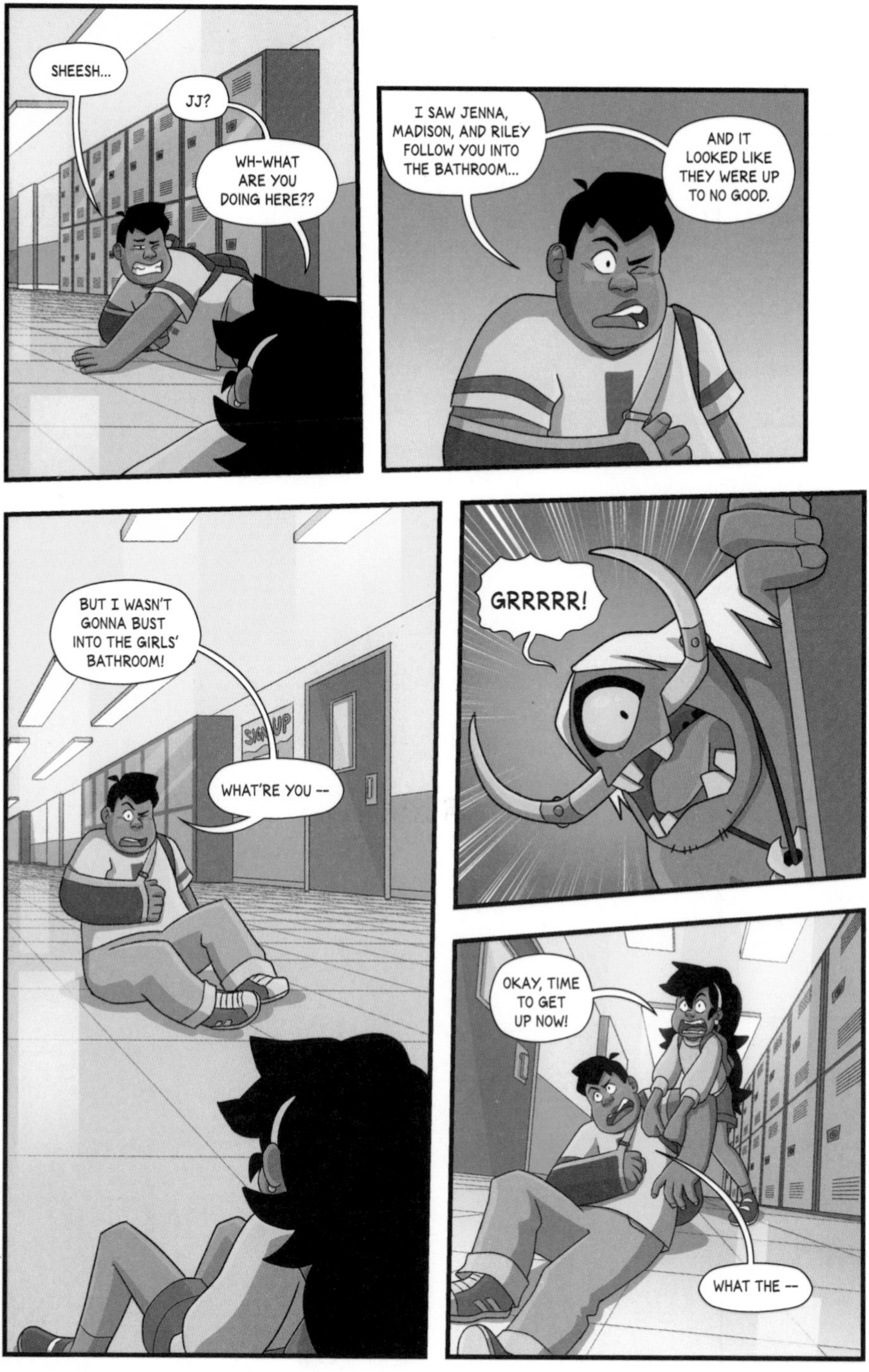
SHEESH...
JJ?
WH-WHAT ARE YOU DOING HERE??
I SAW JENNA, MADISON, AND RILEY FOLLOW YOU INTO THE BATHROOM...
AND IT LOOKED LIKE THEY WERE UP TO NO GOOD.
BUT I WASN'T GONNA BUST INTO THE GIRLS' BATHROOM!
SIGN UP
WHAT'RE YOU --
GRRRRR!
OKAY, TIME TO GET UP NOW!
WHAT THE --

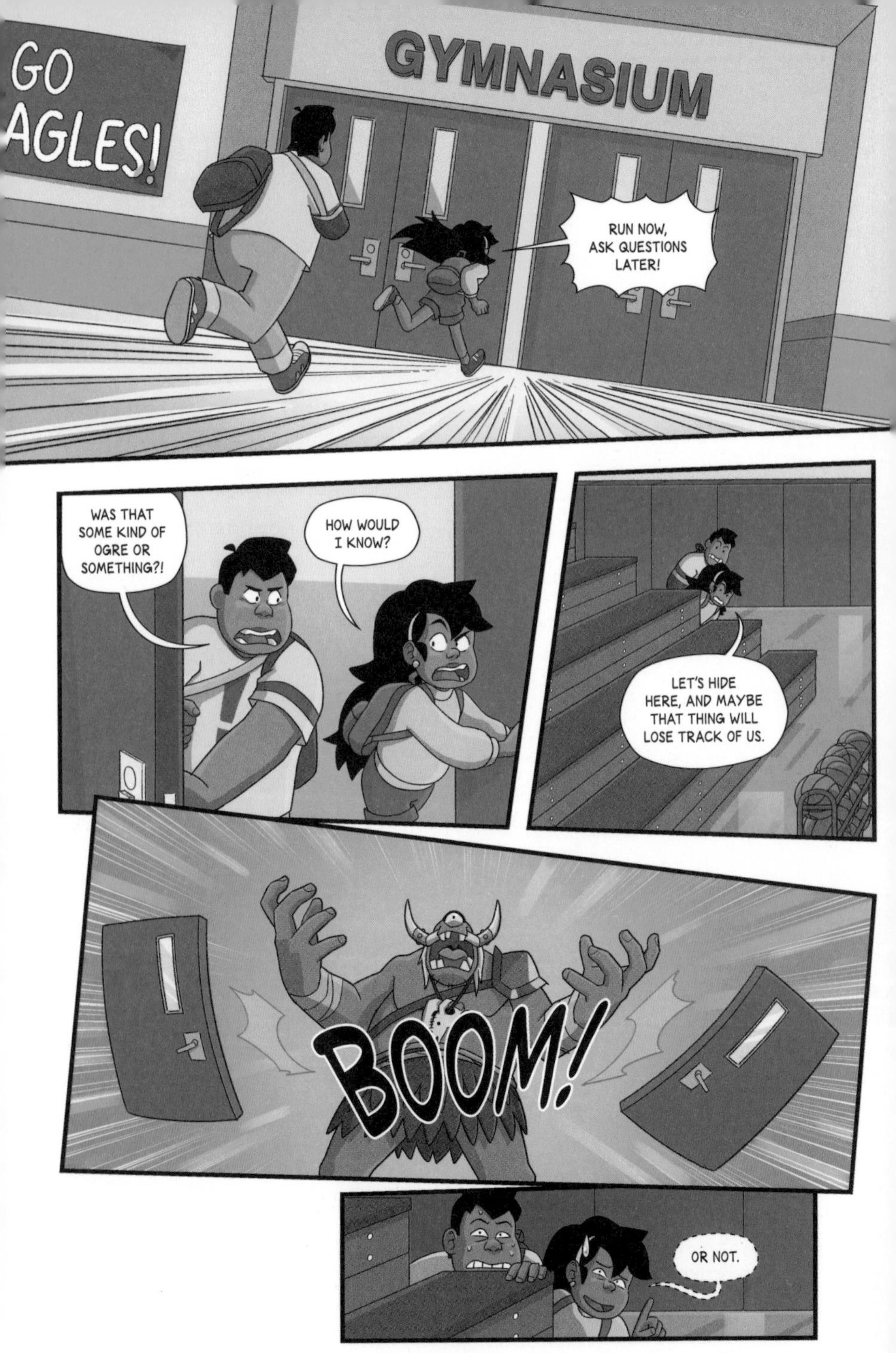
GO
AGLES!
GYMNASIUM
RUN NOW, ASK QUESTIONS LATER!
WAS THAT SOME KIND OF OGRE OR SOMETHING?!
HOW WOULD I KNOW?
LET'S HIDE HERE, AND MAYBE THAT THING WILL LOSE TRACK OF US.
BOOM!
OR NOT.

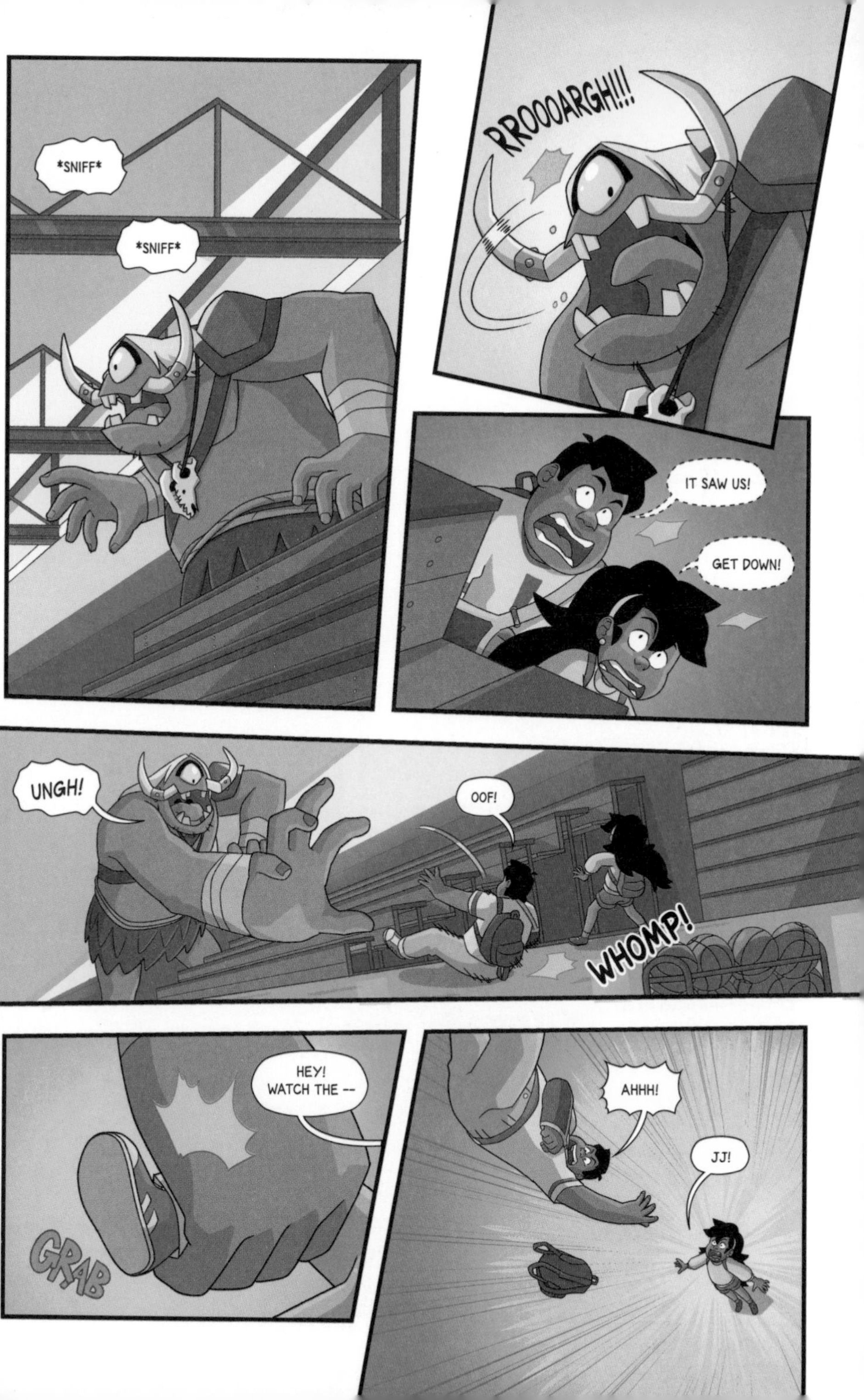
SNIFF
SNIFF
RROOOARGH!!!
IT SAW US!
GET DOWN!
UNGH!
OOF!
WHOMP!
HEY! WATCH THE --
GRAB
AHHH!
JJ!

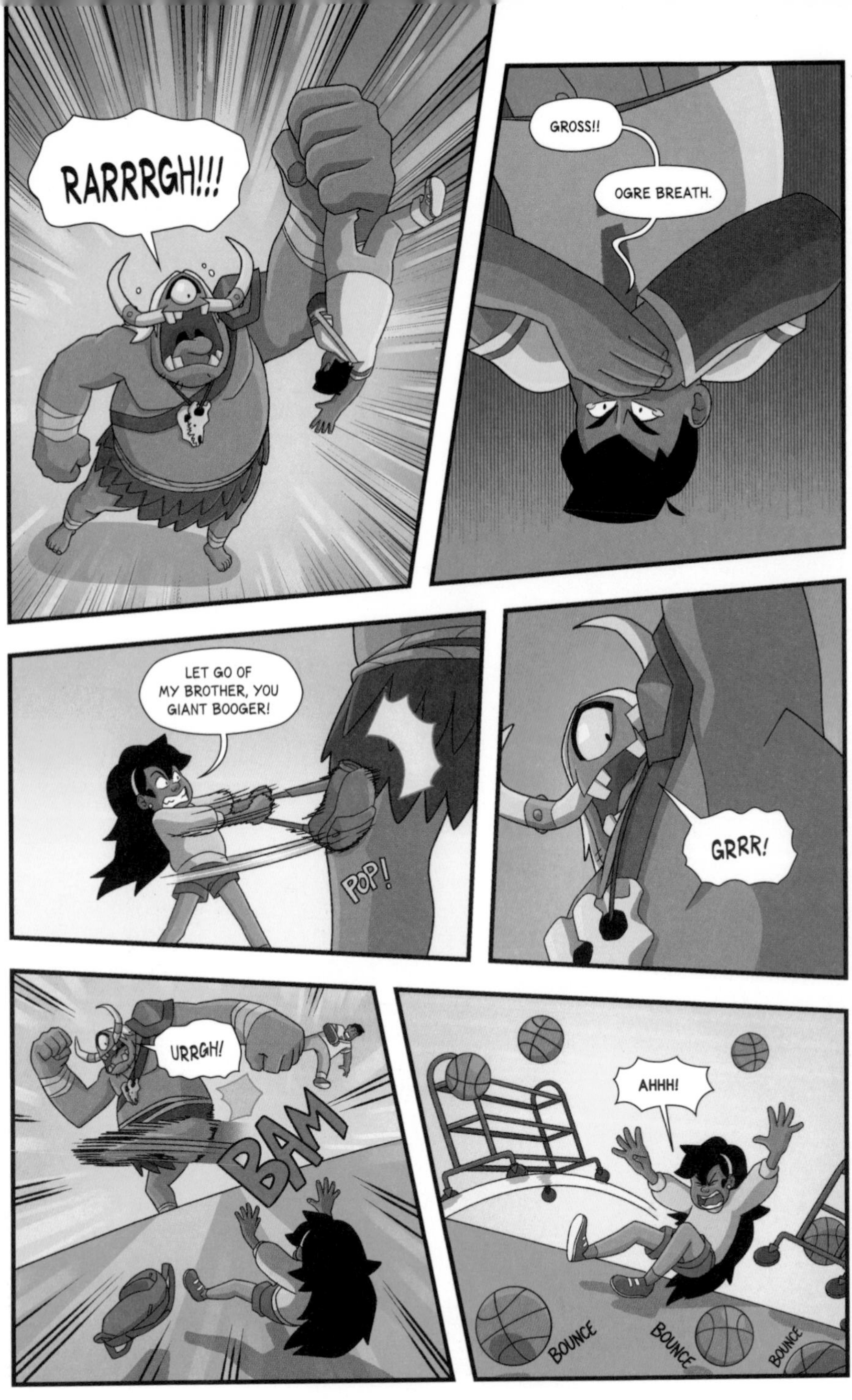
RARRRGH!!!
GROSS!!
OGRE BREATH.
LET GO OF MY BROTHER, YOU GIANT BOOGER!
POP!
GRRR!
URRGH!
BAM
AHHH!
BOUNCE
BOUNCE
BOUNCE

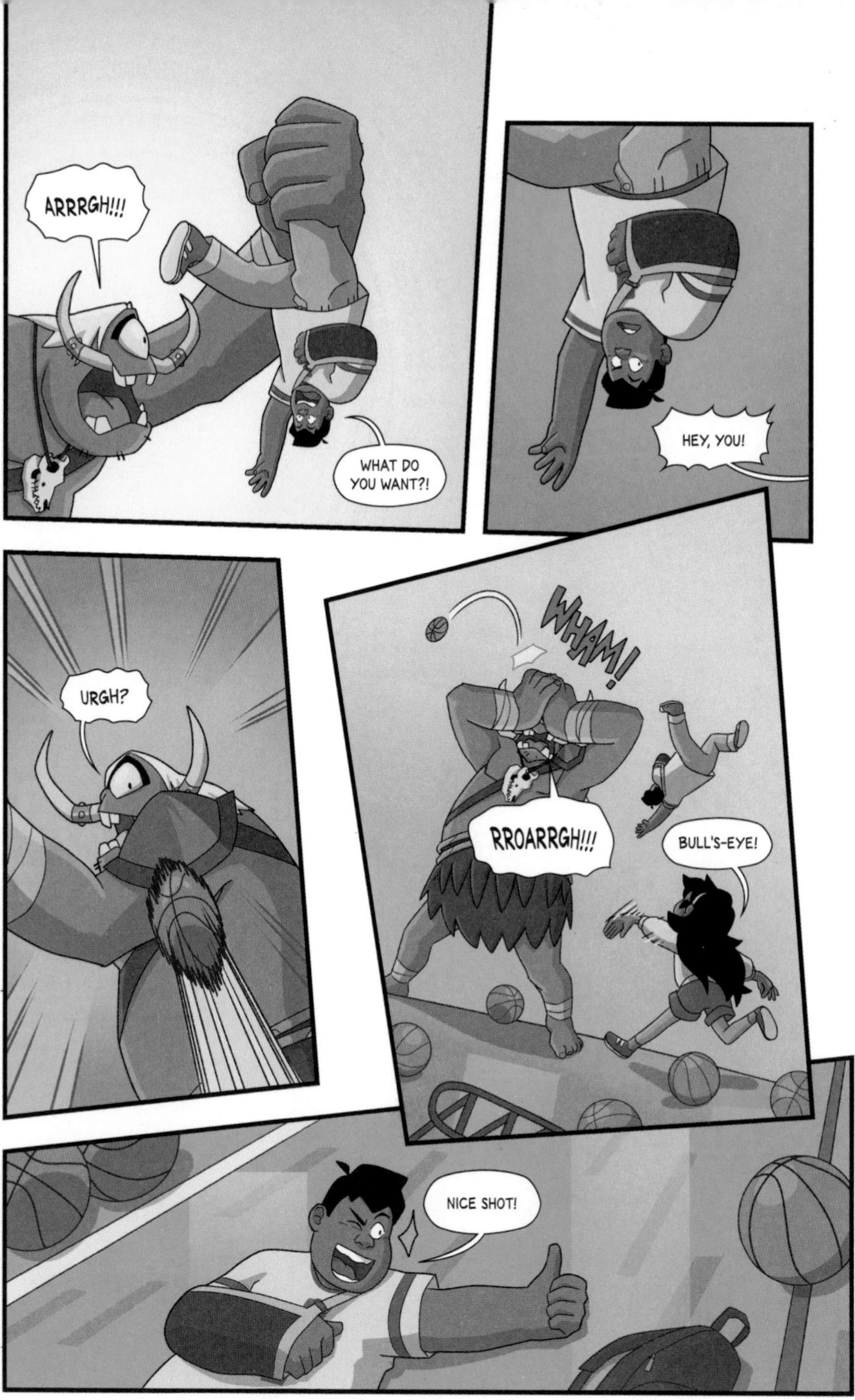
ARRRGH!!!
WHAT DO YOU WANT?!
HEY, YOU!
URGH?
WHAM!
RROARRGH!!!
BULL'S-EYE!
NICE SHOT!

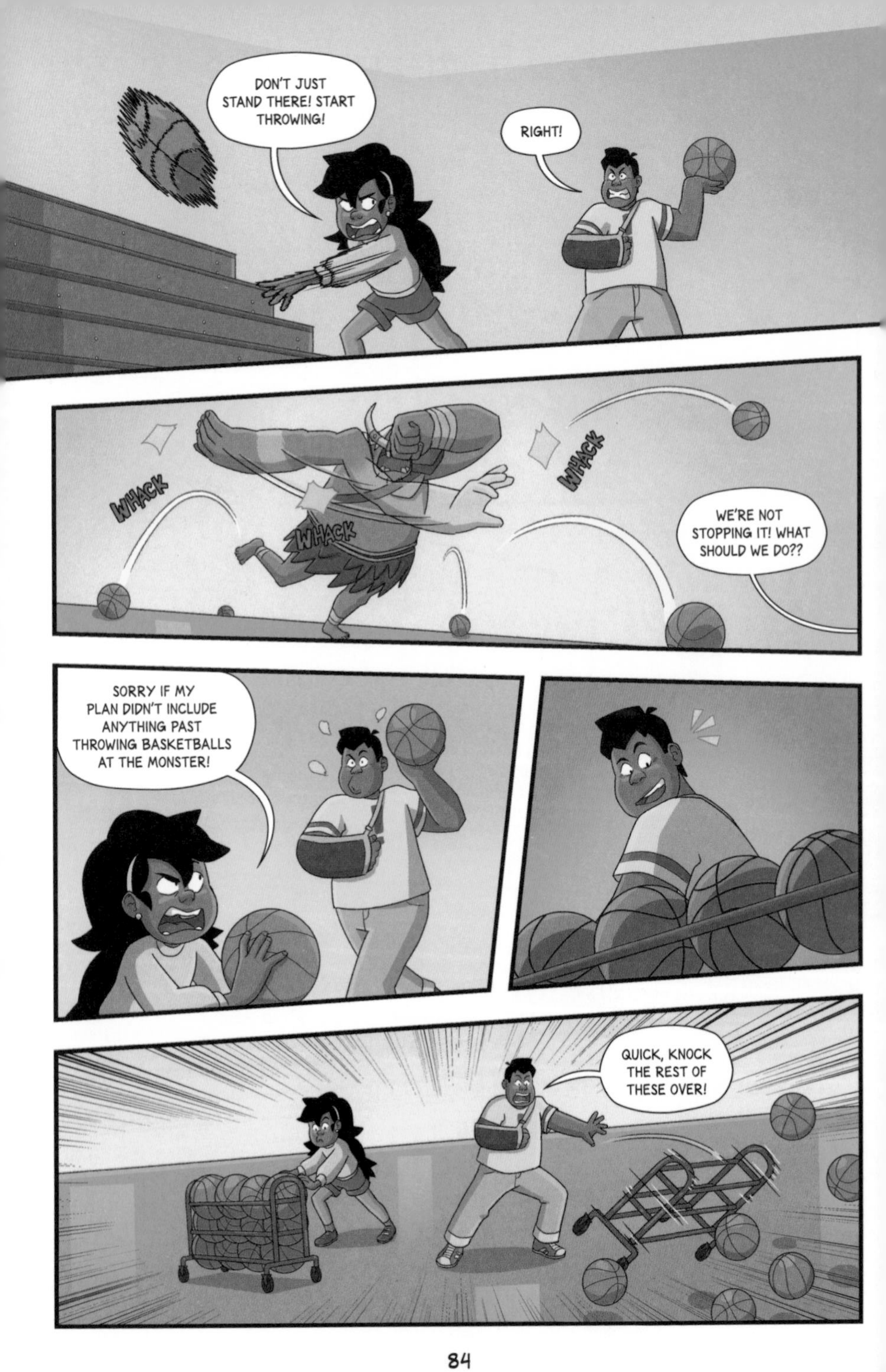
DON'T JUST STAND THERE! START THROWING!
RIGHT!
WHACK
WHACK
WHACK
WE'RE NOT STOPPING IT! WHAT SHOULD WE DO??
SORRY IF MY PLAN DIDN'T INCLUDE ANYTHING PAST THROWING BASKETBALLS AT THE MONSTER!
QUICK, KNOCK THE REST OF THESE OVER!

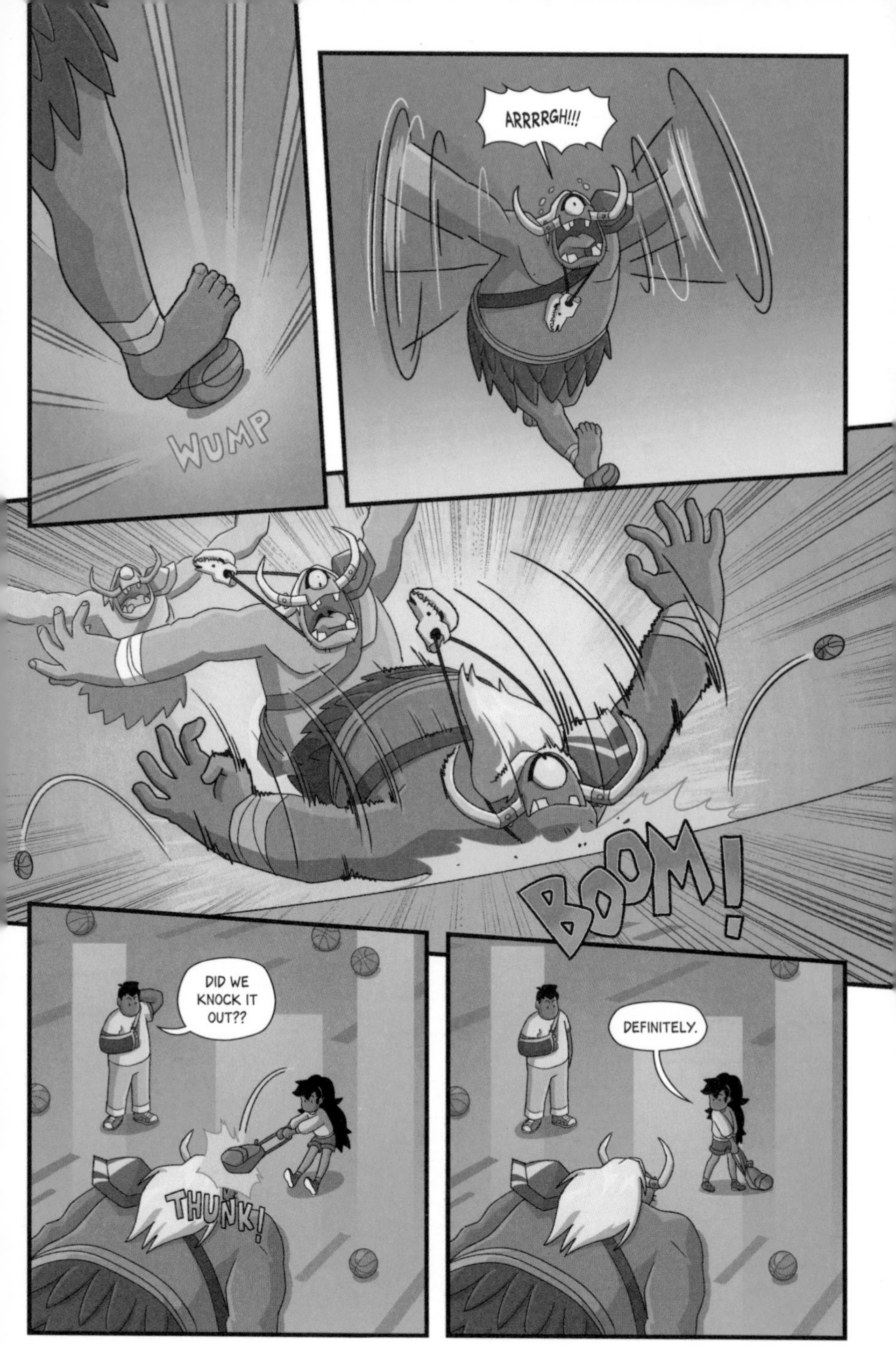
WUMP
ARRRRGH!!!
BOOM!
DID WE KNOCK IT OUT??
THUNK!
DEFINITELY.

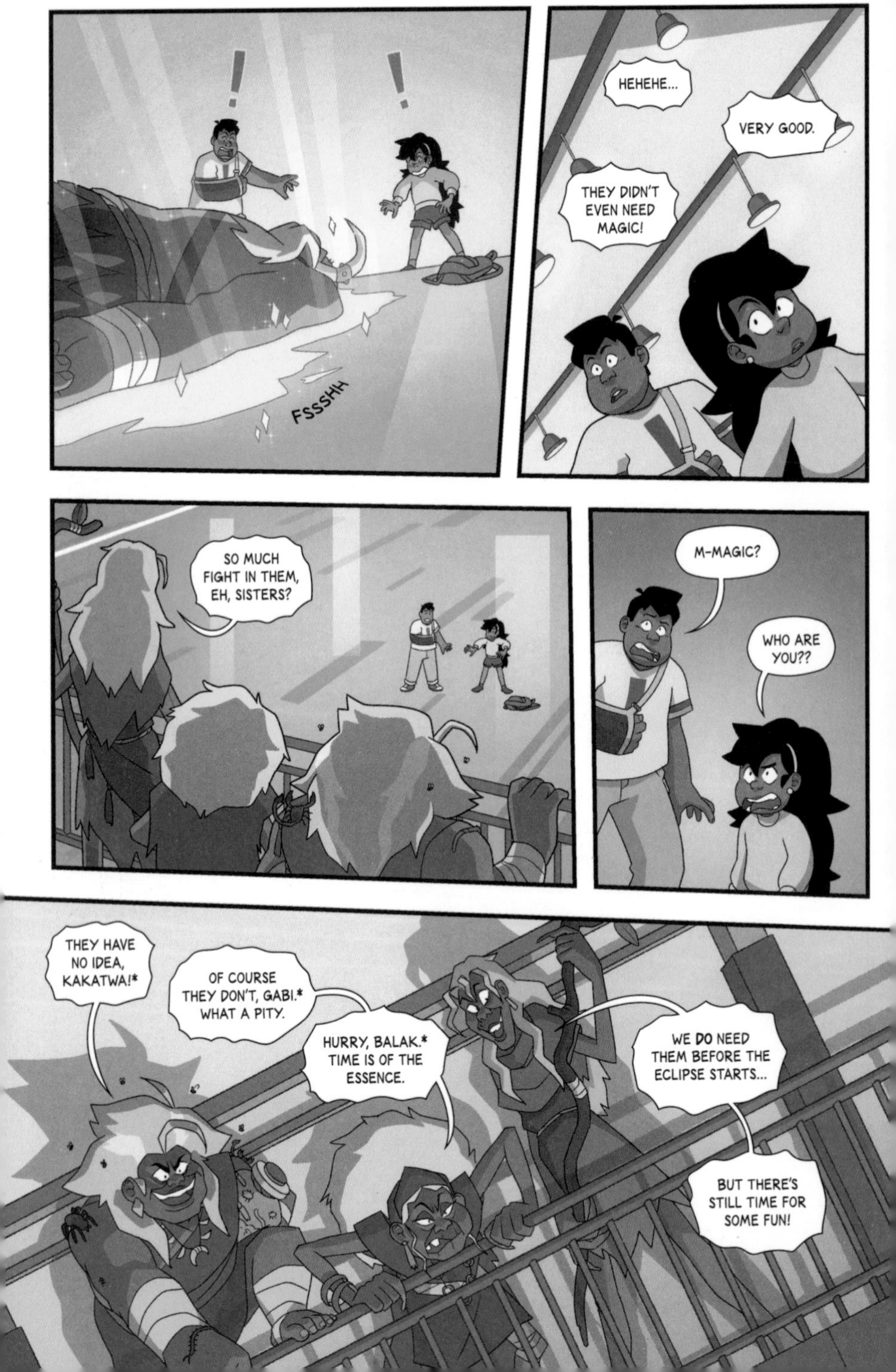
FSSSHH
HEHEHE...
VERY GOOD.
THEY DIDN'T EVEN NEED MAGIC!
SO MUCH FIGHT IN THEM, EH, SISTERS?
M-MAGIC?
WHO ARE YOU??
THEY HAVE NO IDEA, KAKATWA!*
OF COURSE THEY DON'T, GABI.* WHAT A PITY.
HURRY, BALAK.* TIME IS OF THE ESSENCE.
WE DO NEED THEM BEFORE THE ECLIPSE STARTS...
BUT THERE'S STILL TIME FOR SOME FUN!

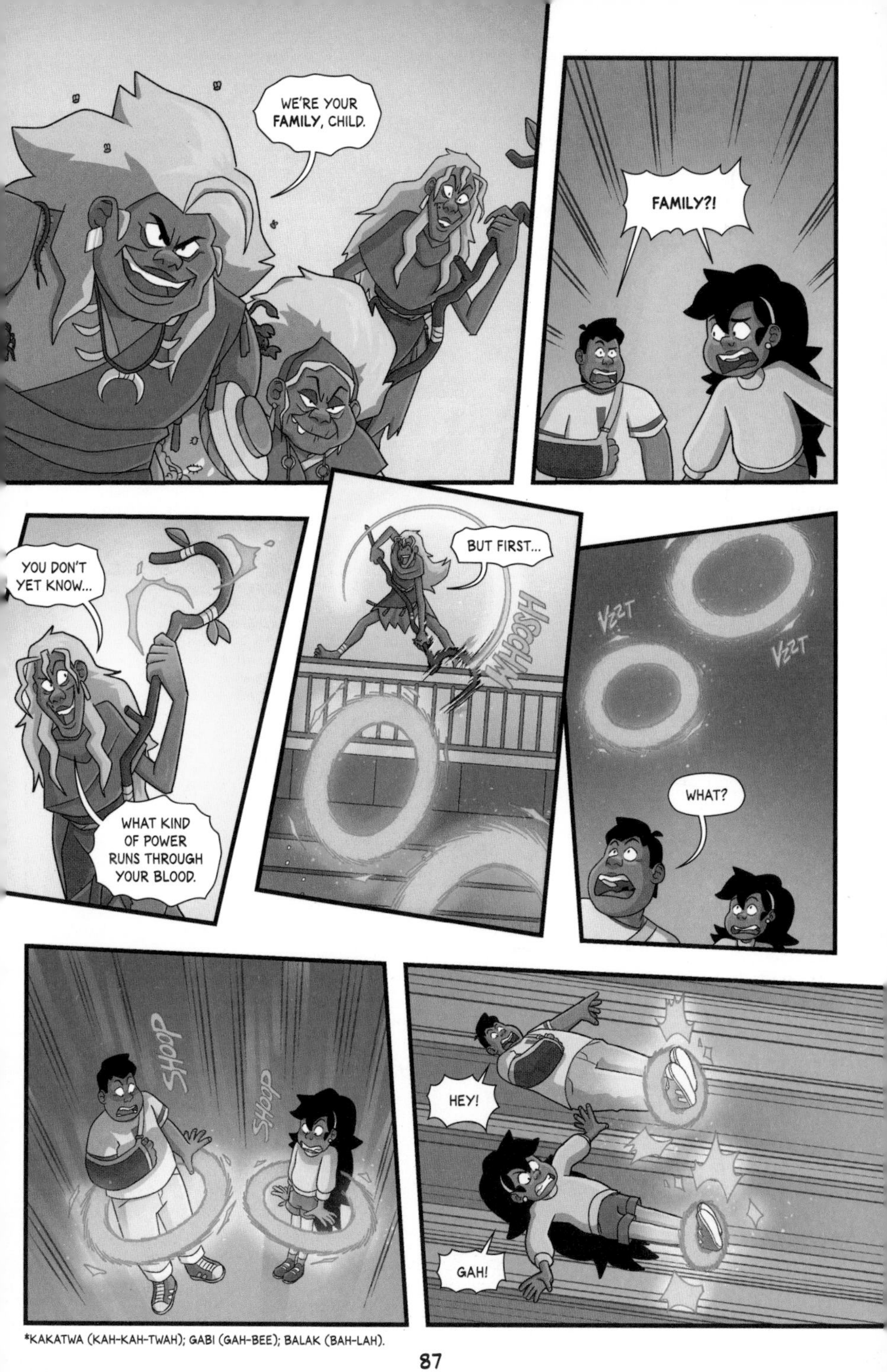
WE'RE YOUR FAMILY, CHILD.
FAMILY?!
YOU DON'T YET KNOW...
WHAT KIND OF POWER RUNS THROUGH YOUR BLOOD.
BUT FIRST...
WHSCHH
VZZT
VZZT
WHAT?
SHOOP
SHOOP
HEY!
GAH!

*KAKATWA (KAH-KAH-TWAH); GABI (GAH-BEE); BALAK (BAH-LAH).

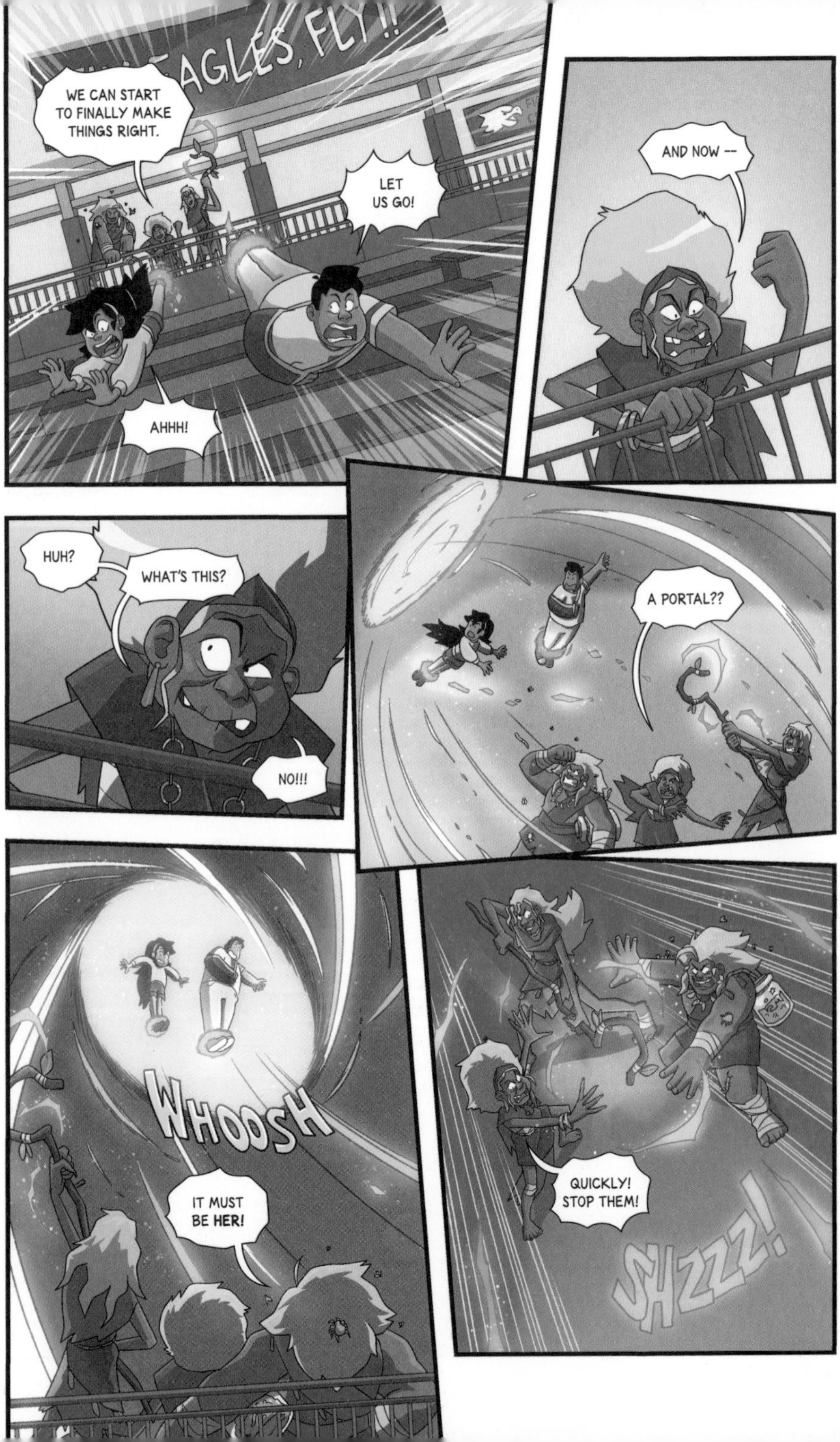
EAGLES, FLY!!
WE CAN START TO FINALLY MAKE THINGS RIGHT.
LET US GO!
AHHH!
AND NOW --
HUH?
WHAT'S THIS?
NO!!!
A PORTAL??
WHOOSH
IT MUST BE HER!
QUICKLY! STOP THEM!
SHZZZ!

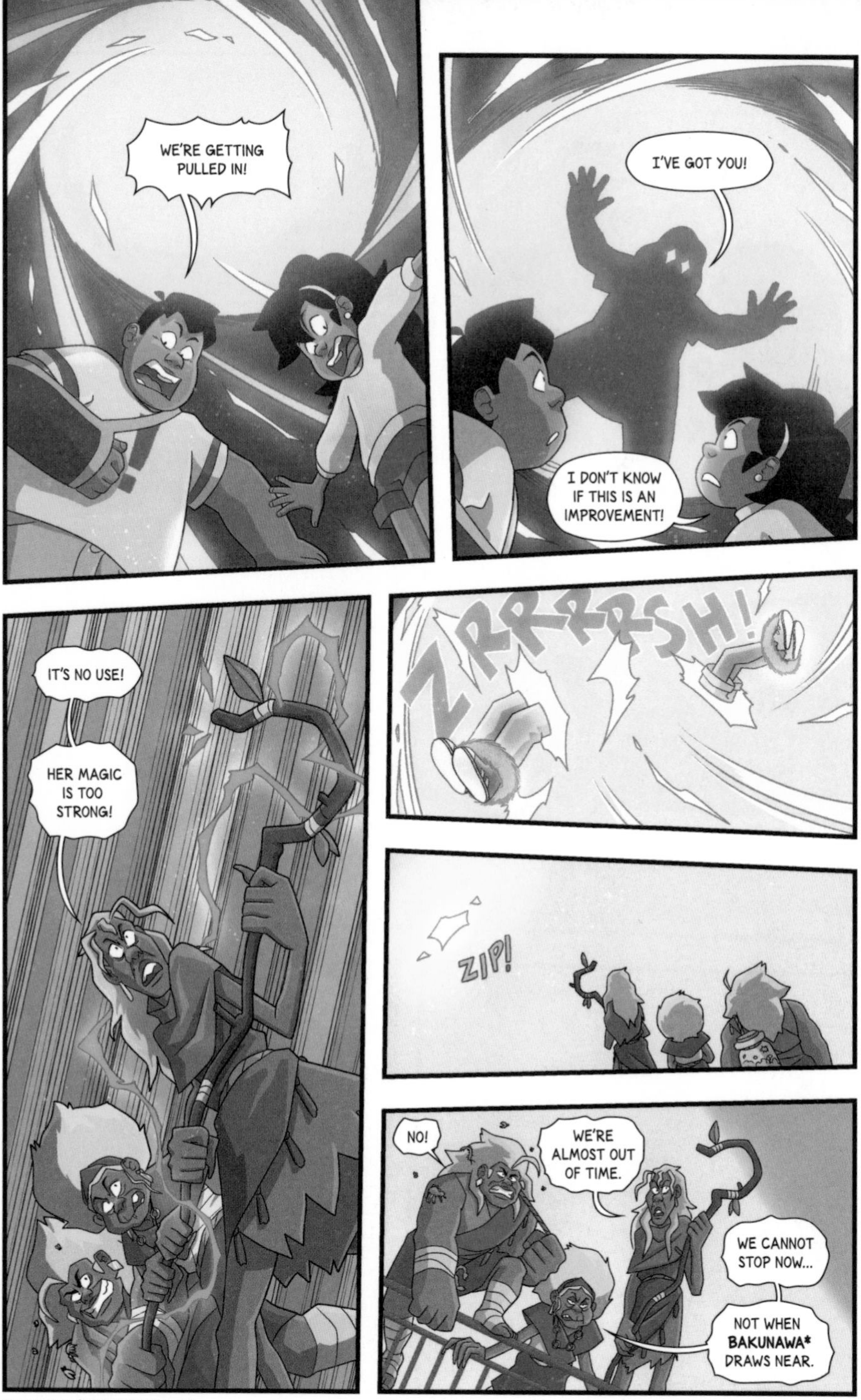

WE'RE GETTING PULLED IN!
I'VE GOT YOU!
I DON'T KNOW IF THIS IS AN IMPROVEMENT!
IT'S NO USE!
HER MAGIC IS TOO STRONG!
ZRRRRSH!
ZIP!
NO!
WE'RE ALMOST OUT OF TIME.
WE CANNOT STOP NOW...
NOT WHEN **BAKUNAWA*** DRAWS NEAR.

*BAKUNAWA (BAH-KOO-NAH-WAH).

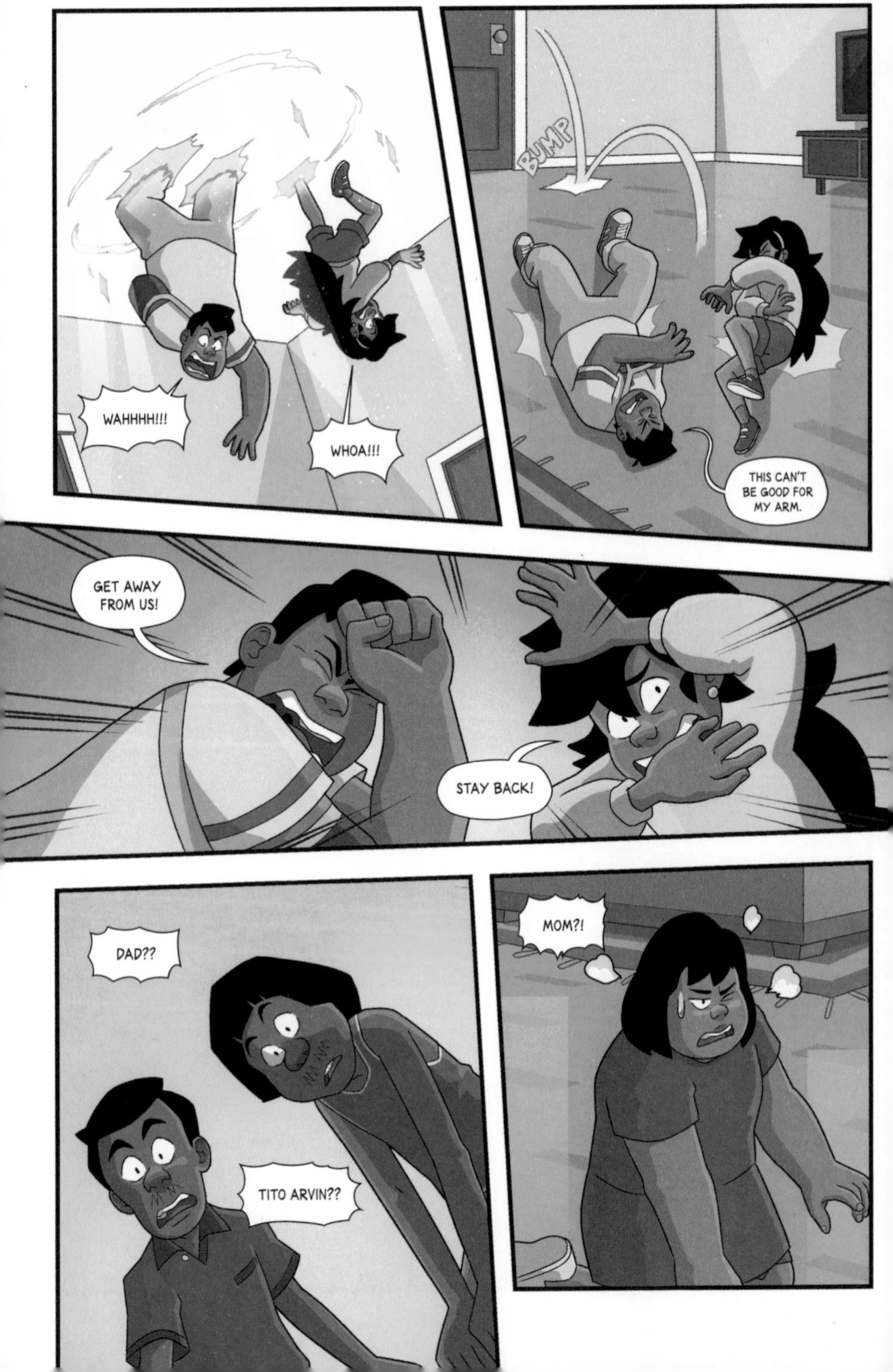
WAHHHH!!!
WHOA!!!
BUMP
THIS CAN'T BE GOOD FOR MY ARM.
GET AWAY FROM US!
STAY BACK!
DAD??
TITO ARVIN??
MOM?!

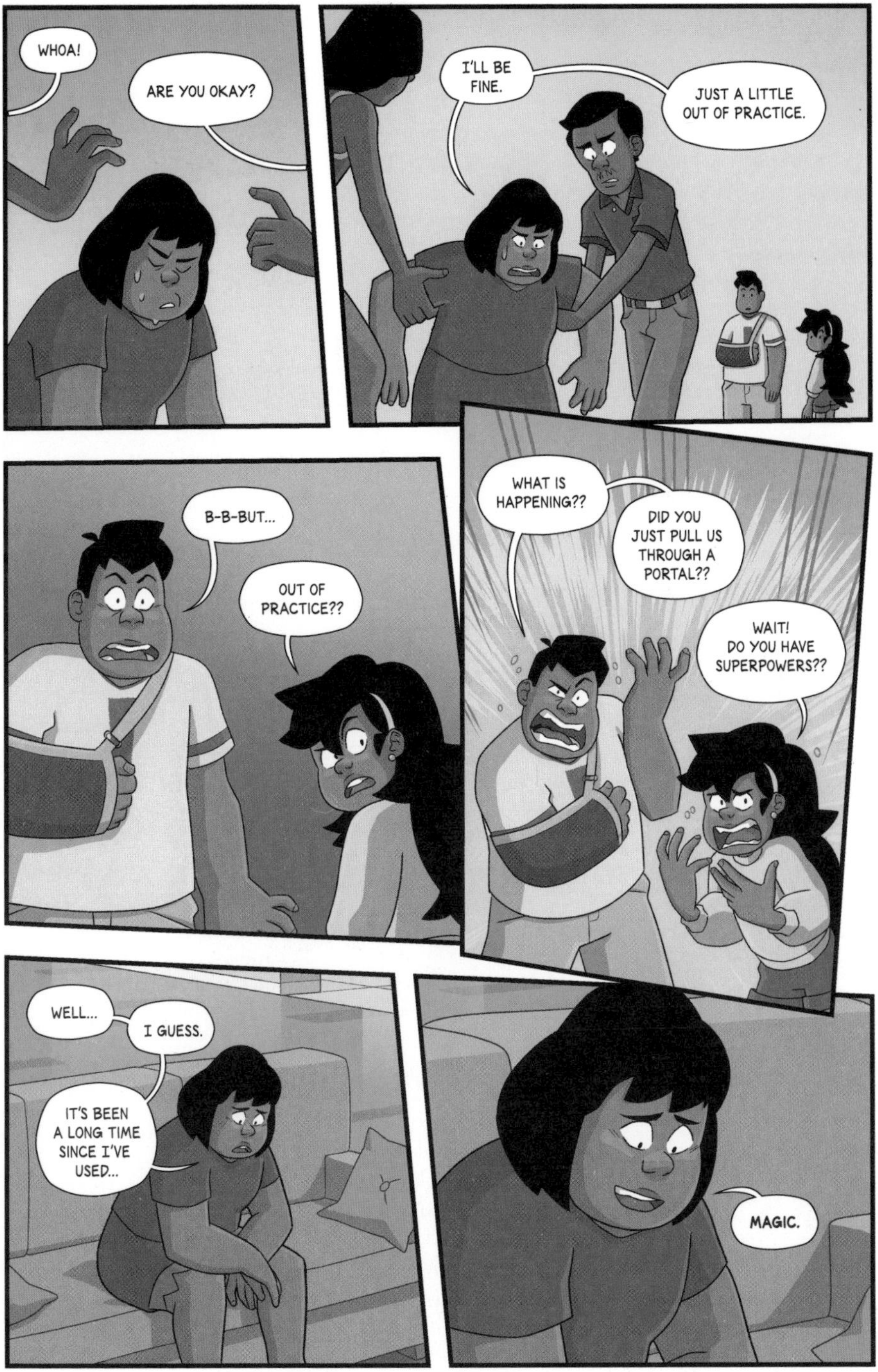
WHOA!
ARE YOU OKAY?
I'LL BE FINE.
JUST A LITTLE OUT OF PRACTICE.
B-B-BUT...
OUT OF PRACTICE??
WHAT IS HAPPENING??
DID YOU JUST PULL US THROUGH A PORTAL??
WAIT! DO YOU HAVE SUPERPOWERS??
WELL...
I GUESS.
IT'S BEEN A LONG TIME SINCE I'VE USED...
MAGIC.

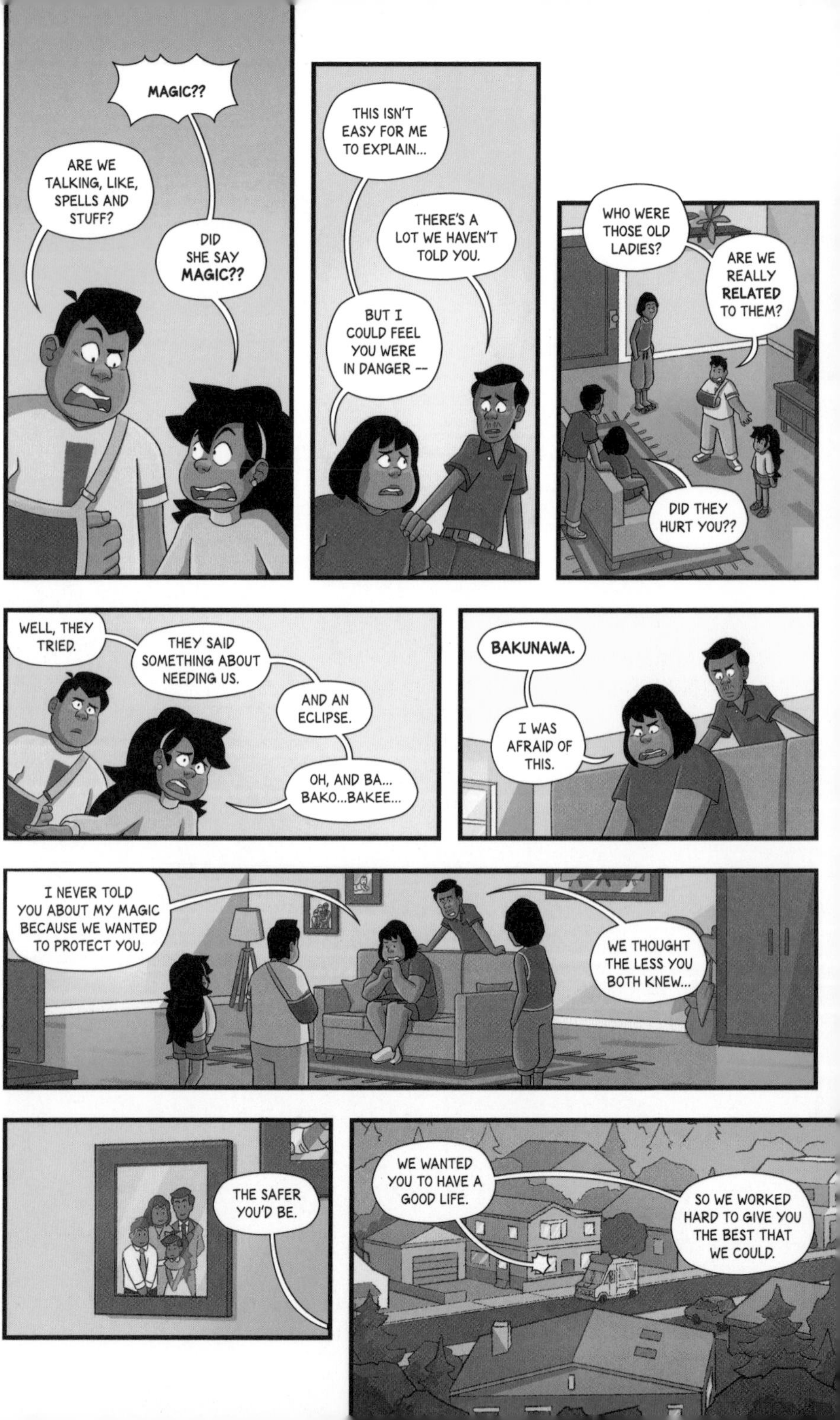
MAGIC??
ARE WE TALKING, LIKE, SPELLS AND STUFF?
DID SHE SAY MAGIC??
THIS ISN'T EASY FOR ME TO EXPLAIN...
THERE'S A LOT WE HAVEN'T TOLD YOU.
BUT I COULD FEEL YOU WERE IN DANGER --
WHO WERE THOSE OLD LADIES?
ARE WE REALLY RELATED TO THEM?
DID THEY HURT YOU??
WELL, THEY TRIED.
THEY SAID SOMETHING ABOUT NEEDING US.
AND AN ECLIPSE.
OH, AND BA... BAKO...BAKEE...
BAKUNAWA.
I WAS AFRAID OF THIS.
I NEVER TOLD YOU ABOUT MY MAGIC BECAUSE WE WANTED TO PROTECT YOU.
WE THOUGHT THE LESS YOU BOTH KNEW...
THE SAFER YOU'D BE.
WE WANTED YOU TO HAVE A GOOD LIFE.
SO WE WORKED HARD TO GIVE YOU THE BEST THAT WE COULD.

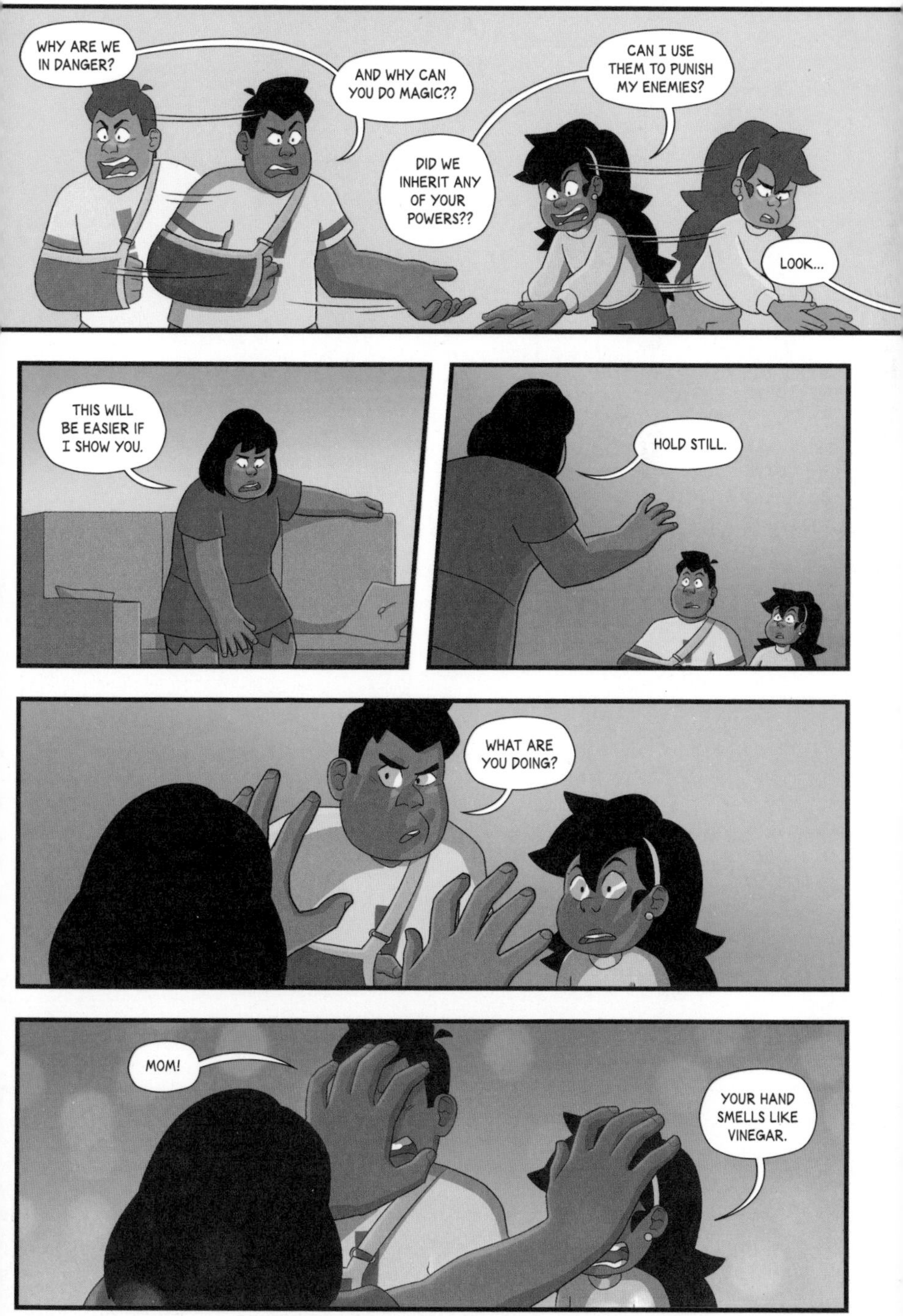
WHY ARE WE IN DANGER?
AND WHY CAN YOU DO MAGIC??
DID WE INHERIT ANY OF YOUR POWERS??
CAN I USE THEM TO PUNISH MY ENEMIES?
LOOK...
THIS WILL BE EASIER IF I SHOW YOU.
HOLD STILL.
WHAT ARE YOU DOING?
MOM!
YOUR HAND SMELLS LIKE VINEGAR.

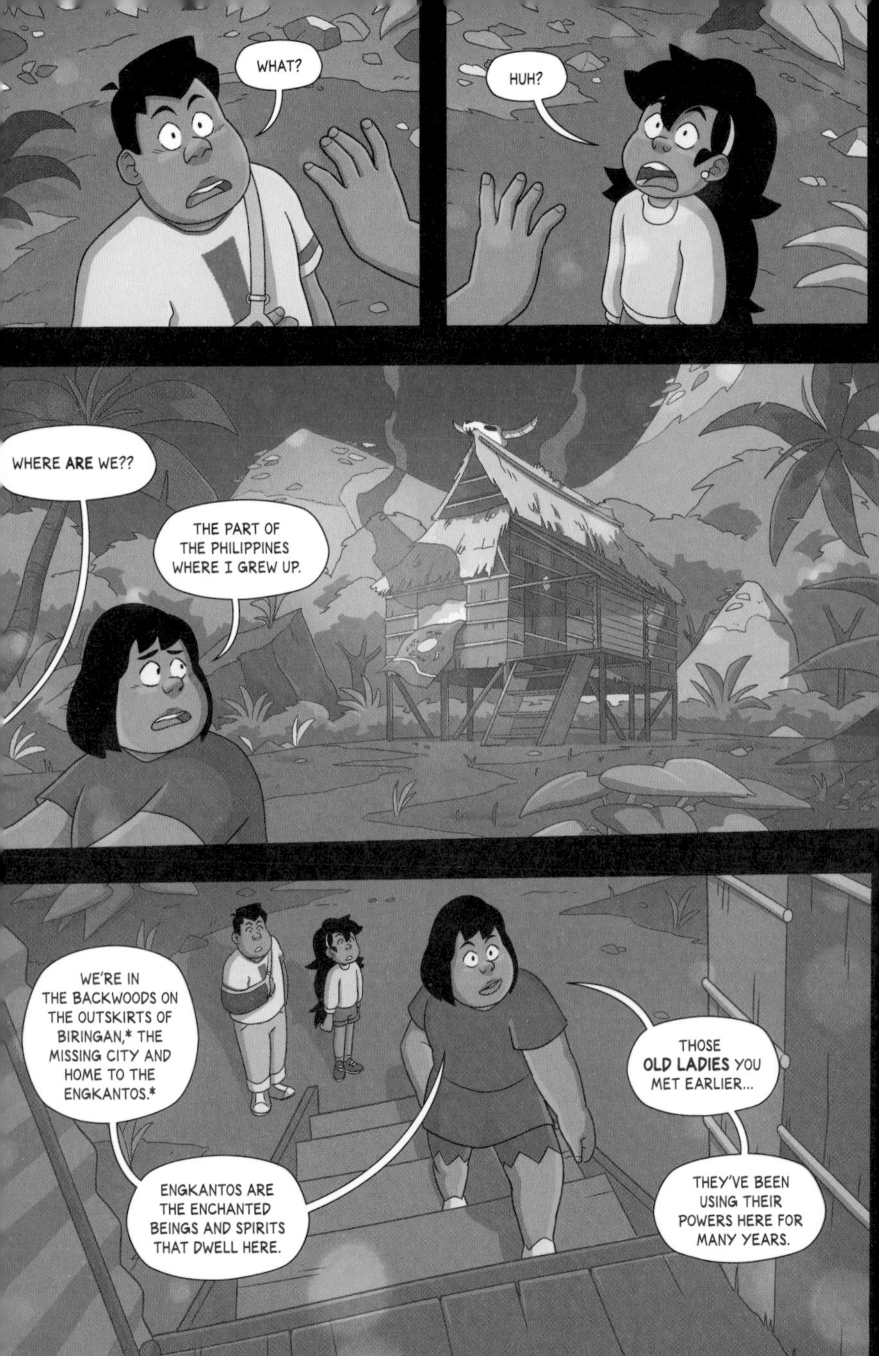
WHAT?
HUH?
WHERE ARE WE??
THE PART OF THE PHILIPPINES WHERE I GREW UP.
WE'RE IN THE BACKWOODS ON THE OUTSKIRTS OF BIRINGAN,* THE MISSING CITY AND HOME TO THE ENGKANTOS.*
ENGKANTOS ARE THE ENCHANTED BEINGS AND SPIRITS THAT DWELL HERE.
THOSE OLD LADIES YOU MET EARLIER...
THEY'VE BEEN USING THEIR POWERS HERE FOR MANY YEARS.

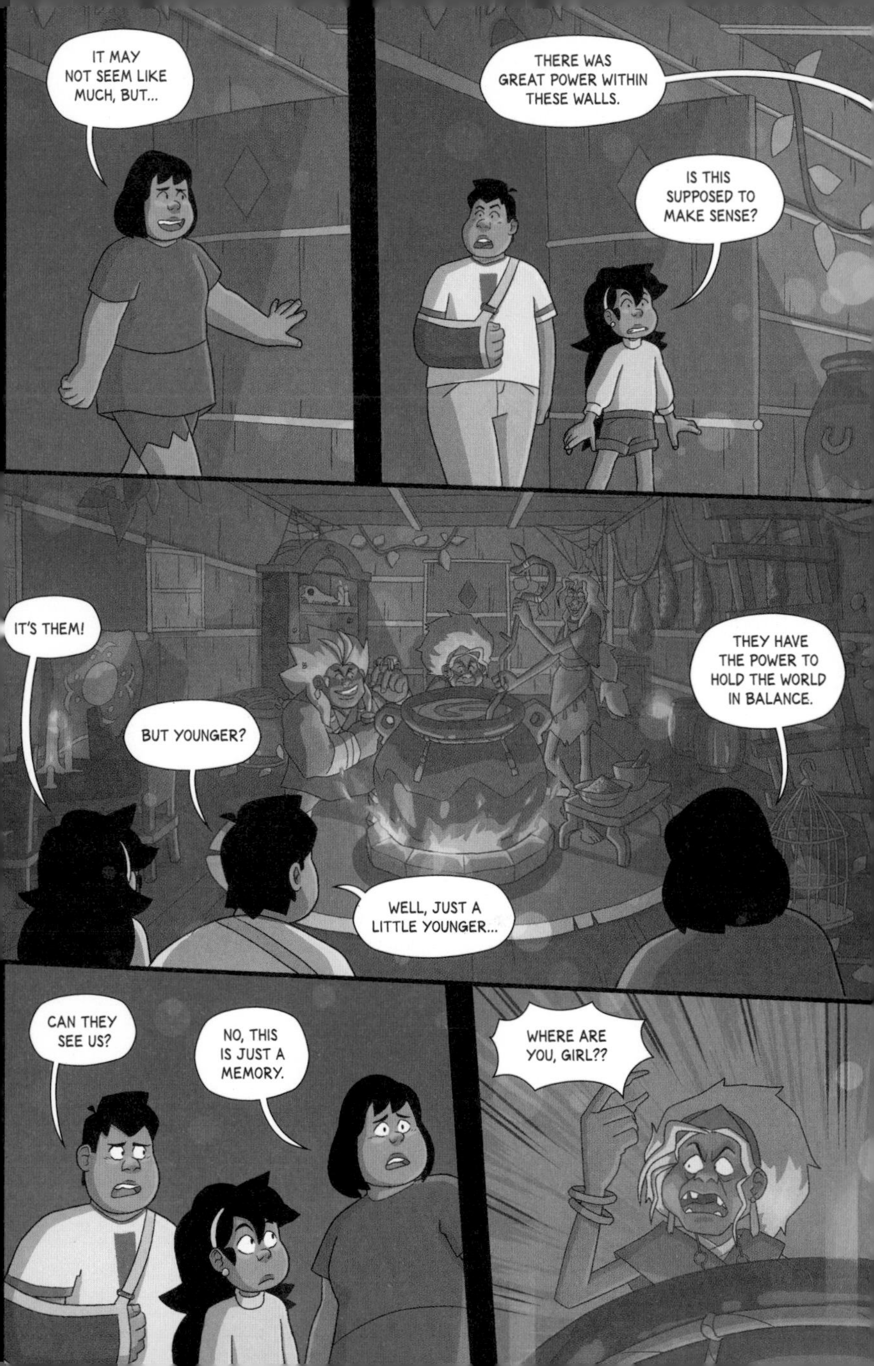
IT MAY NOT SEEM LIKE MUCH, BUT...
THERE WAS GREAT POWER WITHIN THESE WALLS.
IS THIS SUPPOSED TO MAKE SENSE?
IT'S THEM!
BUT YOUNGER?
THEY HAVE THE POWER TO HOLD THE WORLD IN BALANCE.
WELL, JUST A LITTLE YOUNGER...
CAN THEY SEE US?
NO, THIS IS JUST A MEMORY.
WHERE ARE YOU, GIRL??

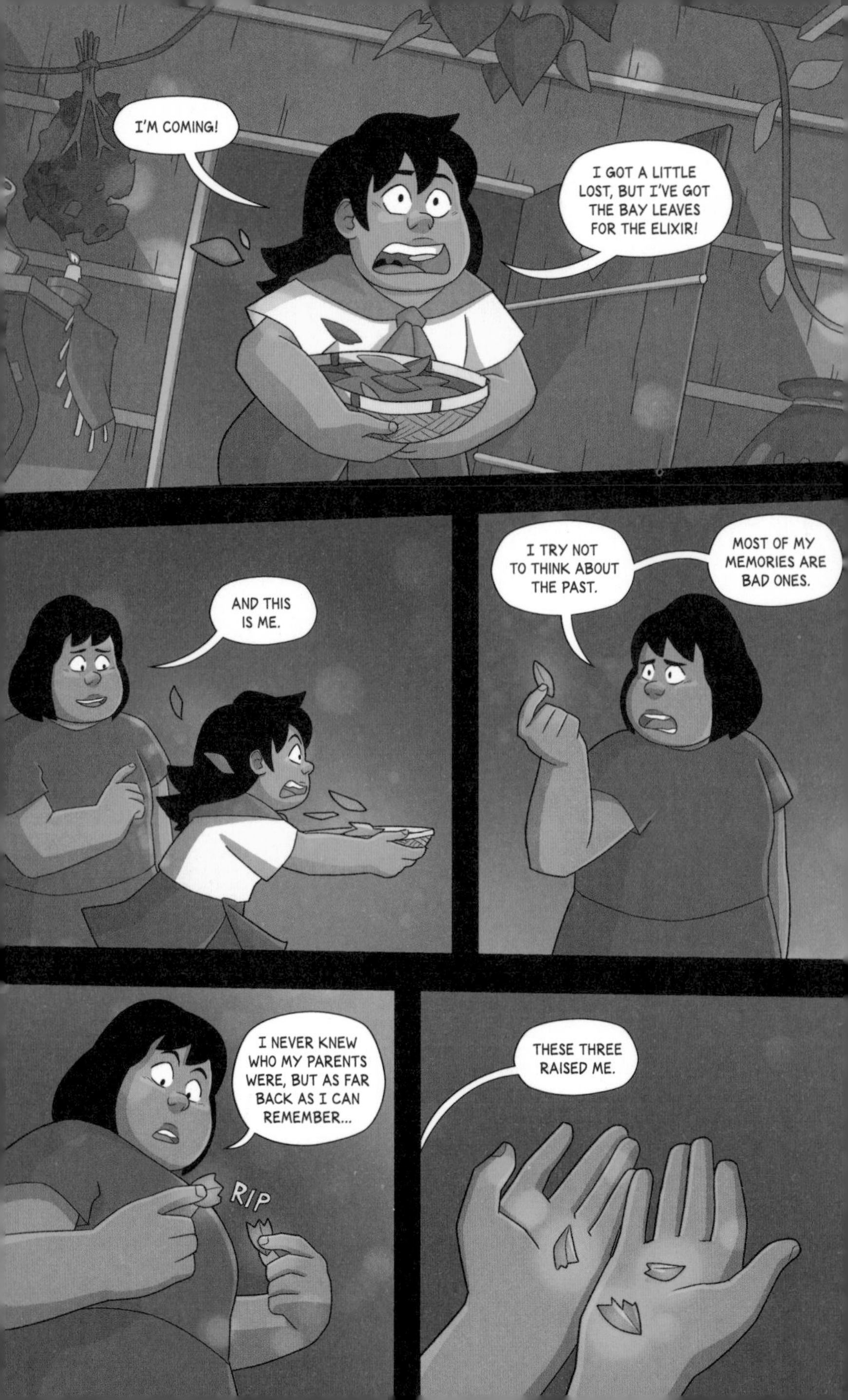
I'M COMING!
I GOT A LITTLE LOST, BUT I'VE GOT THE BAY LEAVES FOR THE ELIXIR!
AND THIS IS ME.
I TRY NOT TO THINK ABOUT THE PAST.
MOST OF MY MEMORIES ARE BAD ONES.
I NEVER KNEW WHO MY PARENTS WERE, BUT AS FAR BACK AS I CAN REMEMBER...
RIP
THESE THREE RAISED ME.

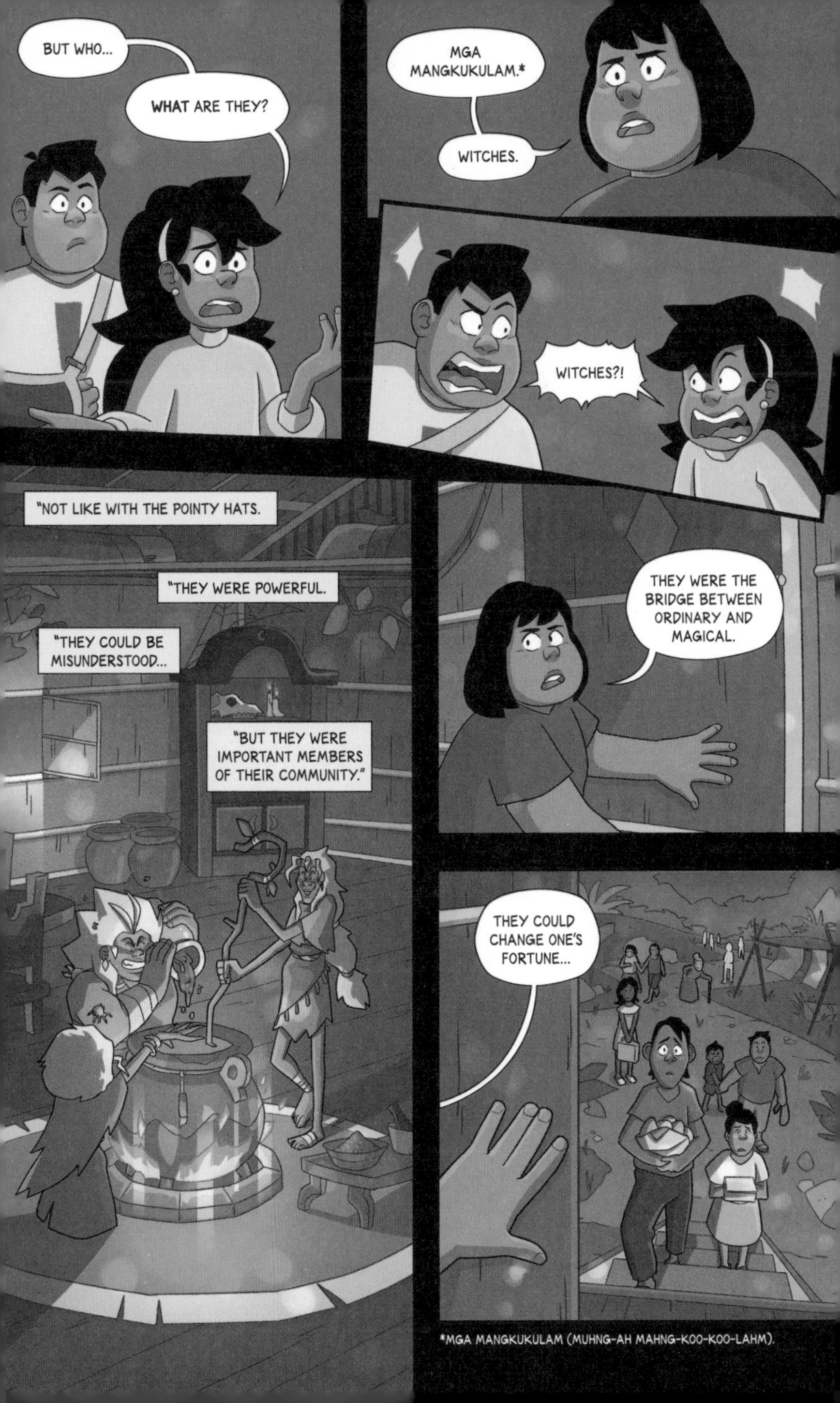

BUT WHO...
WHAT ARE THEY?
MGA MANGKUKULAM.*
WITCHES.
WITCHES?!
"NOT LIKE WITH THE POINTY HATS.
"THEY WERE POWERFUL.
"THEY COULD BE MISUNDERSTOOD...
"BUT THEY WERE IMPORTANT MEMBERS OF THEIR COMMUNITY."
THEY WERE THE BRIDGE BETWEEN ORDINARY AND MAGICAL.
THEY COULD CHANGE ONE'S FORTUNE...
*MGA MANGKUKULAM (MUHNG-AH MAHNG-KOO-KOO-LAHM).

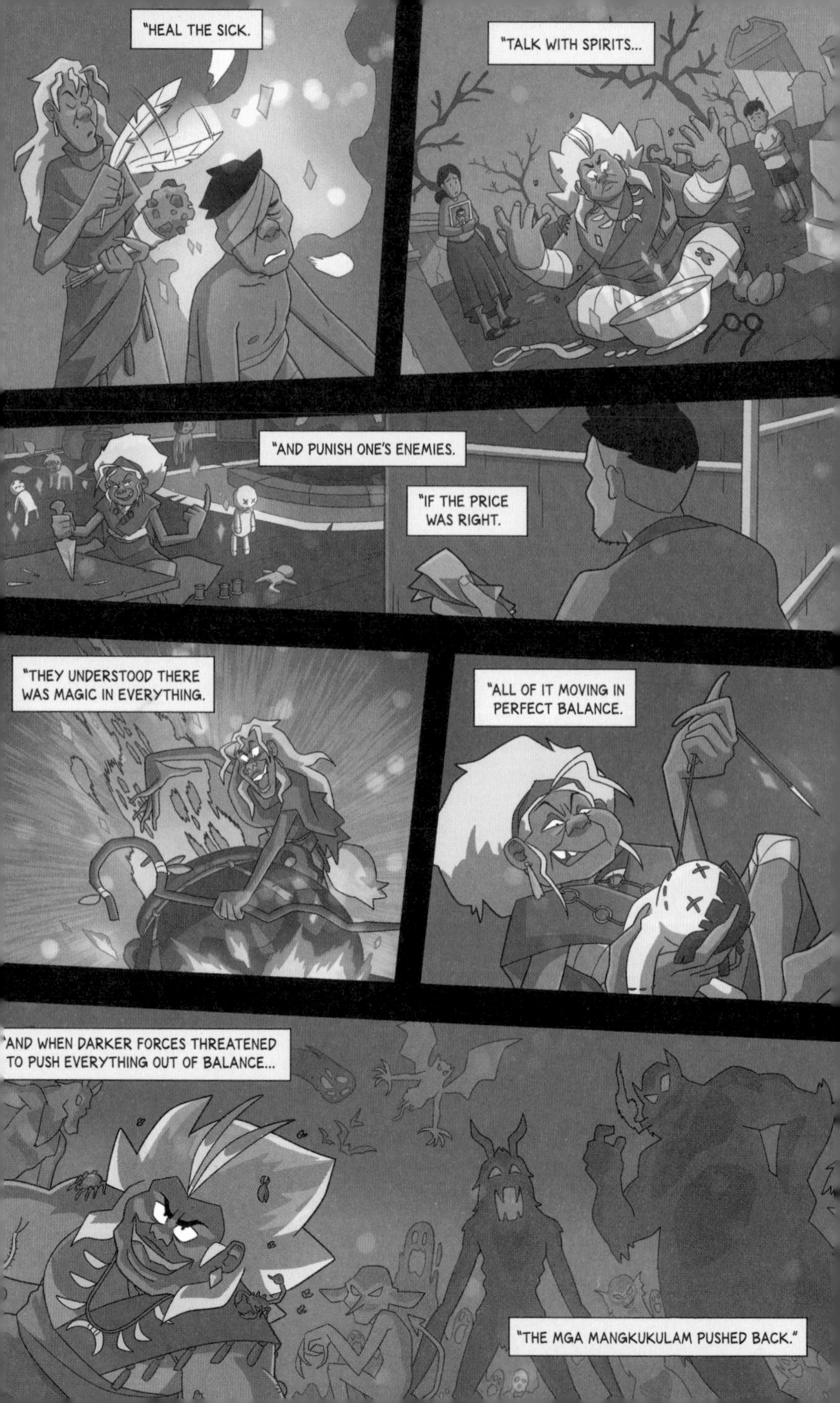
"HEAL THE SICK.
"TALK WITH SPIRITS...
"AND PUNISH ONE'S ENEMIES.
"IF THE PRICE WAS RIGHT.
"THEY UNDERSTOOD THERE WAS MAGIC IN EVERYTHING.
"ALL OF IT MOVING IN PERFECT BALANCE.
"AND WHEN DARKER FORCES THREATENED TO PUSH EVERYTHING OUT OF BALANCE...
"THE MGA MANGKUKULAM PUSHED BACK."

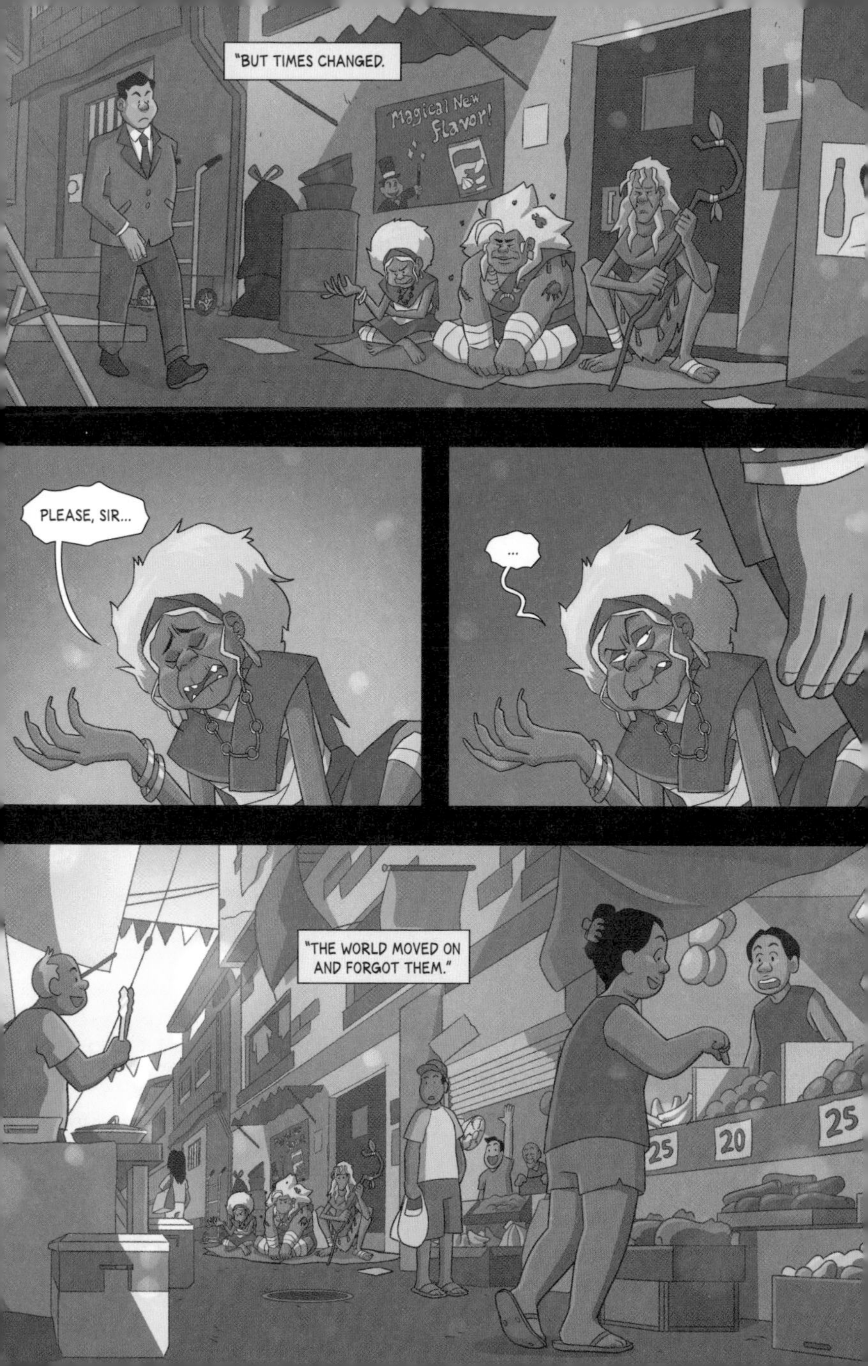
"BUT TIMES CHANGED.
Magical New Flavor!
PLEASE, SIR...
...
"THE WORLD MOVED ON AND FORGOT THEM."
25
20
25

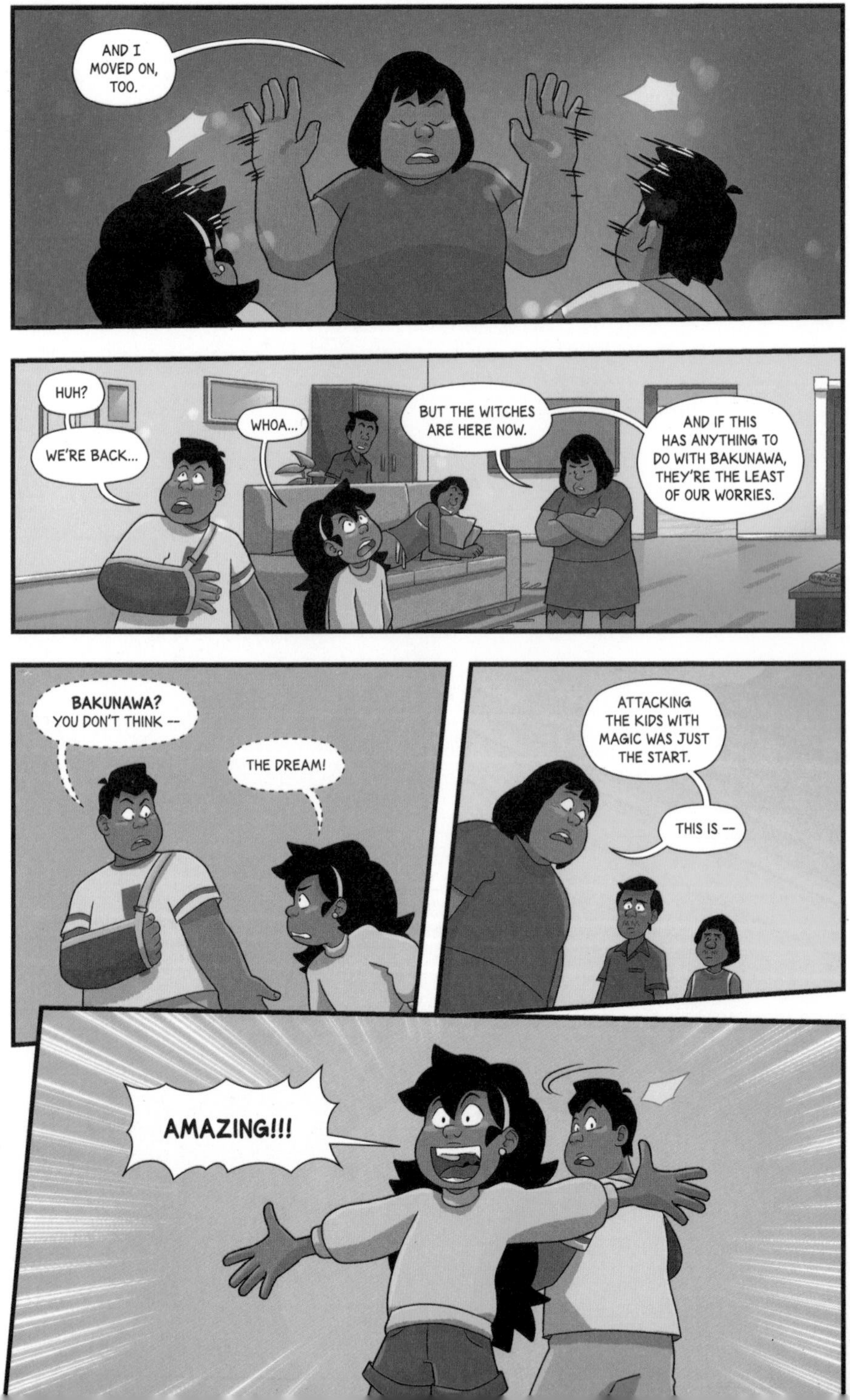
AND I MOVED ON, TOO.
HUH?
WE'RE BACK...
WHOA...
BUT THE WITCHES ARE HERE NOW.
AND IF THIS HAS ANYTHING TO DO WITH BAKUNAWA, THEY'RE THE LEAST OF OUR WORRIES.
BAKUNAWA? YOU DON'T THINK --
THE DREAM!
ATTACKING THE KIDS WITH MAGIC WAS JUST THE START.
THIS IS --
AMAZING!!!

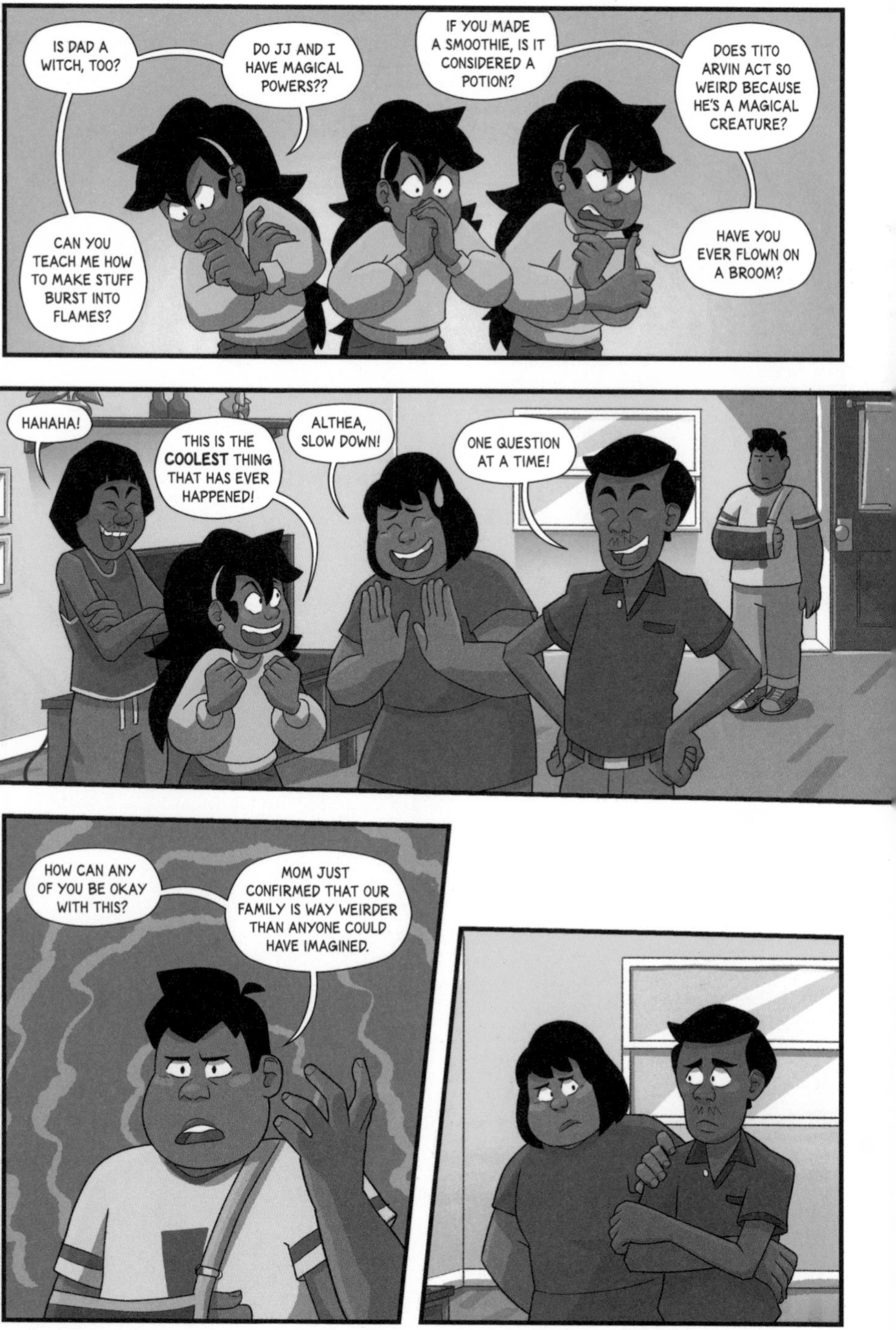
IS DAD A WITCH, TOO?
CAN YOU TEACH ME HOW TO MAKE STUFF BURST INTO FLAMES?
DO JJ AND I HAVE MAGICAL POWERS??
IF YOU MADE A SMOOTHIE, IS IT CONSIDERED A POTION?
DOES TITO ARVIN ACT SO WEIRD BECAUSE HE'S A MAGICAL CREATURE?
HAVE YOU EVER FLOWN ON A BROOM?
HAHAHA!
THIS IS THE **COOLEST** THING THAT HAS EVER HAPPENED!
ALTHEA, SLOW DOWN!
ONE QUESTION AT A TIME!
HOW CAN ANY OF YOU BE OKAY WITH THIS?
MOM JUST CONFIRMED THAT OUR FAMILY IS WAY WEIRDER THAN ANYONE COULD HAVE IMAGINED.

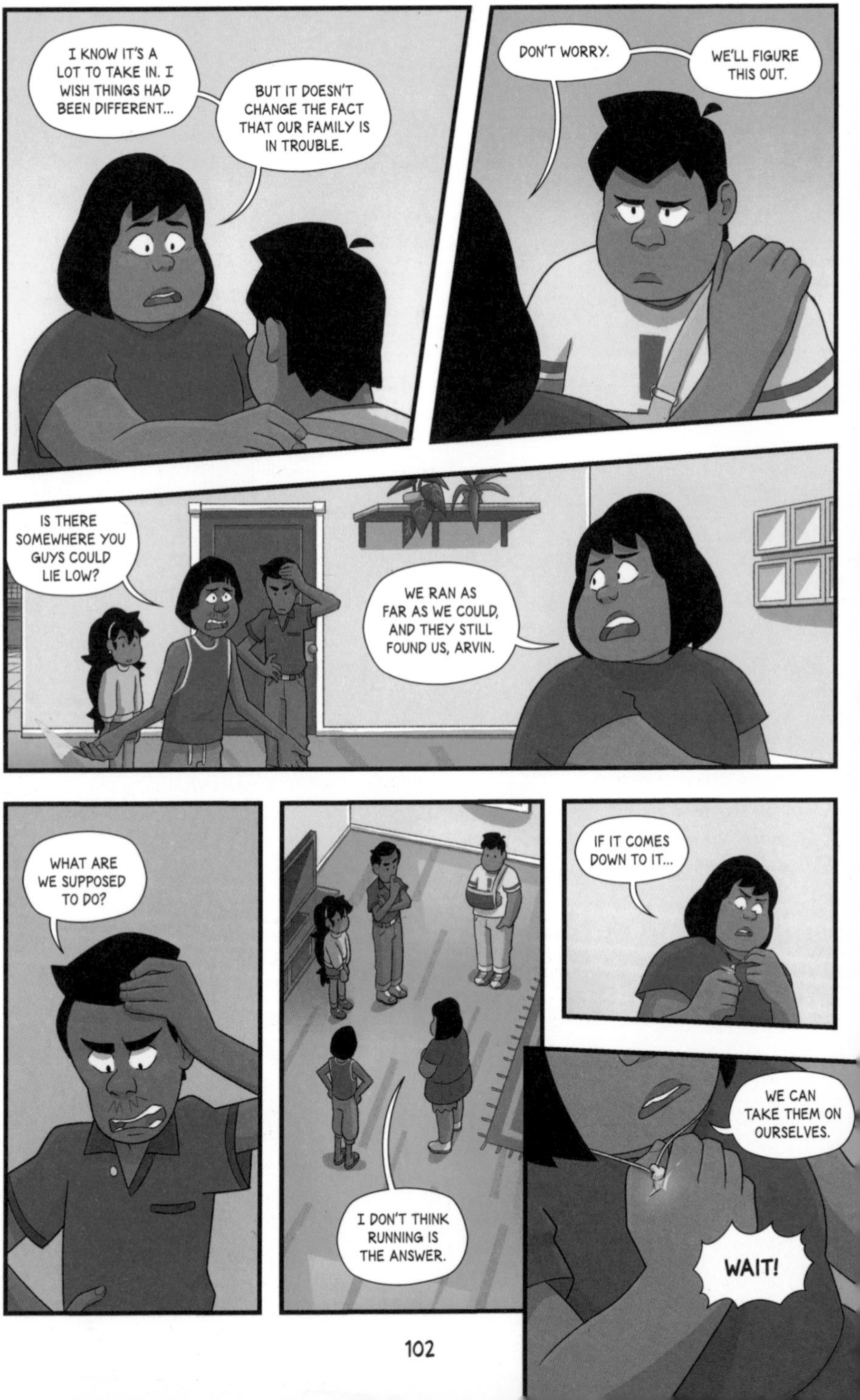
I KNOW IT'S A LOT TO TAKE IN. I WISH THINGS HAD BEEN DIFFERENT...
BUT IT DOESN'T CHANGE THE FACT THAT OUR FAMILY IS IN TROUBLE.
DON'T WORRY.
WE'LL FIGURE THIS OUT.
IS THERE SOMEWHERE YOU GUYS COULD LIE LOW?
WE RAN AS FAR AS WE COULD, AND THEY STILL FOUND US, ARVIN.
WHAT ARE WE SUPPOSED TO DO?
I DON'T THINK RUNNING IS THE ANSWER.
IF IT COMES DOWN TO IT...
WE CAN TAKE THEM ON OURSELVES.
WAIT!

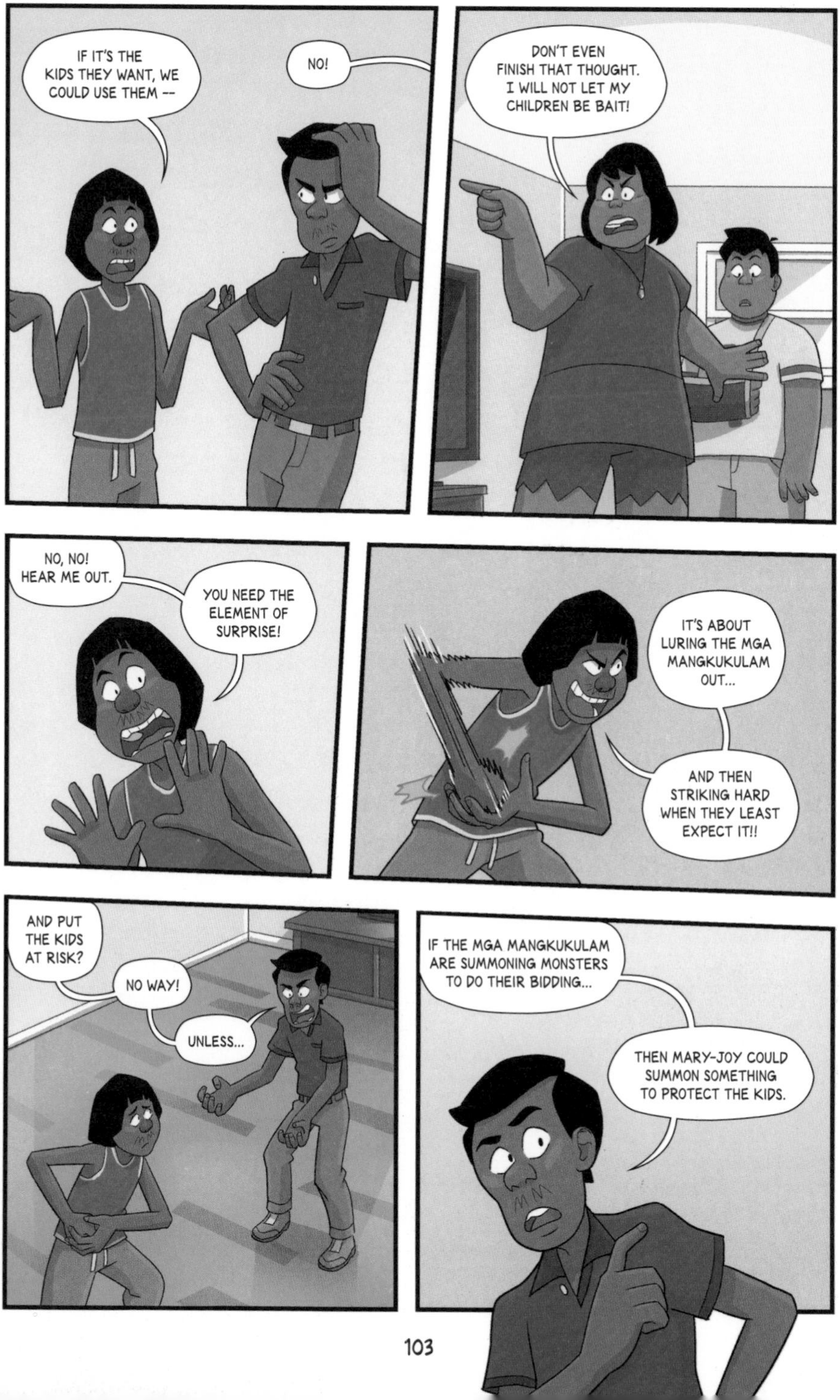
IF IT'S THE KIDS THEY WANT, WE COULD USE THEM --
NO!
DON'T EVEN FINISH THAT THOUGHT. I WILL NOT LET MY CHILDREN BE BAIT!
NO, NO! HEAR ME OUT.
YOU NEED THE ELEMENT OF SURPRISE!
IT'S ABOUT LURING THE MGA MANGKUKULAM OUT...
AND THEN STRIKING HARD WHEN THEY LEAST EXPECT IT!!
AND PUT THE KIDS AT RISK?
NO WAY!
UNLESS...
IF THE MGA MANGKUKULAM ARE SUMMONING MONSTERS TO DO THEIR BIDDING...
THEN MARY-JOY COULD SUMMON SOMETHING TO PROTECT THE KIDS.

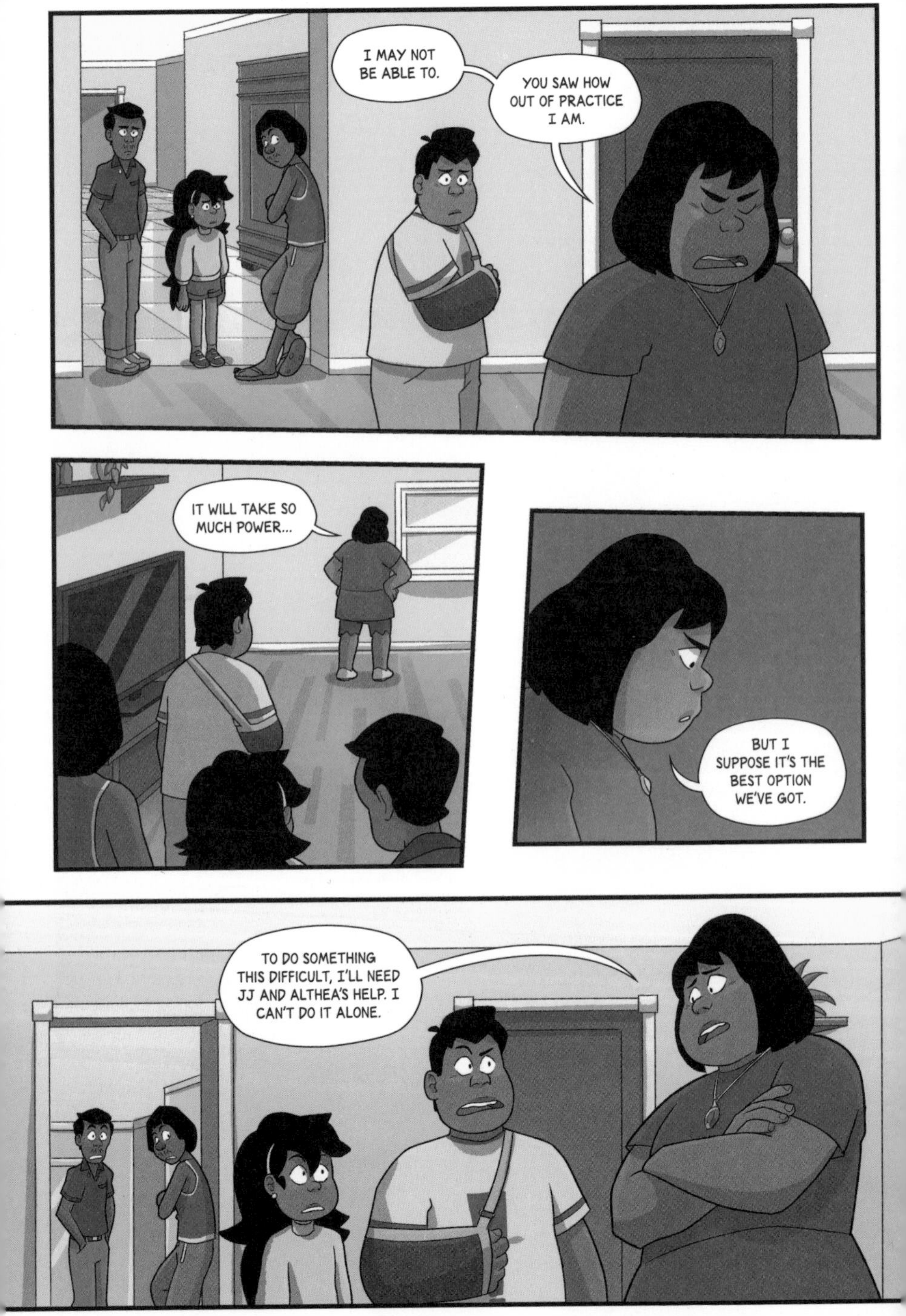
I MAY NOT BE ABLE TO.
YOU SAW HOW OUT OF PRACTICE I AM.
IT WILL TAKE SO MUCH POWER...
BUT I SUPPOSE IT'S THE BEST OPTION WE'VE GOT.
TO DO SOMETHING THIS DIFFICULT, I'LL NEED JJ AND ALTHEA'S HELP. I CAN'T DO IT ALONE.

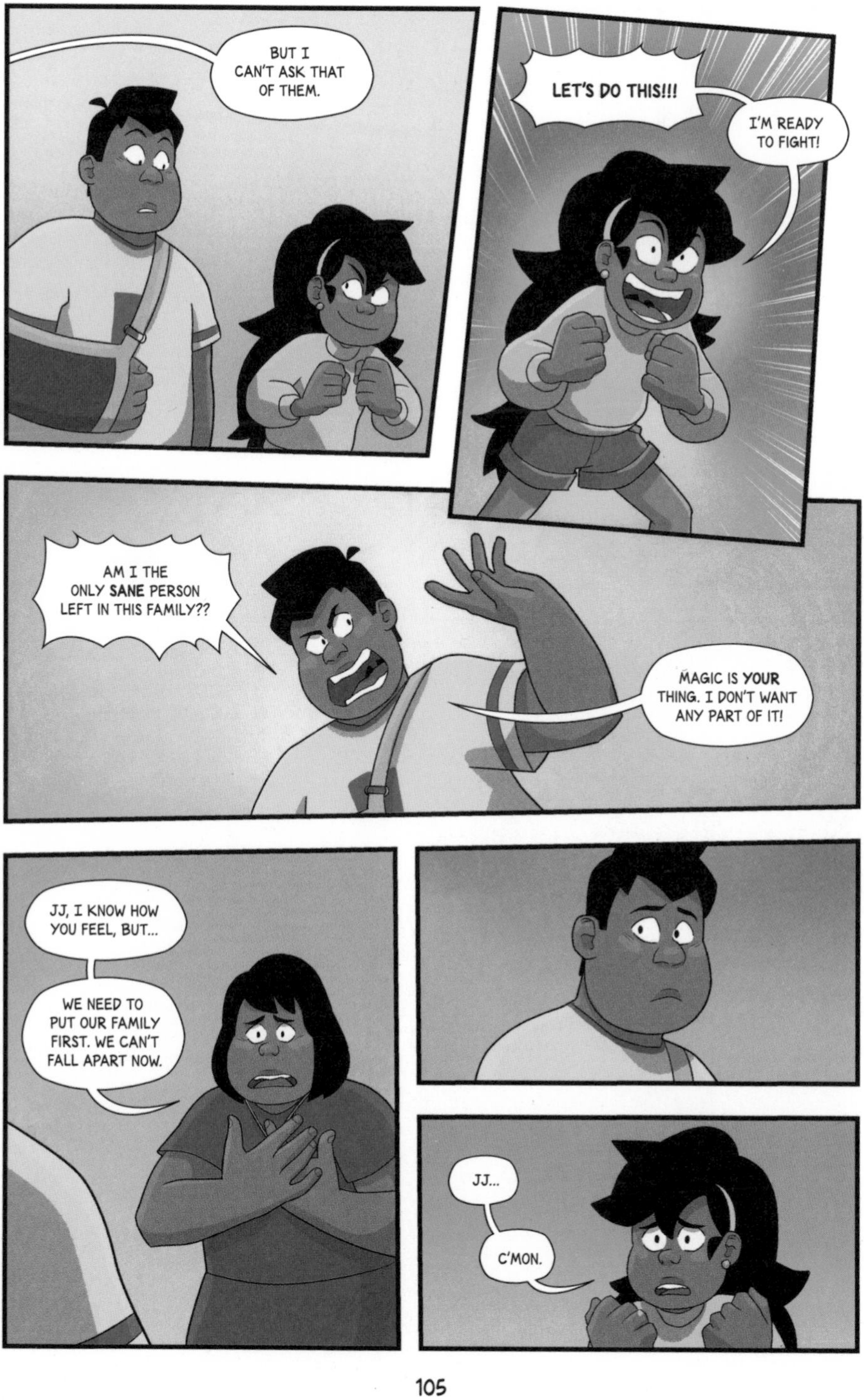
BUT I CAN'T ASK THAT OF THEM.
LET'S DO THIS!!!
I'M READY TO FIGHT!
AM I THE ONLY SANE PERSON LEFT IN THIS FAMILY??
MAGIC IS YOUR THING. I DON'T WANT ANY PART OF IT!
JJ, I KNOW HOW YOU FEEL, BUT...
WE NEED TO PUT OUR FAMILY FIRST. WE CAN'T FALL APART NOW.
JJ...
C'MON.

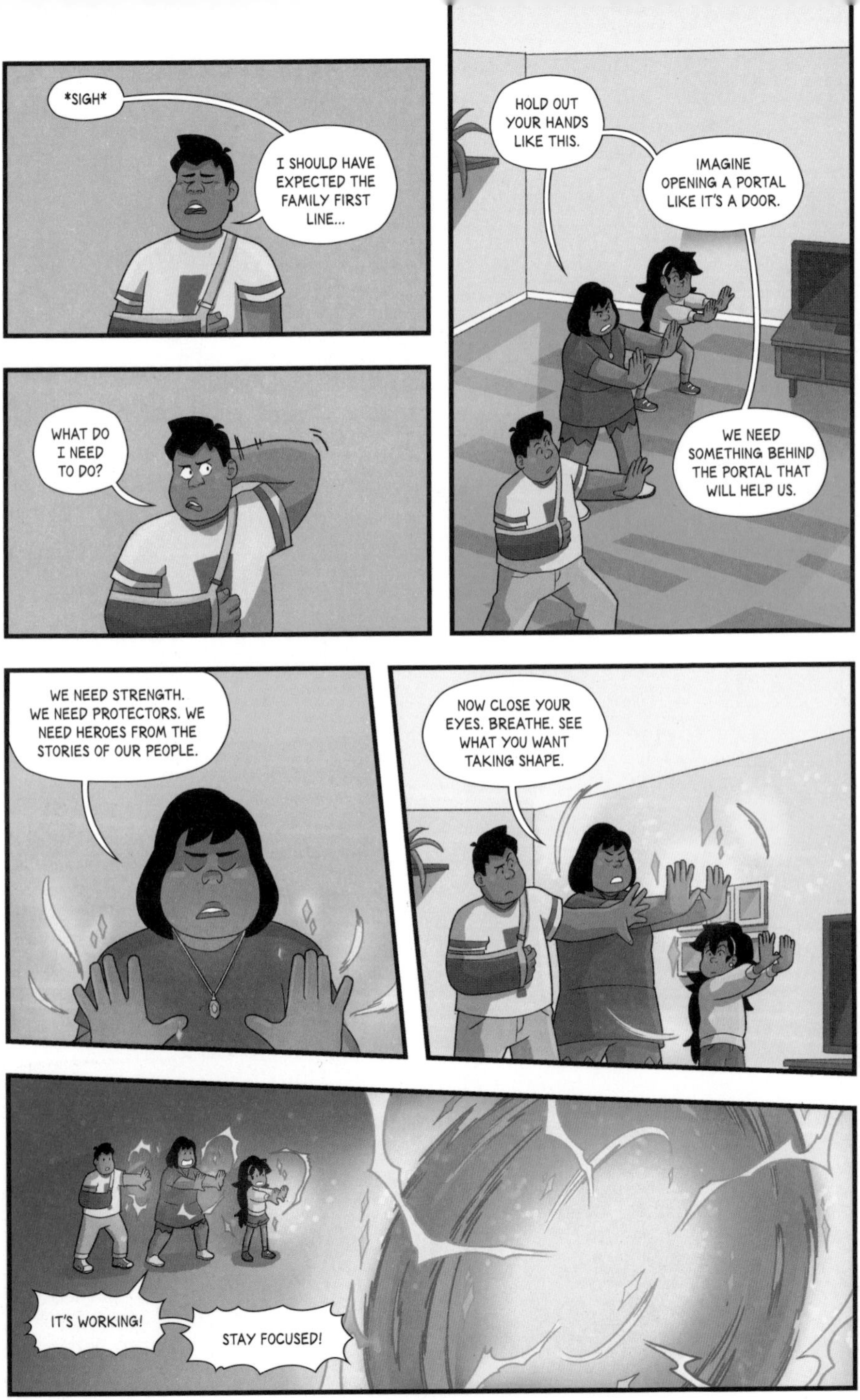
SIGH
I SHOULD HAVE EXPECTED THE FAMILY FIRST LINE...
HOLD OUT YOUR HANDS LIKE THIS.
IMAGINE OPENING A PORTAL LIKE IT'S A DOOR.
WHAT DO I NEED TO DO?
WE NEED SOMETHING BEHIND THE PORTAL THAT WILL HELP US.
WE NEED STRENGTH. WE NEED PROTECTORS. WE NEED HEROES FROM THE STORIES OF OUR PEOPLE.
NOW CLOSE YOUR EYES. BREATHE. SEE WHAT YOU WANT TAKING SHAPE.
IT'S WORKING!
STAY FOCUSED!

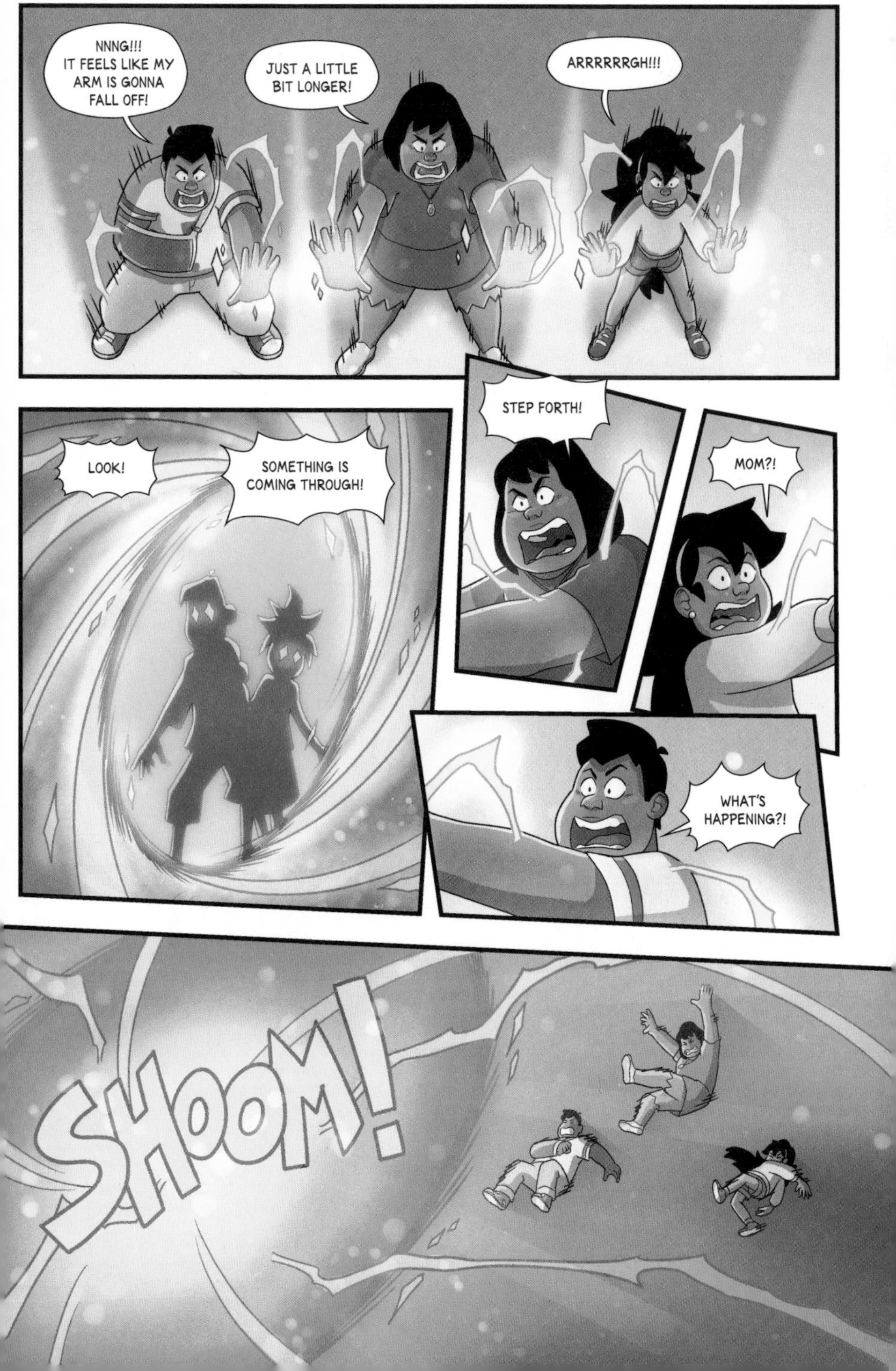
NNNG!!! IT FEELS LIKE MY ARM IS GONNA FALL OFF!
JUST A LITTLE BIT LONGER!
ARRRRRRGH!!!
LOOK!
SOMETHING IS COMING THROUGH!
STEP FORTH!
MOM?!
WHAT'S HAPPENING?!
SHOOM!

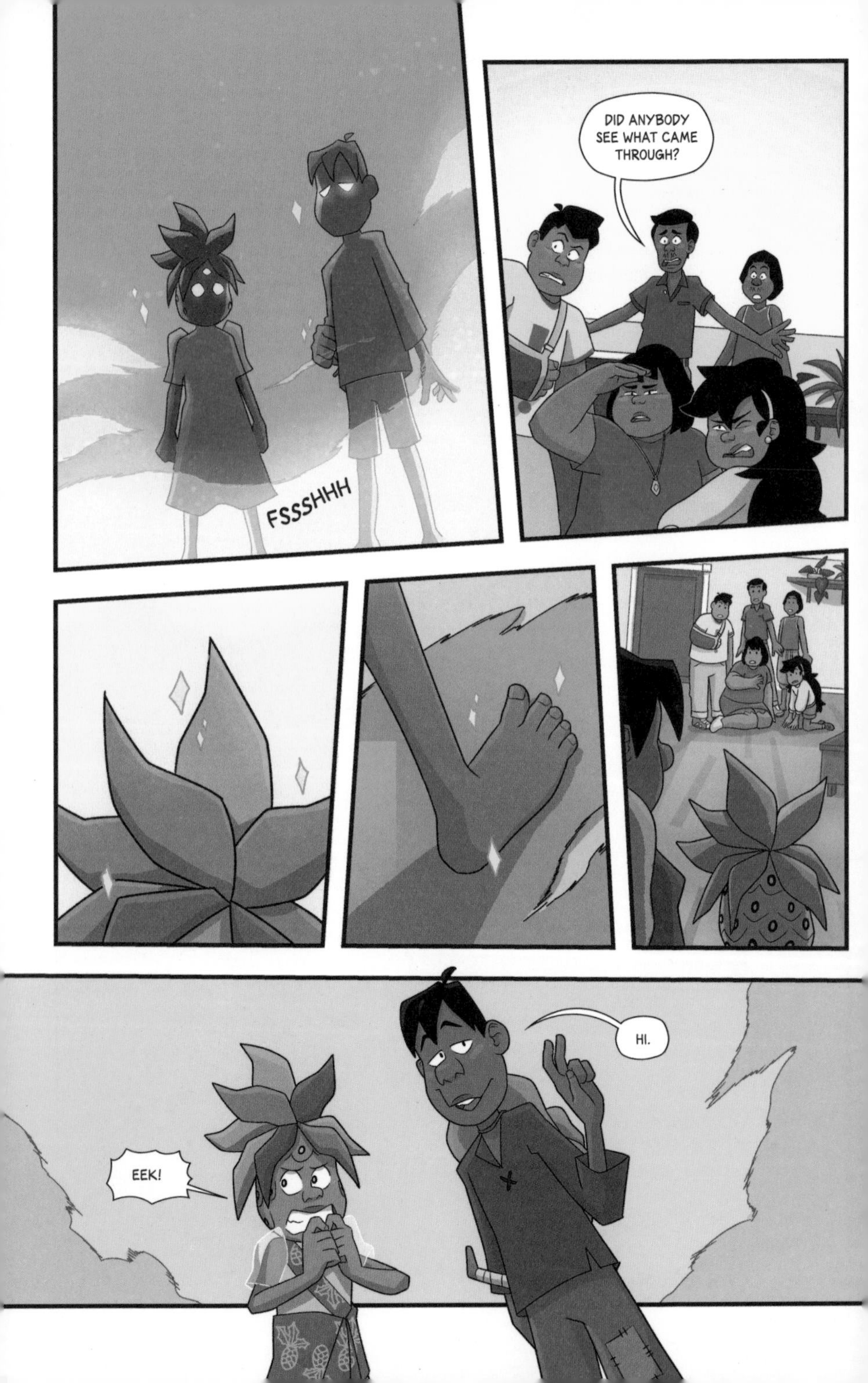
FSSSHHH
DID ANYBODY SEE WHAT CAME THROUGH?
HI.
EEK!

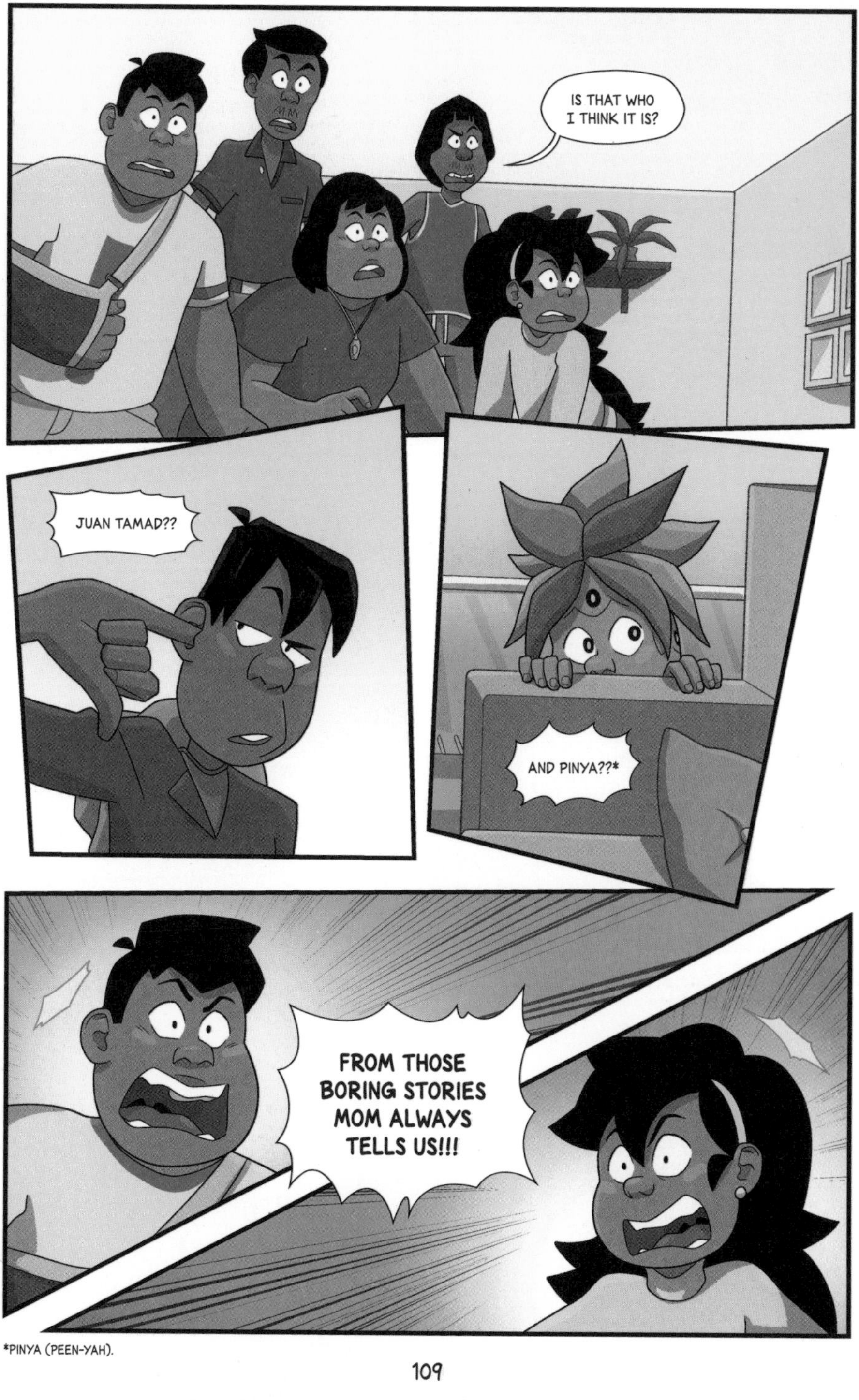
IS THAT WHO I THINK IT IS?
JUAN TAMAD??
AND PINYA??*
FROM THOSE BORING STORIES MOM ALWAYS TELLS US!!!

*PINYA (PEEN-YAH).

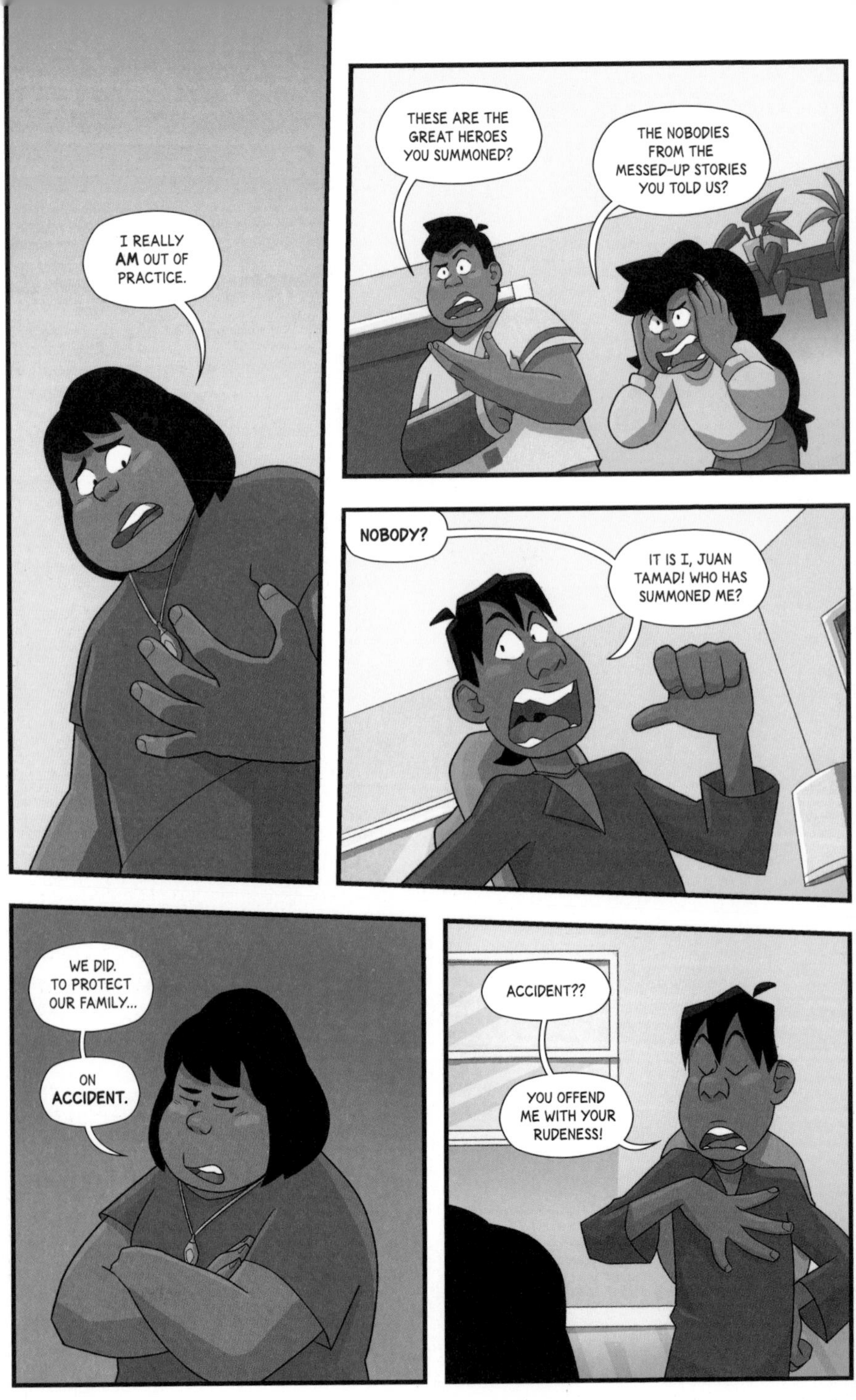
I REALLY **AM** OUT OF PRACTICE.
THESE ARE THE GREAT HEROES YOU SUMMONED?
THE NOBODIES FROM THE MESSED-UP STORIES YOU TOLD US?
NOBODY?
IT IS I, JUAN TAMAD! WHO HAS SUMMONED ME?
WE DID. TO PROTECT OUR FAMILY...
ON **ACCIDENT.**
ACCIDENT??
YOU OFFEND ME WITH YOUR RUDENESS!

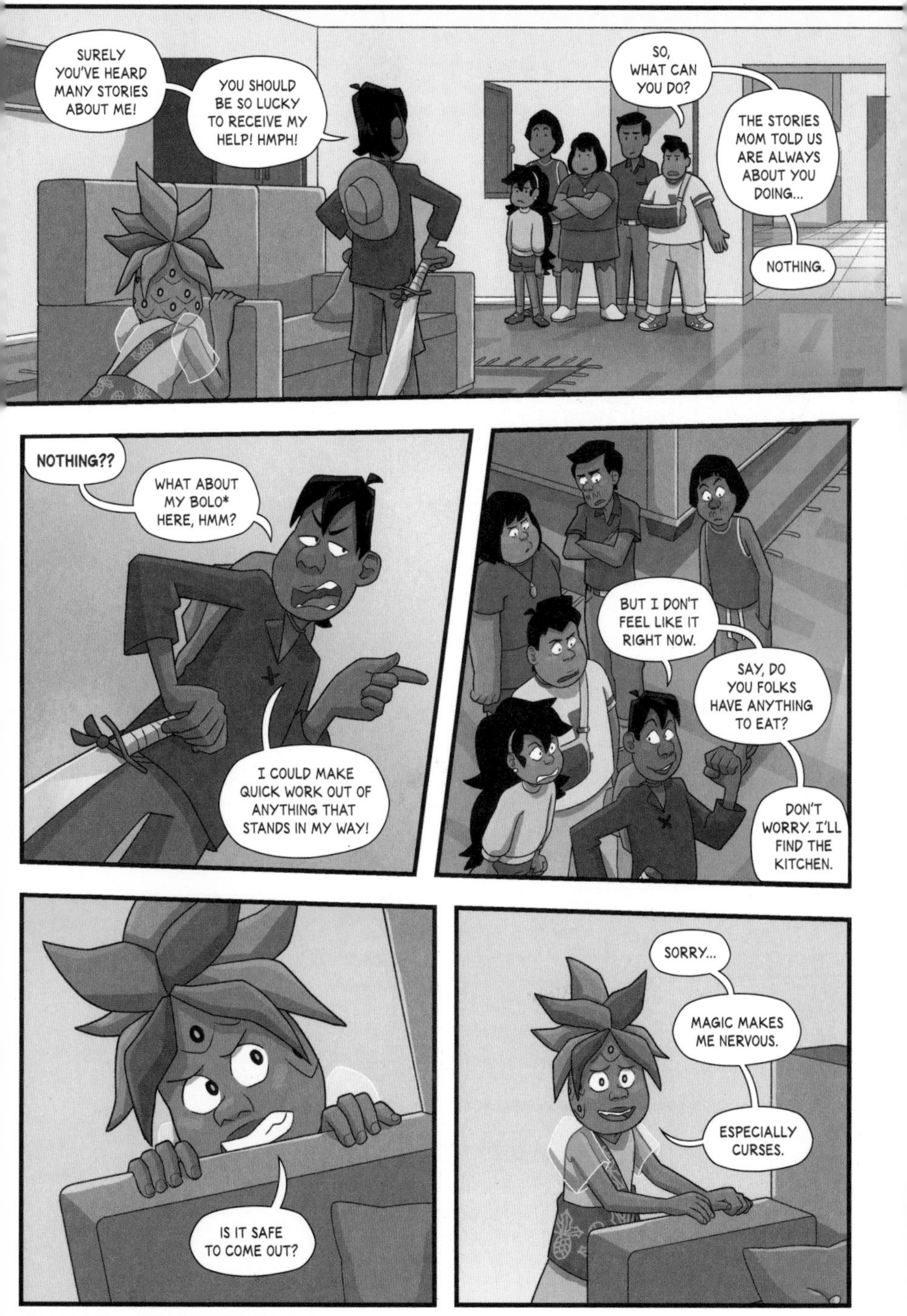
SURELY YOU'VE HEARD MANY STORIES ABOUT ME!
YOU SHOULD BE SO LUCKY TO RECEIVE MY HELP! HMPH!
SO, WHAT CAN YOU DO?
THE STORIES MOM TOLD US ARE ALWAYS ABOUT YOU DOING...
NOTHING.
NOTHING??
WHAT ABOUT MY BOLO* HERE, HMM?
I COULD MAKE QUICK WORK OUT OF ANYTHING THAT STANDS IN MY WAY!
BUT I DON'T FEEL LIKE IT RIGHT NOW.
SAY, DO YOU FOLKS HAVE ANYTHING TO EAT?
DON'T WORRY. I'LL FIND THE KITCHEN.
IS IT SAFE TO COME OUT?
SORRY...
MAGIC MAKES ME NERVOUS.
ESPECIALLY CURSES.

*BOLO (BO-LOH): A LARGE KNIFE OR CUTTING TOOL.

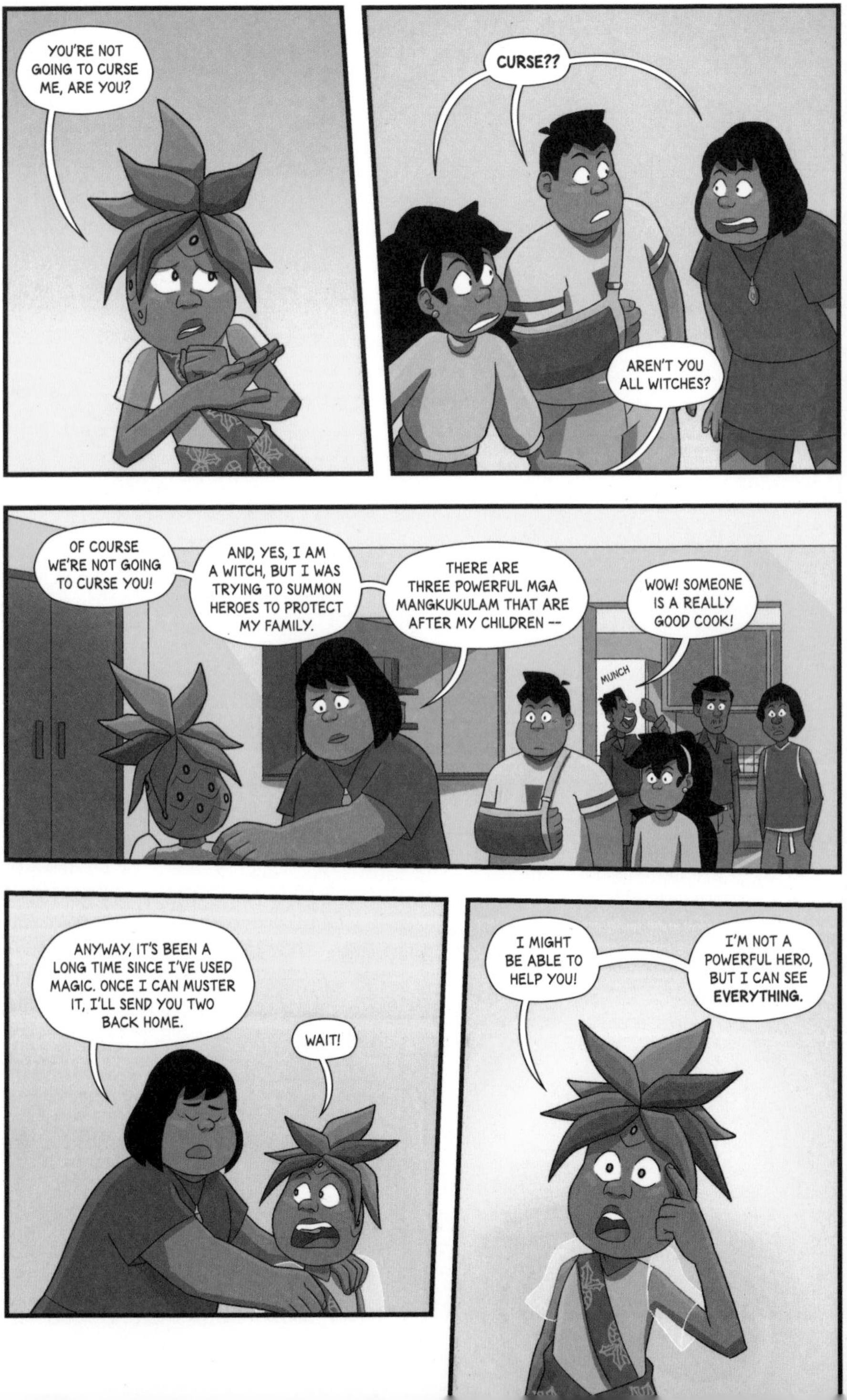
YOU'RE NOT GOING TO CURSE ME, ARE YOU?
CURSE??
AREN'T YOU ALL WITCHES?
OF COURSE WE'RE NOT GOING TO CURSE YOU!
AND, YES, I AM A WITCH, BUT I WAS TRYING TO SUMMON HEROES TO PROTECT MY FAMILY.
THERE ARE THREE POWERFUL MGA MANGKUKULAM THAT ARE AFTER MY CHILDREN --
WOW! SOMEONE IS A REALLY GOOD COOK!
MUNCH
ANYWAY, IT'S BEEN A LONG TIME SINCE I'VE USED MAGIC. ONCE I CAN MUSTER IT, I'LL SEND YOU TWO BACK HOME.
WAIT!
I MIGHT BE ABLE TO HELP YOU!
I'M NOT A POWERFUL HERO, BUT I CAN SEE **EVERYTHING.**

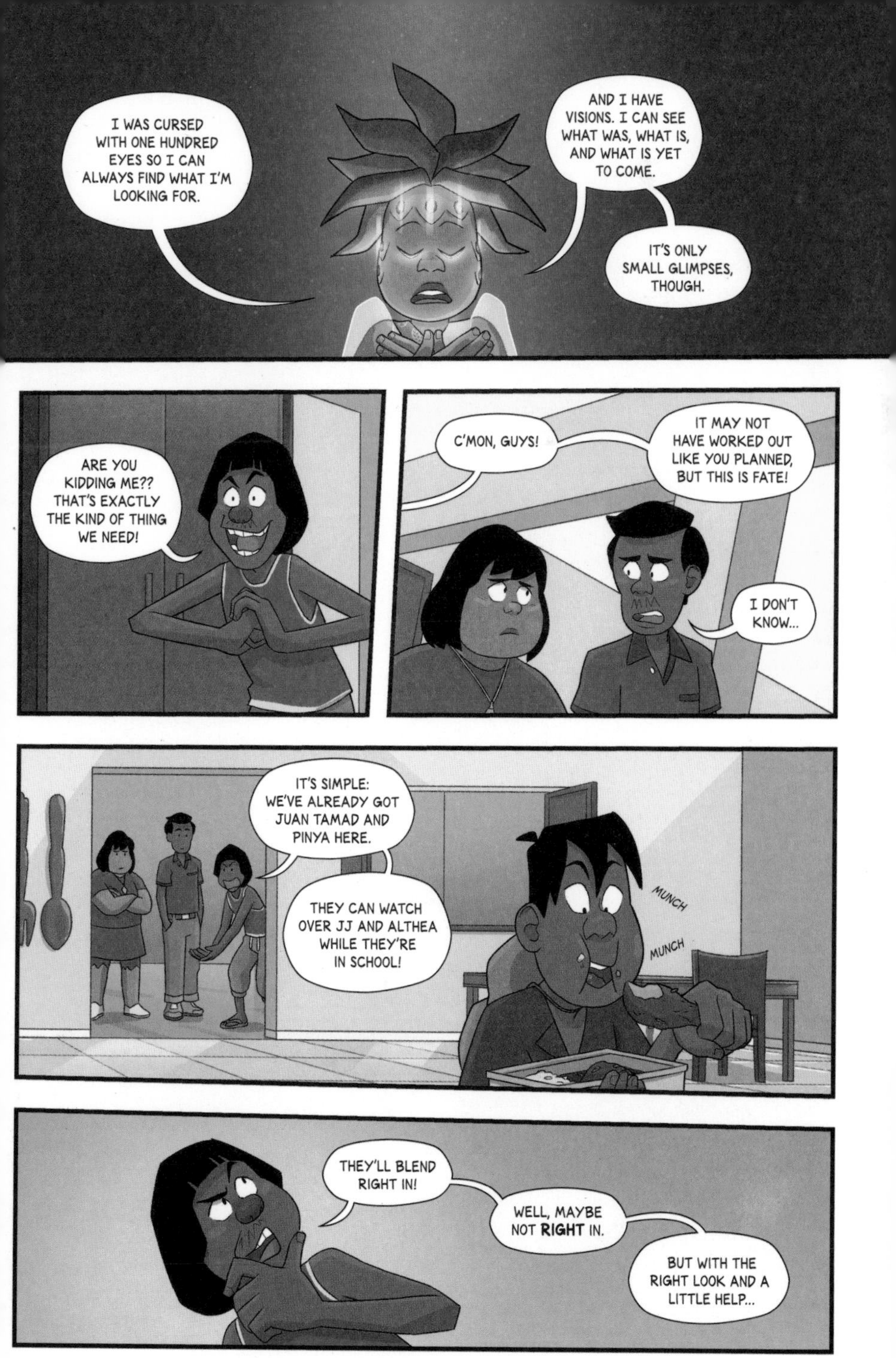
I WAS CURSED WITH ONE HUNDRED EYES SO I CAN ALWAYS FIND WHAT I'M LOOKING FOR.
AND I HAVE VISIONS. I CAN SEE WHAT WAS, WHAT IS, AND WHAT IS YET TO COME.
IT'S ONLY SMALL GLIMPSES, THOUGH.
ARE YOU KIDDING ME?? THAT'S EXACTLY THE KIND OF THING WE NEED!
C'MON, GUYS!
IT MAY NOT HAVE WORKED OUT LIKE YOU PLANNED, BUT THIS IS FATE!
I DON'T KNOW...
IT'S SIMPLE: WE'VE ALREADY GOT JUAN TAMAD AND PINYA HERE.
THEY CAN WATCH OVER JJ AND ALTHEA WHILE THEY'RE IN SCHOOL!
MUNCH
MUNCH
THEY'LL BLEND RIGHT IN!
WELL, MAYBE NOT **RIGHT** IN.
BUT WITH THE RIGHT LOOK AND A LITTLE HELP...

"OKAY, A **LOT** OF HELP."

THIS PLAN COULD NOT BE MORE IDIOTIC.

I'M SUPPOSED TO FIND SOME OLD CLOTHES THAT WILL MAKE YOU LOOK LIKE A REGULAR KID??

I'M SORRY YOU ARE BURDENED WITH THIS TASK.

PSH, IT'S REALLY NO BIG DEAL.

ME AND MY FRIENDS USED TO GO THROUGH ONE ANOTHER'S CLOSETS ALL THE TIME.

WELL, MY **OLD** FRIENDS, THAT IS.

OOOH!

ARE THESE COOL, AMERICAN TEEN CLOTHES?

I DON'T EVEN WANNA SEE WHAT YOU PICKED OUT.

I need a vacation from this vacation!

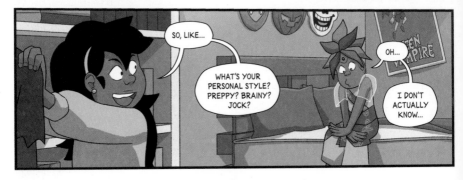

SO, LIKE...

WHAT'S YOUR PERSONAL STYLE? PREPPY? BRAINY? JOCK?

OH...

I DON'T ACTUALLY KNOW...

114

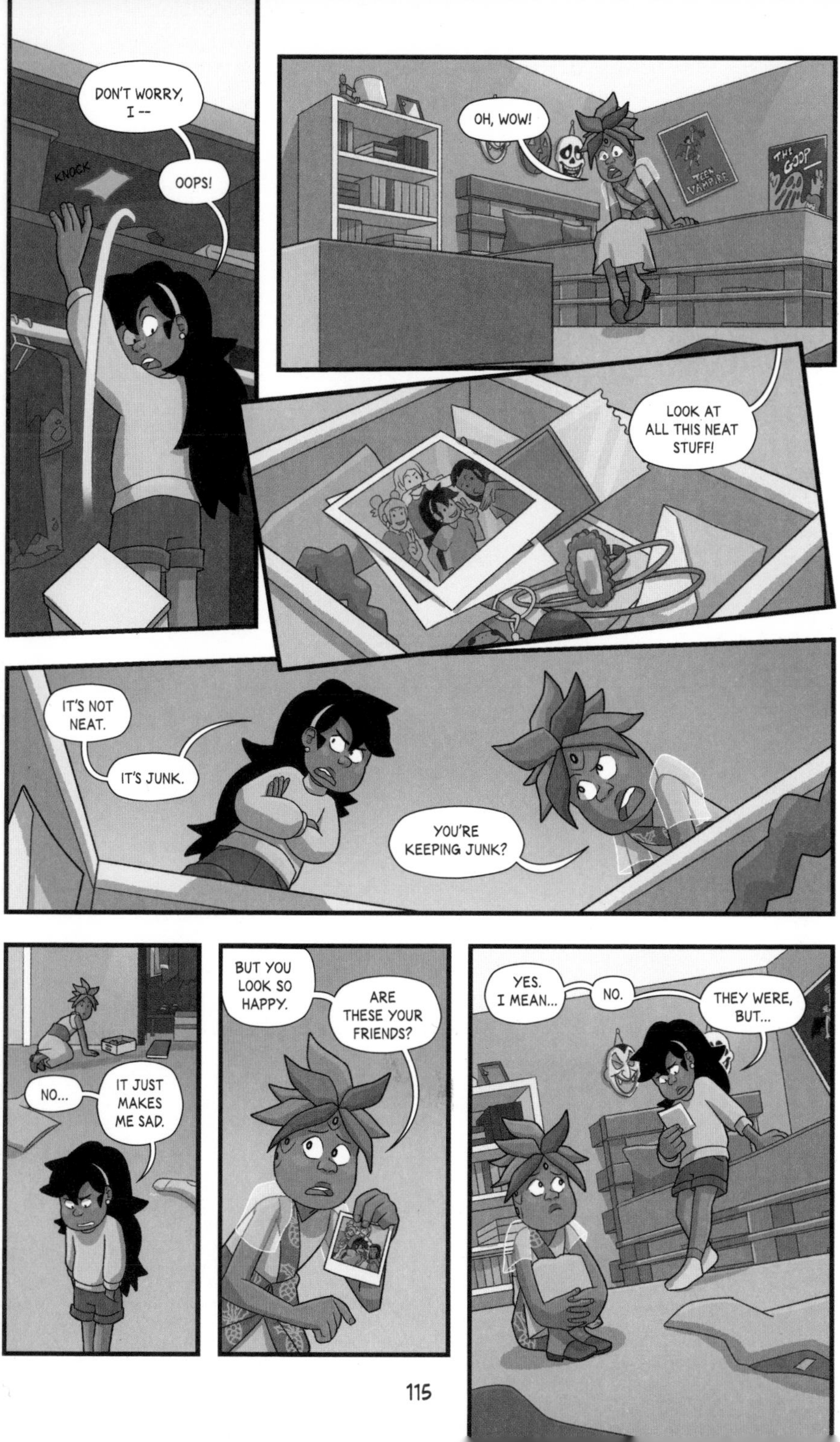
DON'T WORRY, I --
KNOCK
OOPS!
OH, WOW!
TEEN VAMPIRE
THE GOOP
LOOK AT ALL THIS NEAT STUFF!
IT'S NOT NEAT.
IT'S JUNK.
YOU'RE KEEPING JUNK?
NO...
IT JUST MAKES ME SAD.
BUT YOU LOOK SO HAPPY.
ARE THESE YOUR FRIENDS?
YES. I MEAN...
NO.
THEY WERE, BUT...

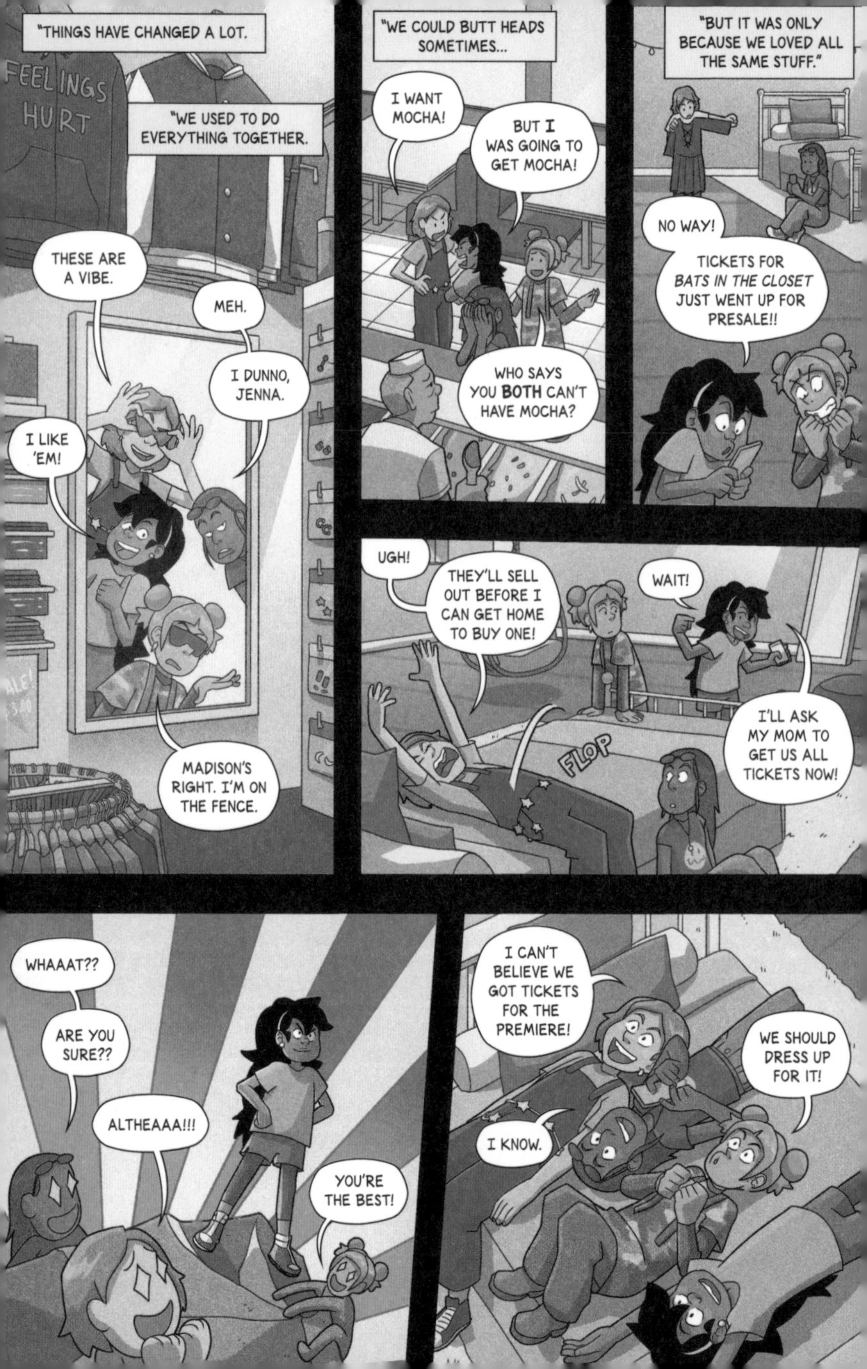

"THINGS HAVE CHANGED A LOT.
FEELINGS HURT
"WE USED TO DO EVERYTHING TOGETHER.
THESE ARE A VIBE.
MEH.
I DUNNO, JENNA.
I LIKE 'EM!
MADISON'S RIGHT. I'M ON THE FENCE.
"WE COULD BUTT HEADS SOMETIMES...
I WANT MOCHA!
BUT I WAS GOING TO GET MOCHA!
WHO SAYS YOU BOTH CAN'T HAVE MOCHA?
"BUT IT WAS ONLY BECAUSE WE LOVED ALL THE SAME STUFF."
NO WAY!
TICKETS FOR *BATS IN THE CLOSET* JUST WENT UP FOR PRESALE!!
UGH!
THEY'LL SELL OUT BEFORE I CAN GET HOME TO BUY ONE!
WAIT!
FLOP
I'LL ASK MY MOM TO GET US ALL TICKETS NOW!
WHAAAT??
ARE YOU SURE??
ALTHEAAA!!!
YOU'RE THE BEST!
I CAN'T BELIEVE WE GOT TICKETS FOR THE PREMIERE!
WE SHOULD DRESS UP FOR IT!
I KNOW.

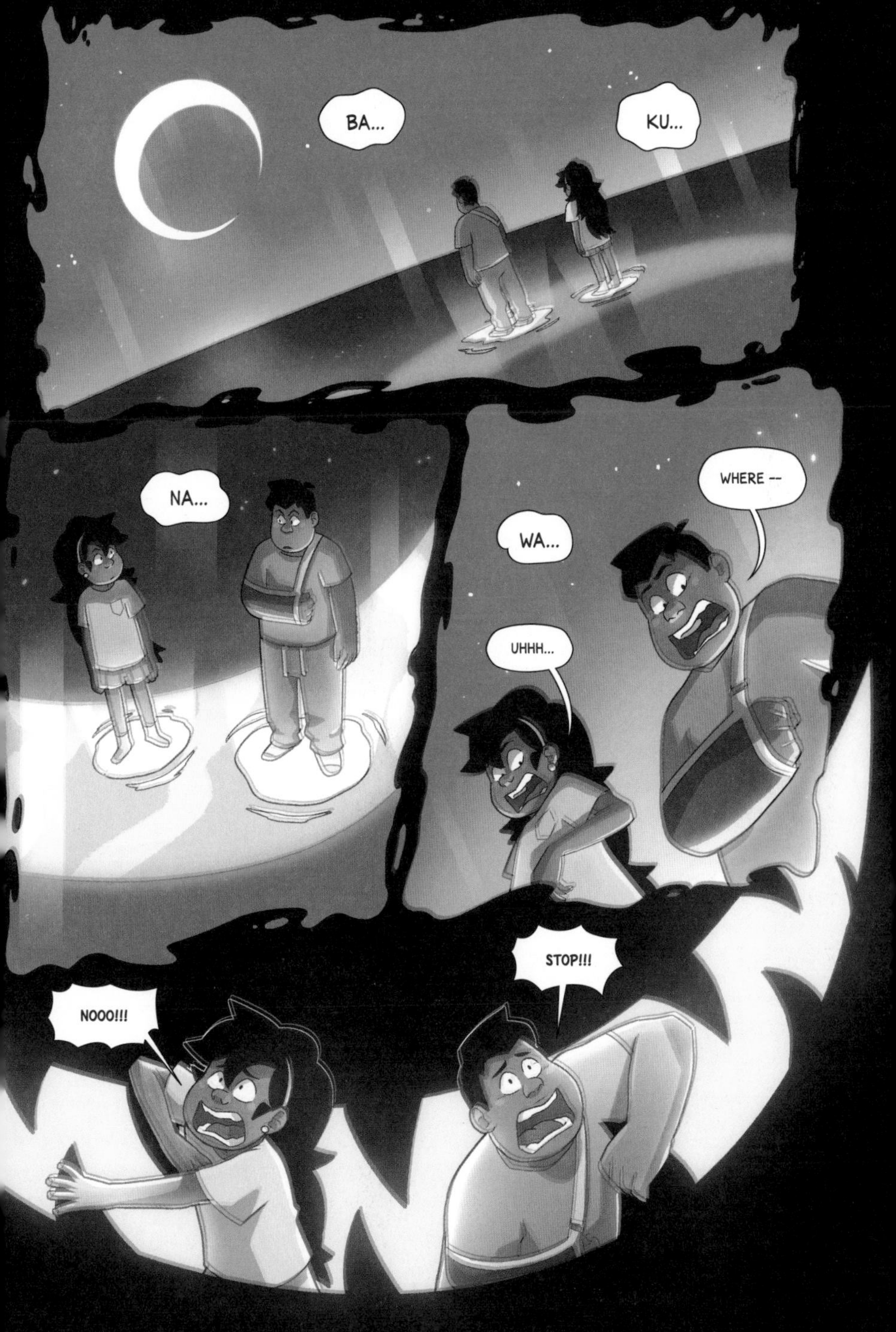
BA...
KU...
NA...
WA...
WHERE --
UHHH...
STOP!!!
NOOO!!!

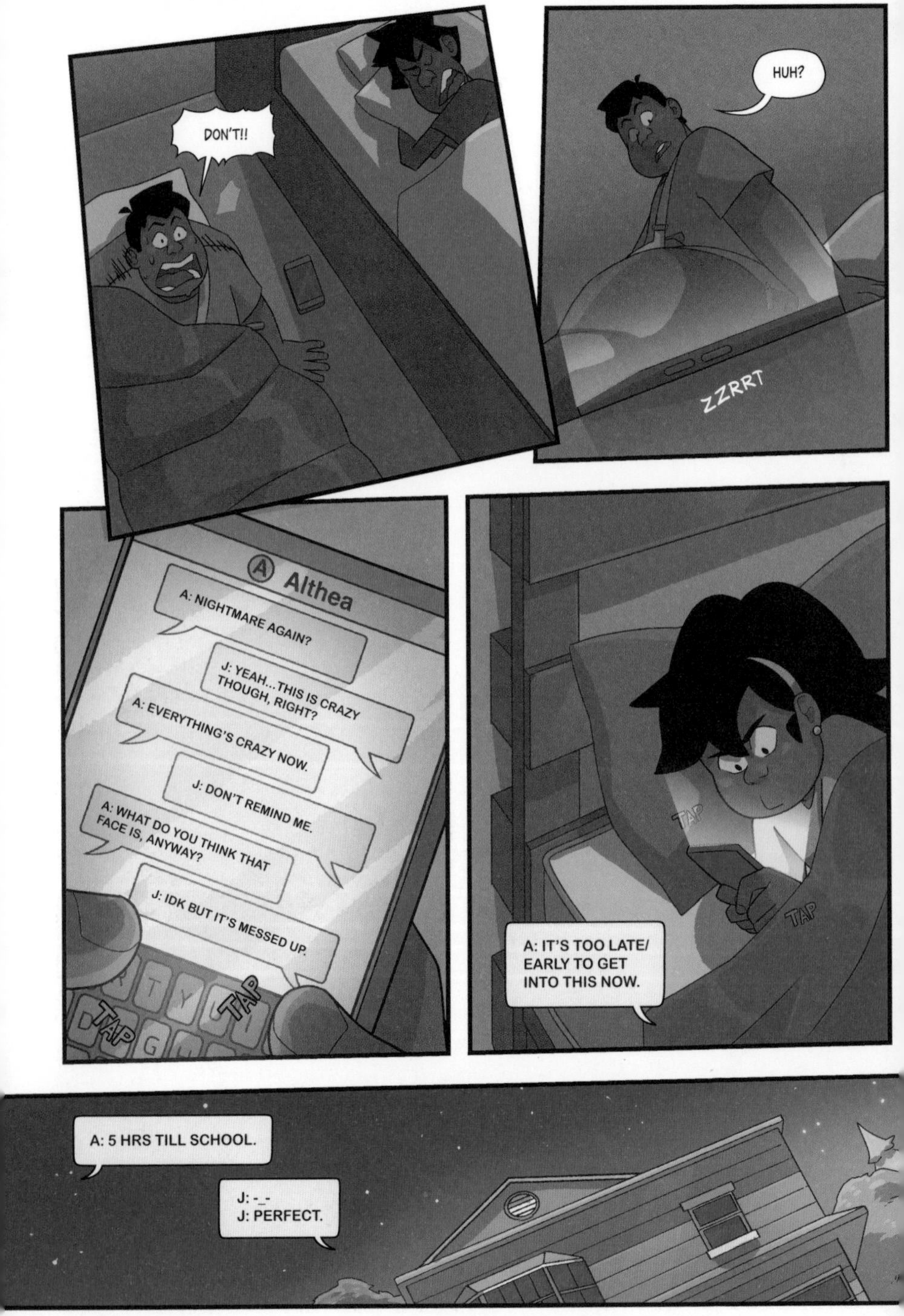
DON'T!!
HUH?
ZZRRT
Althea
A: NIGHTMARE AGAIN?
J: YEAH...THIS IS CRAZY THOUGH, RIGHT?
A: EVERYTHING'S CRAZY NOW.
J: DON'T REMIND ME.
A: WHAT DO YOU THINK THAT FACE IS, ANYWAY?
J: IDK BUT IT'S MESSED UP.
TAP
TAP
TAP
TAP
A: IT'S TOO LATE/ EARLY TO GET INTO THIS NOW.
A: 5 HRS TILL SCHOOL.
J: -_-
J: PERFECT.

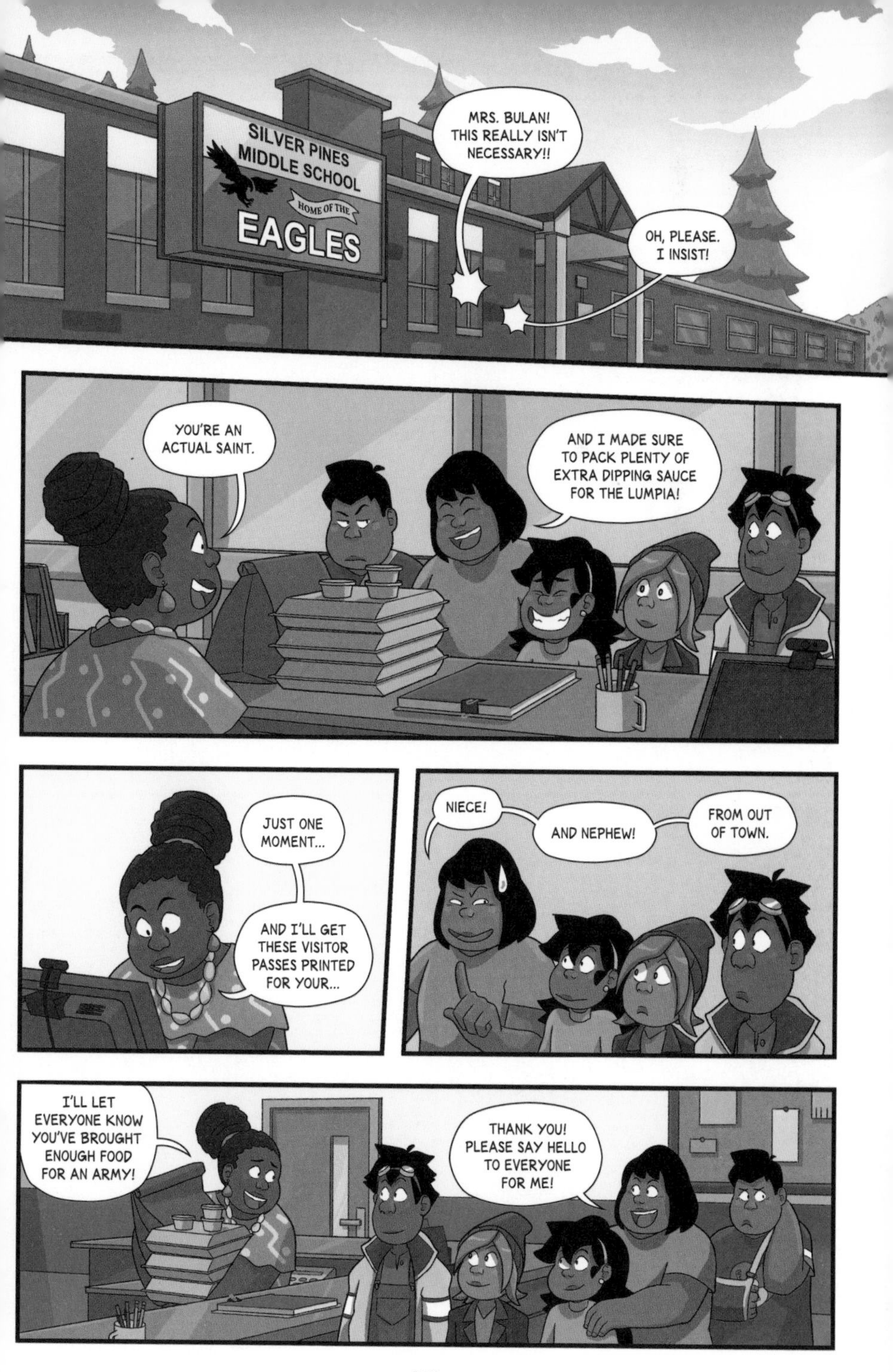
SILVER PINES MIDDLE SCHOOL
HOME OF THE
EAGLES
MRS. BULAN! THIS REALLY ISN'T NECESSARY!!
OH, PLEASE. I INSIST!
YOU'RE AN ACTUAL SAINT.
AND I MADE SURE TO PACK PLENTY OF EXTRA DIPPING SAUCE FOR THE LUMPIA!
JUST ONE MOMENT...
AND I'LL GET THESE VISITOR PASSES PRINTED FOR YOUR...
NIECE!
AND NEPHEW!
FROM OUT OF TOWN.
I'LL LET EVERYONE KNOW YOU'VE BROUGHT ENOUGH FOOD FOR AN ARMY!
THANK YOU! PLEASE SAY HELLO TO EVERYONE FOR ME!

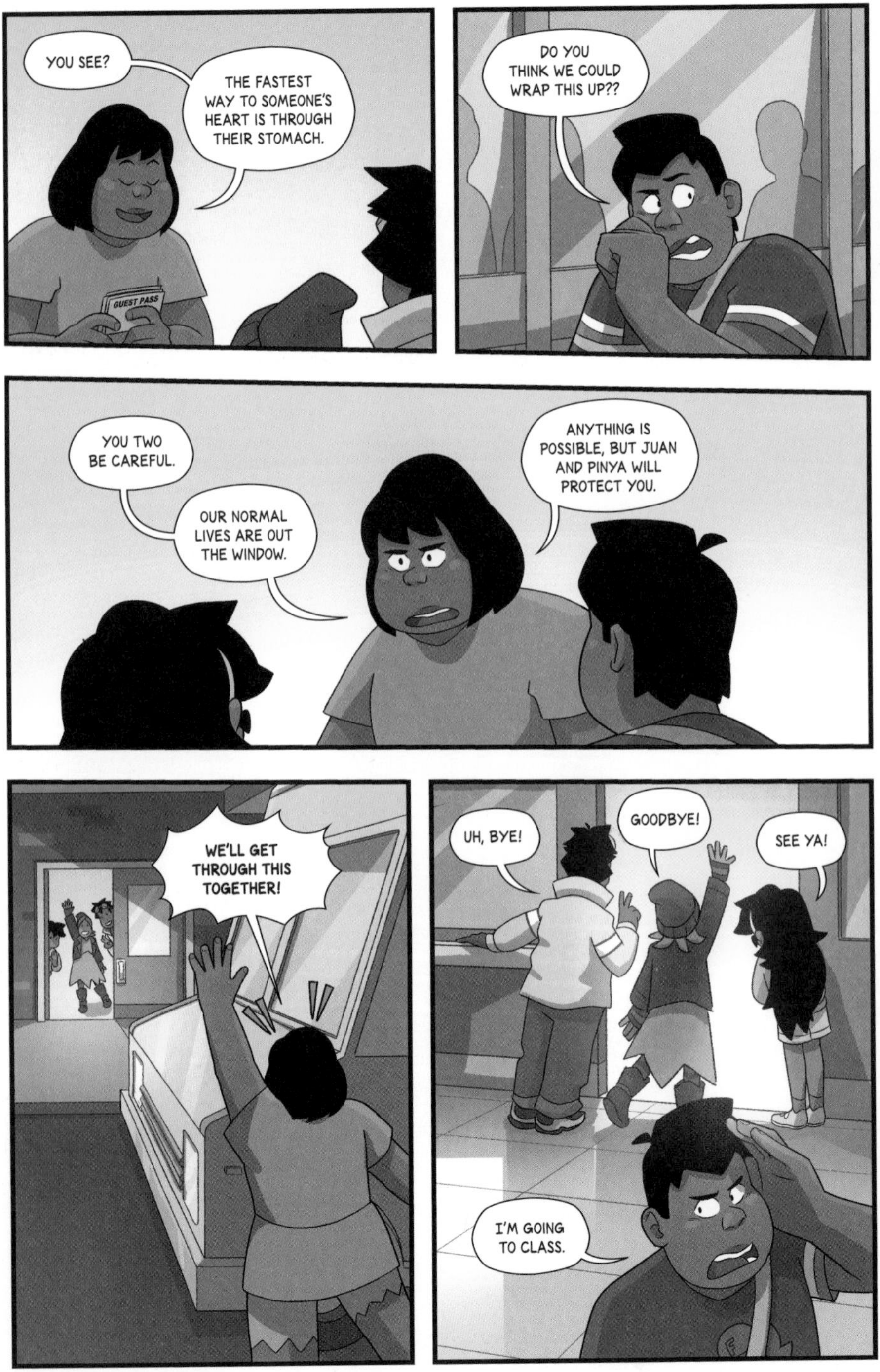
YOU SEE?
THE FASTEST WAY TO SOMEONE'S HEART IS THROUGH THEIR STOMACH.
GUEST PASS
DO YOU THINK WE COULD WRAP THIS UP??
YOU TWO BE CAREFUL.
OUR NORMAL LIVES ARE OUT THE WINDOW.
ANYTHING IS POSSIBLE, BUT JUAN AND PINYA WILL PROTECT YOU.
WE'LL GET THROUGH THIS TOGETHER!
UH, BYE!
GOODBYE!
SEE YA!
I'M GOING TO CLASS.

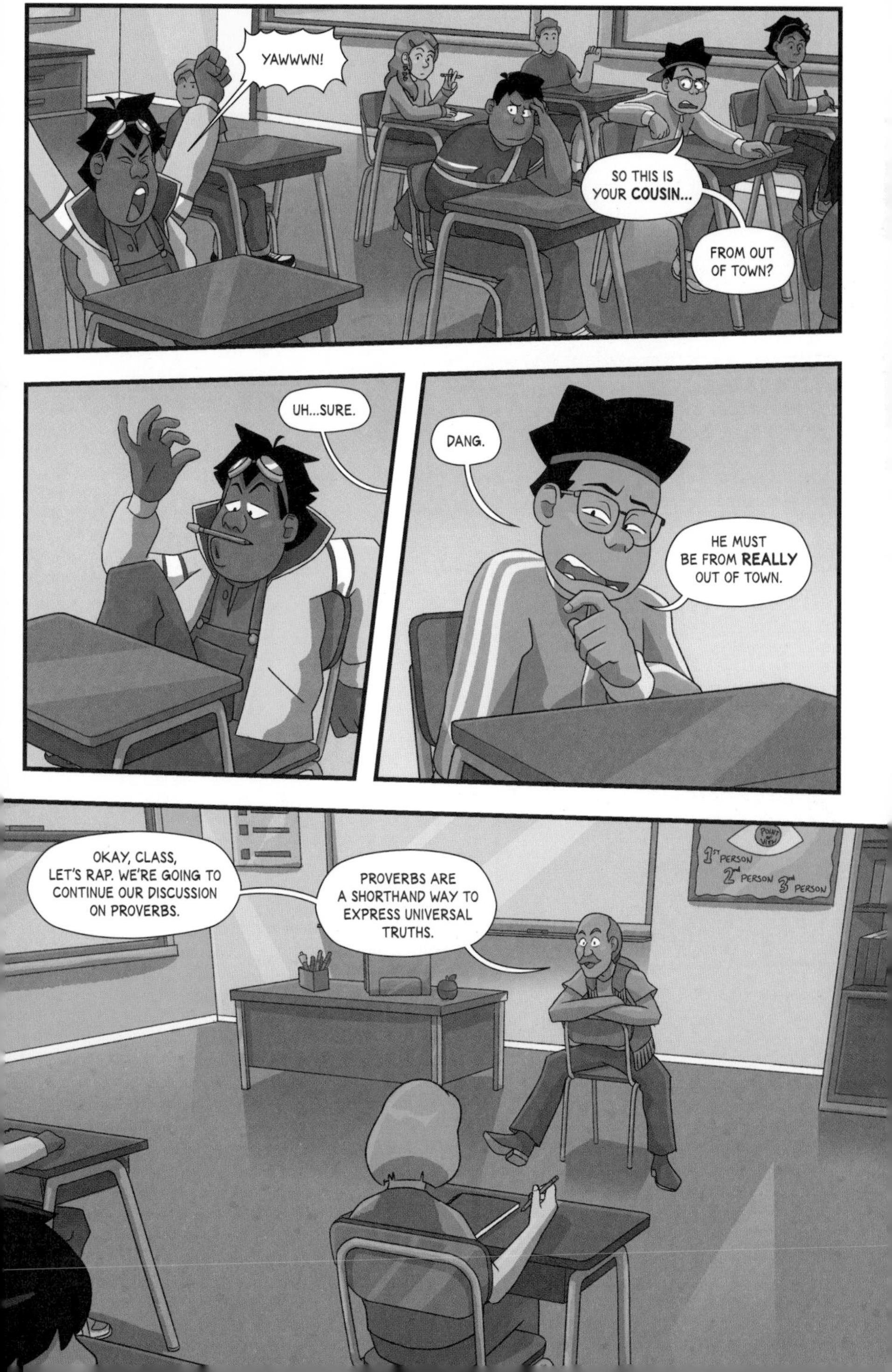
YAWWWN!
SO THIS IS YOUR **COUSIN...**
FROM OUT OF TOWN?
UH...SURE.
DANG.
HE MUST BE FROM **REALLY** OUT OF TOWN.
1ST PERSON
2ND PERSON
3RD PERSON
OKAY, CLASS, LET'S RAP. WE'RE GOING TO CONTINUE OUR DISCUSSION ON PROVERBS.
PROVERBS ARE A SHORTHAND WAY TO EXPRESS UNIVERSAL TRUTHS.

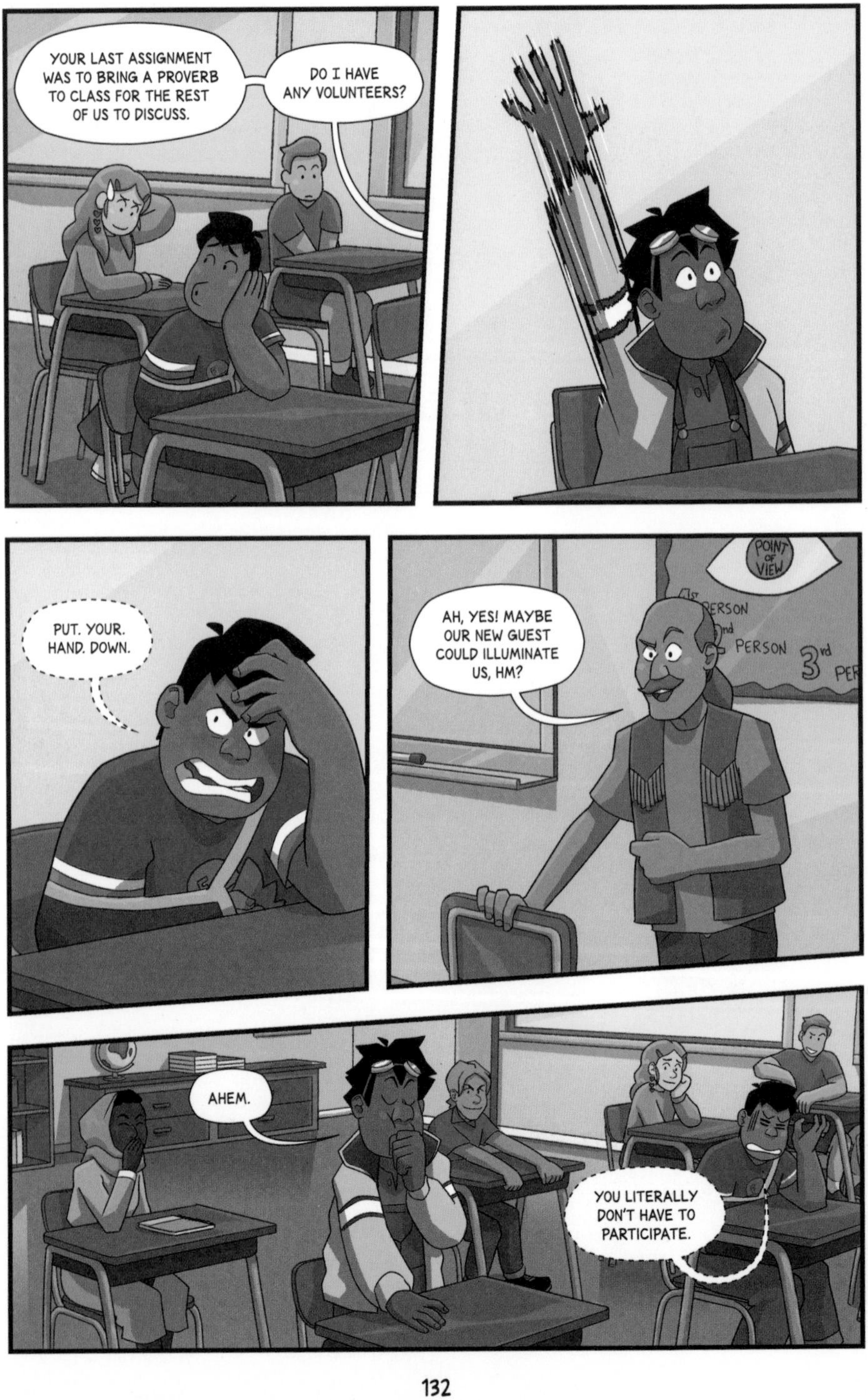
YOUR LAST ASSIGNMENT WAS TO BRING A PROVERB TO CLASS FOR THE REST OF US TO DISCUSS.
DO I HAVE ANY VOLUNTEERS?
PUT. YOUR. HAND. DOWN.
AH, YES! MAYBE OUR NEW GUEST COULD ILLUMINATE US, HM?
POINT OF VIEW
AHEM.
YOU LITERALLY DON'T HAVE TO PARTICIPATE.

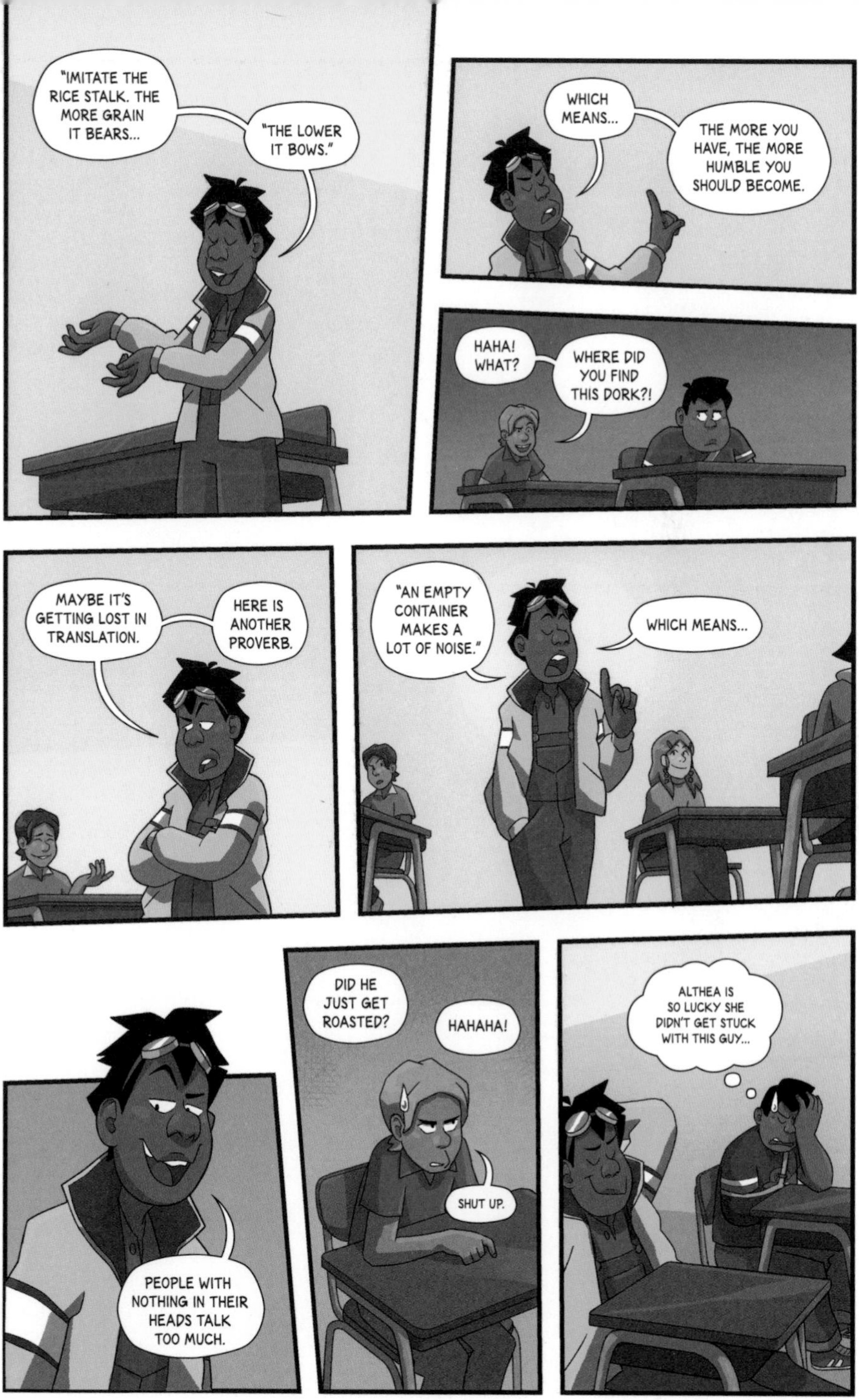
"IMITATE THE RICE STALK. THE MORE GRAIN IT BEARS...
"THE LOWER IT BOWS."
WHICH MEANS...
THE MORE YOU HAVE, THE MORE HUMBLE YOU SHOULD BECOME.
HAHA! WHAT?
WHERE DID YOU FIND THIS DORK?!
MAYBE IT'S GETTING LOST IN TRANSLATION.
HERE IS ANOTHER PROVERB.
"AN EMPTY CONTAINER MAKES A LOT OF NOISE."
WHICH MEANS...
PEOPLE WITH NOTHING IN THEIR HEADS TALK TOO MUCH.
DID HE JUST GET ROASTED?
HAHAHA!
SHUT UP.
ALTHEA IS SO LUCKY SHE DIDN'T GET STUCK WITH THIS GUY...

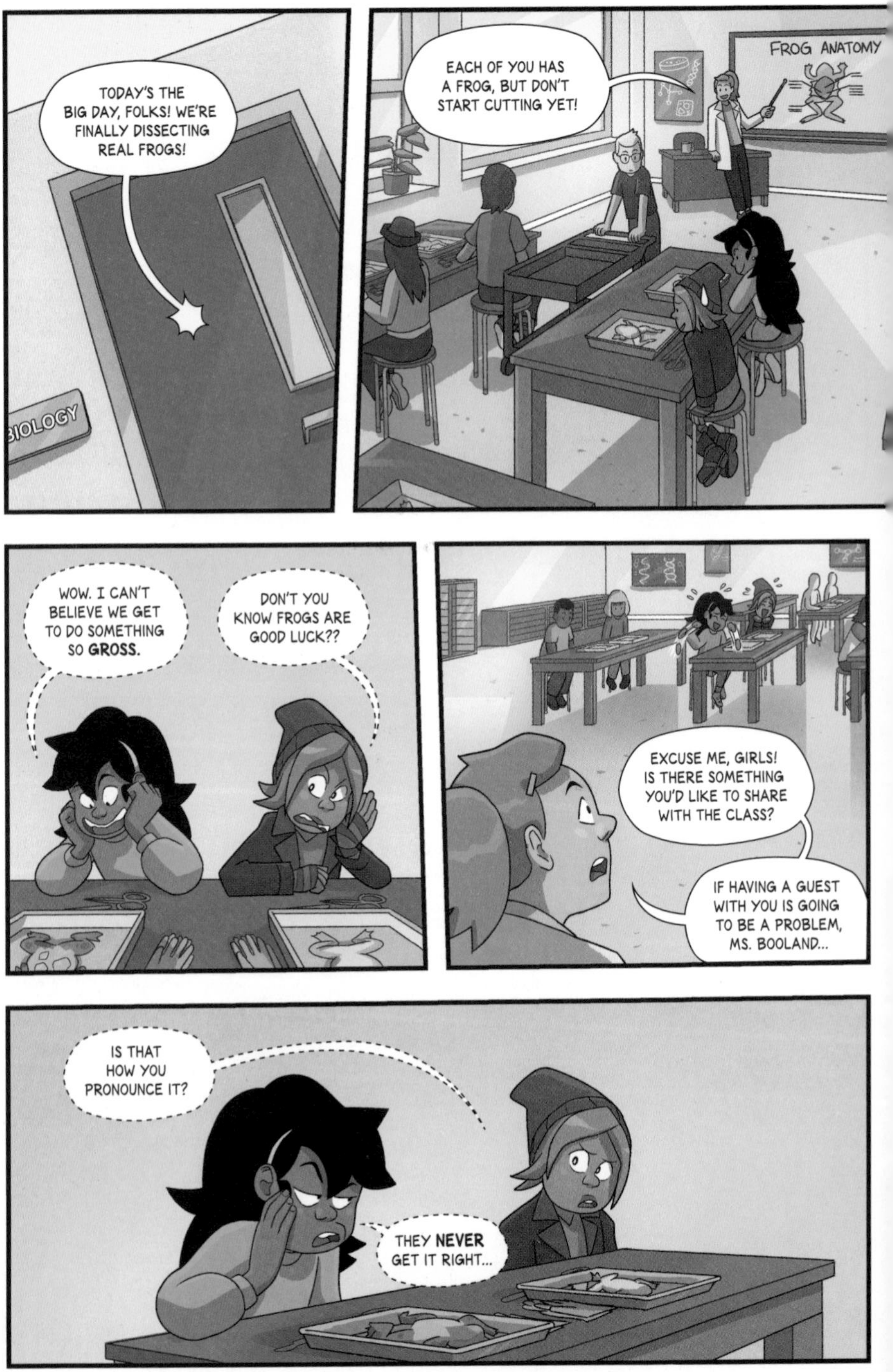
TODAY'S THE BIG DAY, FOLKS! WE'RE FINALLY DISSECTING REAL FROGS!
BIOLOGY
EACH OF YOU HAS A FROG, BUT DON'T START CUTTING YET!
FROG ANATOMY
WOW. I CAN'T BELIEVE WE GET TO DO SOMETHING SO **GROSS.**
DON'T YOU KNOW FROGS ARE GOOD LUCK??
EXCUSE ME, GIRLS! IS THERE SOMETHING YOU'D LIKE TO SHARE WITH THE CLASS?
IF HAVING A GUEST WITH YOU IS GOING TO BE A PROBLEM, MS. BOOLAND...
IS THAT HOW YOU PRONOUNCE IT?
THEY **NEVER** GET IT RIGHT...

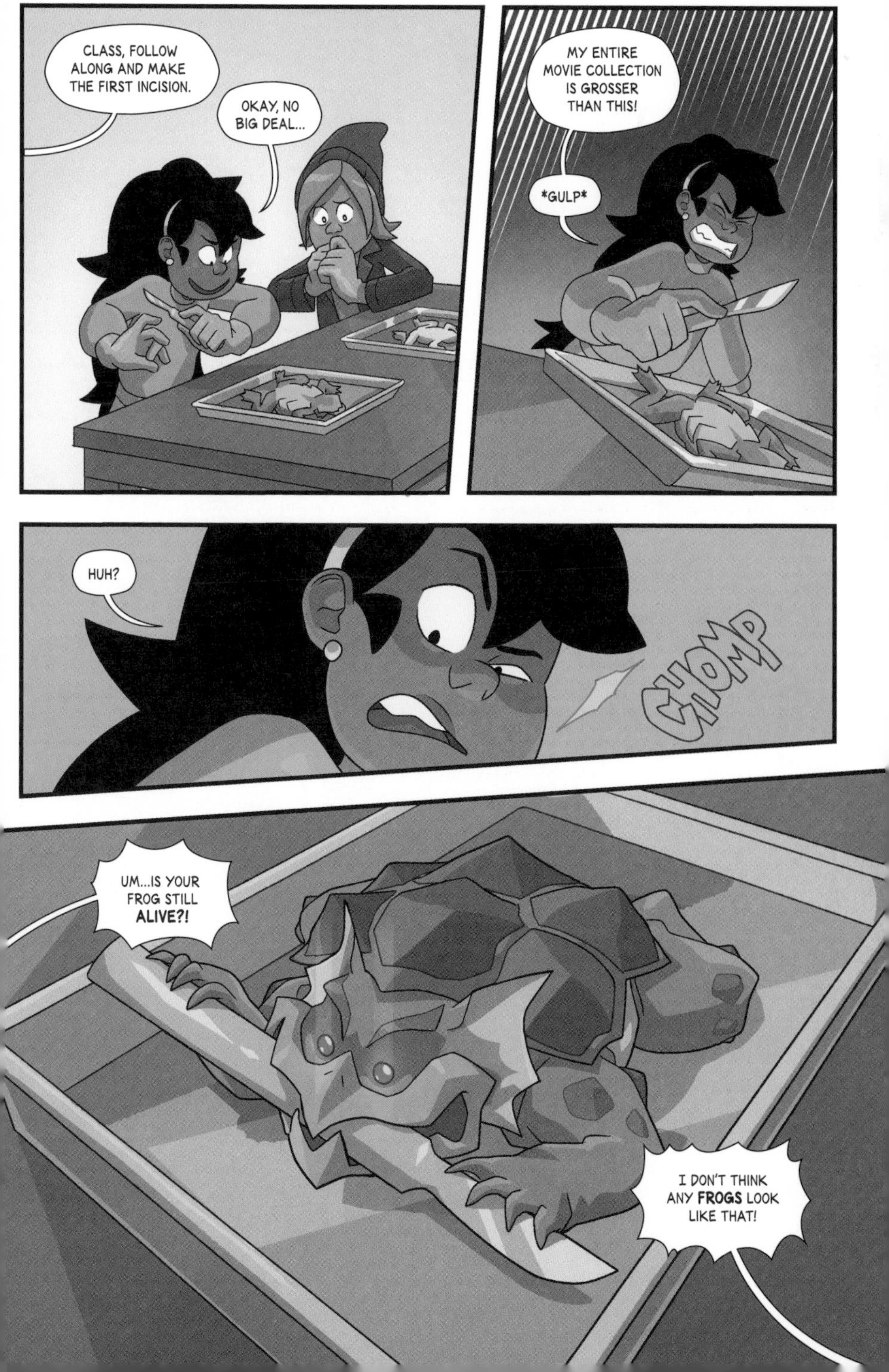
CLASS, FOLLOW ALONG AND MAKE THE FIRST INCISION.
OKAY, NO BIG DEAL...
MY ENTIRE MOVIE COLLECTION IS GROSSER THAN THIS!
GULP
HUH?
CHOMP
UM...IS YOUR FROG STILL **ALIVE?!**
I DON'T THINK ANY **FROGS** LOOK LIKE THAT!

IS THIS, LIKE, A WITCH THING??

NOD
NOD

THE WITCHES MUST'VE SUMMONED ANOTHER ASWANG!*

I THINK IT'S A BERBEROKA!* IT CAN GROW BY DRINKING WATER.

SO AS LONG AS WE DON'T --

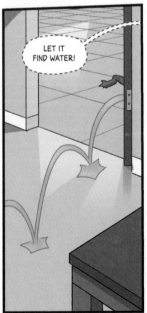

LET IT FIND WATER!

I THINK WE'RE GONNA NEED SOME BACKUP.

WE'LL BE RIGHT BACK, MS. PESTOTNIK!

LOOK, ANDREW, I ADMIRE YOUR MORAL OBJECTION TO THIS, BUT...

PLANT CE

*ASWANG (AHS-WAHNG): SHAPE-SHIFTING, EVIL MONSTERS, CREATURES, BEASTS, ETC., FROM FOLKLORE.
*BERBEROKA (BERR-BEH-ROKAH): A MAN-EATING WATER CREATURE THAT DRAINS RIVERBEDS TO TRICK HUMANS IN ORDER TO DROWN THEM.

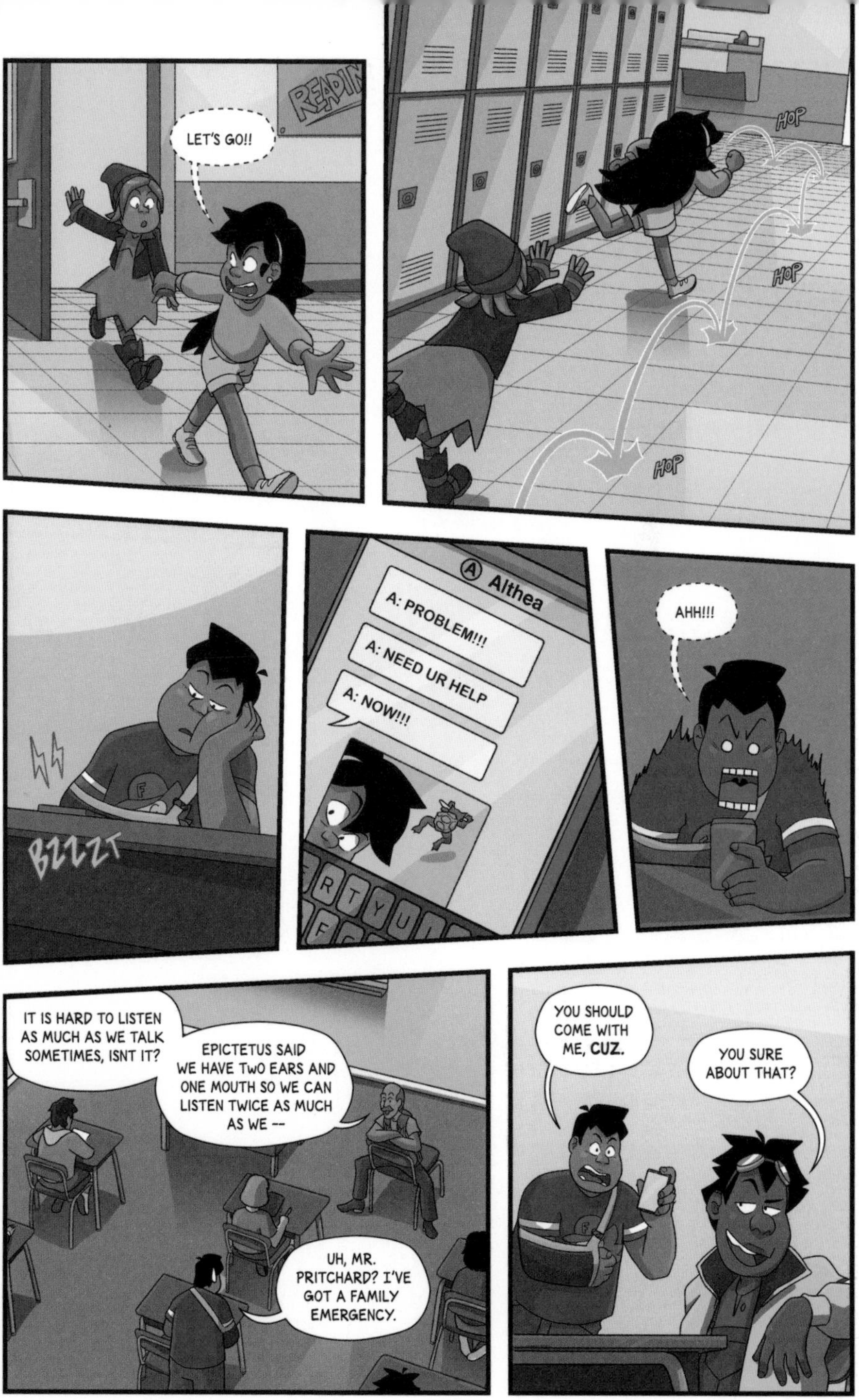
READIN
LET'S GO!!
HOP
HOP
HOP
BZZZT
Althea
A: PROBLEM!!!
A: NEED UR HELP
A: NOW!!!
AHH!!!
IT IS HARD TO LISTEN AS MUCH AS WE TALK SOMETIMES, ISNT IT?
EPICTETUS SAID WE HAVE TWO EARS AND ONE MOUTH SO WE CAN LISTEN TWICE AS MUCH AS WE --
UH, MR. PRITCHARD? I'VE GOT A FAMILY EMERGENCY.
YOU SHOULD COME WITH ME, **CUZ.**
YOU SURE ABOUT THAT?

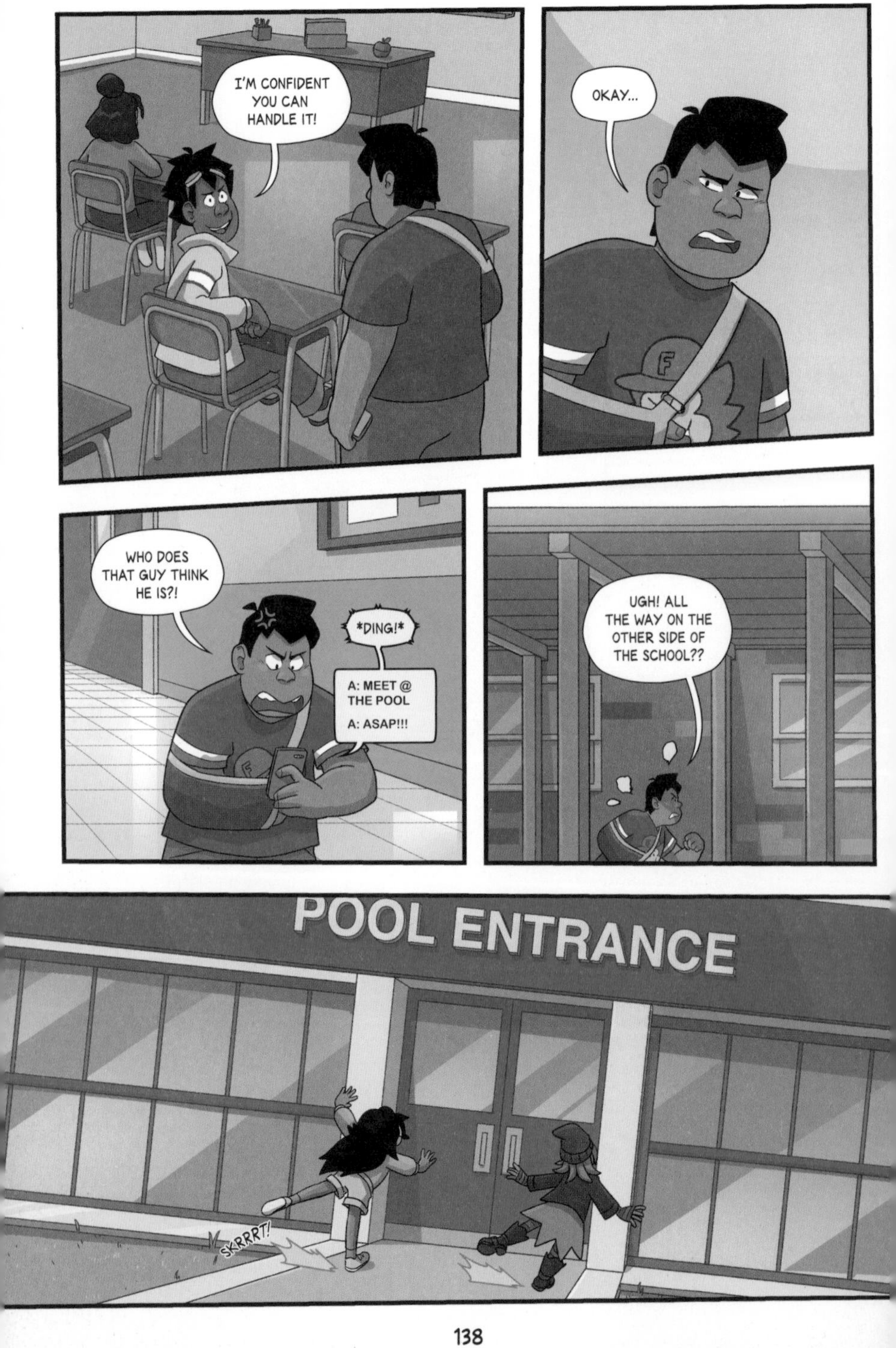
I'M CONFIDENT YOU CAN HANDLE IT!
OKAY...
WHO DOES THAT GUY THINK HE IS?!
DING!
A: MEET @ THE POOL
A: ASAP!!!
UGH! ALL THE WAY ON THE OTHER SIDE OF THE SCHOOL??
POOL ENTRANCE
SKRRRT!

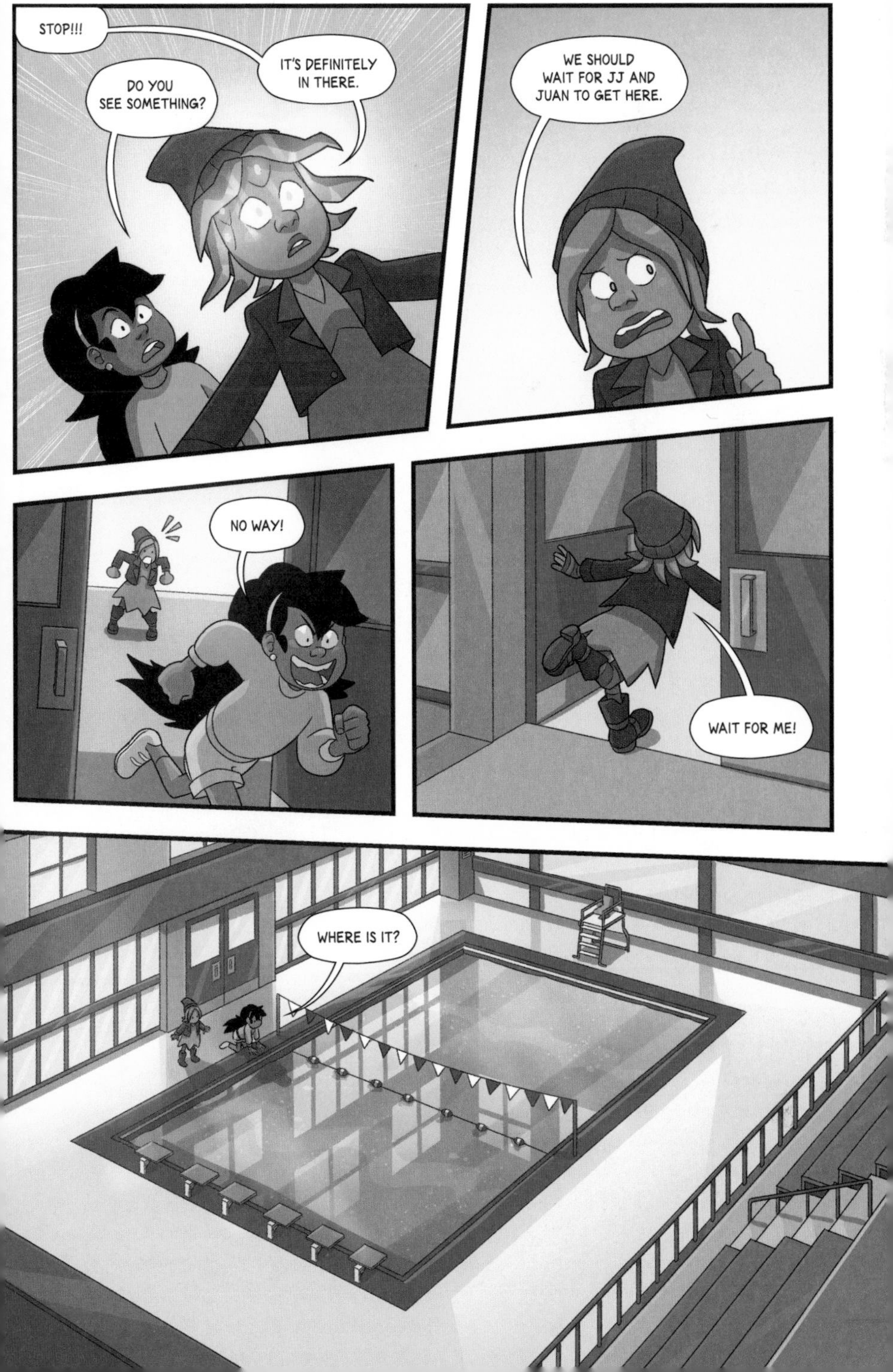
STOP!!!
DO YOU SEE SOMETHING?
IT'S DEFINITELY IN THERE.
WE SHOULD WAIT FOR JJ AND JUAN TO GET HERE.
NO WAY!
WAIT FOR ME!
WHERE IS IT?

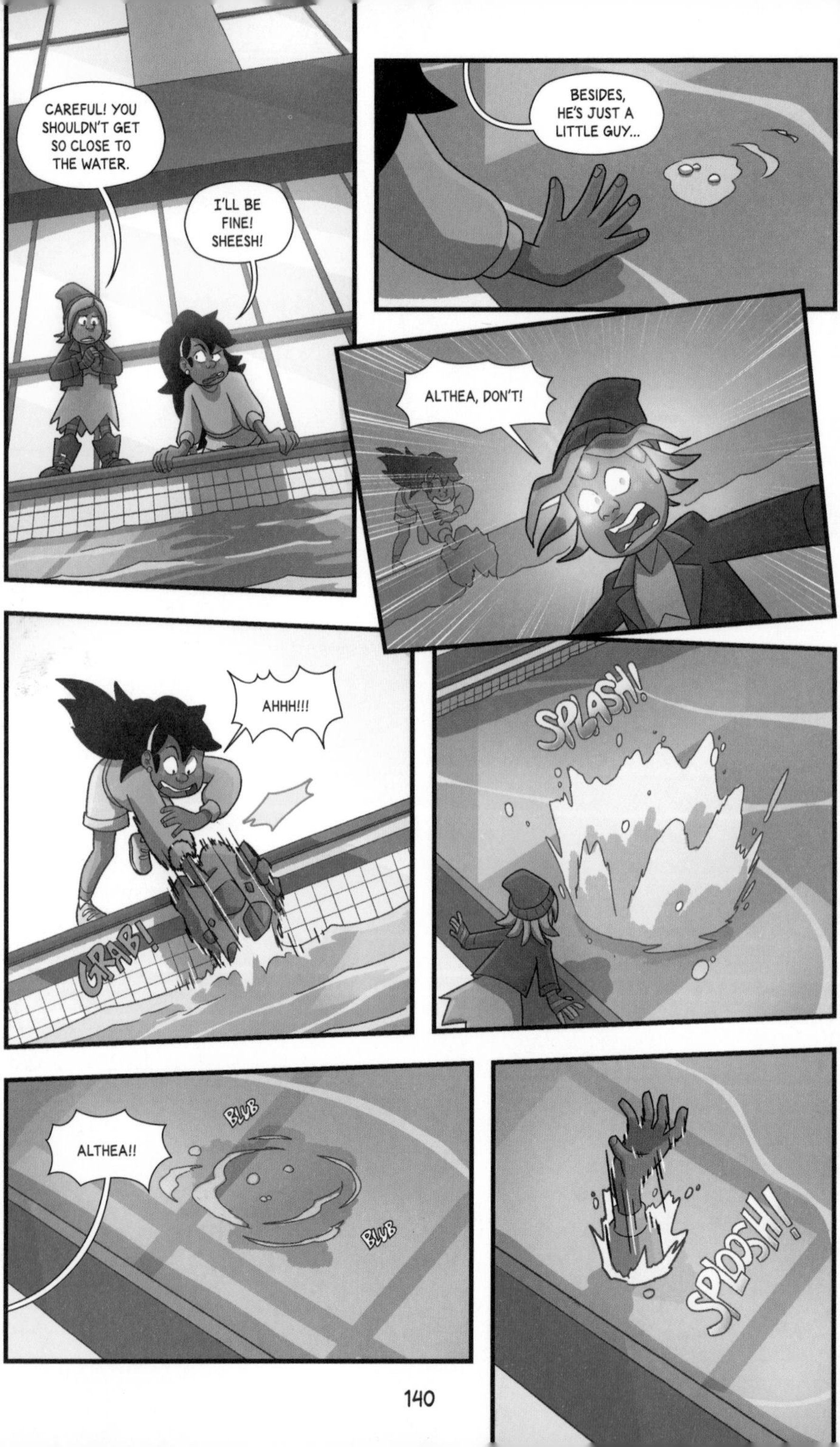
CAREFUL! YOU SHOULDN'T GET SO CLOSE TO THE WATER.
I'LL BE FINE! SHEESH!
BESIDES, HE'S JUST A LITTLE GUY...
ALTHEA, DON'T!
AHHH!!!
GRAB!
SPLASH!
ALTHEA!!
BLUB
BLUB
SPLOOSH!

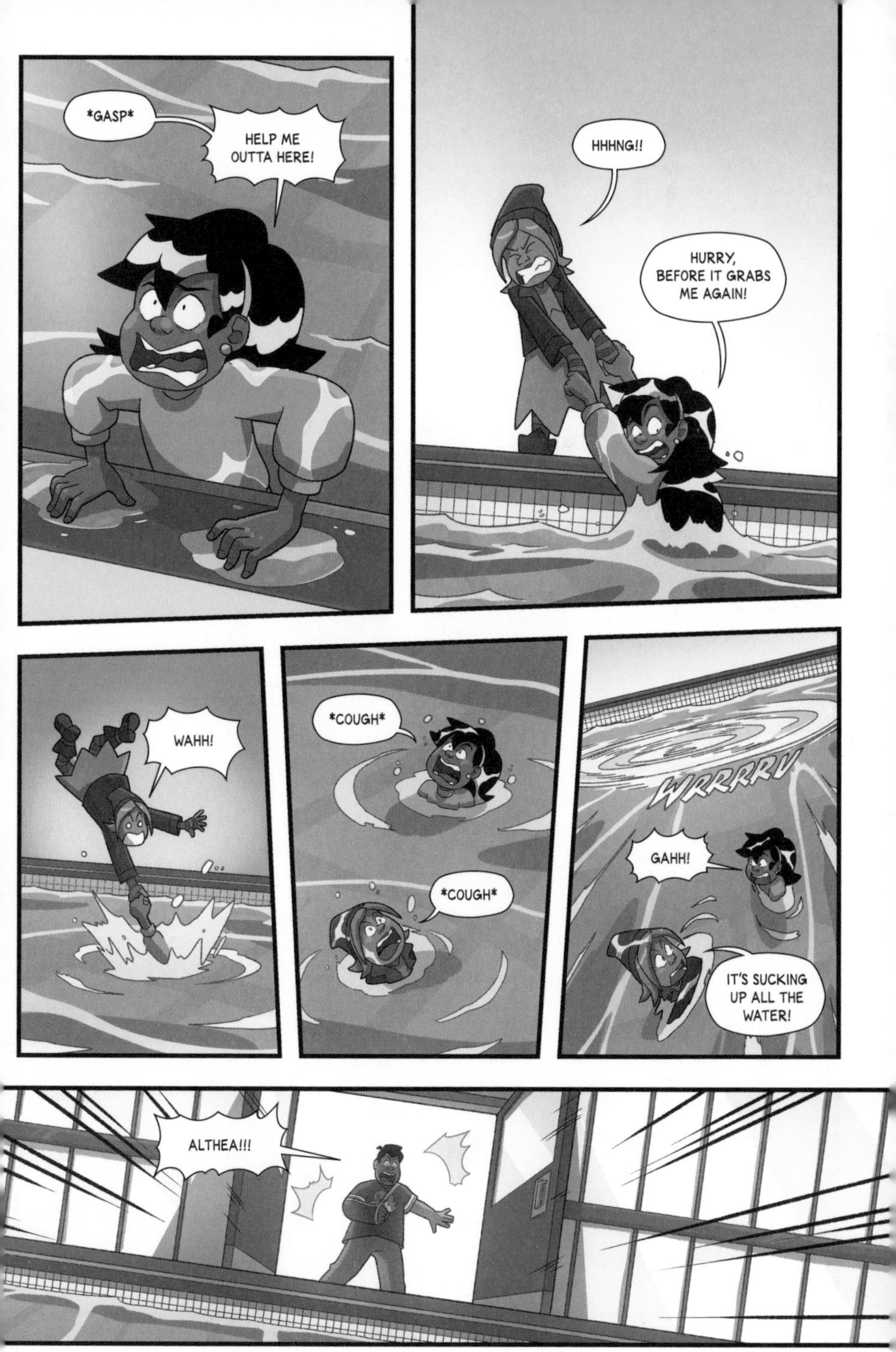
GASP
HELP ME OUTTA HERE!
HHHNG!!
HURRY, BEFORE IT GRABS ME AGAIN!
WAHH!
COUGH
COUGH
WRRRRV
GAHH!
IT'S SUCKING UP ALL THE WATER!
ALTHEA!!!

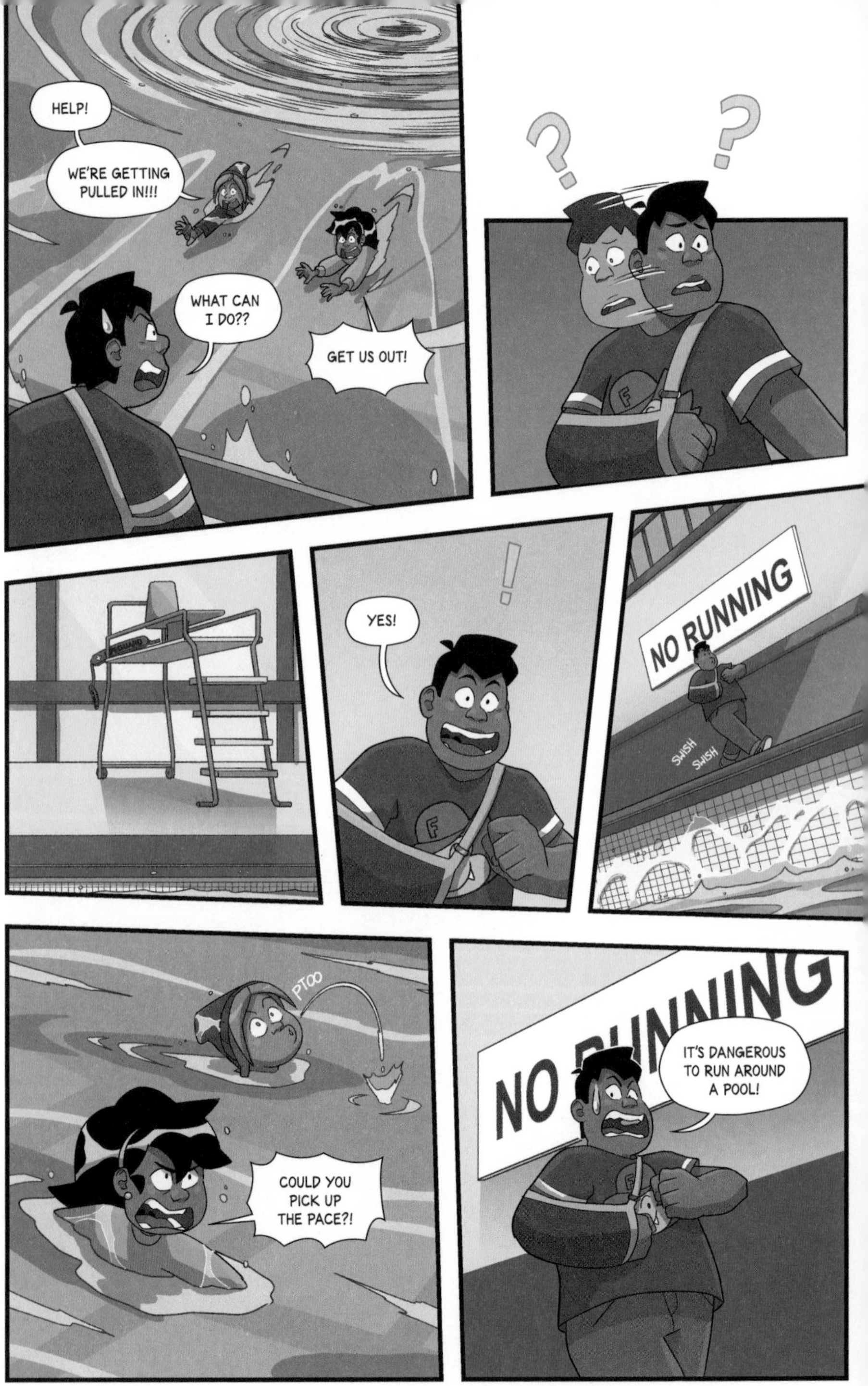
HELP!
WE'RE GETTING PULLED IN!!!
WHAT CAN I DO??
GET US OUT!
?
?
YES!
NO RUNNING
SWISH
SWISH
PTOO
COULD YOU PICK UP THE PACE?!
NO RUNNING
IT'S DANGEROUS TO RUN AROUND A POOL!

WHERE'S JUAN TAMAD?!

WE COULD REALLY USE HIS HELP, TOO!

HE BLEW ME OFF TO PLAY **MR. POPULAR** IN MY ENGLISH CLASS!

THAT GUY...

TOTALLY...

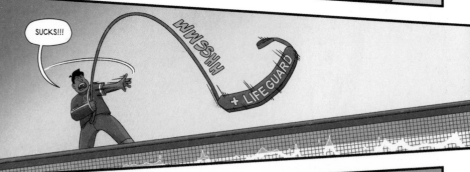

SUCKS!!!

WMSSWW

+ LIFEGUARD

SPLASH

START PULLING!

WHAT DO YOU THINK I'M DOING??

URGH!

PERFECT TIME TO HAVE THE USE OF ONLY ONE ARM!

I GOT YOU.

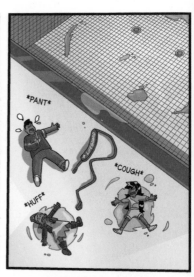

PANT

COUGH

HUFF

WHAT WERE YOU THINKING?! YOU SHOULD'VE WAITED FOR ME --

WHUMP!

?

GRRRRRRR

DOOM!

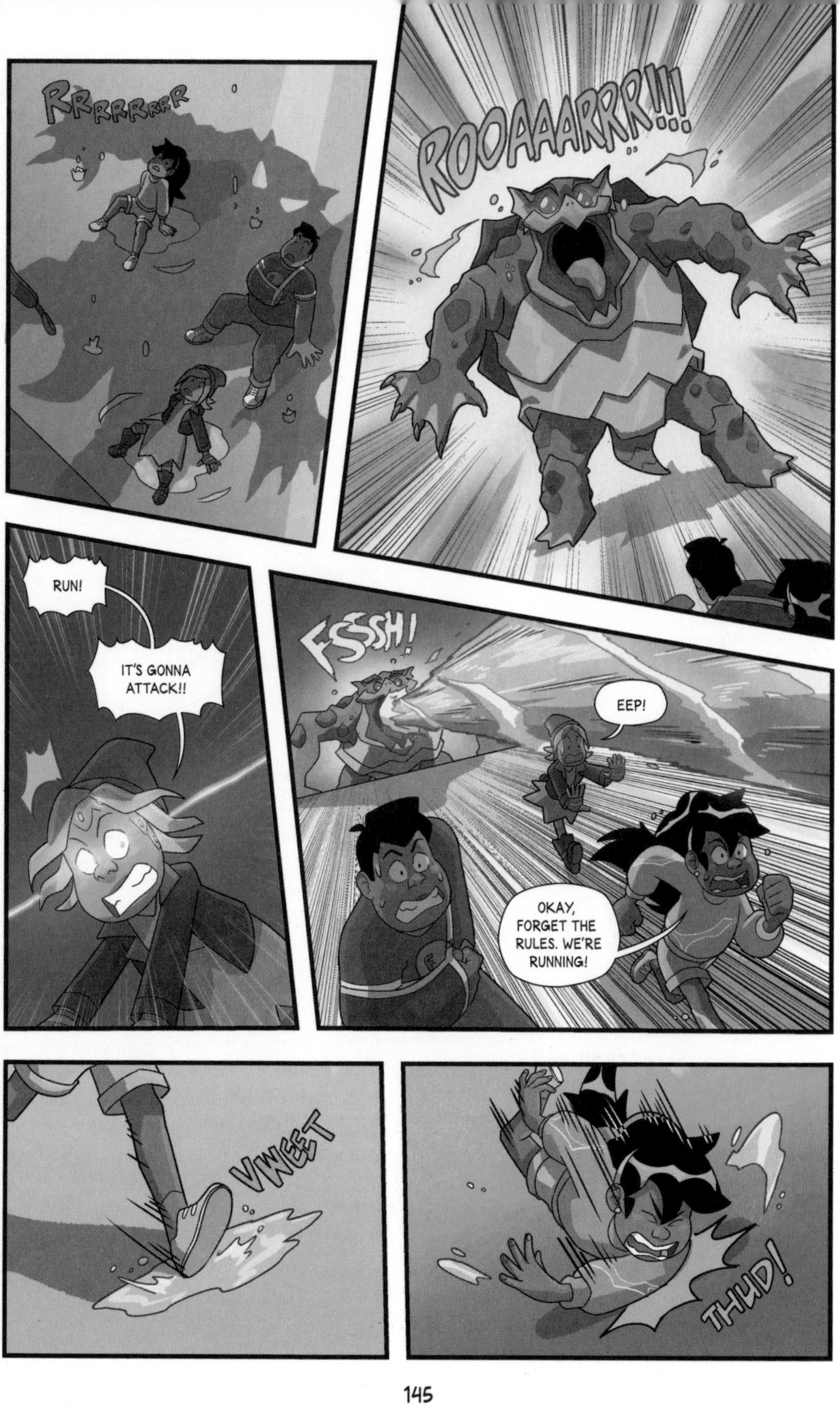
RRRRRRRR
ROOAAARRR!!!
RUN!
IT'S GONNA ATTACK!!
FSSSH!
EEP!
OKAY, FORGET THE RULES. WE'RE RUNNING!
VWEET
THUD!

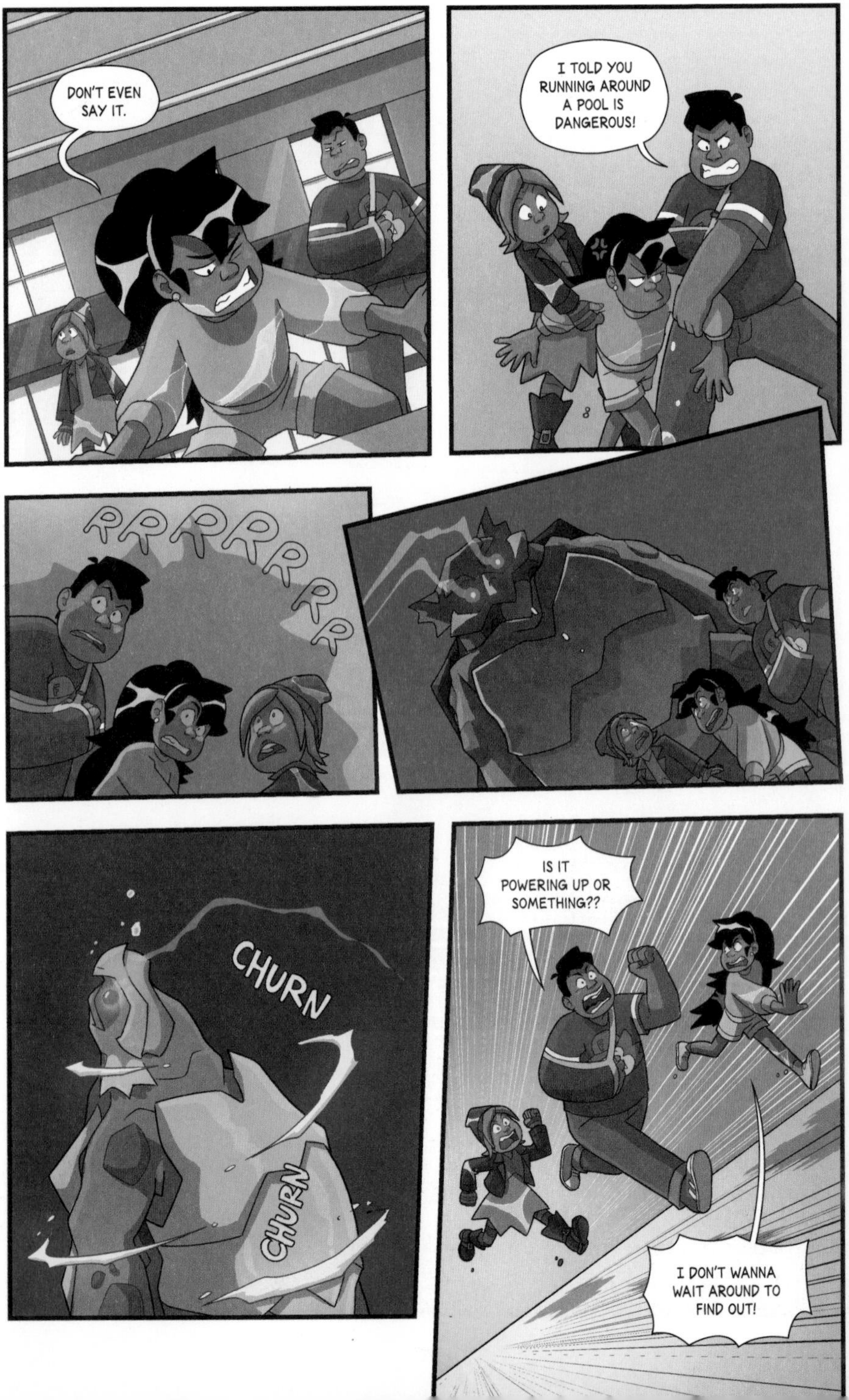
DON'T EVEN SAY IT.
I TOLD YOU RUNNING AROUND A POOL IS DANGEROUS!
RRRRRRRRR
CHURN
CHURN
IS IT POWERING UP OR SOMETHING??
I DON'T WANNA WAIT AROUND TO FIND OUT!

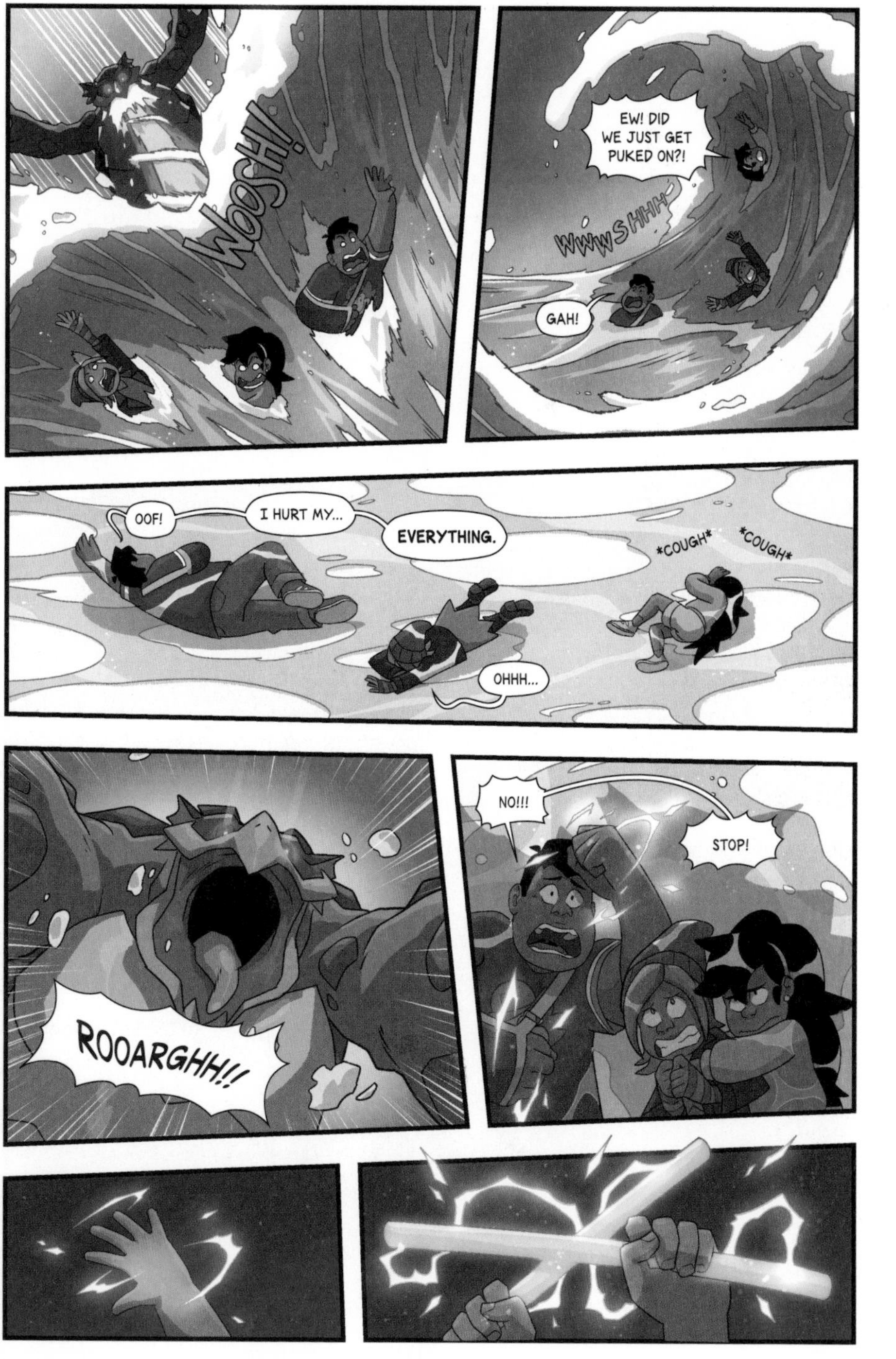
WOOSH!!
EW! DID WE JUST GET PUKED ON?!
WWWSHHH
GAH!
OOF!
I HURT MY...
EVERYTHING.
COUGH
COUGH
OHHH...
ROOARGHH!!
NO!!!
STOP!

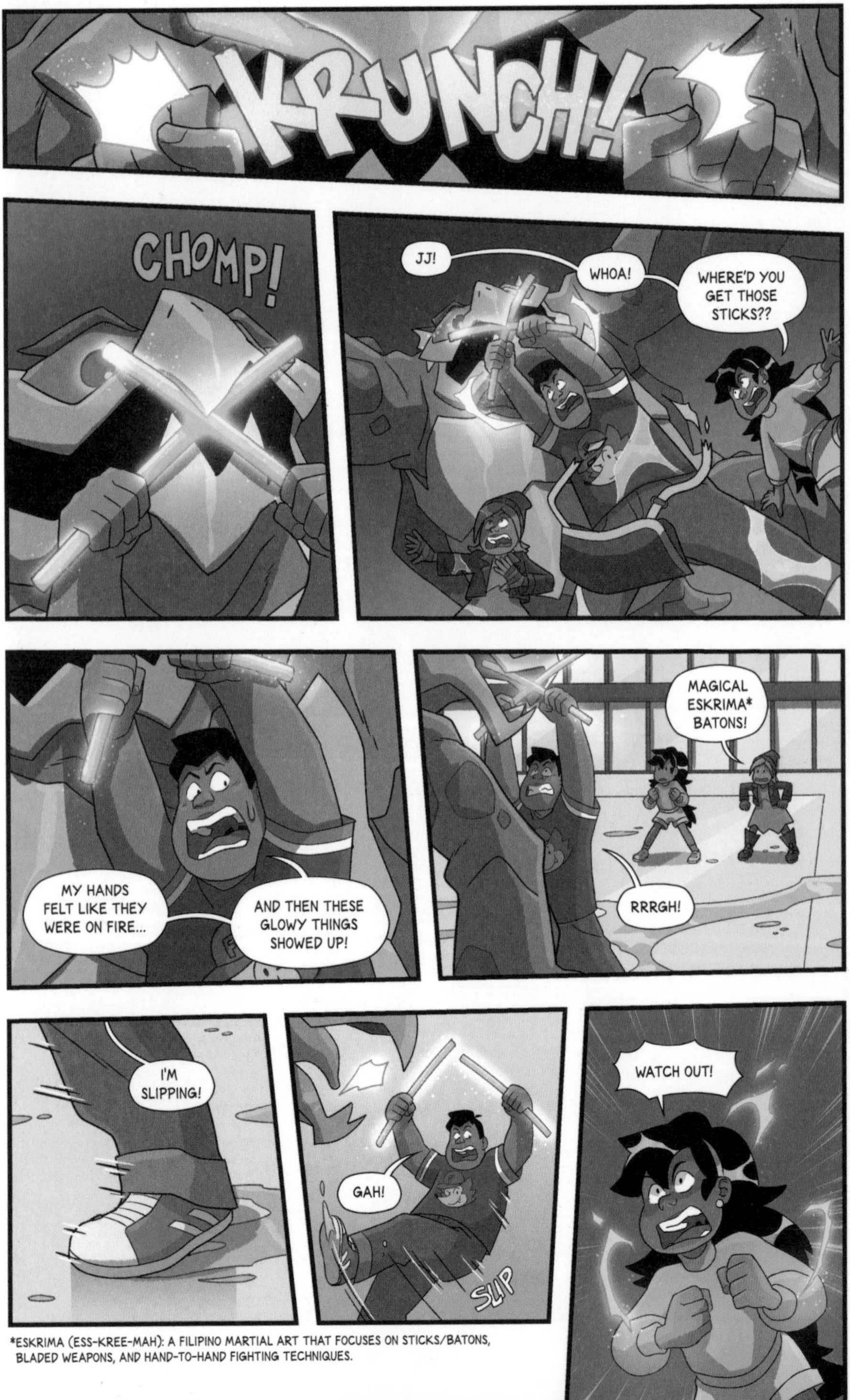
KRUNCH!
CHOMP!
JJ!
WHOA!
WHERE'D YOU GET THOSE STICKS??
MY HANDS FELT LIKE THEY WERE ON FIRE...
AND THEN THESE GLOWY THINGS SHOWED UP!
MAGICAL ESKRIMA* BATONS!
RRRGH!
I'M SLIPPING!
GAH!
SLIP
WATCH OUT!

*ESKRIMA (ESS-KREE-MAH): A FILIPINO MARTIAL ART THAT FOCUSES ON STICKS/BATONS, BLADED WEAPONS, AND HAND-TO-HAND FIGHTING TECHNIQUES.

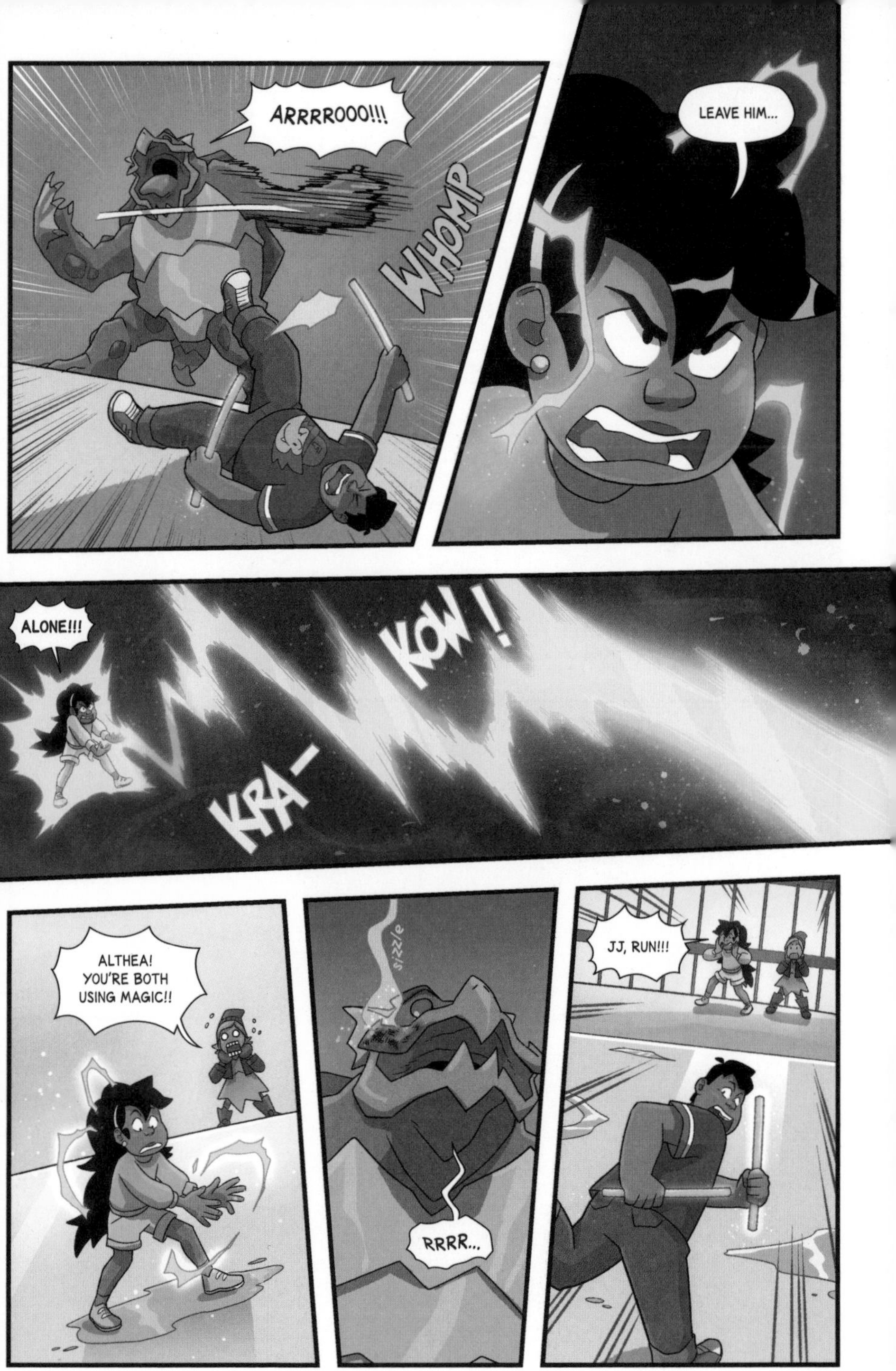
ARRRROOO!!!
WHOMP
LEAVE HIM...
ALONE!!!
KRA-
KOW!
ALTHEA!
YOU'RE BOTH
USING MAGIC!!
sizzle
RRRR...
JJ, RUN!!!

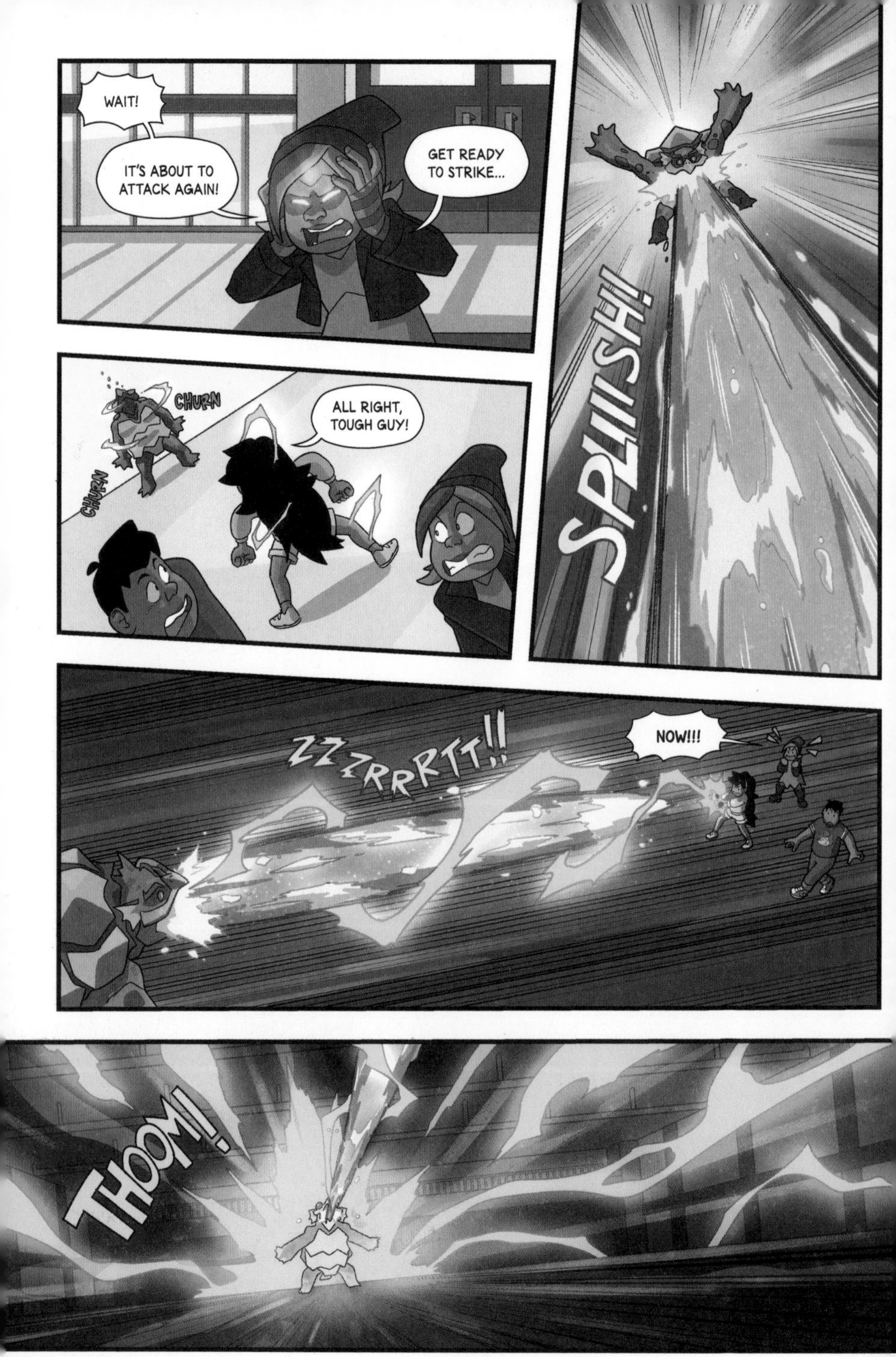
WAIT!
IT'S ABOUT TO ATTACK AGAIN!
GET READY TO STRIKE...
SPLUSH!
CHURN
CHURN
ALL RIGHT, TOUGH GUY!
NOW!!!
ZZZRRRTT!!
THOOM!!

SIZZZ

CRASH!

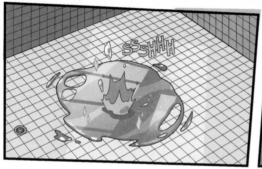

SSSHHH

THE POOL FILLED BACK UP!

AND THAT THING DISAPPEARED, JUST LIKE THE OGRE IN THE GYM!

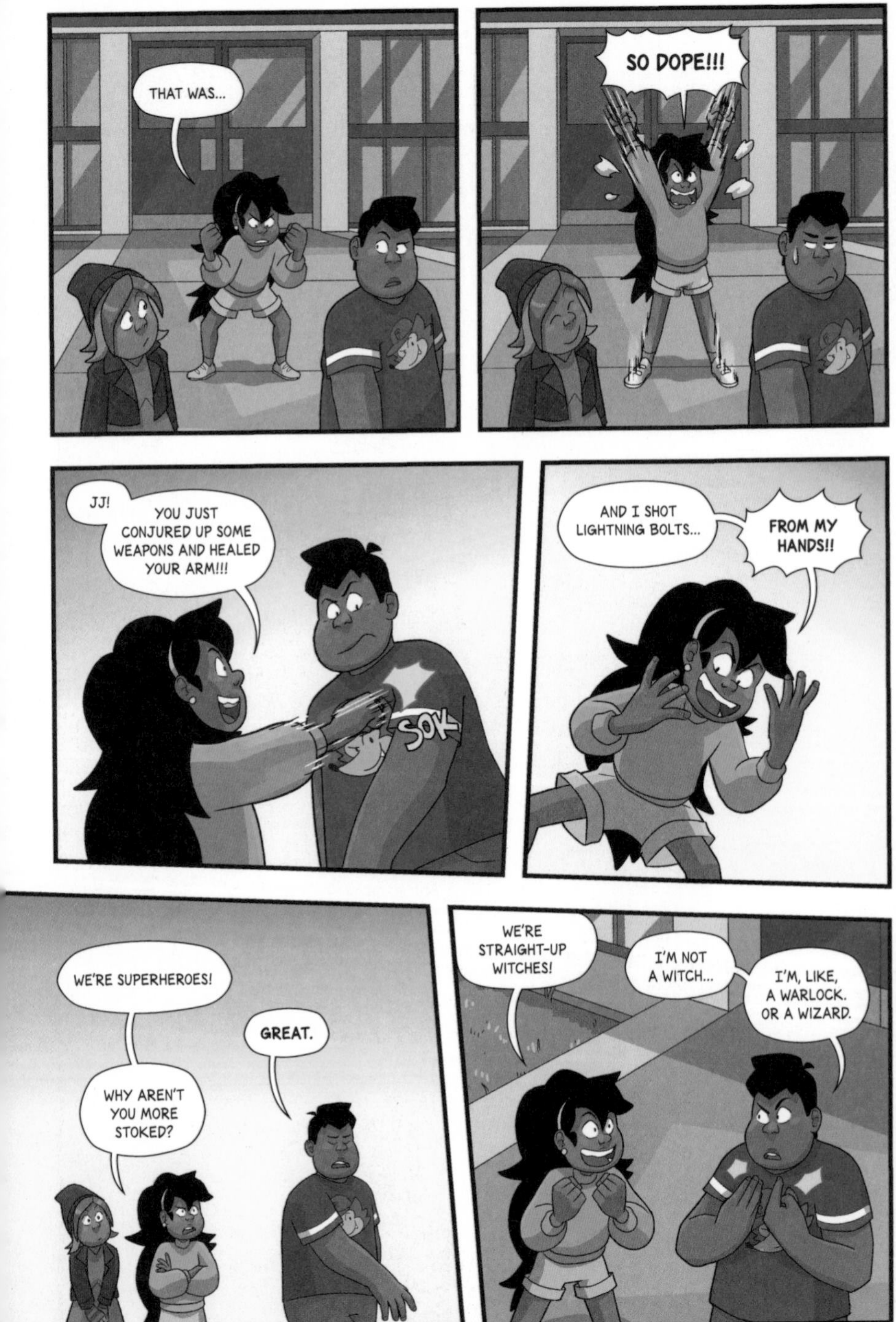
THAT WAS...
SO DOPE!!!
JJ!
YOU JUST CONJURED UP SOME WEAPONS AND HEALED YOUR ARM!!!
SOK
AND I SHOT LIGHTNING BOLTS...
FROM MY HANDS!!
WE'RE SUPERHEROES!
WHY AREN'T YOU MORE STOKED?
GREAT.
WE'RE STRAIGHT-UP WITCHES!
I'M NOT A WITCH...
I'M, LIKE, A WARLOCK. OR A WIZARD.

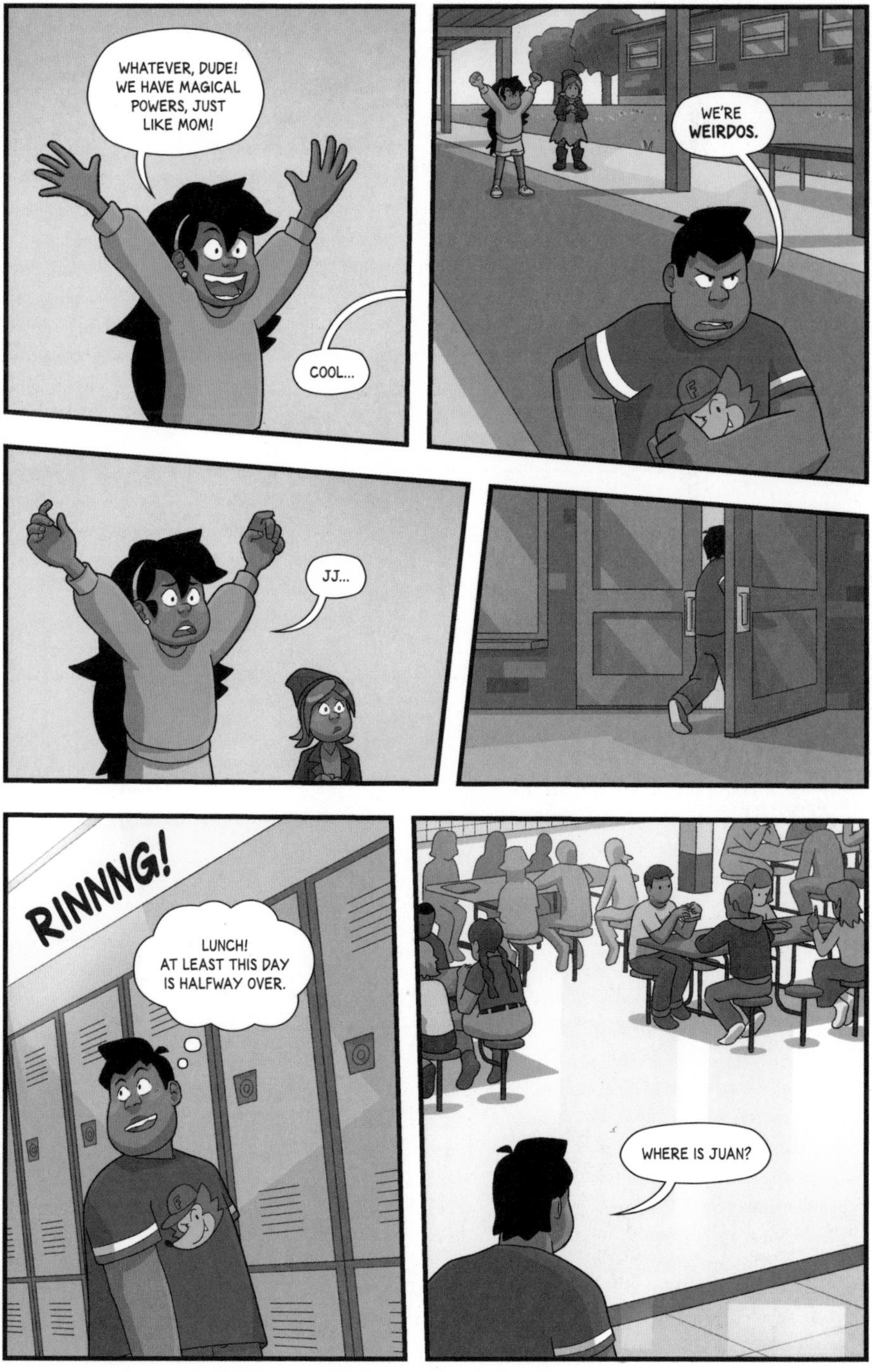
WHATEVER, DUDE! WE HAVE MAGICAL POWERS, JUST LIKE MOM!
COOL...
WE'RE WEIRDOS.
JJ...
RINNNG!
LUNCH! AT LEAST THIS DAY IS HALFWAY OVER.
WHERE IS JUAN?

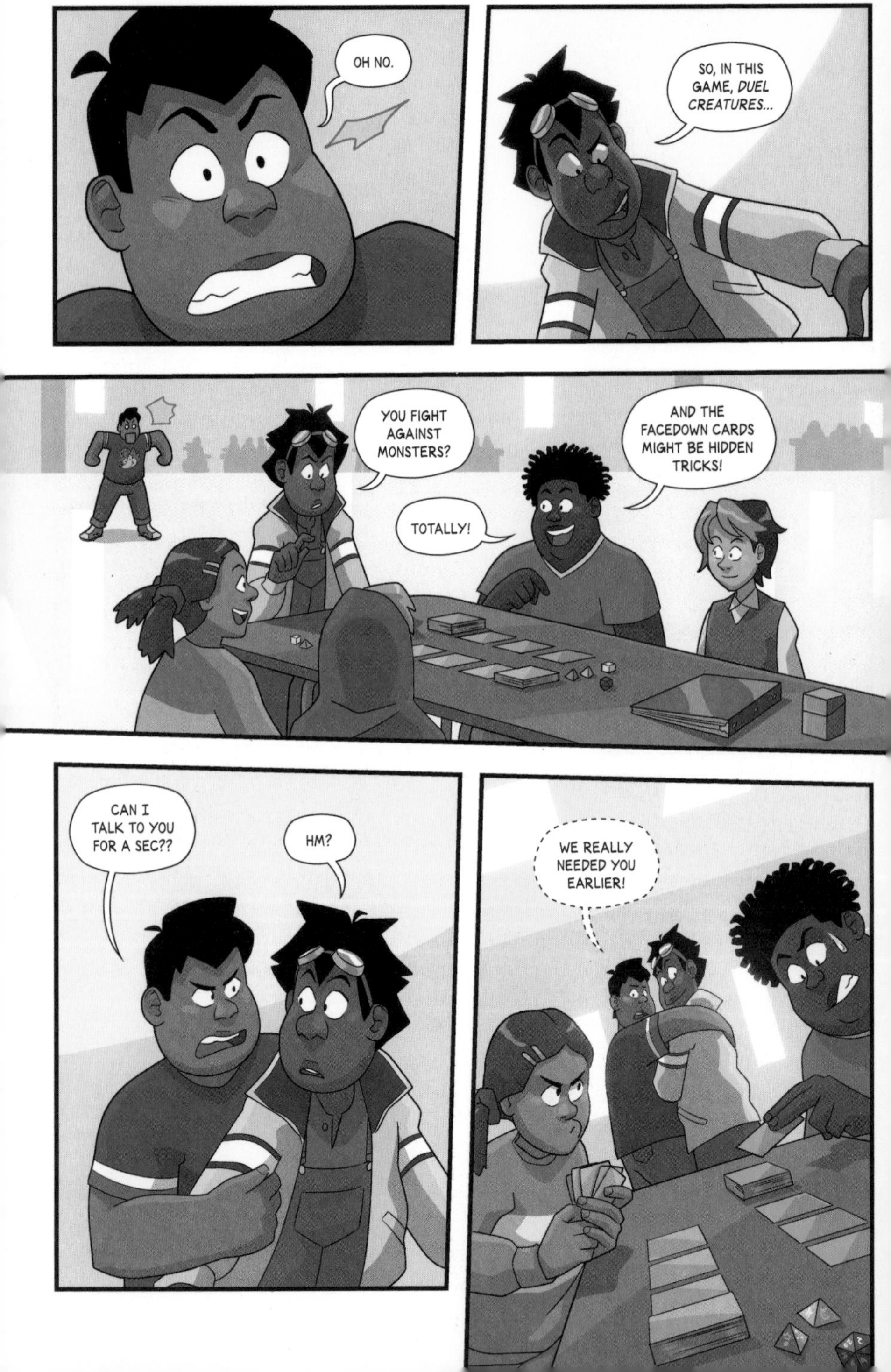
OH NO.
SO, IN THIS GAME, *DUEL CREATURES*...
YOU FIGHT AGAINST MONSTERS?
AND THE FACEDOWN CARDS MIGHT BE HIDDEN TRICKS!
TOTALLY!
CAN I TALK TO YOU FOR A SEC??
HM?
WE REALLY NEEDED YOU EARLIER!

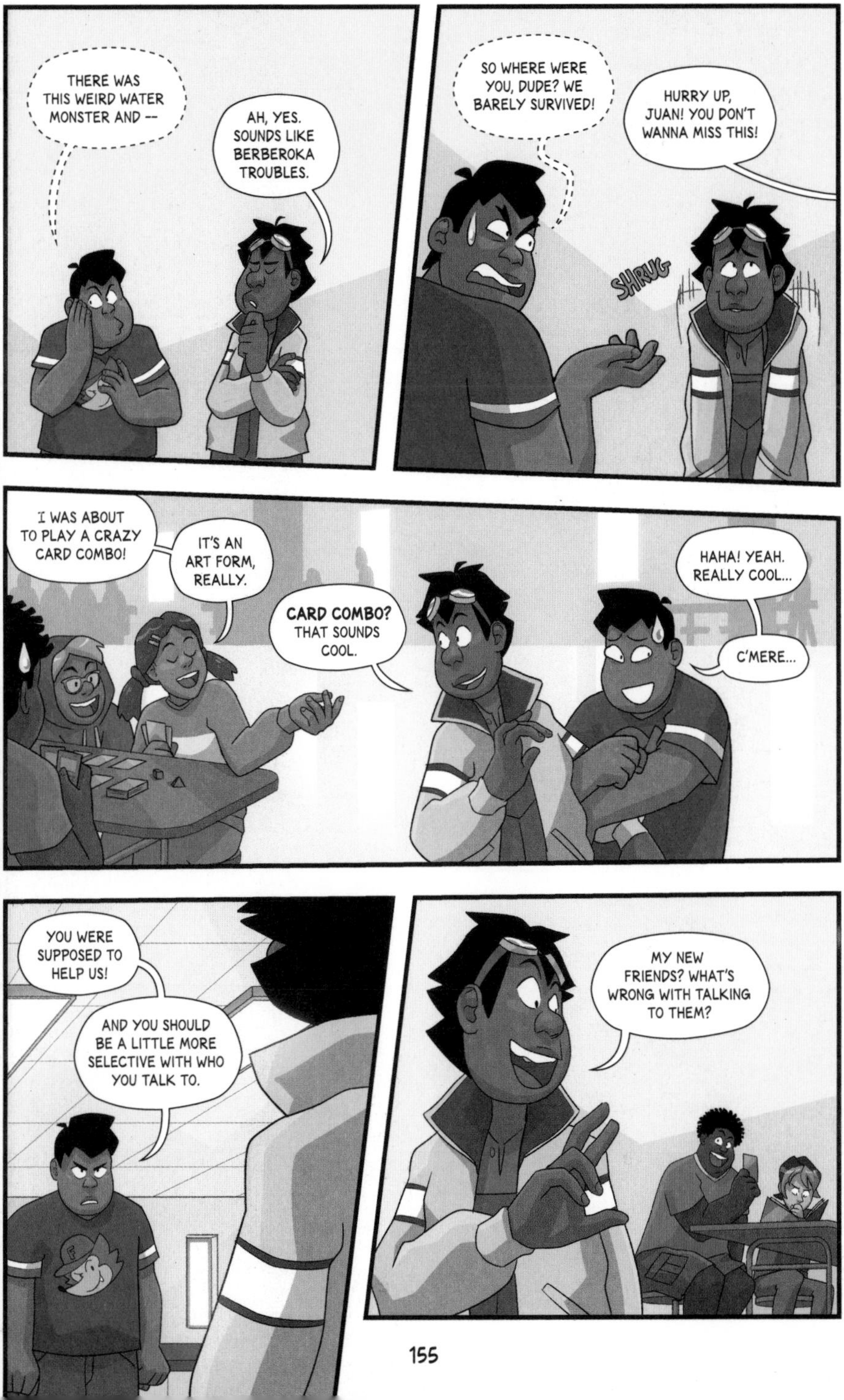
THERE WAS THIS WEIRD WATER MONSTER AND --
AH, YES. SOUNDS LIKE BERBEROKA TROUBLES.
SO WHERE WERE YOU, DUDE? WE BARELY SURVIVED!
HURRY UP, JUAN! YOU DON'T WANNA MISS THIS!
SHRUG
I WAS ABOUT TO PLAY A CRAZY CARD COMBO!
IT'S AN ART FORM, REALLY.
CARD COMBO? THAT SOUNDS COOL.
HAHA! YEAH. REALLY COOL...
C'MERE...
YOU WERE SUPPOSED TO HELP US!
AND YOU SHOULD BE A LITTLE MORE SELECTIVE WITH WHO YOU TALK TO.
MY NEW FRIENDS? WHAT'S WRONG WITH TALKING TO THEM?

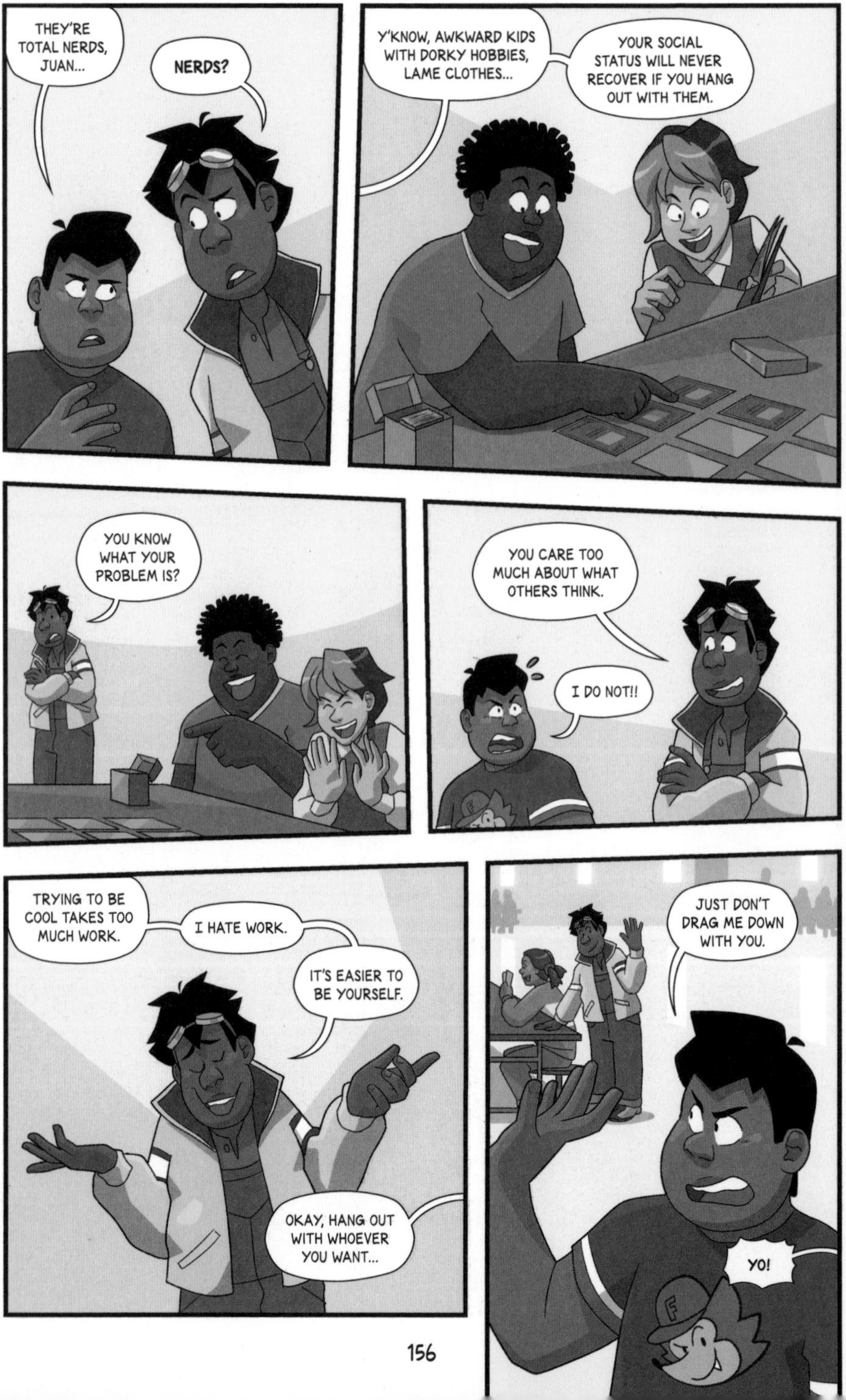
THEY'RE TOTAL NERDS, JUAN...
NERDS?
Y'KNOW, AWKWARD KIDS WITH DORKY HOBBIES, LAME CLOTHES...
YOUR SOCIAL STATUS WILL NEVER RECOVER IF YOU HANG OUT WITH THEM.
YOU KNOW WHAT YOUR PROBLEM IS?
YOU CARE TOO MUCH ABOUT WHAT OTHERS THINK.
I DO NOT!!
TRYING TO BE COOL TAKES TOO MUCH WORK.
I HATE WORK.
IT'S EASIER TO BE YOURSELF.
OKAY, HANG OUT WITH WHOEVER YOU WANT...
JUST DON'T DRAG ME DOWN WITH YOU.
YO!

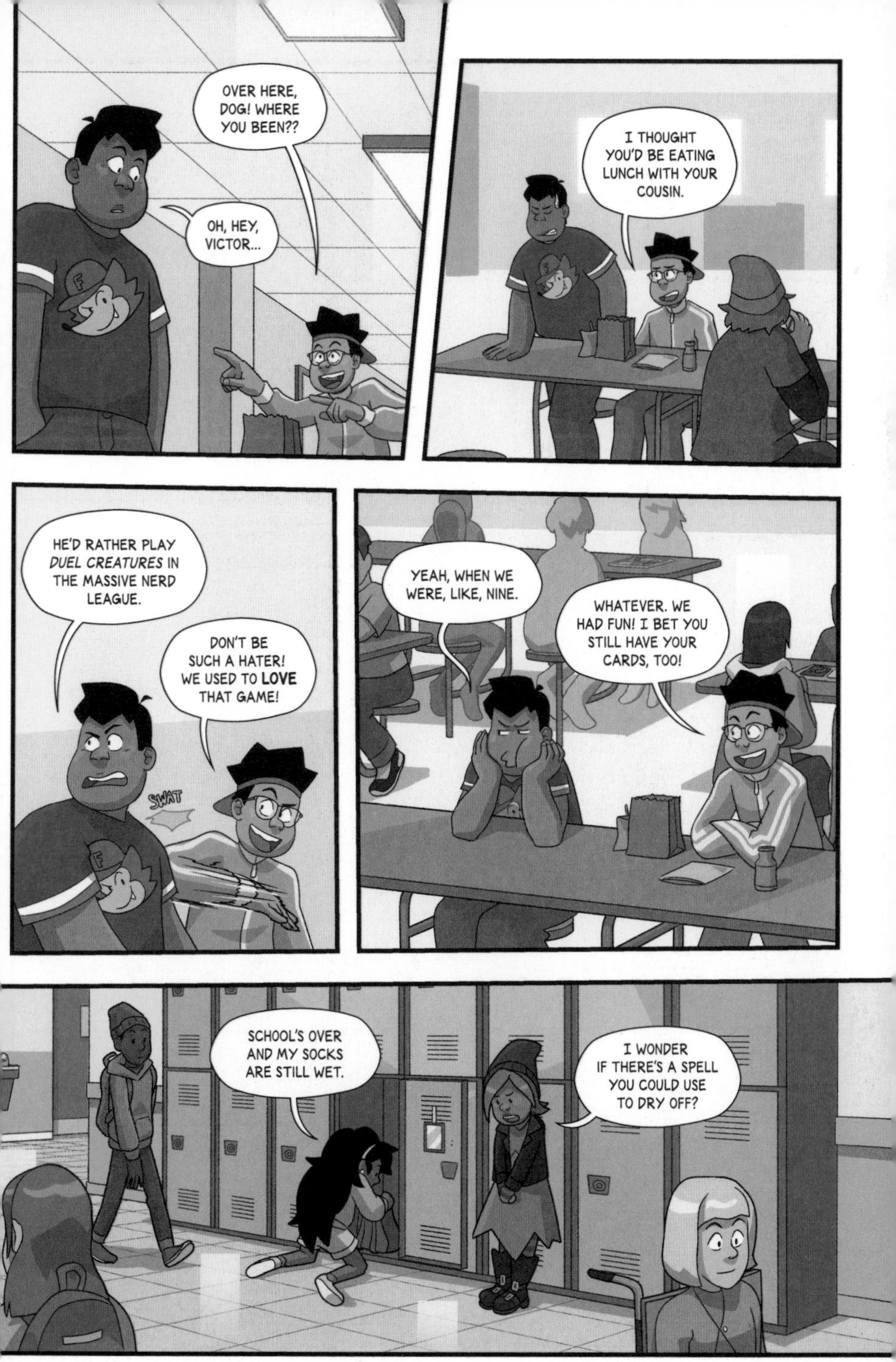
OVER HERE, DOG! WHERE YOU BEEN??
OH, HEY, VICTOR...
I THOUGHT YOU'D BE EATING LUNCH WITH YOUR COUSIN.
HE'D RATHER PLAY *DUEL CREATURES* IN THE MASSIVE NERD LEAGUE.
DON'T BE SUCH A HATER! WE USED TO **LOVE** THAT GAME!
SWAT
YEAH, WHEN WE WERE, LIKE, NINE.
WHATEVER. WE HAD FUN! I BET YOU STILL HAVE YOUR CARDS, TOO!
SCHOOL'S OVER AND MY SOCKS ARE STILL WET.
I WONDER IF THERE'S A SPELL YOU COULD USE TO DRY OFF?

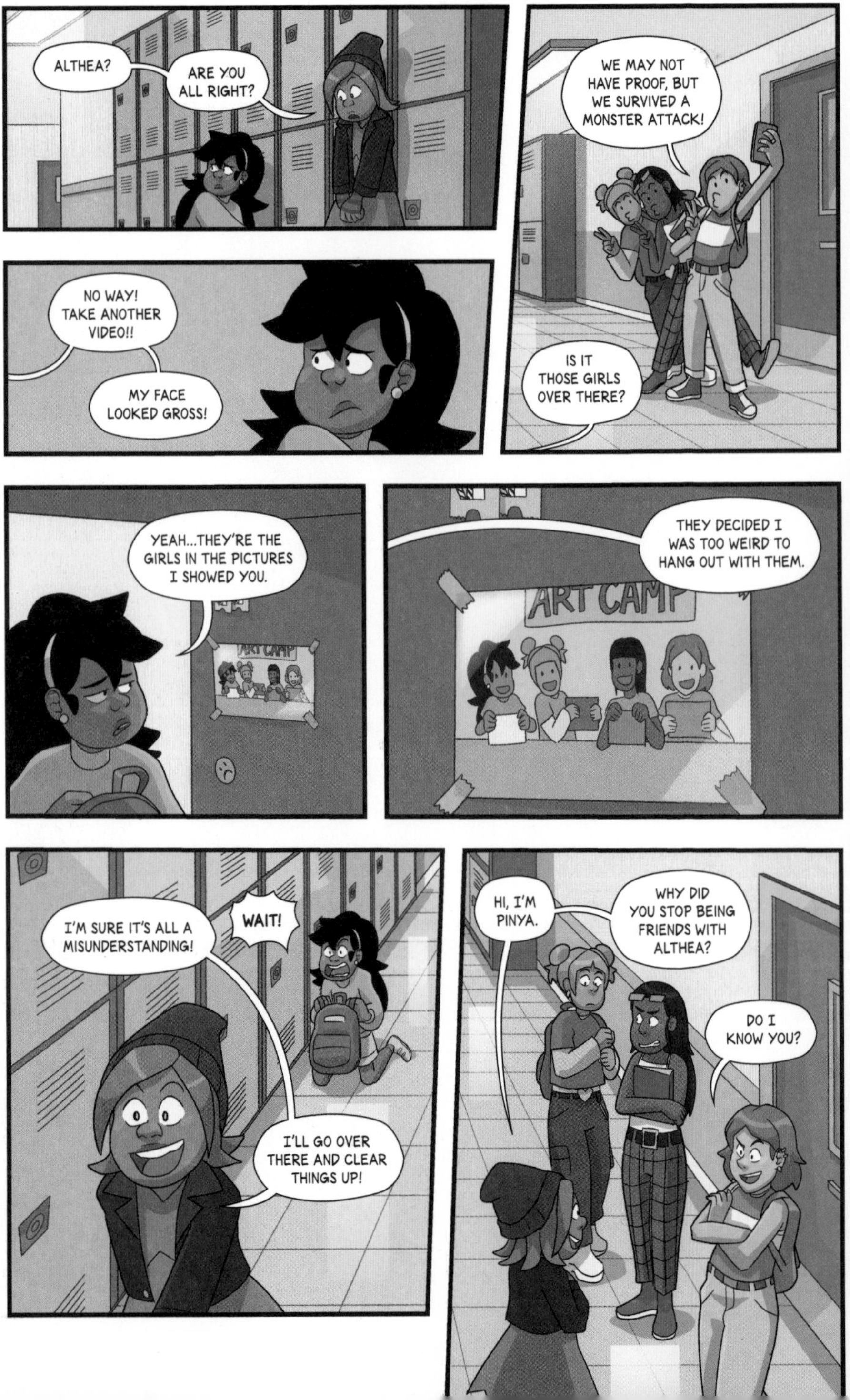
ALTHEA?
ARE YOU ALL RIGHT?
WE MAY NOT HAVE PROOF, BUT WE SURVIVED A MONSTER ATTACK!
NO WAY! TAKE ANOTHER VIDEO!!
MY FACE LOOKED GROSS!
IS IT THOSE GIRLS OVER THERE?
YEAH...THEY'RE THE GIRLS IN THE PICTURES I SHOWED YOU.
ART CAMP
THEY DECIDED I WAS TOO WEIRD TO HANG OUT WITH THEM.
ART CAMP
I'M SURE IT'S ALL A MISUNDERSTANDING!
WAIT!
I'LL GO OVER THERE AND CLEAR THINGS UP!
HI, I'M PINYA.
WHY DID YOU STOP BEING FRIENDS WITH ALTHEA?
DO I KNOW YOU?

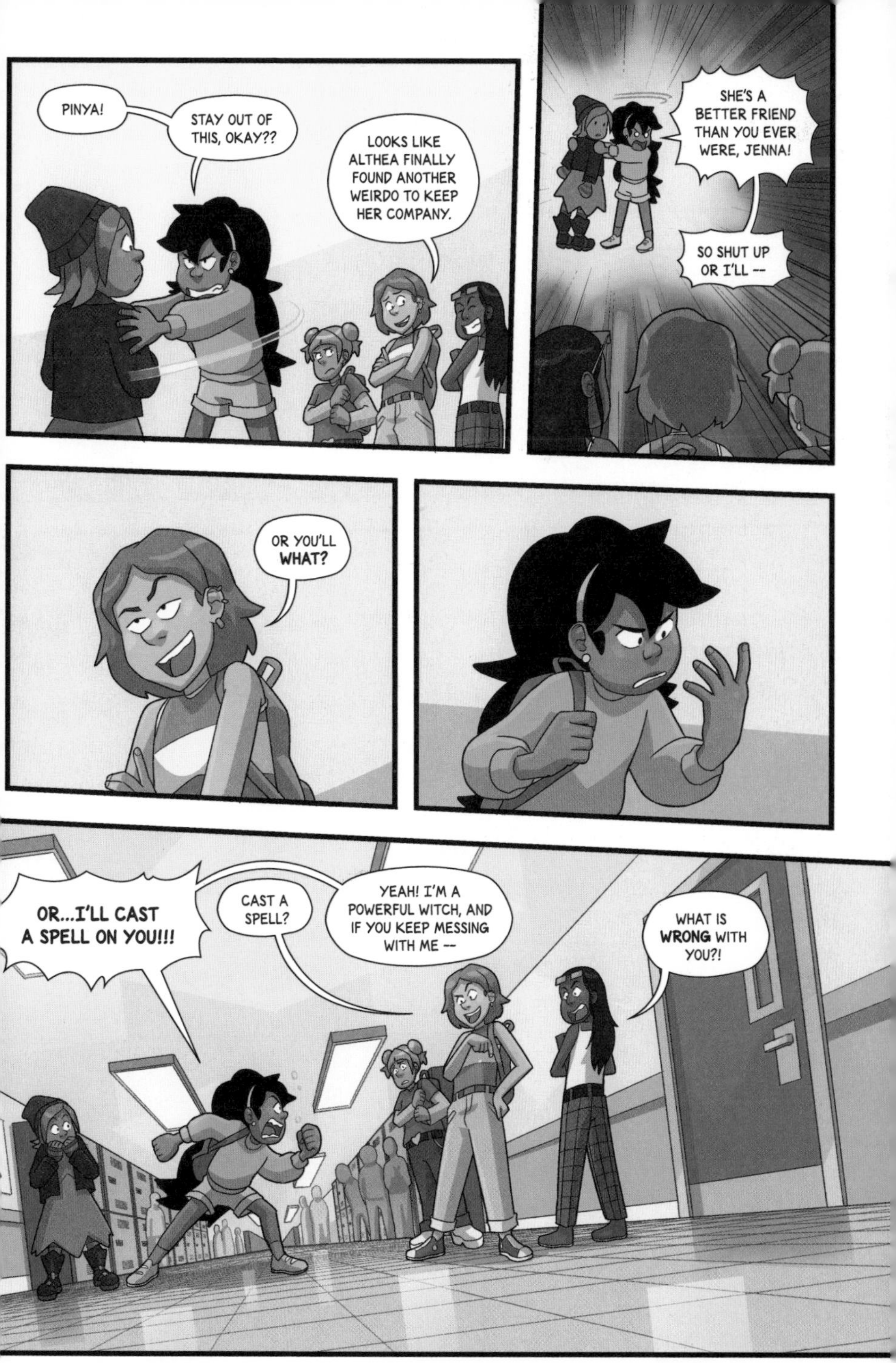
PINYA!
STAY OUT OF THIS, OKAY??
LOOKS LIKE ALTHEA FINALLY FOUND ANOTHER WEIRDO TO KEEP HER COMPANY.
SHE'S A BETTER FRIEND THAN YOU EVER WERE, JENNA!
SO SHUT UP OR I'LL --
OR YOU'LL **WHAT?**
OR...I'LL CAST A SPELL ON YOU!!!
CAST A SPELL?
YEAH! I'M A POWERFUL WITCH, AND IF YOU KEEP MESSING WITH ME --
WHAT IS **WRONG** WITH YOU?!

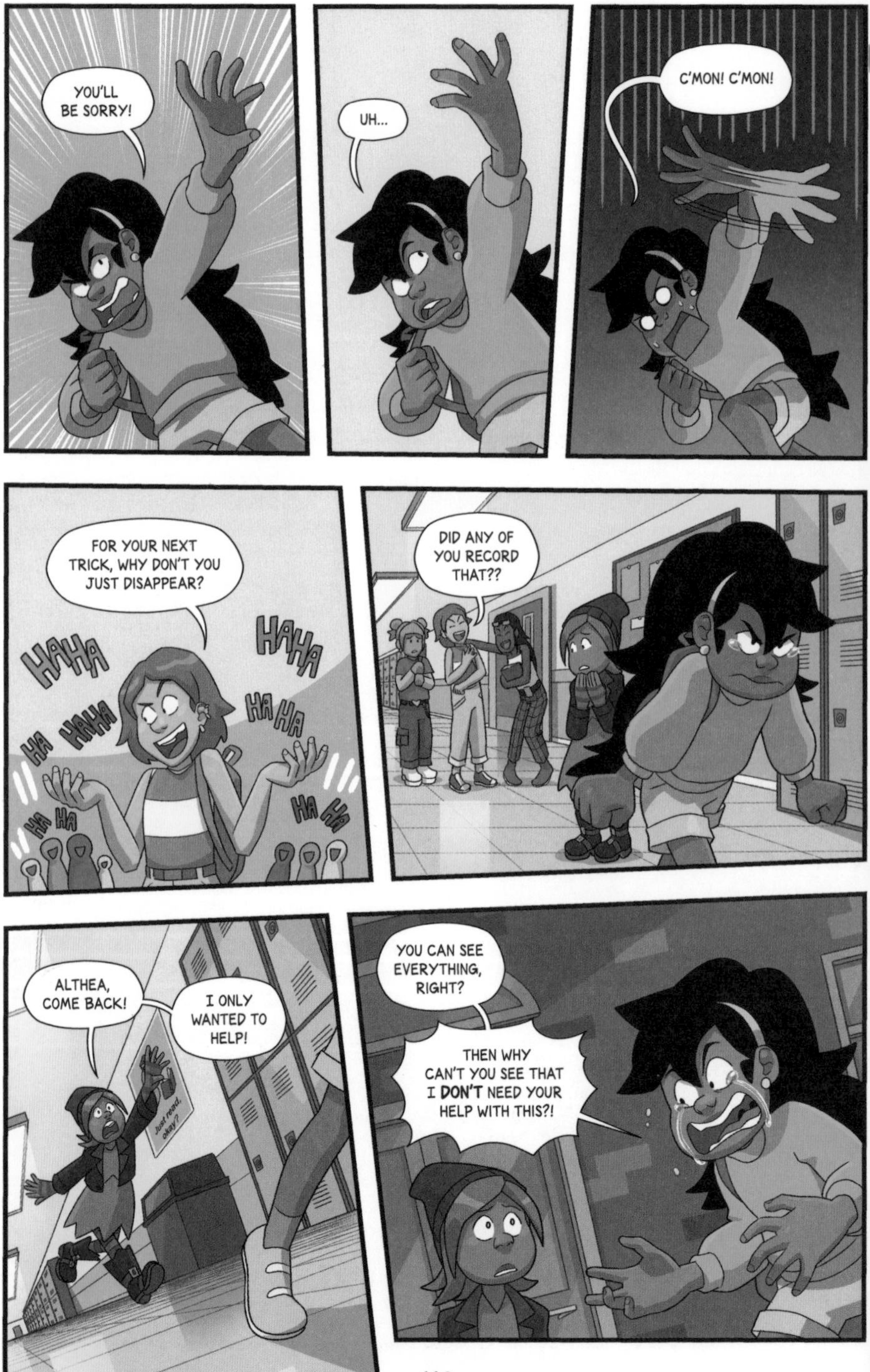
YOU'LL BE SORRY!
UH...
C'MON! C'MON!
FOR YOUR NEXT TRICK, WHY DON'T YOU JUST DISAPPEAR?
HAHA
HAHA
HAHA
HA HAHA
HA HA
HA HA
HA HA
DID ANY OF YOU RECORD THAT??
ALTHEA, COME BACK!
I ONLY WANTED TO HELP!
Just read, okay?
YOU CAN SEE EVERYTHING, RIGHT?
THEN WHY CAN'T YOU SEE THAT I **DON'T** NEED YOUR HELP WITH THIS?!

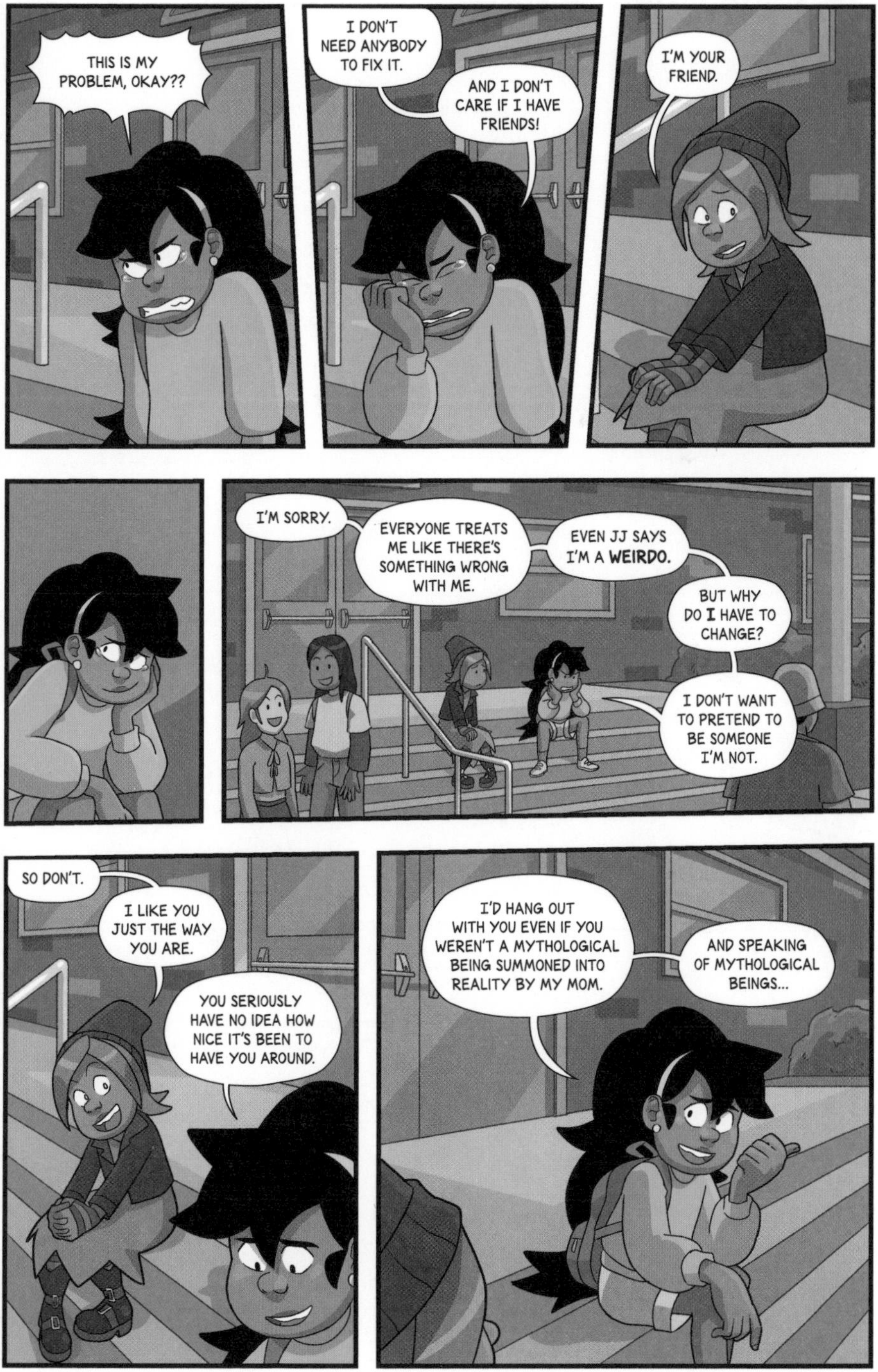
THIS IS MY PROBLEM, OKAY??
I DON'T NEED ANYBODY TO FIX IT.
AND I DON'T CARE IF I HAVE FRIENDS!
I'M YOUR FRIEND.
I'M SORRY.
EVERYONE TREATS ME LIKE THERE'S SOMETHING WRONG WITH ME.
EVEN JJ SAYS I'M A **WEIRDO.**
BUT WHY DO **I** HAVE TO CHANGE?
I DON'T WANT TO PRETEND TO BE SOMEONE I'M NOT.
SO DON'T.
I LIKE YOU JUST THE WAY YOU ARE.
YOU SERIOUSLY HAVE NO IDEA HOW NICE IT'S BEEN TO HAVE YOU AROUND.
I'D HANG OUT WITH YOU EVEN IF YOU WEREN'T A MYTHOLOGICAL BEING SUMMONED INTO REALITY BY MY MOM.
AND SPEAKING OF MYTHOLOGICAL BEINGS...

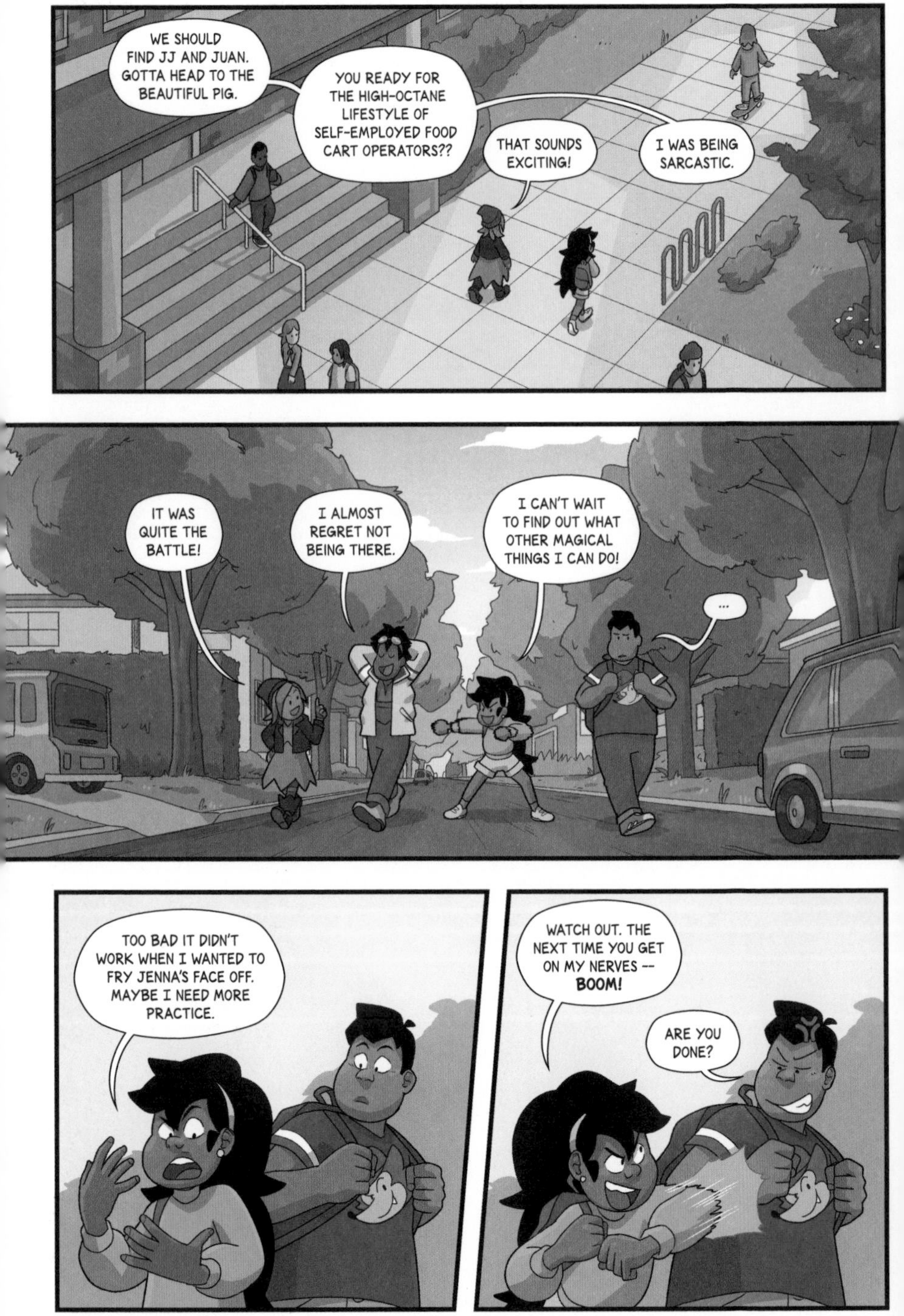
WE SHOULD FIND JJ AND JUAN. GOTTA HEAD TO THE BEAUTIFUL PIG.
YOU READY FOR THE HIGH-OCTANE LIFESTYLE OF SELF-EMPLOYED FOOD CART OPERATORS??
THAT SOUNDS EXCITING!
I WAS BEING SARCASTIC.
IT WAS QUITE THE BATTLE!
I ALMOST REGRET NOT BEING THERE.
I CAN'T WAIT TO FIND OUT WHAT OTHER MAGICAL THINGS I CAN DO!
...
TOO BAD IT DIDN'T WORK WHEN I WANTED TO FRY JENNA'S FACE OFF. MAYBE I NEED MORE PRACTICE.
WATCH OUT. THE NEXT TIME YOU GET ON MY NERVES -- **BOOM!**
ARE YOU DONE?

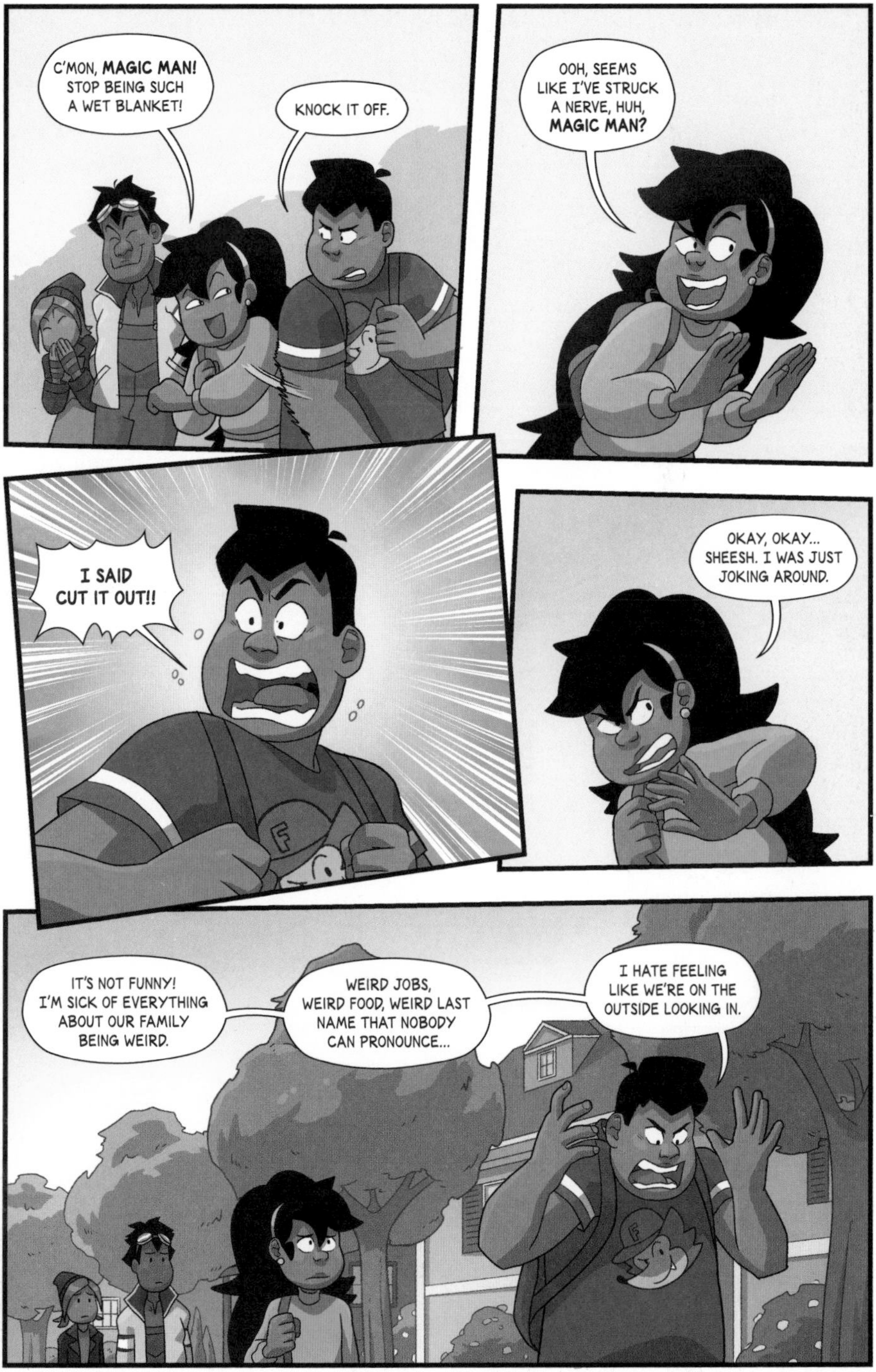
C'MON, MAGIC MAN! STOP BEING SUCH A WET BLANKET!
KNOCK IT OFF.
OOH, SEEMS LIKE I'VE STRUCK A NERVE, HUH, MAGIC MAN?
I SAID CUT IT OUT!!
OKAY, OKAY... SHEESH. I WAS JUST JOKING AROUND.
IT'S NOT FUNNY! I'M SICK OF EVERYTHING ABOUT OUR FAMILY BEING WEIRD.
WEIRD JOBS, WEIRD FOOD, WEIRD LAST NAME THAT NOBODY CAN PRONOUNCE...
I HATE FEELING LIKE WE'RE ON THE OUTSIDE LOOKING IN.

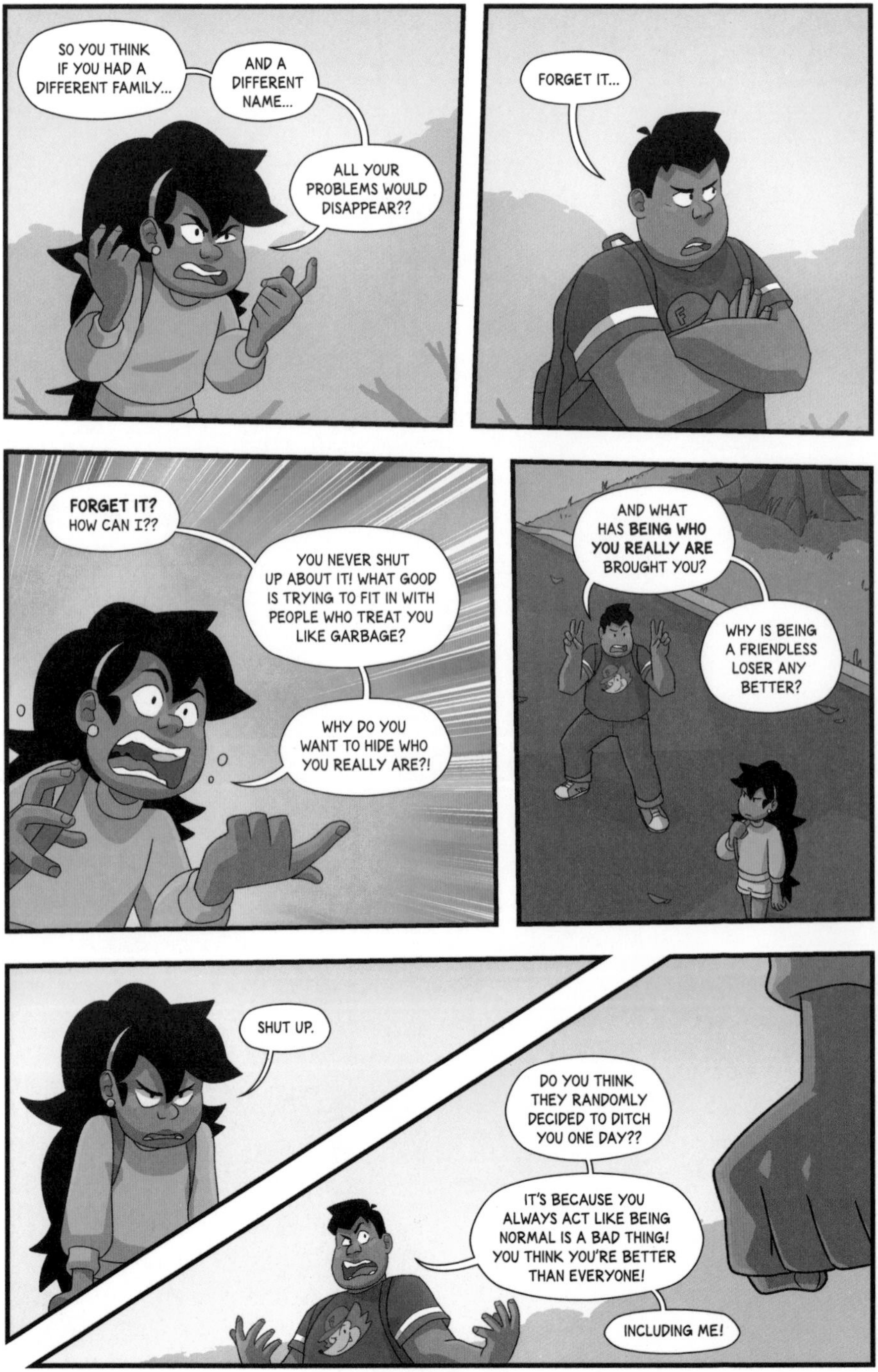
SO YOU THINK IF YOU HAD A DIFFERENT FAMILY...
AND A DIFFERENT NAME...
ALL YOUR PROBLEMS WOULD DISAPPEAR??
FORGET IT...
FORGET IT? HOW CAN I??
YOU NEVER SHUT UP ABOUT IT! WHAT GOOD IS TRYING TO FIT IN WITH PEOPLE WHO TREAT YOU LIKE GARBAGE?
WHY DO YOU WANT TO HIDE WHO YOU REALLY ARE?!
AND WHAT HAS **BEING WHO YOU REALLY ARE** BROUGHT YOU?
WHY IS BEING A FRIENDLESS LOSER ANY BETTER?
SHUT UP.
DO YOU THINK THEY RANDOMLY DECIDED TO DITCH YOU ONE DAY??
IT'S BECAUSE YOU ALWAYS ACT LIKE BEING NORMAL IS A BAD THING! YOU THINK YOU'RE BETTER THAN EVERYONE!
INCLUDING ME!

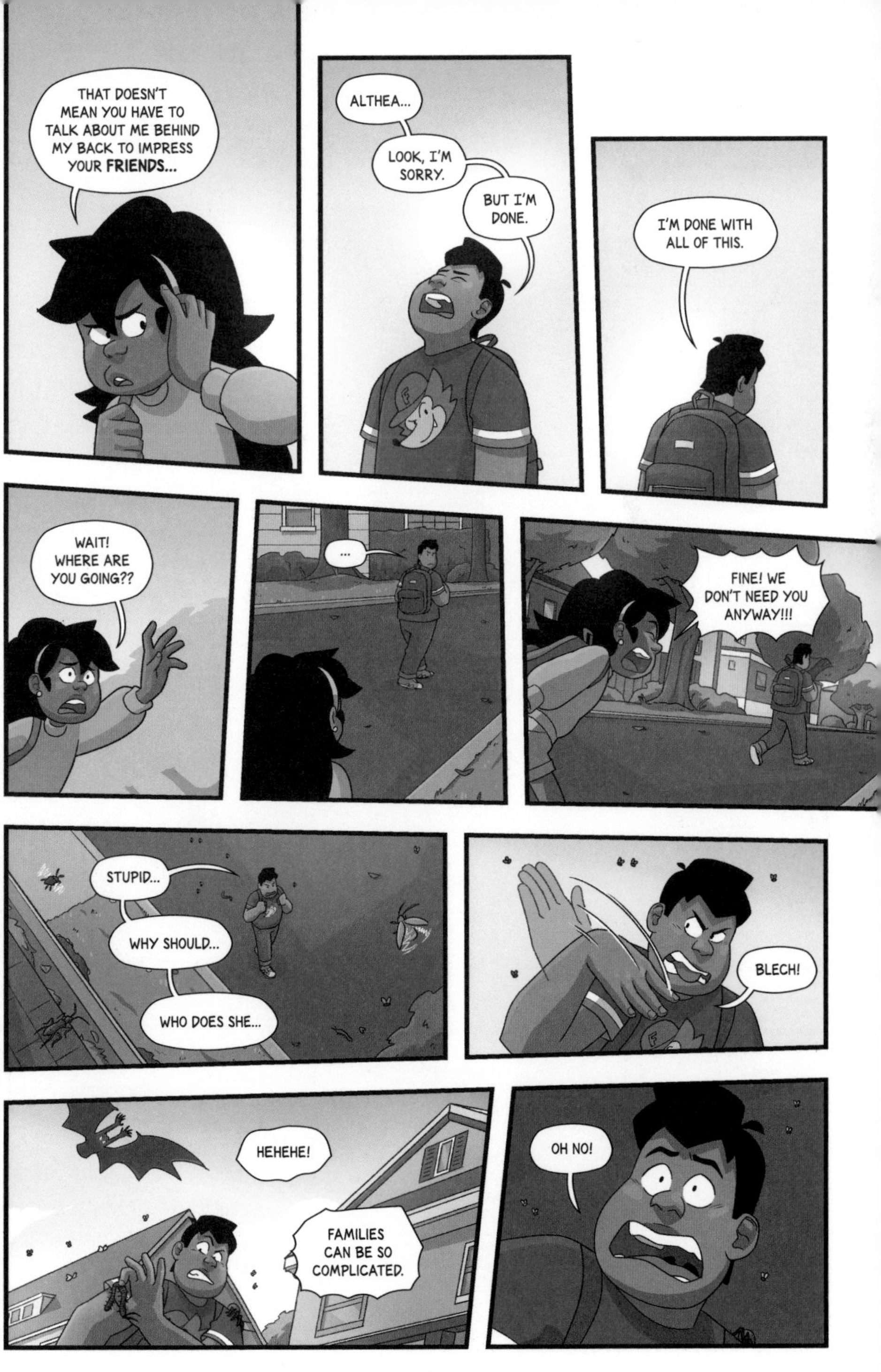
THAT DOESN'T MEAN YOU HAVE TO TALK ABOUT ME BEHIND MY BACK TO IMPRESS YOUR **FRIENDS...**
ALTHEA...
LOOK, I'M SORRY.
BUT I'M DONE.
I'M DONE WITH ALL OF THIS.
WAIT! WHERE ARE YOU GOING??
...
FINE! WE DON'T NEED YOU ANYWAY!!!
STUPID...
WHY SHOULD...
WHO DOES SHE...
BLECH!
HEHEHE!
FAMILIES CAN BE SO COMPLICATED.
OH NO!

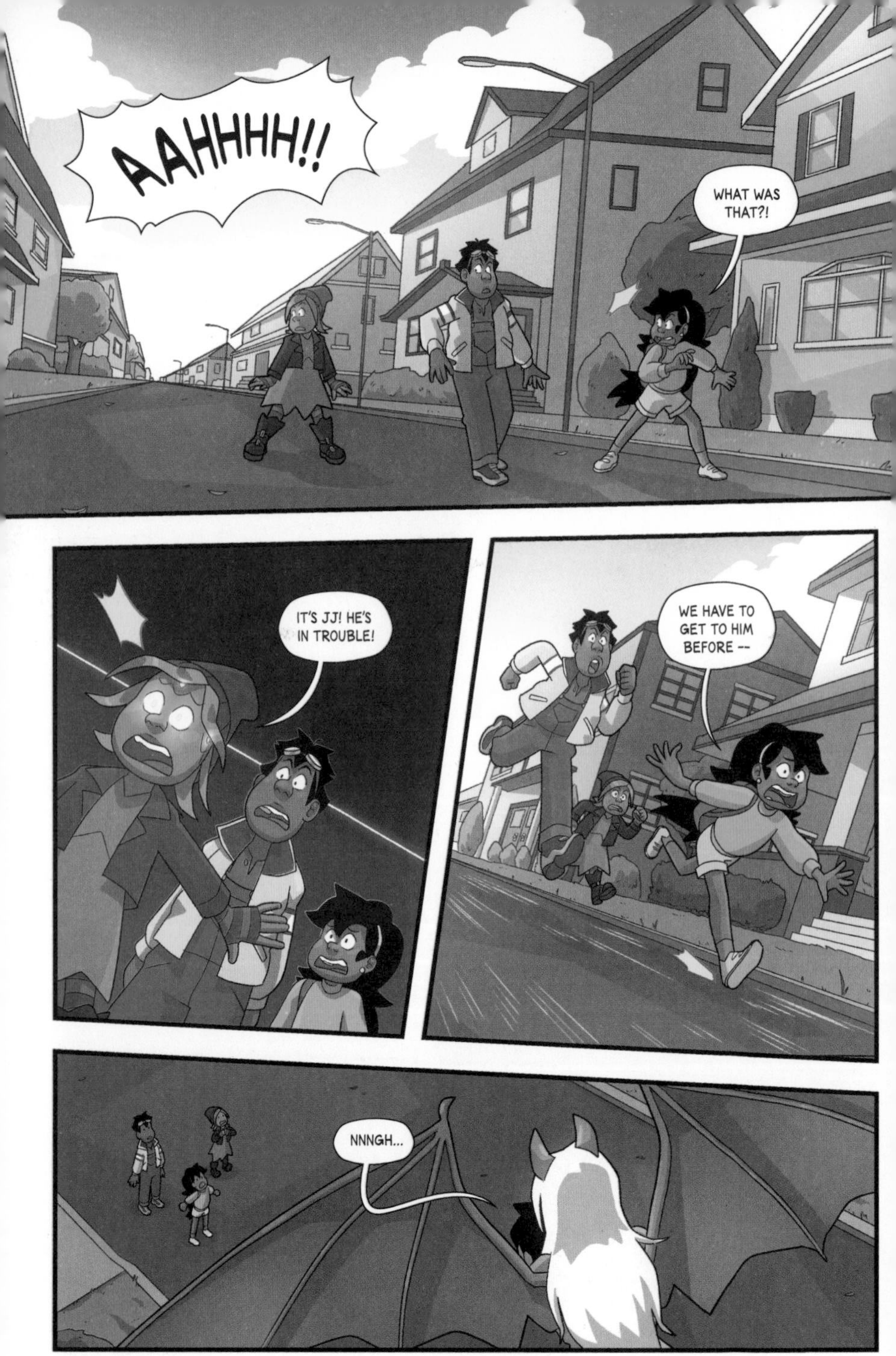
AAHHHH!!
WHAT WAS THAT?!
IT'S JJ! HE'S IN TROUBLE!
WE HAVE TO GET TO HIM BEFORE --
NNNGH...

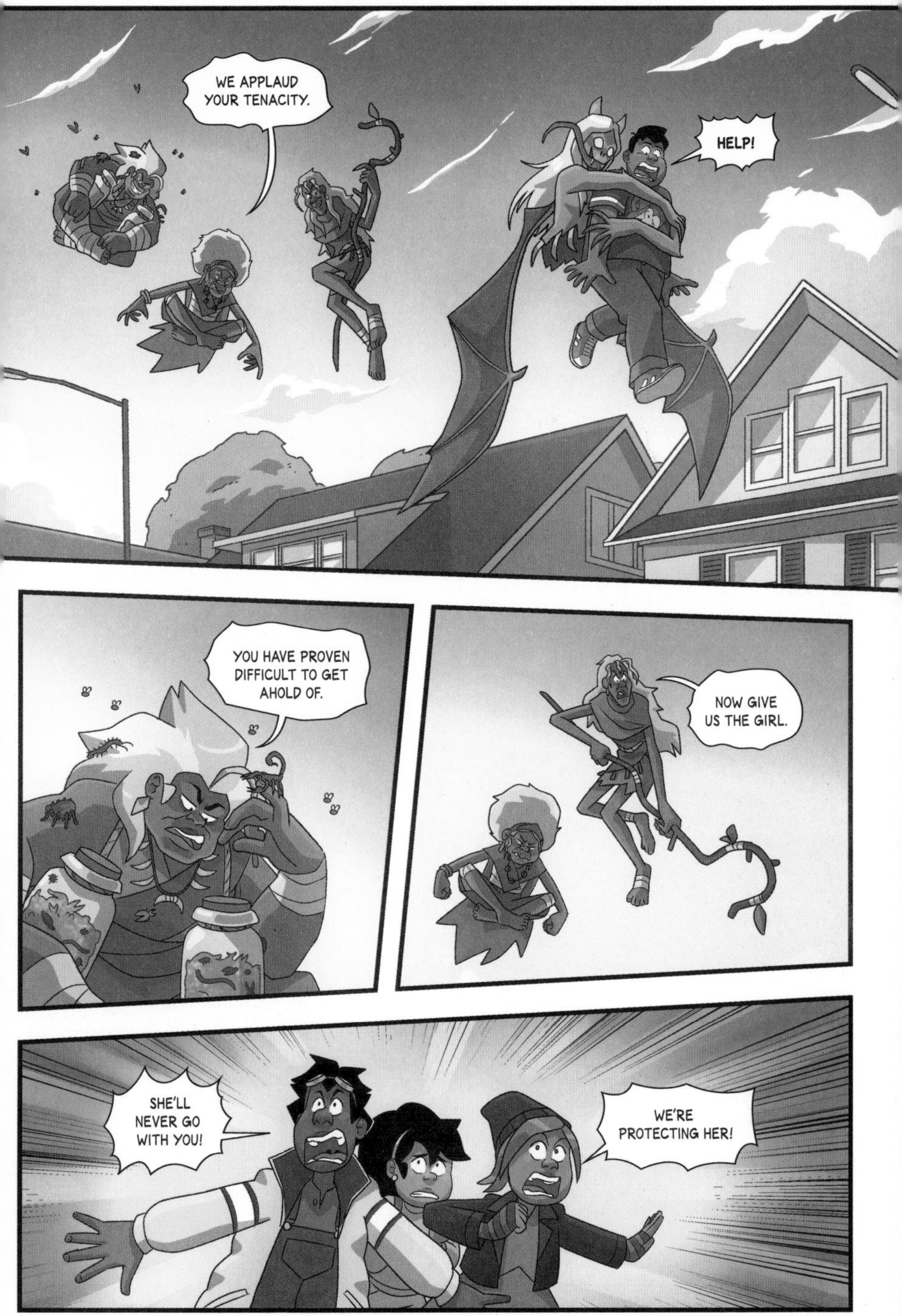
WE APPLAUD YOUR TENACITY.
HELP!
YOU HAVE PROVEN DIFFICULT TO GET AHOLD OF.
NOW GIVE US THE GIRL.
SHE'LL NEVER GO WITH YOU!
WE'RE PROTECTING HER!

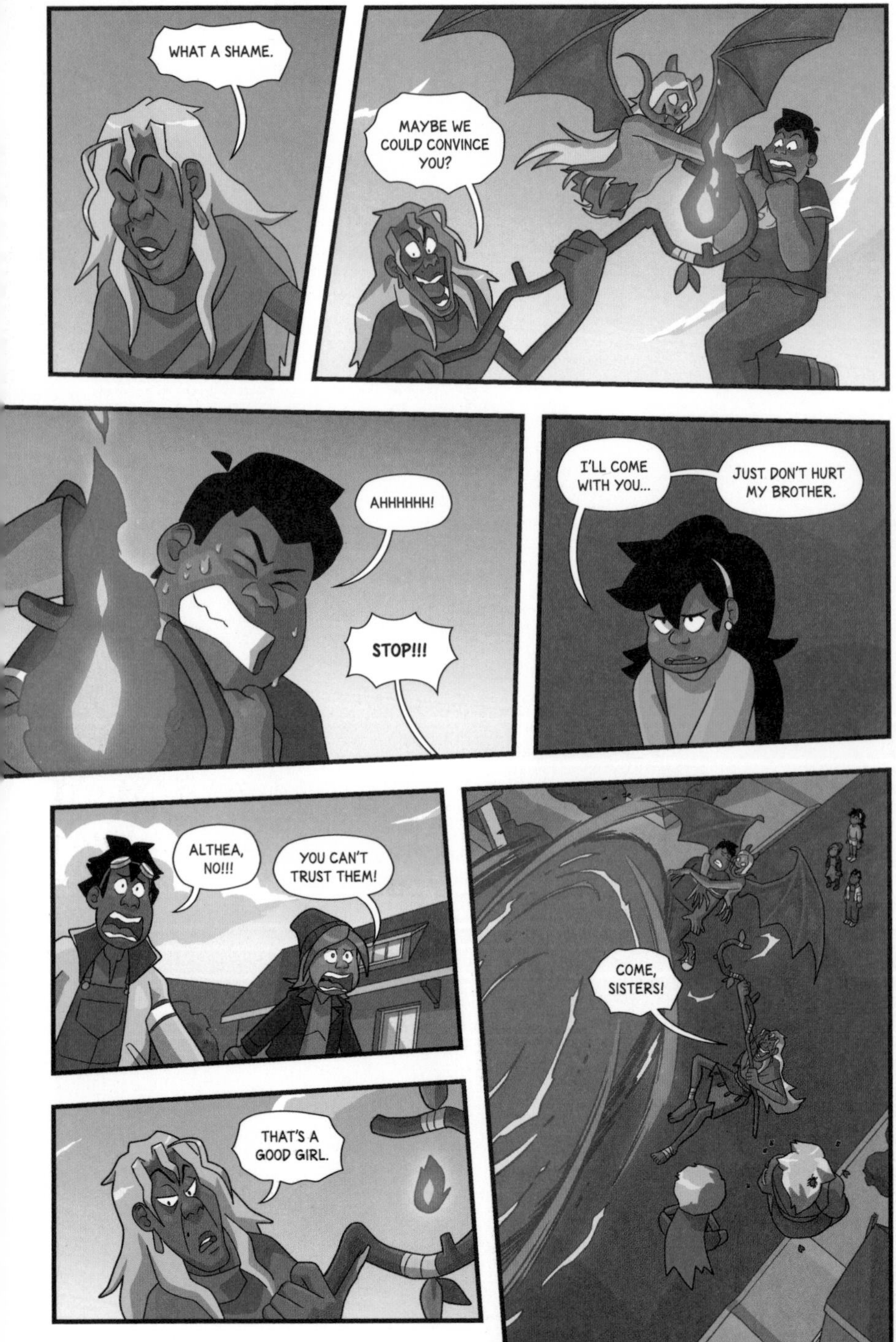
WHAT A SHAME.
MAYBE WE COULD CONVINCE YOU?
AHHHHHH!
STOP!!!
I'LL COME WITH YOU...
JUST DON'T HURT MY BROTHER.
ALTHEA, NO!!!
YOU CAN'T TRUST THEM!
THAT'S A GOOD GIRL.
COME, SISTERS!

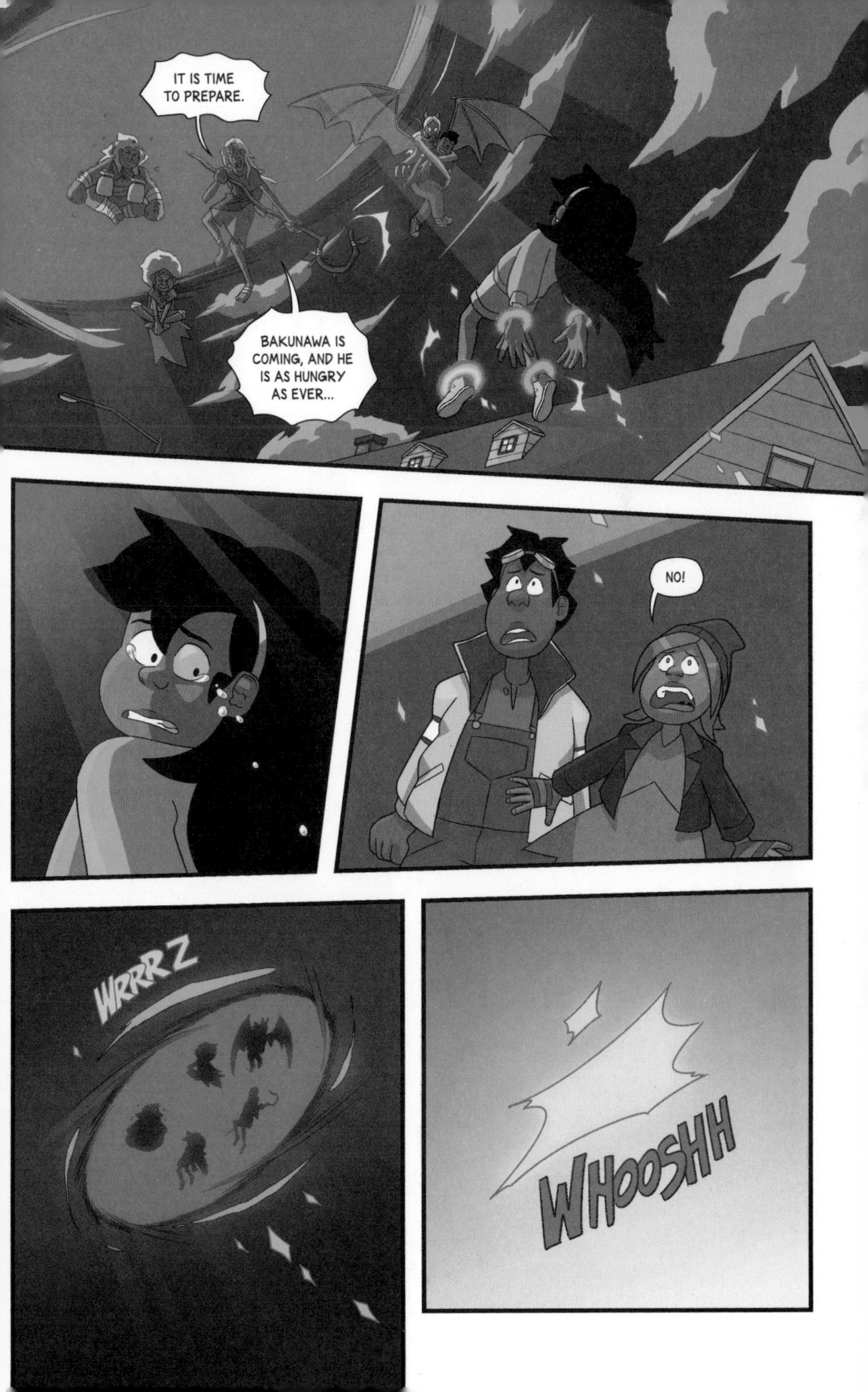
IT IS TIME TO PREPARE.
BAKUNAWA IS COMING, AND HE IS AS HUNGRY AS EVER...
NO!
WRRRZ
WHOOSHH

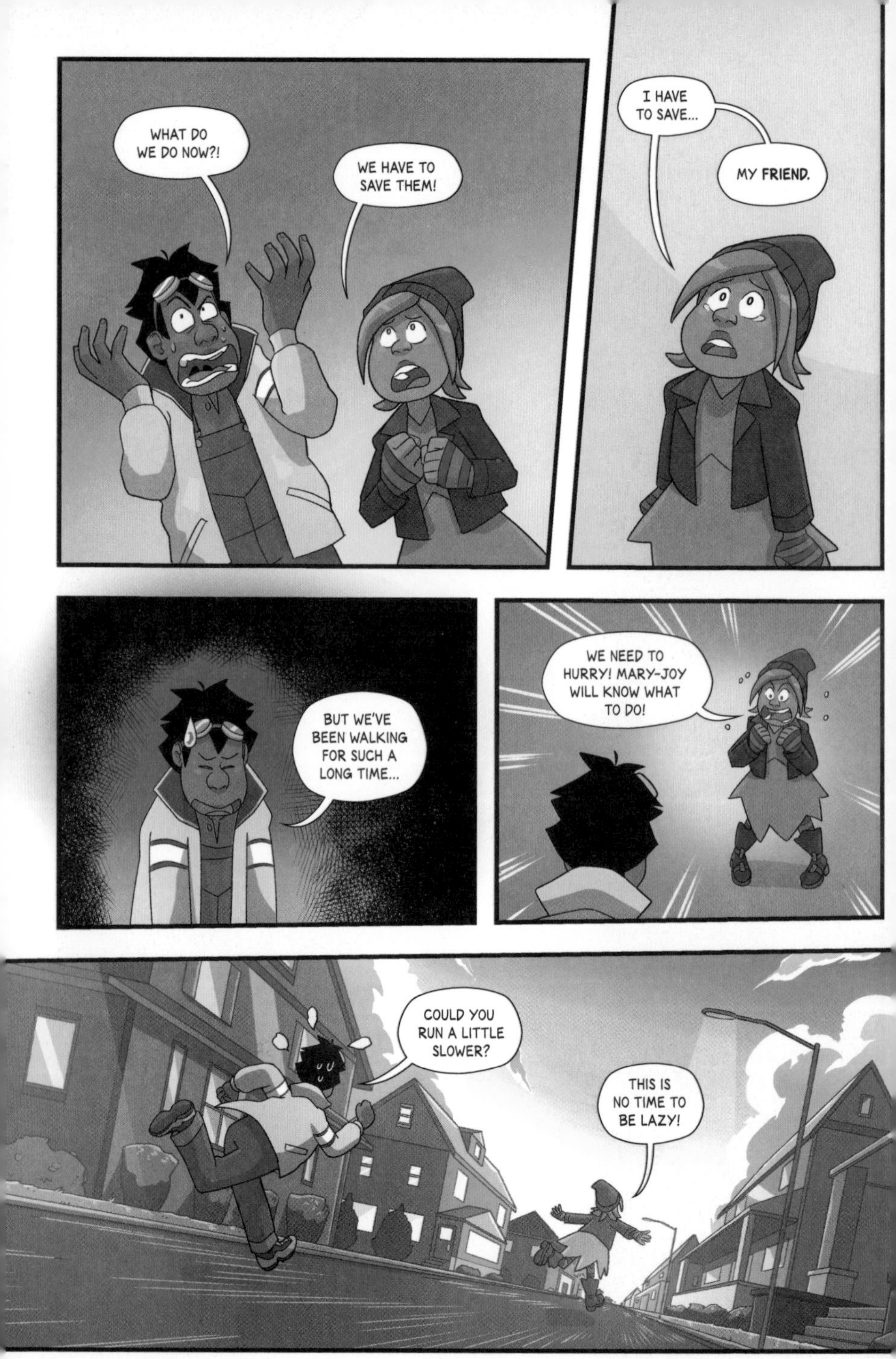
WHAT DO WE DO NOW?!
WE HAVE TO SAVE THEM!
I HAVE TO SAVE...
MY **FRIEND.**
BUT WE'VE BEEN WALKING FOR SUCH A LONG TIME...
WE NEED TO HURRY! MARY-JOY WILL KNOW WHAT TO DO!
COULD YOU RUN A LITTLE SLOWER?
THIS IS NO TIME TO BE LAZY!

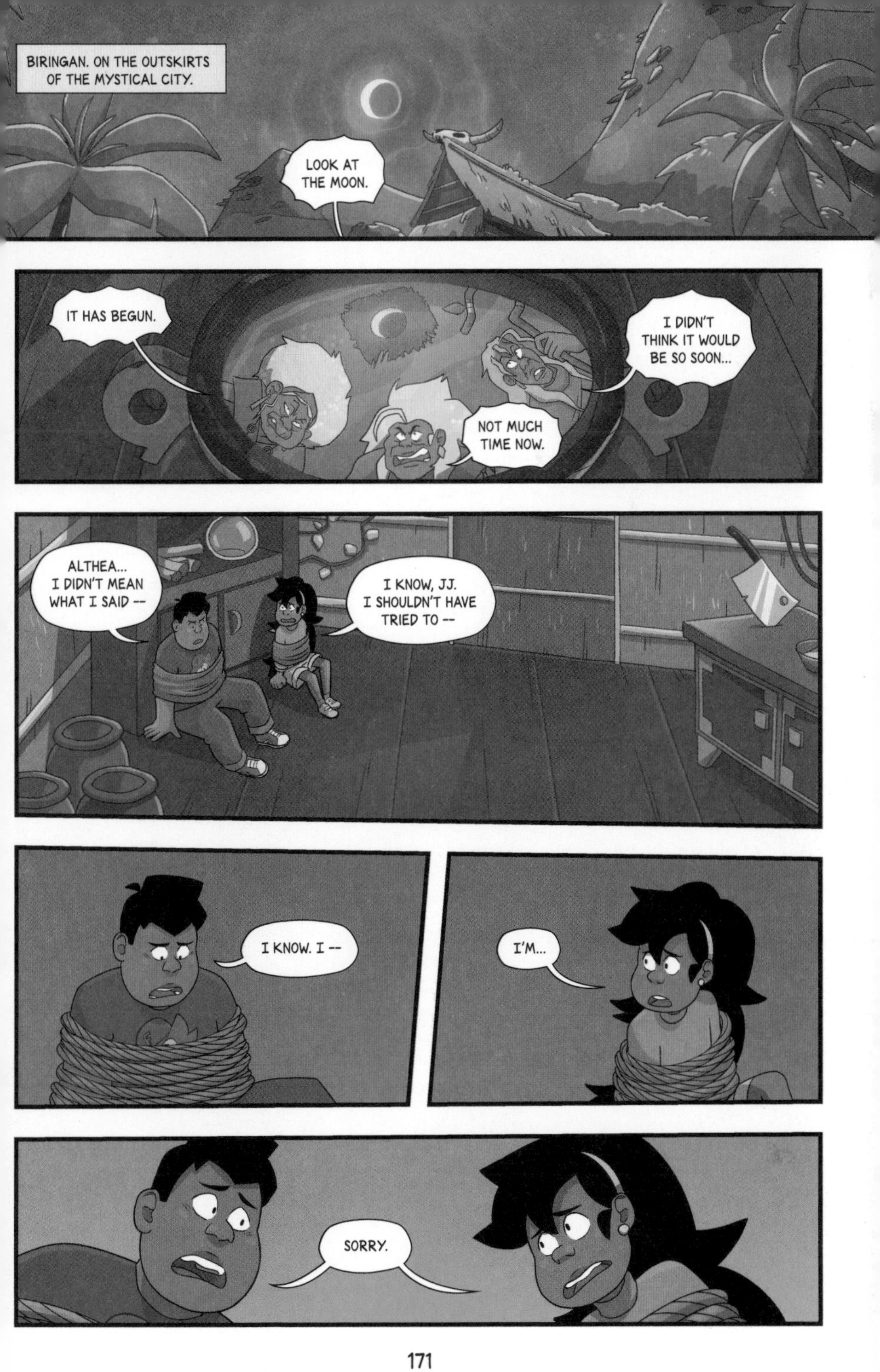
BIRINGAN. ON THE OUTSKIRTS OF THE MYSTICAL CITY.
LOOK AT THE MOON.
IT HAS BEGUN.
I DIDN'T THINK IT WOULD BE SO SOON...
NOT MUCH TIME NOW.
ALTHEA... I DIDN'T MEAN WHAT I SAID --
I KNOW, JJ. I SHOULDN'T HAVE TRIED TO --
I KNOW. I --
I'M...
SORRY.

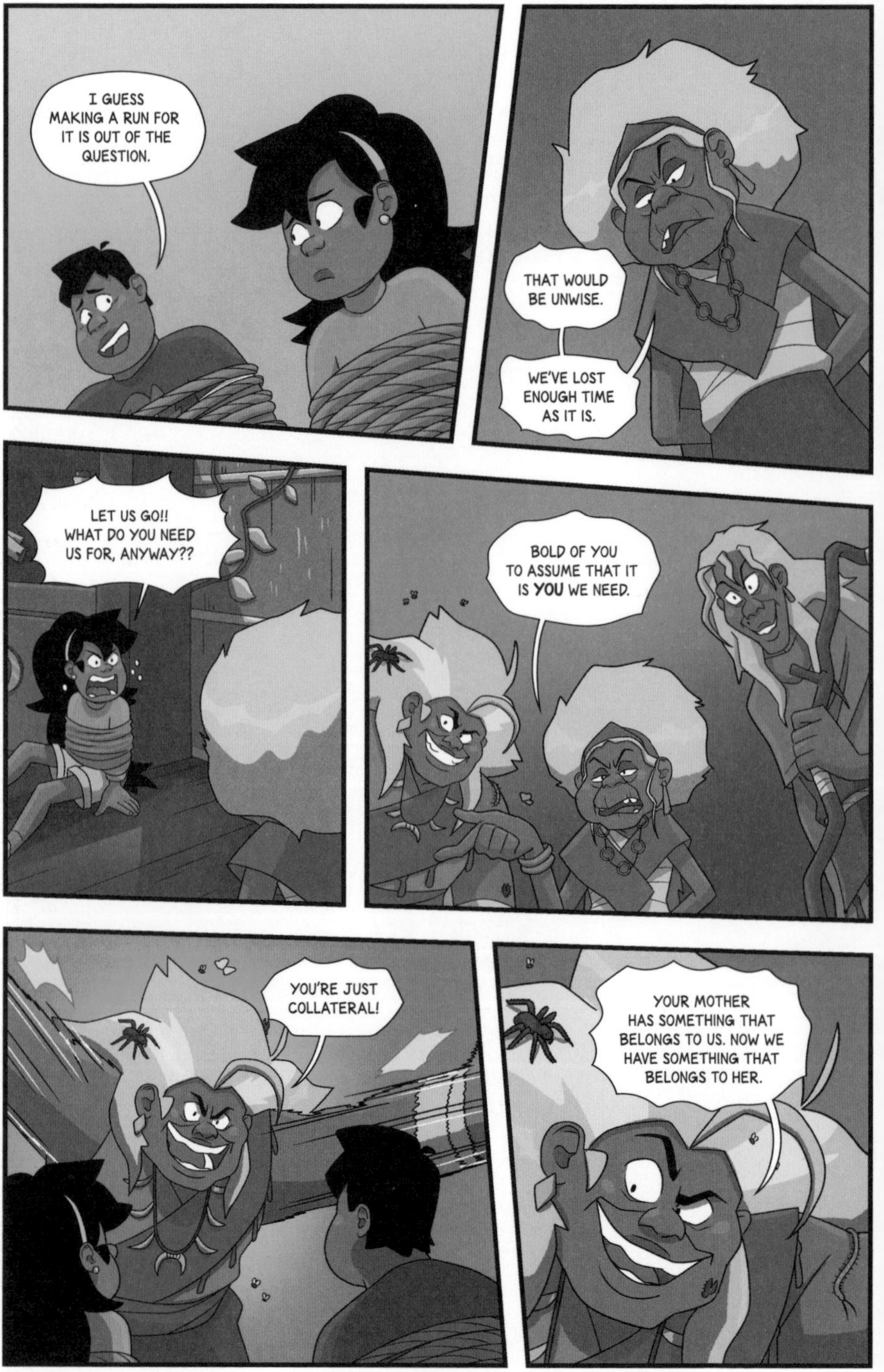
I GUESS MAKING A RUN FOR IT IS OUT OF THE QUESTION.
THAT WOULD BE UNWISE.
WE'VE LOST ENOUGH TIME AS IT IS.
LET US GO!! WHAT DO YOU NEED US FOR, ANYWAY??
BOLD OF YOU TO ASSUME THAT IT IS **YOU** WE NEED.
YOU'RE JUST COLLATERAL!
YOUR MOTHER HAS SOMETHING THAT BELONGS TO US. NOW WE HAVE SOMETHING THAT BELONGS TO HER.

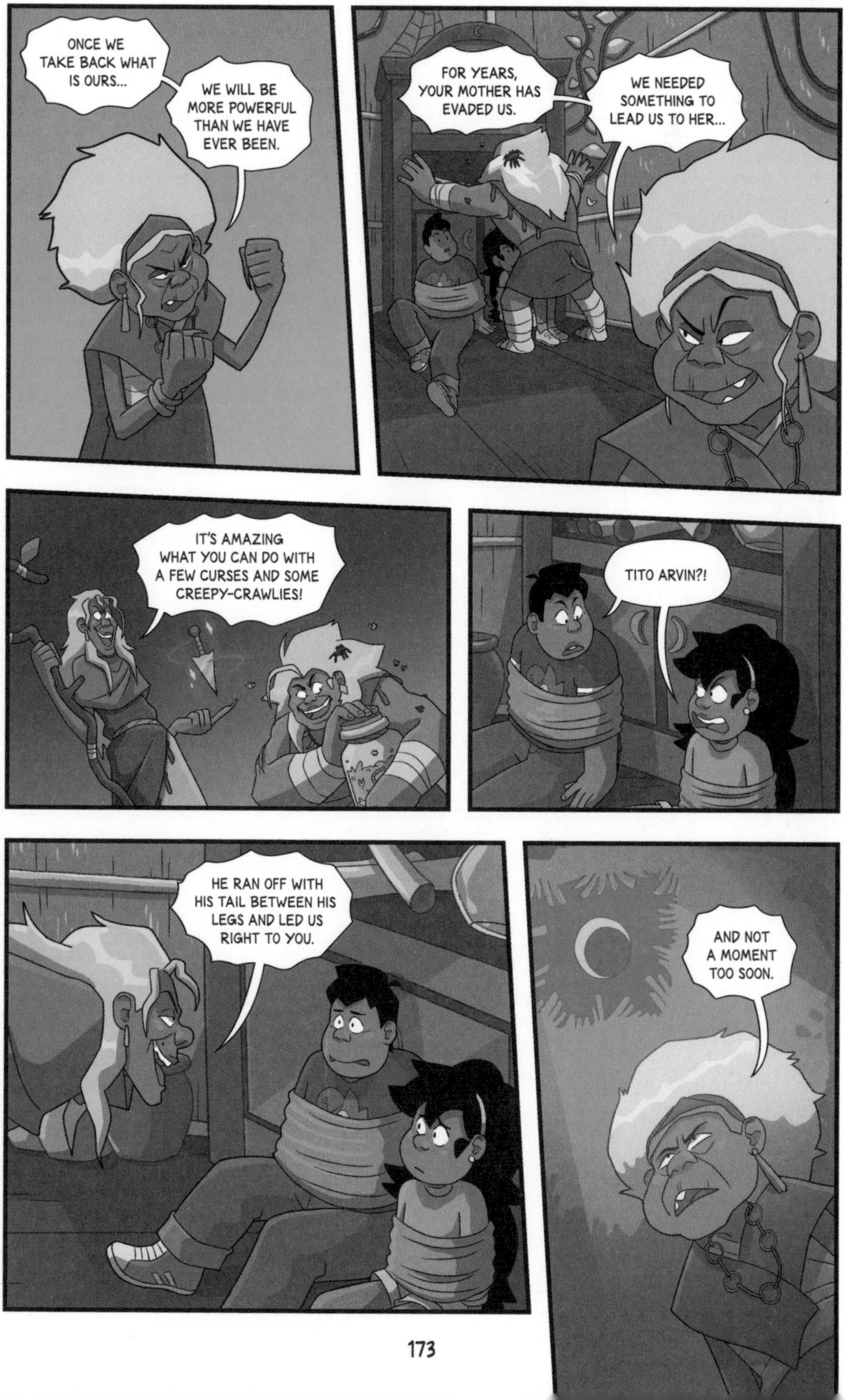
ONCE WE TAKE BACK WHAT IS OURS...
WE WILL BE MORE POWERFUL THAN WE HAVE EVER BEEN.
FOR YEARS, YOUR MOTHER HAS EVADED US.
WE NEEDED SOMETHING TO LEAD US TO HER...
IT'S AMAZING WHAT YOU CAN DO WITH A FEW CURSES AND SOME CREEPY-CRAWLIES!
TITO ARVIN?!
HE RAN OFF WITH HIS TAIL BETWEEN HIS LEGS AND LED US RIGHT TO YOU.
AND NOT A MOMENT TOO SOON.

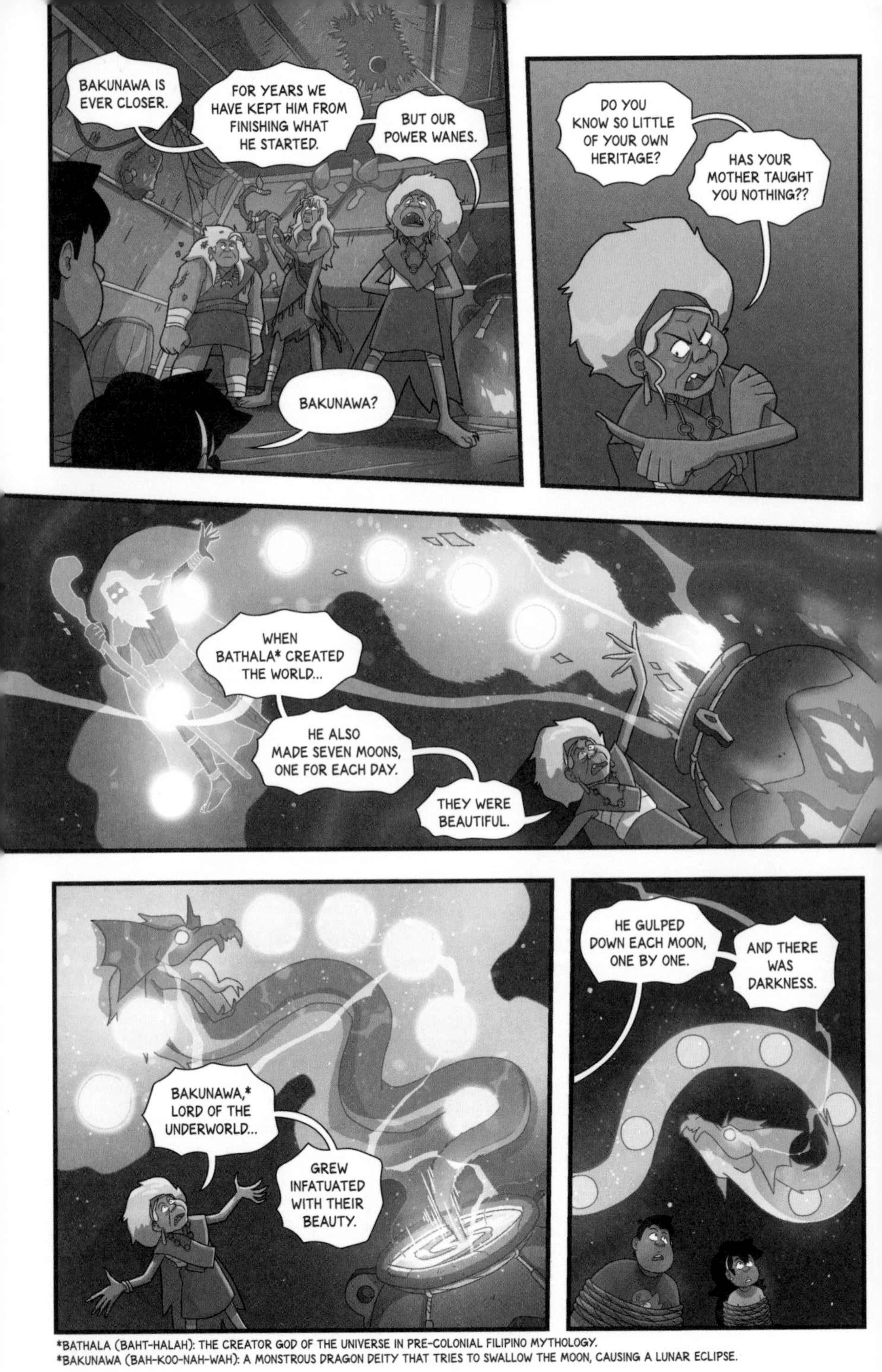
BAKUNAWA IS EVER CLOSER.
FOR YEARS WE HAVE KEPT HIM FROM FINISHING WHAT HE STARTED.
BUT OUR POWER WANES.
BAKUNAWA?
DO YOU KNOW SO LITTLE OF YOUR OWN HERITAGE?
HAS YOUR MOTHER TAUGHT YOU NOTHING??
WHEN BATHALA* CREATED THE WORLD...
HE ALSO MADE SEVEN MOONS, ONE FOR EACH DAY.
THEY WERE BEAUTIFUL.
BAKUNAWA,* LORD OF THE UNDERWORLD...
GREW INFATUATED WITH THEIR BEAUTY.
HE GULPED DOWN EACH MOON, ONE BY ONE.
AND THERE WAS DARKNESS.

*BATHALA (BAHT-HALAH): THE CREATOR GOD OF THE UNIVERSE IN PRE-COLONIAL FILIPINO MYTHOLOGY.
*BAKUNAWA (BAH-KOO-NAH-WAH): A MONSTROUS DRAGON DEITY THAT TRIES TO SWALLOW THE MOON, CAUSING A LUNAR ECLIPSE.

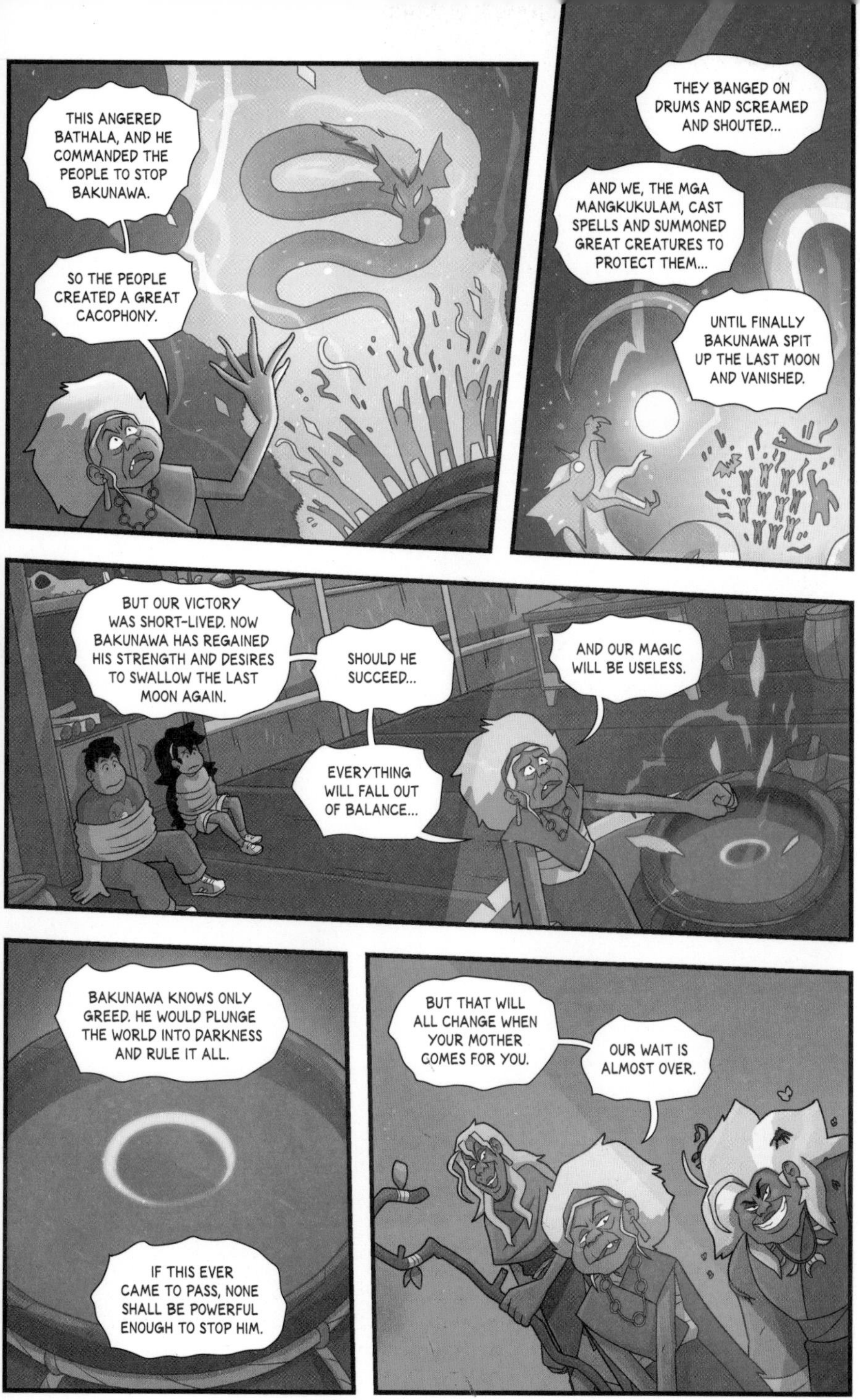
THIS ANGERED BATHALA, AND HE COMMANDED THE PEOPLE TO STOP BAKUNAWA.
SO THE PEOPLE CREATED A GREAT CACOPHONY.
THEY BANGED ON DRUMS AND SCREAMED AND SHOUTED...
AND WE, THE MGA MANGKUKULAM, CAST SPELLS AND SUMMONED GREAT CREATURES TO PROTECT THEM...
UNTIL FINALLY BAKUNAWA SPIT UP THE LAST MOON AND VANISHED.
BUT OUR VICTORY WAS SHORT-LIVED. NOW BAKUNAWA HAS REGAINED HIS STRENGTH AND DESIRES TO SWALLOW THE LAST MOON AGAIN.
SHOULD HE SUCCEED...
EVERYTHING WILL FALL OUT OF BALANCE...
AND OUR MAGIC WILL BE USELESS.
BAKUNAWA KNOWS ONLY GREED. HE WOULD PLUNGE THE WORLD INTO DARKNESS AND RULE IT ALL.
IF THIS EVER CAME TO PASS, NONE SHALL BE POWERFUL ENOUGH TO STOP HIM.
BUT THAT WILL ALL CHANGE WHEN YOUR MOTHER COMES FOR YOU.
OUR WAIT IS ALMOST OVER.

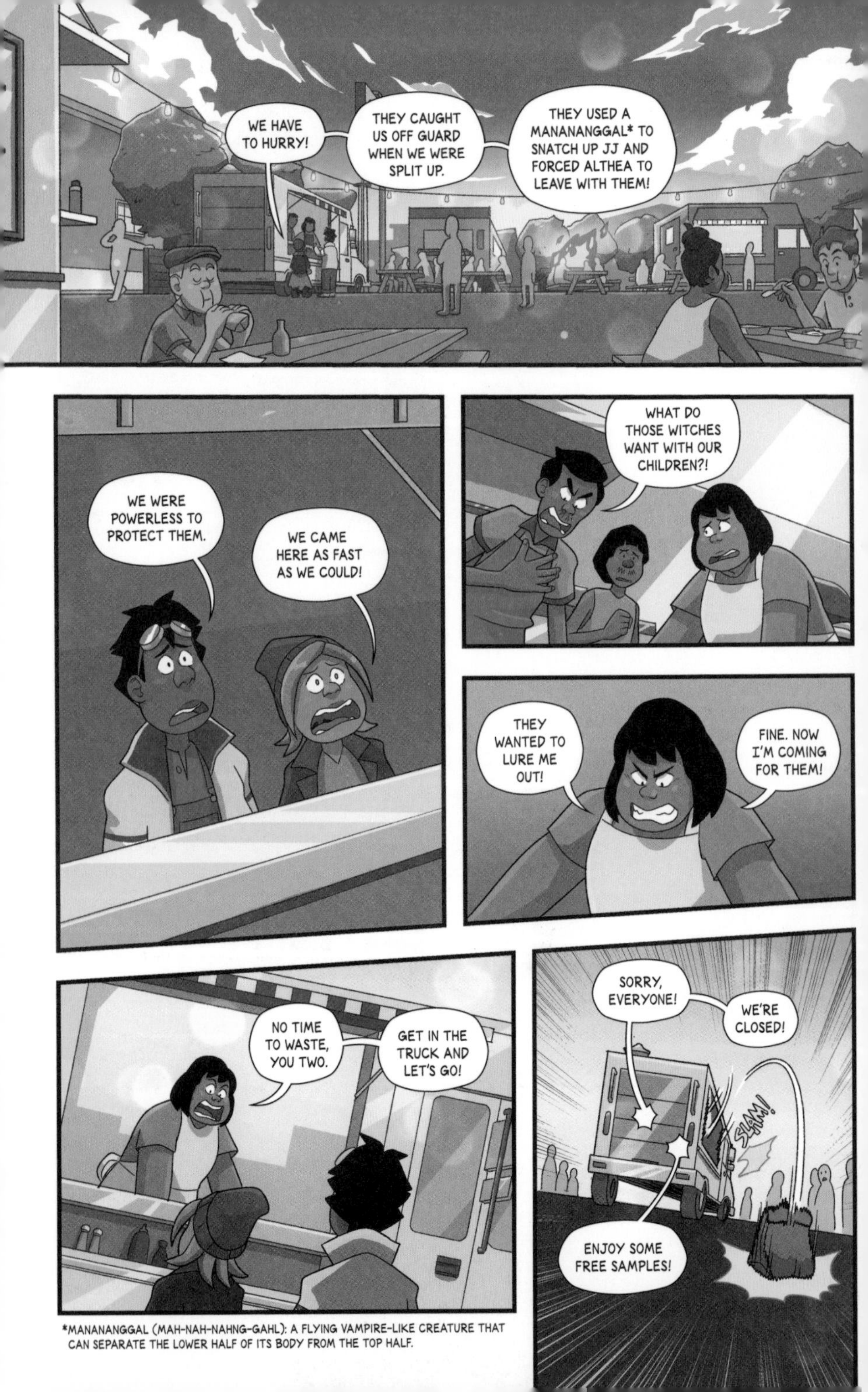
WE HAVE TO HURRY!
THEY CAUGHT US OFF GUARD WHEN WE WERE SPLIT UP.
THEY USED A MANANANGGAL* TO SNATCH UP JJ AND FORCED ALTHEA TO LEAVE WITH THEM!
WE WERE POWERLESS TO PROTECT THEM.
WE CAME HERE AS FAST AS WE COULD!
WHAT DO THOSE WITCHES WANT WITH OUR CHILDREN?!
THEY WANTED TO LURE ME OUT!
FINE. NOW I'M COMING FOR THEM!
NO TIME TO WASTE, YOU TWO.
GET IN THE TRUCK AND LET'S GO!
SORRY, EVERYONE!
WE'RE CLOSED!
SLAM!
ENJOY SOME FREE SAMPLES!

*MANANANGGAL (MAH-NAH-NAHNG-GAHL): A FLYING VAMPIRE-LIKE CREATURE THAT CAN SEPARATE THE LOWER HALF OF ITS BODY FROM THE TOP HALF.

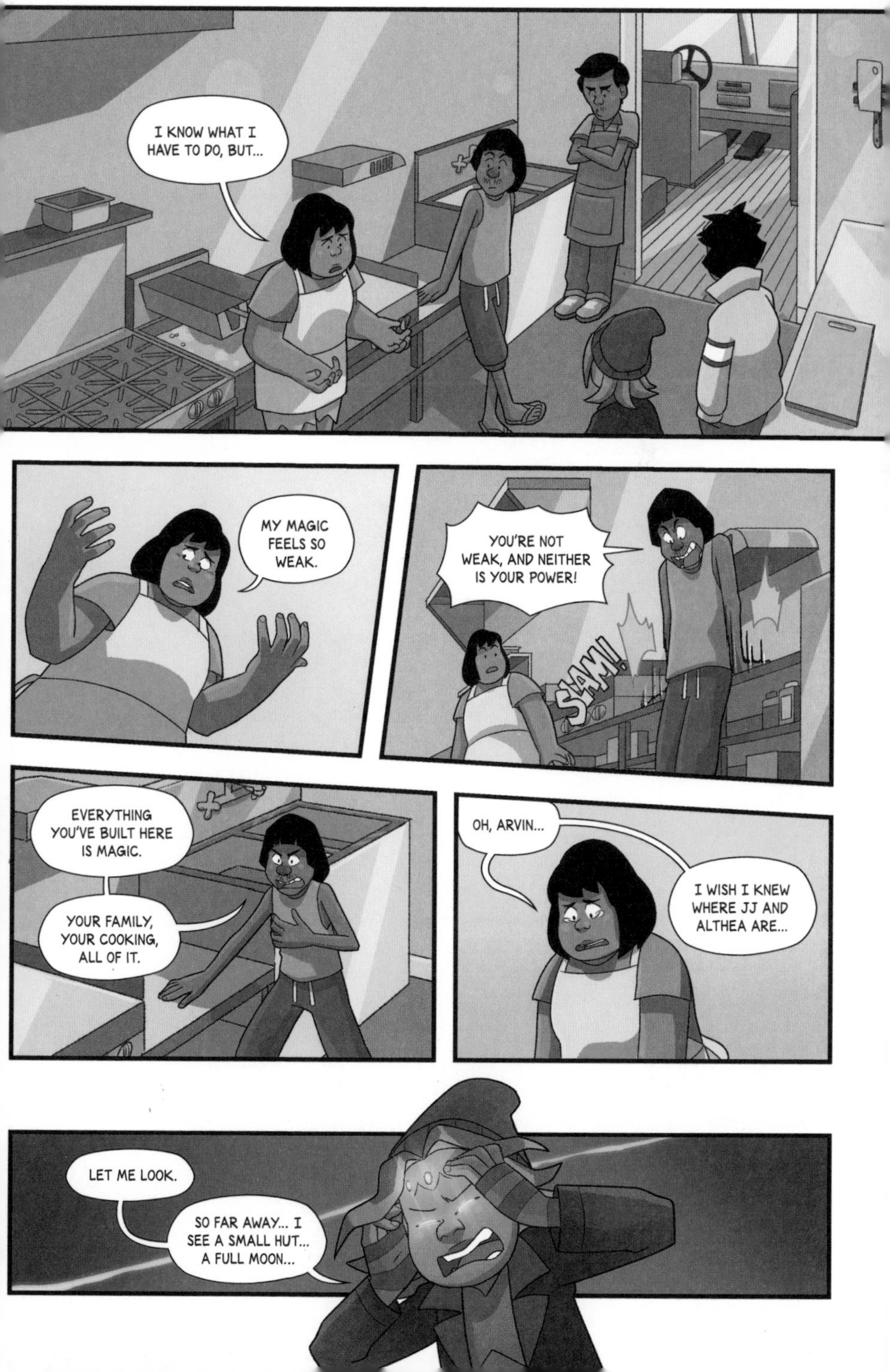
I KNOW WHAT I HAVE TO DO, BUT...
MY MAGIC FEELS SO WEAK.
YOU'RE NOT WEAK, AND NEITHER IS YOUR POWER!
SLAM!
EVERYTHING YOU'VE BUILT HERE IS MAGIC.
YOUR FAMILY, YOUR COOKING, ALL OF IT.
OH, ARVIN...
I WISH I KNEW WHERE JJ AND ALTHEA ARE...
LET ME LOOK.
SO FAR AWAY... I SEE A SMALL HUT... A FULL MOON...

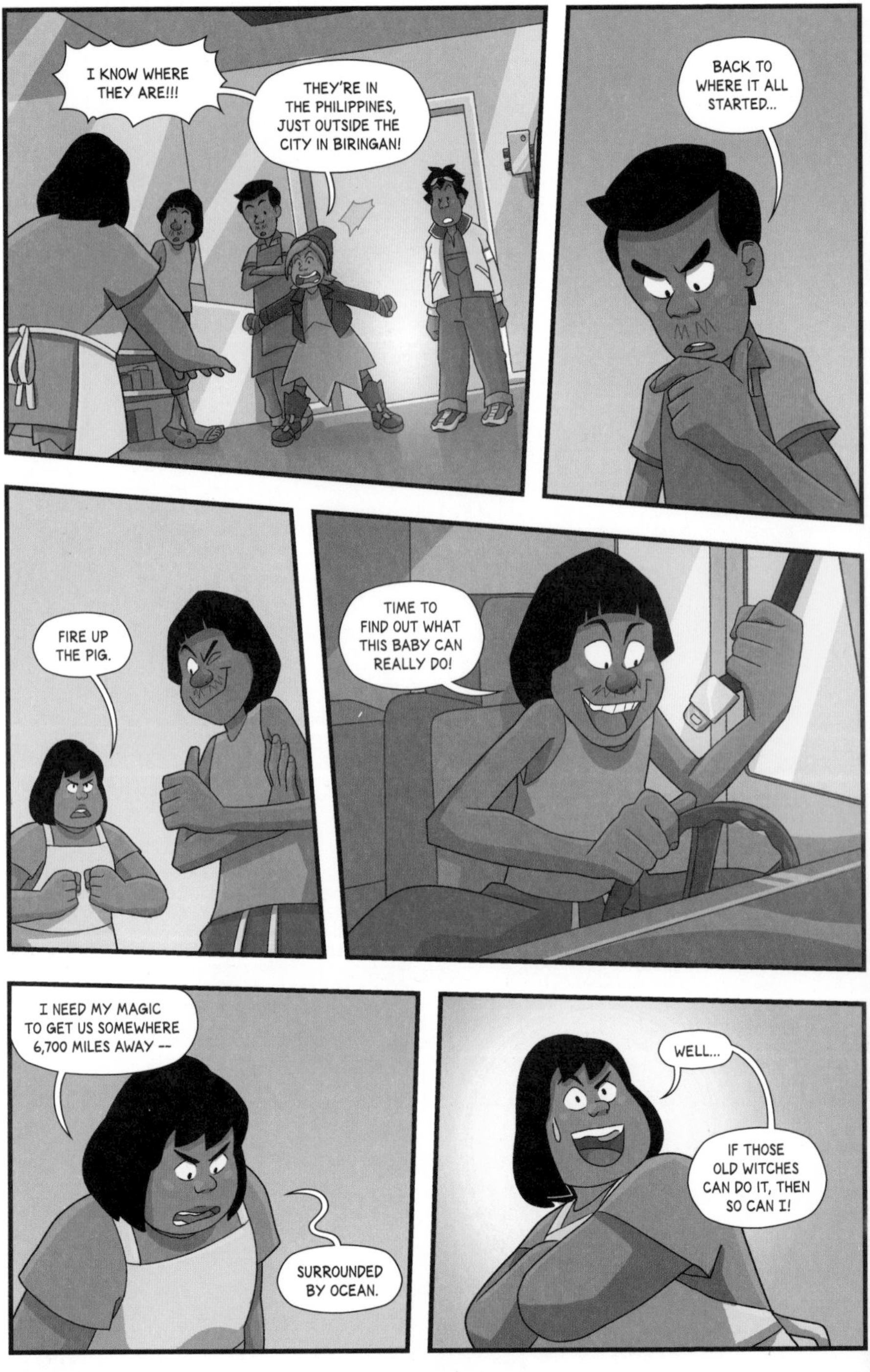
I KNOW WHERE THEY ARE!!!
THEY'RE IN THE PHILIPPINES, JUST OUTSIDE THE CITY IN BIRINGAN!
BACK TO WHERE IT ALL STARTED...
FIRE UP THE PIG.
TIME TO FIND OUT WHAT THIS BABY CAN REALLY DO!
I NEED MY MAGIC TO GET US SOMEWHERE 6,700 MILES AWAY --
SURROUNDED BY OCEAN.
WELL...
IF THOSE OLD WITCHES CAN DO IT, THEN SO CAN I!

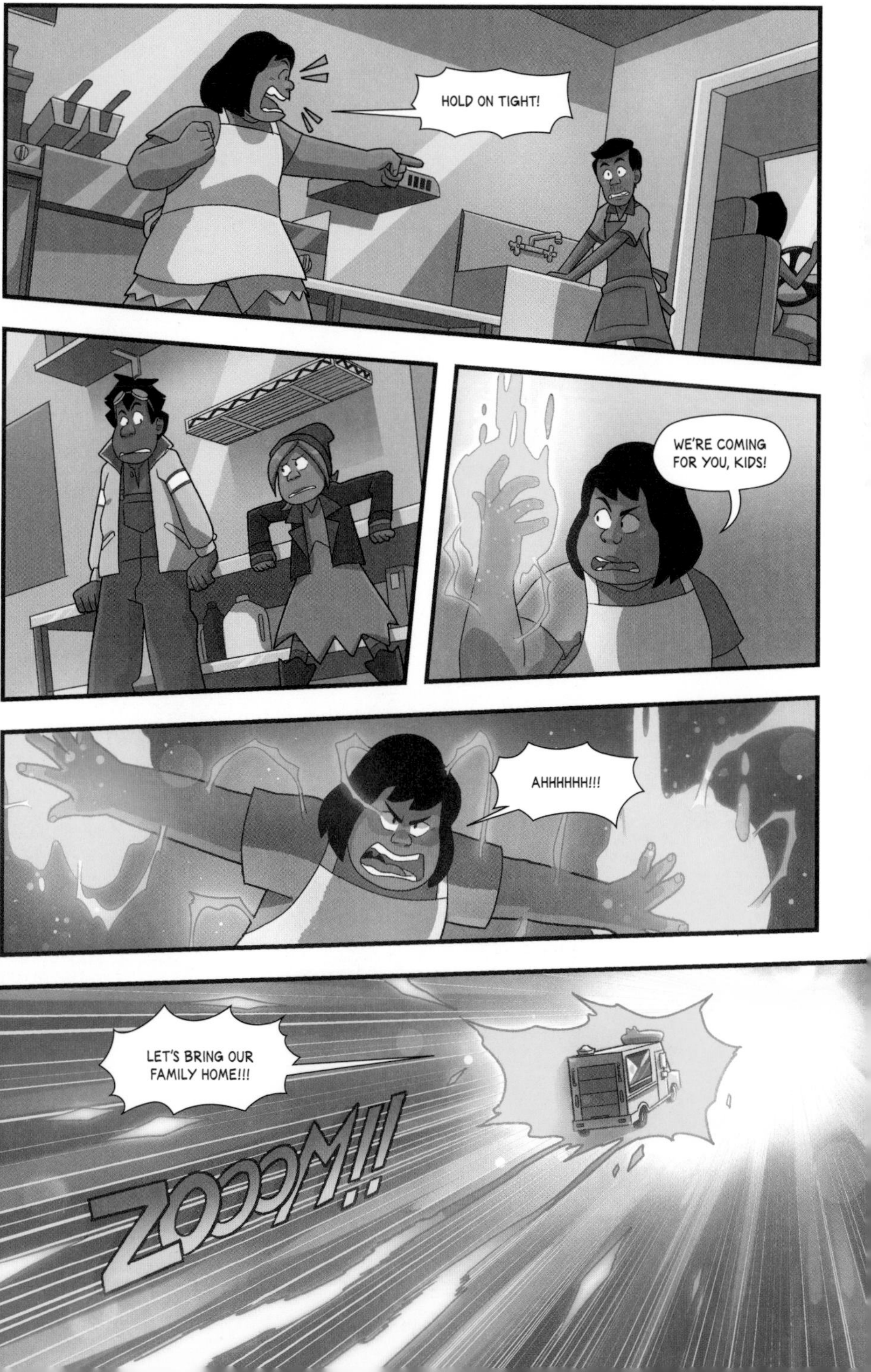
HOLD ON TIGHT!
WE'RE COMING FOR YOU, KIDS!
AHHHHHH!!!
LET'S BRING OUR FAMILY HOME!!!
ZOOOOM!!

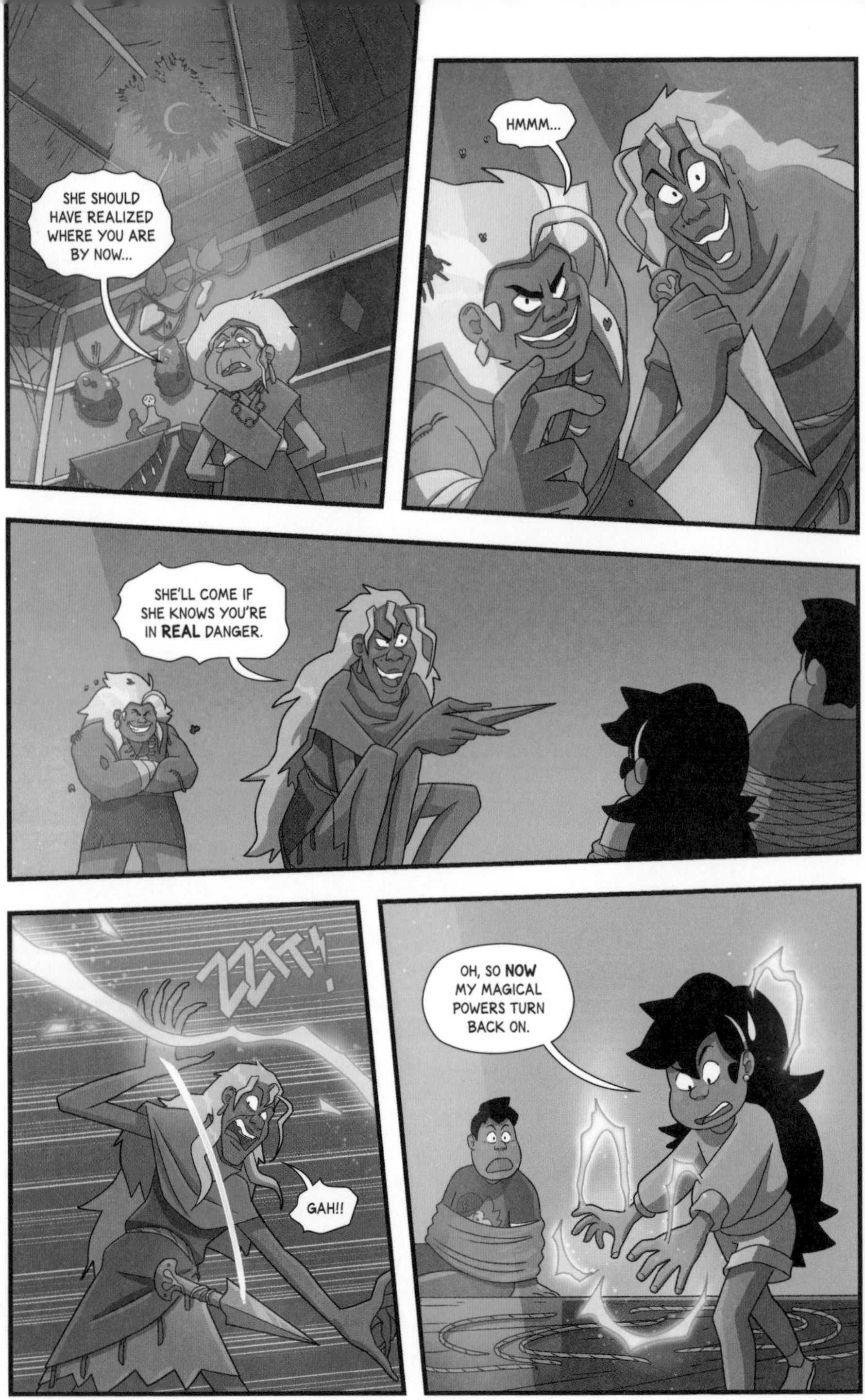
SHE SHOULD HAVE REALIZED WHERE YOU ARE BY NOW...
HMMM...
SHE'LL COME IF SHE KNOWS YOU'RE IN **REAL** DANGER.
ZZTTT!
GAH!!
OH, SO **NOW** MY MAGICAL POWERS TURN BACK ON.

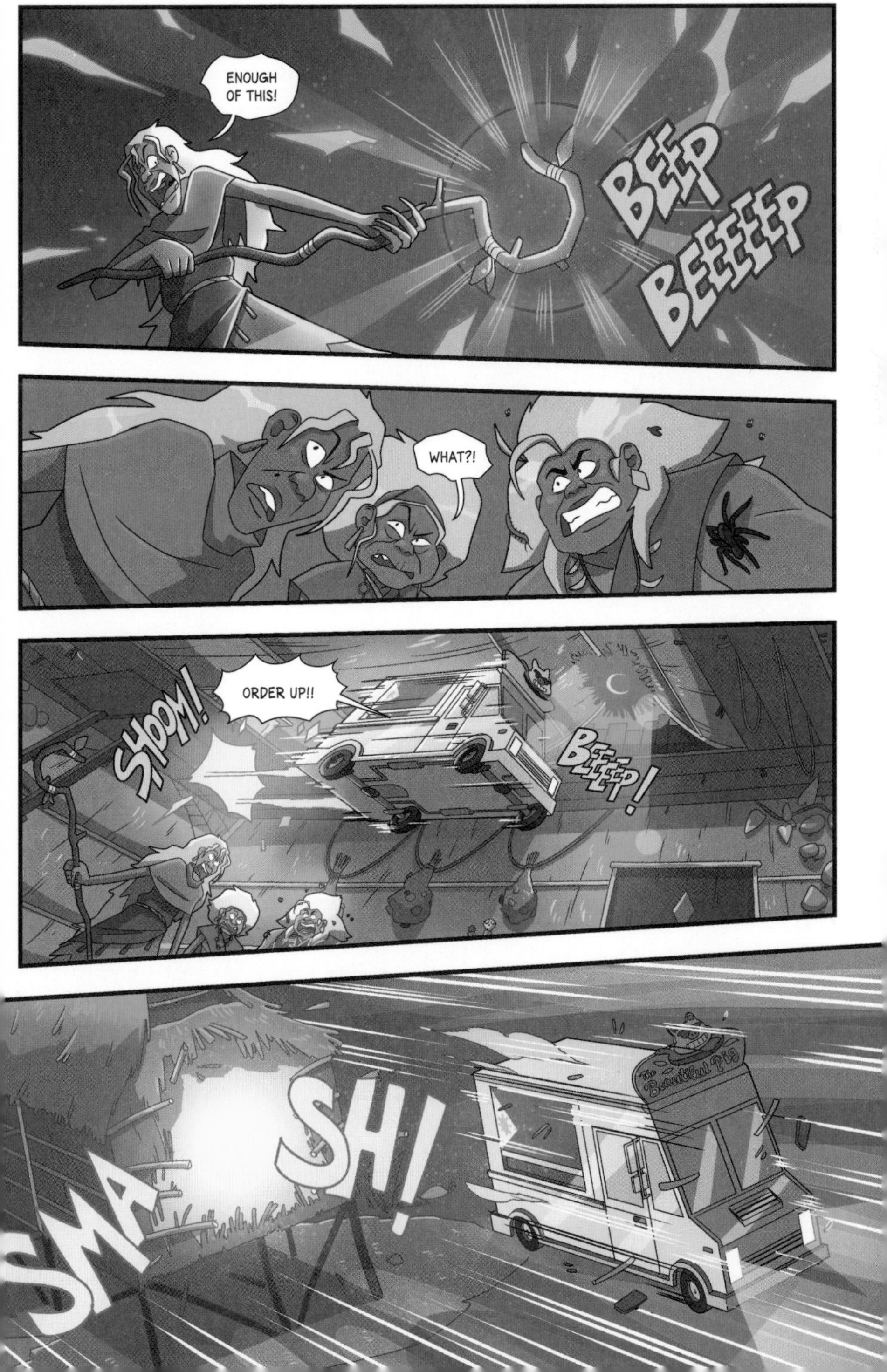
ENOUGH OF THIS!
BEEP BEEEEEP
WHAT?!
ORDER UP!!
SHOOM!
BEEEP!
The Beautiful Pig
SMASH!

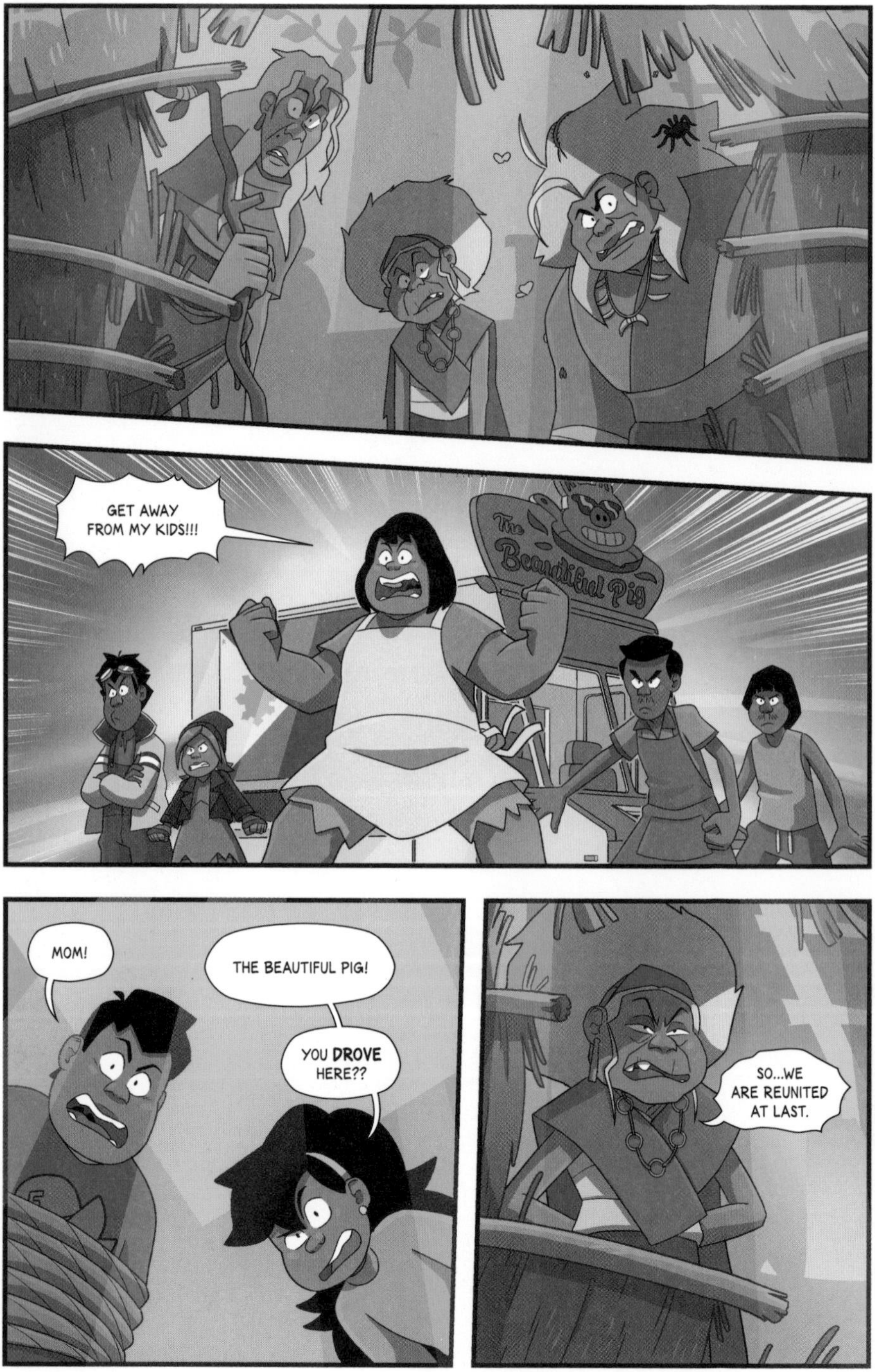
GET AWAY FROM MY KIDS!!!
The Beautiful Pig
MOM!
THE BEAUTIFUL PIG!
YOU **DROVE** HERE??
SO...WE ARE REUNITED AT LAST.

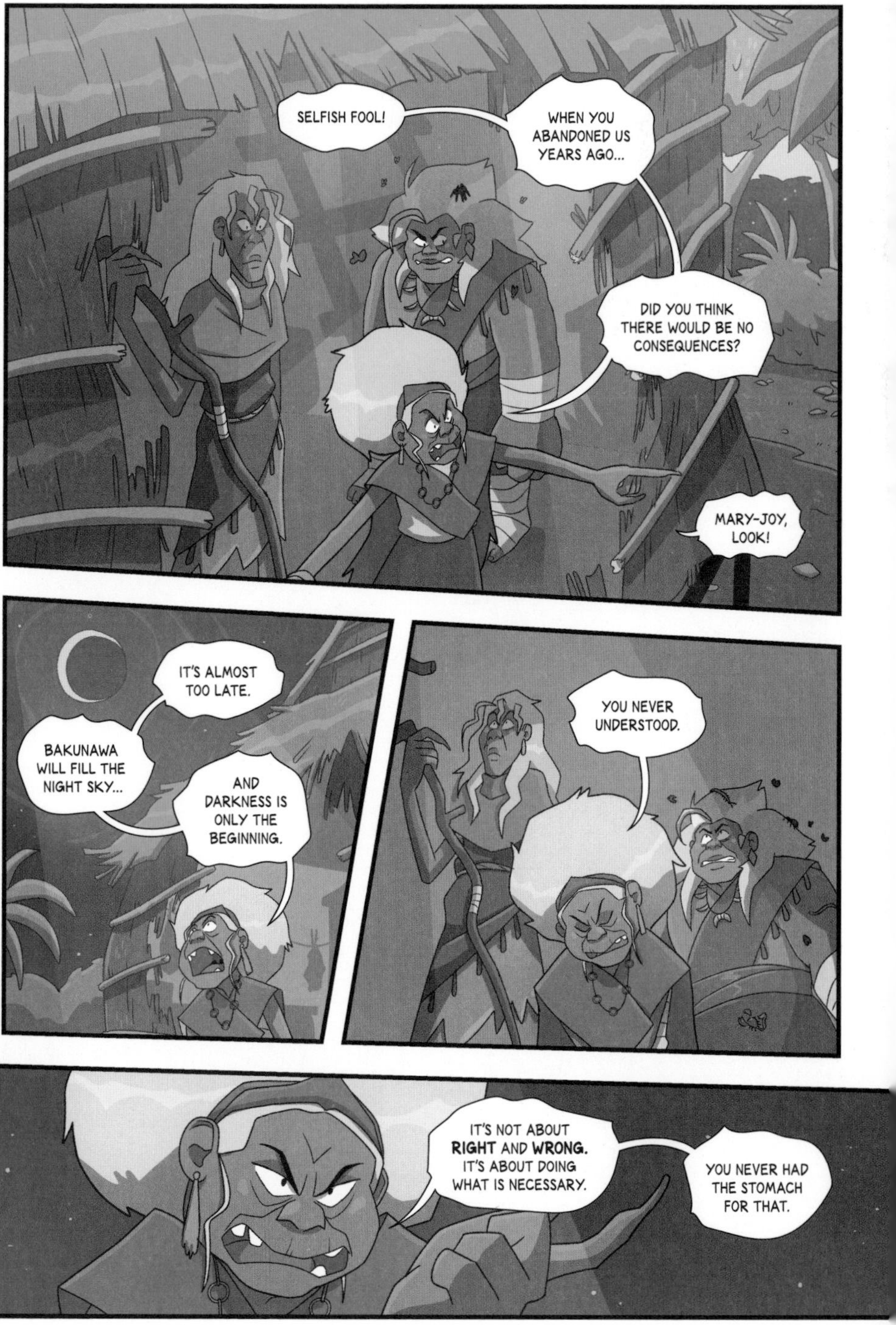
SELFISH FOOL!
WHEN YOU ABANDONED US YEARS AGO...
DID YOU THINK THERE WOULD BE NO CONSEQUENCES?
MARY-JOY, LOOK!
IT'S ALMOST TOO LATE.
BAKUNAWA WILL FILL THE NIGHT SKY...
AND DARKNESS IS ONLY THE BEGINNING.
YOU NEVER UNDERSTOOD.
IT'S NOT ABOUT **RIGHT** AND **WRONG.** IT'S ABOUT DOING WHAT IS NECESSARY.
YOU NEVER HAD THE STOMACH FOR THAT.

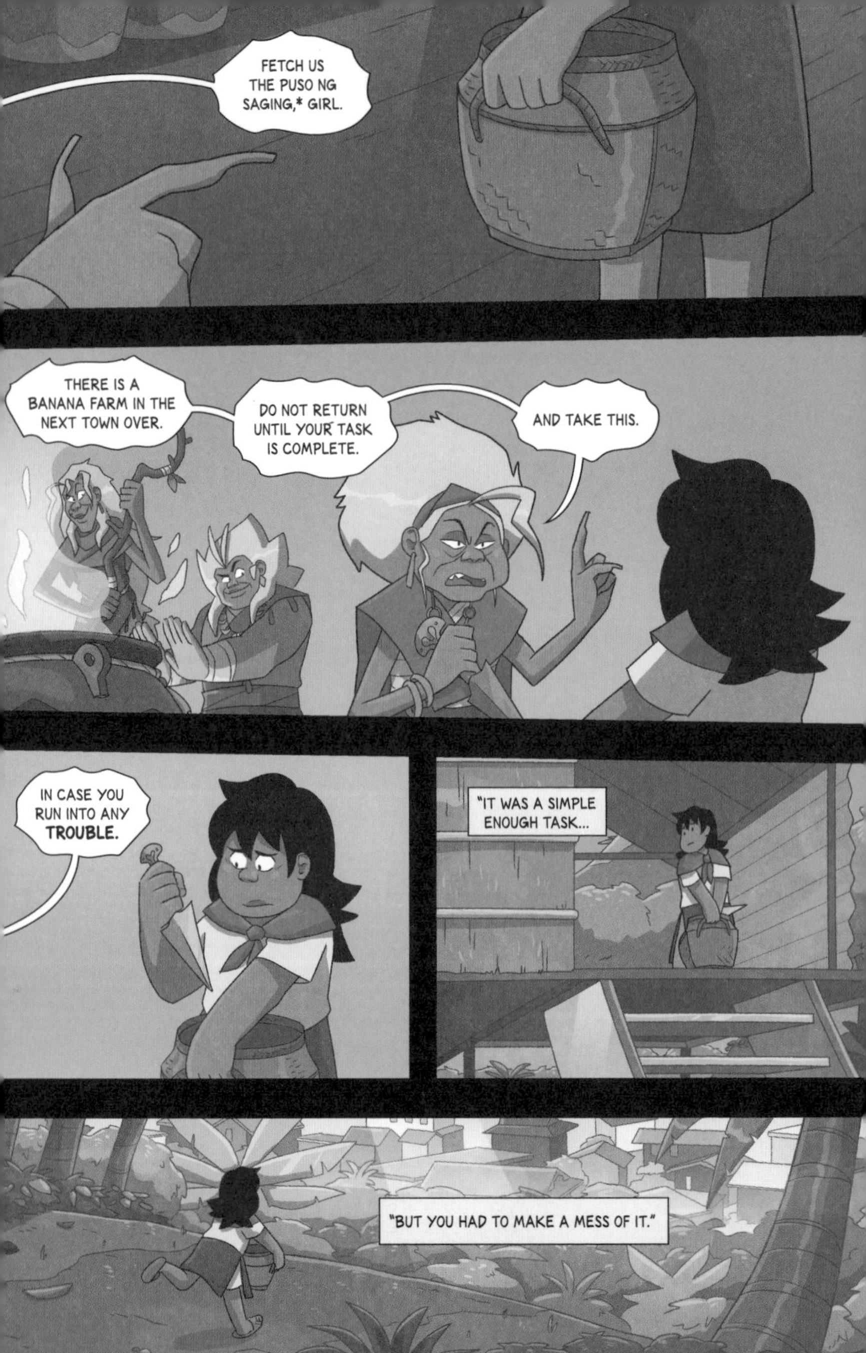
FETCH US THE PUSO NG SAGING,* GIRL.
THERE IS A BANANA FARM IN THE NEXT TOWN OVER.
DO NOT RETURN UNTIL YOUR TASK IS COMPLETE.
AND TAKE THIS.
IN CASE YOU RUN INTO ANY **TROUBLE.**
"IT WAS A SIMPLE ENOUGH TASK...
"BUT YOU HAD TO MAKE A MESS OF IT."

*PUSO NG SAGING (POO-SOH NAHNG SAHG-EENG) TRANSLATES TO "HEART OF THE BANANA," AND IT REFERS TO THE BLOSSOM OF A BANANA TREE.

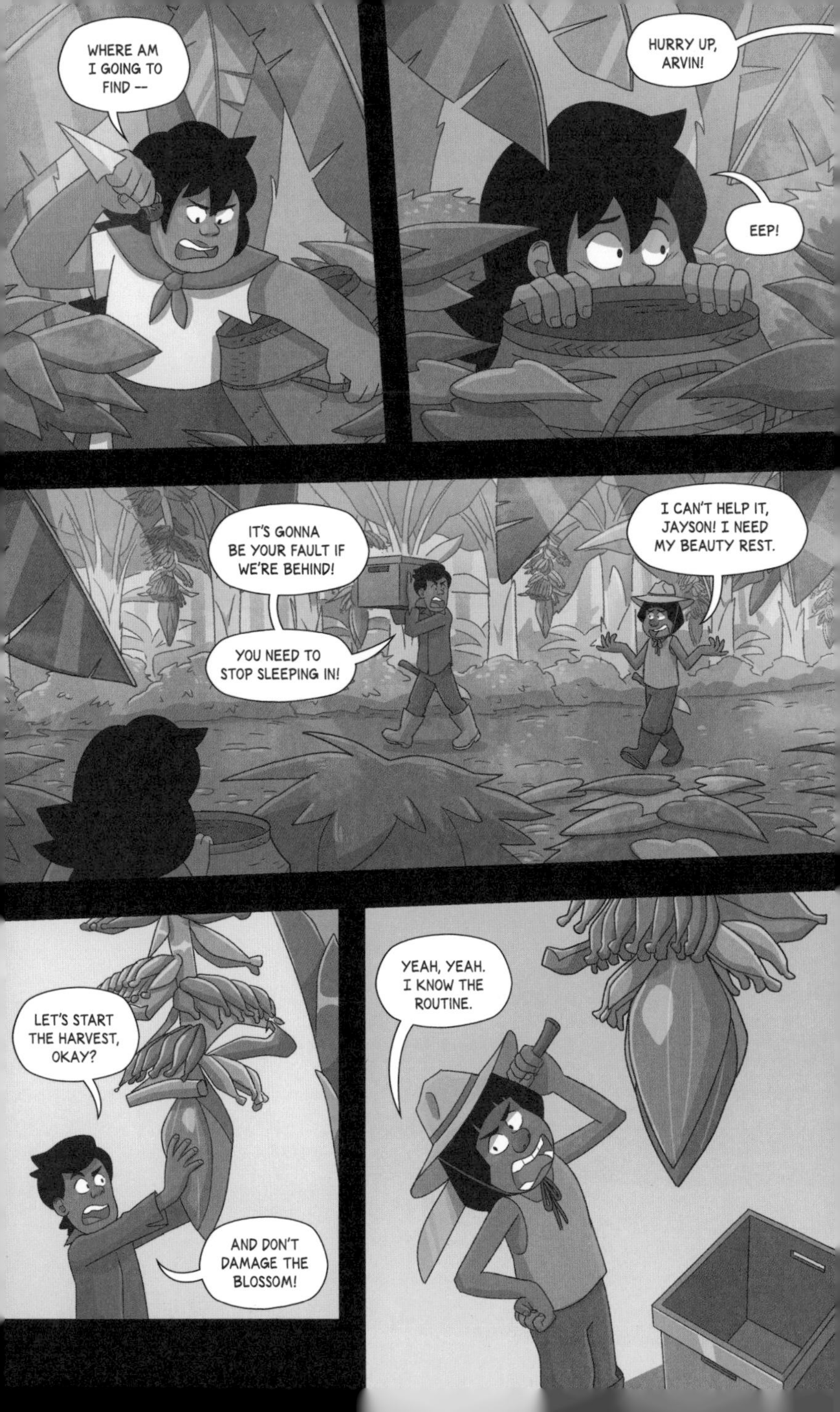
WHERE AM I GOING TO FIND --
HURRY UP, ARVIN!
EEP!
IT'S GONNA BE YOUR FAULT IF WE'RE BEHIND!
YOU NEED TO STOP SLEEPING IN!
I CAN'T HELP IT, JAYSON! I NEED MY BEAUTY REST.
LET'S START THE HARVEST, OKAY?
AND DON'T DAMAGE THE BLOSSOM!
YEAH, YEAH. I KNOW THE ROUTINE.

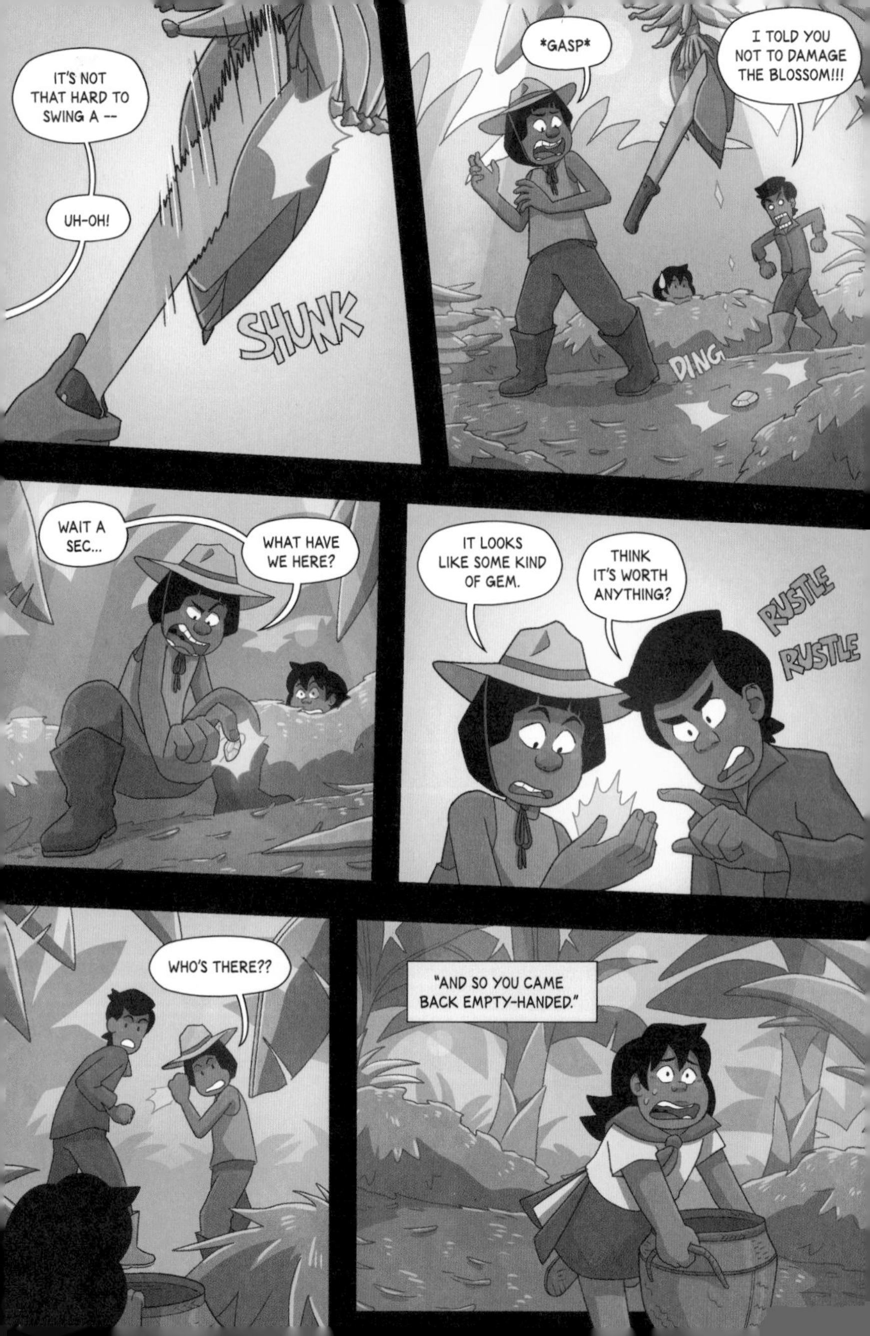
IT'S NOT THAT HARD TO SWING A --
UH-OH!
SHUNK
GASP
I TOLD YOU NOT TO DAMAGE THE BLOSSOM!!!
DING
WAIT A SEC...
WHAT HAVE WE HERE?
IT LOOKS LIKE SOME KIND OF GEM.
THINK IT'S WORTH ANYTHING?
RUSTLE
RUSTLE
WHO'S THERE??
"AND SO YOU CAME BACK EMPTY-HANDED."

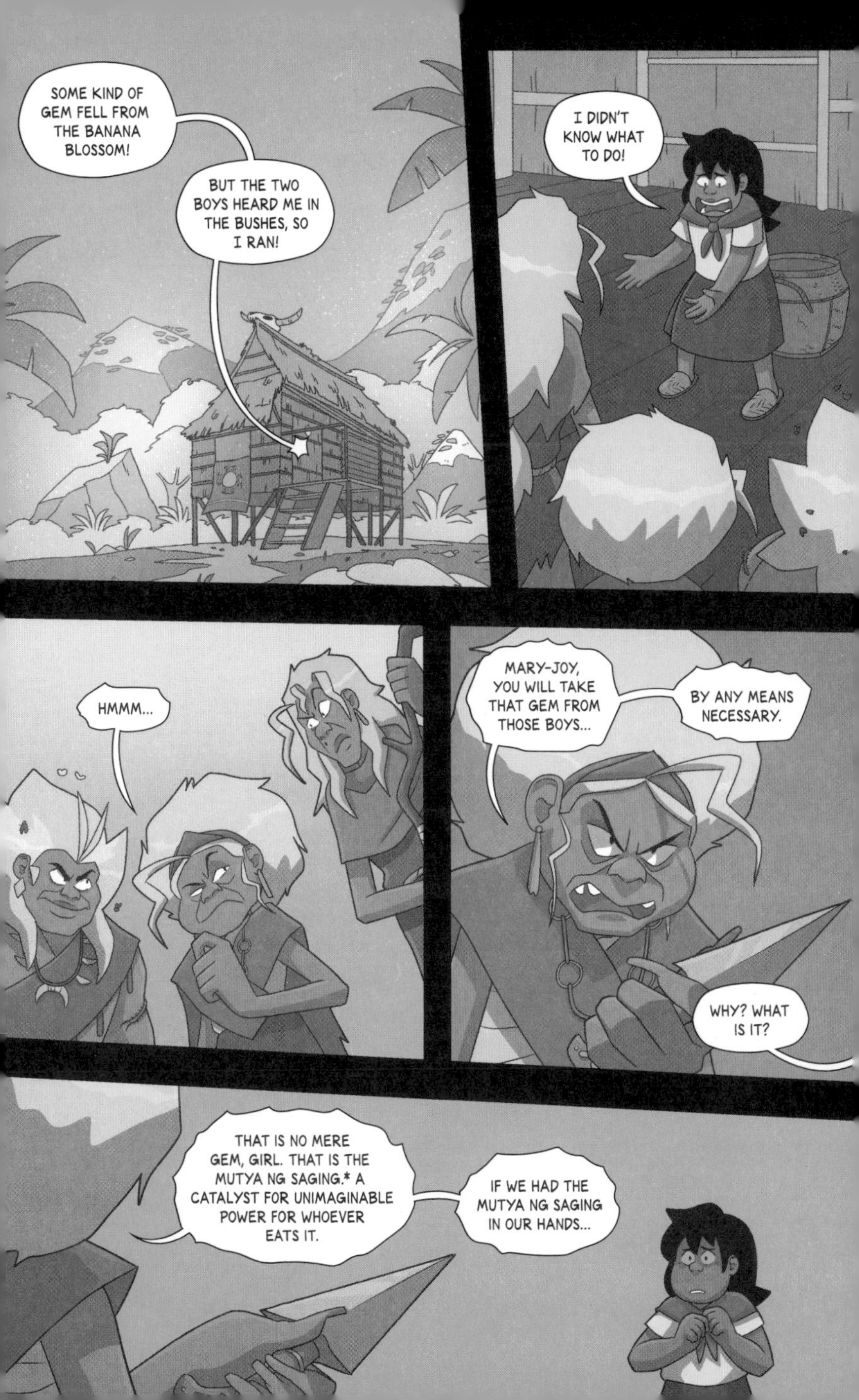
SOME KIND OF GEM FELL FROM THE BANANA BLOSSOM!
BUT THE TWO BOYS HEARD ME IN THE BUSHES, SO I RAN!
I DIDN'T KNOW WHAT TO DO!
HMMM...
MARY-JOY, YOU WILL TAKE THAT GEM FROM THOSE BOYS...
BY ANY MEANS NECESSARY.
WHY? WHAT IS IT?
THAT IS NO MERE GEM, GIRL. THAT IS THE MUTYA NG SAGING.* A CATALYST FOR UNIMAGINABLE POWER FOR WHOEVER EATS IT.
IF WE HAD THE MUTYA NG SAGING IN OUR HANDS...

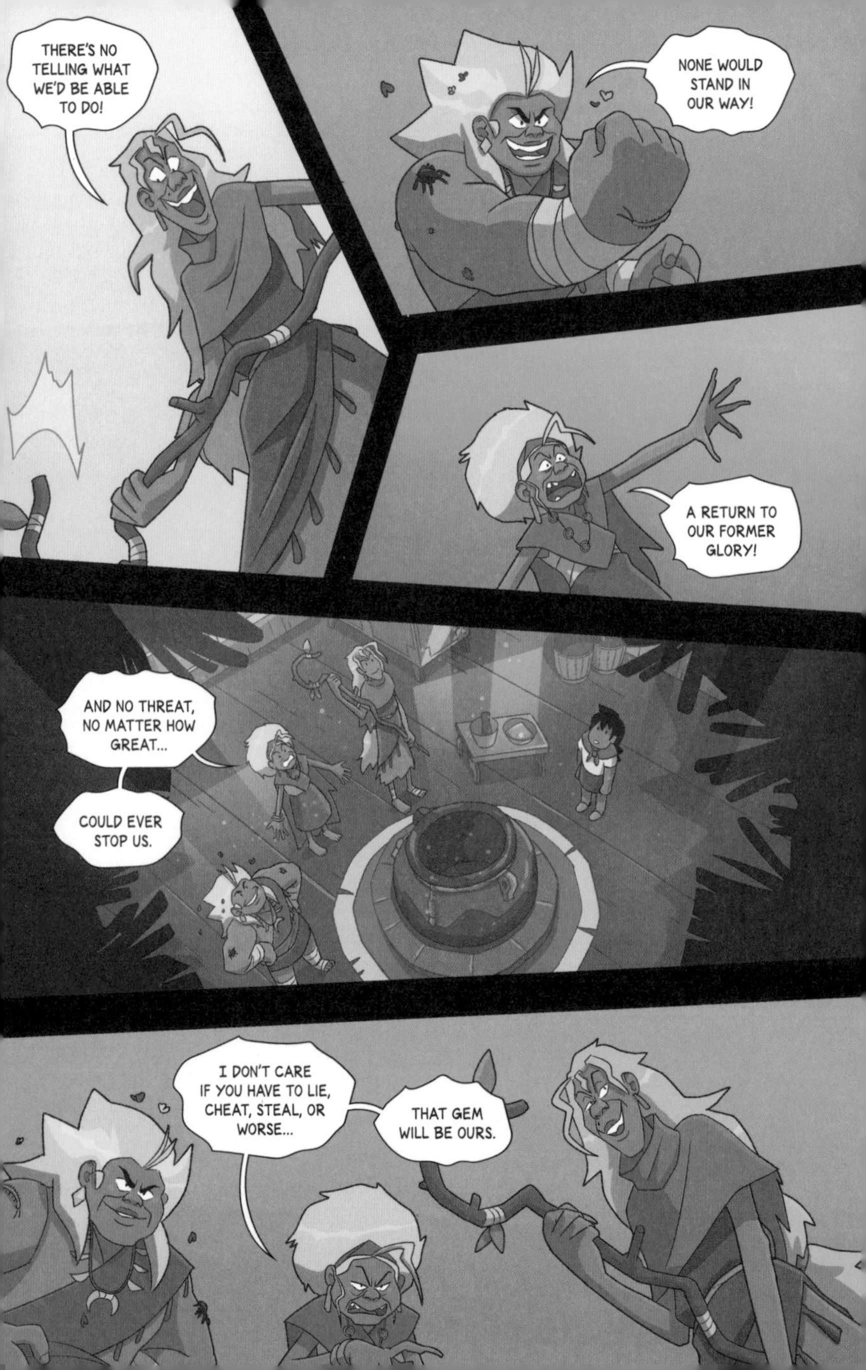
THERE'S NO TELLING WHAT WE'D BE ABLE TO DO!
NONE WOULD STAND IN OUR WAY!
A RETURN TO OUR FORMER GLORY!
AND NO THREAT, NO MATTER HOW GREAT...
COULD EVER STOP US.
I DON'T CARE IF YOU HAVE TO LIE, CHEAT, STEAL, OR WORSE...
THAT GEM WILL BE OURS.

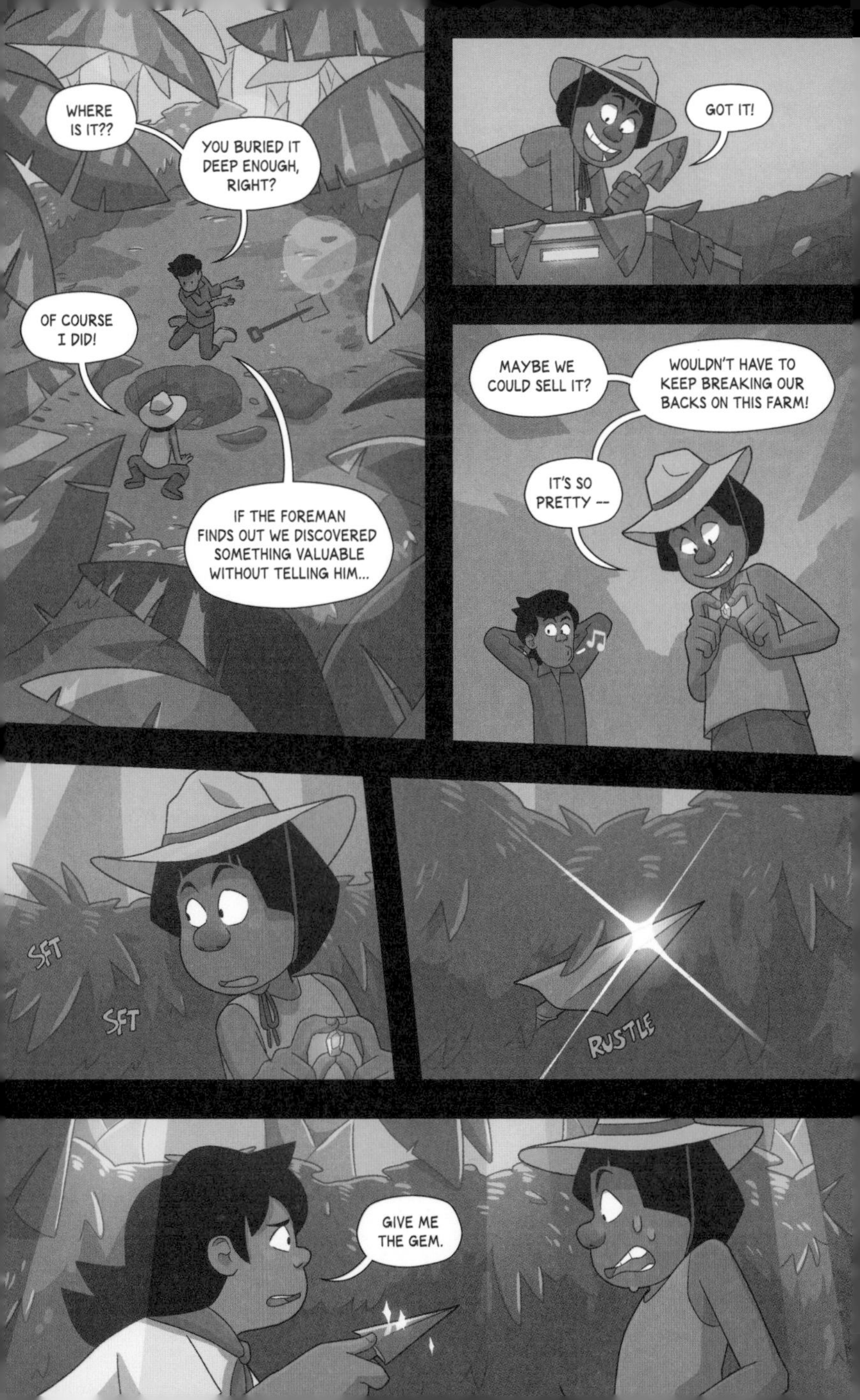
WHERE IS IT??
YOU BURIED IT DEEP ENOUGH, RIGHT?
OF COURSE I DID!
IF THE FOREMAN FINDS OUT WE DISCOVERED SOMETHING VALUABLE WITHOUT TELLING HIM...
GOT IT!
MAYBE WE COULD SELL IT?
WOULDN'T HAVE TO KEEP BREAKING OUR BACKS ON THIS FARM!
IT'S SO PRETTY --
SFT
SFT
RUSTLE
GIVE ME THE GEM.

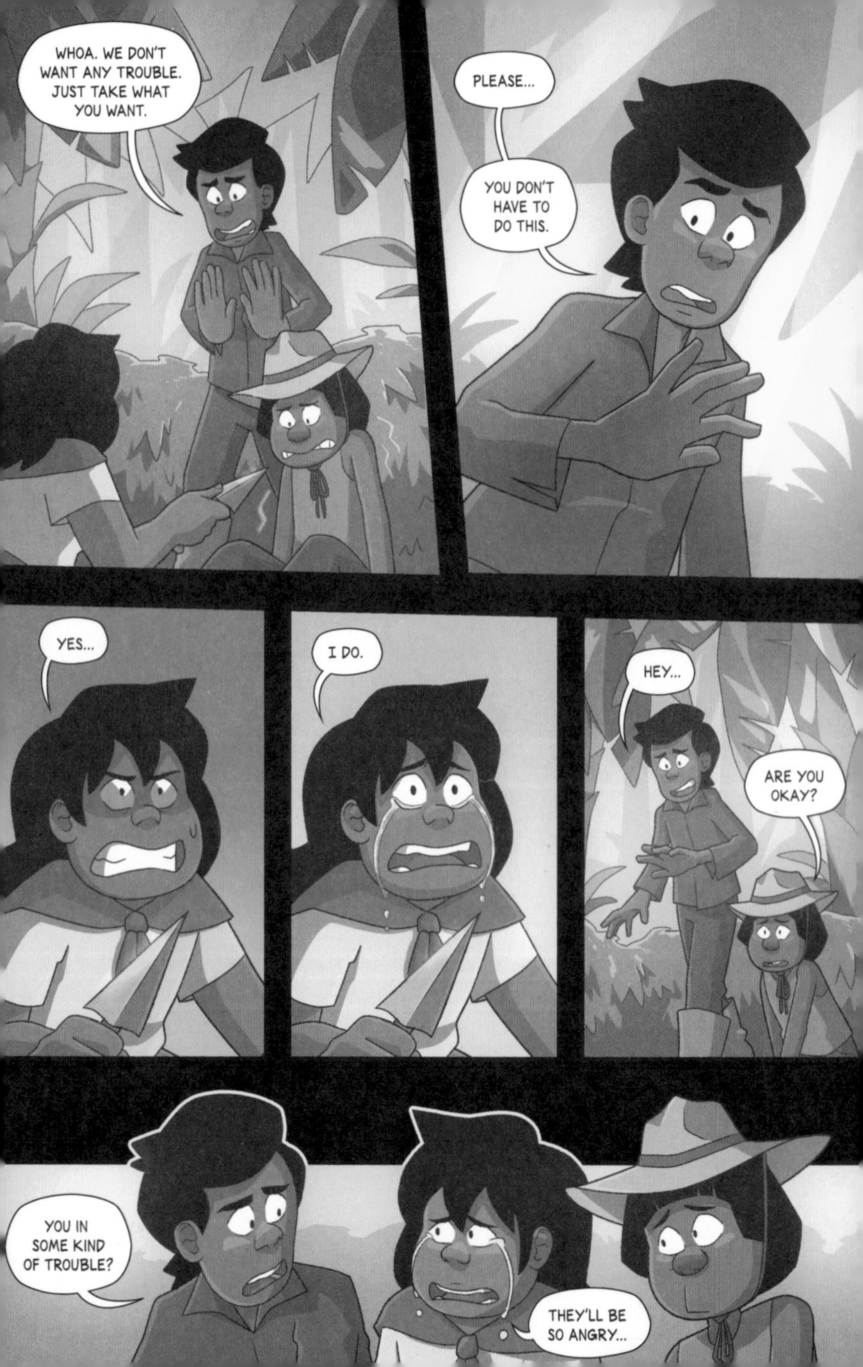
WHOA. WE DON'T WANT ANY TROUBLE. JUST TAKE WHAT YOU WANT.
PLEASE...
YOU DON'T HAVE TO DO THIS.
YES...
I DO.
HEY...
ARE YOU OKAY?
YOU IN SOME KIND OF TROUBLE?
THEY'LL BE SO ANGRY...

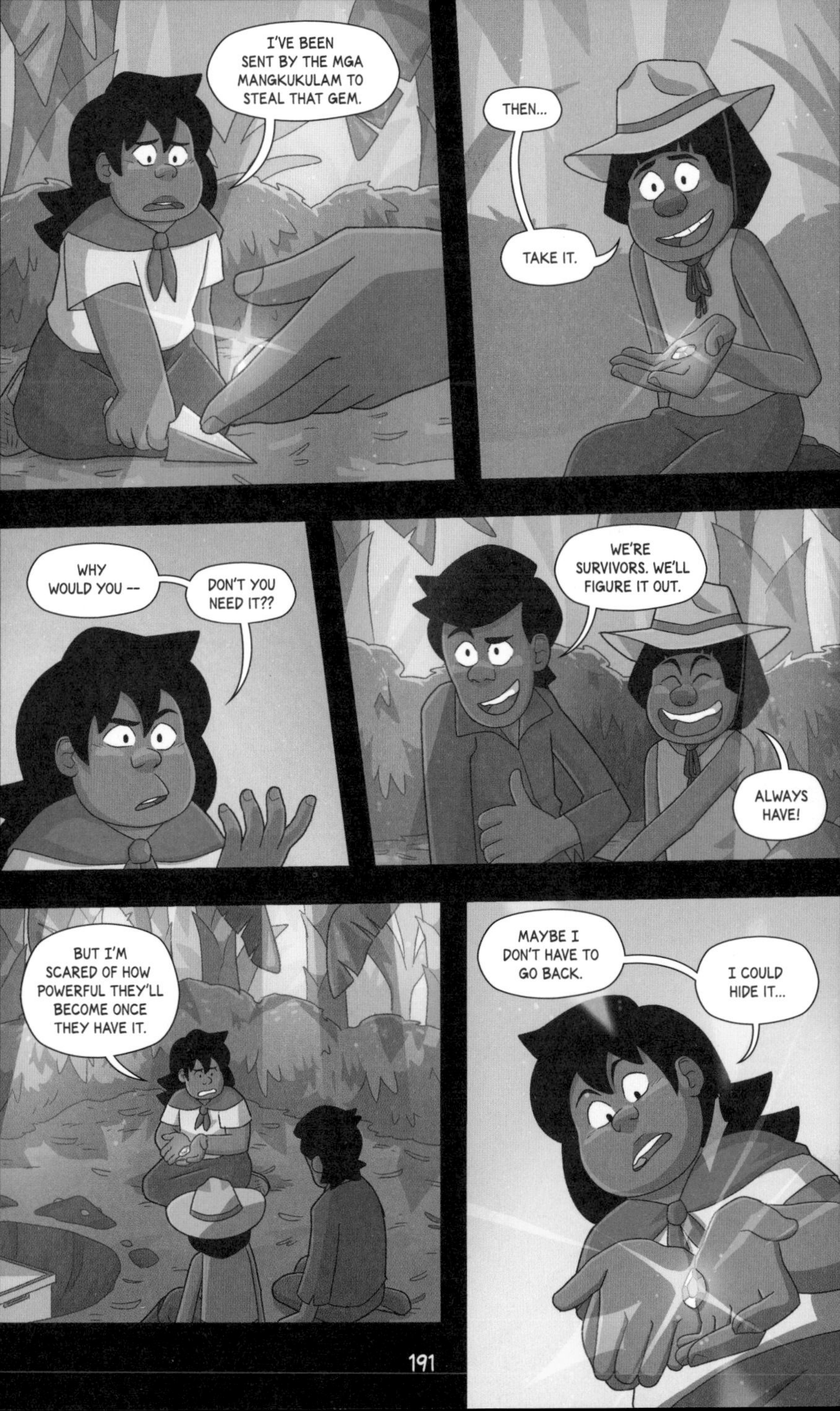
I'VE BEEN SENT BY THE MGA MANGKUKULAM TO STEAL THAT GEM.
THEN...
TAKE IT.
WHY WOULD YOU --
DON'T YOU NEED IT??
WE'RE SURVIVORS. WE'LL FIGURE IT OUT.
ALWAYS HAVE!
BUT I'M SCARED OF HOW POWERFUL THEY'LL BECOME ONCE THEY HAVE IT.
MAYBE I DON'T HAVE TO GO BACK.
I COULD HIDE IT...

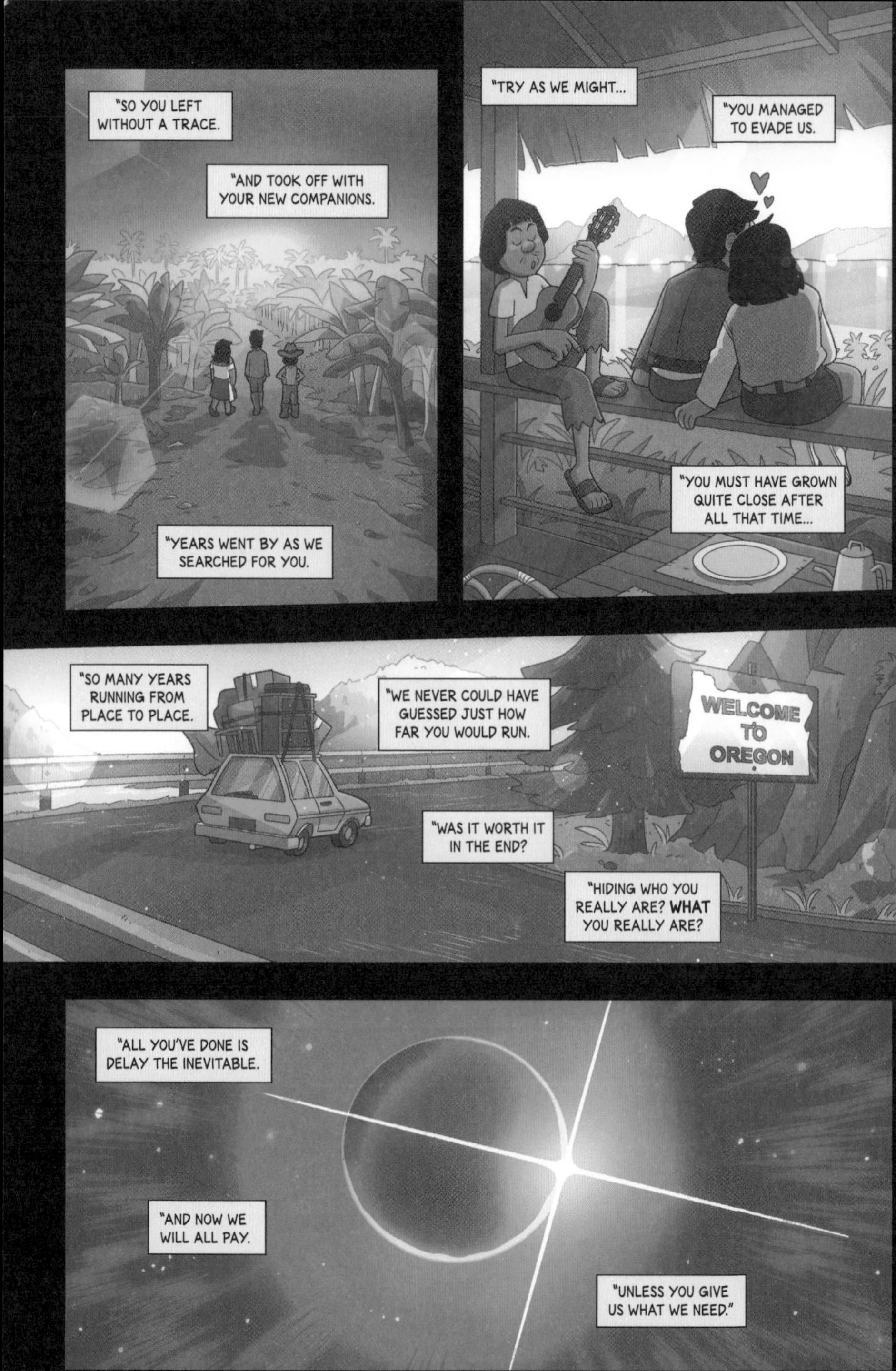
"SO YOU LEFT WITHOUT A TRACE.
"AND TOOK OFF WITH YOUR NEW COMPANIONS.
"YEARS WENT BY AS WE SEARCHED FOR YOU.
"TRY AS WE MIGHT...
"YOU MANAGED TO EVADE US.
"YOU MUST HAVE GROWN QUITE CLOSE AFTER ALL THAT TIME...
"SO MANY YEARS RUNNING FROM PLACE TO PLACE.
"WE NEVER COULD HAVE GUESSED JUST HOW FAR YOU WOULD RUN.
WELCOME TO OREGON
"WAS IT WORTH IT IN THE END?
"HIDING WHO YOU REALLY ARE? **WHAT** YOU REALLY ARE?
"ALL YOU'VE DONE IS DELAY THE INEVITABLE.
"AND NOW WE WILL ALL PAY.
"UNLESS YOU GIVE US WHAT WE NEED."

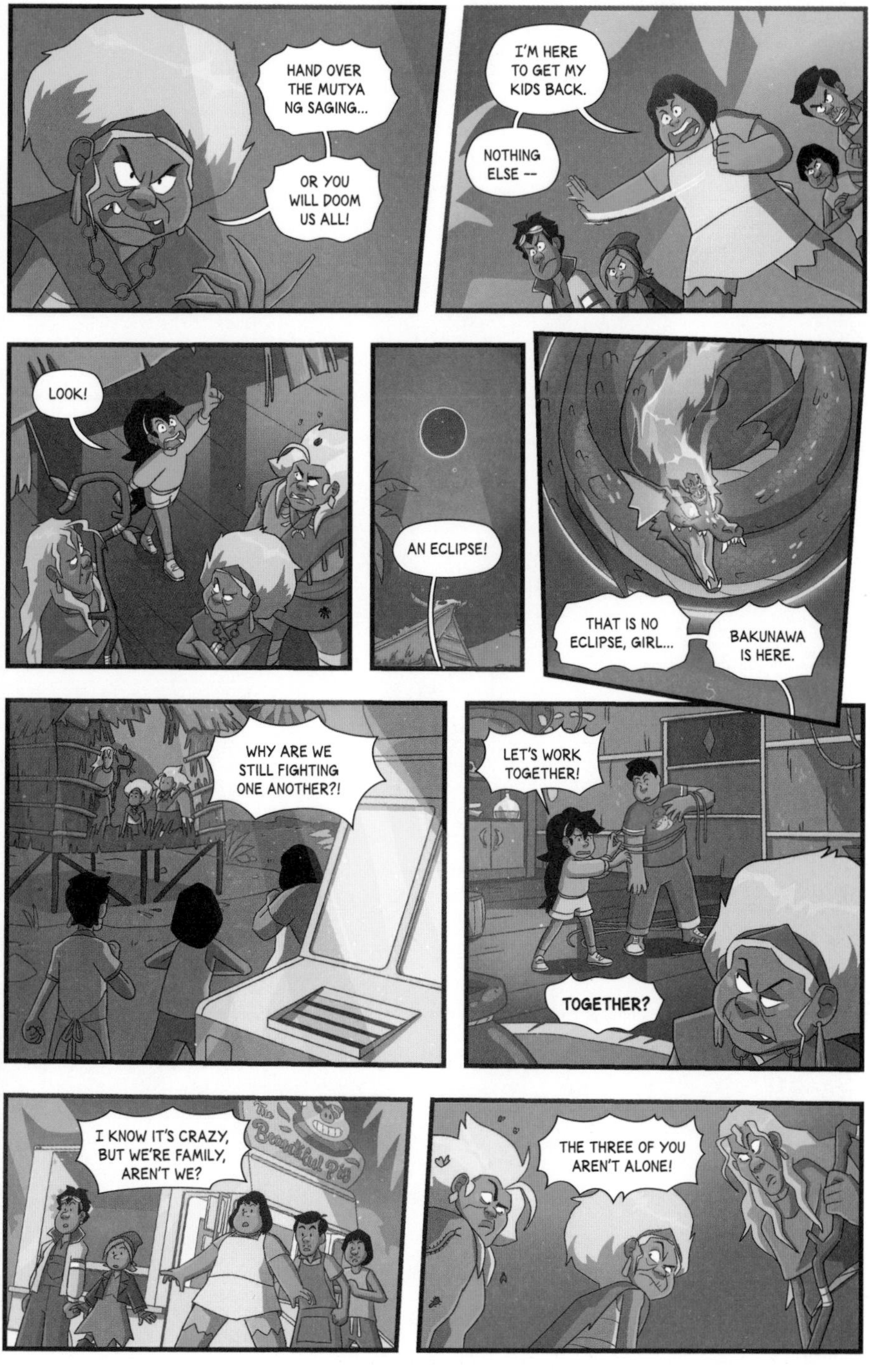
HAND OVER THE MUTYA NG SAGING...
OR YOU WILL DOOM US ALL!
I'M HERE TO GET MY KIDS BACK.
NOTHING ELSE --
LOOK!
AN ECLIPSE!
THAT IS NO ECLIPSE, GIRL...
BAKUNAWA IS HERE.
WHY ARE WE STILL FIGHTING ONE ANOTHER?!
LET'S WORK TOGETHER!
TOGETHER?
I KNOW IT'S CRAZY, BUT WE'RE FAMILY, AREN'T WE?
The Beautiful Pig
THE THREE OF YOU AREN'T ALONE!

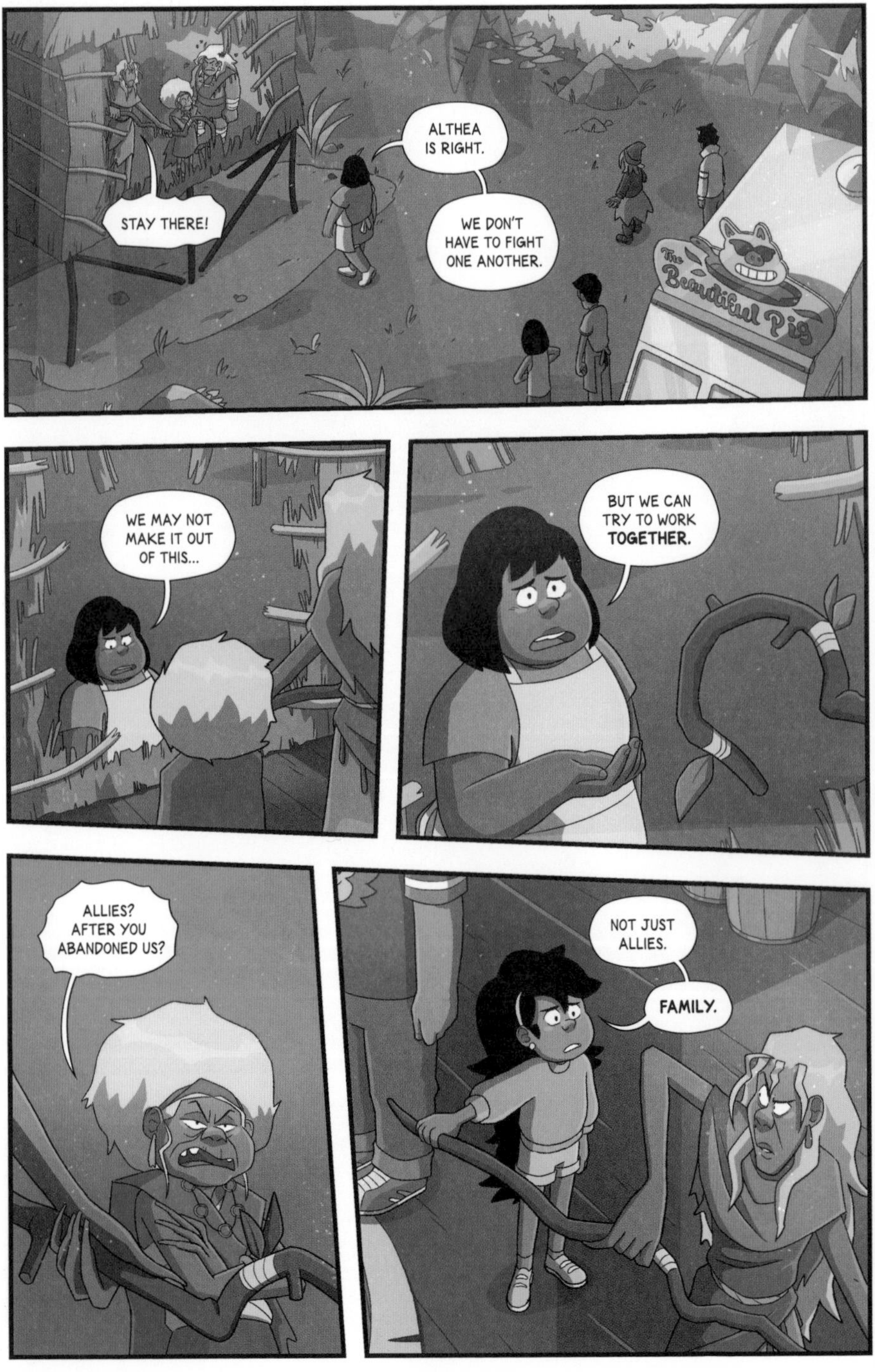
STAY THERE!
ALTHEA IS RIGHT.
WE DON'T HAVE TO FIGHT ONE ANOTHER.
The Beautiful Pig
WE MAY NOT MAKE IT OUT OF THIS...
BUT WE CAN TRY TO WORK **TOGETHER.**
ALLIES? AFTER YOU ABANDONED US?
NOT JUST ALLIES.
FAMILY.

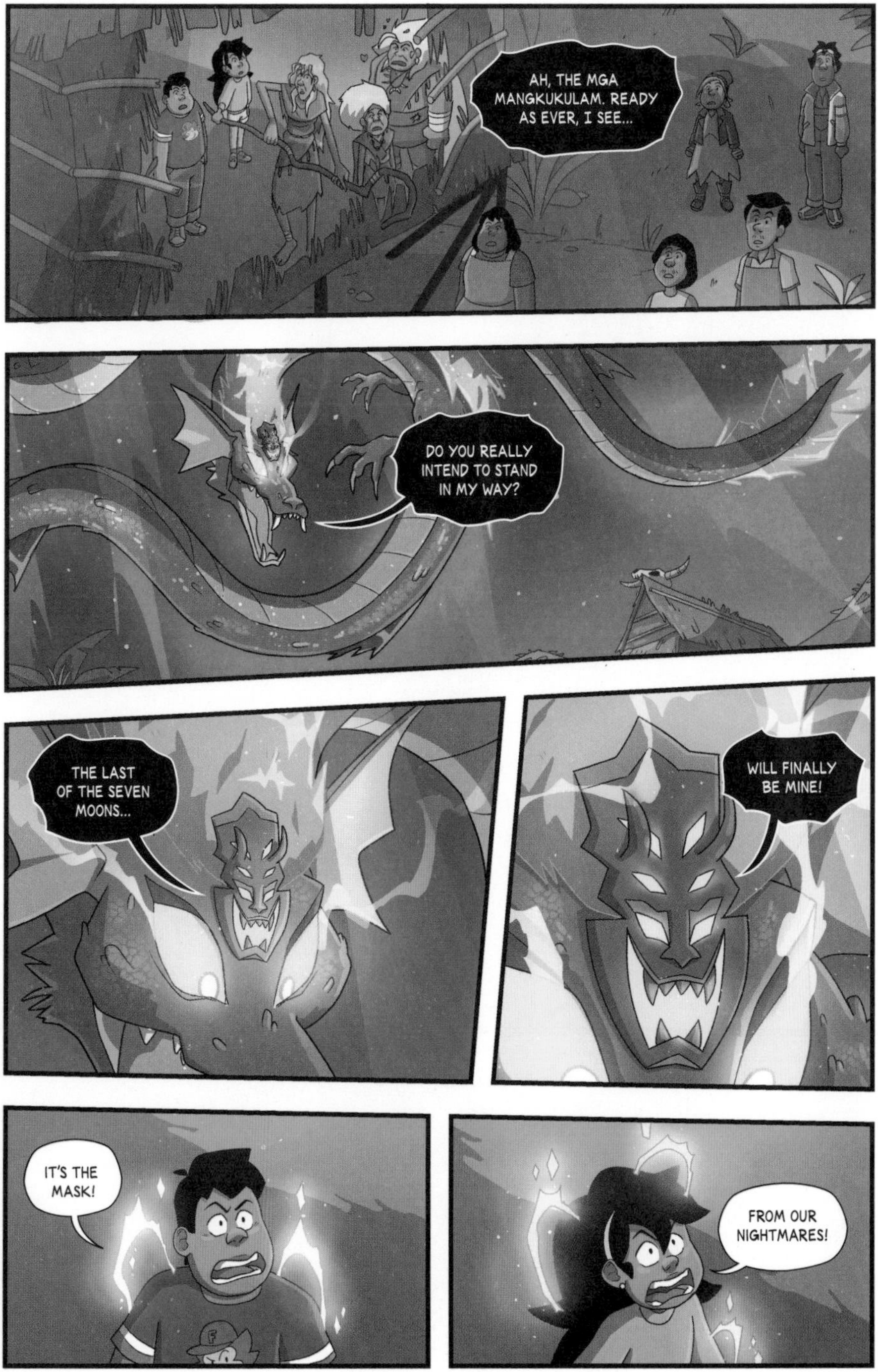
AH, THE MGA MANGKUKULAM. READY AS EVER, I SEE...
DO YOU REALLY INTEND TO STAND IN MY WAY?
THE LAST OF THE SEVEN MOONS...
WILL FINALLY BE MINE!
IT'S THE MASK!
FROM OUR NIGHTMARES!

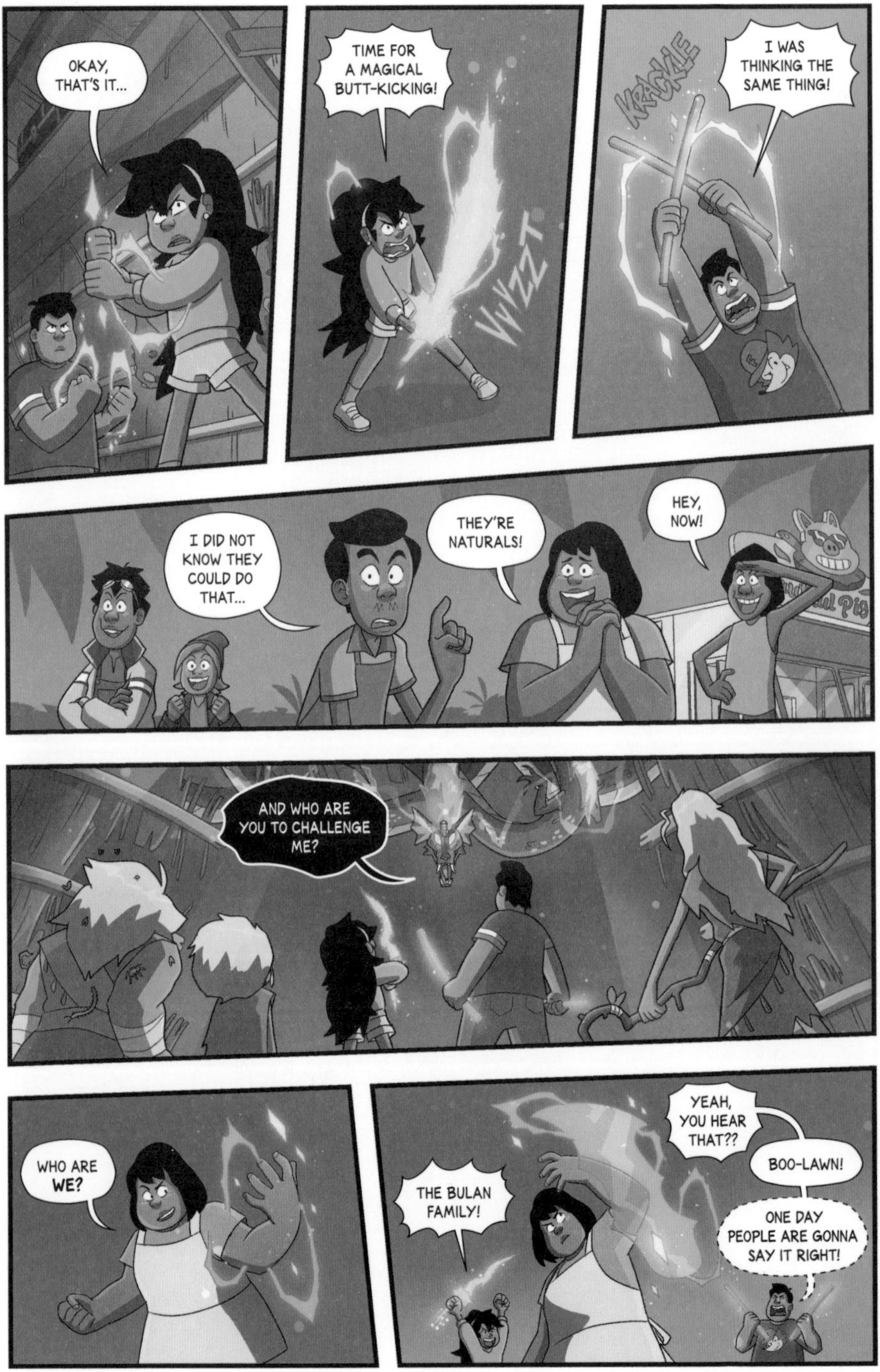
OKAY, THAT'S IT...
TIME FOR A MAGICAL BUTT-KICKING!
VVVZZT
KRACKLE
I WAS THINKING THE SAME THING!
I DID NOT KNOW THEY COULD DO THAT...
THEY'RE NATURALS!
HEY, NOW!
AND WHO ARE YOU TO CHALLENGE ME?
WHO ARE **WE**?
YEAH, YOU HEAR THAT??
THE BULAN FAMILY!
BOO-LAWN!
ONE DAY PEOPLE ARE GONNA SAY IT RIGHT!

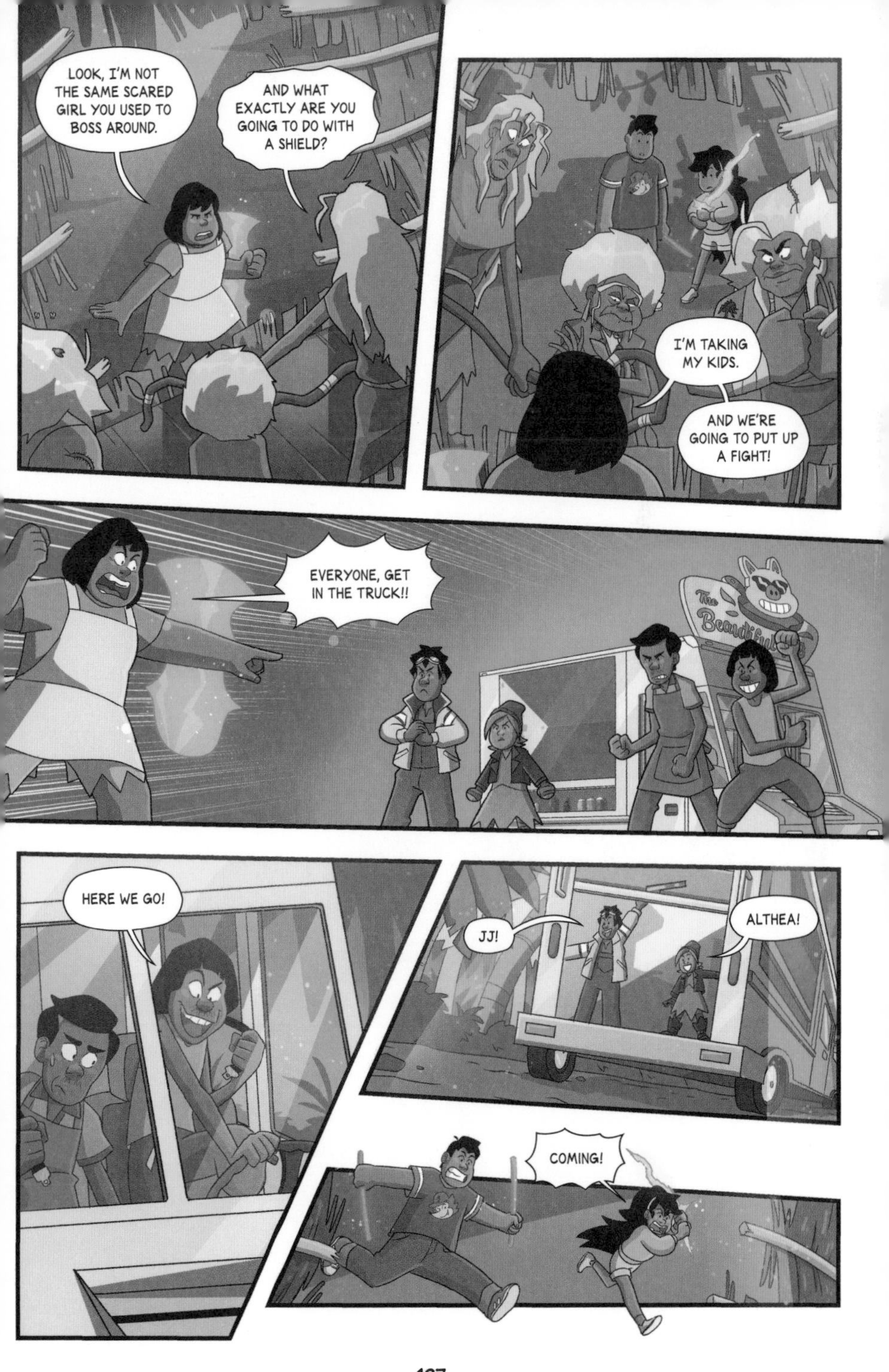
LOOK, I'M NOT THE SAME SCARED GIRL YOU USED TO BOSS AROUND.
AND WHAT EXACTLY ARE YOU GOING TO DO WITH A SHIELD?
I'M TAKING MY KIDS.
AND WE'RE GOING TO PUT UP A FIGHT!
EVERYONE, GET IN THE TRUCK!!
HERE WE GO!
JJ!
ALTHEA!
COMING!

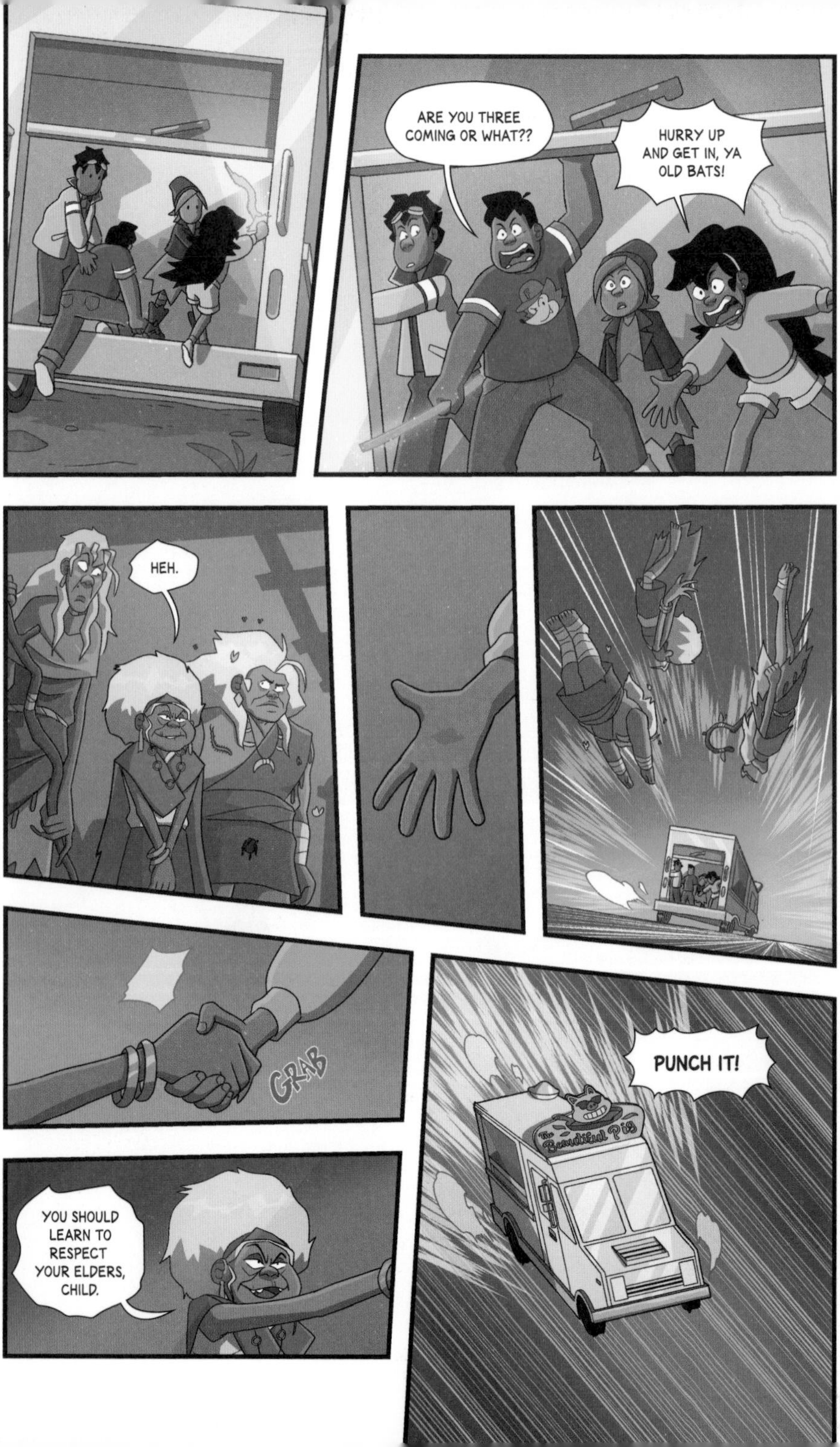
ARE YOU THREE COMING OR WHAT??
HURRY UP AND GET IN, YA OLD BATS!
HEH.
GRAB
YOU SHOULD LEARN TO RESPECT YOUR ELDERS, CHILD.
PUNCH IT!
The Beautiful Pig

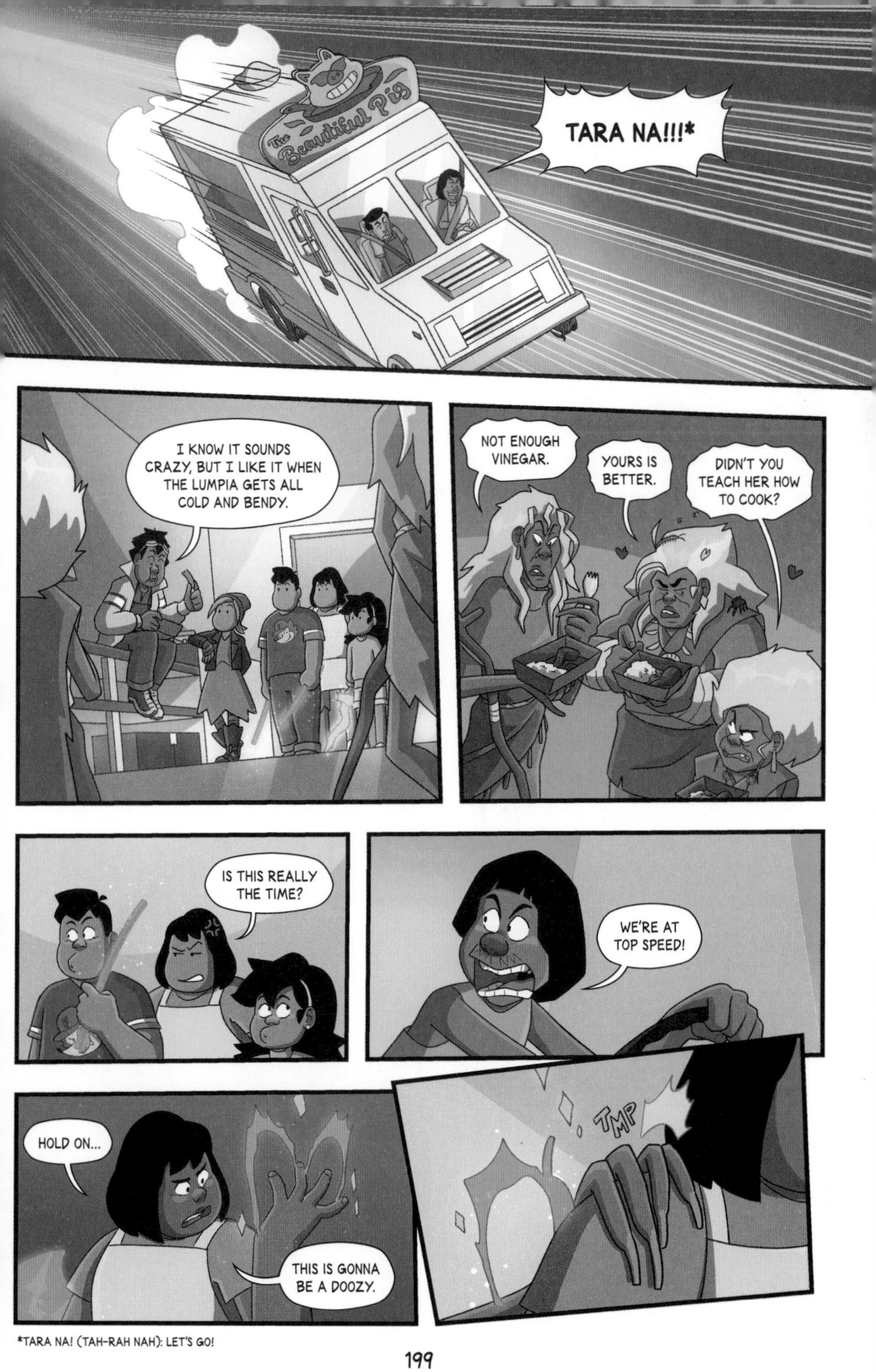
TARA NA!!!*
The Beautiful Pig
I KNOW IT SOUNDS CRAZY, BUT I LIKE IT WHEN THE LUMPIA GETS ALL COLD AND BENDY.
NOT ENOUGH VINEGAR.
YOURS IS BETTER.
DIDN'T YOU TEACH HER HOW TO COOK?
IS THIS REALLY THE TIME?
WE'RE AT TOP SPEED!
HOLD ON...
THIS IS GONNA BE A DOOZY.
TMP

*TARA NA! (TAH-RAH NAH): LET'S GO!

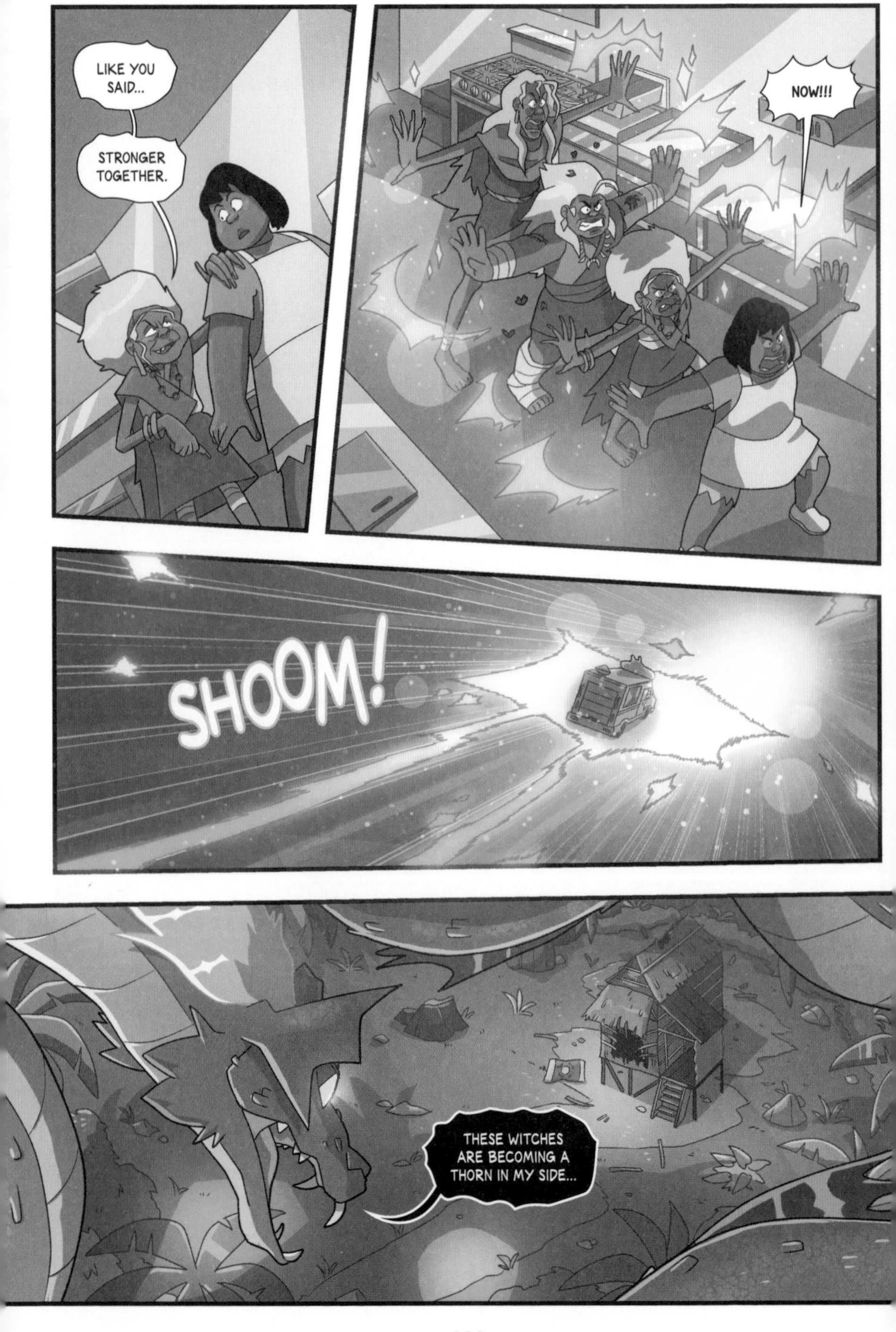
LIKE YOU SAID...
STRONGER TOGETHER.
NOW!!!
SHOOM!
THESE WITCHES ARE BECOMING A THORN IN MY SIDE...

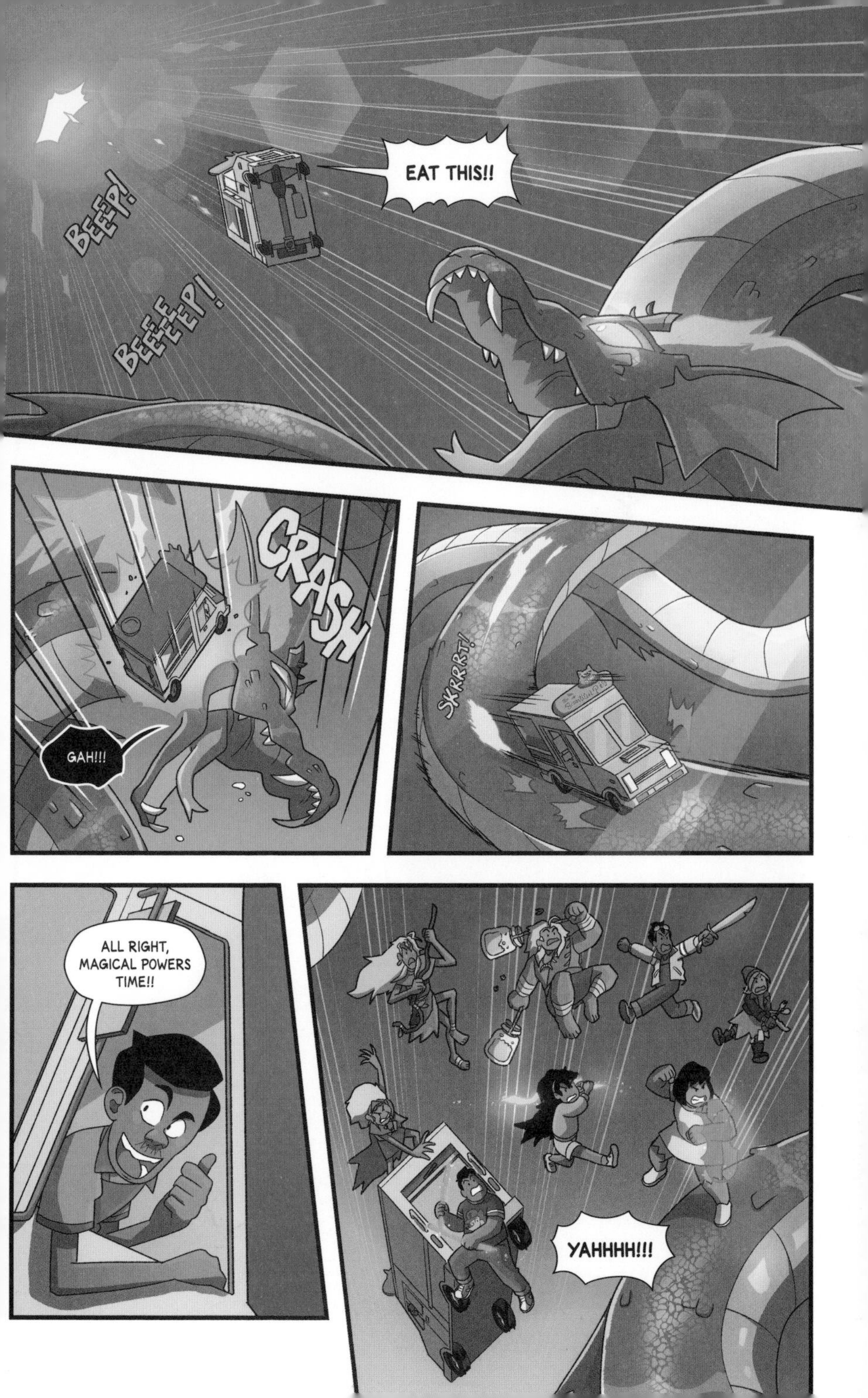
BEEEP!
EAT THIS!!
BEEEEEEP!
CRASH
GAH!!!
SKRRRT!
ALL RIGHT, MAGICAL POWERS TIME!!
YAHHHH!!!

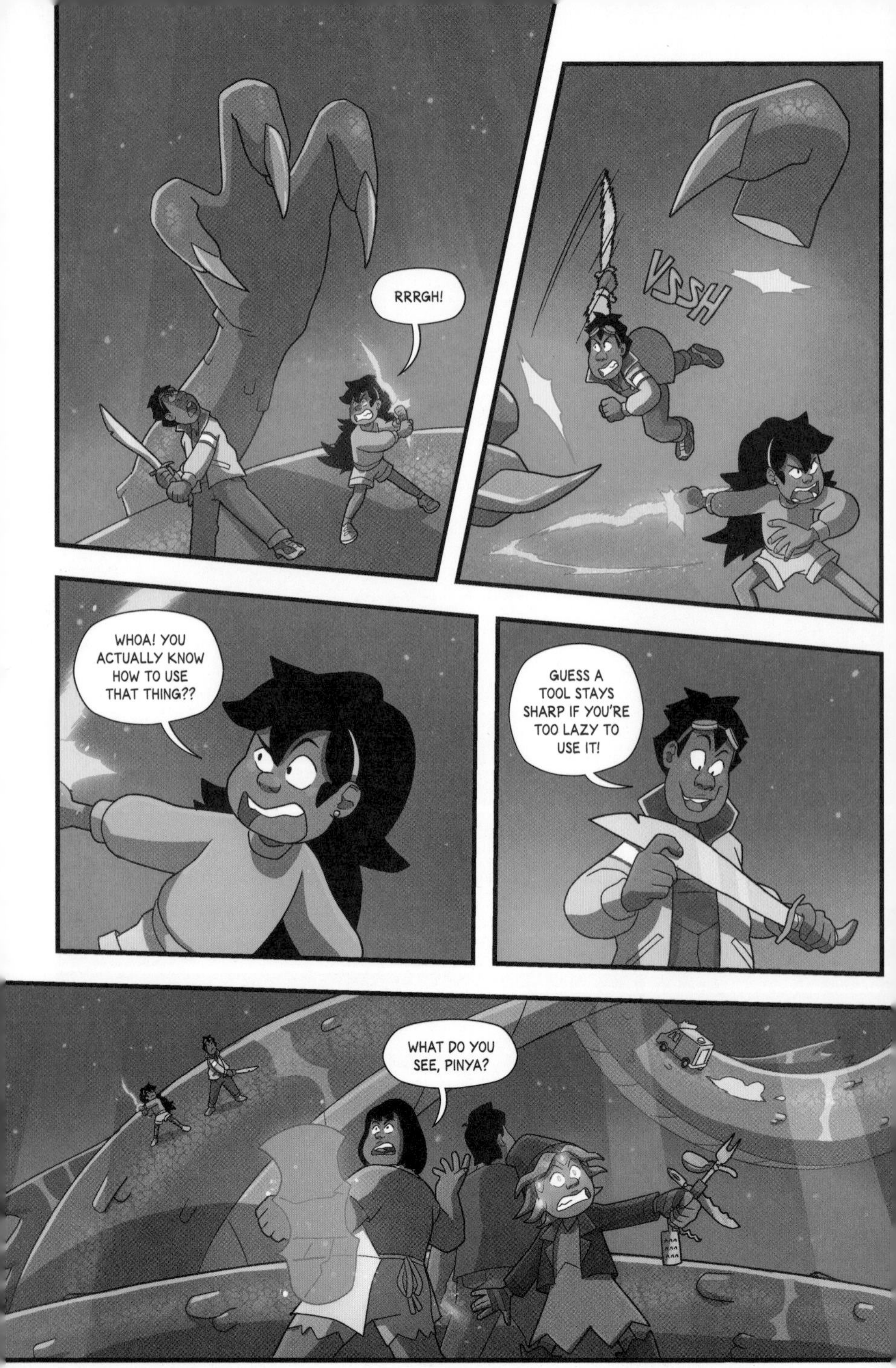
RRRGH!
VSSH
WHOA! YOU ACTUALLY KNOW HOW TO USE THAT THING??
GUESS A TOOL STAYS SHARP IF YOU'RE TOO LAZY TO USE IT!
WHAT DO YOU SEE, PINYA?

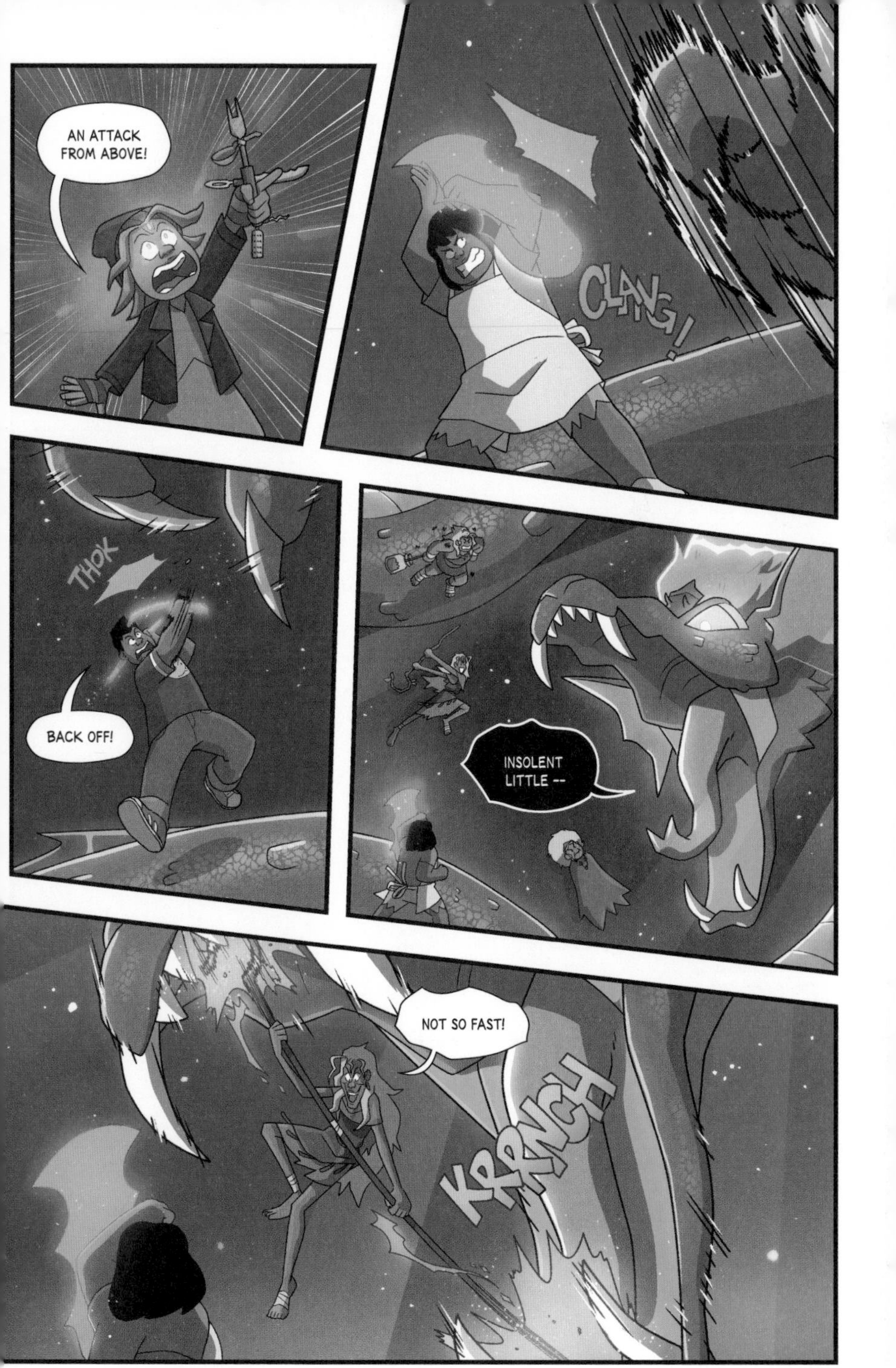
AN ATTACK FROM ABOVE!
CLANG!
THOK
BACK OFF!
INSOLENT LITTLE --
NOT SO FAST!
KRRNCH

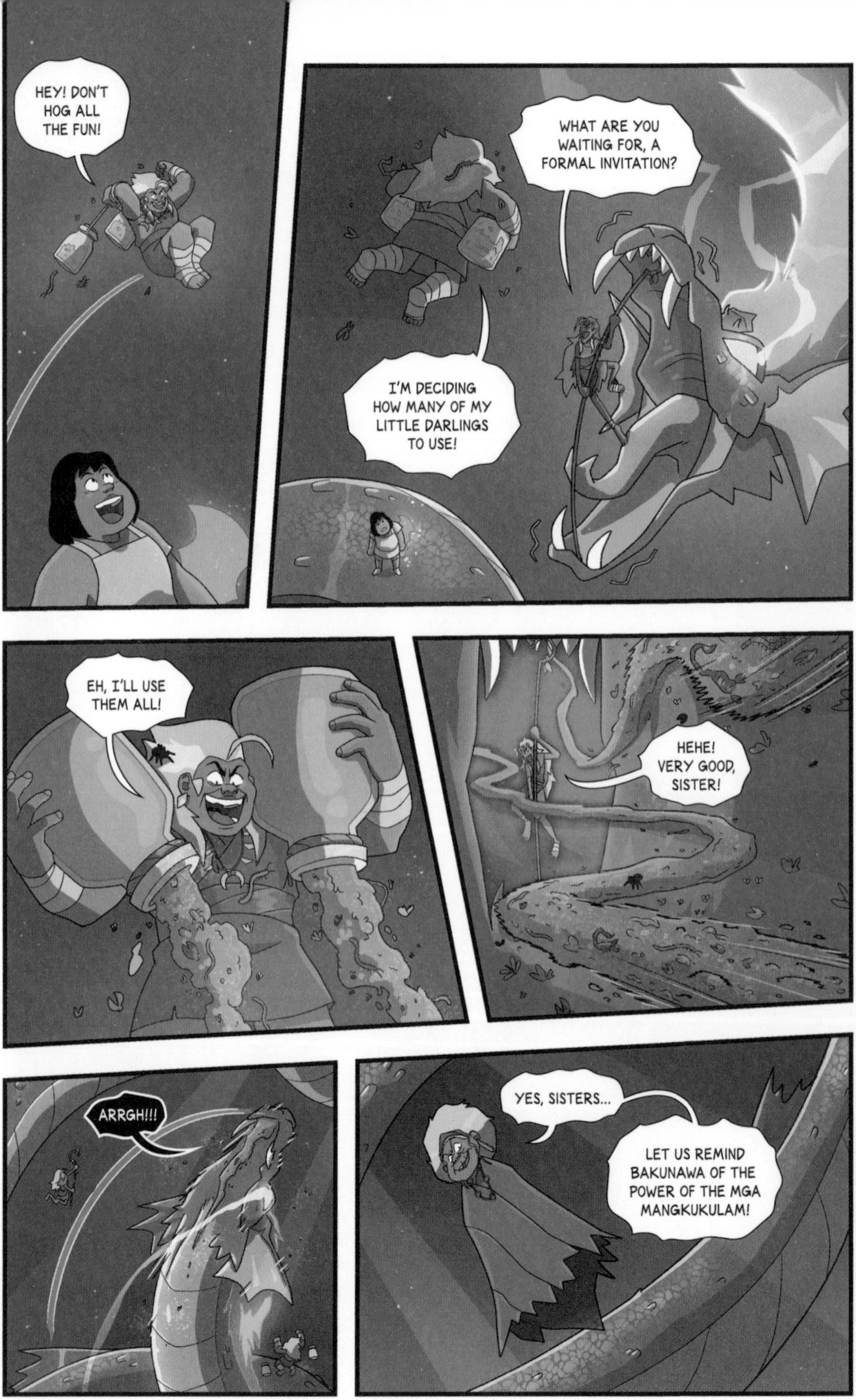
HEY! DON'T HOG ALL THE FUN!
WHAT ARE YOU WAITING FOR, A FORMAL INVITATION?
I'M DECIDING HOW MANY OF MY LITTLE DARLINGS TO USE!
EH, I'LL USE THEM ALL!
HEHE! VERY GOOD, SISTER!
ARRGH!!!
YES, SISTERS...
LET US REMIND BAKUNAWA OF THE POWER OF THE MGA MANGKUKULAM!

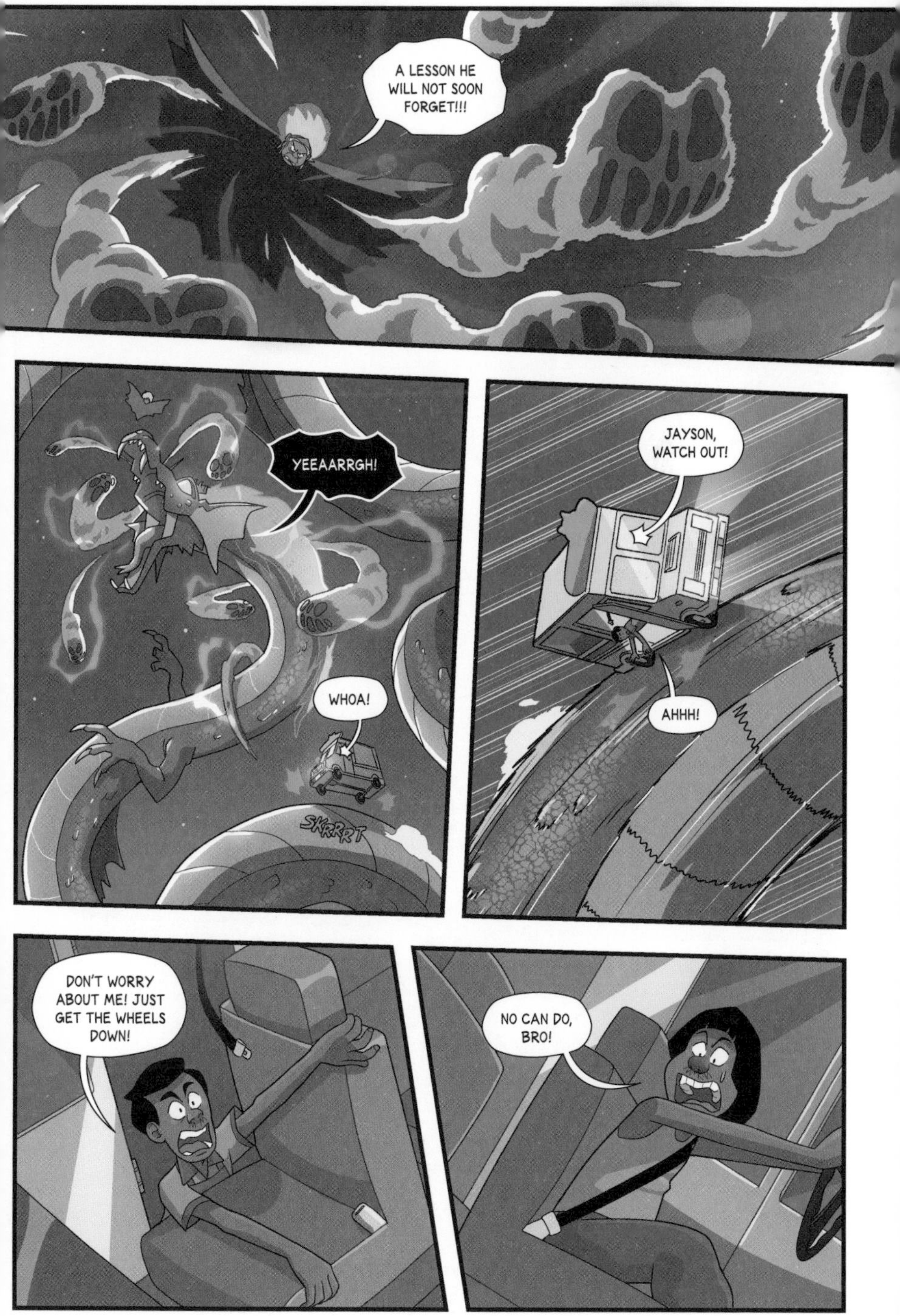
A LESSON HE WILL NOT SOON FORGET!!!
YEEAARRGH!
WHOA!
SKRRRT
JAYSON, WATCH OUT!
AHHH!
DON'T WORRY ABOUT ME! JUST GET THE WHEELS DOWN!
NO CAN DO, BRO!

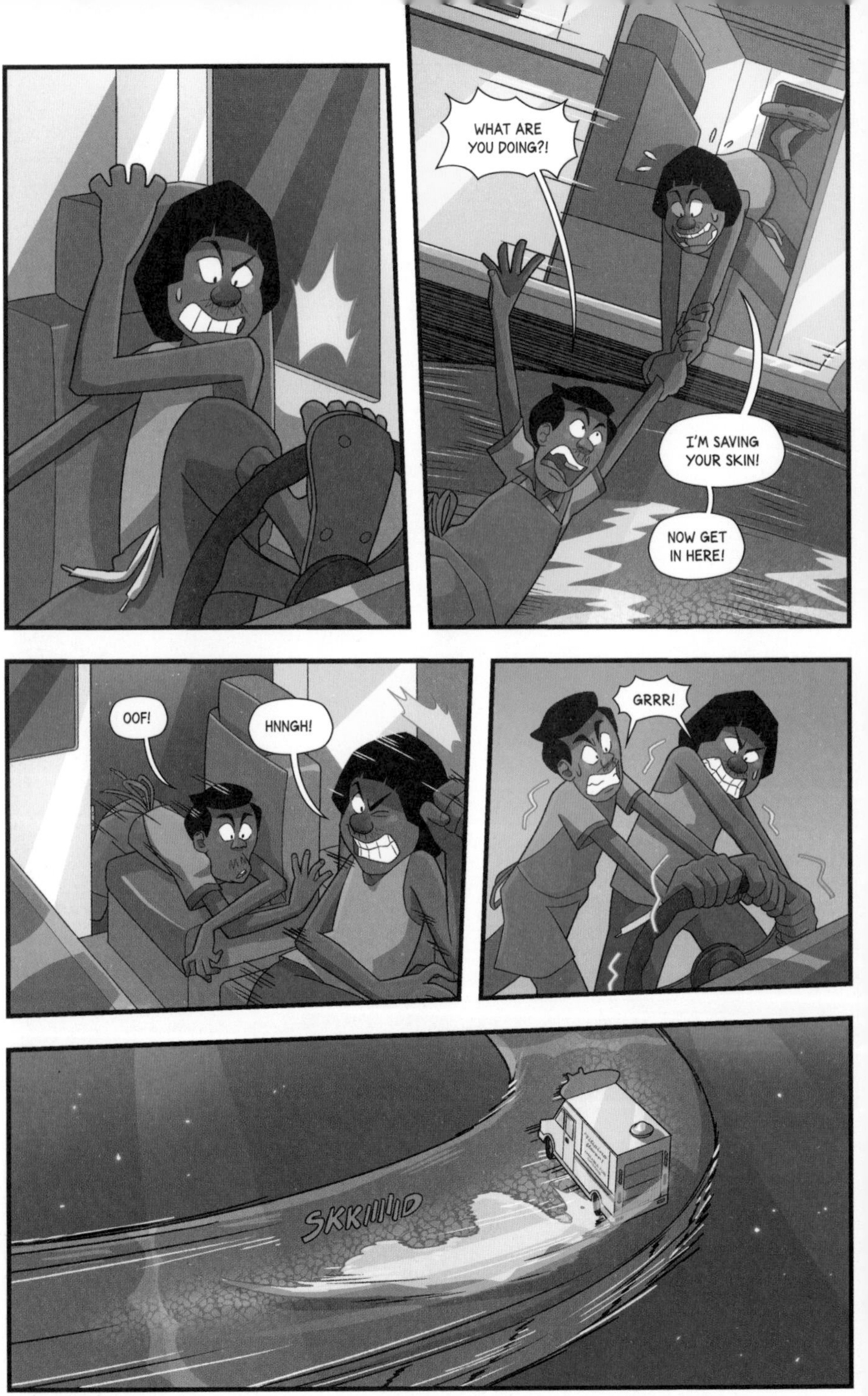

WHAT ARE YOU DOING?!
I'M SAVING YOUR SKIN!
NOW GET IN HERE!
OOF!
HNNGH!
GRRR!
SKKIIIID

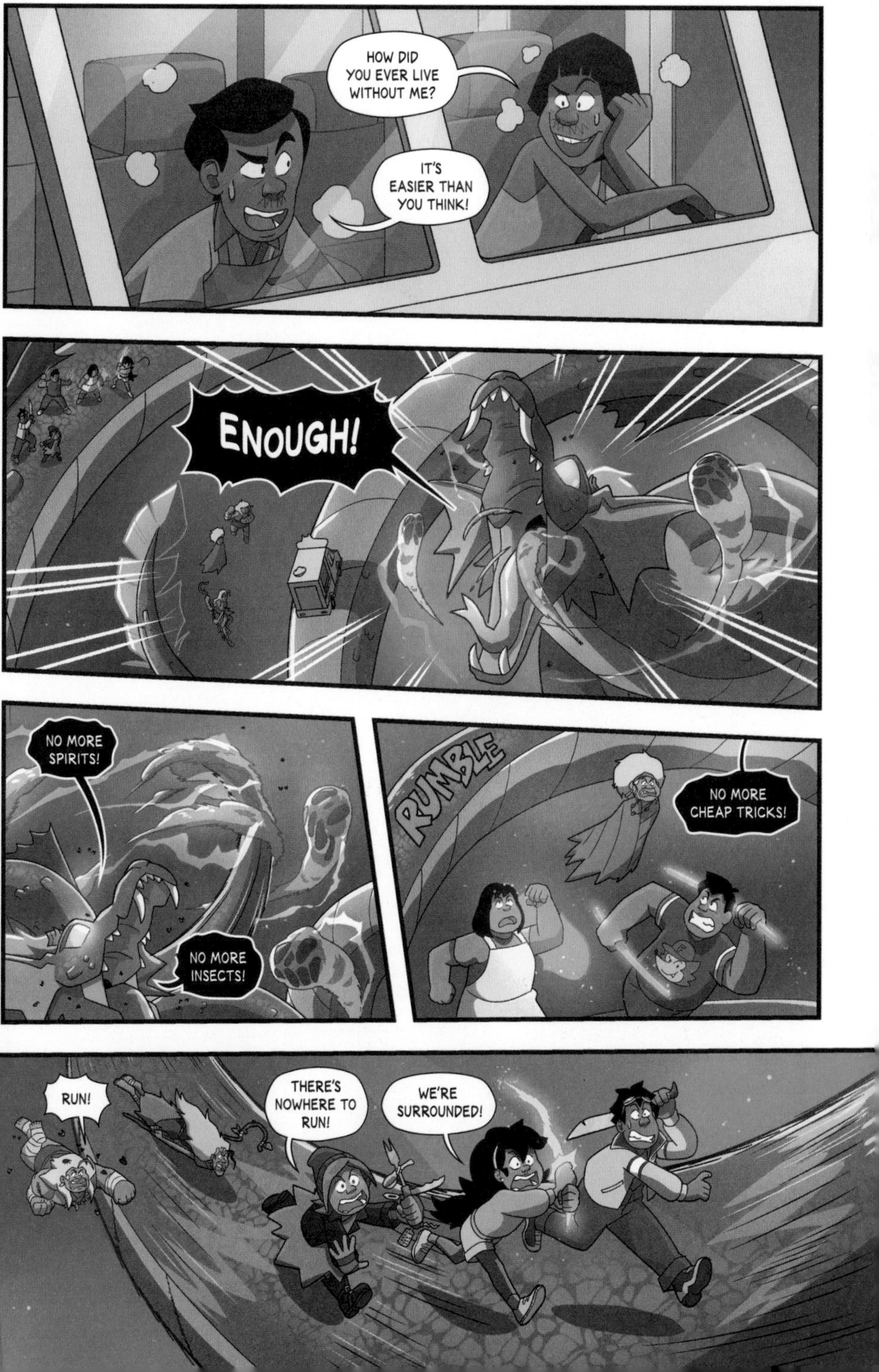
HOW DID YOU EVER LIVE WITHOUT ME?
IT'S EASIER THAN YOU THINK!
ENOUGH!
NO MORE SPIRITS!
NO MORE INSECTS!
RUMBLE
NO MORE CHEAP TRICKS!
RUN!
THERE'S NOWHERE TO RUN!
WE'RE SURROUNDED!

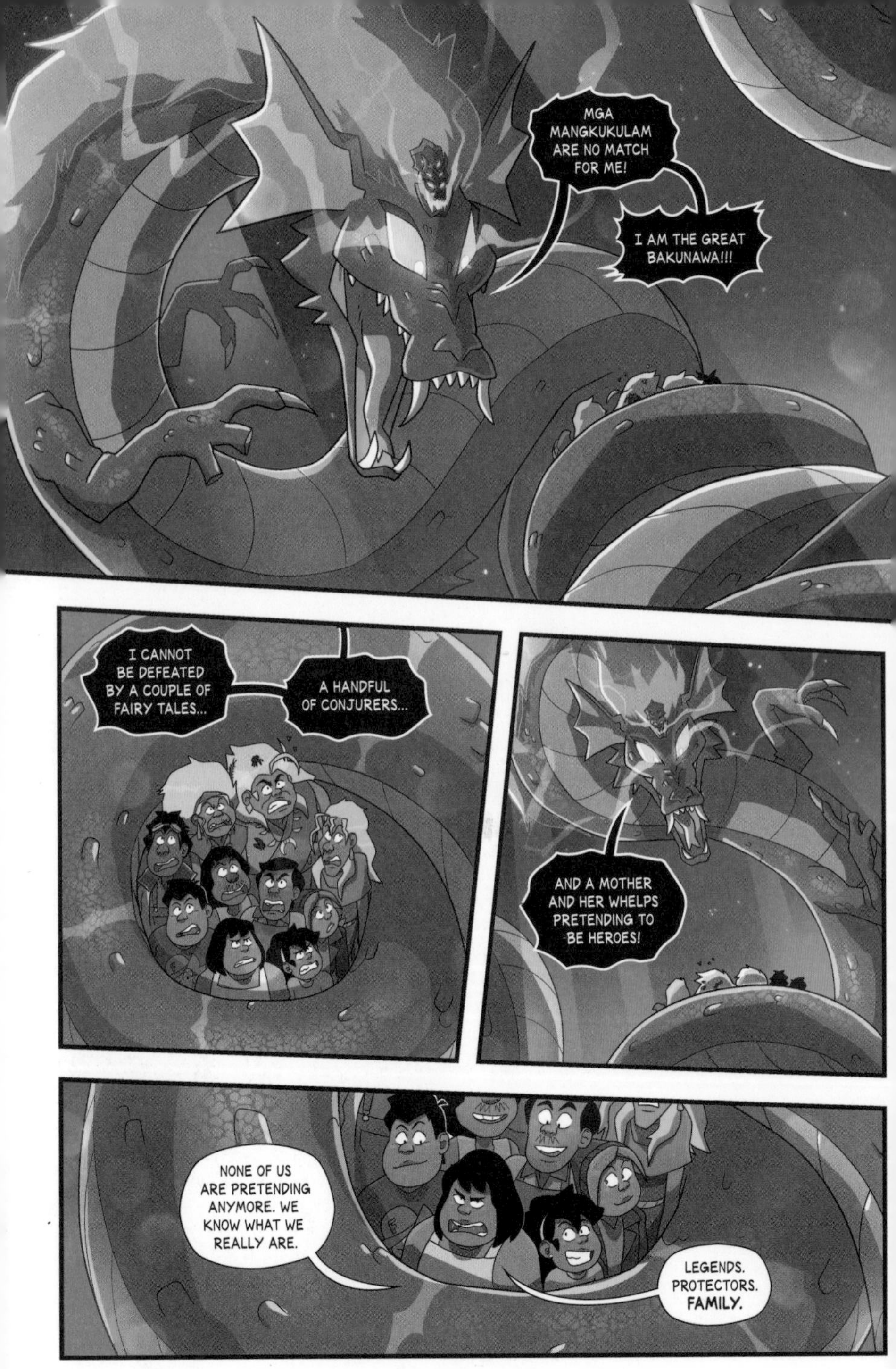
MGA MANGKUKULAM ARE NO MATCH FOR ME!
I AM THE GREAT BAKUNAWA!!!
I CANNOT BE DEFEATED BY A COUPLE OF FAIRY TALES...
A HANDFUL OF CONJURERS...
AND A MOTHER AND HER WHELPS PRETENDING TO BE HEROES!
NONE OF US ARE PRETENDING ANYMORE. WE KNOW WHAT WE REALLY ARE.
LEGENDS. PROTECTORS. **FAMILY.**

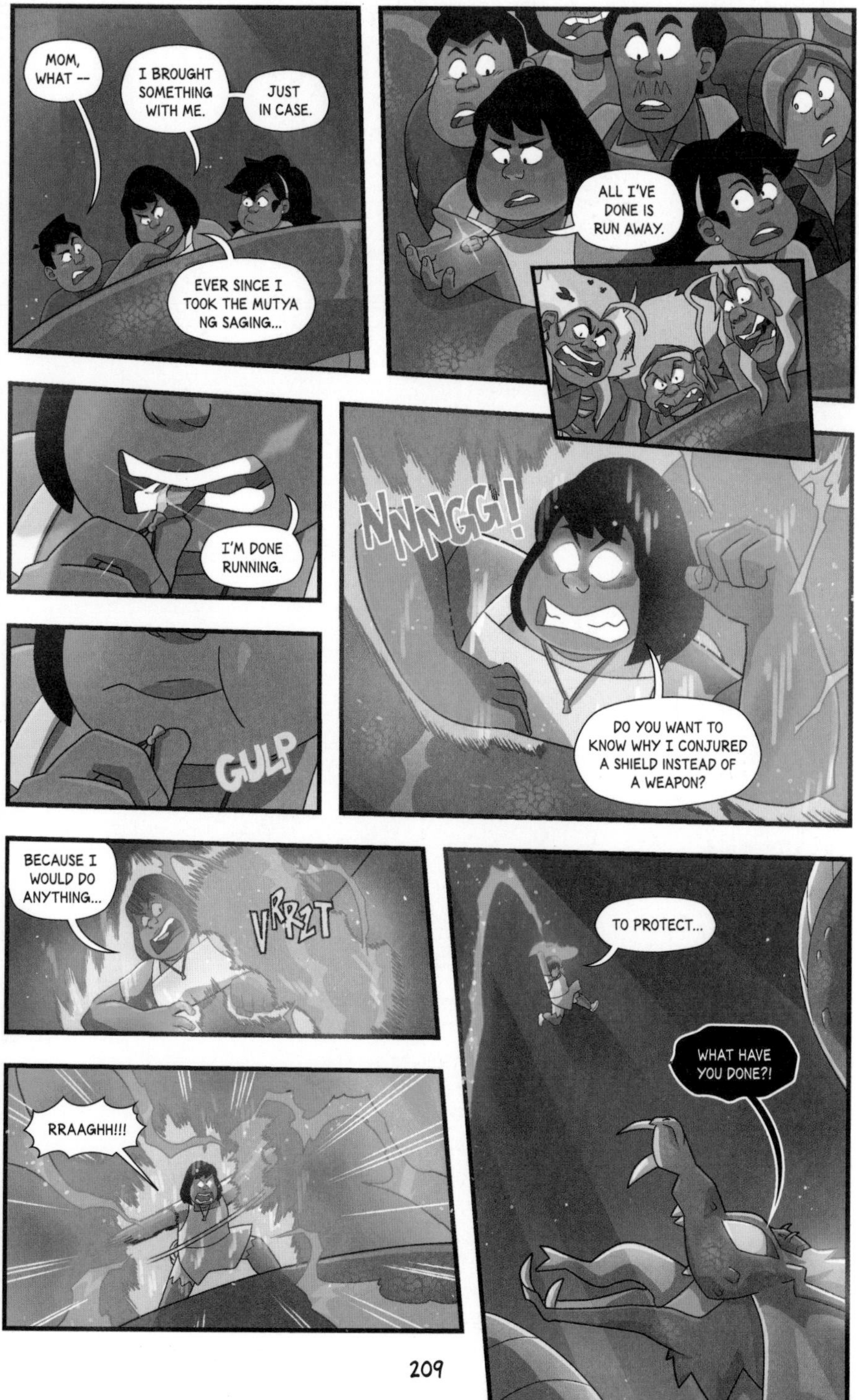
MOM, WHAT --
I BROUGHT SOMETHING WITH ME.
JUST IN CASE.
EVER SINCE I TOOK THE MUTYA NG SAGING...
ALL I'VE DONE IS RUN AWAY.
I'M DONE RUNNING.
GULP
NNNGG!
DO YOU WANT TO KNOW WHY I CONJURED A SHIELD INSTEAD OF A WEAPON?
BECAUSE I WOULD DO ANYTHING...
VRRZT
RRAAGHH!!!
TO PROTECT...
WHAT HAVE YOU DONE?!

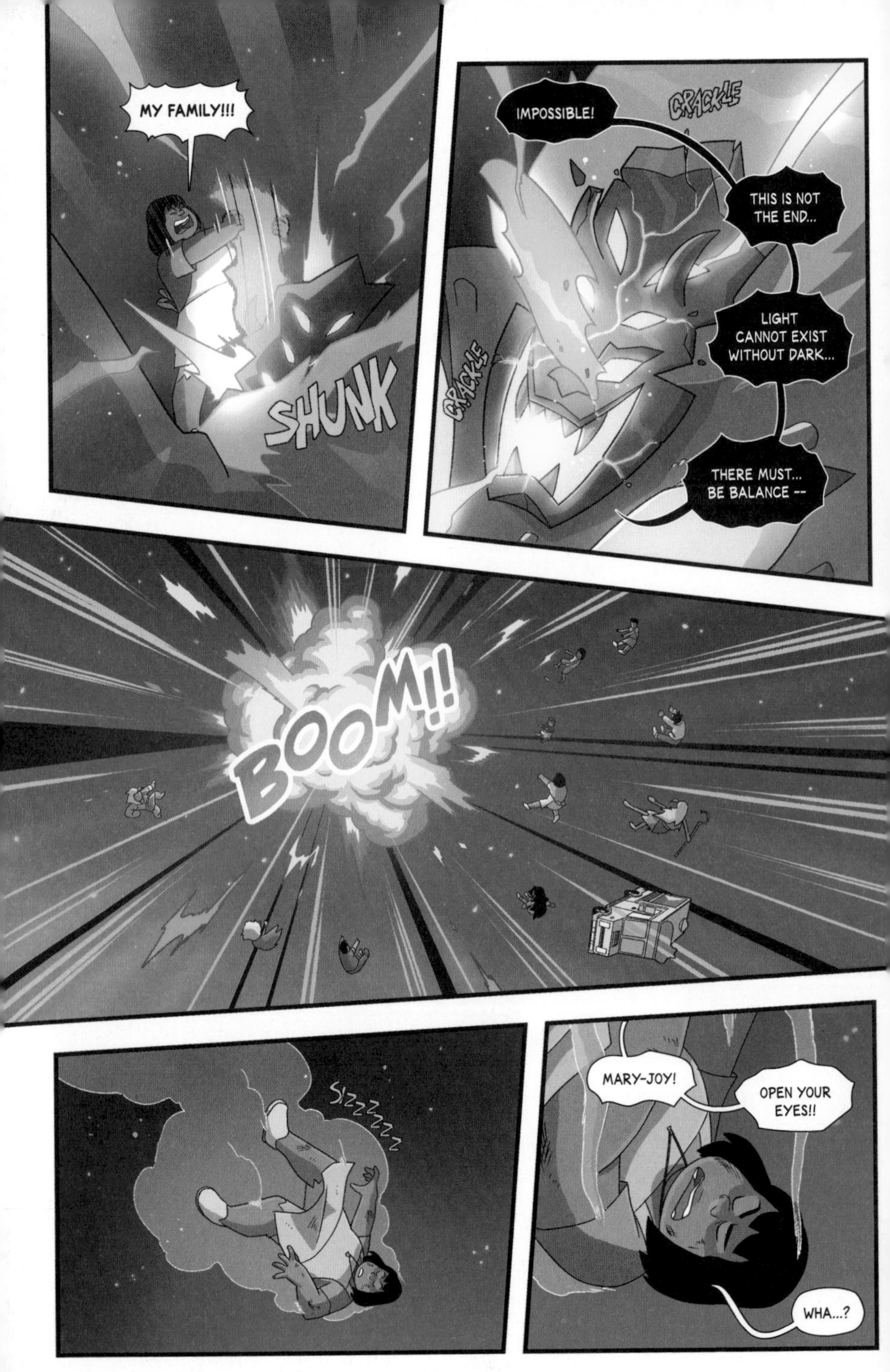
MY FAMILY!!!
SHUNK
IMPOSSIBLE!
CRACKLE
THIS IS NOT THE END...
LIGHT CANNOT EXIST WITHOUT DARK...
CRACKLE
THERE MUST... BE BALANCE --
BOOM!!
SIZZZZZZ
MARY-JOY!
OPEN YOUR EYES!!
WHA...?

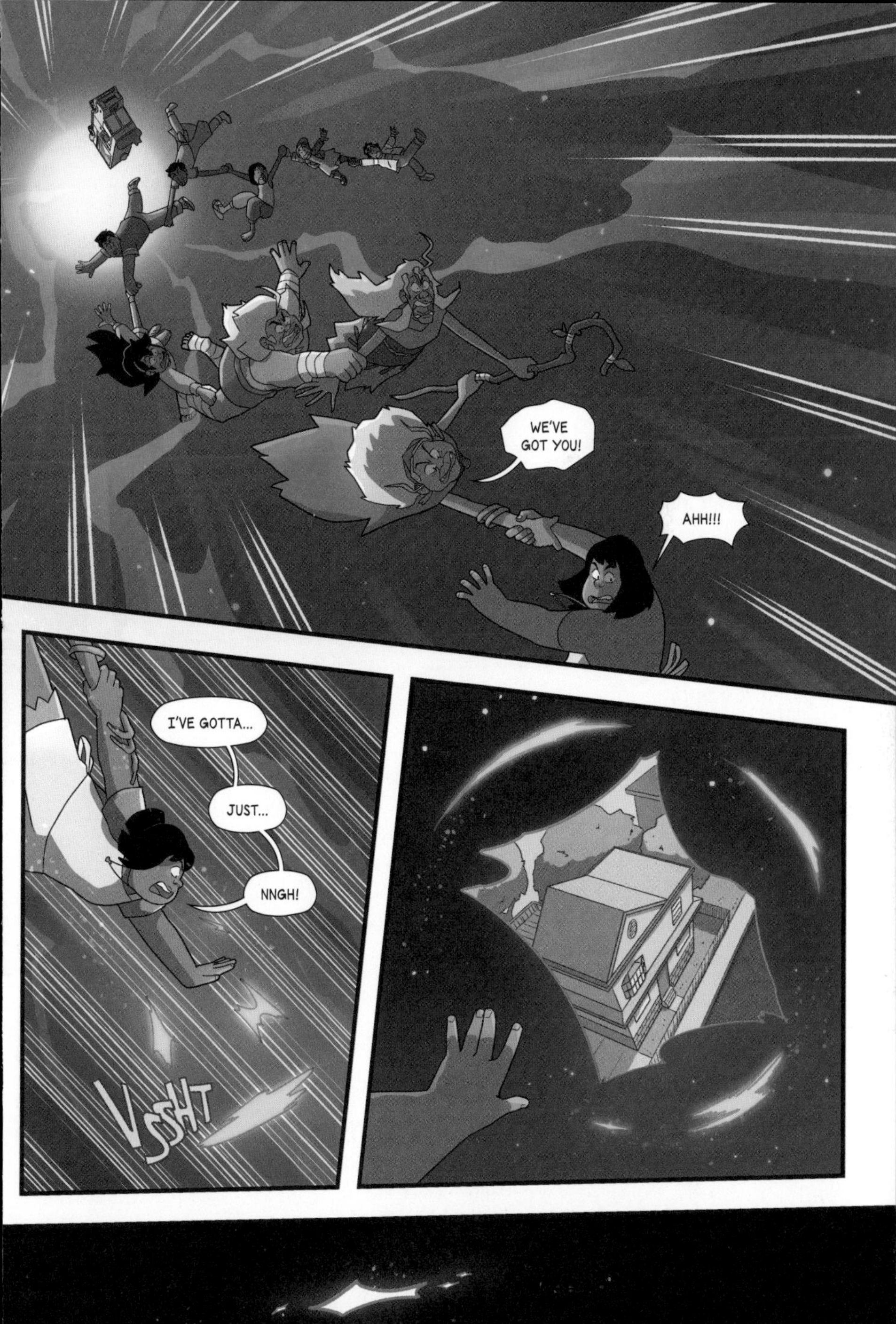
WE'VE GOT YOU!
AHH!!!
I'VE GOTTA...
JUST...
NNGH!
VSSHT

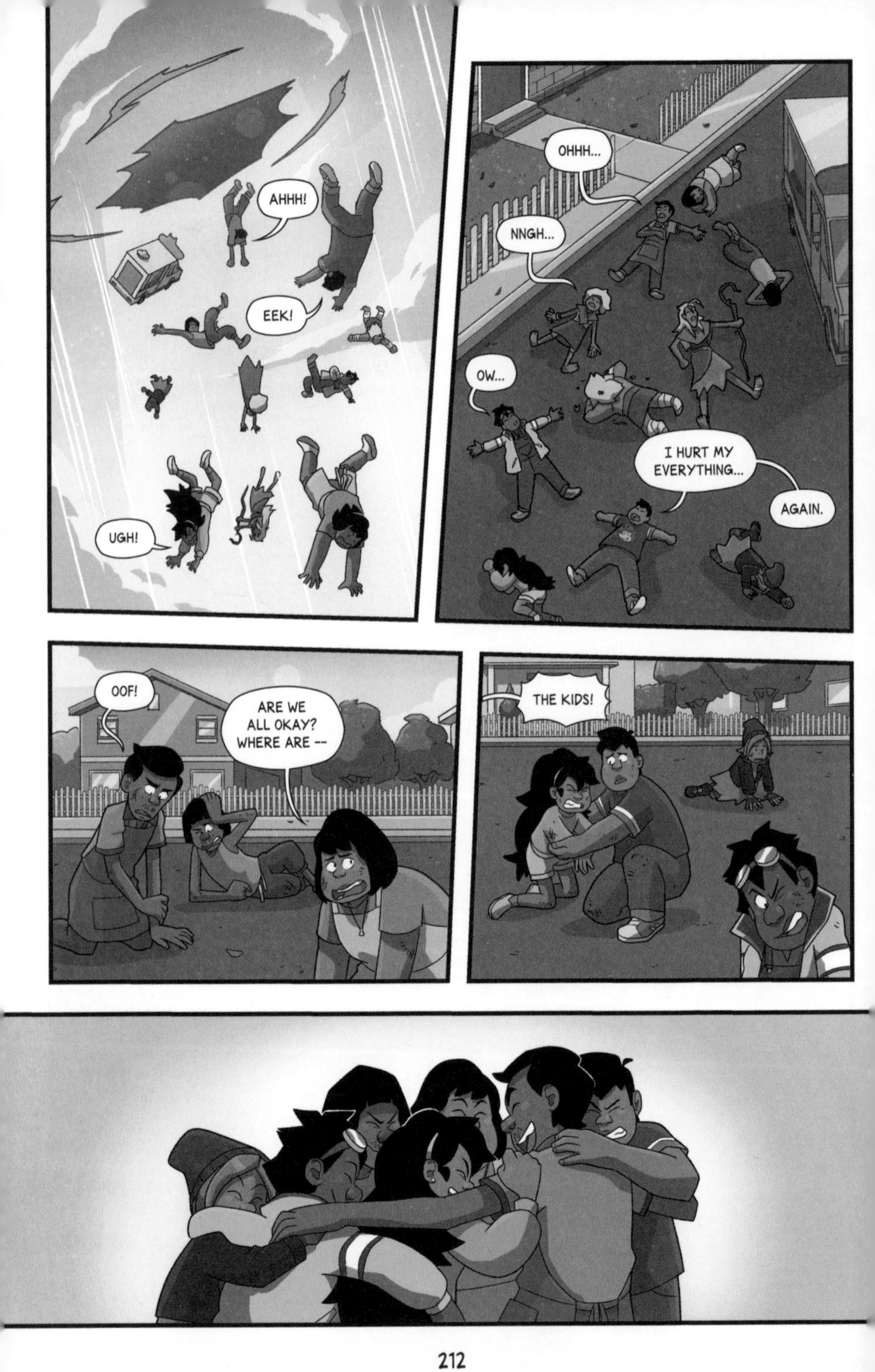
AHHH!
EEK!
UGH!
OHHH...
NNGH...
OW...
I HURT MY EVERYTHING...
AGAIN.
OOF!
ARE WE ALL OKAY? WHERE ARE --
THE KIDS!

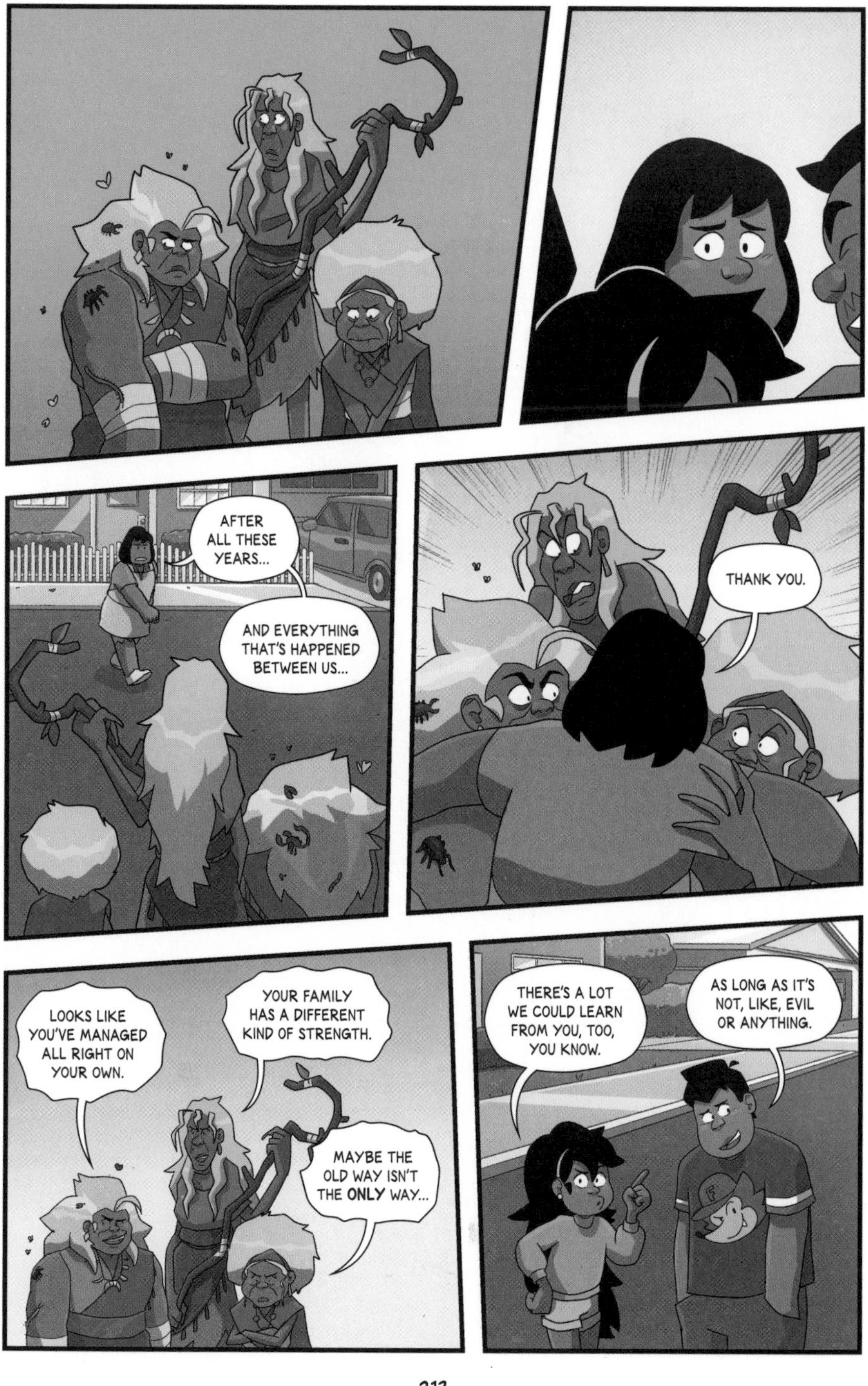
AFTER ALL THESE YEARS...
AND EVERYTHING THAT'S HAPPENED BETWEEN US...
THANK YOU.
LOOKS LIKE YOU'VE MANAGED ALL RIGHT ON YOUR OWN.
YOUR FAMILY HAS A DIFFERENT KIND OF STRENGTH.
MAYBE THE OLD WAY ISN'T THE **ONLY** WAY...
THERE'S A LOT WE COULD LEARN FROM YOU, TOO, YOU KNOW.
AS LONG AS IT'S NOT, LIKE, EVIL OR ANYTHING.

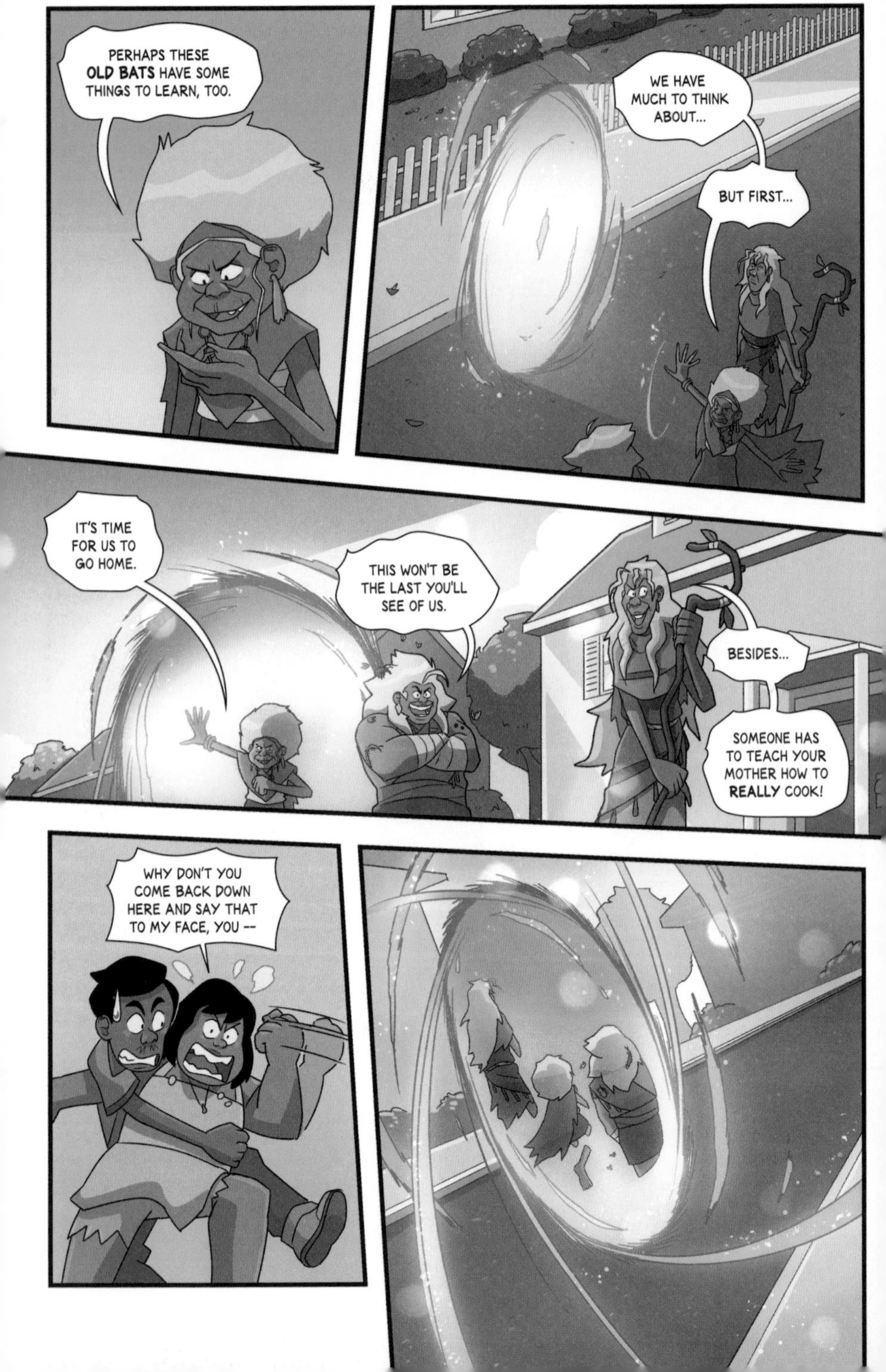
PERHAPS THESE **OLD BATS** HAVE SOME THINGS TO LEARN, TOO.
WE HAVE MUCH TO THINK ABOUT...
BUT FIRST...
IT'S TIME FOR US TO GO HOME.
THIS WON'T BE THE LAST YOU'LL SEE OF US.
BESIDES...
SOMEONE HAS TO TEACH YOUR MOTHER HOW TO **REALLY** COOK!
WHY DON'T YOU COME BACK DOWN HERE AND SAY THAT TO MY FACE, YOU --

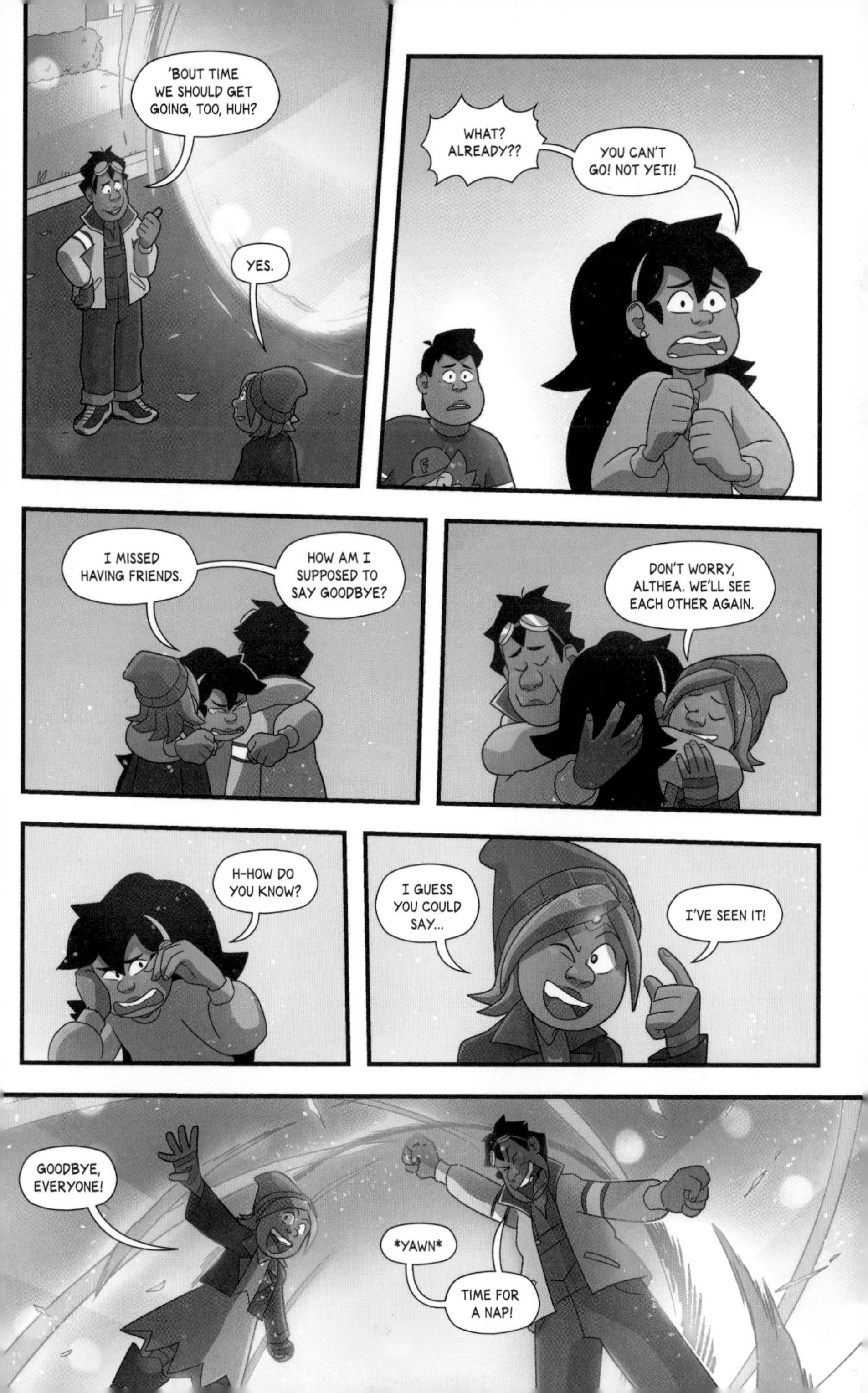
'BOUT TIME WE SHOULD GET GOING, TOO, HUH?
YES.
WHAT? ALREADY??
YOU CAN'T GO! NOT YET!!
I MISSED HAVING FRIENDS.
HOW AM I SUPPOSED TO SAY GOODBYE?
DON'T WORRY, ALTHEA. WE'LL SEE EACH OTHER AGAIN.
H-HOW DO YOU KNOW?
I GUESS YOU COULD SAY...
I'VE SEEN IT!
GOODBYE, EVERYONE!
YAWN
TIME FOR A NAP!

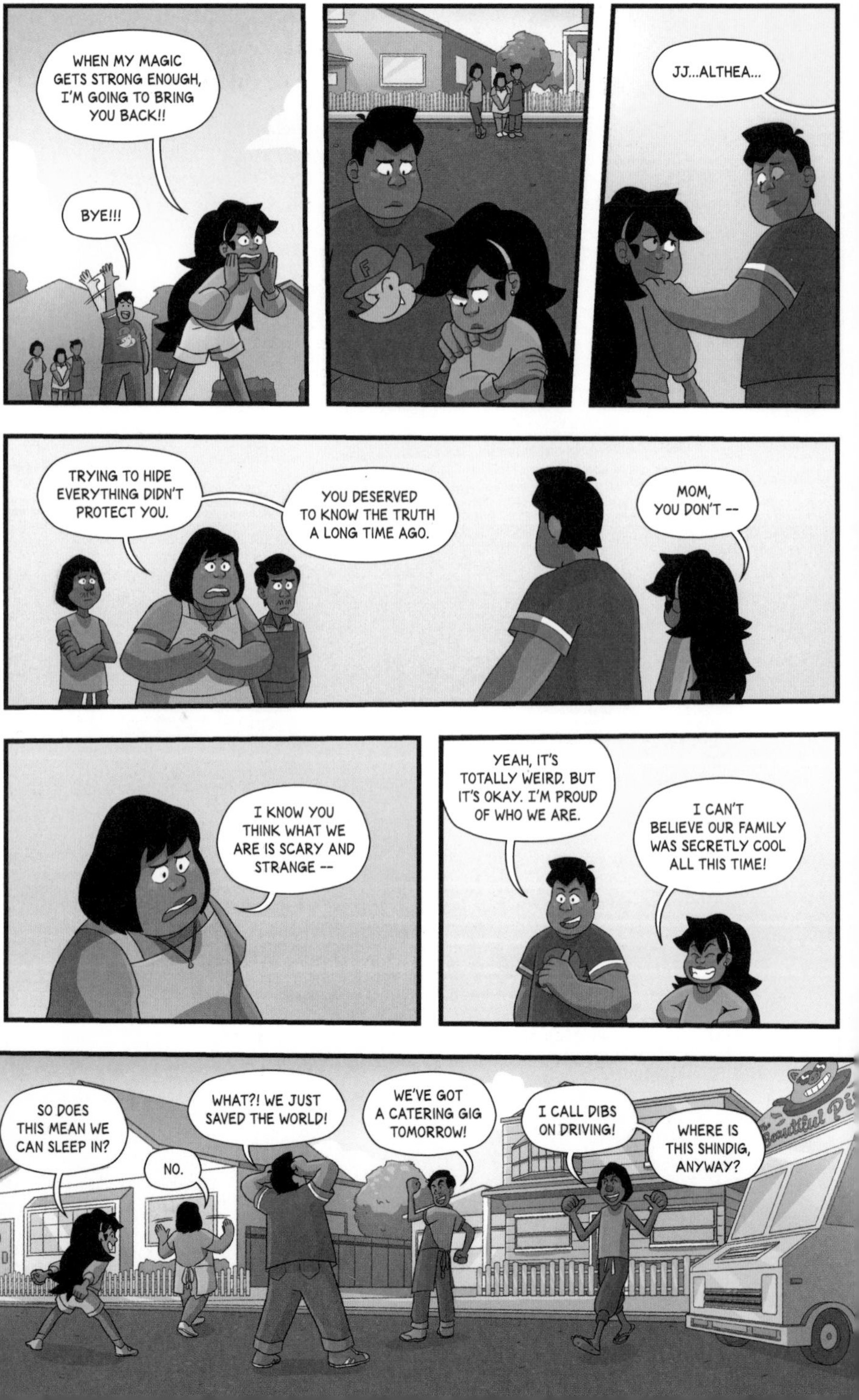
WHEN MY MAGIC GETS STRONG ENOUGH, I'M GOING TO BRING YOU BACK!!
BYE!!!
JJ...ALTHEA...
TRYING TO HIDE EVERYTHING DIDN'T PROTECT YOU.
YOU DESERVED TO KNOW THE TRUTH A LONG TIME AGO.
MOM, YOU DON'T --
I KNOW YOU THINK WHAT WE ARE IS SCARY AND STRANGE --
YEAH, IT'S TOTALLY WEIRD. BUT IT'S OKAY. I'M PROUD OF WHO WE ARE.
I CAN'T BELIEVE OUR FAMILY WAS SECRETLY COOL ALL THIS TIME!
SO DOES THIS MEAN WE CAN SLEEP IN?
NO.
WHAT?! WE JUST SAVED THE WORLD!
WE'VE GOT A CATERING GIG TOMORROW!
I CALL DIBS ON DRIVING!
WHERE IS THIS SHINDIG, ANYWAY?

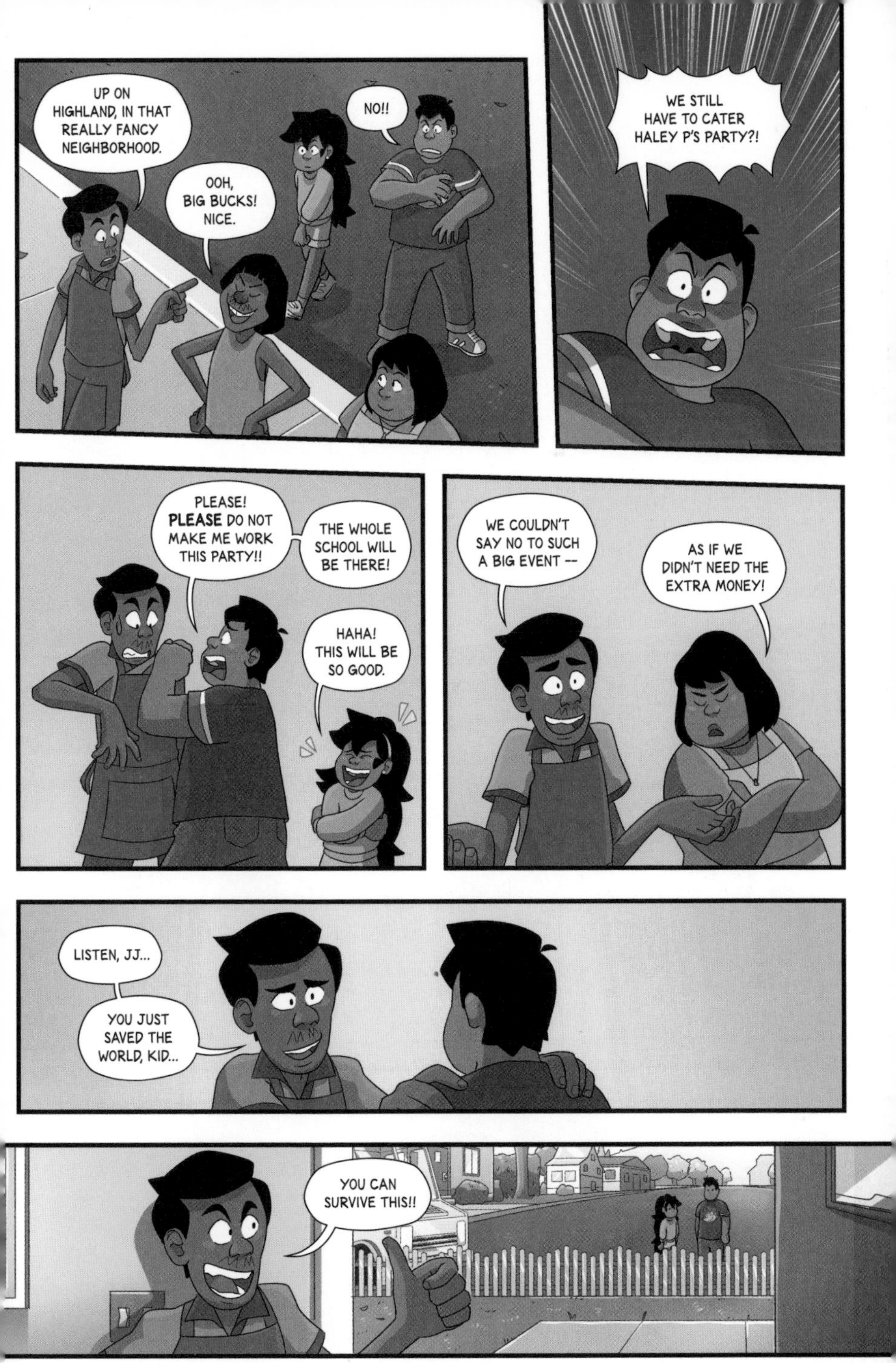
UP ON HIGHLAND, IN THAT REALLY FANCY NEIGHBORHOOD.
OOH, BIG BUCKS! NICE.
NO!!
WE STILL HAVE TO CATER HALEY P'S PARTY?!
PLEASE! **PLEASE** DO NOT MAKE ME WORK THIS PARTY!!
THE WHOLE SCHOOL WILL BE THERE!
HAHA! THIS WILL BE SO GOOD.
WE COULDN'T SAY NO TO SUCH A BIG EVENT --
AS IF WE DIDN'T NEED THE EXTRA MONEY!
LISTEN, JJ...
YOU JUST SAVED THE WORLD, KID...
YOU CAN SURVIVE THIS!!

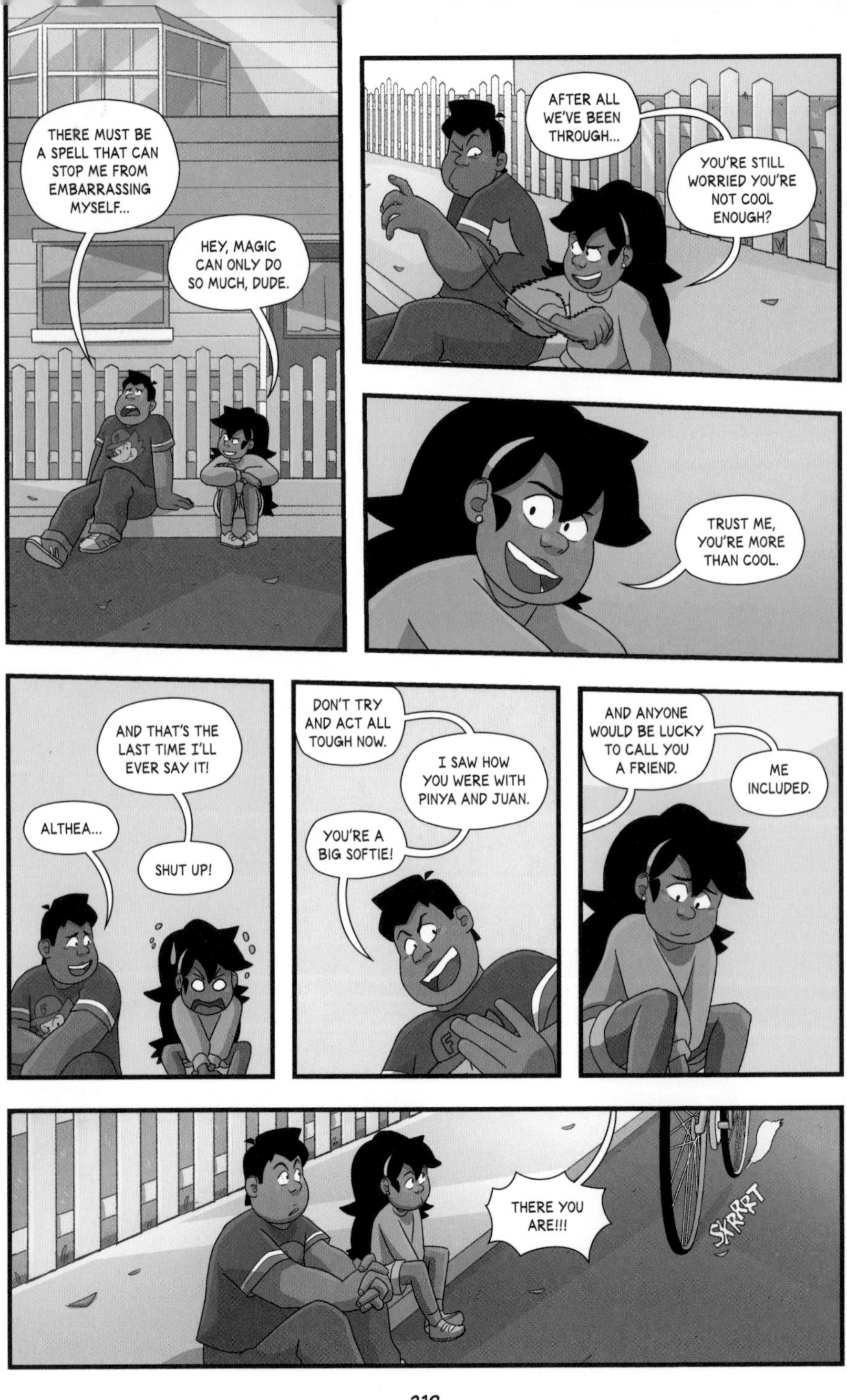
THERE MUST BE A SPELL THAT CAN STOP ME FROM EMBARRASSING MYSELF...
HEY, MAGIC CAN ONLY DO SO MUCH, DUDE.
AFTER ALL WE'VE BEEN THROUGH...
YOU'RE STILL WORRIED YOU'RE NOT COOL ENOUGH?
TRUST ME, YOU'RE MORE THAN COOL.
AND THAT'S THE LAST TIME I'LL EVER SAY IT!
ALTHEA...
SHUT UP!
DON'T TRY AND ACT ALL TOUGH NOW.
I SAW HOW YOU WERE WITH PINYA AND JUAN.
YOU'RE A BIG SOFTIE!
AND ANYONE WOULD BE LUCKY TO CALL YOU A FRIEND.
ME INCLUDED.
THERE YOU ARE!!!
SKRRRT

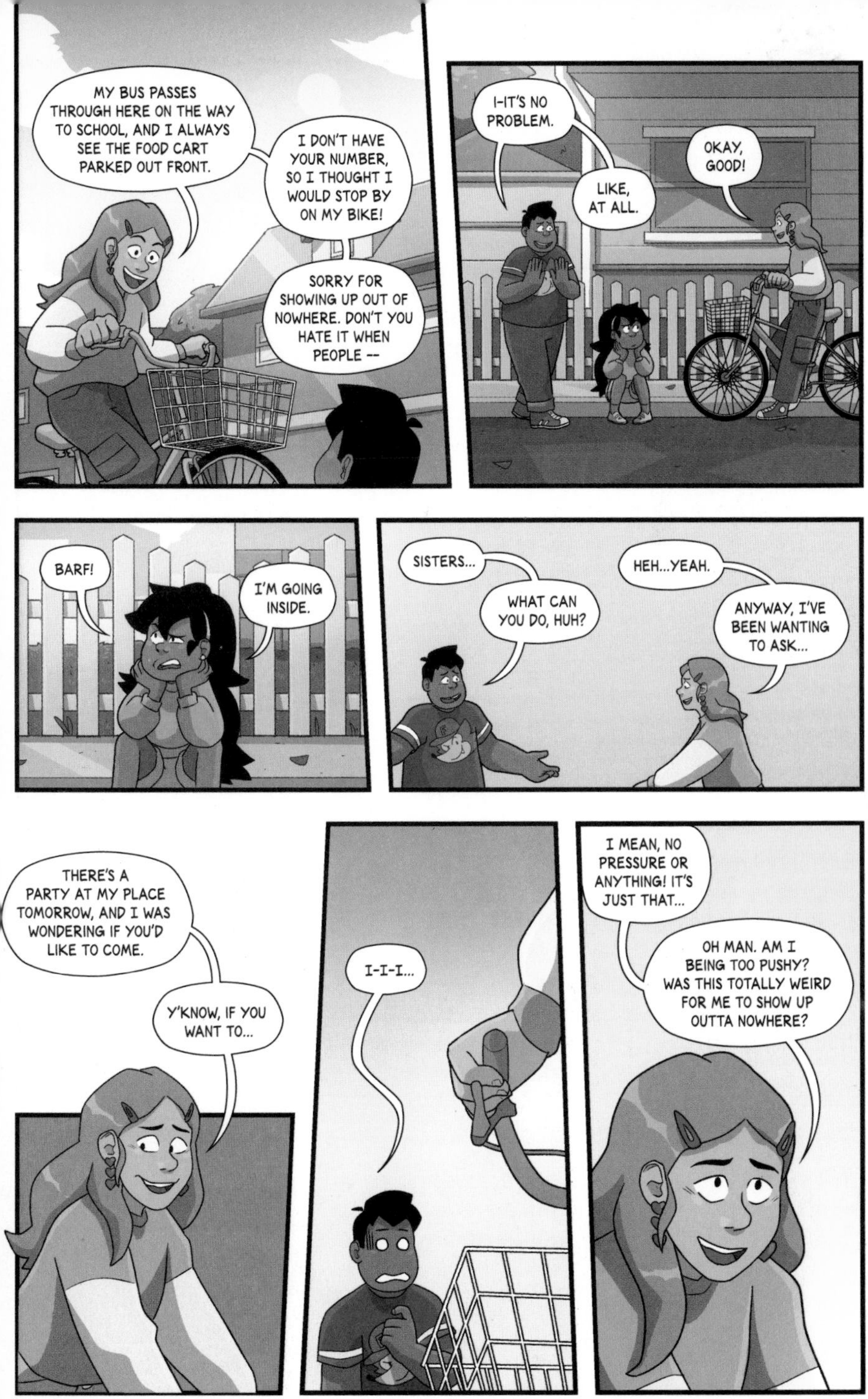
MY BUS PASSES THROUGH HERE ON THE WAY TO SCHOOL, AND I ALWAYS SEE THE FOOD CART PARKED OUT FRONT.
I DON'T HAVE YOUR NUMBER, SO I THOUGHT I WOULD STOP BY ON MY BIKE!
SORRY FOR SHOWING UP OUT OF NOWHERE. DON'T YOU HATE IT WHEN PEOPLE --
I-IT'S NO PROBLEM.
LIKE, AT ALL.
OKAY, GOOD!
BARF!
I'M GOING INSIDE.
SISTERS...
WHAT CAN YOU DO, HUH?
HEH...YEAH.
ANYWAY, I'VE BEEN WANTING TO ASK...
THERE'S A PARTY AT MY PLACE TOMORROW, AND I WAS WONDERING IF YOU'D LIKE TO COME.
Y'KNOW, IF YOU WANT TO...
I-I-I...
I MEAN, NO PRESSURE OR ANYTHING! IT'S JUST THAT...
OH MAN. AM I BEING TOO PUSHY? WAS THIS TOTALLY WEIRD FOR ME TO SHOW UP OUTTA NOWHERE?

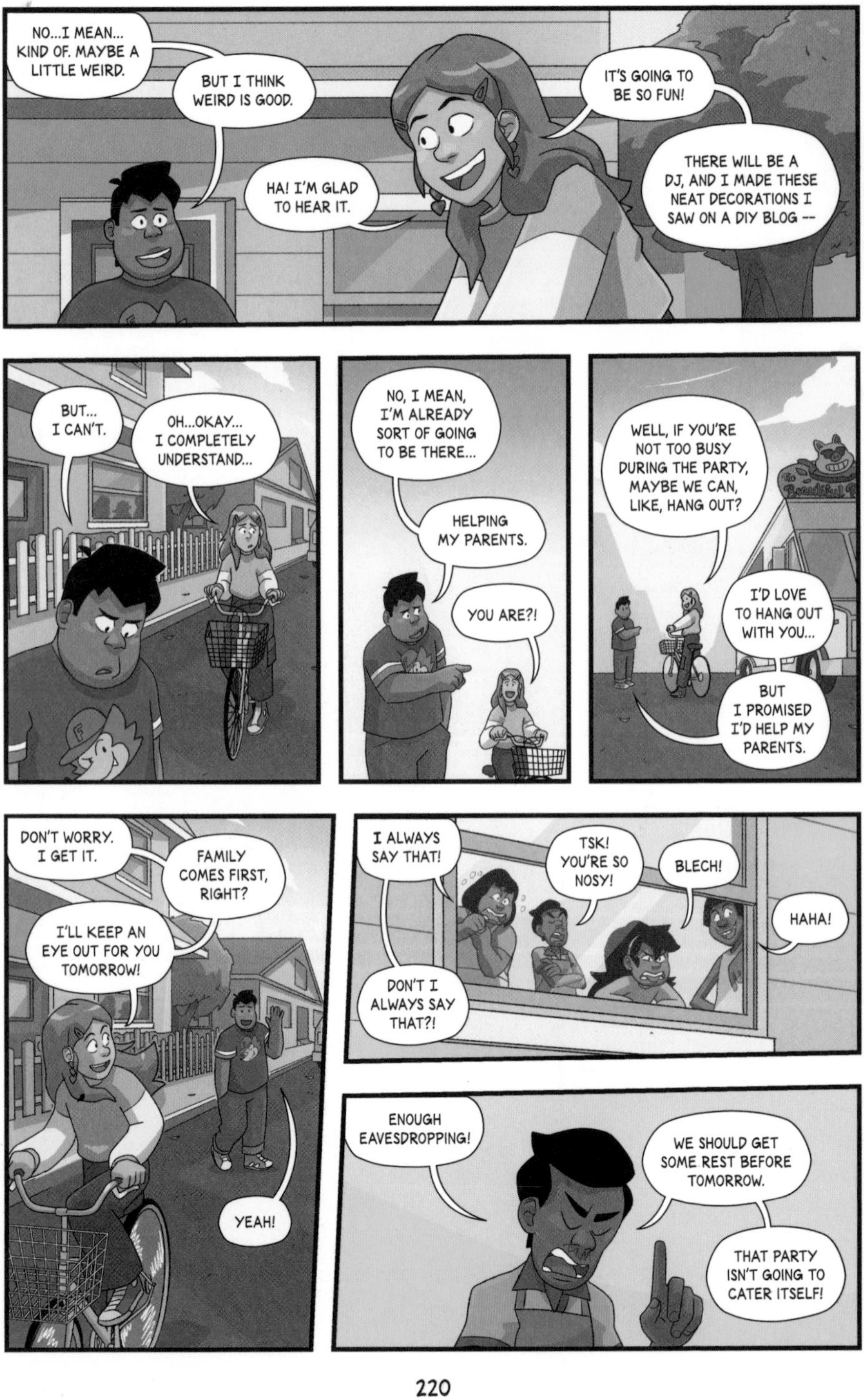
NO...I MEAN... KIND OF. MAYBE A LITTLE WEIRD.
BUT I THINK WEIRD IS GOOD.
HA! I'M GLAD TO HEAR IT.
IT'S GOING TO BE SO FUN!
THERE WILL BE A DJ, AND I MADE THESE NEAT DECORATIONS I SAW ON A DIY BLOG --
BUT... I CAN'T.
OH...OKAY... I COMPLETELY UNDERSTAND...
NO, I MEAN, I'M ALREADY SORT OF GOING TO BE THERE...
HELPING MY PARENTS.
YOU ARE?!
WELL, IF YOU'RE NOT TOO BUSY DURING THE PARTY, MAYBE WE CAN, LIKE, HANG OUT?
I'D LOVE TO HANG OUT WITH YOU...
BUT I PROMISED I'D HELP MY PARENTS.
DON'T WORRY. I GET IT.
FAMILY COMES FIRST, RIGHT?
I'LL KEEP AN EYE OUT FOR YOU TOMORROW!
YEAH!
I ALWAYS SAY THAT!
DON'T I ALWAYS SAY THAT?!
TSK! YOU'RE SO NOSY!
BLECH!
HAHA!
ENOUGH EAVESDROPPING!
WE SHOULD GET SOME REST BEFORE TOMORROW.
THAT PARTY ISN'T GOING TO CATER ITSELF!

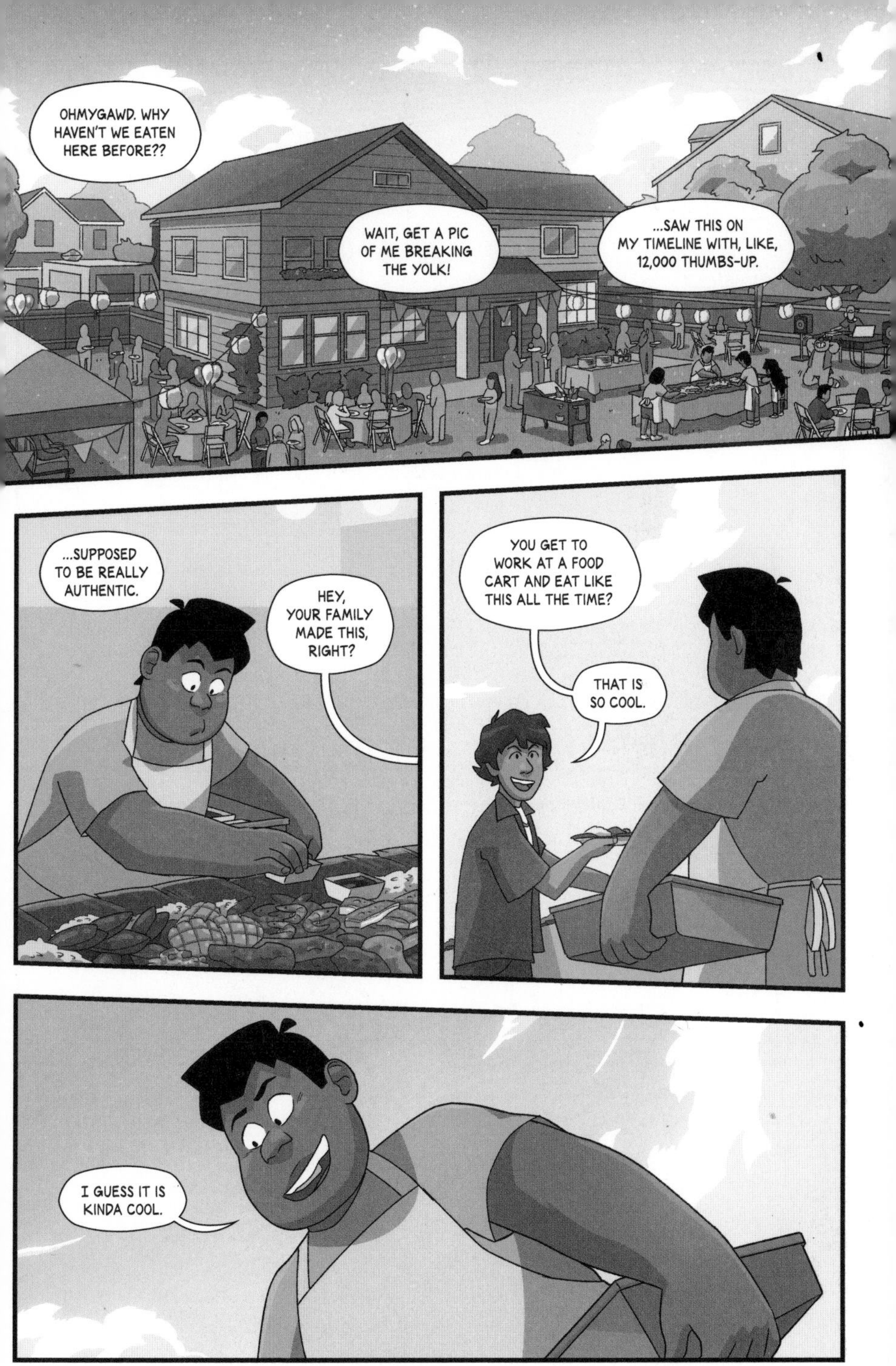
OHMYGAWD. WHY HAVEN'T WE EATEN HERE BEFORE??
WAIT, GET A PIC OF ME BREAKING THE YOLK!
...SAW THIS ON MY TIMELINE WITH, LIKE, 12,000 THUMBS-UP.
...SUPPOSED TO BE REALLY AUTHENTIC.
HEY, YOUR FAMILY MADE THIS, RIGHT?
YOU GET TO WORK AT A FOOD CART AND EAT LIKE THIS ALL THE TIME?
THAT IS SO COOL.
I GUESS IT IS KINDA COOL.

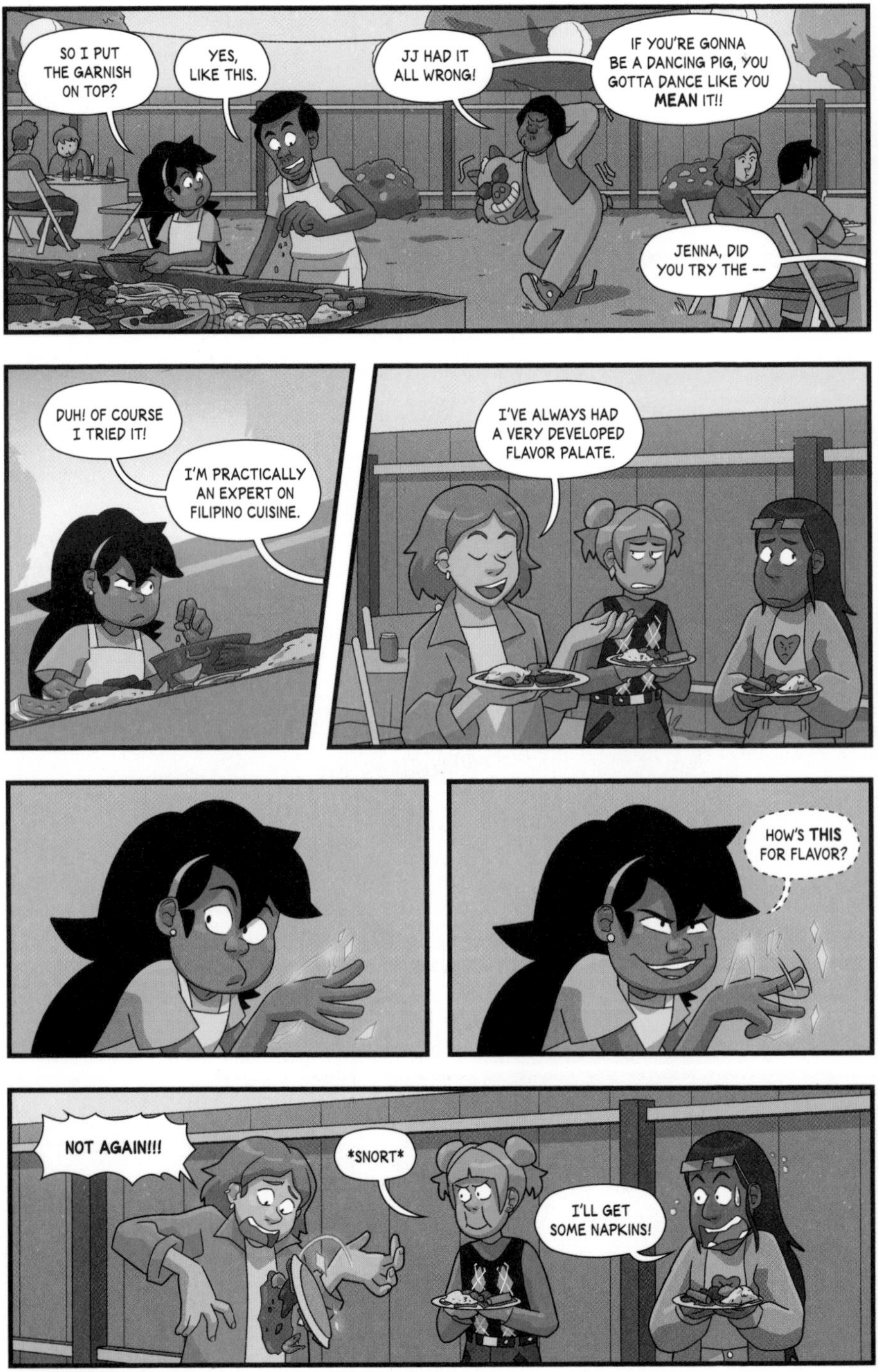
SO I PUT THE GARNISH ON TOP?
YES, LIKE THIS.
JJ HAD IT ALL WRONG!
IF YOU'RE GONNA BE A DANCING PIG, YOU GOTTA DANCE LIKE YOU **MEAN** IT!!
JENNA, DID YOU TRY THE --
DUH! OF COURSE I TRIED IT!
I'M PRACTICALLY AN EXPERT ON FILIPINO CUISINE.
I'VE ALWAYS HAD A VERY DEVELOPED FLAVOR PALATE.
HOW'S **THIS** FOR FLAVOR?
NOT AGAIN!!!
SNORT
I'LL GET SOME NAPKINS!

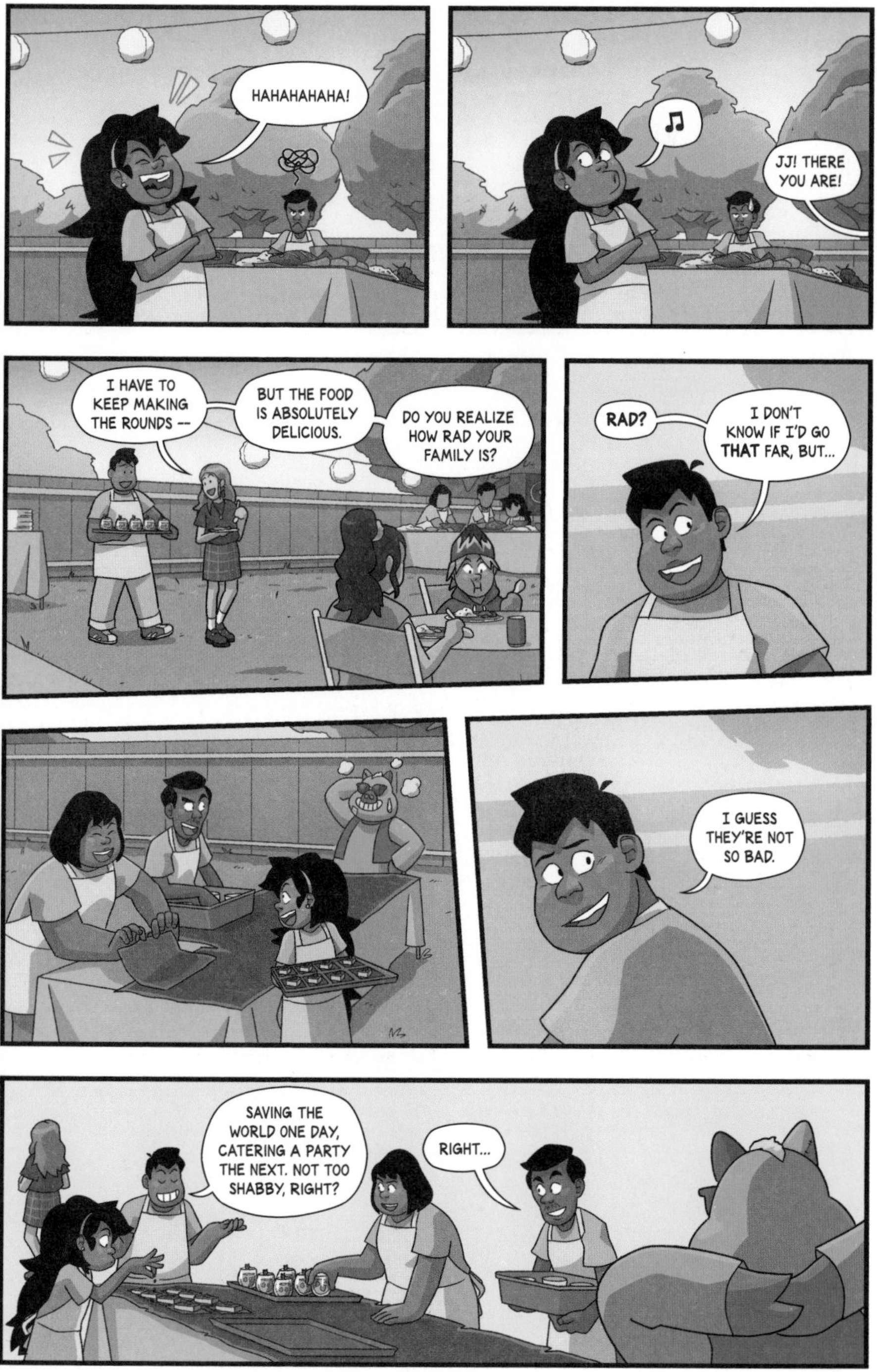
HAHAHAHAHA!
♫
JJ! THERE YOU ARE!
I HAVE TO KEEP MAKING THE ROUNDS --
BUT THE FOOD IS ABSOLUTELY DELICIOUS.
DO YOU REALIZE HOW RAD YOUR FAMILY IS?
RAD?
I DON'T KNOW IF I'D GO **THAT** FAR, BUT...
I GUESS THEY'RE NOT SO BAD.
SAVING THE WORLD ONE DAY, CATERING A PARTY THE NEXT. NOT TOO SHABBY, RIGHT?
RIGHT...

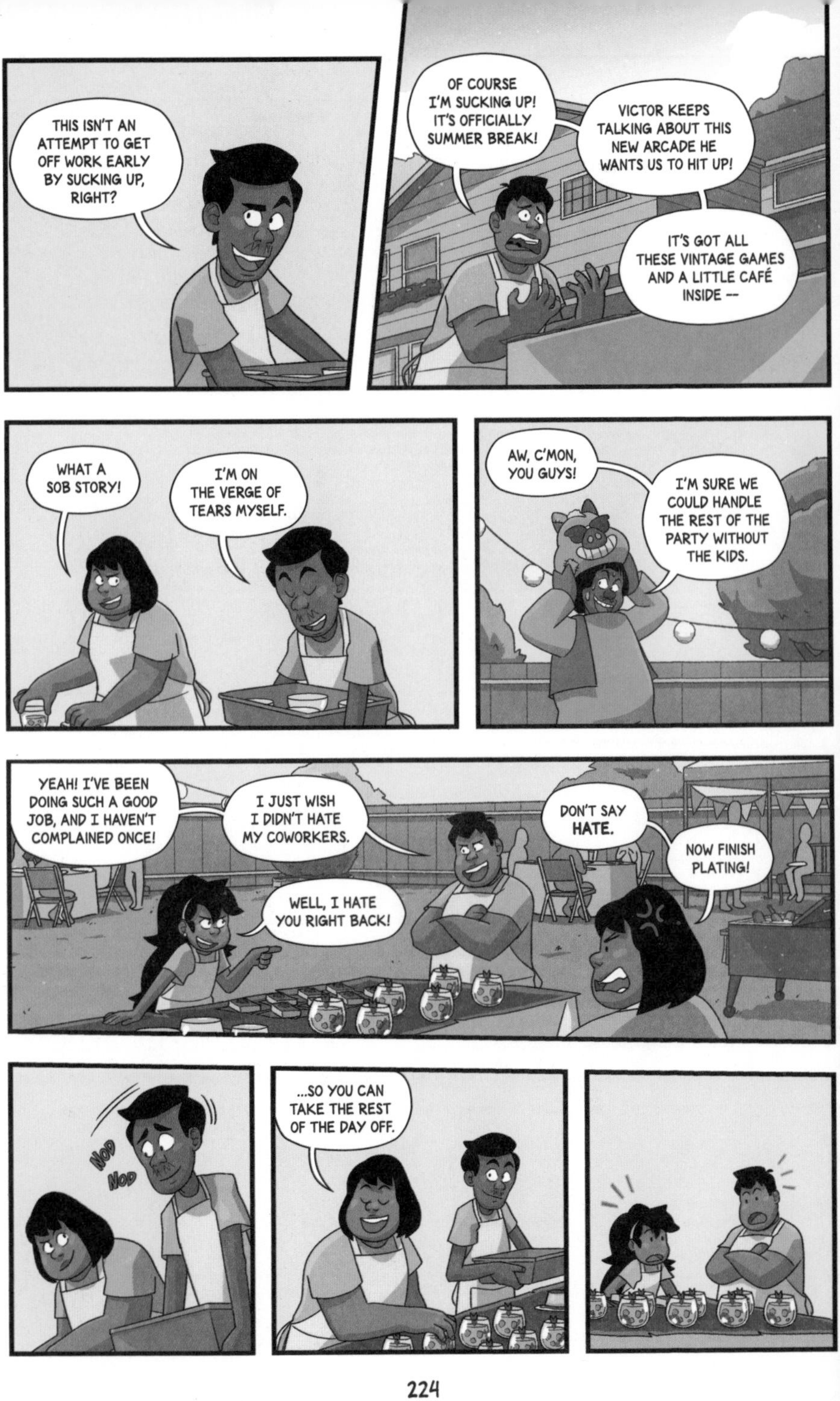
THIS ISN'T AN ATTEMPT TO GET OFF WORK EARLY BY SUCKING UP, RIGHT?
OF COURSE I'M SUCKING UP! IT'S OFFICIALLY SUMMER BREAK!
VICTOR KEEPS TALKING ABOUT THIS NEW ARCADE HE WANTS US TO HIT UP!
IT'S GOT ALL THESE VINTAGE GAMES AND A LITTLE CAFÉ INSIDE --
WHAT A SOB STORY!
I'M ON THE VERGE OF TEARS MYSELF.
AW, C'MON, YOU GUYS!
I'M SURE WE COULD HANDLE THE REST OF THE PARTY WITHOUT THE KIDS.
YEAH! I'VE BEEN DOING SUCH A GOOD JOB, AND I HAVEN'T COMPLAINED ONCE!
I JUST WISH I DIDN'T HATE MY COWORKERS.
WELL, I HATE YOU RIGHT BACK!
DON'T SAY **HATE.**
NOW FINISH PLATING!
NOD
NOD
...SO YOU CAN TAKE THE REST OF THE DAY OFF.

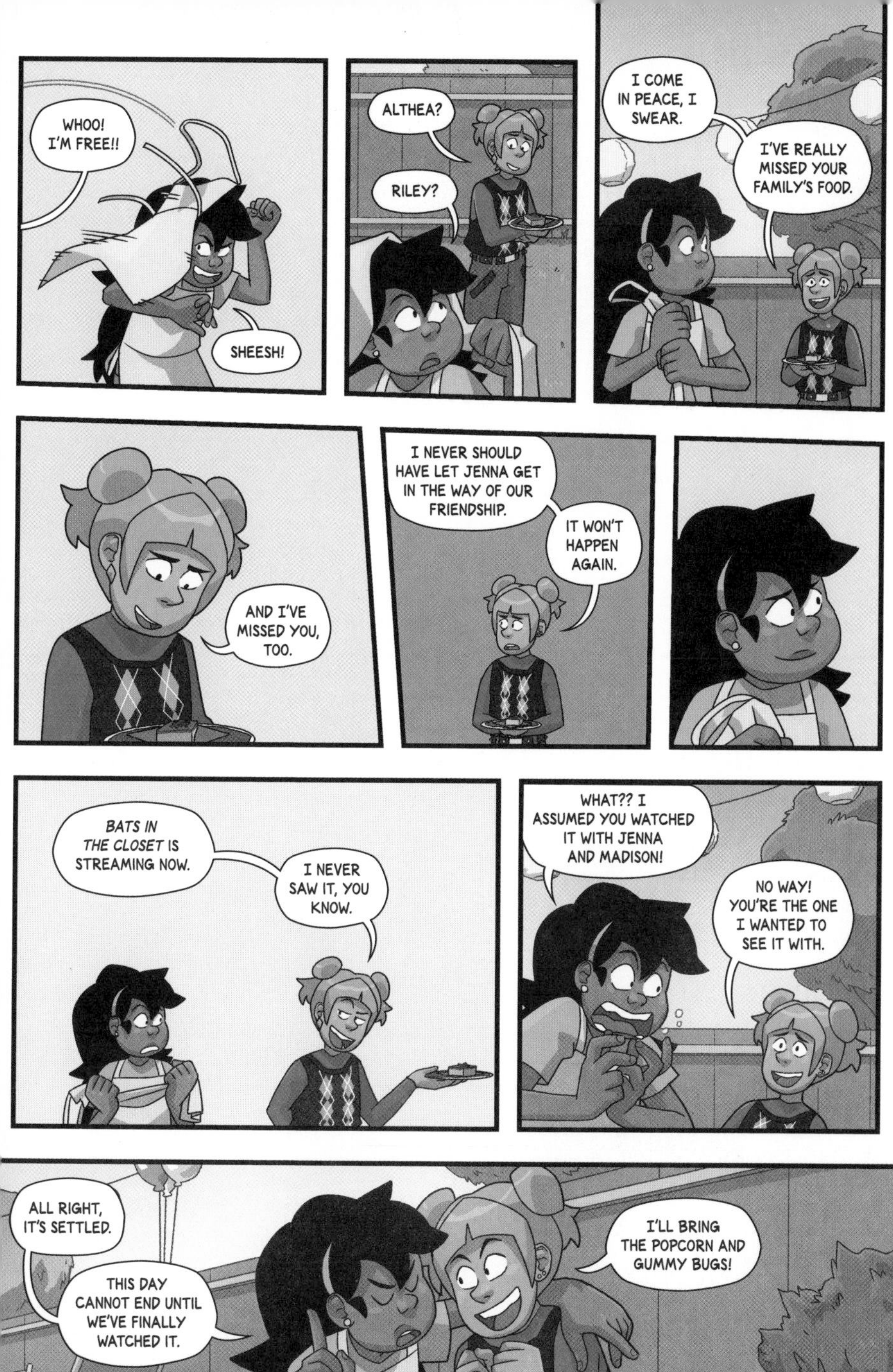
WHOO! I'M FREE!!
SHEESH!
ALTHEA?
RILEY?
I COME IN PEACE, I SWEAR.
I'VE REALLY MISSED YOUR FAMILY'S FOOD.
AND I'VE MISSED YOU, TOO.
I NEVER SHOULD HAVE LET JENNA GET IN THE WAY OF OUR FRIENDSHIP.
IT WON'T HAPPEN AGAIN.
BATS IN THE CLOSET IS STREAMING NOW.
I NEVER SAW IT, YOU KNOW.
WHAT?? I ASSUMED YOU WATCHED IT WITH JENNA AND MADISON!
NO WAY! YOU'RE THE ONE I WANTED TO SEE IT WITH.
ALL RIGHT, IT'S SETTLED.
THIS DAY CANNOT END UNTIL WE'VE FINALLY WATCHED IT.
I'LL BRING THE POPCORN AND GUMMY BUGS!

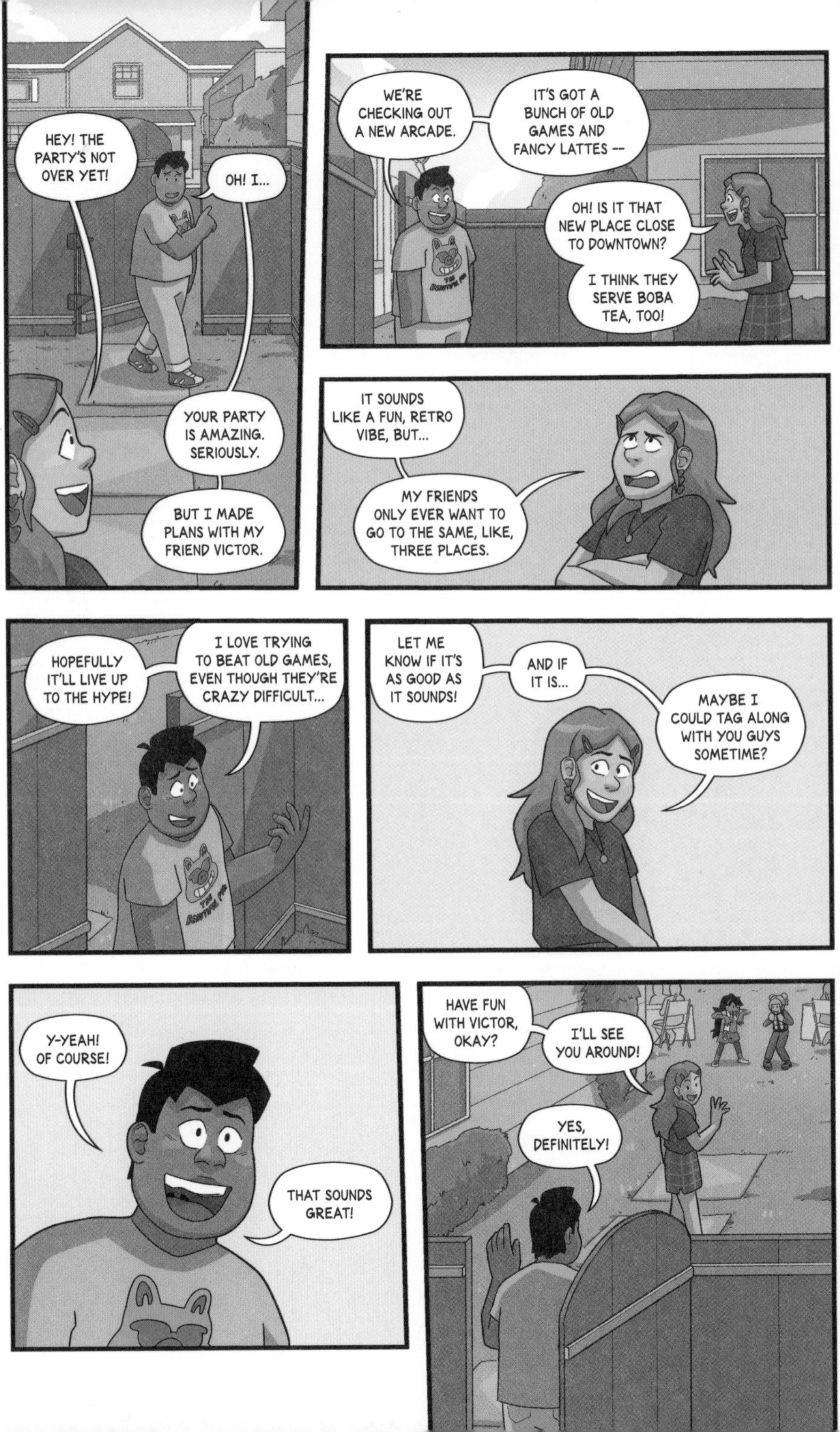
HEY! THE PARTY'S NOT OVER YET!
OH! I...
YOUR PARTY IS AMAZING. SERIOUSLY.
BUT I MADE PLANS WITH MY FRIEND VICTOR.
WE'RE CHECKING OUT A NEW ARCADE.
IT'S GOT A BUNCH OF OLD GAMES AND FANCY LATTES --
OH! IS IT THAT NEW PLACE CLOSE TO DOWNTOWN?
I THINK THEY SERVE BOBA TEA, TOO!
IT SOUNDS LIKE A FUN, RETRO VIBE, BUT...
MY FRIENDS ONLY EVER WANT TO GO TO THE SAME, LIKE, THREE PLACES.
HOPEFULLY IT'LL LIVE UP TO THE HYPE!
I LOVE TRYING TO BEAT OLD GAMES, EVEN THOUGH THEY'RE CRAZY DIFFICULT...
LET ME KNOW IF IT'S AS GOOD AS IT SOUNDS!
AND IF IT IS...
MAYBE I COULD TAG ALONG WITH YOU GUYS SOMETIME?
Y-YEAH! OF COURSE!
THAT SOUNDS GREAT!
HAVE FUN WITH VICTOR, OKAY?
I'LL SEE YOU AROUND!
YES, DEFINITELY!

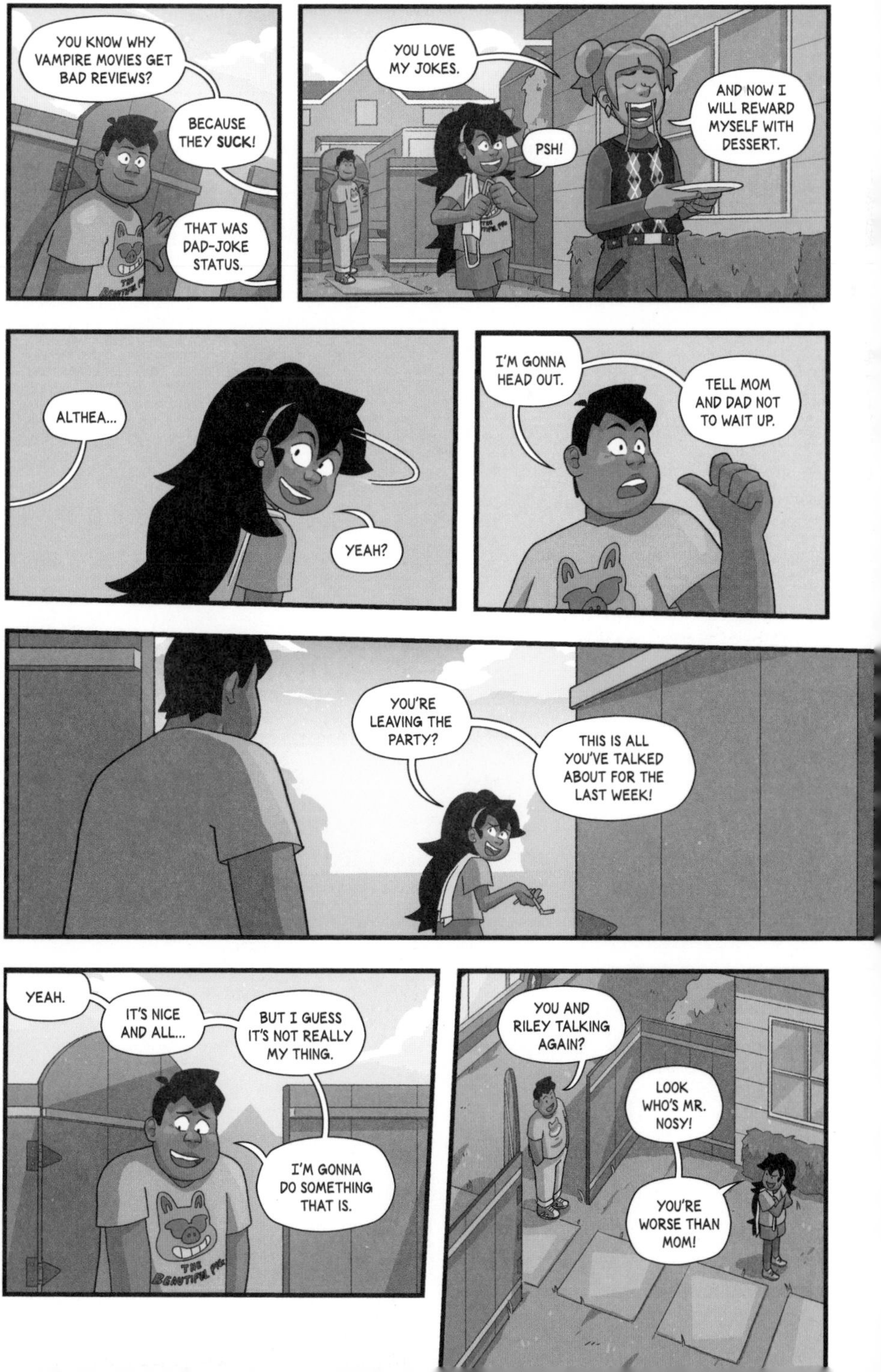
YOU KNOW WHY VAMPIRE MOVIES GET BAD REVIEWS?
BECAUSE THEY **SUCK**!
THAT WAS DAD-JOKE STATUS.
YOU LOVE MY JOKES.
PSH!
AND NOW I WILL REWARD MYSELF WITH DESSERT.
ALTHEA...
YEAH?
I'M GONNA HEAD OUT.
TELL MOM AND DAD NOT TO WAIT UP.
YOU'RE LEAVING THE PARTY?
THIS IS ALL YOU'VE TALKED ABOUT FOR THE LAST WEEK!
YEAH.
IT'S NICE AND ALL...
BUT I GUESS IT'S NOT REALLY MY THING.
I'M GONNA DO SOMETHING THAT IS.
YOU AND RILEY TALKING AGAIN?
LOOK WHO'S MR. NOSY!
YOU'RE WORSE THAN MOM!

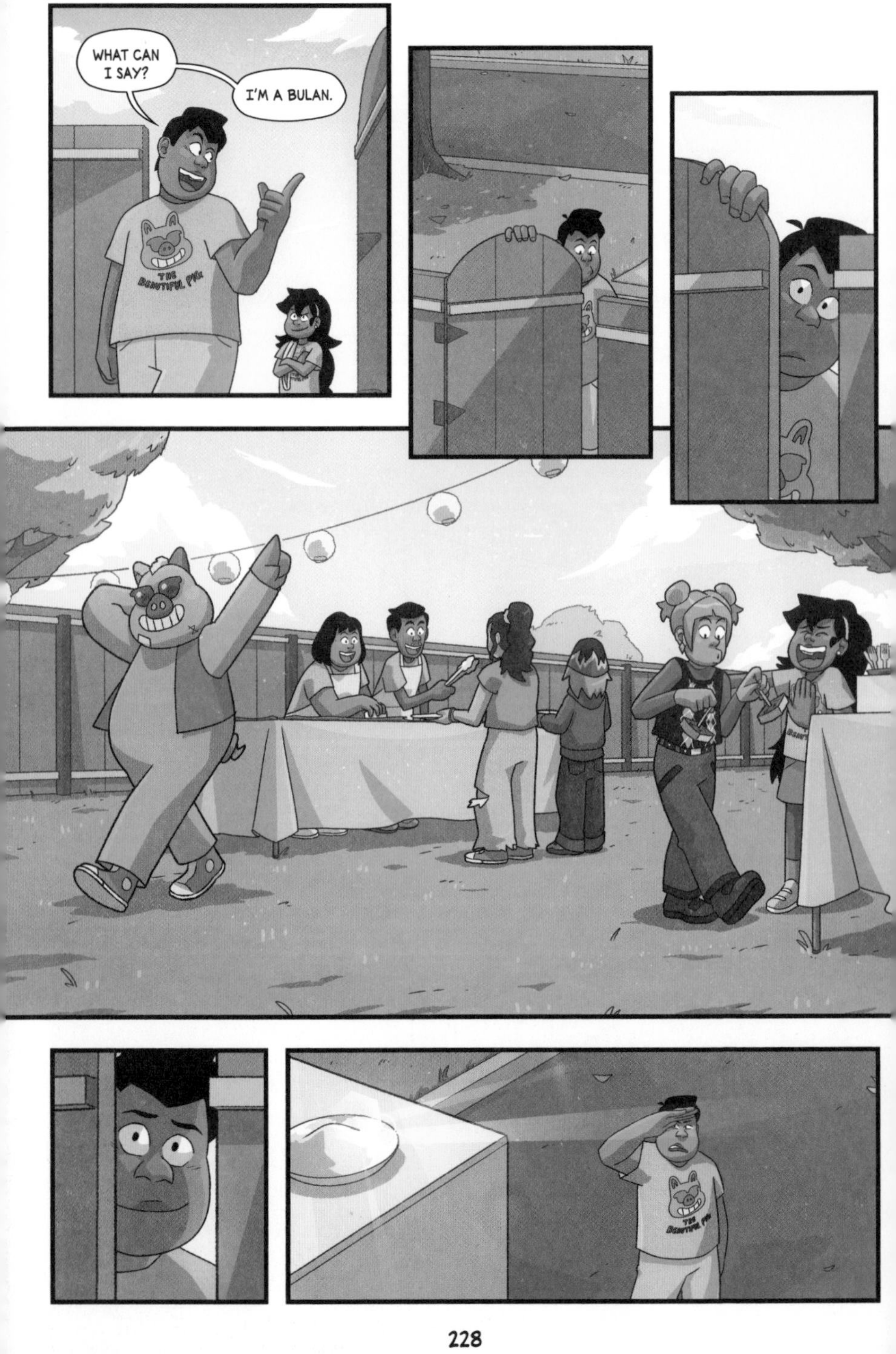
WHAT CAN I SAY?
I'M A BULAN.

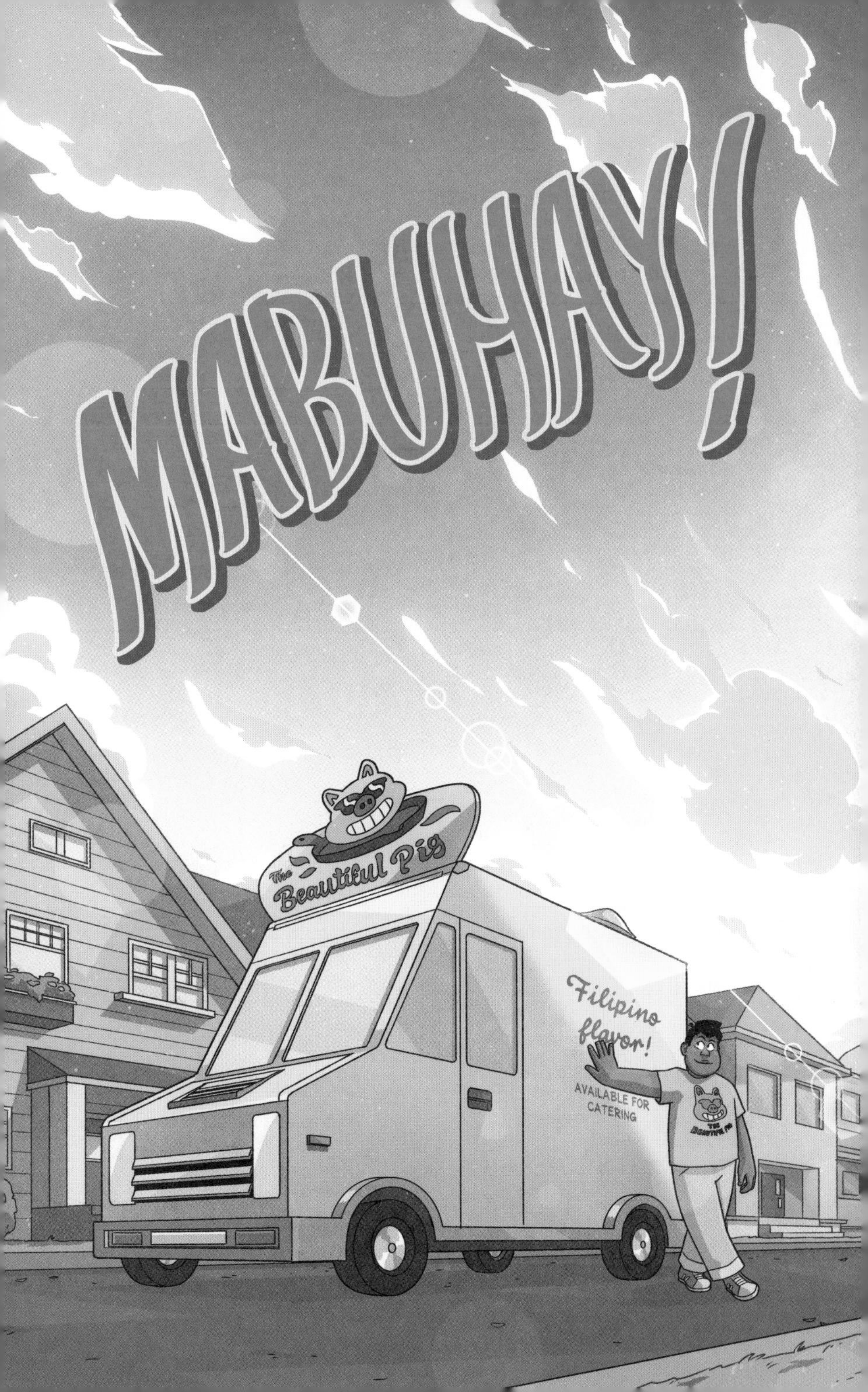
MABUHAY!
The Beautiful Pig
Filipino flavor!
AVAILABLE FOR CATERING

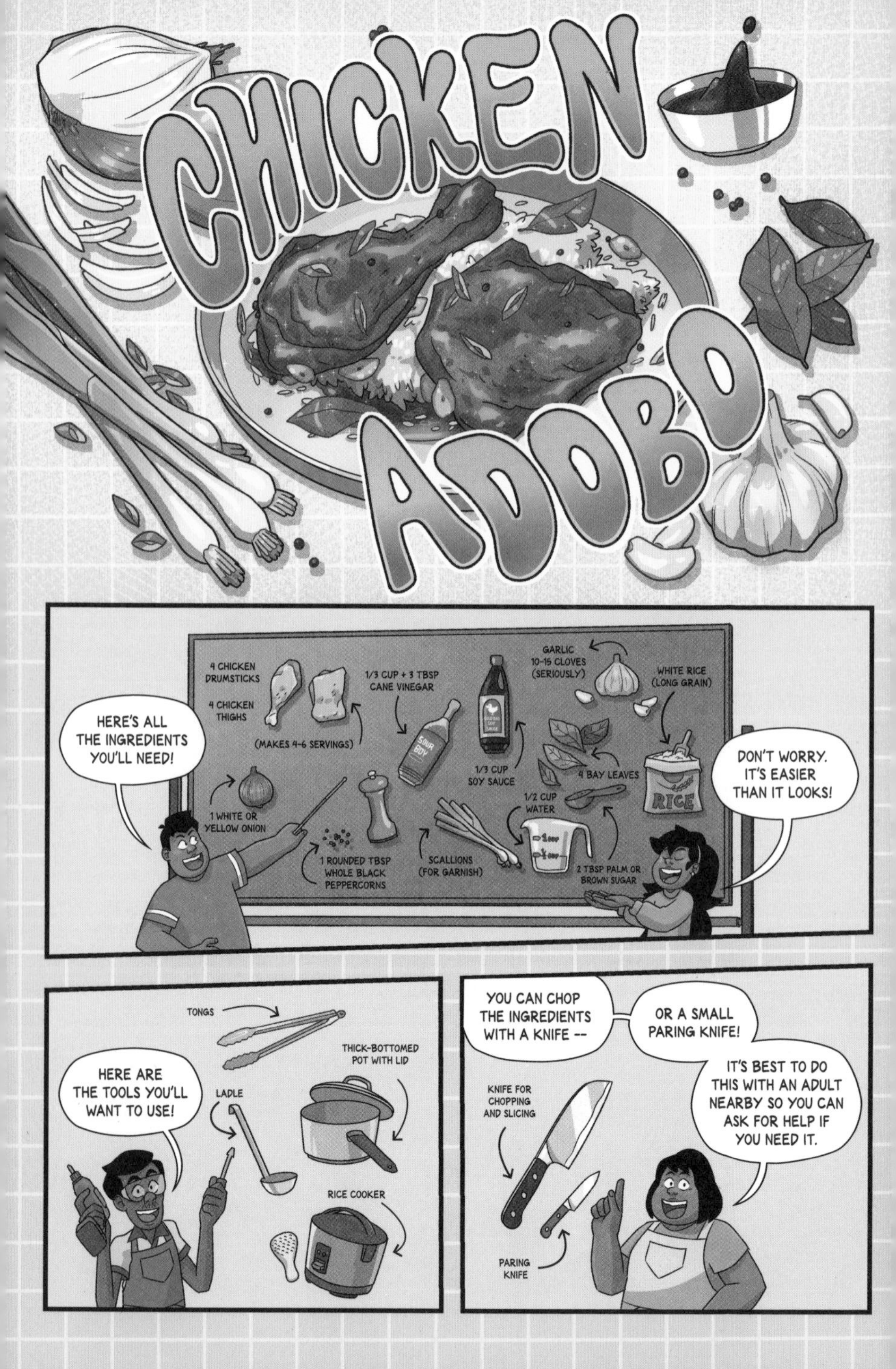
CHICKEN ADOBO
HERE'S ALL THE INGREDIENTS YOU'LL NEED!
4 CHICKEN DRUMSTICKS
4 CHICKEN THIGHS
(MAKES 4-6 SERVINGS)
1/3 CUP + 3 TBSP CANE VINEGAR
1/3 CUP SOY SAUCE
GARLIC 10-15 CLOVES (SERIOUSLY)
WHITE RICE (LONG GRAIN)
4 BAY LEAVES
RICE
1/2 CUP WATER
1 WHITE OR YELLOW ONION
1 ROUNDED TBSP WHOLE BLACK PEPPERCORNS
SCALLIONS (FOR GARNISH)
2 TBSP PALM OR BROWN SUGAR
DON'T WORRY. IT'S EASIER THAN IT LOOKS!
TONGS
HERE ARE THE TOOLS YOU'LL WANT TO USE!
LADLE
THICK-BOTTOMED POT WITH LID
RICE COOKER
YOU CAN CHOP THE INGREDIENTS WITH A KNIFE --
OR A SMALL PARING KNIFE!
IT'S BEST TO DO THIS WITH AN ADULT NEARBY SO YOU CAN ASK FOR HELP IF YOU NEED IT.
KNIFE FOR CHOPPING AND SLICING
PARING KNIFE

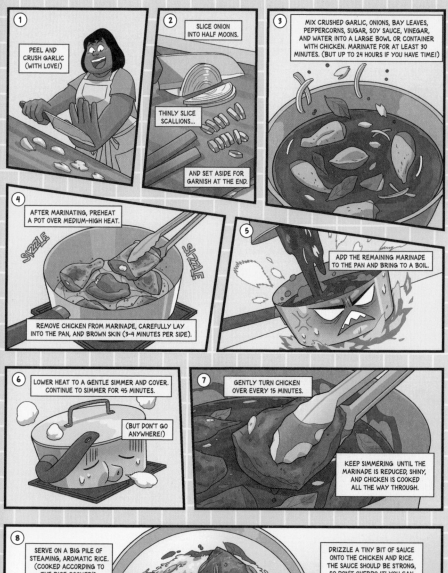

1 PEEL AND CRUSH GARLIC (WITH LOVE!)

2 SLICE ONION INTO HALF MOONS.

THINLY SLICE SCALLIONS...

AND SET ASIDE FOR GARNISH AT THE END.

3 MIX CRUSHED GARLIC, ONIONS, BAY LEAVES, PEPPERCORNS, SUGAR, SOY SAUCE, VINEGAR, AND WATER INTO A LARGE BOWL OR CONTAINER WITH CHICKEN. MARINATE FOR AT LEAST 30 MINUTES. (BUT UP TO 24 HOURS IF YOU HAVE TIME!)

4 AFTER MARINATING, PREHEAT A POT OVER MEDIUM-HIGH HEAT.

SIZZLE SIZZLE

REMOVE CHICKEN FROM MARINADE, CAREFULLY LAY INTO THE PAN, AND BROWN SKIN (3-4 MINUTES PER SIDE).

5 ADD THE REMAINING MARINADE TO THE PAN AND BRING TO A BOIL.

6 LOWER HEAT TO A GENTLE SIMMER AND COVER. CONTINUE TO SIMMER FOR 45 MINUTES.

(BUT DON'T GO ANYWHERE!)

7 GENTLY TURN CHICKEN OVER EVERY 15 MINUTES.

KEEP SIMMERING UNTIL THE MARINADE IS REDUCED, SHINY, AND CHICKEN IS COOKED ALL THE WAY THROUGH.

8 SERVE ON A BIG PILE OF STEAMING, AROMATIC RICE. (COOKED ACCORDING TO THE RICE COOKER'S INSTRUCTIONS.)

GARNISH WITH THINLY SLICED SCALLIONS.

DRIZZLE A TINY BIT OF SAUCE ONTO THE CHICKEN AND RICE. THE SAUCE SHOULD BE STRONG, SO DON'T OVERDO IT! YOU CAN ALWAYS ADD MORE IF YOU WANT!

NOW EAT UP! PART OF FILIPINO COOKING IS MAKING SURE NOBODY LEAVES THE TABLE HUNGRY!

MABUHAY!

To Mom & Pop. This one, and all
of the next ones, are for you.

AUTHOR'S NOTE

Mabuhay! is not an autobiography . . . but it kind of is. There is so much of me in this story and in these characters.

I devoured all sorts of media as a kid—TV shows, movies, comic books, you name it. But when you grow up noticing how little you or your family fits the mold of anything you see on a screen or page, you can't help but feel left out. Even worse, you may start to distance yourself from all the things that make you different.

I wasted so much time and energy trying to be a "regular" kid; pretending I didn't like the nerdy stuff that I secretly *loved*, being embarrassed if I went to school with a jacket that smelled like fried fish, feeling bad about myself because nobody who looked like me was on the cover of a teen magazine. It took time, but I eventually realized that the stuff that makes you feel "different" isn't anything to be ashamed of—it should be celebrated.

At first, I didn't know that celebrating difference was at the heart of *Mabuhay!* I just made a drawing of a Filipino family with a food cart, and it snowballed from there. I remembered the stories my mom and aunties told me whenever they thought I was being lazy or a smart aleck. Later, I wondered what would happen if the folkloric figures and monsters from these tales were *real*. With each page, I drew more and more from my own life: the kind of school I went to, the friends I had, and the food my family cooked. The more I excavated my memories and my culture, the more I appreciated them.

Whether the person who reads this book is the child of an immigrant or just somebody who feels like they're stuck on the outside looking in, I hope they find a piece of themselves here. It took me a long time to appreciate the aspects of myself I attempted to hide, and all I can hope is that maybe *Mabuhay!* will do the same for others. The stuff that makes you "different" is the *best* stuff. I promise.

GLOSSARY

ALL TERMS ARE TRANSLATED FROM TAGALOG, THE NATIONAL LANGUAGE OF THE PHILIPPINES.

ADOBO (*ah-doh-boh*):
One of the most popular dishes in the Philippines, usually consisting of meat — chicken or pork are the most common — cooked in vinegar, soy sauce, garlic, peppercorns, and bay leaves, served with a side of steamed or fried rice.

ALTHEA (*al-tay-ah*):
This is how Filipinos pronounce the name Althea (*not al-thee-ah*).

ARROZ CALDO (*ah-rohz cahl-doh*):
A savory chicken and rice porridge topped with crispy pork skin, fish sauce, and calamansi (*cahl-uh-mahn-see*), a Filipino citrus fruit.

ASWANG (*ahs-wahng*):
Shape-shifting, evil monsters, creatures, beasts, etc., from folklore.

BAKUNAWA (*bah-koo-nah-wah*):
A monstrous dragon deity that tries to swallow the moon, causing a lunar eclipse.

BALAK (*bahl-ahk*):
Plan/intent.

BATHALA (*baht-halah*):
The creator god of the universe in pre-colonial Filipino mythology.

BERBEROKA (*berr-beh-rokah*):
A man-eating water creature that drains riverbeds to trick humans in order to drown them.

BIRINGAN (*beer-eeng-ahn*):
A mythical city said to be in the Samar province of the Philippines.

BISTEK (*bee-stehk*):
Marinated strips of sirloin steak, slowly cooked, and served with steamed rice and sliced onions.

BOLO (*bo-loh*):
A large knife or cutting tool.

BULAN (*boo-lahn*):
The word for "moon" in several languages of the Philippines, as well as a mythological moon deity.

ENGKANTOS (*eng-kahn-tohs*):
Mythical environmental spirits who may take human form.

ESKRIMA (*ess-kree-mah*):
A Filipino martial art that focuses on sticks/batons, bladed weapons, and hand-to-hand fighting techniques.

GABI (*gah-bee*):
Night.

HALO-HALO (*hah-loh-hah-loh*):
Translates as "mix-mix." A layered dessert of shaved ice, fruits, sweetened beans, young coconut, ube ice cream, and condensed milk.

HAY NAKU (*hi nah-koo*; some people say *nah-koh*):
An expression of surprise or disbelief. From "Hay, nanay ko," which literally means "Oh, my mother!"

KAKATWA (*kah-kah-twah*):
Weird/odd.

KARE-KARE (*kah-reh-kah-reh*):
An oxtail stew made with toasted rice, a thick and savory peanut sauce, and vegetables.

LONGSILOG (*lohng-see-lohg*):
A breakfast dish of silog, a common mix of garlic fried rice and eggs, with longganisa (*lohng-gah-nee-sah*), a sausage with varying regional differences, added to it.

LUMPIA (*loom-peeyah*) and LUMPIANG SHANGHAI (*loom-peeyahng shang-hi*):
Crispy fried spring rolls, often filled with ground meat, vegetables, and aromatics, and then dipped in a sweet chili sauce.

MABUHAY! (*mah-boo-hi*):
A greeting, a toast, or a way to wish others luck. The root word *buhay* means "life" or "to live," so saying "Mabuhay!" (literally "Long live!") to someone is to wish good things upon their life.

MANANANGGAL (*mah-nah-nahng-gahl*):
A flying vampire-like creature that can separate the lower half of its body from the top half.

MGA MANGKUKULAM (*muhng-ah mahng-koo-koo-lahm*):
Witches. Also MANGKUKULAM (*mahng-koo-koo-lahm*): Witch.

MUTYA NG SAGING (*moot-yah nahng sahg-eeng*):
A fabled gem that is said to drop from a blossomed banana heart at midnight. If you swallow it, you will be granted amazing strength and magical powers.

PAMANGKIN (*pah-mahng-kheen*):
Nephew or niece.

PANCIT (*pahn-seet*):
Noodles; also, a noodle dish with sautéed vegetables, meat, and seafood. There are many versions with different ingredients, sauces, and toppings.

PASALUBONG (*pah-sah-loo-bohng*):
The Filipino tradition of bringing gifts after traveling.

PINYA (*peen-yah*):
Pineapple.

PESO (*peh-soh*):
The Philippine peso , or PISO (*pee-soh*) in Tagalog, is the official currency of the Philippines.

PUSO NG SAGING (*poo-soh nahng sahg-eeng*):
Translates to "heart of the banana" and it refers to the blossom of a banana tree.

TAMAD (*tah-mahd*):
Lazy.

TARA NA! (*tah-rah nah*):
Let's go!

TITO (*tee-toh*):
Uncle, but also can be used as an affectionate term for an older male family friend.

UBE HALAYA (*oo-bay hah-li-ah*):
A sweet jam made from ube (a purple yam), condensed milk, and butter.

ACKNOWLEDGMENTS

I have worked harder on this story than maybe anything else, but I wasn't alone. In fact, *Mabuhay!* wouldn't be here without the efforts of the many people who brought this book to life and all the friends and loved ones supporting me every step along the way.

A heartfelt thank-you to:

Mom and Pop, you've had my back since day one. You always believed in my art and the stories I wanted to tell. I wouldn't be who I am today without your love and encouragement. A million acknowledgments still wouldn't be enough.

Jess, Ollie, and Sam, for all the times you checked in on me or offered to grab me some groceries from the Asian market because you knew I was slammed with work. Throughout all of this, you never ceased to make sure that I was doing okay.

Auntie Tessie, for all the memories, fairy tales, and stories.

Peter and Alexa, for the life-changing rice cooker you bought for me as congratulations for getting *Mabuhay!* published. I'm not kidding. You two essentially kept me fed throughout the entirety of this book and the quickest way to my heart is through my stomach.

Aubrey, for all the times I paced back and forth bouncing plot points, dialogue, etc. off you, and for all the times that you stopped me from losing belief in myself.

Tanya McKinnon, for not only being an amazing agent full of tenacity and passion, but for all the tough love and growth as a storyteller you helped me achieve.

Shivana Sookdeo, for being incredibly generous with advice and making me feel like a little (just a little) bit less of a baby.

Megan Peace and David Saylor, for helping me look at every facet of my script, character designs, and essentially every inch of *Mabuhay!* You helped me take a rough gem and polish it again and again until it had little anime shines all over it.

Carina Taylor and Phil Falco, for taking on the task of making sure this book looked as good as it could, whether it was through design, art notes, or from the overall amount of work put in to keep the train on the tracks. I'd be a hopeless pile of goo without all your hard work and talents.

Rice Gallardo, George Williams, and Aaron Polk, for your assistance on colors. Your talent is immeasurable and I'm not being hyperbolic when I say that this book would not exist without you. I can't believe how skilled and horrifyingly fast y'all are.

Dr. Maximo D. Ramos, for all your contributions to organizing and categorizing so much traditional Filipino folklore. Your work is unparalleled.

Penny and Ace, for the pets, neck scrunches, and company during the long days and nights. You couldn't ask for a better pair of pups.

Last but certainly not least, I'd like to thank everyone who personally reached out to me over the course of making this book to share encouraging words, excitement, anecdotes, and love. This all started with a little drawing of a family standing in front of a food cart and ever since I shared that drawing, there was no shortage of people asking what *Mabuhay!* was, or when it was coming out, or to tell me how much my characters remind them of their own family members, or how homesick my fictional family made them feel. Every long night, every time I felt exhausted, I was bolstered by the kind words and well wishes you all gave me. Thank you, thank you, thank you.

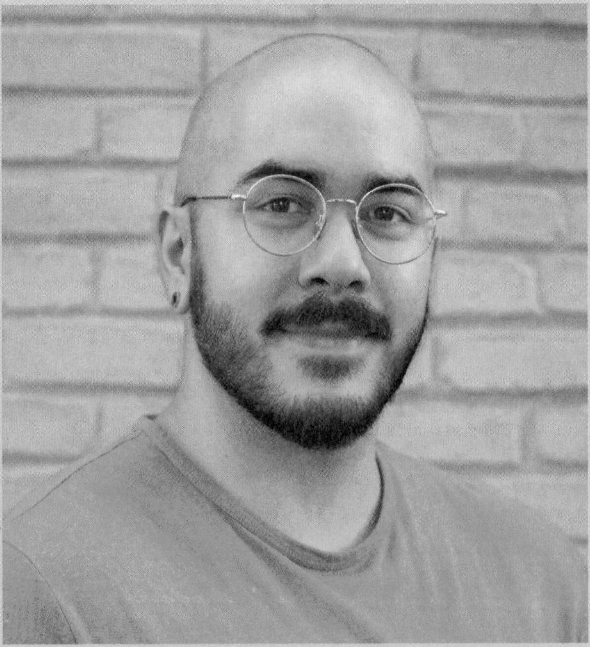

Photo: Aubrey Aiese

ZACHARY STERLING is a Filipino American illustrator, sequential artist, writer, and animation designer. Over the past several years, Zachary has worked on comics and graphic novels for young adult readers as well as animation designs for Frederator Studios and an unannounced project for Netflix. He was born in Torrance, California, but raised in the suburbs of Portland, Oregon — the place he proudly calls home. For more about Zachary, check out zacharysterling.com